The story of Josephine Cox is as extraordinary as anything in her novels. Born in a cotton-mill house in Blackburn, she was one of ten children. Her parents, she says, brought out the worst in each other, and life was full of tragedy and hardship – but not without love and laughter. At the age of sixteen, Josphine met and married 'a caring and wonderful man', and had two sons. When the boys started school, she decided to go to college and eventually gained a place at Cambridge University, though was unable to take this up as it would have meant living away from home. However, she did go into teaching, while at the same time helping to renovate the derelict council house that was their home, coping with the problems caused by her mother's unhappy home life – and writing her first full-length novel. Not surprisingly, she then won the 'Superwoman of Great Britain' Award, for which her family had secretly entered her, and this coincided with the acceptance of her novel for publication.

Josephine gave up teaching in order to write full time. She says 'I love writing, both recreating scenes and characters from my past, together with new storylines which mingle naturally with the old. I could never imagine a single day without writing, and it's been that way since as far back as I can remember.' Many of her previous novels of North Country life are available from Headline and are immensely popular.

'Bestselling author Josphine Cox has penned another winner' *Bookshelf*

'Hailed quite righ⸻ ⸻ ⸻ ⸻n of Catherine Cooks⸻

'Guaranteed to t⸻ ⸻less romantics' *Sunda⸻

Love Me
Or Leave Me

and

Miss You Forever

Josephine Cox

headline

ISBN 0 7553 2655 5

Typeset in Baskerville by Avon DataSet Ltd,
Bidford-on-Avon, Warwickshire

Printed and bound in Great Britain by
Clays Ltd, St Ives plc

Headline's policy is to use papers that are natural, renewable and
recyclable products and made from wood grown in sustainable
forests. The logging and manufacturing processes are expected to
conform to the environmental regulations of the country of origin.

HEADLINE BOOK PUBLISHING
A division of Hodder Headline
338 Euston Road
London NW1 3BH

www.headline.co.uk
www.hodderheadline.com

Love Me
Or Leave Me

When I was signing in Leicester last year, two lovely sisters came to see me.

One of them brought something to show me, and we had a wonderful talk, and a good cry as well.

I know they read all my books so are bound to read this.

Please get in touch. I'm so anxious to know how you got on.

CONTENTS

PART ONE

JULY 1954
THE FARM

Chapter One

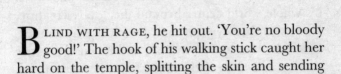

BLIND WITH RAGE, he hit out. 'You're no bloody good!' The hook of his walking stick caught her hard on the temple, splitting the skin and sending dark blood down her shocked face. 'You're too much like your mother!' he screamed. 'Useless. The pair of you.'

Through her pain, Eva looked at him, her quiet green eyes betraying nothing of what she felt. She didn't speak. She knew from bitter experience that to utter even one word would only send him into a greater fury. So, her heart pounding, she stood, head high, unflinching. Silently defiant.

Father and daughter faced each other as they had done so many times over the past two years. Many emotions passed between them: anger, love, guilt, and a sorrow too deep to voice.

He was the first to shift his gaze. 'Where is she?'

She turned away.

His voice followed her, low and threatening, 'Answer me, you bugger.'

She swung round and stared at him, her silence like a painful physical presence.

Momentarily subdued, he could not draw his gaze from hers. The quiet pride in those beautiful green eyes touched his heart. In spite of what she might believe, he had always loved her; always believed she was special. There was a time when his whole world centred round this lovely creature. Now, with her eyes on him, he felt like a criminal. Once she had smiled on him, and he on her. Once there was a close and unique bond between them. Now, there was nothing.

He remembered the child she had been, filled with the joys of life, delighting in all around her; he recalled the sound of her girlish laughter, the way her young eyes sparkled whenever she saw something new – a bright flower peeping through the ground after a hard winter, a glowing sunset that lit the sky with a halo of dazzling colour. And he would never forget the look on her face when he had let her cradle a newlaid chick in the palm of her tiny hand. How gentle and caring she had been, and how desperately he had loved that darling child.

The memories unfolded and the tears were close, but he pushed them deep inside himself. All that was a lifetime ago. Before the accident. Before he ceased being a man. God Almighty! Why did it have to happen? Life was cruel. But then so was he. He had turned his resentment on his wife and only child, tormenting and hurting them as if they were to blame when it was no more their fault than it was his. Guilt overwhelmed him. He alone had destroyed the wonder that lit her eyes.

In a soft, repentant voice that took her by surprise, he asked, 'Do you love me, Eva?'

She hesitated.

'The truth, mind,' he urged. 'I need to know.'

She lowered her gaze. She never wanted to hurt him.

'You've never lied to me,' he persisted. 'Don't lie to me now.' He paused, fearing her answer, yet knowing what it must be. 'Eva, do you love me, like you used to?'

'No, Father.' She raised her eyes. They were immensely sad, the gaze profoundly honest. 'I don't love you the way I used to.' Admitting it broke her heart. 'I'm so sorry, Father.' Once, a lifetime ago, she had loved him like no other being on earth. Now, he was like a stranger.

He bowed his head. 'You hate me then?'

'No, I don't hate you.' Love and hate were powerful, draining emotions. Eva had learned to suppress them well. But the sadness, the regrets, were always with her.

He felt her sorrow, and it was more than he could bear. Pain returned, and with it the rage. 'Where the bloody hell is my breakfast?'

'I'll get it for you now.'

She half turned, only to be stopped by a vicious blow on the shoulder. 'I don't want you to get me anything!' he snarled. 'How do I know you won't poison it?'

Angry that he should have lashed out at her yet again, her response was swift and condemning. 'You're a nasty, spiteful devil. You don't deserve any breakfast.'

'Go and find your mother, damn your eyes.'

'Why should I?'

'Because if you don't, I might just smash everything she values more than she does me.' To make his point, he jabbed his walking stick at a small blue vase until it rocked back and forth on the mantelpiece. 'She wouldn't thank you for not fetching her then, would she, eh?'

Eva caught the vase before it fell to the floor. She gave him a withering glance. 'Hand me the stick and I'll fetch her.' Her voice was low, trembling with anger.

'I'll give you the stick all right, you bugger!' he growled. 'Across your bloody legs, that's where.' Falling back into the chair like an old sack, he began whimpering, 'I'm ill. Fetch her. Tell her she's needed. Go on! Get a move on, damn you.'

Aware that he had the ability to bring on his own crippling pain whenever it suited him, Eva carefully replaced the vase, gave him a glance that warned, 'Don't touch it', and then swiftly departed.

Quickening her steps through the old farmhouse with its damp walls and low wooden beams, she went into the yard, glad to breathe the fresh summer air. She ran down the crooked pathway and on across the field, heading for the long barn beyond the orchard.

Her mother would be there, she was sure of it.

———➤•◄———

A LONE IN THE barn, Colette Bereton swung the axe high in the air, her small, muscular body stiffening with effort before she brought it down again in one long, easy stroke. There was a satisfying thud as the razor-sharp blade sliced through the log in a shower of splinters.

Taking a moment to throw the kindling into the wicker basket, she stretched her aching back, groaning in a soft northern voice, 'God help us! Me bones feel like they've been stretched on the rack, so they do!'

She looked up as the sun disappeared behind dark clouds; the heavens suddenly threatened rain and the air, too, had taken on a cold mood. 'July is always unpredictable,' she muttered. 'One minute blazing sunshine, the next yer arse is freezing.' She shrugged. 'Seems to me we'll be needing more kindling than this little lot.' She glanced at the half-filled basket. 'It's hard work an' no mistake. What I need is a good strong feller to help me out.' She shook her head, thinking of her husband, Marcus, a man she still loved in spite of everything. 'I had the finest man alive,' she murmured, 'but that was a lifetime ago.'

She fell into a deep, brooding silence, not for the first time wishing with all her heart that things had not turned out the way they had. Now, that same 'fine' man was crippled inside and out, heart and soul smothered by pain and resentment. The burden was not only his; it was hers too, and Eva's. He had only made matters worse by being bitter and hurtful towards her and the girl. Two years ago, before the tractor had pinned Marcus beneath it, causing damage to his back and legs, their lives had been fairly comfortable. Now the responsibility of keeping a roof over their heads had fallen to her and Eva, and the burden was a heavy one. Yet she tried to keep a happy heart.

'Get on with yer work now,' she chided herself, 'before the man himself comes crawling after you on his knees.' She knew he was capable of such a thing. She glanced nervously towards the orchard; from here she couldn't see the house, but her thoughts carried her there, to the sitting room where she had left the two of them earlier. 'I hope he's not being too difficult with the girl.' She knew from experience how hurtful he could be.

Determined now to return as quickly as possible,

she raised the axe again and while she worked, she sang.

Like Eva, she loved to sing. There was a time when Marcus used to sit and listen while she and Eva entertained him with folksongs her old granddaddy had taught her. She would always remember those times with delight. Now, though, it was forbidden to sing in the house, so whenever she worked outside, her voice would lift in song to help her through the long, hard days.

She swung the axe in time to the melody, unaware that Eva, half hidden by the trunk of an old apple tree, had paused to listen to her.

The song she sang was 'I'll take you home again, Kathleen'. The words and melody evoked many bitter-sweet memories in Eva. As the poignant words filled her troubled soul, she was transported back over the years to when her mother was young and carefree and her father a strong, wonderful man. On a winter's night he would sit before a warm, cheery fire while his wife and daughter sang to him. Afterwards there would be clapping and laughter, and lots of hugs and kisses.

Now, while her mother sang, Eva cried soft, helpless tears that ran down her face and dampened the collar of her blouse.

After a while she wiped her eyes, composed herself and joined in the song, as she hurried towards her mother.

Colette laughed out loud. 'You never could resist joining in, you bugger! Not even when you were small enough to sit on yer mammy's knee.' Colette gazed fondly at her daughter; she saw such loveliness and promise in Eva. The girl was already a beauty, but not in a bold, striking way. She was a quiet young woman, very self-assured and strong-willed.

Like her mother, Eva was small and strong, but while Colette had light brown eyes, her daughter's were the colour of a deep, calm sea, sometimes green, sometimes darkest blue, always beautiful. Her waist-long hair was the colour of ripened corn, her skin smooth and gently tanned by the many hours she spent outside in God's fresh air. Eva was a simple girl, with simple tastes. She loved the countryside with a fierce, abiding passion. An only child, caught between her parents and with no desire for material things, this place and the countryside around were her only real sources of contentment.

As she studied her, Colette noticed the trickle of blood running from Eva's hairline. Her features hardened. 'Did your father do that?'

'It's nothing.'

Reaching out, Colette pushed back the long fair hair. The gash was deeper than she had thought. 'To the stream,' she urged, and pushed Eva forward.

At the stream, the two of them knelt on the hard ground while Colette used the cuff of her blouse to wash away the blood. 'Sometimes yer father can be a right bastard!'

After a moment or two, Eva drew away. 'It's just a scratch,' she said.

'What's his excuse this time?' Colette asked as they walked back to the barn.

Helping her mother gather the kindling, Eva was careful not to alarm her. 'He wants you home, that's all.'

'Oh, aye? Let me guess. He's thrown his breakfast across the room and threatened to skin yer alive if yer don't do as he says.'

'He says he's ill. He needs you.'

'I see.' With a knowing smile, Colette threw the last of the kindling into the basket. 'Then I'd best get back, eh?' She would have heaved the basket across her shoulders, but Eva took it from her, swinging it easily to her own shoulders.

She said, 'Maybe he really is ill this time.'

Colette shook her head. 'Somehow, I don't think so. Yer father's been hurt and he's often in great pain, but he's never ill.' She looked up wistfully. 'Except in his mind.'

The two of them set off back to the house.

'I thought to leave him sleeping until I'd finished chopping the wood. Did he wake in a foul mood?'

Eva gave a half-smile. 'You could say that.'

'Refused his breakfast?'

Eva nodded.

'Threatened all and sundry if yer didn't fetch me?'

'That's about right.'

'What was it this time?'

'Your best china.' Eva gave her mother a sideways glance, her lips twitching in a smile.

'The vase, eh?'

'The same.'

Colette nodded. 'The wily old bugger knows how to get his own way.' Then she grinned. 'I wonder what the old devil would say if he knew the vase was worth no more than the price of a pint.'

Eva laughed out loud. 'It's not him who's the wily old bugger, it's you!'

'I have to be one step ahead of him,' Colette answered with a wink. 'An' if the ol' misery catches on to the vase trick, I've one or two more up me sleeve, so don't you worry.'

'Oh, I'm not worried.' And she wasn't.

'Never let a man know what yer up to,' Colette said knowingly. 'Keep 'em guessing, that's what I say.' She gave Eva a nudge. 'Did I ever tell yer about the first time me and yer daddy made love?'

'No, you never did.' Shyness flooded her soul.

'It was in a field, right over a hornets' nest. Talk about panic!' She began chuckling. 'I've never heard such language in all me life. An' believe me, if you've never seen a naked man running full pelt through the hedgerows with a swarm of hornets after him, well, you've never lived!'

'Were you badly stung?' Eva couldn't help but smile.

'Stung?' Colette's brown eyes rolled. 'Everywhere yer could possibly think of. Yer daddy came off worse though. One angry hornet attacked his nether regions and he couldn't walk straight for a week.' Taken by a fit of giggling, she fell against a tree. 'It damped his ardour, I can tell yer that.'

'You've a wicked sense of humour,' Eva chided. As they hurried on, the two of them were helpless with laughter and the sound of their mirth echoed through the orchard.

He heard it. And his face went dark with rage.

<hr>

A T THE FRONT door, Colette put her finger to her lips. 'Ssh.' She reached up and took the basket from Eva's shoulders. 'Leave yer father to me,' she said quietly. 'An' when yer chores are done, get yerself ready an' go into town. It's Saturday, an' didn't yer promise Patsy you'd go with her to that new nightclub in Bedford? It'll do yer good to get away from here for a while – put the roses back in yer cheeks.'

Eva had been looking forward to a night out with Patsy but she was worried about her mother.

'I don't like leaving you when he's in this kind of mood.'

Colette sighed. 'Yer not to worry about me an' yer father. I know how to handle the old devil. He'll not get the better of me.' She gave Eva a little push. 'Go on, lass. The sooner you've finished your work, the sooner you can be out of it.'

Eva wasn't so sure. 'We'll see.'

Colette knew better than to press her. Eva was too much like herself to be pushed into doing something she didn't want to do. All the same, it pained her to see how her daughter was beginning to take on more and more responsibility for her and Marcus. When all was said and done, Eva was only eighteen years old, with her whole life before her.

Colette found Marcus seated in his armchair, reading the paper and chewing on a ham sandwich. 'It's cold,' he snapped, peering at her from over the paper. 'The fire wants banking up.'

'Why did yer need to send Eva after me?' Taking a moment to warm her hands before the fire, she chided gently, 'Shame on yer, Marcus. One o' these days you'll really be in trouble an' nobody will believe yer.'

Crumpling the paper between his great fists, he answered in a harsh voice, 'I was feeling badly but you didn't care a sod, did you, eh? Took your bleedin' time getting back here, didn't you? For all you cared I might have been lying face down on the floor, helpless – dying even.'

'Aye, but yer weren't, were yer?' More's the pity, she thought bitterly, and was immediately filled with remorse. 'Oh, now, I didn't mean to sound cruel,' she told him. 'I'm tired, that's all. I was up first light and me back feels like it's broke in two.' Coming to him with a smile, she said, 'I hoped you'd sleep till I got back.'

'Hoped I'd kick the bucket, you mean.' Throwing the half-eaten sandwich to the floor, he snapped, 'No bloody breakfast, and a cold house, that's what greeted me when I got out of bed.'

'The house wasn't cold, Marcus,' she protested. 'I made up a good fire before I left. And Eva tells me she offered you breakfast, but you refused.' In an effort to appease him, she said kindly, 'I'll get you a nice cup of tea and a hot breakfast, how does that sound?'

To her dismay, his face set in a sullen expression. 'Don't want it,' he snarled. 'I woke up feeling fit, feeling like a real man for the first time in ages. I wanted *you*, but you weren't there. You're never bloody well there when I need you.'

Misunderstanding, she answered softly, 'Well, I'm here now, so tell me what I can do for you, an' I'll do it.'

'Get back upstairs.' His face smug, he settled more comfortably into the chair. 'Make yourself ready and I'll be there as soon as I've finished reading my paper.' Slowly and deliberately he began straightening the battered paper.

Now she understood.

With a determination to match his own, she quietly refused. 'No, Marcus.'

'What's that you say?' He couldn't believe his ears.

Colette stood her ground. 'I've been up since first light. I've washed a pile of clothes and hung them out, gathered the eggs, set the shop out ready for Patsy, and chopped enough wood to see us through the week. I've worked myself into the ground. I'm cold and tired, and I need a bath. So when I've got you a hot breakfast, I mean to soak me aching bones. Afterwards, I'll give Eva a hand with the day's chores so she can take herself off for an evening out with Patsy.' Struggling to control her anger, she reminded him, 'God knows, the girl deserves it.'

While she talked, his face grew white, his thick, misshapen fingers gripping the arms of the chair. There was murder in his eyes as he said in a low voice, 'I don't think you heard me, so I'll say it again. *Get upstairs and make yourself ready!*'

Afraid but defiant, she resisted. 'It's no use you getting yerself into one of yer fits. I *won't* go upstairs for you, and I won't make myself ready, as you call it. What I will do is bank up the fire then make your breakfast.' She smiled at him. 'I expect yer feeling a bit miserable, what with me out all hours doing this or that, and the pair of us never being able to sit and talk the way we used to.' She chatted on, looking away as she said, 'With a hot meal inside yer belly, you might be in a better mood.'

She turned to the fireplace and stooped to pile some logs in a semi-circle over the coals. The flames leaped high, licking at the fire-back. 'There now, isn't that cosy?' She turned to the chair where he'd been sitting.

He wasn't there.

For a moment she was confused, then she looked up and here he was, standing to one side of the fireplace, his arm resting on the mantelpiece and his face grinning down on her. 'I can move quick as a snake when I've a mind.'

'I can see that,' she acknowledged suspiciously. 'What else can you do that you've never told me about?'

'That's for me to know and you to find out.'

She didn't reply. Oddly disturbed, she continued to look up at him. There was something about his manner that frightened her; the way he lurked close, the way he spoke, soft yet not gentle. And his eyes – small, dark eyes that she knew like the image of her own face. She had seen those eyes smile on her, and she had seen them crumple in pain, but she had never seen them

17

as they were now, rock-hard and staring, alive with hatred.

'Don't be angry,' she murmured. She often put his needs before her own and gave way to his demands, for the sake of peace, but this time she was so bone-weary she couldn't face having him roll on top of her.

Reaching down, he took hold of her arm, pinching it so hard she gave a small cry. 'You'll never see the day when I'm too crippled to take a woman,' he growled. 'So it's either up in the bedroom or on the floor here and now.' He licked his lips in anticipation. 'What's it to be then, my lovely?'

'Take yer hands off me!' Sometimes, it was more than she could cope with. Marcus was not the same man she had married all those years ago. That man was dead and gone, just as surely as if the tractor had crushed the life out of him. God forgive her, there were times when she wished it had. He should be thanking the good Lord for saving his life but instead he spent every waking minute cursing the hand fate had dealt him. But, for all that, she would never desert him. In spite of his contempt for her, she would stay and make his life as bearable as possible. He was her husband for better or worse, and she had given her vows before God.

As she struggled to free herself, she said what was in her heart, her voice hard with disgust. 'There was a time when I went weak with pleasure at the touch of yer hand, but not now, not any more. Yer not the man I married. You're a lazy, idle bugger and, God help me, I'm stuck with yer. That's a burden I have to live with, like it or not.' There was fire in her eyes as she faced up to him. 'Listen to me, for I mean every word. Yer bullying will get you nothing. I swear to Him above, I'll die before you see me give in to yer demands ever again.'

Stunned by her outburst, he just gaped at her.

She'd gone too far to stop now, and she emptied her heart of all the bad things that had gathered these past years. 'You take pleasure in using me and the girl to wait on yer hand and foot, when all the time yer capable of doing things for yerself. Other men have been hurt and maimed, and they don't lie back and cosset themselves. What kind of coward is it that would blame their family for what's happened? You can walk as well as me when you've a mind, and you still have the strength of ten men when it suits yer.' She held nothing back. 'Yer a bad, lazy feller, Marcus Bereton. Instead of whining an' moaning, why don't yer get out and do some of the hard work round this place? You'd be a happier man for it, and me and the girl would have a better life, and not before time neither!'

'*You dare talk to me like that?*' Marcus roared. She struggled desperately to free herself, but he pinned her down, perilously close to the fire, until the sweat ran down her face and she could hardly breathe. She began to fear for her life.

'Let go of me, Marcus,' she ordered, trying hard not to show her fear. 'Yer won't solve anything by hurting me.'

'That's for me to say.' He spread his legs to balance himself and used his free hand to undo his trousers. 'I can see I'll have to take what I want – unless you want me to get it elsewhere.' His eyes glittered madly. 'The girl hasn't had a man yet. Think on *that* before you refuse me again.'

His words filled her with white-hot loathing and fury, and as he laughingly bore down on her, her strength rose to match her rage. Without thinking of the consequences, she pitted herself against him.

<hr />

IN THE COLD and damp of the shed, Eva shivered. The old wooden building was long past its prime; there were long, widening cracks in the walls and a hole in the roof the size of a man's fist. Eva had meant to patch it up, but somehow there was never the time.

She paused in her work, folding her arms for warmth. The damp had crept right into her bones. Beneath her feet the flagstones felt like hard slabs of ice, and above her head the sky was clearly visible through the sagging roof. 'The old place really needs pulling down,' she mused. 'But where would we get the money for a new one?' The land gave them a living, that was all. There was no money for luxuries.

Stacking the last of the kindling, she turned the basket upside down and hung it on the peg.

She padlocked the door behind her when she left. As she slipped the big iron key into her pocket, she chuckled. 'Anyone would think I was locking up the crown jewels.' The shed contained crates of eggs and a selection of winter vegetables, kindling, sacks of coal and the few tools they possessed. It didn't amount to much, but it was worth more than jewels to them.

Last winter somebody had broken into the shed and stolen a leg of pork and a fat Christmas turkey that Eva had earned picking Brussels sprouts with frozen fingers on a neighbour's land. Colette was furious. She dug out an old padlock and from that day on the shed was secured every night, though she had to agree with Eva that if anyone really wanted to get in, all they had to do was sneeze hard and the whole place would tumble like a pack of cards.

As Eva made her way back to the house, she thought she heard a scream. Unsure, she paused to listen. When she heard it again, she realised with horror that it was her mother's voice. 'Dear God! What's he doing to her?' As she broke into a run, she heard Colette call her name and her heart froze with fear. 'Please God, let it be all right,' she prayed as she flew down the path and burst, breathless, into the house.

S HE COULD SMELL smoke the moment she threw open the door. She rushed to the sitting room and stared, horrified, at the sight that met her eyes.

Kneeling on the floor, with Colette in his arms, her father rocked back and forth, his face buried in his wife's hair. Colette lay limp and quiet, her dress burned, her face smudged and dirtied. Flames licked up the walls, caught hold of the curtains and fired the ceiling. The smoke was suffocating.

'Get out, Father!' Surging forward, Eva took hold of him by the shoulders. 'The fire's out of control, we have to get out!' She tried to loosen his hold on her mother, but his grip was like iron.

'Why wouldn't she listen?' he gasped. The tears ran down his face, making thin pink tracks through the soot on his skin. 'I didn't mean to hit her . . . didn't know she would fall backwards . . . the fire took her.' He could hardly speak for the smoke filling his lungs.

With her own lungs close to bursting, Eva stooped down, slid her arms beneath Colette's small body and, with a strength born of desperation, lifted her mother out of his grasp. She staggered out of the room, into the smoke-filled kitchen and on towards the back door. Behind her, Marcus slumped to the floor. Eva was only conscious of the awful stillness of the weight she carried. She dared not think and, afraid of what she might see, did not look down.

The back door was shut. Kicking out with all her might, she breathed a sigh of relief when it sprang open. Head down, she lunged forward, heat and smoke following. With a surge of fear, she realised the hem of her skirt was on fire.

'It's all right, we've got you!' Voices invaded her head as she fell to the ground, her arms still round her mother's small body. 'Let me have her. You're safe now.' Neighbours had seen the flames and made their way here, anxious to help. In the distance Eva could hear the unmistakable sound of sirens.

'My father . . .' Eva looked about for him. He was nowhere to be seen. Grabbing hold of the nearest person, her eyes wide with fear, she cried, 'My father's still inside!'

'Don't you worry,' the man said. 'A couple of the lads are bringing him out now.'

They laid him on the ground, next to Colette. A woman knelt beside him. Catching sight of Eva's stricken face, she shook her head. 'I'm sorry,' she murmured. 'The smoke was too much for him.'

Marcus was gone.

Colette lived for only a few moments. 'You've been my reason for living,' she whispered, her brown eyes quietly smiling up at Eva's haunted face. 'Try not to remember the bad times, sweetheart.' Her gaze went to the man who had once given her such joy. Reaching out, she touched his hand. Whispering softly to Eva, she said, 'Deep down, your daddy was a good man.' In her eyes shone a great sadness for the wasted years.

They clung to each other in their last moments together, their tears mingling as their lives had mingled. Then, with a gentle sigh, Colette closed her eyes.

Eva held on to that small figure, her grief terrible to see. 'Whatever will she do?' asked one old woman who lived in the valley. 'With all her family gone, where can she turn?'

People shook their heads. They couldn't see a future for Eva.

And, for a long time to come, neither could Eva.

Chapter Two

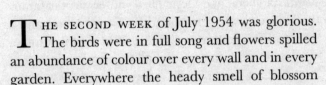

THE SECOND WEEK of July 1954 was glorious. The birds were in full song and flowers spilled an abundance of colour over every wall and in every garden. Everywhere the heady smell of blossom filled the air.

The vicar made mention of it, and tired spirits were lifted by it, but Eva didn't notice. All her senses were focused on the two wooden boxes standing side by side before the altar.

The church was full; people who knew the Beretons had come and so had people who didn't, always mindful of the fact that tragedy could strike anyone at any time. Their hearts went out to Eva, a lovely, hard-working girl who had lost everything. While the vicar prayed for the souls of the departed and asked that their only child might find peace, all eyes were on Eva, so young and alone.

Her gaze never left the coffins of her parents. In her mind's eye she saw it all as it had been, before the accident, before the badness set in. Her heart was full of memories; the images flitted through her shocked mind, touching her with such bitter-sweet pain she could hardly breathe. Occasionally, shining through the sorrow came the touch of a smile, gently lifting the corners of her mouth and lighting her eyes with the brightness of tears.

The years had been kind before love had turned to indifference and then to a kind of hatred. The bad years had been like a long hard winter, yet the family had stayed together, bound by ties of blood and a shared life. Now it was the most beautiful summer and they were parted, and all that had gone before was just a whisper in the wind.

Suddenly the congregation broke into song. Her thoughts shattered, Eva looked up. She could not bring herself to sing; what was there to sing about? Instead, her quiet green eyes roved over the congregation and she wondered why they were here. Most of them were strangers to her. A round-faced woman caught Eva's glance and looked away. A tall, grey-haired man at the end of the pew reverently bowed his head. Eva thought she had seen him once before, when her mother sold the kindling sticks at market. She seemed to recall he bought two bundles and afterwards stayed to pass the time of day.

There were pitifully few relations. The Beretons had been a small family; Marcus had no brothers or sisters and his own parents were long gone. Colette had one sister, who was married with two sons, and an aged aunt. They were all here. Eva had welcomed them only this morning, but it was like welcoming strangers. All but one. Bill. It warmed her heart to see him again.

———❧———

T HE SERVICE WAS over. The mourners filed out behind the coffins, into the pretty churchyard, where the two were laid to rest.

When everyone had gone, Eva stayed behind to speak to her parents. In her heart she did not believe they had gone far away. In fact, she felt closer to her father at that moment than she had at any time over the past few years. She felt that, somehow, these two people who had been her whole life would be with her wherever she went, for as long as she herself was alive.

Her mother had once told her that hate and love were two sides of the same coin. Now she knew what that meant, because the love for her father was still there. 'I love you both so much,' she murmured. 'I will always love you.' The tears came, and she let them fall, her heart sore with pain.

From the doorway of the church, Bill thought how small she seemed standing there, all alone, so vulnerable, so tragic. He wanted to go to her, but his instincts warned him that this was her time. A time to recollect, and mourn. It was not for him to intrude. But he felt for her. Eva had always been special to him, she always would be. And because of what he had learned from his father earlier he knew she would suffer more before the day was through.

God alone knew how hard he had tried to protect her from what was to happen, but his hands were tied and there was nothing he could do. Except maybe warn her. But that was pitifully little.

He continued to look at her, thinking how lovely she still was, and how very young she seemed, though he recalled how fiercely independent she had been as a child. Remembering, he smiled. Would she remember how it was, he wondered, or had she forgotten? He hoped not.

After a time he turned away, murmuring, 'I'm sorry, Eva.'

Eva caught sight of him walking away. The last time she had seen him, they had both been just children, but the years had not changed him all that much; the way he walked was the same, with a kind of long, easy stride, and his dark brown hair still seemed to have a mind of its own.

She looked away. 'It was a long time ago,' she whispered. 'So much has happened since then.' Seeing him had moved her deeply.

She glanced back to her parents. With a brave smile and a small prayer for their safekeeping, she wrenched herself away.

B ACK AT THE farmhouse, Patsy put the finishing touches to the buffet. At thirty years of age, she was a big, handsome woman, with baby-blue eyes and untidy auburn hair. Anxious that everything should be just right by the time the mourners returned, she cleared away the dirty crockery.

She went back into the sitting room. Looking round, she praised herself in a strong Irish voice. 'Sure, I've done meself proud, so I have.'

And she had. On the table were plates of dainty sandwiches, small sausage rolls, sliced ham and squares of cheese, enough new bread and butter to feed an army, and a selection of scones made by Eva the night before. She checked the place settings. 'Plates, knives, cups and saucers, milk and sugar . . .' She squealed with horror. 'Be Jaysus! Sure, I've forgotten to put out the napkins.' She looked frantically about, until her eye caught the pile of blue paper napkins standing on the dresser where Eva had left them. Rushing across, she grabbed them. 'Patsy Noonan, sure you'd forget yer head if it weren't screwed on to yer stupid shoulders.'

After arranging the napkins between each plate, she stood back to survey the scene again. Thanks to the hard work of the neighbours, restoring and replacing treasures after the fire, the room was warm and cosy, with a number of small pictures across one wall – prints of sunflowers and fields, and a pretty flower-framed cameo of Colette and Marcus on their wedding day. Her grin of pleasure faded as she caught sight of the fire-blackened chimney breast. 'It's a sad thing, so it is,' she sighed. 'Now then, it's time to get meself washed and tidy before they come through the door.'

In the hall she glanced at herself in the mirror; staring back was a strong, pleasant face, with small splashes of red plum jam round the mouth and chin. 'Yer a sloppy article, so yer are!' she told herself. But it didn't matter. What mattered was Eva. Patsy loved her dearly and had appointed herself Eva's guardian. It broke her heart to see how her whole world had come to such an end, and she worried about how quiet Eva had been.

When Patsy was worried, she got hungry, and she was hungry now: 'I think I'd better have my share now, before it's all gone.' Turning on her heel, she returned to the sitting room and helped herself to a jam tart. It was gone before she was even halfway up the stairs. Licking her fingers, she continued smartly towards the bathroom.

Outside the main bedroom she stopped. The door was open. She could see the big old bed which Eva's parents had shared. Patsy sighed. 'I hope you've both found a better place,' she murmured, making the sign of the cross on her forehead. She knew that life in this house had not been easy these past two years. 'Oh, Eva!' She brushed away a tear. 'You helped me through a bad time once and I hope

I can help you do the same now.' Eva was the kind of friend that only came along once in a lifetime: 'Yer shouldn't be put through such pain, my love, but it's strange how life punishes the gentlest of creatures.'

Eva had told Patsy she could use her room; a bright, sunny place with chintz curtains and pretty rugs on the floor. After washing in the bathroom, she combed her hair in front of Eva's mirror and then put on the straight black dress which Eva had hung on the wardrobe door.

Regarding herself in the long, oval mirror, she groaned. 'Yer still a fat little thing, even in black. One of these days you'll have to slim down or there won't be a frock to fit yer this side of heaven.' She *would* slim down, but not yet. There was no incentive. Certainly no boyfriend. For some reason she could not understand, young men didn't fancy her.

Downstairs she checked everything again. She brought the kettle to the boil and then threw open the sitting-room window to let in some air – the afternoon sun flooding into the room was making it uncomfortably warm. That done, she went to the door and looked down the lane. 'No sign of them yet,' she muttered. She was half tempted to help herself to another jam tart but thought better of it.

Settling down to wait, she sat on the front step, her chubby legs crossed and her back against the door jamb. The warmth of the sun on her face made her feel sleepy.

Half an hour later, the first car drew up and Eva stepped out. Her gaze was drawn immediately to the front doorstep and the familiar figure curled up there. She couldn't help but smile. Patsy was fast asleep.

'Looks like it's all been too much for her,' the driver chuckled. He was a kindly man, used to ferrying people to and from the churchyard. He had done the job these past twenty years, until now he could almost do it with his eyes closed. On these serious occasions there was little cause for amusement, but seeing that fat little urchin on the doorstep, his old heart was warmed. 'Seems a pity to wake her,' he said to Eva. 'A neighbour, is she?'

'A friend,' Eva gently corrected him. 'A very dear friend.'

He nodded. In his work he got to know most things, and what he knew about Eva was that she had lost her entire family in one fell swoop. Life was a bastard sometimes. 'Do you want me to wait, love?' Often the relatives were in a hurry to get away. Other times they lingered, like vultures over a meal.

Eva shook her head. 'I don't think so,' she told him, watching the other two cars draw up. 'From what Aunt Margaret said, they have everything arranged.'

It surprised her when he took hold of her hand. 'I haven't had a chance to say how sorry I am,' he said. 'The job I do is not a thankful one, and to be honest I'm glad to leave it behind at the end of the day. It isn't often I let myself be affected. I can't afford to, but I'd just like you to know I think you've been dealt a lousy hand, you being so young and all.' As he looked into those strong green eyes, he felt humbled. 'God bless you,' he murmured. 'I wish you all the best.'

Eva didn't know quite what to say.

He understood. 'Right you are then.' Glad to be off home where he could put his feet up for the rest of the day, he shuffled back into the driving seat, started the engine and shifted into gear. In no time at all he had made a tight and difficult turn and was heading in the opposite direction.

Eva watched him for a moment before returning her attention to Patsy. When she saw her Uncle Peter violently shaking the poor girl, she was horrified. 'What do you think you're doing?' Hurrying across the garden, she grabbed him by the arm. 'Leave her alone.' Her voice trembled with anger. 'Please, go inside. I'll see to Patsy.'

'Lazy little bugger!' Straightening his shoulders, he glared at Patsy who had woken in a fright. 'What's she doing lolling all over the step like that? Doesn't she realise there's been a funeral? Has she no respect?'

Wide awake now, Patsy retaliated. 'Yer gave me a bleedin' fright, so yer did!' Scrambling to get up, she almost knocked him over. 'An' if yer ask me, it's *you* who needs to have a bit of respect. You're the one shouting and bawling, so yer are!'

Peter's face turned bright red. 'Do you realise who you're talking to, young lady?'

'No, and I don't wish to, you bad-tempered old sod.'

Muttering under his breath, he squared his small, stiff shoulders and turned to Eva. 'Get rid of her,' he demanded sourly. 'We've important matters to discuss, and they are not for strangers' ears.'

'I'll do no such thing,' Eva replied. 'Besides, Patsy is no stranger. She's my best friend, and Mother loved her as much as I do.'

'Do as you're told, young lady,' Peter snapped. 'I do not want her in this house.'

Eva's impulse was to get rid of *him*. But, mindful of the fact that this awful little man was married to her mother's sister, she remained calm and dignified. 'I'm sorry, Uncle Peter, but I've already explained, Patsy is a friend. She's been here all morning, preparing the food. And, with all due respect, I think you should remember this is *not* your house. Patsy will always be welcome here.'

Sucking air through his nose, he said crisply, 'In spite of her faults, your mother always had good manners. It's a pity you're not more like her.'

'We all have our faults, Uncle Peter. Yourself included, I'm sure.' The sly criticism of her mother hurt Eva deeply. Another time she might have taken issue with him, but not today. This was a day she wanted to remember with dignity. He was her uncle, after all, and he had come all the way from Canada to pay his respects. That at least called for a small measure of restraint.

'Very well,' he conceded with ill grace, 'if you insist she must stay, then I suppose she must.'

Eva's Aunt Margaret had seen and heard it all. Looking ashamed and worried, she gave Eva a nervous smile. Eva smiled back, and the poor woman relaxed.

When the two visitors had entered the house, Patsy spoke her mind with bruising honesty. 'Sly little sod. No wonder yer mammy didn't like him.'

Eva agreed. 'He worries me. I can't believe he's travelled all the way from Canada just to pay his respects.'

'Perhaps yer Aunt Margaret persuaded him to make the trip.'

They peered discreetly into the house, where Margaret was rushing about waiting on her husband, as though she was a servant and he the master. 'I don't think he'd come over here just because she asked him to, do you?' Eva said.

'Happen you're right.'

'Poor woman. She seems frightened of him.' Much like her own mother had grown frightened of her husband in the last two years.

When Peter turned and smiled at her through the window, Patsy whispered, 'Watch him, Eva. He's a bad divil.'

'I know what you mean, but don't worry,' Eva assured her. 'I'm a match for the likes of him.'

'What did he mean when he said you had important matters to discuss?' Patsy had always felt free to speak her mind with Eva.

'Your guess is as good as mine.' It had been years since Uncle Peter had visited England, and for a long time there had been no contact between their two families. Eva couldn't imagine what he had in mind, but one thing was certain, whatever he was up to, it would not be to her advantage. Though she was sure there was nothing he could do to hurt her, Eva couldn't help but feel threatened. He was too confident; too arrogant by half.

'Come on, Patsy,' she urged. 'We'd better go in.'

Patsy groaned. 'Jaysus, look at what he's done.' Raising her arm, she twisted it so she could see the elbow. 'The bugger's skinned my elbow on the wall.'

'It's not too bad, Patsy.' Eva deliberately made little of it. Taking out her handkerchief, she dabbed at the blood. 'There's some Germolene in the kitchen. That should take the sting out of it.' She helped Patsy brush the dust from her dress.

The entire episode had spanned only a few

minutes, but in that time Peter's two sons and the aged aunt had made their way into the house.

'Time to put my best face on,' Eva murmured as she and Patsy went in, 'though to tell the truth, I'd rather just be on my own to think things through.'

Patsy made no comment. She knew exactly what Eva meant, for hadn't she been through something very like it herself?

Peter was the first to greet her. 'You're slipping in your duties, my girl,' he announced with irritating authority. 'You should have been at the door to see everyone in.'

'I would have been if you hadn't caused such a fuss outside,' she reminded him. Turning to Patsy, she told her where to find the Germolene then, mindful of her duties, she approached the aged aunt.

Great-Aunt Judith was the sister of Eva's grandmother. 'How are you, my dear?' she said, greeting Eva with a half-smile. 'Margaret and I have been so worried about you. I couldn't believe it when I heard,' she added brokenly. 'God only knows how hard it must be for you.' In her late eighties now, Judith was small and wizened, with soft brown eyes and a halo of wispy silver hair. There was an air of serenity about her.

'You mustn't worry,' Eva replied fondly. 'I'll be all right.' Her gaze strayed to where Patsy was checking the food. 'Patsy has been a tower of strength to me, and it does help, you being here.'

'I did love your mother,' the old dear murmured. 'She was a sweet little thing, always singing, as I recall.'

Eva was too filled with emotion to speak.

Lost in her memories, the old woman went on, 'She was such a lovely little thing, much like yourself, my dear.' She stroked Eva's long fair hair. 'I remember when she and Margaret were girls. Margaret was the quiet one, while Colette was always up to mischief. Full of fun, she was.' Taking out a snow-white handkerchief, she shook open the newly ironed folds. 'Too young,' she whispered, noisily blowing her nose into the handkerchief. 'Your mammy was too young to be so cruelly struck down.' Big, sorrowful eyes looked at Eva. 'And I'm so old. It isn't right that I should outlive her.'

Eva put a comforting arm round her. 'Don't upset yourself,' she said gently. 'You'll only make me feel worse.'

'Oh, I wouldn't want to make things worse for you, my dear,' Judith answered, a little smile breaking through her tears. 'But . . . whatever will you do now, child?'

Taking hold of the old woman's hands, Eva replied in a quiet, reassuring voice, 'You mustn't forget I'm my mother's daughter.'

The old woman smiled. 'Not only in looks but in spirit too.'

'So you'll stop worrying?'

The old woman nodded.

When Eva leaned forward to kiss her, Judith clung to her. This was Colette's girl and, God willing, she would come to no harm.

———— ⊰⊙⊱ ————

B ILL TURNED FROM looking out of the window just at the moment when Eva and the old lady were embracing. When he saw them, the whisper of a smile touched his dark eyes. Then he lowered his gaze, thrust his hands into his pockets and strolled out of the house, into the sunshine.

Unaware of his attention, Eva drew away from her great-aunt, a bright smile lighting her features. 'Now, how would you like a big slice of cake? I made it last night – one of my mother's recipes.'

'Go on then,' the old woman replied. 'Not too big a slice though. My girdle's tight enough as it is.'

At the table, Margaret spoke to Eva. 'I'm not sure if we've done the right thing coming here,' she said. 'I did so want to see Colette again, but I never thought . . . never dreamed . . ,' She stopped, her voice quivering with emotion. A moment, that was all, and she had her feelings under control. 'I had no idea your Uncle Peter had kept in touch with someone at this end . . . a solicitor . . . name of Dollond, I think. It was he who passed on the awful news, and of course we had to come.' After pausing to gauge Eva's reaction, she continued in harsher tones, 'Your Uncle Peter has a secretive way with him. It can be very unsettling at times.'

Eva recalled Peter's remarks about 'matters of importance'. 'How do you mean exactly?' Somehow, she trusted Aunt Margaret.

'I'm not sure, only he can be devious.' It was obvious Margaret didn't know what was on Peter's mind either. 'I wouldn't blame you for not wanting us here. We're almost like strangers to you now.'

'You mustn't think like that,' Eva reassured her. 'I really am glad you came.' With the exception of Peter, she thought. He was better out of sight, out of mind.

'I'm sorry he behaved like that.' Margaret's gaze momentarily flicked to Peter. 'My husband can be a very difficult man when he sets his mind to it.'

'We're all a bit fraught.' Eva thought it only polite to make excuses for him.

Margaret looked at Eva for a moment, before saying in a soft, kindly voice, 'Peter is a selfish, arrogant man, and I'm more aware of that than most.'

Sensing her sadness, Eva changed the subject. 'I'd better make myself useful,' she said brightly. 'I promised Aunt Judith a piece of chocolate cake.'

'Then you mustn't keep her waiting.'

As Eva turned to go, Margaret called her back. 'Eva?'

'Yes?'

'Thank you.'

Eva nodded. There was obviously more to this family than met the eye; dangerous undercurrents. Margaret seemed a good woman. It was a pity she was tied to a man like Peter.

Eva cut a generous slice of chocolate cake for Judith. Todd, Margaret's younger son and the image of his father, was helping himself to a sausage roll. Eva greeted him politely and then made her way back to the old woman. She could feel Todd's eyes burning in the back of her neck. She didn't like him, any more than she liked his father.

She found Judith sound asleep in the armchair, head to one side, snoring gently.

'Will yer look at that?' Patsy remarked. Before Eva could protest, she took the plate of chocolate cake from her. 'I'll hide it,' she muttered. 'When they've all gone, we'll have it with a cup of tea.'

Silently, Eva wished they would *all* go soon, even Patsy, God bless her. The day seemed never-ending, and the thought of her parents weighed heavily in her heart. But it seemed no one was in a hurry to leave. For the next half-hour, the old woman slept on; Margaret asked Eva if she could see the family photograph album and, once engrossed in that, she was a world away. Deep in conversation, Peter and Todd stood in a corner of the room, far enough away from the others not to be heard.

Patsy busied herself toing and froing, and when

Eva came to help, she was banned from the kitchen. 'Will yer not be told? Tomorrow you can cook us a meal and wash up afterwards. Yer can go through the house like a dose o' salts and wash every curtain in the place if yer like.' Her voice took on a softer tone. 'Yer Aunt Margaret seems a kindly woman, so she does. Why don't yer talk to her? Sure she grew up with yer mammy, didn't she? Mebbe the pair of youse could help each other.'

Eva was leaning, arms folded, against the work-top, her gaze drawn outside to the rose garden, where her mother used to sit and be quiet after a long, hard day.

For a moment Patsy watched her, silent and saddened. She put a comforting arm round her shoulder. 'There's me blabbering away, and yer not even listening, are yer?'

Startled, Eva swung round. 'Sorry, Patsy. What did you say?'

'What I said was . . . Yer look worn out.' Gently she propelled Eva towards the door. 'Why don't yer go out and sit in the garden? It'll only take me a few minutes to clear this lot away. After-wards, I'll get us both a cool drink and we'll sit together for a while. What do yer say to that, eh?'

'I'd like that.' Suddenly she didn't want Patsy to go. Once the others had left and the house was empty, she would be alone. In all her life she had never been really alone. Her mother had always been there. And her father.

Patsy peeped through the door into the front room. 'Yer uncle and the young one are still whispering in the corner,' she told Eva. 'The old woman's still asleep and Margaret's crying over the photos. No sign of the handsome feller, though I don't suppose he's too far away.'

Eva felt ashamed. 'I don't know what he'll think of me, I haven't spoken two words with him yet.' Shyness engulfed her.

'He'll understand, so he will. He seems different from the others. Keeps to himself. I've seen him speaking to his mother and the old one, but he seems to be keeping his distance from the other two. Is there bad blood between him and his father, d'yer think?'

'There didn't used to be. Mind you, I wouldn't have noticed even if there was, not then. Whenever Aunt Margaret came to visit us, me and Bill would be outside. Winter or summer, it didn't matter, we'd fish in the brook or swing from the old crooked tree in the orchard.' The memories were vivid now, as was the affection she'd always had for him. 'We had a secret den in the barn, hidden away between the apple crates and the manure bags.'

'Stink, did yer?' Patsy wrinkled her nose. It was good to hear Eva reminiscing.

43

JOSEPHINE COX

Eva laughed. 'We did stink but we didn't care. You know how it is when you're kids. Mum used to ask where we'd been to get in such a state, but we never told.' It was all coming back, bringing a rush of joy to her heart. 'Oh, Patsy, we did have such good times then.'

'Fond of him, were yer?' Patsy's romantic heart melted. 'Childhood sweethearts and all that?'

Eva shook her head. 'We were only kids.' Her smile was revealing. 'Though I do remember that we used to talk about getting married when we grew up.'

'Did you miss him after he went to Canada?'

'Like mad.' Just for a fleeting moment she felt the pain she had felt then. 'For weeks I cried myself to sleep.'

'Did yer never hear from him again?'

'For a while, yes. When Aunt Margaret wrote to Mam, there'd be a little note inside from Bill. But, like I said, we were only kids, and kids soon forget.'

'*You* haven't.'

'No.' She never would. 'But then I never forget anything.' For a long time, she dreamed that Bill would come back and they could pick up where they'd left off. But that was just a childish dream. 'Anyway, after a time, Aunt Margaret stopped writing and that was that.'

'Why would yer Aunt Margaret stop writing?'

Eva hesitated. Something her mother had confided in her came back to her. 'I think Peter must have ordered her not to keep in touch.'

'Why would he do that?'

Eva shrugged her shoulders. 'Who knows?' She did know, but it wasn't wise to raise the past.

'You're keeping something back, aren't you?' Patsy was like a dog with a bone. 'If it's bad, it's better to share, then it can't hurt you, me darlin'.'

'Between you and me, and nobody else?' Eva knew Patsy would keep on until she'd found out the truth. 'I don't want it known outside these four walls.'

'Ah now, have yer ever known me to gossip?'

'No, I haven't.'

'So get it off yer chest.'

'It's just that Mam told me how Peter tried to flirt with her. No,' she corrected herself, 'it was more than that. He came here one day when Dad was out in the spinney. Mam was upstairs and heard him come in. When he called out, she told him to wait a minute and she'd be right down. But he didn't wait. Instead, he went upstairs and made a pass at her. He got his arms round her waist and tried to push her on to the bed. Mam put him in his place, and he never forgave her. You see, he was used to getting what he wanted.'

'He's even more of a bastard than I thought!'

Eva was quiet for a moment, before confiding, 'That was why he wouldn't let Aunt Margaret keep in touch, in case Mam told her. But she wouldn't have. That wasn't her way.'

'All the same, Margaret was yer mammy's sister. Why didn't she ignore him and write anyway? How would he ever find out?'

'I should imagine he watched her like a hawk. I don't expect things were easy. Just now, she told me he was devious and selfish.'

'I'm surprised he took the old one to Canada with them,' Patsy said caustically. 'He seems the sort who'd make arrangements to have her put down like an old dog. I mean, she'd be a burden, wouldn't she? He might have to feed and house her. My God, sure that's a terrible burden for a foine man to be lumbered with!'

Smiling, Eva shook her head. 'You don't mince your words, do you?' She regarded Patsy fondly. 'And you're right. I can't be certain, but I suppose at the time Aunt Judith was in her early seventies.' It was difficult to know. Aunt Judith's age had always been a bit of a mystery. 'Anyway, according to Mam, Margaret dug her heels in – "First time I've ever known Margaret stand up to him," that's what Mam said. Apparently there was quite a fuss. Aunt Margaret wanting one thing and Uncle Peter wanting another, with the poor old dear stuck between the two.'

'Families, eh?' Patsy tutted. 'Makes you wonder if it's all worth it.'

'Peter threatened to leave Aunt Margaret behind if she didn't toe the line.'

'So how did she persuade him to take Judith in the end?' Patsy leaned across the table, her homely face cradled in large, capable hands. 'Don't tell me, he realised that if Margaret stayed behind, he'd have to wait on himself and there'd be nobody for him to nag at. *That's* why he agreed to take the old woman after all, isn't it?'

'Wrong.'

'All right then, *Bill* threatened to stay behind, and your Uncle Peter hadn't got the guts to go it alone.'

'Wrong again.'

'Then why?'

'Money.'

'What money?'

'Aunt Judith's money. She had a bank account, and she owned her own house, two up, two down, on Hardwick Street. She planned to keep the house and rent it out, in case she didn't like it in Canada. Uncle Peter talked her out of that plan and put one of his own to her.'

'He's the devil's own, so he is!'

'Anyway, she sold the house and handed Uncle Peter a sizeable sum – an investment in his new business, that's what he told her.'

'Well now, she must be worth a bob or two because if he's anything to go by, the business must be doing all right.'

'I'm afraid not, Patsy.' Eva's face was grim. 'The business collapsed and she lost the lot. Aunt Margaret wrote and told Mam how bad it was, and how they might have to come home. But somehow, Uncle Peter got financial backing for another business and he's never looked back.'

'Did he ever repay the old woman?'

'I should think that would be the last thing on his mind.' Eva glanced towards the living room. Satisfied there was no one nearby, she went on, 'This is a clever, cunning man. When he drew up the agreement with Aunt Judith, I dare say he made sure that if anything should go wrong, he wouldn't be held responsible.'

'The man's a bastard, so he is!'

Eva wholeheartedly agreed. Talking about him left a bad taste in her mouth. 'I'm neglecting my duties,' she said. 'I'd better go in and be sociable.'

'Sure they haven't even missed yer.' Once again, Patsy steered Eva towards the back door. 'If they want yer, they know where to find yer. So be off now. I'll follow yer in a few minutes, so I will.'

EVA MADE STRAIGHT for the rose garden. For a while she strolled round it, picking off dead flowerheads and dropping them into a plant pot, the way her beloved mother used to do.

After a while she paused and smiled, her tear-filled eyes raised to the sky. 'Look at me, Mam,' she murmured. 'Following in your footsteps, bringing you as close to me as I can.'

All day she had kept back the heartache, making herself remember the good times and keeping her mind on the family who had gathered here. Now, though, hugging the plant pot close to her breast, she bowed her head and let the heartache take its course.

Sobs racked her body and tears ran down her face. There was so much pain inside. Her mother, and her father, were gone for ever, and she was left with only the earthly things they had left behind. Suddenly the world was incredibly lonely and frightening. How would she cope? What would she do without the love and companionship of that dear, darling woman?

She chided herself for being selfish. What about her mother? So young and vital, with much of her own life before her. And what about her father? Maybe in the fullness of time he would have become a better, kinder man. Now she would never know. But it was her mother she yearned for.

'Wherever you are,' she murmured, 'I'll always

love you, every day, every minute for the rest of my life. But what now? What will I do without you, Mam?'

'*You'll be strong, like you always were, like she would want you to be.*'

Startled, Eva swung round, almost falling into Bill's arms. 'I'm sorry.' Embarrassed and ashamed, she didn't know what to say.

For a moment he didn't reply. Instead he gazed down into those troubled green eyes and his heart went out to her. He had loved Eva when she was small and he loved her now. When the time was right, he would tell her that, but for now she needed comfort, that was all. 'I heard you crying,' he said, 'and I couldn't walk away.' He held on to her, his hands warm and strong about her shoulders. 'I'll go if you want me to,' he offered. 'I'll understand if you'd rather be alone.'

With the smallest of movements she shook her head. 'Please stay.' His nearness was comforting. In that moment when she saw him there, it was as if they were children again. The perfume of roses filled the air and the birds sang, and as they stood there, each heart was filled with joy. 'It's good to see you, Bill,' Eva said, and his slow, easy smile carried her back over the years.

'It's good to see you too,' he replied, 'but I wish it was under different circumstances.'

She glanced down, the grief overwhelming her.

'Eva?'

She looked up, her eyes moist but on her face a look of determination. 'I'd better go back inside.' Her instincts warned her that her uncle was watching her every move. The last thing she wanted was to be less than her mother would have expected. But it was so good to be here in the garden where her mother had been happy, and with Bill beside her she felt a kind of peace she hadn't felt for a long time.

'Don't go back inside just yet.' Gesturing to a rough-bark seat Bill said, 'We could sit and talk over old times. Or just stroll round the garden if you'd rather.' She was so vulnerable, he wanted to put off the moment when he must burden her with more bad news.

'I don't suppose a few more minutes will matter,' Eva decided. 'Let's sit and talk.' Already she was feeling better. It was almost as though her mother was watching and had sent an old friend to ease her grief.

As they walked to the bench, Eva sneaked a glance at him. He had always been a good-looking boy and now he was a handsome man. He still had the same dark, laughing eyes he had had as a boy, though they were sombre right now.

'I'd know you in a crowd,' she said as they sat down.

'Oh? I expect what you really mean is I still

look like that snotty-nosed, raggy-arsed kid you used to chase.'

'That's right,' she said with a laugh. 'You do.'

Patsy was on her way with the cold drinks, but seeing them laughing together, she turned on her heel and made her way back to the kitchen. 'They're in love and don't even know it.' She smiled to herself, then promptly drank both glasses of lemonade.

Bill took hold of Eva's hand. 'I'm so sorry, Eva. Is there anything you'd like me to do? Anything at all?'

'I'm all right,' Eva told him. 'I'm grateful for your offer but there's nothing you can do to help me – nothing *anyone* can do.' Taking a deep breath she told him in a firm voice, 'But you were right when you said I must be strong. I have to get on with my life, just as she would want me to.'

'I know you will,' he said. 'I remember what a determined little thing you were. Whenever we got in trouble, you always insisted on having your share of the punishment.'

She laughed at that. 'You hated it, didn't you? How I'd always own up just when you'd taken all the blame.'

'You were always such an independent little madam.'

'And you always wanted to be my knight in shining armour.'

'I often recall our little adventures,' he said with a smile. 'They were the best part of my growing up.'

'Mine too.' It was such a pity that life had to change.

'Did you know I married?' There was no use hiding the fact.

Taken aback, Eva concealed her disappointment. 'No, but I'm not surprised. Did you bring her with you?'

'She wasn't able to come. Other commitments and all that.'

'I see.' Eva understood. Funerals were difficult, especially when you didn't know the family.

'Eva?' He looked into her face and wanted to hold her tight. But she wasn't his, and they were not children any more.

'What is it, Bill?'

He took a deep breath, ready to explain, but then he stalled a moment longer. 'As I recall, you were always a loner. You said it was hard to make friends. Is it still like that, Eva?'

Eva thought for a moment. It was true what Bill said. As a child she saw very few children of her own age, and on the odd occasion when she did, they seemed so confident and self-assured that she felt inadequate. When she started school, it wasn't any easier, though she desperately wanted to be part of a group, or to find a friend of her own.

'Yes, it's still the same,' she answered. 'I wasn't blessed with the knack of making friends. But I'm luckier than most.'

'Why is that?' He couldn't take his eyes off her. Oh, but she was so delightful. Much prettier than he remembered, and with such a gentle, lovely nature.

'I've had three wonderful friends in my life,' she said. 'My mother. You. And Patsy.' She sighed, a flicker of sadness crossing her features. 'First of all, *you* went. Now my darling mam's gone.' A small smile brightened her face. 'But I still have Patsy who I love dearly. She's like my own sister.'

A frown creased his forehead. 'Patsy? Oh, she's the one who fell asleep on the doorstep, right?'

Eva nodded. 'I know what you're thinking. That I should find a more responsible friend, more my own age.'

'Not at all. A friend is a friend, and should be cherished. Tell me about her.'

'Her name is Patsy Noonan.' Eva chuckled. 'Irish as the Blarney Stone, she is.'

Bill laughed. 'She doesn't mince her words, I know that. I heard her giving my father a piece of her mind, and my God he deserved it.'

Eva was surprised. 'You heard?'

He nodded. 'I didn't intervene because I didn't think you'd thank me for it, and anyway the two of you were giving him a hard enough time as it was.' Delight lit his face. 'It did my heart good, I can tell you.'

'You were right not to intervene. I prefer to fight my own battles.'

'Oh, and don't I know it!' He reminded her of the time they had made a den in the middle of a neighbouring farmer's cornfield. When the farmer ran them off, Eva pelted him with rotten apples. 'He told your dad about it in the pub the next night, and everyone had a laugh. The farmer said he thought you were too dangerous to be let loose.'

For a precious moment their laughter brought them closer together. Then he spoke softly. 'Eva, there is something you must know. Something I must tell you before you go back inside.' The time was right.

Eva looked into his eyes. 'I'm listening.' She wondered if he was about to open his heart to her, tell her how he felt the same way she did. With him so near, it was as if no time had passed and the same strong bond that had drawn them together all those years ago was still there. Still wonderful.

He might have told her just that. He might have told her far more. But, for the moment at least, there were other, more pressing issues. 'Two days ago, I learned something you need to be aware of,' he began. But before he could go on, they were interrupted.

'Eva! Eva, where are you?' Todd's voice cut

through the air. 'Oh, there you are.' Approaching from the direction of the house, he ran towards them, a small, hard-faced young man, wearing a false smile over his air of self-importance; and as he came nearer, it crossed Eva's mind that his father must have looked exactly like that when he was the same age.

'What is it, Todd?' He made her feel as if she had been caught out like a naughty girl hiding away. 'I was just coming back to the house,' she said guiltily.

She was about to get up but Bill reached out to restrain her. 'Not yet,' he softly pleaded. 'There are things you need to know.'

Realising Bill's intention, Todd stepped between them.

'What is it you want?' Bill demanded, glaring at him.

Addressing himself to Eva, Todd explained, 'Father's been looking everywhere for you. He needs to see you now.'

'Well, he'll just have to wait, won't he?' Bill knew why his father wanted to talk to Eva, and it fired his anger.

Still addressing Eva, Todd told her, 'He said to tell you it can't wait, that we have to be away soon.'

In a quiet, firm manner, Bill said, 'Tell him Eva will be along in a few minutes. We have things to discuss first.'

Sensing the tension between the two brothers, Eva intervened. 'It's all right, Bill. Really. We can talk after I've heard what your father wants.' A quick, intimate smile lit her eyes. 'That is, if you still want to.' She couldn't be certain. After all, a lot of water had passed under the bridge since last they met.

He nodded. 'I'd like that,' he said, and the words came from his heart, although he couldn't help wondering if Eva would want to talk once she learned what his father had to say to her. 'I'll wait for you,' he promised.

'Thank you. I'm sure I won't be too long.'

As Todd hurried her away, Bill's face was grim. 'Don't let him destroy you,' he murmured.

<hr>

PETER WAS WAITING in the sitting room, alone. Eva wondered if he'd purposely cleared the room, waking Great-Aunt Judith in the process. His hands were thrust deep into his pockets and his back was to the fire. His face was red from the heat. 'Come in, my dear,' he said as Eva stepped into the room, followed by Todd. Peter gestured to the armchair. 'No need to stand to attention. Make yourself comfortable.'

Eva declined. 'If you don't mind, I'll stand. Just say what you have to say.' There was something about him . . . She felt he was nursing some kind of secret, and it had to do with her, she was certain. It irked her, too, the way he stood with his back to the fire, inviting her to sit in her own chair, in her own house. The man was too arrogant for words.

'Very well,' he conceded, 'though I think it might be better if you sat down.' A smile crept over his shrewish features. 'I'm afraid I have some rather unpleasant news for you.'

'I'm listening.' She sounded calm and composed, but inside her stomach was churning.

'As you wish.' He began pacing up and down. 'It's to do with your future, my dear,' he began. 'What had you in mind, now that your parents are . . . well, now that you're all alone here?'

'Why, carry on of course,' Eva answered without hesitation. 'My parents built up a good business here. I have no intention of throwing it all away.'

'A few acres and a small farm shop – what is it you sell? Eggs, kindling and whatever else you can coax out of this godforsaken land?' Peter's chest puffed out as he began strutting once more. 'Hardly a good business, my dear.'

'Good enough for my parents, and good enough for me. This godforsaken land, as you call it, has provided well for a family of three all these years.'

'Then you must consider yourself fortunate, my dear.' Suddenly he was looking at her in a different way. This was *his* child; born out of rape and lust. If it had suited his purpose to hurt her with the dreadful truth, he would have taunted her with it, but there was nothing to be gained. With a darkened expression and a cutting edge to his voice he said, 'It's time for you to leave all this behind and start a new life.'

Infuriated, Eva replied in a cold, quiet voice, 'I think that's for *me* to decide. This little business might not measure up to your high standards, but it's what I want.' She stepped forward. 'I'm grateful that you saw fit to attend my parents' funeral, but now I think it's time for you to leave.'

'That, my dear, is for me to decide, to echo your own words. There are matters here that need attending to.' He raised his hands to encompass the room.

'What do you mean?'

'None of this is yours. Not the land, or the house, or even the sad little business.' His sly smile enveloped her. 'It's *mine*, my dear. It always has been.' The price he paid for taking Colette by force was to continue providing the roof over their heads. Now though, with Colette gone, he owed this girl nothing.

Eva's face went white with shock. 'You're lying! How can it be yours? My parents bought this house soon after they were married. I've lived here all my life.'

He shook his head. 'Nothing is ever what it seems.'

'I don't believe you.'

'Then you must see your solicitor. He knows the truth.' Impatient now, he strode past her to the door. 'I won't turn you out here and now,' he said over his shoulder, 'but I'll be back tomorrow evening, eight o'clock sharp, by which time I'll expect you to be packed and ready to hand over the keys.'

When he had gone, Eva went to the window and looked out over the land that her mother had loved. 'It can't be true,' she whispered. 'Mam would have told me.' Beneath the big old oak, she could see Bill in angry conversation with his father. Now she knew what he had been trying to tell her. 'He's lying!' she whispered over and over. 'He's lying!' And yet somehow she knew he was not.

'He's *not* lying,' Todd's voice said in her ear. 'I've seen the papers. It all belongs to him.' She swung round, to find his gloating face inches from her own. He dared to put his hand on her shoulder. 'I have some influence with my father,' he murmured. 'Be nice to me, and I'll see what I can do.'

Before Eva could reply, he was violently jerked away. Bill had him by the scruff of the neck. 'I ought to thrash you good and proper, but this is not the time or the place. This is *still* Eva's home, and you'd do well to remember why we're here!' And with that, Bill marched his brother to the door. Todd twisted to glare at Eva. 'It won't be your home for long, not if I know my father!'

'We'll see about that,' Bill hissed. 'He has me to reckon with yet!' With a shove he pushed Todd out of the room. Turning to Eva, he apologised. 'I'm sorry about that. But I meant what I said, I'll do everything in my power to stop him.'

'I can't believe it,' Eva said. 'How could your father get possession of this house? When? And why wasn't I told?'

'I'm sorry, Eva, I can't answer any of your questions. I only found out about this business the day before we arrived, and that was only by accident when I heard the two of them discussing it.' Bill crossed the room and took her hand in his. 'I've tried to reason with him, even offered to buy it from him for you. But he won't listen. For some reason, he flatly refuses any offer I make.' He squeezed her hand. 'But I won't let him get the better of you, Eva. Somehow or other, I'll make certain that you keep what's rightfully yours.'

'Dear Bill, still my knight in shining armour,' Eva said with a brave smile. Then her shoulders slumped. 'I don't understand any of this.'

'Neither do I.' Bill thought back to the journey from Canada, the way Todd and his father had huddled together, furtively plotting. 'What really puzzles me is the way he's gone right against his business instincts. Money is his god. I've made him an offer over and above what he could hope to get for this property on the open market and yet still he refuses.'

'That's because he's a bastard!' As soon as she'd said it, Eva felt ashamed. 'I'm sorry, I shouldn't have said that. When all's said and done, he's still your father.'

'He's *not* my father.' Unsettled, Bill moved away, standing for a while with his back to the blackened chimney. 'I was adopted. I never learned to love him, but I adore Margaret. She's been the mother I never had.' His voice shook. 'He's been a swine to her. I've tried time and again to persuade her to leave him, but she never would – never will.'

Eva's heart went out to him. 'Some women are like that. However badly they're treated, they stay with their man through thick and thin. My mother was like that. She said that when you gave your marriage vows before God, you were duty bound to live by them, especially if there were children involved.'

'Make your bed and lie on it, eh?' he said wryly. 'You don't know what it's been like, seeing her buckle under to his every demand. All these years he's chipped away at her confidence until now she's just a shadow of her old self. The peculiar thing is, when I was man enough to challenge him, Margaret took his side and I found myself out on the streets.' His lip curled. 'Seems I read the situation wrong.'

'She loves you though.' Anyone could see that. 'More than she loves her own son, I think.'

'Why am I telling you all this?'

'Because old friends should be able to tell each other everything.' She deeply valued these moments with him.

Bill made no reply. Instead, he cupped Eva's face in his hands, smiling into her eyes with the look of a man in love. But then, just as she was about to speak, he shifted his gaze and went on. 'Todd has never been any comfort to her,' he confided. 'He's moulded in his father's image. The older he gets, the more he admires him, and the more like him he becomes.'

'I can see that.'

Bill sighed. 'There's something odd here though, Eva. My father's a wealthy man, with more land and property than he knows what to do with. He doesn't need this house, or the land.' He hesitated. 'It's almost as though . . .' He wasn't quite sure how to put into words what he was feeling.

Eva finished his sentence for him. 'Almost as though he has a grudge against me, is that what you're trying to say?' The same thought had occurred to her.

'But it doesn't make any sense.'

'All the same, you're right. It's as though he's trying to punish me.'

'But you were just a child the last time he saw you. What reason would he have for wanting to punish *you*?'

'I think I may know why. There was a time when he took a fancy to my mam, and when she turned

63

him down he was furious.' That was as much as her mother had admitted; praying the awful truth would never emerge.

'But he can't blame you for that.' He wasn't surprised by what Eva had told him. In Vancouver where they lived, his father's weakness for other women was no secret – except maybe to his wife.

'No, he can't blame me,' Eva said, 'but maybe he thinks that by repossessing her home and throwing me out, he's getting his revenge on her.'

Bill nodded. 'It's the sort of thing he might stoop to.'

'I can't help thinking there's something else, though,' she said quietly. 'Why would he hold a grudge all this time? And why did he wait until now to make his move? If he really does own this house as he claims, why didn't he throw us out long ago, while Mam was still alive? That would have hurt her deeply. It has to do with me, I'm sure of it.'

'I think you're wrong. I think it's more to do with his obsession with power. I know it's difficult, Eva, but please, for your own peace of mind, try not to dwell on it for now. You've been through so much already.' He raised her face to his. 'This house, the land, it's very important to you, isn't it?'

Too choked for words, she nodded, her eyes appealing to him.

'Don't worry,' he murmured. 'One way or another we'll get to the bottom of it. For now, let's just concentrate on keeping him at arm's length.' His expression hardened. 'He won't have it all his own way, Eva, I can promise you that.'

Eva squared her small shoulders. 'And I promise, whatever happens, he will never have the satisfaction of bringing me down.'

Bill looked at the way she stood, head high, determination shining from her, and he knew he would never love her more than he did at this moment. 'I've no doubt you're a match for him,' he said, a smile creeping over his handsome features, 'and I've no doubt you mean to leave your mark on him.' The smile gave way to a frown. 'But you must never underestimate him, Eva. I know him too well. He's a very clever, dangerous man.'

'I'm not afraid of him.' Though, there *was* the tiniest part of her that quailed at the thought that he might know something about her that she didn't. 'First thing in the morning I mean to go into Bedford and see the solicitor. Everything my parents ever did was through Dollond and Travers in Ainsworth Street. If anyone can get to the bottom of this, they can.'

'That's very wise,' he agreed, 'but don't be too disheartened if you don't get any joy from them.' He winked conspiratorially. 'I have a few ideas of my own.'

'No, Bill.' For her aunt's sake, Eva hated the idea of deepening the rift in the family. 'I'm not ungrateful, but this is something I have to do on my own.'

'Trust me, Eva.'

'I do trust you.'

'Good!' Taking her by surprise, he kissed her on the mouth. 'Tomorrow night, eight o'clock,' he promised, 'we'll be waiting for him.' And with those few words, he departed, leaving Eva softly touching her lips. His kiss had been a disturbingly pleasant sensation.

IN THE MORNING, Eva and Patsy prepared to drive into Bedford. Eva swore when the car wouldn't start. 'I wish our money could have stretched to a more reliable one,' she groaned. 'But I suppose beggars can't be choosers.' Impatient, she gave the car a kick.

When, with a shuddering sigh, it burst into life, she looked at Patsy and laughed. 'I wonder if a good kick up the backside would do the same for you?'

Patsy was never at her best first thing. 'Fancy dragging me outta bed this time of a morning. Are yer trying to kill me or what?'

'What's wrong with you?' Eva asked, amused. 'It was gone six when I woke you. You've been up earlier than that before.'

'Oh aye! After a drop too much o' the good stuff and the bed won't keep still.'

'Stop moaning and look for a parking place.'

'Look yerself, yer bossy young bugger!' Patsy was thirty, going on ninety. 'I'm that tired, I can't see a hand in front o' me.' As she sank down into the car seat, her bleary eyes peered at the dashboard clock. 'Will yer look at that!'

'What?' Eva kept her eyes on the road.

'It's still only quarter past eight, so it is. What an uncivilised hour for a lady like meself.'

In spite of her worries, Eva had to laugh. 'Some lady. Take a look at yourself in the mirror. Go on!' She glanced at Patsy's sleepy face and unkempt hair. 'You look like something the cat dragged in.'

Patsy stole a look at herself in the vanity mirror, and sure enough she gave herself a fright. 'Ah, sure, I can't be perfect *all* the time!'

'You did insist on coming with me, remember. I would have told you all about it when I got back. After all, I'm fighting for your home as well as mine. If he takes the land, he takes your cottage too. We mustn't forget that.'

'I know.' Patsy glanced in the mirror for a second time. 'And yer right, I do look like something the cat dragged in. But don't you worry, give me a minute an' yer won't believe yer eyes.' Spitting into the palms of her hands, she ran her hands over her hair to flatten it until it looked like an ill-fitting cap. 'There! That's better. Now for a bit of lipstick. Where's yer bag, me darlin'?' Without waiting for an answer, she plucked Eva's handbag from the back seat and began rummaging. 'Jaysus! You've got everything in here but the back door.'

While Patsy groomed herself, Eva negotiated the narrow entrance into the car park. There was one space. 'That's lucky.' Reversing into it, she shifted the car out of gear and switched off the engine. 'You don't have to come in if you don't want to.' Turning to Patsy, she had a shock. 'Good God! Whatever have you done to yourself?'

Patsy's red hair had a mind of its own and it took more than spittle to keep it down. Like a mass of coiled springs that had been suppressed for too long, it framed her head like an electrified halo. Her lips and teeth were covered with lipstick and her long lashes clotted with mascara.

'Oh, Patsy!' Eva didn't know whether to laugh or cry.

'What? Yer don't think it suits me? The truth now, how do I look?'

'Different.' Biting her lips, Eva managed to stem her laughter. 'Yes, that's it. You look different.'

For a long, anxious moment, Patsy examined herself in the mirror. Then, with a solemn face, she turned and stared at Eva. 'I look like a circus clown,' she said, the grin erupting into laughter.

A short time later, sobered by the purpose of their journey, the two of them made their way to the High Street and up towards Ainsworth Street.

'If I remember rightly, their offices are just past the church.'

'Are you sure they'll see us?'

'No, but I'm hoping they can fit us in before they start their appointments for the day. That's why I wanted to get here early. I knew I wouldn't have a hope of getting an appointment at such short notice.'

As it turned out, Eva's instinct was right.

'Ten minutes, Miss Bereton, that's all I can spare. Sit yourself down, before I change my mind.' Thomas Dollond was an elderly man, with a sharp mind and a kind, round face. When the two of them were seated, he carefully eased his old bones into his chair; Eva wasn't certain whether the loud, creaking sound was him or the chair.

'We wouldn't have come without an appointment,' Eva said, 'only it's very urgent.' Patsy tugged at her sleeve. 'Oh, I'm sorry, this is Patsy Noonan.'

'Really?' His surprise betrayed itself for only a second. 'Ah yes, Miss Noonan has been doing your mother's accounts for some time. She also works in the farm shop and rents the field cottage.'

'You know a great deal.' It was Eva's turn to be surprised. As far as she knew, it was some time since her mother had visited these offices.

Patsy didn't know whether to be flattered or annoyed. 'Who told you all that?' she asked him.

'A solicitor is paid to know these things,' he said importantly. Adjusting his spectacles, he added, 'Incidentally, your account ledgers are a pleasure to the eye. Meticulously kept, as I recall, and very commendable, especially as I believe you are not a qualified accountant.' What a wild-looking thing she was, he thought. Not at all what he'd imagined from her neat work. 'Mrs Bereton told me how highly she valued you.'

Turning his attention to Eva, he said, 'You say the matter is urgent?'

'Desperately.'

Leaning back in his chair, he nodded like one of those monkeys on a stick. 'I know about your parents,' he said sympathetically, 'and I'm very sorry. In fact, I dictated a letter only yesterday but in view of the delicate situation I thought it best to delay sending it.'

Eva sat bolt upright. 'What letter?'

He cleared his throat. There were moments when he hated his job. This was one of those moments. 'It's to do with the property, but I think you already know that, don't you?' He was visibly uncomfortable. 'Isn't that why you're here?'

'My uncle says the property is his.' Eva hardly dared go on, afraid of the answer to the question she had to ask. 'It isn't true, is it?'

He sighed.

'I'm sorry,' Mr Dollond's voice was filled with

genuine regret, 'your uncle has owned the property for many years. Long before he went to Canada, in fact.'

'But my parents bought it before he went.' At least that was what she had always believed.

He shook his head slowly. 'Your uncle purchased the property when your parents went through a period of financial difficulty. Your parents then became paying tenants. The agreement was drawn up in this very office. I myself oversaw the trans- action and was given responsibility for its smooth running over the years.' Getting out of his chair, he went to the filing cabinet and took out a buff-coloured file. 'It's all here,' he said, seating himself to thumb through the file. 'Deeds, rental agreement made by your parents, records of pay- ments and such.'

'May I see?'

'Of course.' Handing her the file he explained, 'Your uncle rang me the day he arrived. He was most adamant that, should you ask to see proof of his ownership, as he believed you might, I must have all documents readily available.'

Patsy had heard enough. 'Mercenary bastard!' she muttered.

Mr Dollond leaned forward. 'I sincerely hope you don't mean me, young lady?' Thirty she might be, but compared to him she was a mere babe in arms.

'Er, no, sir.' Patsy went red with embarrassment. 'I meant Eva's uncle from Canada.' Her embarrassment didn't last long. '*He's* the mercenary bastard!'

The old gent smiled. 'Then, as long as you don't quote me outside these four walls, I wholeheartedly agree. The fellow is a scoundrel!' Such a personal comment went against his many years of professional discipline. But he was due to retire soon and these days he found himself speaking his mind more and more.

Eva perused the file. With every page her heart sank deeper. At last, despairing, she handed back the file. 'All this time,' she murmured, 'and I never knew it was all his.'

'I'm sorry, but he has the right to evict you.'

'Is there nothing I can do?' Eva felt close to tears.

'I'm afraid so.' He dared not give her any false hopes. 'I've spoken with your uncle at great length. He's adamant he won't keep you as tenant.' He ventured an idea. 'Perhaps *you* might be able to persuade him.'

'I would rather die.'

'Then I'm afraid there is nothing to be done. The harsh truth is, your uncle is here to reclaim his property and I'm duty bound to assist.'

Eva wondered why he was 'duty bound'. If he really didn't want to act on behalf of her uncle, he should say so. To her mind, he was no better than her uncle. Money was a powerful leveller, she thought cynically.

'I tried everything,' he said. 'I did think he might let you buy the property from him but he flatly refuses to sell any part of it, to you or to anyone else.'

'Not even to Bill.' Her mind kept harking back to him; her heart too.

'I'm sorry, I didn't hear that.'

'His son, Bill – adopted son,' she corrected herself. 'He made a very generous offer for the property and was refused.' Eva would always be grateful to him for trying. 'Bill is a good man. He had an idea that he could buy it and then sell it to me at a price I could afford. But my uncle would have none of it.'

'I see. Well, I'm afraid it only confirms what I've said. For whatever reason, he means to reclaim this property for himself.'

'Can I fight him through the courts? Tenants' rights or something like that?' She was grasping at straws.

He shook his head. 'A waste of time. It was your parents who were the tenants, not you.'

'What if I refuse to budge?'

Patsy answered her. 'The bugger will send in the bailiffs and have you thrown out, and your belongings behind you.'

'She's right, I'm afraid.' Nodding his head in that peculiar way of his, Mr Dollond added grimly,

'In the end he will win, and you'll be left with bitter memories.' He seemed embarrassed. 'You probably think I'm as heartless as your uncle, but it isn't that simple. Unfortunately, your parents and I were bound by the same agreement and now, however unpleasant it might be, it's left to me to tie up all the loose ends.'

In fact there were very few 'loose ends'. He had kept the records straight over the years, and Colette Bereton had looked after the house and land exceedingly well. Her loving care of the place had greatly added to its value. To his mind, Peter Westerfield's spiteful treatment of Colette's daughter bordered on wickedness. But who knew what lay behind the man's decision, and anyway, who was he to question it, especially when he was being paid, and had been paid, very handsomely indeed?

Eva was silent. It seemed like only a heart-beat ago she had a father and a mother, a home and security; and Patsy, too, had been settled and content for the first time in years. Now it was all being snatched away, and there was nothing she could do to stop it. 'I'm sorry you couldn't help,' she said eventually. 'I'm sorry we've wasted your time, and ours.' There was bitterness in her voice, and a certain amount of condemnation.

'I'm sorry too.' Getting out of his chair, Mr Dollond came round to sit on the desk in front of her. 'I *have* tried to reason with your uncle.'

'I'm sure you have.' Eva relented. 'I don't hold you responsible for any of this, though I wish I hadn't been kept in the dark all this time.'

'Look, I may be an experienced solicitor, but I'm also an old man coming towards the end of his career. I'm fortunate to have children and grand-children, and it would break my heart to see them treated in the shocking way your uncle is treat-ing you.' He coughed and scratched his chin, and seemed to be struggling with his thoughts. 'I've been more fortunate than most. I own a few acres of land, and a small cottage set aside for the new gardener. But he isn't due to start for a month. You're welcome to stay there for a few weeks. It will give you breathing space, time to think and make plans.'

'Thank you. It's a very generous offer and I'm truly grateful.' Eva was deeply touched by his gesture. 'But I can't accept.' It was no solution. She had to stand on her own two feet or she might never move forward.

'But what will you do?' Suddenly he felt guilty. Had he really done enough to help her? More to the point, in view of the huge fee he was being paid, had he really wanted to?

'I'm not quite sure what I'll do,' Eva answered softly. 'But one thing I do know.' She stood up then, her shoulders straight, her expression harder than Patsy had ever seen it. 'My uncle can take the roof from over my head and leave me destitute, but he will never break my spirit.'

The old man admired her courage. 'I can believe that,' he said, 'but it's a sorry day when families fall out among themselves. Still, once he's returned to Canada, I don't suppose you'll ever need to have any contact with him again.'

Eva looked solemn. 'There are things here I still don't understand, but I will. One day, I'll find out the reason behind his spite. Meanwhile, just as it's up to you to tidy up all the loose ends, it's up to me to prevent *him* from ever again setting foot in my mother's house.' Her quiet smile was unnerving.

'What do you mean by that? I've already told you what will happen if you insist on staying there. He'll have no choice but to send in the bailiffs and they can be very aggressive – and they have the law on their side!'

Digging into her purse, she asked, 'How much do I owe you?'

'Well, nothing . . . I mean . . .' Her calm, collected manner flustered him.

Eva closed her purse. 'Thank you for your time,' she said and left the office with Patsy before he could say another word.

➤➤●◄◄

'WHERE *will* we go?' Subdued by the outcome, Patsy was only now beginning to realise the seriousness of their situation.

Once outside the office, Eva slowed her steps. 'I don't know,' she admitted. 'We need to talk about it – what to do, which direction to go. We need to pool what resources we have and draw up some kind of budget.'

'Ah, sure, *I* can do that.' Patsy was beginning to feel useful. 'But it's the *other* things. I don't own much more than the clothes on me back, but there's some lovely things belonging to your mam in that cottage, and in the house too. And what about all her precious ornaments? That delightful little clock that sits on the mantelpiece and chimes the quarter hour, all her blue china, and the wooden dolphin yer daddy carved for her when you were born?'

Eva smiled at that. Her mother had told her how he had sat, night after night, working on that dolphin. Oh, but he must have loved her in those early days.

'Yer mammy wouldn't want yer to leave that behind.'

Drawn into the past, and deeply troubled by the present, Eva lapsed into silence.

Patsy gabbled on. 'We'll have to ask your uncle for time to send in the removal van. We can't leave it all behind. The bugger would only sell it for what he could get, and you'd never see a penny of it!'

'I'll see to it, Patsy. Don't worry.' Eva didn't want to talk about it right now. What she needed was time to think, to get her mind in order. So much had happened and it was all bearing down on her, like a great, heavy weight.

'Such lovely things,' Patsy persisted. 'Yer uncle will *have* to give us time to get them out, so he will.'

'I don't want any favours from him.' Eva's heart ached. 'Besides, they're just things. Holding on to them won't bring her back, will it?' Mr Dollond had been her last hope; now it was all up to her. Even Patsy was counting on her to forge a future for them both. The more Eva thought about it, the more she wondered if she was up to the responsibility.

Patsy linked her arm through Eva's. 'No, me darlin',' she conceded, 'having her things won't bring yer mammy back. Nothing will. But we have each other, and that's something to be grateful for, isn't it?'

Eva clasped her hand over the podgy fingers. 'Oh, Patsy,' her eyes shone with affection, 'you're all I have now. And you're right, about the furniture and things. I have no intention of leaving them for him to get his hands on. They belonged to my parents, their lives were wrapped up in them.'

Shrugging, she gave a deep sigh. 'I can't leave them, and I can't take them. We have to travel light. We don't even know where we're going, or how we'll earn a living, or even whether we'll have a roof over our heads.'

'You make it sound frightening.'

'We'll be all right,' Eva said confidently. 'We're not afraid of hard work, and we've done all manner of things – accounting, stock-keeping, running a shop, maintaining a smallholding. Besides, we're young and strong enough to tackle anything.'

Patsy laughed out loud. '*You* might be young,' she cried, 'but I'm way past my prime and far too fat to *tackle* things.'

'Give over, Patsy. You're only thirty.'

'Well, I'm still too fat.'

'I shouldn't worry too much about that,' Eva grinned. 'If we have to starve for a few days, the weight will fall off you.'

'I don't intend to starve, I can tell you that now,' Patsy said stoutly. She loved her food.

'You know, Patsy, I really believed the solicitor would say my uncle was lying and that everything was all right.'

'But it isn't, is it?'

'To tell you the truth, Patsy, I am frightened.'

Patsy was shocked. 'Sure, I never thought I'd see the day when you were frightened of *anything*.'

'Deep down, we're all frightened of something.'

And for once, Patsy didn't argue. She, more than anyone, knew the wisdom of those words.

⟶•⟵

B Y LATE AFTERNOON, Patsy had divided her worldly possessions between a small suitcase and a cardboard box. 'Well, that's it,' she declared, carrying them to the car. 'Where do you want them?'

'Stack them in the car boot with my stuff.' Eva stared at the suitcase and box. 'Is that all?' she asked. 'Are you sure you haven't forgotten anything?'

Patsy shook her head. 'It's all there.' She swung the suitcase up and into the back of the boot, then wedged the box on top. 'Anyway, I thought you said we had to travel light.'

'Oh, look at that!' Eva pointed to the top of the copper beech and there, trembling on the lower branches, two baby pigeons were preparing for flight. 'Aren't they lovely?'

'Ugly, yer mean. I've never seen such ugly things as baby pigeons.'

Captivated, Eva couldn't take her eyes off them. 'Oh, Patsy, look again,' she urged. 'Look at their bright, shining eyes and fluffy new feathers, and think of the courage it takes to fly off into the unknown.' She would miss it here, in this lovely, quiet place.

Patsy looked again at the birds. 'Well, mebbe.

But you would be excited, wouldn't yer? I know how long you've waited for them birds to fledge. Now they're ready to leave, yer must be feeling like a mother hen, watching her babies take to the skies.'

'They're ready to spread their wings, just like us.'

Patsy felt a great sadness. She wasn't at all ready to spread her wings. In her lifetime, she had travelled to many places, and whenever she moved on, it had always been with a sense of adventure and excitement. But not this time. This time she had put down roots and pulling them up was painful. And if it was painful for her, then she couldn't begin to imagine how Eva must be feeling.

'Eva?' Patsy so much wanted to help but she didn't know how.

'Yes?' As Eva turned, the light caught the gleam of tears in her eyes, and all her sorrow and pain were written there.

Patsy's words of comfort stuck in her throat. Instead she said lamely, 'I think we both need a cup of tea. What do you say, me darlin'?'

'It's best if we go quickly,' Eva replied. 'That way we won't be prolonging the agony.' There was another reason too. 'I don't want to still be here when he turns up.' The thought of her uncle gloating as he saw them off the premises was too much to contemplate.

'But it's only six o'clock. He won't be here for

another two hours. Anyway, didn't Bill say he might find a way for us to stay here?'

'That's what he said.'

'Then shouldn't we wait? At least until eight o'clock?'

'No.' Eva had already decided. 'I'm sure Bill would move heaven and earth if it meant we could stay, but we can't, and it's no good fooling ourselves. There is nothing he can do to make my uncle change his mind. He won't be budged by anyone, not by the solicitor, not by Bill, and especially not by me.'

'Will we ever come back, do you think?' Patsy's voice shook.

Eva looked at her, her own heart aching terribly, and in a moment they were seeking comfort in each other's arms. 'Don't worry,' Eva said through her tears. 'We'll be all right. We'll look out for each other, just like we've always done.' Simple words, softly spoken, but they soothed Patsy, and that was enough. 'Go and tidy the cottage,' Eva suggested. 'I'll finish off in the house and then we'll be gone from here.'

Patsy was confused. 'What about your mam's things? I thought you'd arranged for the man from the charity to come and collect them?'

'I changed my mind.'

'Why?'

'Please, Patsy, not now.' She didn't feel like explaining every move she made. Besides, she knew

Patsy would never agree with what she had decided. Best not to tell her until afterwards, she thought.

While Patsy busied herself tidying the cottage, Eva did the same in the house. 'Must leave it all as Mam would have wanted,' she said to herself as she went about her work. First she washed and stacked the few dishes she and Patsy had used over lunch; then she dusted and hoovered, and last but not least, she collected together all her mother's smaller possessions and packed them into her father's tatty leather hold-all.

Gazing at a photograph of her mother, she murmured, 'I'm only taking these few things, Mam.' For a while her loss overwhelmed her. 'I don't need anything to remind me of you, Mam,' she said. 'I'll carry you in my heart for ever.'

The photograph showed her mother sitting on the swing beneath the apple tree. It was a sunny day, and Eva had been trying out her new camera. Neither she nor her mother thought the photograph would be much good, because the sun was in the wrong position and Colette was making her laugh. Just as Eva snapped the picture, her mother swung towards her, hair flying in the breeze and skirt lifted high. 'I'm sorry, sweetheart,' she said afterwards, 'but I felt like a little girl again, and oh, it was such fun. I didn't mean to waste your film.'

And yet, as it turned out, it was the best picture Eva ever took. Colette was delighted. Eva bought a frame and sat it on the mantelpiece where it had been ever since. Even Marcus had liked the picture. 'You didn't have to show your arse though,' he complained, but there was a twinkle in his eye every time he looked at the photograph.

Now, taking it down from the mantelpiece, Eva gazed at the picture for a long, precious time, reliving the day, moment by moment.

When it was too painful to look any longer, she carefully undid the back of the frame and lifted the photo out. It seemed like an act of sacrilege.

———✦———

BILL MADE ONE last, desperate plea to his father. 'For years you've been after that piece of land I secured in Whistler,' he said. 'I'll make a deal with you. Sell the Bereton place to me, and we'll talk about the Whistler land.' They were in the office of a suite of rooms Peter had taken in Bedford's grandest hotel.

Peter's eyes glittered with greed. 'What? You mean you'd consider selling that to *me*?' He couldn't believe why Bill would do such a thing. 'Good God, man! It cost you an arm and a leg to secure that land. It must be worth a small fortune now – right at the foot of the Rockies and ripe for development. If it got out that you were prepared to sell, you'd have people biting your hand off.'

'Well, do you want to talk, or don't you?'

'How good a deal will it be for me?'

Bill thought he had him hooked. 'It'll be good enough, but I can tell you now, I don't intend to give it away.' He knew how badly Peter wanted that land. He wanted it too, but it was Eva's needs he had in mind now. Besides, with the right investment, the Bereton place could be a little gold mine, and if it was what Eva wanted, he was more than prepared to inject the capital needed.

'I can't believe you're really offering that land to me,' Peter said. 'You've known all along how badly I wanted it. I had planned to develop it myself, or sell it on for a handsome profit. Thanks to you, all that went right out the bloody window.' His weasel-like features lifted in a sly grin. 'You didn't get it all your own way, though, did you, eh? At least I had the satisfaction of forcing up the price. I was the one bidding by proxy. You never knew that, did you?'

'I had an idea it was you,' Bill said easily. 'Don't forget, I know the way you operate. So. Name your offer for the Whistler plot, and I'll see if it's good enough.'

'Why do you want the Bereton place?'

'That's my business.'

Peter grinned. 'You always were soft on her, weren't you? For weeks after we took you to Canada you couldn't settle. She was on your mind then, and she's still on your mind. Even when you married and settled down, I bet you still hankered after her.'

He knew how to hit hard. 'I wonder what your wife would say if she knew you were making a play for your own cousin.'

Incensed, Bill fought to retain his dignity. 'That's enough!' Everything Peter had said was the truth, he couldn't deny that. But he had never once been unfaithful to Joan, and he had no intention of being so now. Eva was special to him, and always would be, but he suspected she didn't feel the same towards him. Moreover, their lives had long ago gone their separate ways. 'I spent many happy hours on the Bereton place when I was a boy,' he admitted. 'Eva will always be part of that time. I just don't want to see her thrown out of her own home. That's my reason for coming to you now, and only that.'

Peter was still sneering. 'After all, you and the Bereton girl aren't blood cousins. You're one of the unknowns, dumped by your own mother, whoever she was. And fool that I was, I took you in. Ten years of marriage and I still had no heir. How wrong I was. I picked you. I needn't haven't bothered. Within two years I at last had a son who was my own flesh and blood.' He paused; Eva was his own flesh and blood too, but she would never know it. 'So if you wanted to set up home with the Bereton girl, what's to stop you? Not the law, that's for certain, and not me, because I couldn't care one way or the other what you do with your life. In fact, all I want you to do is to get out of my sight, for good! Now!'

Bill frowned. 'I thought we had some business going here.'

'I wouldn't do business with you if you got down on your knees and begged me – though it might be a pleasing sight.'

The bastard means it, thought Bill with a sinking heart. 'I thought you wanted the Whistler land.'

'Oh, I want it right enough, make no mistake about that. I'll have it too.' His voice stiffened. 'But I'll have it on my terms.'

'Over my dead body!'

'Don't tempt me,' Peter snarled. 'Anything can be arranged.' Striding to the door, he called out, 'Todd, your brother is ready to leave.'

Todd promptly appeared. 'What's wrong?' His bulbous stare went from his father to Bill.

'See him out,' Peter ordered.

Todd looked at Bill. 'It seems you've outstayed your welcome.' He put a hand on Bill's arm.

White-faced, Bill shrugged him off. 'Move away.'

Todd glared at him, his face filled with hatred. 'You're not one of us. You never will be.' With that he swung his fist. Bill caught it and roughly thrust Todd aside. He lost his footing and fell at his father's feet in an undignified heap.

'You bastard!' Todd shouted.

'Maybe so,' Bill answered quietly. 'But there are bastards and bastards. And you two are the worst kind. I'm glad you think I don't belong.' He stared at them with contempt. 'I'm only sorry I'm branded with the same name.'

On his way out, he was shocked to see Margaret in the adjoining room, head down and softly crying. 'I'm sorry you had to hear that.' He put his arm round her and drew her close. 'I love you dearly. You know that, don't you?'

She nodded, looking at him with pained eyes. 'I know,' she said, 'and I know how badly they've always treated you.'

'Why don't you come with me? I'll take care of you.'

When she shook her head, his heart sank. 'Oh, Mother. You'll never leave him, will you?'

'Not yet,' she whispered. 'One day though . . .'

'I'll keep in touch,' he promised her.

Chapter Three

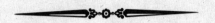

'WE'VE ONLY HALF an hour before they arrive, so we have.'

Patsy was panicking. Now that she had accepted they had no choice but to leave, she was anxious to be gone. 'I don't want you to see that awful man again,' she told Eva. 'Come on, me darlin', we've done all we can, and now it's time to go.'

'I won't be long, Patsy. Just another few minutes.' Her whole life was in this house, she thought wistfully. Leaving it all behind was the most agonising thing she had ever had to do.

'Did yer say the solicitor phoned?'

'About ten minutes ago. He wanted me to take the house keys to him after we've locked up.'

'And will you?'

Eva looked round the room. 'I keep thinking I've forgotten something.' She didn't want to talk about handing over the house keys.

Patsy took the hint. 'Did yer phone the furniture man?'

'I did.'

'And yer say he offered yer a fair price for yer mammy's lovely things?'

'I've already told you.'

'So we're to collect the money from the shop then?'

'That's what he said.'

'We're to take the key to the shop and wait there, have I got that right?'

'Don't worry about it, Patsy. It's all organised.' She wished Patsy would leave it alone. The more questions she asked, the more Eva felt obliged to lie. Although not all of it was lies. She had phoned the man, and he had made a fair offer, subject to seeing the articles. They were to take the key to him and he would come straight up to view and collect the goods. When he returned to the shop, if he was happy with the deal, he would pay out the agreed sum. The only thing was, Eva had already decided to turn down the man's offer. But she daren't say anything, or Patsy would only start worrying all over again.

Patsy ran her hand over the pine rocker where Colette used to sit in the evenings. 'Sure, it's a sin and a shame, so it is,' she muttered.

Eva's heart was close to breaking and Patsy was only making matters worse. All Eva wanted was a moment or two alone. All of her life was here, within these four walls. Leaving it was tearing her apart.

'Patsy, will you do something for me?' She had

to be diplomatic. The last thing she wanted was to make Patsy feel unwanted. She owed her so much. All through this dreadful time, Patsy had been a rock to her, even though she was losing her own home and livelihood. Friendship like that was rare.

Happy to help, Patsy grinned. 'Just say the word an' it'll be done in the wink of an eye.'

Eva beckoned her over. 'Look there, Patsy.' Pointing to the hen enclosure and the few proud creatures strutting about in ignorance, she said, 'I've been wondering what to do about the poultry. If I sell them to the farmer, he's bound to wring their necks, and if we leave them here I've no doubt Peter Westerfield will do the same, but with a great deal more enjoyment.' Her features hardened. 'I'll never forgive him for turning us out of here. Mam always used to say we shouldn't harbour grudges, but he's a wicked man. I won't forget what he's done. I know my father was very difficult, and sometimes he was spiteful. But that was because he'd been struck down in his prime and he couldn't cope with it. Uncle Peter has no such excuse. He's just bad through and through.'

'I can't understand why yer mammy never told yer he owned this property.'

'I've no idea why she would keep something as important as that from me.' Eva had agonised over it, but she could think of no reason to explain the secrecy. 'We used to talk about everything, or at least I thought we did. But I mustn't think about it too much. There's nothing I can do to change things, and I don't want it to mar my memories of her.' Although nothing could ever do that, she thought. 'If Mam chose not to tell me, then I can only think she had good reason.'

'Yer right.' Patsy felt better for knowing that Eva was as puzzled by the question as she was. 'Now then, me darlin', what do yer want me to do about these wretched hens?'

'Let them loose, Patsy.'

'What? Yer mean just open the gates and let them run off?'

Eva nodded. 'Yes. Why not?'

'Well, at least that'll give them a chance to survive. And while I'm at it, I'll see if they've laid any eggs since this morning.'

'Good idea.' The two of them had already loaded the trailer with fruit, vegetables, eggs and kindling, and hooked it to the back of the car.

Through the window, Eva watched her hurry across to the enclosure. With her wild, red hair and that funny way she had of bobbing along, arms swinging, her trousers looking as if she'd jumped too far into them, she was always a sight. 'You're a mess,' Eva chuckled, 'but whatever would I do without you?'

She laughed as Patsy tried rounding up the birds; they led her a merry dance and one even had the gall to flutter on to her shoulders and squirt down her back. 'Gerroff, yer scrawny parrot!' she screeched, doing a lively jig to frighten it away. 'Or I'll wring yer bloody neck meself, so I will!'

Eva laughed so much the tears ran down her face. Then she turned round and the empty house was like a dark blanket thrown over the sunshine.

Quickly now, before Patsy could return, Eva hurried about the task she had set herself. 'I'm sorry, Mam,' she muttered, 'but it's better this way.'

First she went into the hallway to collect all the bits and pieces she had decided to keep – small things she didn't have the heart to leave behind, like the notebook her mother used to jot ideas down in, and the little rag peg bag she had made with her own hands. Small, inconsequential things that wouldn't take up too much room and were an integral part of Eva's memories.

After making certain that everything the two of them were taking was safely stacked in the car boot, she satisfied herself that Patsy was still at war with the poultry – though she needn't have bothered looking because the squawks and shouted abuse told its own story.

Back in the house, she took pen and paper and wrote a note. It was a difficult note to write, and one which she had given much thought to.

Dear Bill,

I hope you find this note. I daren't leave it at the house.

Like you, I've never forgotten where we played as children, nor the happy times we had then. But that was a lifetime ago; we both know there comes a day when you have to put it all behind you, and try to survive in the real world. I have to go away from here now, and I don't know if I shall ever be back.

I just want to say thank you, Bill, for the happy times we had when we were children, and for what you are trying to do for me now. But please understand when I say I would rather you didn't cross swords with your father because of me. I would not want that on my conscience, especially when your relations with him are already strained.

Please don't worry about me, and don't come after me. If I don't learn how to make my own way in the world, I will never amount to anything.

Goodbye, Bill. Give my love to Aunt Margaret. I know you will both understand why I had to do what I did. Have a safe journey back to your wife.

Be happy, Bill. I will never forget you.

Love,

Eva

P.S. If you have any thought for me at all,
please respect my wishes.

Folding the note into an envelope, she made her
way out, through the kitchen and along the path to
the barn, where she and Bill used to play. 'Nothing's
changed,' she murmured, entering the barn and
lingering by the door, 'and yet *everything's* changed.'
Nostalgia swept over her. 'The magic of childhood
doesn't last long. You blink, and it's all gone.'

In her mind's eye she could see herself and Bill
in this old barn. She could imagine them climbing
the apple crates and building the den they were
so proud of. She looked at the low timber beam
where the two of them sat and gazed out of the
window, unseen by the world. 'I was wrong,' she
said, smiling, 'the magic hasn't gone. It's still here.'
She laid the palm of her hand across her heart.
'It's all still part of me. Part of my life.' It was a
comforting feeling.

She stuck the note on an old nail in the timber
beam and stared out of the window at the very same
scene she and Bill used to look at. She raised her
gaze to the sky. 'Please let him find the note.' If
he didn't, he would always believe she had gone
away ungrateful. That was no way to say goodbye
to a friend. As it was, a few hastily scribbled words
were small return for what he had tried to do for
her, but it was all she could offer. If things had

been different and he hadn't had a wife, maybe they could have seen each other, talked over the old times and renewed a very special friendship. But, the way things were, it was better to let sleeping dogs lie.

For a time she let her thoughts wander. 'It's no good dwelling in the past,' she told the bare walls. 'I have to forge a life for myself and Patsy.' Though how she would do that she had no idea as yet. 'Bill already has a life,' she whispered with the smallest tinge of regret. 'Once he's home he won't give me a second thought' – though somehow she couldn't really bring herself to believe that.

'Pull yourself together, Eva,' she told herself grimly. 'You know what you have to do.'

As she left, she closed the barn door behind her; she didn't want her Uncle Peter or that obnoxious son of his to wander in. 'Though I'm sure they'll get around to it eventually,' she said scornfully. 'But not before Bill finds the note, I hope.' On the way back to the house, she went into the shed and took out a number of articles which she crammed into an old sack.

Patsy caught sight of her going back into the house. 'Next time yer want any monsters set free, yer can do it yerself!' she called. 'The buggers don't want to go. Sure, I reckon they'd rather have their necks wrung than take their chances out there.' All around her the birds fluttered and panicked, and the more she went after them, the more frantic they became. 'See what I mean? There's not a penn'orth o' brains between 'em!'

Reluctant to cross the yard with her sack, Eva called back, 'Keep still, Patsy. You're making them panic.'

'It's *me* that's panicking!' Patsy replied. All the same she did as Eva suggested and stood still, and in no time at all the birds strutted away in orderly fashion, out of the pen and into the field. 'Yer deserve to be eaten alive!' Patsy shrieked at them.

Eva hoped they would be safe. 'Keep your wits about you,' she whispered to them as they disappeared from sight. 'It's a dangerous world out there.' As she and Patsy would find out soon enough, she thought anxiously.

'Wait for me in the car,' Eva told Patsy. 'I'll only be a minute.'

'I'll just clean meself up first,' said Patsy, heading for her cottage. 'Messy buggers, those parrots.'

Once inside the house, Eva carefully secured the door before undoing the sack. Laying the articles on the sitting-room carpet, she checked to see if she had forgotten anything. No. It was all there – a half-filled petrol can, old newspapers and oily rags. Her hands were trembling as she undid the top of the can.

There was a moment when she almost abandoned the idea, but thoughts of her Uncle Peter taking possession of this lovely house where she had been so happy were more than she could bear; and the idea of him pawing over her mother's things hardened her resolve. 'I have to do it, Mam,' she murmured, 'and may God forgive me.'

She waited, her gaze locked on the window. 'Come on, Patsy!' she muttered. 'Hurry up, or I won't have the courage to do it.' She daren't set light to the place until Patsy was safely in the car. Eva suspected Patsy would not be able to cope with what she was about to do.

Washed and tidy, with her hair scraped into a pigtail, Patsy emerged from the cottage and hurried to the car. 'Ready!' she called, seeing Eva looking from the window.

Eva smiled and waved, relieved when Patsy looked away.

One last check through the house and Eva was horrified to see she had almost forgotten her mother's photograph, which was still on the mantelpiece. Quickly now, she popped it into her skirt pocket. Taking a deep breath, she screwed the newspaper into soft balls and set them before her mother's chair; that done, she piled some kindling on top and soaked the mound in petrol. She then dipped an oily rag into the petrol and trailed it from the mound to the door, treading warily as she retreated.

She let the rag fall to the floor, then stepped back to a safe distance, struck a match and dropped it directly on to the rag. At first, it seemed she might have to do the whole thing again, but just as she took a step forward, the rag ignited. Alarmed, she jerked backwards, unaware that the photograph of her mother had tumbled from her pocket.

For a moment her stricken gaze followed the narrow trail of fire as it slowly meandered across the room. It should take a while before it reaches the chair, she thought. Then she hurried out of the house. She had already made sure that every window was closed and now she locked the front door and ran to the car, praying that the fire would not show itself before she and Patsy got away.

'Where've yer been?' Patsy demanded.

'Just making sure the house is secured. I don't want to leave it too easy for that bastard to get in.'

'Have yer got the keys?'

Eva started the car and shifted into gear. 'They're in the dustbin,' she answered. 'If he wants them, he can grovel about in there.'

Patsy laughed. 'Yer a girl after me own heart, so yer are.'

At the bottom of the lane, Eva sneaked a look back. There was no sign of the fire having got a proper hold yet, thank God. All the same, her heart felt like a lead weight inside her as she drove on.

'What's wrong, me darlin'?' Patsy knew her every mood.

Coming to the crossroads, Eva headed towards the churchyard. 'Just thinking,' she said.

Patsy understood, remaining quiet for the short journey to the church. Once there, she let Eva go to the graveside alone. 'Ah, sure, you've a lot to think about an' all,' she murmured, wiping away a tear. 'We've neither of us got anybody else. That's why we've got to look out for each other.'

Alone in the pretty churchyard, Eva felt as though she was the last person alive in the whole world. Empty of words, she let the tears fall freely, easing the awful grief inside. Then she dried her eyes, stooped to caress the flowers that were still fresh on the grave, and promised softly, 'As soon as I've made enough money, I'll get you the loveliest headstone I can find.' Then she turned and walked back to the car.

<hr />

As THEY HEADED into town, not a word was spoken. Patsy was thinking about her own parents somewhere in Ireland, yet just as lost to her as if they, too, were in some remote and pretty churchyard. Eva was still too full of emotion to speak. And yet they were perfectly comfortable with each other's silence.

Eventually they turned into a narrow back street. It wasn't an easy task, driving the bulky trailer down it, but Eva wanted to sell to someone out of the way, where she was sure she wouldn't be recognised. The wholesaler she had chosen, a little red-faced man, was in a foul mood. 'Mind you don't knock me bleedin' premises down,' he shouted as she drew up outside.

'Watch yer tongue, yer little weasel!' Patsy snapped indignantly. 'I'll have you know, Eva's as good a driver as any man.'

'Bloody women, who needs 'em! What do you want? State your business then bugger off.'

'I've got produce for sale.' Eva got out of the car and uncovered the goods on the trailer. 'Eight crates of fresh eggs, a dozen baskets of firm apples and pears, straight off the trees, and enough kindling to satisfy your customers for a month.' She picked out a full, round cabbage. 'And you won't find better greens than this if you search from one end of the country to the other.'

Eva was justifiably proud of the harvest she and her mam had gathered. The land they had farmed was good and fertile, but it was muscle and heart that coaxed the food from the ground. 'Flowers too,' she said. 'Freshly picked. And roses like you've never seen.'

'You'd make a good salesman,' the man quipped, 'but I've learned not to trust anybody, however pretty they might be.' His eyes roamed over Eva's face, noting the fine chiselled features and soft, full mouth. But she was a woman, and he'd had enough of them to last a lifetime. 'It don't matter how wonderful *you* think this 'ere stuff is,' he told her crossly, 'I like to see for myself.'

With his fat hands straining his pockets and his flat cap askew, he strolled round the trailer, occasionally plucking out an apple or a pear and sinking his teeth into it, sticky juice dribbling down his chin. 'Hmm. Not bad. Not bad at all.'

Ever mindful of what she had done back at the house, Eva was impatient to get away. 'Well, are you buying or not?' she demanded. 'If you're not, we'll be on our way. There are plenty of other merchants looking for good produce.'

'I'm buying, but I took delivery of fifty boxes of roses and chrysanths only this morning. So I don't need the flowers.'

'It's everything or nothing.'

'How much for the lot then?'

'Make me an offer.' Eva had a figure in mind but she wasn't going to reveal it in case it was less than he was prepared to pay.

'Twenty.'

Without a word, Eva climbed back into the car.

'Hey!' He scurried round the trailer and flung open her door. 'Don't be in such a bleedin' hurry!' It took him a full minute to recover his breath. 'All right, twenty-five.'

Eva closed the door. 'Sorry, I haven't got time to haggle.'

Just as she finished speaking, the sound of a fire siren screamed out. Her heart leapt. They've found the fire, she thought. We've got to get away.

'Thirty,' she told the merchant. 'And that's my last word.'

'What about the trailer? My bugger's knack-ered.'

'Sixty the lot.'

'Fifty-five, and that's *my* last word.'

'Cash?'

'If that's what you want.'

'It is.' She had closed her bank account. If she was to start afresh, it had to be from scratch.

'Go on then, it's a deal, but you're a hard bugger to do business with.' Secretly he admired her stubbornness. He had an idea she might be in some kind of trouble, especially since she seemed to be in a desperate hurry to get away. Either she was short of a bob or two, or this little lot had fallen off the back of a lorry.

Eva hopped out of the car. 'You get the cash,' she suggested, 'while we unhitch the trailer.'

'I'll give you a good price for the car, if you're interested in selling that as well.'

One stern look from Eva was enough to send him on his way. 'Bleedin' women!' he muttered as he went. 'Steal the arse from your trousers if you let 'em!'

Ten minutes later, Eva was on the road again. 'If

I'd had more time, we could probably have squeezed more out of him,' she told Patsy, 'but I want to get away from here as quickly as I can.'

Suspicious, Patsy stole a sideways glance at her. Eva was looking unusually pale, she thought. 'Eva, you worry me,' she said.

'What do you mean?'

'I don't know. It's just that you seem in an almighty hurry all of a sudden.'

'I've told you, Patsy. I don't want to be around when my uncle turns up at the house.'

'I know that, but we're not at the house now. And will yer slow down! You're doing seventy, so yer are.'

Eva eased her foot off the accelerator. 'I'm sorry,' she apologised. She must be careful not to make Patsy suspicious. What she had done back there at the house was a crime. It was better if Patsy knew nothing about it. That way she could not be implicated. 'We'd better decide exactly where to make for.'

'I thought we'd agreed to go south.'

'Yes, but where south? Which is the best area for us to find work? More to the point, what kind of work are we looking for?'

'Anything that pays a wage or puts a roof over our heads.'

'It won't do, Patsy. We have to be more specific.'

'What then?' Patsy was good at figures but hopeless at making plans.

Eva concentrated her mind. 'First, we need to choose a place and head for it. Then we should book into a hotel or guest house for the night. In the morning, when we're fresh and rested, we'll have a good look round. If we like the place enough to put down roots, we'll go to the labour exchange and see what's on offer. How does that sound?'

'Sounds all right to me.' Patsy's thoughts were driven by her stomach. 'Maybe we should find a cafe and get something to eat while we look at the map.'

'Okay. If you're that hungry, we will. But I'd rather look at the map now and keep going. We've a long journey ahead of us.'

Patsy didn't understand. 'Have we? I thought we didn't know where we were going yet.'

'I'm wondering if we should go north rather than south.' Somewhere her uncle would never think of looking.

Patsy's eyes opened with astonishment. 'North?'

'It's just a thought.'

When Patsy thought of 'north', she thought of Ireland. And when she thought of Ireland, she thought of the council home she'd run away from. 'I'm not sure,' she said. 'How far north?'

'Wherever we go,' Eva assured her, 'we both have to agree. Would you rather we slept on it?'

Patsy nodded. 'I'm too hungry to think straight anyway.'

'All right, we'll find somewhere to eat. Then we'll make for Leighton Buzzard since we're heading that way and find a guest house.'

'Can we afford to stay in a guest house?' Patsy was a born worrier. 'Nothing's cheap, is it?' She had just five pounds. 'I was never one for the saving. Earn it, spend it, that's the way I am.'

'Then you'll have to change your ways,' Eva suggested kindly. 'At least until we're settled.'

Eva had thirty pounds from her bank account, and fifty left from her parents' money; there had been more but the cost of burying them had taken the lion's share. With the merchant's money, she had one hundred and thirty-five pounds altogether.

'We've enough to get us a meal, a night at a respectable guest house, and a good start wherever we decide on,' she said.

'That's grand,' Patsy declared.

And, feeling lighter of heart, the two of them drove on to Leighton Buzzard.

THE FIRST THING Peter Westerfield saw as he turned off the main road was a column of grey smoke above the skyline. Not for a moment thinking it would have any bearing on his own plans, he drove on, down the narrow lane, through the thicket, and on towards the Bereton place. 'She'd better be packed and ready for off,' he grunted. 'It's mine now, lock, stock and barrel.' He laughed, a dark, sinister sound. 'Do you hear me, Colette?' he murmured. 'Your precious daughter's been shown her marching orders. I warned you there'd come a day of reckoning. *This* is the day.' There was a time when he had loved her. Now he felt nothing but hate. 'You made me pay for my bit of pleasure,' he snarled. 'Maybe I should have let the truth be known and beggar the consequences.' Yet he knew that all hell would have been let loose if she had talked. 'Pity it cost me for keeping your mouth shut!'

Bill had arrived earlier. When he drew up, the firemen were frantically trying to extinguish the fire. 'Stand back, sir,' he was ordered. 'The roof could go at any minute.'

No sooner had the fireman spoken than the roof collapsed into itself with a deafening roar. Great timbers jutted into the sky like huge stiff fingers, the flames licking up and around. Another ear-splitting roar and the entire structure caved in like a pack of cards, spewing up a mighty shower of sparks and debris. The once pretty house had become no more than a pile of burnt rubble.

Bill had been devastated to find Eva gone and the house in flames. Convinced that his father might have done it, and maybe even harmed her, he searched the grounds high and low, calling Eva's name. But she was nowhere to be found. Helpless, all he could do was stand and watch while her home burned to the ground. It was a sad and terrible sight. In spite of all their efforts, there was nothing the firemen could do; the house was already beyond saving when they were alerted.

Bill became aware of Peter rushing towards him, his face drained of colour. 'My God!' He stared at the ruins, then at Bill, his face darkening with fury. 'That bitch!' He raised his hands, fingers bent, as if ready to strangle someone. '*She* did this! It's her way of making sure I never lay my hands on it.'

Until then it had not entered Bill's head that Eva could have set light to her own home, but now he realised his father might be right, and he was deeply concerned. If Peter believed she was responsible, he wouldn't rest until she was brought to account.

Bill didn't betray his feelings. 'It's strange you should think it was Eva who did this,' he said. 'I thought it might be you who'd fired the place.'

Peter was startled. 'What the hell do you mean?' he demanded. 'I've been nowhere near, and anyway, why would I go to all the trouble and expense of getting back my own property, only to set light to it?'

Having planted a seed of fear, Bill decided to nurture it. 'You've got every reason to fire the place,' he insisted. 'You told me yourself you've no intention of selling the property, and you flatly refused to rent it to Eva. You won't be here to keep an eye on it yourself since you're returning to Canada soon, so it stands to reason the place would have fallen into disrepair.' He gave Peter a knowing look. 'That being the case, its insurance value is its only asset. I expect you've got it insured to the hilt. I know the way you think – set fire to it, then collect the money.'

He glanced towards the firemen who were now crawling all over the ruins, making certain there were no dangerous pockets of heat that might start the fire up again.

'You're out of your mind!' Peter was visibly shaking with anger. Everything Bill said made sense; to an outsider it was all too plausible, and it put the fear of God in him. 'You know as well as I do, she did this.'

'Well, *I* might believe you, but I doubt anyone else will. You know what insurance companies are like, always suspicious. And the fire service will no doubt want to ask you some questions.'

Peter glanced apprehensively towards the chief fireman who, satisfied that the fire had run its course, was now taking off his helmet and looking their way.

Bill was enjoying himself. 'Could be days, *weeks* even, before the whole thing's sorted out and they let you go home, which won't help your business interests. I mean, how can you control your business when you're this far away? And you've made quite a few enemies over the years, haven't you? You know what they say, when the cat's away, the mice will play. It wouldn't surprise me if they got up to all manner of tricks behind your back.' Then a final dig. 'I shouldn't think they'd want to question me though. So if Todd wants to stay here with you, don't worry, I'll look after your interests back home. You can count on me.'

'Like hell I will!' The chief fireman was making his way towards them. 'Keep your mouth shut,' Peter muttered. 'Least said soonest mended.'

———◦———

T HE FIREMAN ASKED whether they had reported the fire.

'We've only just arrived,' Peter told him. 'This is my property and I was due to meet my niece here.' In a sombre voice he added, 'She's just lost both her parents, you know, and now we're the only family she's got.' He feigned sympathy. 'We arrived a few days ago from Canada, for the funeral, you understand. And now this. Terrible business. Poor girl.' He shook his head and sighed.

'Is she here now?' The fireman glanced about, a look of anxiety in his face. He was an old hand at putting out fires, but he had never learned how to cope with human tragedy.

It was Bill who answered. 'She's gone away for

a few days, with an old friend. My cousin has been through a bad time, as you can imagine.'

'Of course.' He returned his attention to Peter. 'But you're the owner, are you, sir?'

'I've already said.'

'Have you any idea what might have happened here?'

'No idea at all. Like I say, I only arrived a few minutes ago.'

'And you've no idea who made the emergency call?'

'None whatsoever.'

Another voice spoke out, a stranger's voice. 'It were me that placed the call, officer.' The farmer had been a neighbour of the Beretons for many years. 'I only wish I'd got you here earlier, but I'm not as young as I were. I were out rabbiting when I saw the smoke. I knew right away it must be the Bereton place.'

'How did you know that?'

'I'm not senile yet, you know!' the old man retorted. 'The reason I knew it must be the Bereton place is because, as a rule, I can see the rooftop from where I was standing, and all I could see were black smoke swirling to the heavens. Besides, this is the only smallholding in this vicinity, apart from mine, o' course.'

'I see, sir.'

'I had to run all the way home to use the phone.'

Taking his hat off, he wiped the sweat from his brow. 'An' as you can see, I'm not all that nimble on me old legs.' As round as he was tall, he had short, bowed legs and walked with a peculiar dipping motion.

'Did you see anyone else in the vicinity?' The fireman was sure the blaze had been started deliberately.

'Nope.' The old man turned his gaze on Peter. 'Just now, when I were approaching from the spinney, I heard you and the young man talking.' He paused, his eyes never leaving Peter's face. 'I never knew young Eva had an uncle, and I'm sorry this has happened, on top of everything else. Nice girl. Lovely family, they were.' His expression hardened. 'I'd hate to hear anyone bad-mouthing 'em.'

Peter looked away, uncomfortable under the farmer's scrutiny.

The old man rammed his hat back on his head. 'I've said me piece, so, if you've finished, I'll get back to me rabbiting.' He turned and walked away with that peculiar bobbing motion.

'Strange old bird,' said the fireman with a smile. He told the two men he would have to put in a report to the local police station and then rejoined his crew.

Peter climbed into his car, slammed shut the door and wound down the window. 'I'll make her pay for this!' he snarled at Bill. 'The pair of you. You're probably in this together. You tell her from me, she's going to rue the day she crossed swords with Peter Westerfield.'

'Hurt her, and you'll answer to me,' Bill said grimly. It was all he could do to keep his hands to himself, but he knew violence would solve nothing.

Peter sniggered. 'You ought to be very careful about getting too protective of the lovely Eva. You have a wife waiting for you back home, don't forget.'

'Don't ever underestimate me,' Bill warned quietly. 'I'm more than a match for you. If it wasn't for my mother, I'd have finished you long ago. The Whistler plot was a prime example. You wanted it, and I took it. Remember that.'

'And you remember this. Better men than you have tried to finish me off and failed miserably, to their cost.' Peter slammed the car into gear and sped away with a screech of tyres.

⇒•◦•⇐

IN THE SHORT while before he must leave, Bill strayed to the barn. Pushing open the door, he peered inside, a bitter-sweet smile shaping his handsome features. He wandered about, touching this and that, his eyes taking in all the familiar things. 'Dear Eva,' he murmured. 'Thinking of you, and the times we shared, kept me sane when I was at my lowest.' Going to the corner beam where he and Eva used to sit, he looked out of the window at the view that Eva had gazed at only a short time before.

Thoughts of his wife filled his mind, and another kind of love came into his heart; Joan was a sweet person, but she was not Eva. It was odd how life sometimes steered you along, taking you into situations that were not of your making. As a man of principle, he would not break his wife's heart to fulfil his own desires. 'For better or worse', those were the vows he had made. His path had been chosen a long time ago, and however much he wanted to, he was too far down that path to change direction now.

As he turned, he saw the note pinned to the beam. Taking it down, he opened it.

As he read Eva's letter, all manner of emotions swept through him. When at last he finished, he carefully folded it and laid it tenderly on a broken crate. 'I can't take you with me, Eva,' he murmured. He looked out at the blue sky and the way the clouds were beginning to curl overhead. 'But I'll be thinking of you, wherever you are.' Closing his eyes, he sighed deeply. 'Keep safe, my love.' It would take all of his willpower not to search her out.

His heart heavy, he went out into the warm sunshine.

As he approached the pile of black rubble that had once been Eva's home, the acrid smell of burning stung his nostrils and coated his tongue. He stood and surveyed the damage. Nothing had been saved. Everything had been either burned to ash or charred beyond redemption. He bowed his head, wondering what Eva must have felt when she set light to this lovely house. He couldn't even begin to imagine what it must have cost her to do it.

As he turned to leave, something caught his eye, a small piece of paper right at his feet. Intrigued, he bent to pick it up, astonished to see that it was a photograph of Eva's mother, older than when he knew her, but little changed. The edges of the photo were scorched and crumbling, but the face was intact. It was a pretty face, much like Eva's, with a bright happy smile and eyes that shone with the joy of life. 'You shouldn't be here to see this,' he murmured. 'I can't believe Eva would have wanted to leave you behind.'

He wondered about that. Had she simply forgotten it? No. Eva was devoted to her mother. What then? He searched his mind. Of course. In her haste to leave she must have dropped the photo. That could explain why it was not in a frame and lying close to the door.

Carefully, he peeled away the charred edges, then he took out his wallet and placed the photo inside, hoping that one day he might be given the opportunity to return it to Eva.

PART TWO

OCTOBER 1955
NEW FRIENDS

Chapter Four

PATSY WAS TOO excited to work. 'Ah, sure, yer a sly wee bugger, Eva Bereton. I *know* yer planning something for me birthday. Yer might as well tell me.'

Eva continued stacking the freshly laundered linen into the cupboard.

'It's no use yer ignoring me, because I won't go away until I know what's going on.' Persistent to the end, she put down her tray of dirty crockery and placed herself between Eva and the linen basket. 'Well? Are yer gonna tell me or what?'

Reaching round her, Eva drew out two perfectly folded white sheets. 'Nothing to tell,' she lied.

'Aw, go on! I saw you and Frank whispering in the corner the other day. When yer saw me coming yer looked guilty as thieves. Before I could say a word, yer shot off in different directions, so yer did.'

'Rubbish. We did no such thing.' Eva wondered how she was ever going to keep the truth from

Patsy until the day of her birthday. She was as stubborn as a mule. The whole staff were planning a surprise, but it would all be spoiled if Patsy got wind of it.

Patsy's fertile mind was working overtime. She leaned closer, whispering intimately, 'If yer weren't planning something for me, yer must have been planning something else.' Glancing about furtively, she leaned even closer. 'There's something going on between you and Frank, isn't that the truth? Go on, me darlin', yer can tell me. Sure, I'll not say a word.'

Blushing to the roots of her hair, Eva pushed her aside. 'Give over!' she said. 'You know very well there's nothing going on between me and Frank.' Though if he had his way, there would be, she thought. He was a nice enough man, and good-looking into the bargain. She liked him, but with Bill still on her mind, she wasn't ready to get involved with Frank, or anyone else.

'Yer blushing, so yer are.'

'No, I'm not.' Collecting her linen basket, Eva came out of the cupboard and closed the door, turning the key in the lock.

Blackpool hotels had suffered a spate of break-ins lately. The proprietor here took it very seriously, fitting sturdy locks to every cupboard and putting Eva, recently promoted to housekeeper, in charge of their safe-keeping. She had a dozen keys hanging

from her belt, which she put on in the morning
and kept on until she returned to her room in
the evening. She often commented that it was like
carrying a sack of coal round her waist. She had a
permanent bruise on her leg where the keys dangled
and bumped as she walked.

'Frank *does* fancy you though.' Patsy prided
herself on knowing everything.

'It doesn't mean I fancy him, does it?' Eva
didn't mind discussing the subject. At least it had
taken Patsy's mind off her birthday, which was in
two days' time.

'He'd be a good catch, so he would, what with
his mother owning this grand hotel an' all.'

They went down the back stairs and on towards
the kitchen. 'Will you stop trying to marry me off.'
Pairing her with a good man seemed to be Patsy's
sole aim in life. 'I don't doubt Frank would be
a good catch for anyone who might be on the
lookout for a man. But don't look at *me*.' She
batted her hands as if trying to fend off something
threatening. 'You know I'm not interested in men
at the minute.'

'That's because yer won't let yerself forget Bill
Westerfield.'

'Maybe.' She couldn't deny it. Not to Patsy
anyway.

'Holy Mother of Jaysus!' Drawing in a long, loud
breath, Patsy let it out in a withering sigh. 'Will yer

never learn? The man's in Canada, so he is. And he's happily married. Sure, it's been fifteen months since we were forced out of house and home. If yer haven't heard from him in all that time, what makes yer think yer ever will?'

Arriving at the kitchen door, Eva stopped and turned. 'Don't forget he doesn't know where I am.'

'All the same, if he wanted to find out where you were, I'm sure he wouldn't let anything stand in his way. Sure, the man's got money, hasn't he? And money talks, so it does.'

'You don't understand, Patsy.'

'Is that so?'

Eva knew if she didn't put Patsy straight, she'd never get any peace. 'I don't want him to find me. Like you say, he's happily married and far away in Canada.' Momentarily closing her eyes, she saw his face as clearly as if he was in front of her. Recalling every word in the letter she had left him, she told Patsy, 'Nobody knows better than me that Bill would never try to find me.'

'Because he doesn't want to, yer mean.'

'No.' Eva had never told Patsy the truth. She thought this might be the time to do so. 'Because I asked him not to.'

'What are yer saying, Eva?'

Eva told her how she had left Bill a note in the barn where they used to play as children. 'For a time, I wondered whether he might not have found it. Now, after all this time, I know he did.'

'And now yer sorry, is that it?'

Eva shook her head. 'No. I'm glad he found the note, and I'm glad he respected my wishes not to come in search of me.' She sounded so definite, yet in truth she harboured just the tiniest regret.

'All the same, yer love him, don't yer?' Quieter now, Patsy felt ashamed for pressing the point.

Her heart aching, Eva looked into her friend's eyes, and for a brief moment she was tempted to bare her soul, but some deep instinct held her back.

'Well?'

'Nothing.'

'Yer meant to say something. What was it, me darlin'?'

Eva put on her brightest smile. 'How do you fancy going out tonight?' Left to herself, she would much rather curl up in bed with a hot water bottle and a cup of steaming hot chocolate.

'Out? In this weather?' Aware that Eva had deliberately changed the subject, Patsy played along. 'It's enough to freeze the balls off a brass monkey out there. If yer think I'm walking along the seafront, you've another thought coming, so yer have!'

'No, Patsy. I don't mean walking along the

seafront. Besides, the front will be packed with tourists, here for the illuminations. I meant dancing at the tower. What do you say to that?' Eva was suddenly warming to the idea of going out. After all, it was Saturday night, and it was weeks since she and Patsy had done anything exciting. Working all hours to earn money so they could buy a roof over their heads didn't allow time for enjoyment.

Like a child, Patsy clapped her hands with pleasure. 'What a brilliant idea!'

'You're game then?'

'I'll say!'

'Good. I'll meet you in the lobby at quarter to nine, and don't be late.'

'I have to get bathed and changed, and I'll need time to make myself up, so I will. I mean, who knows what talent might be there?' Grinning like a Cheshire cat, Patsy rolled her eyes. '*You* might even find yerself a feller.'

Eva said nothing but gave her a disdainful look. It was enough.

'All right then, nine o'clock on the dot, and yer can have me hide if I'm a minute late.'

'What time, Patsy?' There were occasions when Eva felt she could cheerfully strangle this delightful Irish bundle, but there were other times, like now, when it was all she could do not to laugh out loud.

'Aw, all right then. Quarter to nine it is.'

<hr />

IN THE KITCHEN, Cook was dishing out more helpings of food. 'Thank God another day's nearly over,' she groaned. 'It seems everybody wanted to eat in tonight. The dining room was packed to the hilt. I've been on my feet since four o'clock and I haven't stopped since.' She glanced at the wall clock. 'And here it is five minutes past eight.'

'It's the illuminations, so it is.' Coming into the kitchen, Patsy took the tray to the sink and began unloading it. 'I looked out the window upstairs and the streets are crawling with traffic. I should think every hotel in Blackpool is full right through October.'

Eva agreed. 'Give it another week and it will be so quiet we'll be wishing they were back.'

Patsy's tray clattered to the floor. She bent to pick it up and knocked over a teapot, which went the same way, and shattered. 'Whoops.' She looked sheepishly from Cook to Eva. 'I'll have it cleared away in no time at all, so I will.' She dived into the cupboard for the dustpan and brush.

'It'll cost you to replace that,' Cook reminded her. 'Mrs Dewhirst's rules – breakages have to be paid for by them that does the breaking.'

'That'll leave a big hole in Patsy's wages,' Eva said.

Cook liked these two girls. Patsy was a lovable Irish rogue, who wore you out just watching her. She took each day as it came and bore few responsibilities. Eva, though, was the kind of girl who took the world on her shoulders. A deep-down sort, with a heart of pure gold.

She relented. 'Oh, well, accidents will happen, I suppose. As far as we know, the teapot just fell to the floor, all by itself, isn't that so?'

Patsy and Eva nodded solemnly.

'I'd rather have the tourists here,' Patsy said as she dropped the shards into the bin and replaced the dustpan and brush. 'Remember last winter when we worked so hard we were knackered by the time the tourists started coming in again? All that wallpaper stripping and scrubbing, it fair wore me out. I'd rather rush about cleaning rooms and changing beds, so I would.'

Cook shook her head and pointed to the sink, piled high with crockery. 'Just look at that little lot.'

Eva looked around the room. 'Where's Libby?'

Flicking a wayward greying hair from her face, Cook explained, 'Libby's had to help out with the serving. Billy's still away with the flu and poor Rose couldn't cope, so I had to let Libby loose.' Sniffing, she added, 'It's a good job we've got enough crockery, or I'd be pulling my hair out.'

'I'll help,' Eva offered.

Cook would have none of it. 'Me and the girls didn't start till half past seven this morning, and we had it easy right up to six o'clock tonight, whereas you two started at half past five and you've been run off your feet all day, so be off with you. You look worn out, the pair of you. Go on to your beds.'

'We're going dancing,' Patsy announced.

Cook laughed out loud. 'Dancing, is it?' Plopping a generous helping of cabbage on the plate, she tutted and sighed. 'By! What it is to be young.'

'We can't leave you in a mess like this,' Eva protested. 'It won't take me and Patsy long to clear it away.'

'I said be off with you. Enjoy yourselves and don't come rolling home in the early hours, or Mrs Dewhirst will have something to say. And if you oversleep in the morning, she'll have your guts for garters.'

'My feet ache too much to dance,' said Eva. Besides, dancing usually meant being held in a man's arms, and she wasn't in the mood for that. 'Patsy can dance and I'll watch, but come midnight I'll be ready for my bed.'

'Oh, I'll be snoring long before that,' Cook said as the two of them left the kitchen.

Up in her room, Eva took a moment to relax. Seated on the edge of her bed, she kicked off her shoes and flexed her toes. It was a good feeling. Before she knew it, she had fallen back on the bed and was lying there, eyes closed and arms cradled behind her head.

Relaxed and comfortable, she let her mind wander. She went over everything they had been through since leaving home. She worried in case the fire had been discovered in time and Peter had been able to stand in her mother's house, gloating. She wished she hadn't lost the photograph of her mother. That, more than anything else, had given her many sleepless nights. It wasn't long before she'd discovered the photo was missing, and for one moment she was tempted to drive back to the house and look for it. But that was impossible, of course. She thought about Bill, and her heart turned somersaults. If only things could have been different for them.

She let her mind sink into sleep. Her eyes became heavy, and her arms limp.

The sound of a door banging shut woke her with a jerk. Rubbing her eyes, she mentally shook herself. 'Patsy will kill me!' Eva was suddenly wide awake. The clock on the wall told her she had twenty minutes. It was time enough.

Grabbing a towel and robe she ran out of her room and along the corridor to the bathroom. This cramped part of the hotel was given over to resident staff, with only one bathroom between the four of them. Cook travelled in daily, as did her two assistants and the receptionist. Frank had his own house some half a mile away, and his mother lived in the fancy quarters at the front of the hotel.

The bathroom door was locked. 'Who's in there?' She prayed it wasn't Patsy.

Back came the familiar voice. 'Who the devil d'yer think it is? Sure, I thought you'd already been in and out, so I did.'

'How long will you be?'

'I've only just got in here and I want to try out this new bubble bath. It's supposed to make you smell like something out of heaven. I'm telling you, Eva, the fellers won't be able to keep their hands off.'

'Aw, come on, Patsy. How do you expect me to get ready if you're hogging the bathroom?'

'Use the main one on the next floor down.'

'You know that's not allowed.'

'So?'

'If I get caught, it's instant dismissal.'

'Frank would never let his mother dismiss you.'

'Patsy!'

'Go away, why don't yer?'

'Right!' Eva could be just as stubborn. 'If you're not ready in ten minutes, I'm going back to bed.'

There was a quiet moment, before Patsy started singing. Angry though she was, Eva had to smile. 'You bugger!' she muttered, making her way down the winding stairs to the lower floor.

Unfortunately, the maid was changing the towels there. 'Oh, it's you, miss.' A small young thing with big frightened eyes, she had been working at Sealand Hotel for only two days. 'I'm ever so sorry, miss, I thought you said to change them once in the morning and again at night, while most of the guests are in the dining room.'

'Yes, Meg, that's right. Don't worry. You carry on.' Like a schoolgirl caught smoking behind the bike shed, Eva slunk off. 'I'll never be ready in time,' she muttered, running up the stairs. 'It'll be so late by the time we get there, everyone else will have gone.' And, the way she felt right now, that would suit her very well.

<hr />

TWENTY MINUTES LATER, in spite of everything, Eva made her way downstairs; she had on her best black patent shoes with a bow at the side, a grey swinging skirt, pale blue blouse, and a short jacket in a darker blue.

'Well now, don't you look lovely?' Annie Dewhirst was a tall, slim woman, with short dark hair and a look of authority. The sharp tone of her voice belied her ready smile. 'Where are you off to?'

'Patsy and I are supposed to be going dancing at the tower, but if she's as late as she usually is, it probably won't be worth going.'

'Of course it will be worth going,' Mrs Dewhirst

said. 'You work very hard, Eva, and you need to socialise more. You haven't even got a young man. An intelligent, pretty young lady like yourself, it doesn't seem right.'

'I'm not in the market for a young man,' Eva answered warily. 'I'll leave all that to Patsy.' There were times when she wondered about this woman's probing comments. She got the feeling that beneath that smart, friendly surface lurked a nature that was less than pleasant.

'I see.' The smile disappeared. 'Well, make sure you're in at a respectable time, and mind how much you drink. I don't take kindly to members of my staff coming home the worse for drink.'

'You don't have to worry about that, Mrs Dewhirst.' Eva was deeply offended. 'I have never been the worse for drink, and as for Patsy, she's not as irresponsible as people like to think.'

Annie Dewhirst felt rebuked by Eva's quiet dignity, and suddenly old and drab before her youth and beauty. She could see only too well why her son Frank was so besotted with her, and it was almost more than she could bear. She felt obliged to make amends. Frank would never forgive her if she upset this girl.

'I didn't mean to imply anything,' she apologised. 'You're the last person I would want to criticise. I mean, I'm very grateful for the way you stood in when my housekeeper left in such a hurry. I might even go as far as to say you're the best housekeeper I've ever had.'

'Thank you.' Eva was flattered but not duped.

'You keep yourself to yourself, and I've had no cause at all to complain about you. Patsy, though – well, she can be a bit unpredictable, wild even. At her age I should have thought she might have more sense, but there you are, some people never grow up, do they?'

'Patsy won't be a problem.'

'Just keep an eagle eye on her. I don't want this hotel getting a bad reputation. It's taken me years to establish its good name.'

To Eva's relief, Patsy chose that moment to come hurrying into the hall. 'Hello, Mrs Dewhirst,' she said, all smiles. 'I expect Eva's told you we're going dancing.'

'Yes. I was just saying you should both enjoy yourselves.' She might have repeated her warning about not coming in late, or getting drunk, but thought better of it. What she had told Eva about her being the best housekeeper she had ever employed was the truth. Considering that Eva was not yet twenty, she was surprisingly conscientious. Until such a time as she could get rid of these two and replace Eva with someone equally reliable and competent, she would have to curb her tongue.

Tugging at Eva's sleeve, Patsy said, 'Come on, Eva. Let's go.'

Eva was only too happy to oblige.

Annie Dewhirst watched them leave, one so slim and elegant, the other plump and loud. 'The sooner I get rid of you two, the better,' she muttered. 'As for you, Eva Bereton, keep your hands off my son. I'm saving him for a better catch than *you*!'

———◆———

'Y OU WERE LATE,' said Eva as they stepped into the street. It was cold outside and she buttoned up her jacket.

'I'm really sorry.' Patsy didn't look sorry. 'A bath is still such a luxury after living in the cottage for all that time, I like to make it last.'

'Oh, you did that all right.'

'I think yer look lovely, Eva. Do I look nice? Will the fellers fancy me?'

'I can't speak for the men, but yes, you do look nice.'

Patsy was dressed in a tight black skirt and red blouse under her black coat, and black suede shoes. Impulsively, she did a twirl and almost fell over. Eva grabbed her arm to steady her, and looked at her suspiciously. 'Have you been drinking?' Leaning forward she sniffed at Patsy's face. Sure enough, the faint smell of alcohol wafted up. 'Oh, Patsy!'

Mortified, Patsy lowered her eyes. 'Aw, sure, it were only a wee drop at the bar to give me courage.'

'Just think yourself lucky Mrs Dewhirst didn't

smell the drink on you. You know her views about staff drinking in the bar; only last week she sacked a porter for doing just that.'

'I haven't forgotten.' Patsy made her best Annie Dewhirst face; the voice, too, was good. 'No member of staff to drink in the hotel bar at any time.'

'You're nothing but trouble.'

'I know.'

Eva laughed. 'I must be as mad as you because I love you all the same.'

'Sure, I know that too. I should be ashamed o' meself, so I should.'

'It's no good you playing for my sympathy.' She looked at Patsy's face and couldn't help laughing. 'Come on you,' she said, throwing her arm round Patsy's shoulders. 'Let's enjoy ourselves like the woman said.'

'Now you're talking,' Patsy grinned, and they made their way on foot to the seafront like two excited children.

Thousands of colourful illuminations hung from the street lamps. They were strung across the road, making a zig-zag promenade all of their own, from one end of the Blackpool Mile to the other. There were all kinds of weird and wonderful shapes, figures and caricatures, in colours and patterns of every description, each casting its own special glow. People thronged the promenade and there was an air of excitement all around.

When they got to the tower, Eva was relieved to see there was still a lively crowd in the place. 'That should please you,' she told Patsy, shoving her through the door. 'There's bound to be some fellers on the lookout for a spare woman.'

'They'll be looking at you, not me, so they will.'

'Don't be daft!'

'I'm telling yer. There won't be anyone in this place to touch yer.' She regarded Eva with pride. 'The fellers will be all over yer an' no mistake.'

'No they won't, because, unlike you, I won't be giving them the come-on. Now go on. Hand your coat in and get your ticket, then we can go inside.'

'If a good-looking man asks yer to dance, yer won't say no, will yer?' Patsy never gave up.

'Chance would be a fine thing,' the girl behind the cloakroom counter butted in through her chewing gum. 'I've been on this desk since seven o'clock and I ain't seen *one* good-looking feller all evening.'

Patsy just glared at her and handed in her coat. Then Eva passed her jacket across and they went into the dance hall.

'That silly arse wouldn't know a good-lookin' feller if she saw one,' Patsy announced. 'Experience, that's what counts.'

'You'd know all about that then, would you?' Eva asked, heading for the nearest chair.

'Of course.' Patsy was full of herself. 'Men are no strangers to me.' In the blink of an eye her mood changed. A shadow crossed her face as she recalled one man in particular. 'Mind you,' she added soberly, 'once they've got yer in their clutches, it's hard to escape.'

Realising that Patsy was losing herself in the past, Eva told her, 'Just remember, you're here to enjoy yourself.' Flopping down in the chair, she dug into her purse and took out a one-pound note. 'I'll have a packet of plain crisps and a Babycham, please. You get what you like. My treat.'

'I think I'll have a pint.' Patsy drank like a man.

While Patsy pushed her way to the bar, Eva relaxed. 'My feet feel like hot puddings,' she sighed, taking off her shoes and stretching her toes under the table. 'Ohh, that's better.' Leaning back in the chair, she closed her eyes. 'What I wouldn't give to be in bed right now,' she groaned.

As she spoke the music stopped and her words were clearly audible to the young man at the next table. He leaned over with a smile. 'I'm available,' he said. 'Your bed or mine?'

With an embarrassed smile, Eva shifted her chair away from him. But she could feel his eyes burning into the back of her neck.

That young man wasn't the only one to notice Eva. 'I like your friend,' the barman told Patsy.

He was in his late twenties, short and thick with a coarse face and staring eyes. Sliding the drinks towards her, he said, 'I'm off duty in half an hour. What do you think? Would she mind me chatting her up?'

'She'd probably love it,' Patsy told him. 'She's a devil for the men. But I wouldn't if I were you – unless yer fancy a spell in the hospital, like all the others.'

He turned pale. 'What others?'

'The men she chases. It drives her husband mad, so it does.'

He went paler still. 'She's got a husband then?'

'Built like a bull and with a temper to match.'

'Jesus! I can do without that kind of trouble. What flavour crisps did you want?'

On the way back to the table, Patsy saw how other men were eyeing Eva. 'It's always the same,' she muttered, but there was no malice there. In fact, she was pleased; wherever they went, Eva drew the interest, and Patsy capitalised on it. But it wasn't just that. She had always been proud to be with Eva. As different as day and night, they complemented one another. It didn't matter that there were twelve years between them. They laughed together, cried together, and talked about the kind of things they could never confide to anyone else.

'Took you long enough, didn't it?' Eva was glad

to see her. She felt conspicuous sitting on her own. 'It's a good job you're not a waitress, a girl could die of thirst before you appeared.'

Patsy plopped the Babycham in front of her. 'Here. Get that down yer and think yourself lucky it's all there.' Gazing woefully at her own pint, she grumbled, 'I lost half of mine when a big-footed ape knocked into me.' Choosing a three-legged stool to sit on, she almost lost her balance. 'Jaysus! Can't the buggers afford a stool with four legs?' She pushed it aside and dropped on to a sturdier seat. 'First I lose half me pint, then the bloody stool collapses under me.'

'Didn't you make the bloke buy you another pint?'

'I did.' Patsy winked. 'He's bringing it over now.'

Eva laughed out loud. 'You did it on purpose, didn't you? It wasn't him that knocked into you, it was you that knocked into him.'

Shrugging her shoulders, Patsy chuckled, 'Desperate needs call for desperate measures.'

The man in question was big and muscular. 'I'm sorry again,' he apologised, placing the drink before Patsy. 'I'm not usually that clumsy.' He looked over at the dance floor. 'I'm not that good a dancer but would you like to give it a go?'

'Why not?' Before he could change his mind, Patsy was on her feet and leading him on to the floor. 'Don't go helping yerself to me drink,' she warned Eva. 'I'll know if you have!'

Eva chuckled softly to herself. 'Didn't take you long to get yourself a man, did it, eh?'

For a while, she watched them dancing; the man wasn't as bad as he'd led them to believe. He moved with surprising grace, unlike Patsy who kept treading on his feet, making him wince with pain. Eva tried not to laugh out loud.

'I'm glad she's not dancing with me.' From his place at a nearby table, Frank Dewhirst had been watching Eva for some minutes, before deciding to approach her.

Surprised by his sudden appearance, Eva looked up. 'Frank!' To his mother's fury, they had been on first-name terms for some time now. 'I didn't realise you were back. Your mother said you'd be away for a week at least.'

'Ah, she underestimated my negotiating skill.' At thirty years of age, tall and slim, with brown hair and browner eyes, he had a boyish charm. 'I got the business of buying over much quicker than anticipated. Work on the new foyer will start the second week in January, our quietest time.'

'Your mother says she wants a grand winding stairway.'

'And the rest.'

'I rather like it the way it is.' Eva thought the entrance had a homely, welcoming look.

'So do I, but it's what she wants.' Gesturing to Patsy's seat, he asked, 'Mind if I steal a minute of your time?'

'Of course I don't mind.' She really liked him, though she thought he ought to stand up to his domineering mother a bit more. 'Don't drink Patsy's pint though,' she joked, 'or it will be more than your life's worth.'

Together they watched Patsy and her partner. 'Make an odd couple, don't they?' Frank remarked with a grin. 'How did she latch on to him?'

'She bumped into him on purpose. He spilt her pint and she made him buy another.'

'Was it Patsy's idea to drag him on to the dance floor?'

'No, that was his idea, but I think he's regretting it.' Patsy seemed totally oblivious of her partner's distress. 'I've been wondering whether to rescue the poor devil, but he's such a big, ugly ox, I'm not sure. And anyway, my feet are still aching from a long walk after a long day.'

'Let him take his punishment like a man,' Frank remarked. 'I'd rather you stayed here with me.' In the soft light he thought how beautiful she was, and how childlike. From the first moment he had seen Eva, he was lost. 'There are things I want to ask you.'

Eva was intrigued. 'What things?'

He didn't know how to start. What he really

wanted was to ask her to be his wife, but it was too early. He knew instinctively she didn't feel that way towards him, though he was sure of her affection. It was only a small shift to love, and he could wait; though not too long.

Noticing his hesitation, Eva gently pressed him. 'Is something troubling you, Frank? If helping with Patsy's party is taking up too much of your time, I don't mind doing it all, honestly.'

'No, it's not the party,' he assured her. 'Besides, I offered to help, and I'm having fun.'

'If it isn't the party, what is it?'

'It's you.'

Eva felt apprehensive. 'What about me? Has your mother complained? I know we have words now and then, but I thought she was happy with my work.'

He touched her hand, a thrill running through him. 'No,' his voice was caressing, 'she hasn't complained.' When, embarrassed, Eva drew her hand away, he assumed a casual, businesslike air. 'One thing about Mother, she knows quality when she sees it.' And so do I, he thought. 'You could run that hotel with your eyes closed and she knows it.'

'I don't run the hotel,' she said, though it sounded like a wonderful idea. 'I look after the linen and oversee three young girls.'

'Don't undervalue yourself, Eva. You do much more than that. Since you've been housekeeper, the whole place seems to run like clockwork. You know what they say, if the wheels turn from the bottom, everything is easy. The staff think the world of you, and they're much more content these days.'

'Frank, where is all this leading?'

'Just tell me, Eva, do you intend staying with us a long time, or have you got plans to move on?'

That set her thinking. These past weeks she had grown restless; she didn't see herself as a hotel housekeeper for the rest of her days and she wondered what she might find out there in the big wide world. Patsy, too, was beginning to get restless. But she didn't want to get involved in a discussion about herself and Patsy, so she simply said, 'I haven't given it too much thought.'

'I consider you a friend, Eva.' He felt she was fobbing him off. 'Anything you tell me will remain strictly between the two of us.'

It was true. Frank was a good friend, and he deserved an honest answer. 'I'll admit there have been times lately when I've been tempted to set off and look for something else,' she told him. 'I may have a good job, but it isn't what I wanted. Besides, Patsy isn't cut out to wait on people and clear away their leftovers. We started out with higher hopes, and I feel I owe it to her as well as to myself to set my sights a bit higher.'

His face lit up. 'I was hoping you'd say that,

because I have a proposition to put to you.' His heart said marriage, but his head said wait.

'What kind of a proposition?'

Moving closer he lowered his voice. 'Some time back, I got talking to some men who stayed at the hotel. They were agents, men who scoured the country looking for cheap land. They buy it for next to nothing, hold on to it for a time, and then sell at a handsome profit. "Money for old rope", that's how they described it.'

'Maybe. But you need money to make money. Even I know that.' That was the only thing holding her back. Since she and Patsy had been in work, they had scraped together a tidy sum, but it wouldn't take them far. A number of ideas had gone through her mind, and always it came back to the same argument. There was never enough money.

'What if I were to put in all the capital needed?'

'I'd have to say no.' Bill had offered to help her, and she had refused. She would stand on her own two feet.

'Why not?'

'Because I don't want to be beholden to anybody. It doesn't mean I'm not grateful for the offer, but the answer has to be no, thank you all the same, Frank.'

'A loan then? Pay me back when we start making a profit.'

She shook her head. 'No.'

'Won't you at least think about it? I know we could make a real go of it, Eva, you and me.' The idea was like a worm in his insides; first business partners, then marriage. 'Please don't dismiss it out of hand.'

'All right, I promise I'll give it some thought.' But she knew her answer would be the same.

'That's all I'm asking.' For now, he thought.

———⟫◦⟪———

IN SPITE OF her earlier reservations, Eva enjoyed the evening. She and Frank chatted, mostly about Patsy's birthday party, which was to be held in the local pub. And they danced a few times. As always, they were relaxed in each other's company. Patsy was a hit with her new friend, and though Eva urged her to come and join them, she and her 'big feller' kept clear of them. 'Sure, I'm not playing gooseberry. I can see you and Frank have something cooking.' She winked in that irritating way she had, when she was totally wrong and would not be told otherwise. 'Don't think I haven't seen the two of youse, heads bent and whispering all the while.'

Embarrassed that Frank might overhear, Eva made an excuse to go to the ladies. She knew Patsy would follow.

'There is nothing between me and Frank,' she told Patsy firmly, 'and I'll thank you to remember that.'

'All right, yer not sweethearts. So what were youse whispering about?'

'Can't tell.' Eva mentally crossed her fingers that Patsy wouldn't start on about her birthday again. 'What do you know about that man?' she said to distract her.

'What man?'

'Your new boyfriend.'

Patsy rolled her eyes dreamily. 'Well, he's good-looking—'

'That's a matter of opinion.'

'He's a big, strong hunk—'

'I won't argue with that.'

'An' he's taken a real shine to me, so 'e has.'

Hesitating, Eva wasn't sure how to say what was on her mind, but say it she must. 'I don't like him, Patsy. There's something about him that gives me the shivers.'

'Aw, yer jealous, so yer are.' Dabbing on her lipstick, she got some on her teeth. 'Now, look what you've done!' she cried, throwing her lipstick down. 'Give us a tissue and stop bullying me. It's a long time since I've had a man, and here yer are, making me feel bad.' The trouble was, Eva had struck a raw nerve. There *was* something about the man that was unsettling, but Patsy chose to believe it was the 'chemistry' between them that made her nervous.

Handing her a tissue, Eva said, 'Be careful,

Patsy, that's all I'm asking. Don't let him get you drunk.'

'I can look after meself. You just keep yer mind on Frank. Sure, the two of youse are getting on like a house on fire. It's the first time in ages I've seen you easy with a feller, so it is.' As she went to the door, she remarked, 'I'm going for a walk with me new sweetheart, but I'll not be long, I promise.'

'Don't go too far. I'll be making my way back soon.'

Returning to the table, Eva conveyed her fears to Frank. 'I know she's old enough to take care of herself, and I know I shouldn't poke my nose in, but I can't help feeling she's jumped in at the deep end with this man. I'm sure he just wants to have his way with her.'

'You're a cynic.'

'You think I should mind my own business, don't you?'

'In a word, yes.'

Eva laughed. 'Well, at least you're honest.'

Somehow his rebuke seemed to calm her fears and she contentedly sipped her drink.

Frank talked about the contractors he had signed up to refit the hotel foyer. 'I've seen some of their work,' he said. 'It's quality, and it doesn't cost the earth. In fact, some of the other contractors I talked to were almost double the price on certain fittings. For instance, I've made a saving of fifty pounds on the new balustrade. And the counter front will be in finest walnut – a warm wood, I always think.'

'If you don't mind me asking, does the hotel have a big enough turnover to warrant such expense?'

'You're very astute,' he said. 'That's why I want you with me on that business project. I just know we could make a lot of money.' Seeing her frown, he put up his hands as if in surrender. 'Sorry! I won't mention it again.'

'I'm not saying the hotel doesn't have a good turnover. I know it does. But I wouldn't have thought it was making huge profits.'

'And you would be right.' He had no reason to hide the truth from Eva. 'You're in as good a position as anyone to know the number of guests that come and go. You know the prices, and you can probably make an educated guess about outgoings. I've argued with Mother about spending money on a perfectly respectable foyer, but will she listen? Not her. She has a mind like a woodcutter's axe: once it's been cast, there's no going back.'

Eva smiled at his description but tactfully said nothing. She tapped her foot to the music and watched the dancers, twisting and turning to the rhythm, their bodies close. 'I sometimes wonder where I've been all this time,' she said wistfully. 'I don't ever remember dancing like that.'

'I've never seen you dance,' Frank said. 'You work all hours and when you're not working you sit on the beach looking out to sea. I've seen you there, and I've always thought it would be a sin to disturb you. You seem so deep in thought.' He knew very little about Eva, she hardly ever spoke of her past.

'I have a lot to think about,' she confessed. Where to go from here, what to do, how to live. How to rid herself of the impossible love she felt for Bill. And, above all, what would she do with the rest of her life? Her one great comfort was that her mother was always with her. Wherever she went, whatever she was doing, her thoughts were never far from that beloved woman. She would think of her father too, but there was never the same depth of feeling there. Frank is right, she thought. I work and sleep, and in between I'm all alone. There were times when even Patsy couldn't help.

Frank was quietly observing her, aware that there were depths to Eva he might never fully know. The knowledge was not welcome, but he hid his displeasure. 'You're something of a mystery to me,' he said. 'You never talk about yourself, Eva. You're always holding back, as though you're afraid to be hurt.'

Smiling wryly, she told him, 'We're all afraid to be hurt.'

Growing bolder, he asked, 'Were you hurt, Eva? Did you love someone once?'

She looked away. 'I've never had a deep relationship,' she answered truthfully.

'But you loved someone?'

Eva lapsed into silence, surprised that he should ask such a personal question. And when she answered, it was with simple truth. 'I never loved anyone in that way. I never really thought about it.' Not until Bill came back, she thought.

'Was it a lonely life, on that farm of yours?'

'We kept chickens and grew farm produce, but it was a small place, only a few acres.'

'Sounds like hard work.'

'It was. But it was so beautiful, Frank, unspoilt by the rush and panic of life. I'm not saying it wasn't busy, but there was a tranquillity there, it was a sort of quiet haven where only the changing seasons marked the passage of time.'

'Sounds wonderful.' Not for him though. For him the bright lights and rush of city life. That was where the money was, and that was where he meant to be; Eva, too, only she didn't know it yet.

'One day I'll have it all again,' she went on. 'Just like it was – a small cottage with gardens all around, and an orchard, and fields with a running brook beside them.' It was her goal in life. Her mother's place was gone for ever, but somewhere, in a quiet and lovely place, she would find what her heart desired. Until then, she would have to be patient and do what she had to do to keep body and soul together and make sure she and Patsy had a roof over their heads. But her time would come, she was determined on it.

'I've never had that kind of contentment,' Frank confided. 'My father died when I was very small, and Mother has always been the core of my life.' His expression darkened. 'The trouble is, she still thinks she can rule me. She won't let go. Everything she does, every plan she makes, it's all centred round me.'

'That's only natural, surely.' Eva couldn't understand his animosity. 'You're her only son. It's plain to me that she loves you very much.'

'It's not love,' he said sharply. 'What she feels for me is not natural. She wants to *own* me, control me, like she does everyone else she comes into contact with. Every time I try to strike out on my own, she uses all her wiles to keep me under her wing.'

Eva couldn't disagree; certainly, she was aware that Annie Dewhirst resented her friendship with Frank and did what she could to discourage it in all sorts of subtle ways. 'How old were you when your father died?' she asked.

'He died on my third birthday, a vicious flu virus. He couldn't fight it off, pneumonia set in and he was gone in a matter of days. I have no memories of him at all.' He clenched and unclenched his fists, his eyes cast downwards. 'You've no idea what it's like, growing up without a father and having a mother who tries to dominate your every thought.'

'I know what it's like to be at odds with one of your parents,' she admitted. 'My father was a wonderful man until a tractor overturned on him and he was crippled. After that he changed. He hardly ever smiled, and neither I nor my mother could do anything to please him. In the end we gave up trying. Sometimes life can do that to you.' She sighed deeply. 'One minute you can be a loving, happy family, and the next you're divided and life is never the same again.'

For a while they sat quietly, listening to the music. Frank never took his eyes off Eva. She haunted him. He wanted her so much he was prepared to kill for her. 'Patsy tells me you've done all kinds of work since leaving home.'

Tearing her gaze from the band, Eva smiled. 'You could say that. We stayed in more places than I can remember – Leighton Buzzard, Buckingham, Aylesbury, and others I can't even recall because we were in and out so fast.'

'Did you never want to stay?'

Eva's mind went back to the few weeks they had spent in Leighton Buzzard. 'There was a place. It was a big rambling house, owned by a car dealer; his wife was a dental surgeon working from a room at the back of the house. They were a large noisy family, four boisterous children, two ponies, a Siamese cat, and a German shepherd with a new litter of puppies.'

'Sounds like mayhem.'

'It was, but it was such fun. I looked after the children, while Patsy did the gardening. We were paid well, and on top of that we had a rent-free cottage overlooking the canal. In the evening we could see the barges travelling up and down, the men with their big burly arms and the women in their colourful turbans. We were really happy there, but they decided to sell up and move away. Six weeks we were there, and it was one of the happiest times I can remember.' Except for the memories of home, she thought.

'What else did you do?' He wanted to know everything about her.

'We've turned our hands to all kinds of work. Some of it was hard, and some of it badly paid. But occasionally we got paid well and enjoyed the work. We've washed up in cafes, cleaned offices and, would you believe, we even worked in a zoo for a time, taking money at the ticket kiosk.' She chuckled. 'Once, we got paid a couple of bob each for sweeping the pavement outside Woolworths.'

'My God!' He couldn't help but admire her. 'I don't mind telling you, I'm impressed. And, more to the point, you've managed to impress my mother, and I can tell you from experience, that is *not* easy!'

Eva laughed. Frank was so easy to talk to. He had the knack of making you feel special, as though what you did really mattered. He seemed to take a genuine interest; some men just took pleasure in belittling a woman's achievements. But Eva did not believe she had achieved very much. She was no closer to realising any of her dreams and aspirations. Yet it wasn't for the want of trying.

'Has it been very difficult, Eva?'

'Difficult enough,' she answered thoughtfully, 'but there have been a few laughs along the way, and we always managed to get back on our feet, even when things went wrong. One of the best jobs we had was serving in a baker's shop. We had two rooms above the shop as part of our wages, and as many pastries and pies as we could eat.' She chuckled at the memory. 'Trouble was, Patsy began eating away all the profits. The owner had a word with her, she took offence and the upshot was a blazing row. The next morning, we were thrown out.'

'It seems to me Patsy must be a burden at times.'

'She's *never* a burden,' Eva said immediately. 'Patsy is like a sister to me.'

'I understand.' He didn't though, and he was just the tiniest bit jealous.

'She worked for my mother, did you know that?'

'I believe she mentioned it when she was being interviewed for the job at the hotel.'

'She did the accounts, and helped at the farm

shop. She was a godsend. When my parents died, I was devastated. It was Patsy who got me through it. She was always there. Always supportive.'

She didn't tell him about the other times; how, when her father was at his worst, Patsy would carry them all along as though everything was normal. It was that kind of spirit that kept them going. Life was often impossibly difficult, but Patsy could always make them laugh. 'Oh, no,' Eva said emphatically, 'Patsy could never be a burden. Not to me.'

'She told me you are very like your mother.'

Eva smiled softly. 'I like to think so.'

'She also told me about the fire.'

Shocked, Eva asked, 'What else did she tell you?'

He cast his mind back. 'Only that your parents died because of the fire.'

Tears involuntarily sprang to Eva's eyes, and she was silent.

'Eva, I'm so sorry.' Still she was silent. 'What happened to the house? Did it burn down?'

Suffused with shame, she shook her head.

'Why didn't you stay there if you loved it so much?'

With every word he uttered he opened up old wounds. 'I don't want to talk about it,' Eva said, standing up. Surreptitiously she wiped away her tears. 'Patsy's been gone too long. I'd better go and find her.'

He didn't want her to go, especially not when he was just getting her to open up about herself. 'Patsy won't thank you for going after her,' he argued. 'She'll come back when she's ready. Stay here with me. Please. There is so much more I want to ask you.'

'I'm ready to go home.' Eva couldn't deny she had enjoyed herself, but now she felt tired. It had been such a long, hard day. Besides, Frank was too probing, and she had spent too long trying to put all that behind her. 'If I don't let her know I'm leaving, she'll come back and wonder where I've gone.'

'I'll come with you, and then I'll walk you home.' Fearing he might be rushing her, he swiftly added, 'If you'd like me to, that is. We still have a few things to decide about Patsy's party.' He didn't care a jot about Patsy's party; in fact it was a bloody nuisance. As if he didn't have better things to occupy his time! But it brought him into contact with Eva, and that was good enough for him.

<hr />

OUTSIDE, PATSY WAS fighting her new man off. 'I said no!' Flattening both her hands against his mighty chest, she managed to shove him back a step; being full of drink, he wasn't all that steady on his feet, but then neither was she.

'You're a bloody tease, that's what you are. It were you that led me out here. You wanted it as much as I did, and now you think you can cry

off! Well, you can't! Not when you've got me all
worked up.' Pushing his rough hands up the hem
of her skirt he propelled her back to the wall. 'And
don't yell out, 'cause I can silence you with one
blow.' Licking his lips, he grinned inanely. 'Stop
fighting. Let yourself enjoy it. I've never had any
complaints yet.'

'Touch me and I'll have the authorities on you,
so I will!' Patsy sounded confident, but inside she was
trembling. She had badly miscalculated this oaf. He
was big and strong, and against him she was like a
fly in a gale.

Ignoring her protests, he tore her skirt from
hem to waist. When, terrified, she screamed out,
he pressed a rough hand over her mouth. 'I warned
you!' He smashed his clenched fist into her face and
she slumped unconscious in his arms. He laid her on
the ground. Then with big clumsy fingers he began
removing her undergarments.

<hr>

EVA WAS FRANTIC. 'I *know* I heard her call
out.'

'You must have been imagining it.' Frank hadn't
heard a thing, and was hoping he wouldn't. He
wanted to walk Eva home alone.

'Ssh!' Through the silence of the night, Eva
imagined she heard a kind of scuffling. 'Listen,
Frank. I know she's here somewhere and I'm not

leaving until I've made sure she's all right.' She ran towards a disused building a few yards away. 'I think the sounds came from somewhere round here.' Frank ran after her.

As soon as they turned the corner of the building, they saw him.

'Piss off, you!' Stinking drunk, the burly man was having trouble getting astride Patsy. 'Can't you see we're busy?'

Eva ran forward. 'Quick, Frank! He's hurt her!' Lying beneath him, Patsy's bloodied face stared up, her eyes grey and pained, as though she was trying to make sense of what was going on.

'You cowardly bastard!' Frank yelled. He grabbed the fellow by the collar and forced him to his feet; the big man could hardly stand.

'She asked for what she got,' he slurred.

Struggling to sit up, Patsy leaned heavily on Eva. 'Please, Eva,' she muttered, 'tell Frank . . . let him go.' Eva opened her mouth to protest, but Patsy shook her head. 'He's right . . . I did . . . lead him on. Please . . .'

'Let him go,' Eva reluctantly told Frank, and to the man she said, 'If it was up to me, you'd be marched off to the police station, but for some reason Patsy says no. I'll tell you this though,' she warned. 'If you ever show your face round here again, or come anywhere near Patsy, you won't get off so lightly.'

They watched him go, unsteady and aimless, lurching from one side of the road to the other. 'He deserves a damned good whipping!' Frank said, though he was glad he hadn't had to do it. He was relieved, too, that the police weren't going to be involved. He didn't want to get caught up in anything tawdry.

'Let's get her home,' Eva said. She was worried about Patsy. 'Or maybe we should take her straight to the infirmary. She looks terrible.' In the glow from the street lamp, she noticed that Frank's nose was trickling blood. 'Are you all right?'

With the back of his hand he wiped away the blood. 'It's nothing,' he told her. 'I caught a glancing blow, that's all.' It got better, he thought. Blood on his face made him a real hero. 'Don't worry about me, it's Patsy who needs tending.'

Patsy heard, and put on a brave face. 'I'll be right as rain, so I will,' though her jaw ached as though it had been run over by a steam roller, and her legs felt like jelly. 'A good wash, that's all I need. There's nothing broken.'

'All right, Patsy, if you're sure. We'll get a taxi.' Eva turned to Frank. 'See if you can find one, will you, Frank?'

'I'm not leaving you two in this alley. If I remember rightly, there's a taxi rank just round the corner.'

With Patsy between them, supported on either

side, the three of them slowly made their way back to the road.

'You're lucky we found you when we did.' Frustrated because his chance with Eva was gone for tonight, Frank was annoyed with Patsy. 'He could have killed you, don't you realise that?'

'He didn't though, did he, eh?' Through one swollen eye she peered at Eva. 'I'm sorry, gal. If ye had any sense, you'd send me packing, so ye would.'

Eva shook her head forlornly. 'I've never had any sense where you're concerned.'

'I'm pissed as a nook.'

'I can see that.'

'Sure, I wouldn't blame ye if ye bawled me out.'

Eva's only concern was for Patsy's well-being. It was no time for recriminations. Tomorrow maybe, but not now.

<hr/>

BACK AT THE hotel, Annie Dewhirst was frantic. 'It's gone midnight!' She had been pacing her bedroom floor since eleven thirty. 'Wherever is he?'

She went back and forth, head bent and eyes blazing. Occasionally she would glance out of the window, muttering to herself. '*She's* not back either. If he's with her, he'll not hear the last of it. Scheming little baggage. If she thinks she can get her grubby

JOSEPHINE COX

little hands on this hotel and my money, she's got another think coming.'

She grabbed the phone receiver and rang reception. 'Margaret?'

'Yes, Mrs Dewhirst?'

'Have you seen my son?'

'No, Mrs Dewhirst. Not since he went out some hours ago.'

'Has Eva Bereton come back yet?'

'I haven't seen her, and I've been at the desk the whole time. She and Patsy have gone dancing, I believe.'

'You're sure they're not back?'

'Well, yes. If they'd come through the front door I would have seen them.'

Annie slammed the receiver down and began her pacing again, then stood by the window, wringing her hands. Her eyes bulged out of her head when she saw Frank and Eva carrying the dishevelled Patsy between them. What was worse, Patsy was in full song, her voice ringing out in the clear night air: 'Catch me if yer can, my name is Dan, and I'm yer man . . .'

But Annie wasn't smiling. 'Bastards!' She ran to the door and down the stairs.

'You're not coming in here,' she screeched, flinging open the front door. 'Take her in the back way. When she's safely out of sight, I want to see you, my boy!'

'Patsy needs a doctor,' Frank argued.

Forgetting the professional front she had perfected over the years, she hissed at him, 'I don't give a bugger *what* she needs!' She kept her voice low. 'You are not bringing that drunkard in through this front door. The back way, I said, and be quick about it. If anyone sees her in that state, our reputation will be destroyed.'

Shaking with temper, she glared at Eva. 'Trouble, that's what you are. Real trouble, the pair of you!' Then she quickly closed the door in their faces and leaned on it to gather her composure.

'Are you all right, Mrs Dewhirst?' Margaret asked timidly. She had heard every word exchanged at the front door and prayed her employer wouldn't turn her anger on her.

'Of course I'm all right!' Glancing up at the large clock over the reception desk, she saw that it was almost 2 a.m. With great deliberation, she turned the key in the lock. 'Keep your eye out for any latecomers,' she told the nervous receptionist, 'and mind who you let through that door. Do you hear?'

'Yes, Mrs Dewhirst. Whatever you say.'

SWINGING THE HAPLESS Patsy on to her bed, Frank groaned. 'I had no idea you weighed so much.' Leaning over the bed to recover his breath, he looked straight into her bruised but mischievous face. 'You've knackered me.'

'Well now, it don't take much to knacker you, does it, eh?' She managed a naughty chuckle. 'Ye can stay and see me in me nightie if ye like, but I warn ye, I'm not a pretty sight, even at the best of times.'

'In that case, I think it's a pleasure I'll refuse, if you don't mind. I've seen enough of you for one night.'

As Eva walked him to the door, Patsy called out, 'Don't forget yer mammy wants to see ye – *my boy*!'

Her remark struck home. He stiffened, but made no comment.

'I'm sorry about Patsy,' Eva apologised. 'She means no harm.'

'It's all right,' he lied. 'No offence taken.'

Before Eva closed the door, she kissed him gently on the mouth. 'Well, *I* want to say thank you. Honestly, Frank, if you hadn't been there, I dread to think what might have happened.'

From down the corridor, Annie saw the kiss, and she could hardly restrain herself from calling out. But she chose to remain hidden. Presently, she hurried to her room to wait for Frank.

He didn't come, and she seethed with anger.

Her resolve to get rid of Eva and Patsy hardened into a plan of action which would achieve her aim without Frank ever knowing of her part in it.

———»•○•«———

FRANK DIDN'T SLEEP well that night. Filled with thoughts of Eva and tasting her kiss until the morning light, he began to make his own plans to woo Eva and get her down the aisle as soon as possible. After all, she had kissed him, hadn't she? And what was a kiss if it wasn't an expression of love?

To Eva though, the kiss had been no more than a friendly thank you. 'That was a cruel and unnecessary jibe,' she chided Patsy. 'How could you say a thing like that after what he did for you?'

'Don't know what yer talking about.' With the drink beginning to wear off, Patsy was getting sulky and difficult.

Propelling her to the bathroom, Eva was severe. 'You know what I'm talking about all right,' she said angrily, 'but we'll say no more about it tonight. Let's get you washed and cleaned up, and into your bed. Tomorrow we'll decide what to do.'

Instantly, Patsy was alert. 'What do ye mean, decide what to do?'

'Nothing.' Eva didn't want to talk about anything right now; she felt dead on her feet. But she had no doubt that neither she nor Patsy would be welcome here any more. It was such a shame, especially when she was beginning to understand the hotel trade from top to bottom.

─────※◦◦◦◦───

IN THE MORNING, Annie was all sweetness and light. 'Of course I was angry,' she told Frank, who had come to see her in her office. 'The three of you intending to come in the front entrance like that, whatever would the guests think?'

'You're right, Mum. It was a stupid thing to do. It won't happen again, I can promise you. By the way, where is Eva?' He hadn't been able to find her on the way here.

'I've given her the day off,' Annie said benevolently. 'It's one of our quieter days and I can manage without her for a while. I've been in to see Patsy, and she looks terrible. Her face is swollen like a football.' She shuddered with distaste. Then her expression changed and she bestowed a wide, proud smile on him. 'Eva told me what you did. I'm so proud of you.' Secretly she thought he was a fool. What if he'd been hurt? Killed even? God Almighty, it didn't bear thinking about!

'I didn't do much,' he said lightly. 'There's nothing pressing you want me for, is there, Mum?' he asked. 'I'd like to make sure they're all right.' It was Eva he wanted to see. As for Patsy, he couldn't care if he never clapped eyes on her again.

'I'm afraid they'll have to wait. There's a bit of a crisis and you're the only one who can sort it out.'

'Not today. I've enough to do as it is.' Asking Eva to marry him was top of the list.

'Palmer's have just been on the phone. They're refusing to deliver the tablecloths and decorations for tomorrow's wedding party. If I don't get them by this afternoon, I'm in real trouble.'

That focused his attention. 'Palmer's? There's been some stupid mistake. I placed that order myself weeks ago. Get them back on the phone,' he urged. 'I'll have a word with them, find out what the devil they're playing at.'

'It's no good,' she lied. 'I've been on the phone half an hour with them already this morning. With Carson away for a week, the whole place seems to be falling apart at the seams. I've been passed from office to office, and nobody seems to know what they're doing.'

'Maybe it's time we dropped Palmer's and went elsewhere. Have you phoned any of the other suppliers?'

'Every one and they can't help. Besides, Palmer's are the best. You know that, Frank. When he gets back, Carson will shake that place up like you've never seen. Heads will roll, I can promise you that.' She leaned over the desk towards him. 'There's no other way, Frank, you'll have to go round. You placed the order, and it's you who has to sort it out. Get them to deliver, or we're in real trouble. It won't take you long.'

'But they're forty miles away.'

'An hour there and back, that's all. Please, Frank.'

He sighed. 'But I've got to see Eva before I go.'

'You can't.'

'Why not?

'Because she's driven Patsy to the doctor's and they may have a long wait before he'll see her on a Sunday. Don't waste time, Frank. Sort this thing out with Palmer's, and Eva will be here when you get back. I'll tell her there's been a crisis and you're seeing to it.' A happy thought entered her head. 'I'm sure Eva realises there are times when only you can put things right.'

It worked. He nodded. 'You're right, Mum. A crisis, you tell her that.'

Well satisfied, Annie watched him hurry off. Then she made two calls. The first was to Palmer's. 'Mr Carson's secretary,' she requested officiously.

The two women had a very curious conversation, the upshot of which was that the secretary would expect her 'payment' soon, and that yes, everything would be ready when Frank arrived.

'It's always good to have friends in low places,' Annie chuckled as she put down the phone. 'Especially ones who owe you a favour or two.'

Her next call was to send for Eva and Patsy; they had not gone to the doctor but were in Patsy's room, where Eva was tending her bruises.

When, a few moments later, they were standing before her, Annie regarded them with contempt. She might well have taken to Eva, had it not been for the fact that Frank had taken to her first. She was so lovely and bright, her fair hair falling loose about her shoulders, her green eyes looking at her expectantly, and a trifle warily. Patsy was bruised and sore, her top lip grotesquely swollen and her nose puffed and red. They were a strange pair, Annie thought.

'I want you out of here in half an hour,' she said brusquely. 'Pack your bags. Be off, and don't ever come here again.'

'Jaysus!' Patsy was shocked to her roots. 'Surely to God ye ain't throwing us out?'

Eva's shock was short-lived; this was no more than she had expected. 'I understand,' she said. 'We'll be on our way. The last thing we want is trouble.'

'Good. That's all I have to say. Now, get out of here.'

Patsy half turned, but Eva held her back. 'Hang on, Patsy. I think Mrs Dewhirst has forgotten something.'

Annie stiffened. 'And what might that be?' she asked tightly.

'Our back pay and holiday money, Mrs Dewhirst.'

Annie's face went pale with anger. 'There'll be no back pay or holiday money for you two, not after what happened here last night.'

'Then we'll have to wait for Frank and see what he has to say,' Eva bluffed. 'He was with us last night, after all.' She wondered where he was. Probably despatched on an errand to get him out of the way.

Annie couldn't help but feel a stab of admiration for Eva. Realising she had met her match, she conceded. 'Very well. I shall expect you back here, with your bags packed, in half an hour. I'll have your money ready.'

When Eva and Patsy returned to the office, coats on, bags in hand, Annie paid over what was owed. The only words spoken were by Eva, as she was leaving. 'Frank is a good man,' she said to Annie, her tone gentle. 'I like him a lot. But I wasn't trying to steal him from you.'

With those profound words she made her departure. Behind her, Annie was left to wonder about this young woman who had come into her life and gone out of it in so short a time. 'Maybe you weren't trying to steal him,' she murmured to herself, 'but you were a danger that had to be removed. I have never seen my son look at any woman the way he looked at you.'

Annie sat at her desk and studied Eva's signature on the wage receipt. Then she took pen to paper and laboriously copied it over and over, until she had almost perfected the lettering. 'I could have done this for a living,' she chuckled.

A short time later, she read the letter she had written back to herself.

Dear Frank,

I have to leave. I meant to tell you last night, but there was no opportunity.

I know this will come as a shock to you, but I lied to you, Frank. There is someone else. I treated him badly, but it's time for me to face up to my responsibilities. I still love him, you see.

You've been a good friend. I won't see you again, so take care of yourself.

Eva

When Frank came home, full of his accomplishments and eager to see Eva, his mother handed him the note. 'I'm sorry,' she said. 'Eva told me before she left.'

While he read with a stony face, she hoped and prayed it would turn him against Eva.

When a moment later he screwed the letter into a tight ball and threw it on the fire, she breathed a sigh of relief. Eva was out of their lives and he had learned his lesson.

PART THREE

---❦---

JUNE 1960
OLD FRIENDS

Chapter Five

———❦❧———

BILL NEVER LIKED travelling by air. He preferred to have some control over his fate. If anything unexpected happened up in the air, he would have no say at all in the way his life ended.

But when business took you from Vancouver to Victoria, you either took the ferry, or you flew. The ferry was undoubtedly the more relaxed way, and some claimed the most scenic, which was certainly true as the land was not obscured by clouds, but it was slow, and for Bill, time was precious.

The sky was cloudless today; it was a glorious morning in June. The sea stretched beneath them like a deep blue, shimmering carpet. Here and there islands speckled the water, with tiny white-sailed yachts bobbing between them. This part of British Columbia was breathtaking.

'It's so wonderful!' Sheila stretched her neck to look out of the window.

Bill smiled in agreement. 'However many times I see this view, I always feel humble, insignificant.'

'Yes,' she replied, keeping her eyes on the waters

below, 'I know what you mean.' She shifted her gaze to sneak a look at some of their fellow passengers. One of them had his nose stuck in a business paper; a young couple had eyes only for each other; another man was slumped down in his seat, eyes closed and head nodding. 'Though I don't think *they* understand what you mean,' she chuckled.

Bill's eyes followed her gaze. 'Too early in the morning for him, poor devil.' He looked at his watch. 'Half past eight. I wouldn't have minded a lie-in myself this morning.' They had got to bed last night at midnight for the third night in a row, and still they had two days' hard graft in front of them before they could begin their long journey home to Vancouver.

He glanced at Sheila. 'I expect you're tired too, aren't you? You've worked alongside me all through, and never once complained.'

Three years his secretary and two years his friend, Sheila was a godsend to him. She had been forty-seven when he took her on in preference to umpteen young things with feather brains and long legs.

His wife had been surprised when she met Sheila. 'You must be mad, choosing her over some-one younger,' she told Bill, but secretly she was delighted. Sheila, though pleasantly attractive, with a slim figure and good legs, would not pose a threat to her.

Bill had never regretted his choice. Sheila worked hard and was unswervingly loyal. Her reputation brought plenty of attractive offers from other property agents, but she always dropped them into the nearest wastepaper bin. Bill knew what a gem she was, and treated her well. Whenever he went away on business, it was with the knowledge that he would return to an orderly office, with every crisis taken care of. When he went on a business trip involving a string of meetings over a period of time, he would take her along and put an experienced temp in to hold things back in Vancouver. This didn't happen often and so far the arrangement had caused no great upheaval.

'Sheila?'

'Hmm?'

'You seem far away. I just wondered if you regretted being away from the office.'

Her kindly face crinkled in a smile. 'How could I regret seeing all this?' she asked, gesturing to the islands below. 'Of course I'm not regretting it. You know I like to accompany you from time to time. Someone has to keep an eye on you.' She grimaced. 'All the same, I hope that young woman isn't messing up my files!'

Bill laughed. 'She wouldn't dare! Not after the lecture you gave her before we left.'

She stared at him. 'Shame on you, Bill Westerfield. You were eavesdropping.'

'I should think everyone within a five-mile radius heard you laying down the law.' When she looked mortified, he added, 'Only kidding.'

'It was only a short lecture,' she said. 'You have to make sure these temps know their place.' She looked out of the window again. 'We're nearly there, I think.'

As she gazed out of the window, Bill took quiet stock of his secretary. He had grown very fond of her. Slim to a fault, with greying hair and robust outlook on life, nothing seemed to faze her, not even his father. One day she would leave, he knew it was inevitable. Her only living relative was a younger sister who lived in Scotland, and Sheila always said that when she was old and weary, she would go home to be with her sister. Bill hoped that day was still very far away.

His thoughts turned to England, and Eva, and almost without thinking, he took out his wallet and opened it. There, smiling back at him and looking exactly as he remembered Eva herself, was the scorched picture of Colette.

He had been sorely tempted to ignore the plea in Eva's letter and search her out, but he hadn't, in spite of his love for her. His conscience stopped him. He was a married man. The marriage might not be a happy one for him, but he believed his wife loved and needed him, especially since the loss of their only child. Besides, Eva didn't love him in that way. She was probably married herself by now.

'Penny for them?' Sheila's voice broke into his thoughts.

'Just thinking.' Quickly folding his wallet, he returned it to his pocket, drawing her attention to the world outside. 'We're landing,' he observed.

Sheila's heart went out to him. She knew of the photo; it wasn't the first time she'd seen him looking at it, though she had no idea who it was.

Bill was a good man, one of the best. But he was not content. He had not been content for a very long time. The situation at home was fraught, what with the loss of their child last winter, and now his wife's drinking. There had been all kinds of cruel rumours, as there often were about a tragedy. Whispers were growing that Bill's wife was responsible for their son's death because she had left the infant wandering the gardens alone while she entertained a man friend.

Thankfully, Bill seemed unaware of the rumours, but they were spreading, and sooner or later he was bound to hear them. Sheila dared not dwell on it too much. True or not, they could well destroy a marriage that was already struggling to survive. But then, if the marriage were to end, it might not be such a bad thing, she thought, for Bill in particular.

—→◆←—

THEIR LIMOUSINE WAS waiting; long and black, with tinted windows, it had a sinister appearance. 'I hate these things,' Sheila said as she scrambled into the car. 'Everyone stares as you drive along.'

Bill climbed in after her. 'It's human nature. When the windows are blacked out, people naturally want to know who's inside.'

'I feel like a fraud.' Settling down in the luxurious seat, Sheila looked round. The floor-covering was thick and plush; there was a small television, a cocktail bar encased in walnut, and above that a neat row of expensive crystal glasses. 'I'm not used to this. Whatever would people say?'

'Pretend you're a celebrity,' Bill laughed. 'Wind down the window and wave as you go by.'

Wisely ignoring him, she changed the subject. 'How far to the railway station?'

'About twenty minutes, if my memory serves me right.'

The railway waiting room was packed; there were tourists in shorts, children running around, and also, much to Bill's interest, a number of serious-faced men in suits.

'I expect they're here for the same reason as we are,' he remarked to Sheila. 'Whistler is an up and coming area. The development potential is growing, and land prices have taken off again.'

'I wonder if your father will be there.' Sheila voiced what was already on his mind.

'If he is, I'll be ready for him.'

Sheila knew what lay behind Bill's grim tone. Without going into any detail, Bill had told her that his father had made the Bereton girl homeless, and that she had disappeared before he could help her. But Sheila knew Bill well enough to realise there was more to it than that. She even suspected he might be in love with Eva, but she never pried. If there ever came a time when he might want to talk, he knew she was there, and he knew she would never sit in judgement. Until then, Bill's secrets were his own.

'I'm glad I hung on to that parcel of land.' Bill focused his mind on the business in hand. 'It's a hard decision to make, whether to hold on for a bit longer, or develop it now.' He lapsed into thought.

'Follow your instincts,' Sheila told him. 'They haven't let you down yet.'

She was right. It seemed that everything he touched turned to gold. He was sitting on a small fortune with the land at Whistler, and he had made a huge profit from selling off a string of commercial properties in Vancouver. Four years ago he got them for a song because they were rundown and nobody seemed prepared to take them on. Everyone said he was mad, but within two years the whole area had taken off. It was where every businessman wanted his offices located.

The train pulled into the station and everyone began to move towards it.

'Now, *this* is more my cup of tea.' Sheila settled down near a window, with Bill beside her. 'I love trains, and I've always wanted to ride through the Rockies.' She was more excited than the children with their noses pressed to the windows.

Trying not to smile, Bill said, 'You're here to work, my girl, not to enjoy yourself.'

But she did enjoy herself, and so did he.

They ate a hearty breakfast. Sheila had cornflakes with milk and sugar, followed by a fresh croissant and strawberry jam, washed down with a cup of tea. Bill opted for a fried breakfast – egg, tomato, sausage, crispy bacon, the aroma of which permeated every carriage – and plenty of strong black coffee. 'To clear my mind,' he told Sheila, who chided him for drinking so much coffee.

'Bad for your health,' she responded.

The journey was a memorable experience. They passed lakes and forests that were older than Methuselah, and more magnificent than words could describe. The tumbling waterfalls and extraordinary rock formations were an awesome sight, and growing right up to the track were the prettiest flowers of every shape, colour and size.

Some way along the track, the train began to slow down. 'What's happening?' Sheila asked.

A passing guard heard her. 'Look out of your

window to the right.' Smiling knowingly, he moved on.

When Sheila cried out with excitement, Bill leaned over her shoulder. 'Brandy Wine Falls,' he told her; he had seen them on his last trip. 'The water falls from high up in the mountains.' He paused. 'There can't be many sights like that on God's earth.'

Eyes glued to the window and hands clasped together, Sheila whispered, 'It's amazing!'

Falling away from beneath the rails, the rush of clear, sparkling water roared down towards the rocks, where it swirled and meandered before flowing into the forest like a silver snake going to ground. 'I've never seen anything so wonderful!' Sheila murmured. And Bill had to agree.

All too soon, the journey was over. Through the train window, Bill read the station sign, Whistler. 'Now it's down to work.' He was ready. Work took his mind off Eva for a time, but always she returned to haunt him. In his deepest heart, he knew one day he would have to find her. When the time was right.

⟫⟩◦⟨⟪

THE HOTEL WAS small but comfortable. Bill had instructed Sheila to ask for rooms with a mountain view, and that was exactly what they got. Sheila's was on the ground floor, while Bill had opted for a loftier view.

After satisfying himself that she was comfortable, he made his way upstairs to his own room. It was pleasant enough, big and square, with a pine bed and dresser, and a brightly painted bathroom.

Placing his overnight bag on the bed, he took off his jacket and went to the window. This was not the first time he had stayed here, but the grandeur of these mountains always made him feel humble. 'No one should build here,' he murmured. But it was too late for regrets. Already there were numerous buildings – small shops and general supply stores, all catering for the people who came here from all walks of life. There were those who wanted to escape the routine of everyday life and there were the enterprising people who had settled here as soon as it had begun to open up to the outside world; others came for the ski-ing, and many came merely to admire the natural beauties that Whistler had to offer.

At 2 p.m., Sheila and Bill met in the foyer. Bill ordered coffee to be brought through to the lounge. Once there, he and Sheila got straight to work.

'Three meetings,' Sheila reminded him. 'The surveyor at two fifteen, with the architect joining you both on site half an hour later. I booked a quiet room here in the hotel for your discussions afterwards. I've checked at the desk and there's no problem.' She grimaced. 'It's just a small room overlooking the gardens, which they put aside for business meetings, though I'm told they have a full conference room planned for next year.'

'Have they given me the two hours I asked for?'

'What with the auction and all, the room is apparently booked solid from midday, but yes, you've got your two hours.'

The waitress brought the coffee and Sheila shifted her papers to the sofa. 'I've put the schedule and all relevant documents in here.' She handed Bill a slim plastic folder.

He glanced through it. 'Thorough as usual,' he commented, giving her a grateful smile.

'It's what you pay me for.'

'It's make your mind up time,' he said. 'By the end of the day, big decisions will have to be made. If I make the wrong ones, I may well live to regret it.'

'That won't happen.'

He laughed. 'You never doubt, do you?'

'Not where you're concerned.' She had often wished things might have been different. Sometimes life cast a dark shadow and it was hard to get out from under it. Bill was more a part of her life than he would ever know and that was how it should be.

'I'll have to keep my wits about me, that's for sure,' Bill remarked thoughtfully.

'You've tangled with them all before. They know they'll get no change from you.'

'I need you there,' he told her. 'Take notes. Miss nothing. I don't want surprises.'

'Trust me.'

'Don't I always?'

His remark made Sheila feel ashamed. As for not wanting surprises, he would be shocked to his roots if he knew the truth. And, oh, how she longed to tell him. The temptation was never far away, but conscience and fear were stronger, so she remained silent.

———◆———

THE DAY WAS perfect, warm and bright, with a cool breeze falling from the mountains. The surveyor commended Bill on his choice of site. 'This whole place must have been wide open when you bought this,' he observed. 'You had the choice, and you settled on what I reckon is the best piece of real estate in the whole area.'

'I did my homework.'

'I can see that.' Now and again a man like Bill Westerfield came up from nothing to take on the old veterans. It took a younger, more agile mind to see into the future. All the same, the surveyor felt a tinge of regret. 'It seems a pity to build stores and such here,' he remarked, for a moment letting his heart rule his head. 'Such a tranquil place. Still, I suppose we have to move with the times. Or stand still and be trodden underfoot.'

'No, you're right,' Bill answered thoughtfully. 'It does seem a pity, and to tell you the truth, I'm not entirely convinced that "stores and such" are the right way forward. That's why I wanted you and the architect here at the same time. I have several ideas I want to chew over.'

For a moment they stood at the foot of the mountains, gazing at the site and projecting their minds forward to what might eventually stand here. Now, it was a vast empty area, pitted with ancient dips and rises. Boulders, delivered from the mountains at some time in the distant past, dotted the landscape. The ground swept upwards towards the mountains; on one side was a brook, on the other a dramatic, curving swath of pine trees. Directly in front was a panoramic view of the small community below, and beyond that a wide shimmering lake. The site itself lay like a precious jewel in a timeless garden.

'There are men who would pay an absolute fortune for this,' the surveyor remarked enviously.

'They're too late.' Bill thought of his adoptive father. 'They missed their chance long ago.'

With Sheila always two steps behind, the two men strode about, measuring, discussing, bandying ideas, and though he was alert to the task in hand, Bill's heart was with Eva.

There was something here, in this quiet, beautiful place, that reminded him of her. He could build her a home here, which she would cherish; they could have a wonderful life, blessed with children, God willing, and live here for the rest of their days. A lifetime in paradise, he thought.

He laughed inwardly. What was he thinking of? Things like that were the stuff of fairy tales.

Some time later, the architect joined them, and the discussions took on a new dimension. 'It's going to be a viable, commercial proposition,' he advised Bill. 'But we might have to cut deep into that area there.' He gestured towards the swath of trees.

'That's not an option.' Bill was adamant. 'We're not here to destroy. *If* I decide to build rather than sell, it must naturally complement what's already here. To spoil it would be sacrilege.' From out of the corner of his eye, he caught Sheila's quiet smile of approval.

When the outdoor work was concluded, they retired to the hotel. The room booked for the meeting was soulless, with harsh green walls and a large central table surrounded by straight-backed chairs. It was not very welcoming, but conducive to business.

Bill placed himself at the head of the table, with the surveyor and architect on either side of him. Sheila remained close by, pen and pad at the ready.

'Down to business,' Bill declared. 'Before we leave this room, I need to know that we're all of the same mind.' The surveyor and architect began emptying their briefcases on to the table. 'Put away your notes and plans,' Bill told them. 'We're starting from scratch.'

———◆———

WHENEVER BILL WAS away, Joan Westerfield was never lonely. 'Don't you feel ashamed?' she teased, stroking the man's erect penis.

Groaning, he pushed up to her. 'Why should I feel ashamed?'

She giggled. 'Not many men would make love to their son's wife – in his bed, too.'

'He's *not* my son!'

She laughed softly, opened her legs and drew him down on top of her.

Unable to resist, he smiled wickedly. 'You're a devil!'

'Devils together,' she whispered and pushing her tongue into his mouth, gave herself up to him.

The following evening Bill returned. 'I've missed you,' Joan murmured, meeting him at the door with open arms. 'You've no idea how lonely it can be when you're not here.'

That night they made love. For her it was a triumph. For Bill, though he was a man, with a man's needs, it just made him want Eva all the more.

Tonight, as always after he and Joan had made

love, he went downstairs and made himself a cup of strong coffee. 'If I thought Joan could be happy without me, I'd go right now,' he whispered. But believing that he was the one at fault because of his love for another woman, he swept aside his secret longings.

In her cosy apartment, Sheila, too, was finding it difficult to sleep. Seated in an armchair in her sitting room, she gazed at the photograph. Tears ran down her face. 'I should never have let it happen,' she muttered. 'Why did I let it happen?'

The photograph was of two babies; one a boy, the other a girl. 'I made one mistake,' she whispered, clasping the photograph to her breast, 'and I'll be punished for the rest of my life.'

Chapter Six

'TAKE YOUR FRIEND home, before I kick her out on the end of my toe!'

Eva gave the man a withering glare. 'It was the waitress who started the argument. Patsy was only defending herself.'

'Out, I said!' With a dozen customers looking on, he was in no mood for listening. 'It's not the first time she's caused trouble in here, and now I'm barring her.' He paused, looking into Eva's defiant face and thinking how lovely she was. 'You're welcome any time,' he said more kindly, 'but not her. Not that one!' For good measure he gave Patsy a little shove towards the door, and received a mouthful of abuse in return.

'If you bar Patsy, you bar me,' Eva told him.

He shrugged. 'As you like.' He ushered them out and on to the pavement.

The waitress who had goaded Patsy made a rude gesture. Patsy saw it. 'The little bastard, I'll rip her eyes out!' she shrieked, and Eva had to physically restrain her from barging back inside.

'One of these days, Patsy Noonan . . .' Giving up, Eva sighed. 'What's the point? You'll never change.'

'Sure, it weren't my fault!' With her lip dragging the ground, Patsy trailed behind. 'Didn't ye see how she kept on at me?'

Eva paused for Patsy to catch up. 'Can you blame her?'

'What d'ye mean by that?'

'You know perfectly well what I mean, Patsy, telling the poor girl how you'd spent the night with her young man. And not content with that, you had to go into every sordid detail.'

'Serves her right. She's no good for him anyway.'

'Oh? How do you know that?'

Sulking now, Patsy retorted, 'I don't want to talk about it.' She began going at a faster pace, forcing Eva to keep up with her. 'If she can't take the truth, it's not my fault, is it?'

'Wait a minute!' Catching Patsy by her coat sleeve, Eva drew her to a halt. 'Is this the same man you said you were serious about? The one you thought might walk you down the aisle?'

'I said I don't want to talk about it.'

'He's dropped you, hasn't he? Like all the other men you take a shine to, he's had his fun and games, and now he doesn't want to know.'

'All right! Go on, say it!'

'What?'

'"I told you so." Say it, I don't mind. It's what I deserve.'

Now, everything was clear. Eva felt desperately sorry but at the same time she did wish Patsy would be more careful with the men she chose. 'Oh, Patsy, when will you ever learn?'

As they walked along, Patsy was broodingly silent, and Eva kept her own counsel, thinking how true it was that men seemed always to be at the root of a woman's problems. As for herself, she had never lost sight of Bill. He was always in her mind. In her heart.

Eva drew Patsy into a tiny cafe opposite the castle. 'Let's go in here,' she suggested. 'We never did get around to ordering food.'

'Don't want to.'

'You're not hungry then?'

'I didn't say that.'

'They do a delicious ham and salad roll in here, remember?' Eva was starving. This was their lunch break and there would be no more time for food until they finished at six tonight. 'Come on, Patsy. We have to be back at work in half an hour.'

'If I do come inside, I'm not talking.'

Eva despaired. When Patsy was in this mood, it was like trying to shift a mountain. 'That's okay. Whatever you want.'

In the event, the lunch was very enjoyable; hot

ham rolls with salad on the side, and a steaming mug of strong coffee topped off with cream. 'I don't love him.' Patsy had a mouthful of ham and a piece of cucumber in her mouth. 'He was just a passing fancy. Somebody to take me out and treat me like I was special.'

Eva made no comment.

'He *did* dump me,' she confessed, 'like I was nothing at all.'

Still Eva made no comment.

Unperturbed, Patsy went on, chewing and chatting at the same time. 'We were getting on like a house on fire, I told ye that, didn't I? Then, out of the blue for no reason, he told me he was going back to *that* little sourpuss!' She made a sour face. 'That's what I can't understand.' Her eyes grew round. 'What the devil does he see in *her* when there's me for the taking?'

Eva took a bite out of her ham roll. She knew that whatever she said, Patsy would disagree. If she let Patsy talk without interruption, she could get it all off her chest and hopefully they would have a peaceful afternoon.

'What's wrong with you?' Patsy demanded. 'Are ye deaf or what?'

'Afraid to open my mouth, that's all.'

'Why?'

'In case I get my head bitten off.'

'Don't be so bloody daft!'

'Patsy?'

'Don't go asking me about him, 'cause I'm not talking!'

'No. I was just thinking, about us.'

'What about us?'

'I've been wondering if it's time to move on.' In fact, Eva had thought of nothing else this past year. Now they had a healthy sum of money saved, she felt an irresistible urge to try and build a business of their own.

'I thought you liked it here in Wales. Especially Cardiff. One of the prettiest places you've seen, that's what you said.'

'And I meant it. The people are very friendly too.' Sometimes it was a real wrench moving away. 'But our contract has nearly finished. In three weeks' time, the site will be completed and we'll be out of a job.'

'Jaysus!' Wrapped up in her personal trials, Patsy had never given it a thought. 'What about the house? Will we be turned out?'

'It was part of the contract, Patsy. Several years' work and a house for the duration. In three weeks, it all comes to an end.'

'What will we do?'

'There are two things we can do, Patsy,' Eva answered. 'We can stay here and scout about for work and a place to live. Or we can go and search out something altogether different. Go somewhere

Josephine Cox

where no one can ever turn us out. Find something that really belongs to us – bought and paid for.'

'What? Like our own house, you mean?'

'And maybe our own business.' Excitement filled Eva's soul. 'Oh, Patsy, it's what we've scrimped and saved for these past years. We've got a tidy sum put by, not a fortune but it might get us a little business of our own. We'd have to keep our sights low at first, borrow from the bank too I expect, but if we could make a start, oh, Patsy, wouldn't that be something?' A dream come true, that's what it would be.

'Do you really think we could do it? A house and everything?'

'We'd have to go on sharing a house for a time, but if we do well, it wouldn't be long before you could have your own place, Patsy. Think of that.'

Suspicious and insecure, Patsy rounded on her. 'Why should I want my own place? Haven't we been content enough under the same roof? Are you trying to get rid of me, is that it?'

'You know that's not the case, Patsy.' Sometimes Eva longed for a little house of her own. All these years, she and Patsy had lived under each other's feet and though she loved Patsy, she found herself dreaming more and more of her own place. She wanted space to think. Space to be alone with her thoughts and memories. 'I'm thinking of you as well. What if you meet someone special? You might be glad to have your own place.'

Patsy's face lit up. 'You might be right at that. I could fetch him home and we could make all the noise we wanted, instead of being afraid to wake you.' Leaning over the table, she wiped the crumbs from her mouth and clenched her fists in the air. 'It sounds good. So tell me what the plans are.'

While Eva outlined her ideas for their future, Patsy ordered another ham roll, and to hell with the time!

<hr />

T HE NEXT THREE weeks flew past.

'I wish I could keep you both on.' A tall willowy man in his early sixties, Larry was the owner of the Castle Construction Company. 'But I promised myself that this would be the last project.'

The three of them stood in his portable office, staring out of the window at the sprawling new housing development. Wide roads and landscaped gardens lent an air of grandeur to the rows of mock Tudor houses, every one sold by Larry and Eva, with the help of Patsy's exuberant telephone manner. 'Now that it's finished, and I'm still in good health, thank God, I mean to retire.'

He looked from one to the other. 'You can stay

on in the house for a few weeks if you like, but after that I'll need to sell it. I have to rake in as much as I can for my retirement.'

Eva thanked him but declined. 'You've been very good to us,' she said, 'but we've got plans of our own.'

Satisfied, he shook hands with them, then handed each a small brown envelope. 'It's just a small token of my appreciation. With Patsy's flair on the phone, and your genius in selling to anyone who showed an interest, Eva, I feel I owe you. And don't say it's what you were paid for, because there are others who are paid the same and don't give a monkey's.'

They left the office and Eva made her way across the site to the foreman.

'You're away then, the two of you?' Mick Forester was a kindly soul, short in stature with a wiry frame and a laugh that would frighten donkeys, but he had a heart of gold, and it was full of aspirations for a life with Patsy Noonan.

'The place won't be the same when you're gone,' he sighed. 'Me and the lads will be here for at least six months, landscaping and tidying up. But I wish you all the best.' His blue eyes strayed to where Patsy was waiting for Eva. 'Take care of the lass,' he said. 'It's a job I'd willingly do, if only she'd let me.'

Eva said what was in her heart. 'Patsy's a

fool. She wouldn't know a good man if she fell over him.'

'Where will you go?'

'Blackburn, I think.' In fact, she was certain.

'Why Blackburn?'

'Because Lancashire is not too far away, and I've heard there's a lot of new enterprises opening up.'

He chuckled. 'Looking to make a fortune, are you?'

Eva smiled. 'I can but try.'

'Look after yourselves,' he called, and Patsy, tormenting as ever, blew him a kiss.

'You're heartless,' Eva chided, 'breaking his heart the way you did.'

'Not him,' Patsy replied. 'It was over between us almost as soon as it got started.'

'That's a shame.'

'No, it's not. He's too quiet, too easily satisfied with his lot – work every day, home every night and out once a week. I need something more exciting out of life.'

'It's not because he's a widower with a small daughter, is it?'

'Maybe, I don't know. But I can't say I relish the thought of being tied to a kitchen sink or looking after a snotty-nosed brat.'

'That's a bit harsh. Mick's child is a sweet little thing.'

'You're right, she's a little darlin'', but I'm not ready to play Mammy.' Patsy's own hard childhood had coloured her vision of family life. 'Anyway, I'm too irresponsible and set in me ways to settle down, so I am.'

'He adores you, Patsy, anyone can see that.'

'I know it. But I don't want kids and I don't need a husband.'

In fact, Patsy had taken a real shine to Mick, until he began to talk of marriage. It had unnerved her and now she was afraid to go anywhere near him. 'To tell you the truth,' she murmured, 'I hope he forgets all about me.'

Eva knew there were times when you spoke your mind, and other times when you let Patsy be. This was a time to let her be. 'So, we're off to Blackburn then, are we?'

'Whatever you say.' Patsy was not one for making decisions. 'But why Blackburn?'

'Some time ago Frank told me about men who make a killing on buying and selling land. It sounds perfect, and the north is a very lucrative area. I just have a good feeling about it.'

Patsy's mind had already turned to other matters. 'What did old Larry give us?' She took out her brown envelope and tore it open. She gasped when she saw the small bundle of notes nestling there. 'Jaysus! Will ye look at that?' Quickly she counted them. 'Sixty quid!'

When Eva counted hers, she was astonished to find one hundred pounds in crisp new notes. 'He's obviously very grateful.'

'Sure, the old sod must have made an absolute fortune!'

'And good luck to him,' Eva declared. 'Now, God willing, it's our turn.'

Patsy dreamed of new high-heeled shoes and black stockings, of nightclubs and men who wouldn't get too close. As for Eva, she could see herself and Patsy with their own thriving business. That was her dream.

She had another dream too, and it clouded her visions for the future. The face was handsome, with laughing eyes and a lock of hair that fell mischievously over his forehead.

The man was Bill. A man with a wife and probably children by now, a family in which she played no part.

Their last sight of Wales was the shimmering river and the hills beyond. 'I'll never forget this lovely place, and its people,' Eva said. 'One day we'll come back.'

'When we're stinking rich,' Patsy added.

Eva smiled. 'Money isn't everything. Always remember that.'

Chapter Seven

O N THE FIRST day of November 1965, Eva
and Patsy arrived in Blackburn.

'Where are we going?' Patsy asked, clambering
into the taxi Eva had hailed.

Eva took out a folded note from her coat
pocket. 'Number fourteen, Albert Street, please,'
she told the driver, reading from the note. Then
she turned to her impetuous friend. 'Let me do the
talking, Patsy. And if she tries to up the rent she's
already agreed on, don't start swearing, or we'll
find ourselves sleeping in the park tonight.'

'Anybody would think I were a blabbermouth,
so they would,' Patsy complained. 'Don't ye think
I know when to behave?' She grinned and gave
the driver a wink in his mirror.

Albert Street was narrow and cobbled, with
terraced houses on either side, and a lamppost
in front of every other door. 'Couldn't ye find
something a bit posher?' Patsy was disappointed.
'We've got money now. We're important.'

'We're no more important than when we set

out from me mam's place,' Eva reprimanded her. 'We've just been luckier than most. Besides, we haven't got money to waste, Patsy. Not if we want to find a place of our own and set up a little business.'

As they drove past the houses, Eva thought how well kept they were; the front doorsteps were scrubbed and the net curtains glowed like white teeth from every window. 'You can always tell when a house is loved,' she remarked, drawing Patsy's attention. 'See how they sparkle?'

'Pretty,' replied Patsy, her eyes on the driver, who by now was sure he was on a promise.

Eva wondered what their new landlady was like. Old? Young? Married or single? Was she crotchety or good-natured, and how did she come to advertise in a Welsh regional newspaper? 'No men need apply,' it said, and 'No dogs, ornamental or otherwise.' Nothing about rent in advance though, and, as a rule, landlords always demanded a month's rent in advance.

Number fourteen stood by itself at the end of the road; it was tiny with two windows upstairs and two downstairs. It had a brown wooden door and a wrought-iron balustrade which hid the cellar steps. On one side of the house was a pretty bridge over a brook, and on the other an empty space where a house had been demolished. From the look of the rubbish piled in the middle, it seemed someone had a mind to build a bonfire. A stuffed bird stood in one of the downstairs windows of number fourteen.

'Jaysus! A dead parrot.' Patsy was horrified. 'Ye didn't say we were lodging with Long John Silver.'

A thin, waif-like boy, with protruding ears and a mop of lank brown hair, answered the door.

'Could I please speak to your mother?' Eva asked.

'What's it about?' He had a strong Cockney accent, which took Eva aback.

'Is your mother in?'

'Are you from the social?' He looked quickly up and down the street, his startlingly blue eyes filled with fear.

'No, we're not,' Eva assured him. 'Could you tell your mammy her new lodgers are here?'

He visibly relaxed. 'Are you Eva Bereton and Patsy Noonan?'

Eva nodded.

'Me mam ain't 'ere.'

'Is it all right if we come in anyway?' Producing the letter she'd received from the lady of the house, she explained, 'We've already agreed terms.'

'No! Yer can't come in.' Agitated, he began to close the door.

Patsy promptly stuck her foot out to block it. 'You cheeky little sod!' she exclaimed. 'Turning away paying folk – I hope yer mammy clips yer ear when she comes back.'

Both Eva and Patsy were stunned when he began to weep. 'She ain't coming back,' he sobbed. 'Me mam's dead an' buried, an' me dad's buggered off. Tell the authorities if yer like but they'll not put me away 'cause they'll never find me.' He pushed past them and fled down the street.

'Good God above!' Eva's heart ached for him. 'Stay here,' she told Patsy, 'I'm going after him.' And before Patsy could object, she too was gone, running down the street as though her life depended on it.

With Eva gone and the door wide open, Patsy began calling, 'Hello. Is anyone home?'

No answer.

She leaned into the corridor. 'Hello?'

She almost jumped out of her skin when a tabby cat darted out from behind the door. 'Jaysus, Mary and Joseph! Are ye trying to finish me off or what?' Shooing the cat away, she decided to wait for Eva before going inside. 'This place gives me the creeps, so it does,' she muttered, inching the door shut until it was only open a crack.

Patsy noticed that the downstairs net curtains in the house opposite were twitching; it was obvious someone was watching. 'Nosy old sods!' she grumbled. 'Mind yer own bloody business.' She glared at the window, and whoever was peeping

seemed to go away. Satisfied, Patsy drew the two
small suitcases closer and sat astride them, legs
apart and arms folded. 'Don't be too long, Eva,'
she whispered. 'Me arse isn't built for straddling
suitcases.'

⟴

EVA FELT AS though her lungs would burst.
Having followed the boy across two streets,
then over a bridge and down a bank, she found
herself beside a stream. There was no sign of the
boy, but she sensed he was near. 'I only want to
talk,' she called out. 'I don't mean to hurt you. I'd
like to help, if I can.'

'Go away!'

Eva turned towards the direction of his voice
and spotted him. Crouched low and peering fear-
fully round the trunk of a tree, he darted back when
she caught sight of him. 'It's all right,' she said,
edging nearer. 'I really do want to help you.'

'Stay back!' There was a sob in his voice and,
like her, he was out of breath.

Eva stopped in her tracks. 'It's not fair,' she said,
hoping he wouldn't up and flee again. If he did, she
didn't think she could race after him any more.

Her comment had confused him. He stayed
silent and hidden.

'It's not fair,' Eva said again. 'You know my
name and I don't know yours.'

Silence.

'Will you tell me?'

A slight movement, but no answer.

'I'll guess.' After all that running, her legs ached. She moved cautiously towards a large round boulder. 'I'm not going away,' she told him. 'I'm going to sit down here, and we can talk.' From the boulder she had good sight of the boy. He was facing her, his face stained with tears.

'I bet you're called Bill, aren't you?' Shocked that this particular name had come to her without thinking, she went on, 'When I was your age I knew a boy called Bill. He and I were best mates, and I was very sad when he went away.' Sadder now than she was then, she thought.

'Me name ain't Bill.' With the back of his hand he wiped his tears away.

Encouraged that he hadn't yet taken flight, Eva asked, 'Is it Jack then?'

'I'm not telling yer.'

'I bet it's Michael.'

'Don't be daft!'

'I give up. What is it then?'

Silence.

'Me mam says she called me after a film star. He can sing and dance and everything.'

'Frank Sinatra?'

'Naw.'

'Dean Martin?'

'Never 'eard of 'im.'

'Mickey Rooney?'

'I'm glad she didn't call me that. The kids at school would have called me Mickey Mouse.'

'Fred Astaire?'

'That's me dad's name, Fred.' His voice caught in a sob. 'He left us. That's what made me mam poorly. I could hear her, every night, crying herself to sleep.' Unable to hold back his tears, he bent his head and wept again.

Eva slowly got up and moved closer. He made no attempt to run.

'I want me mam,' he groaned, looking up at her with big sorrowful eyes. 'Please. I want me mam!'

Without a word, Eva sank down beside him and gathered him in her arms. For what seemed an age she let him cry, holding him tight, sharing his pain.

After a time, she looked down and said, 'My mother died too. I missed her so much – I still do. Just like you miss your mother.' Placing a kiss on the top of his head, she went on in a whisper, 'It's hard to lose someone you love, and sometimes it makes you feel so sad you think you can never smile again. But you do, you know, even though the pain is still there, deep down.'

'I'll never see her again, will I?'

She had faced the same question herself after her own mother died. 'I don't know,' she answered truthfully, 'but in your heart you'll always see her. She'll be there every time you think of her, even years from now. You have to remember her when she was smiling, when she was happy. Can you do that?'

'I'll try.'

Eva hugged him. 'That's right,' she said. 'And besides, she wouldn't want you to be sad all the time, would she?'

'No.'

'Do you want to go home now?'

'You won't let 'em put me away, will yer?'

'We'll work something out.'

'Promise?'

Eva nodded.

'What about your friend?'

'What about her?'

'She doesn't like me.'

'What makes you say that?'

'She swore at me.' He gazed at her with his blue eyes. '*She* might tell the authorities.'

Eva laughed. 'She swears at me too sometimes, but it doesn't mean she wants to put me away.'

A few minutes later they were on their way back to Albert Street. 'You won't run away again, will you?' Eva asked anxiously. 'Not now we're friends.'

'Depends.' He jumped over a pavement crack. 'On what?'

'Whether Patsy Noonan tells the authorities.' Tucking one leg up, he hopped on to the next flagstone.

'Patsy won't tell.' Taking his hand, Eva propelled him across the road.

'I'm old enough to get across the road.' Indignant, he drew his hand away.

'How old are you?' He looked about twelve, but he was so undernourished, he could be older.

'Old enough,' he said. 'I used to fetch stuff from the market when me mam got too bad to go out.' Close to tears again, he fell silent.

'What was your mother's name?'

'Mary.' He smiled as though saying her name gave him pleasure. 'Her name was Mary, and she was beautiful.'

'That's a lovely name.'

He wasn't jumping the pavement cracks any more. And he wasn't talking. He was quietly brooding.

Eva tried to jolt him out of it. 'You still haven't told me your name.'

'I need to trust yer first.'

'I thought you did.'

'Not yet.' He gave her a wary glance. 'Me mam said I weren't to trust nobody. She said some folk could knife yer in the back and smile at yer while they were doing it.'

'Unfortunately that's true.' Peter Westerfield sprang to mind. 'I knew a man like that once.'

The boy was wide-eyed. 'You mean he knifed you in the back?'

Eva smiled. 'No. What your mother meant was that some people will do you harm even when they pretend to be your friend.'

'I'd like a friend.'

'Everybody needs a real friend, someone who will stay by them through thick and thin. I'll be your friend, if you'll let me.'

'I might.'

'If I meet with your approval, is that it?'

'Mebbe.'

Eva laughed. 'You're a hard man to do business with.'

With a proud smile he said, 'Me mam said I've got the makings of a landlord.'

It was all Eva could do to contain her laughter.

She suspected his mother's comment was a teasing compliment. As she knew from experience, a landlord could be both sharp and kind-hearted. And, from her brief knowledge of this little bundle of manhood, she thought his mother's description was perfect.

When they got back to Albert Street, the door was closed and there was no sign of Patsy. 'She's run off,' the boy said, 'just like me dad.'

'No, she wouldn't do that.'

'Where is she then?'

The door flew open. 'Come inside, why don't ye?' Patsy invited them, eyeing the boy with suspicion. 'The kettle's on, and I've made a fire.'

The boy sprang forward and rushed past her, down the passage and into the back parlour. The fire was roaring and spitting, warming the room like it used to when his mam was here. 'I were saving that coal!' Angry, he rounded on Patsy. 'I only make a fire at nighttime.'

'Ye ungrateful little bugger,' Patsy snapped. 'The house were freezing cold. I thought I were doing you a favour, so I did.'

'Well, yer weren't, and I don't want yer here, neither of yer.' He glanced at Eva and there were tears in his eyes. 'I told yer she didn't like me!'

Behind his back, Eva gestured for Patsy to leave them be. When Patsy flounced into the scullery, Eva spoke firmly to him. 'She didn't mean any harm. I know she should have asked you before coming into your mother's house, but she was only trying to help. Patsy sometimes makes mistakes, like any of us. She's a good, kind soul really.'

'She shouldn't have done it.'

'I know, and we're both very sorry.' Going to him, she asked softly, 'Do you want us to leave? You've only to say the word and we'll be gone before you know it. We can always find other lodgings.'

Behind her back she kept her fingers crossed, praying he wouldn't turn them away; not for their sake, but for his. 'Well? Would you like us to go?'

He didn't look up. '*You* can stay, but not her.' His gaze went towards the scullery.

'Do you remember what I said? About being your friend?'

'Yes.'

'Well, Patsy has been *my* friend for a long time. When my mother died, she helped me to smile again. She stayed with me when everyone else went away. I won't desert her now.'

'She doesn't like me.'

'Do you like her?'

'No.'

'Then what shall we do?'

He thought awhile. 'Will she do what yer tell her?'

Eva gave a small laugh. 'Not always, but I can try.'

'Will yer tell her not to shop me to the authorities?'

'She won't do that, I promise. And I'll do everything in my power to keep you here, in your own home. Will that do?'

'Do you want her to stay?'

'I'm afraid we come as a pair.'

'All right. She can stay. But only because you want her to.'

'Thank you.' She paused. 'You still haven't told me your name.'

'It's Tommy.' He seemed embarrassed. 'Tommy Johnson.'

Eva held out her hand. 'Hello, Tommy Johnson.' Wrapping his small fist round hers, he said shyly, 'Tomorrow I'll show yer where they took me mam.'

Eva felt highly honoured.

From the scullery doorway, Patsy watched the tender scene, her eyes moist. 'You'll never know,' she whispered sadly.

<hr>

W HILE PATSY WENT off to the shops to buy food and a small bag of coal, Eva and Tommy set about cleaning the house.

Like all the houses down the street, the Johnson place was very cramped: three tiny bedrooms, a small, square bathroom and a steep staircase with steps so narrow that you had to walk down it sideways. It had a parlour with a large range, and a scullery that was big enough to take a table and chairs. There was a front room for best, and curtains at every window. But it was filthy dirty.

'Me mam couldn't get about like she used to,' Tommy said, 'and I didn't have no time for

213

cleaning.' Giving the big brush a push, he sent a swirl of dust into the air. 'When me dad ran off, I were the man of the house and I had to fetch money in.'

'How did you manage that?' Little by little, Tommy was opening up.

'Selling old paper to the paper merchant fetched a bit, and there was always the market on a Saturday. The stallholders used to pay me for sweeping, picking up fallen fruit and veg, things like that. Me and me mam used to eat the fruit of an evening, then on Sunday she'd put the veg into a big stewpot.' He licked his lips. 'It were good, and sometimes it lasted all week.'

'What about school?' When he didn't answer, Eva persisted. 'How long have you been on your own, Tommy?'

Still wary, he shrugged. 'Don't know.'

'It's all right,' she assured him, 'but we'll have to talk about it all sooner or later, you know that, don't you?'

'S'pose so.' Disturbed, he put away the brush and disappeared into the back yard where he sat hunched up on the step. He didn't come in again until long after Patsy was back with the shopping, and only then because he couldn't resist the smell of cooking. He ate in silence and then disappeared upstairs.

'I should think it's the first time in a long while

that he's gone to bed with a full stomach,' Eva remarked. 'Did you see him wolf that food down?' It had done her heart good to see it.

Patsy was unusually quiet.

'Cat got your tongue?' Eva asked.

'I don't think we should stay here.' Patsy stared into the fire. 'I think we should go now, while the going's good.'

Eva didn't understand. 'What is it, Patsy? What's wrong?'

She raised her eyes, and they were troubled. 'I don't like this set-up, that's all. How come he's still loose? Why hasn't the social got their hands on him?'

'How come you've taken such a dislike to him?' It wasn't like Patsy.

'He's not our responsibility.'

'So we should leave without trying to help him, leave him to fend for himself, is that what you're saying?'

Patsy's mood deepened as she stared into the flaring flames. 'The boy's trouble, and he's not our problem.'

Eva couldn't believe this was Patsy talking. She was about to say so when there came a knock on the front door. 'Who the devil's that?' Her first thoughts flew to the boy. 'Could be his father. Maybe he heard his wife died and he's come for the boy.'

'Or it could be the authorities,' Patsy said, 'come to take the responsibility off our shoulders.' Impatient, she got up and went to the front door, reappearing a minute later with three women in tow: a tall, skinny being in a long coat that reached the ground; a small, round body wearing a hat and gloves; and a third, homely and smiling. Her name was Maggie Bell, and she was the spokeswoman. 'We've come because we're concerned about the boy,' she said.

'It's the neighbours,' Patsy explained. 'I'll go and pack.' Without another word, she departed upstairs, leaving Eva to deal with them.

Eva invited them to sit down. She learned that the Johnsons had moved into the area just a few months ago. 'In no time at all, the boy's father cleared off,' Maggie Bell said. 'Soon after that the wife fell ill. We all did what we could, but she was a proud, independent sort. The lad seemed to be coping well, and so we let things drift.'

'Have you told the authorities?'

'None of us would want to do that.' Maggie looked Eva in the eye. 'Are you related?'

'No, I'm a lodger.'

'That doesn't matter. All we want to know is, do you mean to look after the boy?'

When Eva answered yes, she had every intention of taking care of Tommy, and that he would come to no harm, Maggie nodded, smiled, and said,

'That's all we wanted to know, and if you need our help, you've only to ask.'

After they'd gone, Eva went upstairs. 'You don't have to pack,' she told Patsy. 'We're staying. And if you two can't get along, then you'll have to learn how to stay out of each other's way.'

Patsy clearly wasn't happy, but she made no protest.

Later, when they were all in bed, the boy's crying was clearly audible.

Eva went to comfort him while Patsy, for reasons known only to herself, lay in her room, pretending not to hear. Like the boy, she could not hold back the tears.

Chapter Eight

THE SUNDAY CHURCHGOERS didn't even notice them. It was too cold for lingering; heads down they hurried away, the biting November wind cutting through their Sunday best. Numbed to the bone, all they had in mind was to get home as quickly as possible, make a cup of tea and sit beside the fire with their knees bared.

Kneeling beside his mother's resting place, the boy fumbled to arrange the flowers – long-stemmed white roses and a scattering of pinks. 'I can't do it,' he said, looking up pitifully at Eva. 'They won't stand up in the vase.'

Rolling back her coat sleeves, Eva knelt beside him. 'That's because they're too long,' she said, taking them out of the vase. 'We'll have to shorten the stems.' One by one she carefully broke them and Tommy arranged the flowers in the vase.

This was the third time Eva had accompanied him to the churchyard, and each time his heart broke anew. Today, though, he didn't cry, and Eva was glad of that. He sat on the hard, cold ground, staring at the name on the headstone; Eva had asked Patsy if they could pay to put the stone over Mary Johnson, and begrudgingly Patsy had agreed. 'It'll come out of *your* money when we start making profits,' she'd retorted.

'It's lovely, ain't it?' Tommy smiled, blinking in the wintry sunshine. 'It feels good to see me mam's name there. Before when I came here, it were all bare and horrible, and I wanted to tell her it weren't my fault. Now she's got pretty flowers and everything.' He gulped back a sob. 'One day, when I'm rich, I'll pay you and Patsy back. Every penny, you see if I don't.'

'Oh? You mean to be rich then, do you?' Eva had an instinct that he probably would turn out all right, in spite of everything.

'I'm gonna have a big, flashy car and drive you anywhere you want to go.'

'What about Patsy?' No matter how hard she tried, Eva couldn't get these two together. There was a barrier between them, put there by Patsy.

'I'm not bothered about her.' His face always darkened when Patsy's name was mentioned. 'I'll only let *you* come in my car.'

'Thank you, but I've got a better idea.'

'What's that?' He scrambled to his feet.

'I'll buy my own car, not a big flashy one but a smart blue one with leather seats and lots of shiny chrome.'

He laughed. 'That's a poncy car!'

Throwing her arm round him, she walked with him from the grave. 'How about if I clip your ear?' she joked.

'Me dad used to say that.' His mood instantly changed. His feet began to drag and he seemed to lose interest.

'Tommy?'

He looked up.

'Why don't you tell me about your dad?' Eva had brought him close to the subject a number of times, but always he backed off.

'He's no good.'

'Is that what you really think?' It seemed a harsh thing for a lad to say about his own father, but on the face of it he had good reason.

'He ran off and left us. If it hadn't been for him, me mam would never have took poorly.'

'Is that what your mam told you?' Sometimes Eva felt Tommy loved his father more than anything in the world. Other times, like now, there was bitterness in his voice when he spoke about him.

'Me mam was always soft. She said he wasn't a bad man – he's a bit of a gypsy, that's what she said. He couldn't stay in one place for long at a time, she told me, and he didn't make her poorly, that's what she said, but he did. I know he did.'

'Would you forgive him if he came back?'

'He won't come back. He's gone back to his

precious London and I won't be clapping eyes on him again.' He clammed up after that, and nothing Eva could say would persuade him to divulge any more.

On the way back to Albert Street, Tommy grew excited. 'Do you want to see my den?'

Frozen to the bone, Eva wanted nothing more than to get home.

'It'll only take a minute,' he promised, taking off at a run. 'Come on!'

Eva went after him. 'Slow down!' she called. Under her breath she muttered, 'It's a long time since I was your age.' Her thirtieth birthday wasn't too far off.

Running, walking and occasionally stopping for breath, the two of them went towards Preston New Road, where the big houses were. At the bottom of Corporation Park, Tommy stopped. 'This is where the posh people live,' he said knowledgeably. 'Dr Franklin lives in that house.' He pointed to a large, red-brick house set back in pretty gardens. 'One night when me mam was really bad, I had to run up here and fetch him.' His chest swelled with pride. 'I got to ride in his big car – like the one I want when I'm rich.'

Gasping for breath, Eva could only nod.

'Come on then,' he cried, and took off again, doubling back to Park Street. 'All the solicitors and important folk live here.' Standing in the middle of the pavement, his arms spread wide to encompass the grand old houses, he had the confident air of an estate agent making a sale. 'Some of these have been made into old people's homes,' he said. 'Me mam said it's really nice for 'em, living near the park.'

Exhausted, Eva sat on a low brick wall. 'I'm not going any further,' she said. When she had started out her nose was numb with cold and her skin proud with goosebumps. Now she was hot and bothered, her underslip sticking to the sweat on her back. 'Just where is this den of yours?'

'In there!' Laughing, he dashed into the front garden of a derelict house. 'It's all right, it's been empty for years.' He opened the front door and went inside. 'Tramps sleep here. I've seen one of 'em lighting a fire an' all.'

Intrigued, but a little wary, Eva followed.

In the hallway, she stood and stared. 'What a terrible shame,' she muttered. 'I bet this house was beautiful in its prime.' In a strange way, it was still beautiful.

Before her were many doors, two to the left and more to the right, and directly in front another, all hanging sadly on their rusted hinges. The ceiling was high, its plaster cracked. Through one corner you could actually see right into the room above. A damaged chandelier creaked dangerously on its chain.

Eva shifted her gaze. A wide stairway wound up to the gallery. There was a window on the half-landing, its stained glass unbroken, remarkably.

Daylight filtered through the green and blue panes, illuminating the hallway eerily.

Eva and Tommy wandered round the house. The oak-panelled walls in the living rooms were missing huge chunks. No doubt that's what the tramp that Tommy saw was burning, Eva mused.

The kitchen was vast. Surprisingly, all its cooking facilities remained intact. There was a long, narrow walk-in pantry at one end, and cupboards reaching to the ceiling over one wall. The windows were smashed and the walls stained with damp. There were holes in the floor, and a pungent smell from the burst pipes beneath the sink. But for all that, Eva thought, it was a bright, pleasant room.

Upstairs the story was the same: neglect and violation, the elements taking over, and in one bedroom creeping ivy had found its way in through the decaying walls.

Taking Eva by the hand, Tommy led her past the main bedrooms towards the smallest room right at the back of the house. 'This is my den,' he said proudly, pushing back the broken door. 'When they took me mam away, I stayed here for two whole nights.'

Eva wanted to ask him what had happened when his mother was taken away – who organised her burial, and who paid for it? Why was he allowed to roam about without being taken into care? But now was not the time. Later, when he got to trust her more, she would find out. Maybe the neighbours knew more than they were saying. Perhaps she should talk to Maggie Bell again.

Eva was astonished by Tommy's den. The view from its window was breathtaking. 'Oh, Tommy! It's beautiful.' It was like coming into heaven from the darkest corner of hell. 'I never dreamed this dilapidated house could be hiding such a view.'

The house stood in extensive grounds. There was a pond filled with green algae; a magnificent stone statue stood in the centre, its nose broken and one arm lying half submerged by its feet. Beside the pond was a decaying set of garden furniture – a round table with fancy legs and four barrel-backed chairs with rotting cane seats.

The grounds led down to a valley, beyond which was a forest and a lake. For one magic moment, Eva's thoughts went back to her mother's house and the fields where she had played and worked. A great sadness filled her lonely heart.

'Ain't it lovely?' Tommy was bursting with pride. 'An' it's all mine. There ain't nobody who knows about it except me and those tramps, an' I ain't seen them for ages.' He wrinkled his nose. 'Phew! They didn't 'alf stink, like summat gawn bad.'

'Who owns this house, Tommy?'

'Nobody.'

Ruffling his hair, she laughed. '*Somebody* must own it.'

'I ain't seen nobody.' He glanced out of the window. 'Except her. She's always telling me to clear off.'

Careful not to touch the broken glass, Eva peered out of the window. A small, round woman was hanging out washing next door. 'I think I'll go and talk to her.'

With Tommy in tow, she hurried down the stairs. The back door was nearest. 'What's she called?'

'I don't know her name.' Tommy hung back. 'Dunno why yer want to talk to the old witch anyway,' he snorted. 'She'll only tell yer to piss off.'

Eva told him he wasn't to use such language, and that he was to stay quiet while she talked to the woman. 'I don't want her thinking we're here to cause trouble.'

Parting the overgrown hedge, Eva called out, 'Excuse me!'

Startled, the woman swung round. 'Who's that?' she shrieked. 'Piss off or I'll fetch the police!'

'Told yer!' Tommy sniggered. 'That's what she always says.'

Taking her courage in her hands, Eva pushed her way through the hedge, emerging dishevelled and scratched. 'I just want a word,' she started, but before she could say any more, the woman flew at her with the line prop.

'Get away from here!' she screeched. 'Bloody tramps!' Catching sight of Tommy loitering behind, she went red in the face. 'You! I've told you before, you little sod! Clear off!'

'No, you've got it wrong.' Eva waved her hand in protest. 'We're not tramps. I want to talk to you, about the house.'

The woman was not convinced. 'If you come a step nearer, I swear I'll run you through.' She brandished the line prop as if it was a bayonet.

'Please, I mean you no harm, I promise you,' said Eva.

The line prop bayonet wavered.

'I wouldn't be bothering you at all, but I really am interested in the house next door. Who owns it, do you know?'

The woman decided that maybe she had overreacted. She put the line prop down. 'You should have come to the front door,' she said. 'You're trespassing, coming through that hedge.' She pointed to Tommy. 'And what's that little bugger doing here?'

'Do you know who owns the house?' Eva persisted.

The woman regarded Eva, wondering whether she could trust her. With the lady of the house gone away and all manner of work to catch up on, she could do with a bit of company. She made her decision. 'You'd best come inside,' she said, shivering. 'It's enough to freeze your insides standing here. The wind whistles up this valley day and night, winter and summer,' she grumbled as she led them to the back door. There she turned and pointed at Tommy. 'You, boy. Either wipe your feet and come in, or be obstinate and stay out. It seems like me an' your mam's got things to talk over.'

Neither Eva nor Tommy corrected her assumption that Eva was Tommy's mother. Somehow it didn't really matter.

When Tommy's feet were wiped clean and Eva's too, the woman continued on into the kitchen.

'Cor!' Tommy's nose twitched in the air. 'Meat pie! Me mam used to bake meat pies. Yer could smell 'em right through the 'ouse.'

The woman surprised them both by smiling. 'Do you want a slice?' She was proud of her culinary skills and to have them appreciated was a real treat. Certainly, the lady of the house never gave her much praise.

'Yeah!'

'Haven't you forgotten something?' Eva said.

'Please.'

'Right.' The woman pulled out a chair. 'Sit yourself at the table, me lad, and I'll get the pie out the oven. It should be done to a turn by now.'

The woman was, what, forty-five, fifty? Eva couldn't be sure. She had greying hair and a slight limp. When she wasn't scowling, she had a face that could pass for pretty. Her eyes were deepest brown, with a bright, merry twinkle.

'I'm Olive, the housekeeper here,' she introduced herself as she pulled a huge pie out of the oven and placed it on a wooden server. She cut a generous slice for Tommy. The pie crust was crisp and light, crumbling as the knife sliced through. Dark brown gravy spilled out, spearing the air with a warm, delicious aroma.

'It's bubbling hot,' Olive warned Tommy. 'Blow on it before you bite or it'll stick to your mouth and have the skin clean off.' She turned to Eva. 'Would you like a slice?'

Eva's mouth was watering. But she mustn't be tempted, she told herself. Patsy would have a meal ready for them when they got back. Tommy might relish two meals, but she couldn't. Not wanting to offend Olive, however, she answered, 'Yes, please, but just a tiny piece to taste.'

While Olive cut another slice, Eva glanced round the room. It reminded her of her mother's kitchen – warm and cosy, with a large sideboard dressed with blue china, and all manner of copper hanging over the fireplace.

'It's old-fashioned, I know.' Olive caught her looking. 'If I had my way, I'd have the whole lot torn out and a new kitchen put in. There are no mod cons here, you know. The house hasn't been changed since the mistress's grandmother was alive.'

When all three were seated round the table, she talked as though she hadn't seen a human being in years. 'The mistress is a kind soul,' she revealed, 'but she's never really been happy since the master and their only daughter were killed in a car crash. Dreadful thing. Her daughter was twenty-two . . . lovely girl.'

'Has she any other children?' Eva asked.

'No, there were no other children, just Rosie. Adopted as a baby, she was, but you'd never have known she wasn't their blood kin.' She frowned. 'Funny how like the mistress she was, same dark eyes and hair, same wide smile.' As though talking to herself, she muttered, 'Like she was made to order.'

'So she lost all her family? That's a terrible thing,' said Eva sadly, memories rushing back to haunt her.

'You talk as if you know a thing or two about losing someone you love.' If Olive hoped for an answer, she was disappointed. Eva quietly ate her pie.

'Cor! This pie's even better than me mam's.' Tommy had scoffed his slice and was looking for a second. With gravy running down his chin he asked hopefully, 'Is there any more going spare, missus?' Snaking out his tongue he sucked the gravy into his mouth.

'No, Tommy,' Eva intervened. 'You've had more than enough.' He and Patsy were already at loggerheads. It would do no good if he was to turn his nose up at her cooking when they got back. 'Besides, you've been very well looked after by this kind lady. A thank you wouldn't hurt.'

'Thanks, missus.' Tommy gave Olive a smile to warm her heart.

'A drop of sarsaparilla to wash it down, that's what the boy needs.' Olive fetched it from the pantry cupboard. 'Now then, m'dear,' she said to Eva, 'what was it you wanted to know about the house next door?'

Eva had many questions, but Olive could not answer them all. The house had been empty these past five years, and all manner of vagabonds and no-goods had slept there. 'We even had them folks with sandals on their feet and bells round their necks. Played fiddles all night, they did. In the end the police ran 'em off.'

'Hippies,' Tommy contributed.

'If you say so,' said Olive. She didn't know who owned the house. It had been put up for sale years ago, but there had been no takers, as far as she knew. 'If anybody has bought it,' she remarked, 'they're certainly taking their time doing anything about the place.'

'Who was handling the sale?' Eva asked. 'Do you know?'

Olive frowned with thought. 'It was a local estate agents. Dunmore . . . No, not Dunmore, Dunnon. That's it, Dunnon and something. I can't remember the second name.' And with that, Eva had to be content.

Soon afterwards, Eva and Tommy rose to leave.

'If I remember any more about the house, I'll let you know,' Olive promised as she showed her visitors out. 'Come and see me again, won't you?' Lonely and often neglected by the woman she worked for, Olive had taken to Eva, and Eva to her.

———

PATSY WAS BESIDE herself. 'Where the devil have ye been?' she demanded as they came into the back room. 'I've been imagining all sorts of terrible things, so I have!'

Eva apologised profusely. 'I've lots to tell you,' she said excitedly. 'I think I might have found us our little business.'

'Not before time either,' Patsy snapped. 'We've been here weeks and it's doing us no good living on our savings.' Her gaze went involuntarily to Tommy who was wolfing down his egg and chips. 'Especially when we've been lumbered with another mouth to feed.'

The spiteful comment silenced Eva. She knew there was something chewing away at Patsy, but for the life of her she couldn't imagine what it was. Each time she commented on it, Patsy denied it and flounced out of the room. The more Patsy protested, the more Eva felt certain there was something behind this hostility towards Tommy. He could be cheeky, yes, and there were times when she had to reprimand him, but Patsy had never even given him a chance.

From that first minute she'd clapped eyes on him, she'd been hostile, and Tommy was all too aware of it, which only made matters worse.

It was eight thirty when Tommy made his way upstairs. 'Goodnight, God bless.' As always, too shy to kiss her, he touched Eva's shoulder as he passed.

'Goodnight, Tommy.' Eva rested her hot drink on the fender. 'Don't forget to wash and clean your teeth, will you?'

At the bottom of the stairs, he paused. 'Can I come with you to find the agent?'

'We'll see.'

'Goodnight then.' He made no move to leave. Instead, he shuffled his feet, bringing his uncomfortable gaze to Patsy, who was in the armchair, pretending to read. 'Goodnight, Patsy.' It was the first time he'd tried to breach the barrier she'd put up between them.

For one heart-stopping minute, Eva really believed Patsy might warm to him. She looked up and stared at Tommy, her features momentarily softening as she studied his eager face and small, wiry form. Opening her mouth to say something, her face suddenly stiffened and she turned away. 'Get off to bed,' she muttered. Her voice was unyielding, her face the same.

Shoulders hunched, he glanced sadly at Eva before he, too, turned away. With slow, weary footsteps, he made his way upstairs.

Eva followed.

In his room, Tommy sat, dejected, on the edge of his bed. 'Why does she hate me?' he asked. 'I ain't done 'er no 'arm, have I?'

Eva sat beside him and put her arm round his thin shoulders. 'No, you haven't done her any harm, Tommy.' Normally he didn't seem to care whether Patsy liked him or not. Tonight, though, he was different. More vulnerable somehow.

'Sometimes, like just now when she told me to get off to bed, she reminds me of me mam.' His voice trembled. 'I really want her to like me, Eva. I want us all to be good mates.'

'So do I,' said Eva with feeling.

'I wish me dad hadn't run off.'

'Have you no idea where he might be?'

A dark mood settled on him. 'I don't care if I never see him again!' Staring down at the bedclothes, he twiddled them between finger and thumb. 'I hate him.'

'Look at me, Tommy.'

The boy looked into her eyes. 'I mean it,' he said sombrely. 'I hate him for what he did to me and me mam.'

'Hatred is a terrible thing, Tommy,' Eva said gently.

'He shouldn't have left us. He *made* me hate him! But I ain't done *nuffin'* to make Patsy hate me.'

234

'I'm sure she doesn't really hate you, Tommy. I'll talk to her again, try to find out what's wrong.'

'You really like that house on Park Street, don't you?'

Eva nodded. 'I think it's beautiful.'

He laughed. 'It's falling down!'

'I know.'

'I'm tired.'

'We've had a busy day. I expect you'll sleep like a log.' She ruffled his hair. 'But not before you've had a wash, I hope.'

Grimacing, he shook his head. 'Goodnight, Eva.'

'Goodnight, Tommy.'

Going out of the room, she glanced back. Tommy was bending over the dresser, taking out a towel. In the mirror she caught sight of his unhappy face and her heart twisted. Poor Tommy. Patsy was being so unfair to him.

Downstairs, she wondered how to confront Patsy about her feud with Tommy. Her previous attempts had proved fruitless, and Patsy was in such a foul mood tonight. Still, the evening was young. She'd leave it till later and hope that Patsy's mood would mellow.

Taking up pen and paper, she began working out some figures. If she was going to persuade Patsy to accept her ideas about the house on Park Street, she needed a strong, convincing argument to put before her.

There was so much she didn't yet know. For instance, what was the agent asking? How much would it cost to renovate the place? They wouldn't have nearly enough money of their own, so how much would it cost to borrow the rest, and who could they turn to? The bank manager had been all sweetness and light when they had made that large deposit, but how would he feel about lending them money to get a business project off the ground? More to the point, would he think her idea was even viable? Patsy, too, would want to know the answers to all these questions.

As Eva tried to do some calculations, she occasionally glanced at Patsy reading her paper, hoping she might show some interest. She wanted Patsy to make the first move, given the mood she was in.

Patsy discreetly watched her from behind her newspaper. 'What's the little bugger up to now?' she wondered. When she could bear it no longer, she got out of her chair. 'Do you fancy another drink?' Waiting for an answer, she stood over Eva, arms folded, peeping at what she had been scribbling but unable to make any sense of it.

'Let me get the cocoa, Patsy. After all, you cooked the dinner.' Eva made to get up, but was pushed back down.

'You stay right there, ye bugger!' Patsy pointed a finger at the sheet of paper. 'I want to know what all this is about. And while you're at it, ye can tell me what you and the boy have been up to half the day. And what were ye talking about just now, up the stairs, eh? It's like a bloody conspiracy round here, so it is!'

'Forget the cocoa, Patsy. Why don't we just sit and talk?'

'Ye know very well I think better with a drink in me hand,' Patsy retorted. 'As there isn't a decent drop of anything else in the place, I'll have to settle for cocoa. So, do ye want one or not?'

Eva nodded, afraid to open her mouth.

When the two of them were seated beside the fire, Eva told her everything. She explained how Tommy had taken her to see his den, and that she had been astonished to find it was a big old house in need of repair.

Patsy regarded her suspiciously. 'Yer after buying this place, aren't ye?'

'Maybe.'

'Where's it at?'

'Park Street.'

'An' where's that?'

'Alongside a beautiful park.' Eva grew excited. 'Oh, Patsy! It's a lovely area, tree-lined streets and big, posh houses. The house has a big garden and the most fantastic view. You'd love it, I know you would.'

'Yer a mad woman, so ye are,' Patsy chuckled.

237

'One minute yer off taking flowers to Tommy's mam, and the next yer full of cock-eyed ideas about spending our hard-earned money on a big house in a tree-lined street.'

'Only if you're agreeable.'

The smile slipped from Patsy's face. 'Ye said something about it being in need of repair. What exactly d'ye mean? The walls want painting? A new bathroom? Just how bad is this place?'

Taking a deep breath, Patsy admitted, 'It's virtually derelict.'

Patsy was horrified. 'Ye *are* bloody mad!'

Undeterred, Eva went on, 'Oh, Patsy, it's really lovely. In its day it must have been the best house up there. There's a pond and a statue, and you should see the land behind. There's the most beautiful valley, which runs into a forest. There's a lake, and the view is just magnificent.'

'Forget it, me darlin'. We're not ready for a big house with a pond and a magnificent view. We'll have to settle for a house something like this one, and a little business too. Have ye forgotten that's why we came here? To get a business going and earn ourselves a tidy living?'

'I think the house can be where we both live *and* work. There's a real business to be had there, Patsy, I'm sure of it.'

'What kind of business are we talking about?'

'I don't even know if we can do it. There's so

much to be gone over. Formal things like finance, and permission for change of use.'

'Eva! Will ye answer me? What kind of business are we talking about?'

'A hotel.' There, it was said, and as she had suspected, it stunned Patsy.

'Jaysus, Mary and Joseph!' Patsy stared at her. 'With the money we've got, we might just be able to open a cafe in the bus station. But a hotel? Jaysus! I thought *I* was the dreamer.'

Grabbing her by the hand, Eva told her, 'We can do it, Patsy, I know we can!'

'I don't see how. Where would we get the money? And even if we could get the house in order, just think of all the other things we'd have to find.'

Eva refused to give in. Grabbing her sheet of paper, she shoved it under Patsy's nose. 'It's all here, what we need – furniture, crockery and cutlery, linen—'

'Beds and towels,' Patsy interjected, 'pots and pans, a reception desk, a till, hotel stationery, receipt books. And staff. Sure, we'd never run a hotel on our own, not a respectable one.'

Eva felt Patsy's excitement growing and she knew she had her. 'It won't be easy, I know, and at the end of the day we might be disappointed, but we have to try, Patsy, or we might always regret it. I've been thinking about it ever since I came back, and I have some ideas.'

'Go on.' Patsy settled into her chair. 'I'm all ears, so I am.'

Collecting her thoughts, Eva got out of her chair and began pacing the room. 'We haven't got anywhere near the kind of money needed but we do have a few thousand pounds, and it's a start.'

Patsy laughed. 'A drop in the ocean compared to the money we'd have to find. And where would we get that, I ask ye?'

'From the bank.'

'Sure, that's like getting blood from a stone. An' even if, by some miracle, we *did* get finance, how would we pay it back? The interest alone would cripple us before we got off the ground.' Patsy knew about money. It was her strength.

'Like I said, it won't be easy. Nothing worthwhile ever is. But look at it this way, Patsy. We have to buy somewhere to live, don't we?'

'A terraced house, that's what we said. Something that would leave us enough money to start a little cafe or a shop.'

'Yes, but if we got the house on Park Street cheaply enough, we might even have enough left over to renovate the place, and there's your collateral. Wouldn't the bank go for that?'

'I'm not sure. They're not very favourable to women opening a business. But you're right, Eva, if we got the house cheaply enough, we might have something to bargain with.' Holding out her hand for the sheet of paper, she said, 'Let me see the figures.'

Reluctantly, Eva handed it over. 'It's just scribble,' she said, 'a few ideas. I'm not good on finance and accounts, you know that. That's your department.'

'If we're serious, we'll have to persuade the bank manager, and to do that, we'll need to show him a financial forecast. If he's not convinced, that's the end of that.'

Eva hugged her. 'Oh, Patsy, I'm sure we can do it!' Suddenly there was something to aim for. Something that would make everything worthwhile.

So it was decided that, first thing in the morning, they would visit the estate agent for the house. Eva had found only one with the name Dunnon in the telephone book for Blackburn – Dunnon and Haines. There seemed little point in Patsy going to look at the house before they knew for certain it was still on the market. Eva was a little apprehensive about what her reaction would be when she saw the state it was in, but she would deal with that when, or if, the time came.

Patsy had one condition about their plans for the morning. 'I don't want the boy tagging along.'

'Why not? He's no bother. Give him a chance, Patsy,' she pleaded. 'He so much wants you to be friends with him.'

'Sure, there's no chance of that.' Collecting the two mugs, Patsy hurried into the scullery.

Eva went after her. 'Don't you think it's time we talked about this?'

'I don't know what ye mean.'

'I think you do. Ever since we came here you've been dead set against that boy. Why? What's behind it all, Patsy?'

'I'm off to me bed.' Patsy made to push by, but Eva held firm.

'Talk to me, Patsy. We've always shared things. There's something very wrong here, and I need to know what it is. I can't help if you won't talk.'

'Sure, there's nothing to talk about.'

'It's not fair on Tommy, and it's not like you to be so hostile.'

Patsy kept her gaze lowered. 'Mebbe it's time you went to the authorities about the boy. He should be at school, out from under our feet, so he should.'

'You know as well as I do they'll put him away. Do you really want that on your conscience?'

'What do you mean to do about him then?'

'I'm going over to talk to Maggie Bell. She seems to care about what happens to Tommy. Maybe she'll have a few ideas. But I'm not going to the authorities.' Eva's voice grew hard. 'And neither are you, Patsy Noonan!'

Patsy turned on her. 'If you think I'd snoop on him, you don't know me,' she snapped.

'Then I'm sorry for jumping to conclusions, but what am I supposed to think?'

For a long moment, Patsy looked at her, thinking what a kind heart and loyal nature Eva had, and she felt ashamed. She would have given anything to confide in Eva, as Eva had always confided in her, but she couldn't bring herself to do it. There were things here that she could never share with anyone; awful, sad things that had haunted her for too long. 'Oh, Eva, I don't want us to fall out. We've been through too much together to let that scrap of a boy come between us. Let him come with us tomorrow if it means that much to you. But don't let him think he'll be living with us. And don't expect me to be friends with him, because I never could be.'

Eva was about to speak, but Patsy shook her head. 'Please, Eva,' she begged, 'leave it at that.'

She made her way across the back room, and on up the stairs, her heart sore, and her eyes filled with tears.

Eva sat in the armchair. What *was* the matter with Patsy? In all the time Eva had known her, Patsy had never taken against anyone like this unless they richly deserved it. But there was nothing she could do if Patsy refused to confide in her.

Eva glanced at the clock. It was almost 10 p.m. 'I wonder if it's too late to go knocking on Maggie Bell's door,' she muttered. There was so much she needed to ask that kind soul. She ought really to go to bed, but there was so much playing on her mind she probably wouldn't sleep anyway. So she quietly put on her coat and crept out of the house. 'Ten minutes, that's all it should take,' she promised herself. 'Twenty at the most.'

———※◆※———

'THIS IS A fine time of night to come calling.' Maggie Bell stood at the door, her figure silhouetted in the hallway light. Her hair was wrapped in curlers and she had obviously taken out her dentures to soak overnight. 'Whatever it is, can't it wait till morning?'

'It's about Tommy.'

'Oh aye, I might have known.' Rolling her eyes, she tutted. 'You'd better come in then.'

The house was surprisingly modern. The furniture was teak and colourful rugs covered the floors. The old range had been taken out and there was a new fire surround, with a chrome clock on top of it and wall lights either side.

'D'yer want a brew?' Without waiting for Eva to answer Maggie went off to put the kettle on. 'Come in here and tell me what the little bugger's been up to,' she called from the kitchen.

'He's a good lad, Mrs Bell—'

'Maggie to my friends.'

'Right, Maggie. He's not been up to anything. It's just that I can't imagine how he's managed on his own, or how he didn't get taken into care. I was hoping you could fill me in a bit more.'

'There's folk round here that don't trust the authorities, and we've all looked out for him.' When the kettle began to whistle, she took the lid off the teapot, poured in a small amount of boiling water and swilled it round. 'He doesn't look it, but the lad's gone fourteen. He'll soon be able to work, then he'll be nobody's responsibility.'

'He doesn't look older than twelve.'

'He's small-boned, like his mam. And he's had a hard time of it, poor little bugger.' Pouring out the tea into two flowered mugs, Maggie asked Eva, 'Do you want him off your hands, is that it? Because if you do, you'll not be allowed to stay in that house. You'll need to find fresh lodgings, you do realise that, don't you?'

'No, I'm not trying to get him off my hands. I've grown very fond of him. I just need to know more, and I've got a feeling you can tell me a lot more than you're letting on.'

Maggie laughed aloud. 'You're a cheeky young bugger! But you've a right to know, seeing as you've been fair enough with the boy.' She carried the tray into the sitting room. 'He looks well,' she declared. 'I've been keeping a crafty eye on him.'

'Tell me about his parents.'

Eva was told to sit down.

'Right.' When Maggie was sitting opposite, she

took a great swig of her tea before launching into a very detailed account of the Johnson family. 'Mary was a northerner born and bred. Her husband, Fred Johnson, was a southerner. He was also a restless, moody man, given to disappearing for days on end and turning up when it suited him.' She gave a snort of disapproval. 'The pair of them were ill-suited, you could see that a mile away. He never did settle here, as far as I could tell.' She sniffed, took another gulp of her tea and added, 'He was a Cockney, and that was where his heart remained. The north was where Mary was born, so she was pulling one way and he was pulling another. But I suppose he wasn't a bad man, just unhappy.'

'But he left his wife and child, so he couldn't have been much good, could he?'

There was a moment when it seemed Maggie might clam up, but then she relented and opened her heart, and what she had to say was a shock to Eva. 'He didn't leave of his own accord. Mary threw him out, bag and baggage. Two o'clock in the morning, it was, and the two of them out in the street, arguing. She said he couldn't come back inside unless he promised to settle down and make a proper home for her and the boy. He said he could make no promises, but he'd try his best. Mary ran inside and fetched a suitcase and an armful of clothes. She threw the lot at him. "Bugger off out of it, and good shuts!" that's what she said.'

'Good God! Where was Tommy while all this was going on?'

'In bed I should think, fast asleep.' She recalled the night it happened. 'He must sleep unconscious,' she remarked, 'because the row woke the street, I can tell you.'

'So Fred Johnson never knew his wife died, and the boy was left all alone?'

'How could he? He's never set foot in the street since that night, and I know Mary never heard from him again.' She sighed, a deep weary sigh. 'Poor Mary, she had a temper as bad as his. The two of them parted bitterly, and the lad ended up taking the brunt of it all. I might well have tried to contact his dad, but I had no idea where to look, and besides, the boy seemed dead set against seeing him again. He blamed Fred for everything, when of course it was six of one and half a dozen of the other.'

'How did you manage to keep the boy out of council care?'

'With difficulty and determination.' Leaning forward she asked, 'Did the boy tell you I had him living here for a time?'

'No.'

'Did he tell you his mam inherited the house from her father, so by rights it now belongs to him?'

Eva was astonished. 'No, I had no idea.'

'There's a lot more you don't know either.'

'What? Things that Mary told you, you mean?'

Eva had taken a liking to Maggie. 'I expect you were a good friend to Tommy's mam, weren't you?'

Maggie laughed. It was an empty sound. 'Enemies, more like. After they arrived here, I never exchanged one word with her. I went out of my way to avoid her, and she did the same when she saw me.'

'But why?'

'It's a long story.' A slow, easy smile spread over Maggie's old face. 'But, if you've got time, I wouldn't mind getting it off my chest after all these years.'

'I've got all the time in the world,' Eva answered, and settled back in her chair.

Chapter Nine

PATSY WAS FLABBERGASTED. 'What?'

'It's true, Maggie Bell is Tommy's aunt.'

'Why didn't she tell us this before? And why isn't she looking after him instead of parking him on us? Anyway, how do *you* know all this?'

'After you and Tommy went to bed last night, I went over there. I had a few questions to ask, and she told me everything.'

Falling into the armchair, Patsy stared at her. 'Then you'd better tell me, hadn't ye?'

Eva related what Maggie had confided in her. 'Mary was Maggie's sister. She was brought up here in Blackburn, in this very street. She was born in this house. She left home when she was sixteen and travelled about for a time, working in nightclubs and bars. She met Tommy's father when she took a job in the East End of London. When Mary became pregnant, they got married. When Mary's father, a widower by then, fell ill, he became desperate to see her again, Maggie says. Being the youngest she was always his favourite and it broke his heart when she left and cut off all contact with her parents. When her mother died, Mary didn't know, because she couldn't be found. Her father didn't want the same thing to happen with him. He wanted to see her again before he died, but it wasn't to be. He didn't know where to begin to look for her. In his will he left Mary everything – this little house which he and his wife had bought soon after they were married, all the furniture, and a sizeable amount of money that he had saved.'

'What did he leave Maggie?'

'Just enough money to bury him beside his wife.'

'Why in God's name would he do that?'

Eva shrugged. 'Who knows? Maggie says it took her years to forgive him. His grave went untended and she couldn't even bear to hear his name. She had given up the idea of marriage to look after her mother when she became ill, and then she stayed on to take care of her father. She nursed them both through their ailing years, and in all that time there was never a word from Mary.'

'How did she find her sister?'

'The solicitor did that, through the Salvation Army, Maggie said.'

'So, when Mary came back to live here, Maggie bought a house over the way?'

'No. She had no money to buy a house. She found a job at the local hospital and rented the place across the street. Apparently the landlord had let the house go to rack and ruin and most of her wages went into making it a home. Two weeks before Mary returned, Maggie was pensioned off with a small sum of money, which she spent on her home. She's got nothing else. In fact, as she told me, she lives day to day, and asks nothing from anybody.'

'Does Tommy know all this?'

'No. Maggie never told him she was his aunt, and she asks that we don't tell him either. When her father cut her out of his will in favour of Mary, he hurt her deeply. When Mary came back, Maggie tried to make friends, but her sister sent her packing. "If you're after some of what our dad left, you can think again," she said. She wouldn't even let her over the doorstep. Then, when she threw Fred Johnson out—'

'Threw him out?' Patsy sat up. 'I thought the boy said he ran off?'

Eva shook her head. 'No. Apparently she threw him out when he wouldn't promise to settle down. After he'd gone, Mary took to the bottle. In no time at all the money was all gone, and she went downhill. The rest you know.'

'Why did Maggie bother to keep an eye out for the boy when she'd been treated so shamefully?'

'Because she's a good woman, Patsy, that's why.'

'So if we got a place of our own, she could take care of him and you need have no conscience about it.'

'It's not that easy, Patsy. She's done her duty, and now she doesn't want to know. She took the boy in and kept him out of council care. When he asked if it was right what they'd said, that she was his aunt, Maggie told him she had lied to them so they wouldn't put him away. Afterwards, she watched out for him when he came back to this house, but now she's washed her hands of him. He'll be fifteen soon, she said, and out at work.'

'After what that family did to her, I can't say I blame her.'

'Tommy's done her no harm.'

'Maybe not.' Patsy's expression hardened. 'But if we get our own place, I still don't want him living with us.'

Eva said nothing. There seemed little point. But she refused to give up hope that Patsy would change her mind.

———◆———

M R HUGHES OF Dunnon and Haines ushered Patsy and Eva into his office and bade them sit down. 'I'm just having coffee,' he said, his bird-like face jutting from his shoulders as though he was about to peck. 'Would either of you like a cup?'

Patsy looked at Eva and Eva answered for them both. 'No, thank you all the same.' Tommy wasn't with them. In the event, there had been no more argument about whether or not he accompanied

LOVE ME OR LEAVE ME

them to the estate agents because he had asked if he could go to the museum to see the stuffed animals instead. Eva agreed, and told him to meet them outside the estate agents at twelve o'clock. Excited as a puppy, he'd gone away whistling.

'Could you please tell us what the position is with regard to the unoccupied house on Park Street?' Eva asked Mr Hughes. 'I understand you were handling its sale.'

'Well now, let me see.' Mr Hughes scratched his nose until it resembled a ripe cherry. 'As I recall there *was* someone very interested in that property, but for some reason or another, the sale never did go through. The gentleman in question said he would come back, but he never did.'

'Who owns the house?' Eva wondered how Dunnon and Haines managed to stay in business with agents as vague as Mr Hughes seemed to be.

'I'll have to look that up,' said Mr Hughes with an apologetic smile. 'It's been some time since anybody enquired about the place.'

Rising from his chair, he skirted round Patsy and began delving in a tall metal filing cabinet by the door. 'Robinson . . . Roberts . . . I'm sure it was something like that.' His fingers alighted on a blue folder. 'Ah! That's it! Roman, Francis Roman, Acacia Lodge, Park Street. Here we are.' Placing the folder before him on his desk, he thumbed through it. 'No, it seems the house was never sold. The owner has since died and the house is scheduled to go to auction in six weeks' time.'

'Auction!' Eva's heart sank. 'That means we'll be up against lots of other buyers.'

'Auction is often the ideal way to buy a property like this.'

'Why do you say that?'

'Not everyone has the ready cash or the means to borrow. Those that have can pick up real bargains if they're lucky.'

'Jaysus!' Patsy was out of her depth. 'We've neither of us ever been to an auction, except for the fruit market on a Saturday, but that's a different kettle of fish from buying a house, so it is.'

'Well, the executors will consider any offers made before the auction.'

'What is the reserve price?'

'There isn't one. Having tried, and failed, to sell the house in the usual way, the executors will take what they can get for the property. However, the original asking price was six thousand pounds, and only an offer in that region would secure the property. Otherwise, the executors will take their chances at auction.'

Eva's heart sank. 'We only have limited funds.' She glanced at Patsy. She seemed too stunned to speak, which was probably just as well. 'Certainly not enough to buy the place outright,' Eva went on. 'We have ideas about developing the house, and that would take even more money.'

'Could you borrow?' asked Mr Hughes. 'The banks might well be interested.' Privately, he doubted that any bank would give these two obviously inexperienced women the time of day, but it wasn't his job to discourage potential buyers. 'A number of these properties have been converted to small, select apartments. It's a good area, close to the park and within easy reach of the town centre.'

'Well, we can certainly try,' said Eva, trying to sound a lot more positive than she felt. She stood up. 'Thank you for your time, Mr Hughes. We'll be in touch.'

'The bugger!' Patsy exploded as soon as they were in the street. 'The place is falling down, you said. How can he ask so much for it?'

'It's got potential,' Eva replied. She scanned the street, looking for Tommy, but he was nowhere in sight. Still, it wasn't quite twelve yet. 'Maybe we should take our chances at the auction. What do you think, Patsy? We might get lucky.'

'Have yer taken leave of yer senses? What chance would we have against professional property developers? None at all, that's what.'

Eva couldn't argue with that. She wasn't going to tell Patsy, but the thought of bidding thousands of pounds in a room full of sharp businessmen terrified her anyway. 'We'd better go and see the bank manager, then.'

'First,' said Patsy firmly, 'I want to see this dream house of yours for meself.' Her face suddenly stiffened as she saw Tommy loping down the street towards them.

'Did you buy the house?' he asked breathlessly as soon as he came to a halt in front of them.

'It's not as easy as all that,' Eva laughed. 'But it's still on the market, and that's a good start.'

On the day Eva took Patsy to see the house, Tommy stuck to them like glue. Patsy declared how he was 'A bloody nuisance, and why did he have to come along in the first place?'

When Eva argued that it was Tommy who found the house, and had every right to be there, Patsy grudgingly conceded. 'All right then,' she grumbled, 'but I don't want him showing me this and that. Nor do I need the pair of youse trying to persuade me into your way of thinking. I'll make me own mind up, so I will!'

On first seeing the house, she gave a groan. 'Jaysus, Mary and Joseph! It's a dreadful ruin, so it is!'

For one awful minute, Eva thought Patsy would turn and run. 'Just look inside,' she pleaded; taking Patsy's arm she drew her closer to the door. 'You've always been better than me at seeing how a place can be improved,' she lied. 'Please, Patsy!

Just a peep? Now we've come this far, you can't not go inside.'

'Just a peep then.' Delighted by Eva's flattering remark, how could she refuse? 'Don't bully me,' she warned, 'or I'm off! And keep that little bugger from under me feet.' Giving Tommy a scowl of a look, she allowed herself to be taken forward.

At the door she shook her head. 'Like I said,' she tutted, 'it's nothing but a ruin. Be Jaysus! It'll take a bloody fortune to put this lot right, so it will.'

As she ventured further into the house, looking into one room and then the other, and after a while going up the stairs, Eva followed and wisely said little. She was afraid to, in case she said the wrong thing and Patsy took off.

Picking out all the faults; the sagging ceilings and the rotting floors, and the way every nook and cranny had been worn by the elements, Patsy sounded as though she hated every inch of the place.

And yet, deep down, Eva suspected Patsy was warming to the house.

Once or twice Tommy looked as if he might take Patsy up on a point or two, but when Eva silenced him with a determined shake of her head, he scurried off into his den and didn't show his face until Patsy had led Eva outside again. 'It's worse than I thought,' she said. Then a smile appeared and Eva knew she liked it. 'You've a good eye, Eva me darling,' she confessed. 'And sure, it isn't me that knows a thing or two about how to bring a place back to life . . . it's you, so it is, and well you know it.'

So, they were in agreement. The place had real possibility.

'But we've got our work cut out, so we have,' Patsy remarked as they made their way home.

Eva made no comment. She knew, possibly more than Patsy did, how much of an uphill battle it would be.

<hr />

FOR THE NEXT couple of weeks, Eva and Patsy threw themselves into drawing up a financial forecast. They checked out the price of furniture, linen, carpets, kitchen and dining necessities, studied hire-purchase terms, and calculated running costs. They also visited the house a number of times with various builders to obtain estimates of renovation costs. At last Patsy had enough facts and figures to draw up a comprehensive financial projection. They dropped it off at the bank and then waited, and hoped. A week later they received a letter from the bank manager suggesting they meet at the house. He wanted to see the place for himself.

They duly met him and watched as he wandered about, making copious notes and muttering to himself. When the three of them stepped out into a bitterly cold day; Eva asked his opinion, but he declined to comment until he'd discussed the situation with senior colleagues at the bank. He asked them to come into the bank at three o'clock the following day. When they agreed, he merely nodded, looked from one to the other, and hurried away.

'We'll get nothing at all from that one,' Patsy said with a snort.

Eva felt the same, but she wouldn't give up. 'What makes you say that?'

'Sure, the bugger couldn't get away quick enough.'

'I hope you're wrong,' Eva said, but deep down she wasn't hopeful.

The following day, her fears were confirmed. 'I'm sorry,' said the manager, 'the bank isn't prepared to take such a risk. I'm afraid we will have to say no.'

'But why dismiss it out of hand like that?' Eva demanded. 'You haven't even talked through our business proposition.'

'This is your first business venture. Your financial projections are pure guesswork. And you have no collateral. If the business failed, the bank would be liable for all your debts.'

'If it was two men sitting here, it would be an altogether different matter,' Patsy scoffed.

He shifted uncomfortably in his seat. 'I assure you, the bank's decision is based on financial issues alone. We believe it's too big a venture for two people with no business experience, and too great a risk without collateral, as I've already said. Now, if you don't mind, I have another appointment.' With that he stood up and strode to the door, which he opened for them. 'If you were to hit on a less ambitious idea, we might possibly talk again.'

'I don't think so,' Eva answered calmly. The next time she and Patsy walked into this bank, it would be to close their account. 'If you'd had the decency to read through our forecast properly, you would have learned that I *have* run a business before, my parents' business, and Patsy kept the books. She probably understands figures better than you do.'

Outside, Patsy rounded on Eva. 'I told you it was a crazy idea but you wouldn't listen.'

'Oh, Patsy, he's not the only one in the world to lend money. We can try elsewhere. We've got time, the agent said so.'

Patsy would have none of it. 'No, Eva. The bank manager's right. It's too big a venture. We'd only end up broke – years of hard work, with nothing to show for it.' She paused, looking at Eva's stricken face. 'I know how much you'd set your heart on it, me darlin', but it wasn't right from the start.'

'It *is* right, Patsy. That house is perfect for a small hotel. We both know it. Don't let him turn you against the idea.'

'I don't want us to lose everything on that place. There'll be other opportunities. Maybe that arrogant bastard was right. Maybe we should lower our sights.'

'I can't force you to go along with it,' Eva said. 'It's as much your money as it is mine, and whatever we do, I want it to be for the two of us. But please, Patsy, won't you give it one more try? Maybe the agent can help us find a backer. Let's go and see him before we throw in the towel.'

'No.' There was something else preying on Patsy's mind. 'The boy obviously thinks he's coming with us when we move. I know you think I might change my mind, but I won't. The further away from me he is, the better I'll like it.'

Eva was shocked. 'Do you really hate him that much?'

'I don't hate him.' Patsy turned away.

'Is that the real reason why you're refusing to try again for the Park Street house, because you're afraid we might have to take Tommy with us?'

'All I'm saying is forget the house on Park Street. It would never have worked out anyway.'

'He's living with us now, so what's the difference?'

'That's another thing. I know we're only weeks away from Christmas, and it's a bad time for house hunting, but as soon as the New Year is over, I want us to start looking for a place of our own. Something we can afford without breaking the bank.'

Patsy's mind was made up, and nothing Eva could say would change it.

Later that night, Eva heard Patsy's fretful footsteps pacing up and down, back and forth. Climbing out of bed, she went along the landing and tapped on her door. 'Are you all right, Patsy?'

The door opened. 'Go to bed!'

'You're not to worry about the house,' Eva told her. 'I didn't realise you were so against it. But it's all right. We'll forget it, like you said.' From the look of Patsy's red eyes, Eva was sure she'd been crying. 'We'll find something else, so you're not to worry, you hear?'

Reaching out but keeping the door only inches open, Patsy took hold of Eva's hand. 'You're a good friend,' she murmured. 'I don't deserve you.'

'Try and get some sleep, Patsy. Goodnight.'

Patsy closed the door and Eva returned to her room.

Neither of them slept much. Eva felt responsible for pressing Patsy into something she didn't feel comfortable with. Acacia Lodge was a real find, she knew that. But if Patsy wasn't happy with the idea, then she had no right to pursue it. She smiled wryly. If she had money of her own, wild horses wouldn't hold her back.

Seated on her bed, Patsy held the photograph in the palm of her hand. For a long time she stared at the images there: a woman, a man and a boy. The man had one arm round his wife, and the other round the boy's shoulders. The boy was Tommy. Patsy assumed the woman was Mary.

It was the man who held her attention. Tall and

rugged, he seemed to be in his early to late forties, with the kind of smiling brown eyes that instantly befriended you. Wearing a chequered shirt and cord trousers, he looked fit and able. The sunshine dappled his face and, in the split second the photograph was taken, the boy was looking up at him with adoring eyes.

As she looked, the tears ran down Patsy's face.

Carefully, she put the photograph back in the envelope and replaced it in the bedside drawer where she first found it.

Chapter Ten

A CACIA LODGE WAS due to be auctioned on
4 December. 'I'd like to attend the auction,
wouldn't you?' Tommy was fast asleep in bed. Eva
and Patsy were sitting by the cheery fire, while Patsy
mended her long coat.

Patsy looked up in surprise. 'What for?'

'I just want to see what kind of a person buys it.
I'd hate to think of it going to someone who might
tear it apart or, worse still, pull it down and build a
monstrosity in its place.'

'What would it matter? It won't be us that buys
it.' Swearing under her breath, Patsy made another
attempt at tidying the sleeve of her coat.

'It *would* matter, Patsy. It's a beautiful house and
deserves better.' Eva lowered her voice. 'I only wish
we could have given it a new lease of life.'

'It's only a house when all's said and done. Yer
too sentimental, so ye are.'

'So you won't come with me?'

'I've got better things to do, so I have,' Patsy
tutted.

'Like what?'

'Like going to the shops for a new winter coat.' With a snort of disgust she threw the garment aside. 'I've had this one for ever. Just look at it!' Raising the sleeve of the coat, she pointed to the frayed cuff. 'It's falling apart, so it is. It's time I treated myself to a new one.'

Startling them, Tommy appeared at the door, his small frame shivering and trembling, more from fear than cold. 'It weren't my fault.' Making a beeline for Patsy, he leaned over and stroked her shoulder, his voice breaking into a sob as he begged, 'Don't hit me, will yer, Mam? Please. I won't do it again.'

Patsy leaped to her feet. 'I'm not yer mam!' she cried. When Tommy seemed not to have heard and just stood there, softly crying, she turned to Eva. 'Jaysus! What's wrong with him?'

Eva had rushed to his side. 'Ssh!' Looking at Patsy, she put her finger to her lips. 'He's sleep-walking.' Tenderly, she turned him round and walked him to the door. 'Quick, Patsy, he's freezing cold. Fetch a blanket out of the linen cupboard, will you?'

Patsy did as she was asked. 'I'm not cut out for this sort of thing,' she protested, though her gaze was constantly drawn to Tommy. 'He put the fear of God in me, so he did!'

And the fear of God stayed with her until she

had gone to her own bed and closed her eyes to sleep.

———⟫◆⟪———

THE AUCTION ROOM was packed to capacity. Eva stayed at the back, though she would rather have been at the front bidding with the rest of them.

Several parcels of land were to go under the hammer: half an acre in the middle of town; a disused generation plant; a block of vandalised garages; and other miscellaneous items which no one seemed to want.

When item number seven came up, there was a buzz of excitement. 'Acacia Lodge,' the auctioneer announced. 'A grand old place, in need of repair but not beyond saving. With eight acres of prime land behind, and a magnificent view, this is a very desirable property.'

'It wants a bloody fortune spent on it.' The portly man close to Eva was talking with his colleague. 'You mark my words, it'll go for a song.'

He was wrong. The bidding was lively and Acacia Lodge was sold for seven thousand pounds, to a man Eva couldn't see properly. He was half hidden by a column at the side of the room.

People began filing out. Eva went forward, curious to see the man who had stolen her dream. But he had already gone. Feeling cheated, she followed the others out and headed towards Albert Street.

Behind her, the business of the day was concluded. 'You've got a good buy there,' the auctioneer told the man. 'A property like that comes up only once in a while.'

The man smiled. 'I've gone above my budget,' he confessed, 'but I've been looking for a long time for a property in this area. This one fits the bill, and I didn't want to let it go.'

'Ah, well, some get what they want,' the auctioneer said wryly, 'and others go away empty-handed.' His gaze went to a balding man who had bid strongly for the house. 'John Lowes is a builder hereabouts. Not a very nice man,' he confided, 'I enjoyed seeing him struggle. You're the first one who's snatched a property from under his nose in a very long time.'

'John Lowes, eh? What did he intend doing with it, do you know?'

'There's only one thing he does with the properties he buys, knocks them down and builds tight little developments that sell for a fortune.' He regarded the man in front of him. Tall and slim, with brown hair and inquisitive eyes, he had the air of someone who knew what he wanted. 'What business might you be in, sir? If you don't mind me asking, that is.'

'I'm a hotelier. My mother died some years back and left me a thriving business. Since then I've built up a network of hotels right across the country.' He pulled out his chequebook.

'Hotels right across the country, eh? What name do you go under?'

Looking up with a smile, the man handed over his cheque. 'Frank Dewhirst,' he answered. 'I'm not known hereabouts.'

The auctioneer passed him a receipt, and all documents relating to Acacia Lodge.

As Frank walked away, the auctioneer muttered, 'Not known hereabouts, eh?' He chuckled. 'I've a feeling you'll be known well enough before too long.'

<hr>

WHEN EVA WALKED in the door, Patsy saw how preoccupied she was. 'Ye shouldn't have gone,' she chastised her. 'Sure, that place wasn't meant for us, me darlin'.'

'Maybe.' Taking off her coat, Eva gave a deep sigh. 'Maybe not. But it doesn't matter now anyway because it's been sold.'

Patsy paraded up and down in her new astrakhan coat. 'Does the coat suit me? I paid more than I wanted but I tried it on and had to have it.'

'It looks lovely,' Eva answered honestly. In fact Patsy looked very attractive. She was made up and her shoulder-length hair shone like roasted chestnuts.

Taking off the coat, Patsy threw two more pieces of coal on the fire. 'Jaysus, yer look frozen to the bone, so ye do.'

Rubbing her hands in front of the fire, Eva looked round. 'Where's Tommy?'

'Gone to the market, that's what he said.'

'How long ago?'

'Can't be sure – an hour, maybe longer.'

'It's half past six. He shouldn't be out in the dark, especially on a cold night like this.'

'I'm not his keeper.'

'Oh, Patsy! He's only a kid.'

'He's fourteen. When I were fourteen, I had to find me own way in the world, so I did. Nothing came easy, and there was no one to worry where I was neither. Stop fretting, will ye? The boy will be back when he's good and ready, so he will. Now then,' she flopped into the armchair, 'will ye tell me what happened at the auction, or what?'

Still concerned about Tommy, but trying not to show it, Eva related the events of the afternoon. 'I don't know who the man was, but he meant to have that place, I can tell you.'

'You're bitterly disappointed, aren't ye?'

'I'll get over it.' She glanced nervously towards the door. 'He should be in by now.'

'Like I said, he'll be in when he's good and ready.'

'You didn't have an argument, did you?'

'We never argue because we never talk.'

'I wish you would.'

'What? Argue?'

'You know very well what I mean.'

Wary, Patsy changed the subject. 'We'll soon be looking for a place of our own,' she reminded Eva. 'A business, too. Christmas will be on us before we know it and, to tell you the truth, I'll be glad when it's over. What with thinking of turning a derelict house into a hotel, and then all this unnecessary worry about a boy who isn't even our responsibility, sure, I reckon we've wasted enough time here. We came here to set ourselves up in home and business, and we've done neither.'

'We could have done both if only you'd listened to me.' Eva hated herself for saying it, but it was the truth. 'Sorry, Patsy. That was unfair.'

'Sure, I can't blame ye. I know what it's like to set yer heart on something only to have it snatched away. In the past, whenever we've had a difference of opinion, you've been right every time.' Patsy gave praise where praise was due. 'But not this time,' she said determinedly. 'This time, you were wrong an' I was right. And I'm making no apologies.'

The door opened and Tommy staggered in with a large Christmas tree. 'I had to fight another lad for this,' he said. 'The man on the stall gave it to me for helping load his lorry. After he'd gone, Billy Bully from Montague Street tried to take it off me, but I gave him a thrashing and he ran off.' Peering out from beneath the branches of the tree, he grinned with pride, his black eye beginning to shine blue, and his face stained with blood. 'It's a grand tree, ain't it?'

'It certainly is,' said Eva, taking part of the weight from him.

Patsy made her excuses and left the room.

'Let's have a look at that face of yours,' Eva said, propping the tree in the corner. 'You should have let the bully have it.'

'I did!' Tommy's chest swelled with pride. 'I gave him a bloody nose and ripped his shirt half-way up his back.' He giggled. 'His mam's got a terrible temper. She'll half kill him when he gets home.'

Seeing that he wasn't badly hurt, Eva had to smile. 'When I said you should have let him have it, I didn't mean . . .' She laughed out loud. 'Oh, never mind. Wash your face and I'll get you something to eat.' With Tommy, there was never a dull moment.

While he sat by the fire, scoffing his cheese sandwich, Eva went upstairs. Knocking on Patsy's door, she asked, 'Are you coming down?'

Patsy opened the door. 'You can come in if you want.'

Entering the room, Eva caught sight of a brown envelope lying on the bed. Patsy quickly tucked it into the drawer, her face red with embarrassment. 'What's that little bugger been up to?'

'He's been fighting over a Christmas tree.'

'Huh!' Going to the dresser Patsy took out a brush and began running it through her hair. 'I'm not coming down.'

'Why not?' Lately, Eva couldn't fathom her. 'I've brewed a pot of tea and made us a cheese sandwich. It's that new crusty bread from the corner baker's.'

'Ten minutes then. But I'm having nothing to do with the boy, or the Christmas tree.'

The evening was painful. Tommy tried time and again to involve Patsy in the conversation, but she would have none of it until, at nine o'clock, she marched off up to her room. Exhausted, Eva wished she hadn't persuaded Patsy to come downstairs. 'You'd best get off to your bed now,' she told Tommy.

He kissed her goodnight on the cheek. 'She wants to take you away from me,' he said soulfully.

'Why do you say that?'

'I just know. I try to be nice to her, but she'll never like me.'

'Go to your bed, Tommy,' Eva urged. 'Tomorrow we'll go and find some decorations for the tree.'

That put the smile back on his face.

After he'd gone to his room, Eva stayed downstairs for a while. But there was no smile on her face.

She looked at the tree slumped in the corner. 'You look like I feel,' she laughed, wondering how Tommy had managed to get it home. 'All the same, we'll dress you up and make you sparkle. Then, with a bit of luck, we might *all* feel more Christmassy.'

———◆———

BRIGHT AND EAGER the following morning, Tommy seemed to have put Patsy out of his mind. 'Where are we going now?' he asked as he and Eva went away from the town centre where they'd stocked up on shiny baubles and tinsel.

'Going to look for some holly.' She swung into Preston New Road.

'But *where?*'

'You'll see.' Eva quickened her steps.

'This is the way to Corporation Park.'

'That's right.'

'Park Street too.'

'Right again.' She had come to know the area very well.

'Are we going to see Olive?'

'If she's there.'

'Do you think she'll offer us some of her delicious pie?'

Eva laughed. 'I hope not. It's Patsy's turn to cook the evening meal, and you know how stroppy she gets if we don't eat every last crumb.'

He thought about that. 'Is she really your best friend?'

'Yes.' Playfully chucking him under the chin, she added, 'And so are you.'

'I wouldn't want her for *my* best friend.' Suddenly his mood had darkened.

Eva slowed. Looking him in the eye she asked, 'Are you sure about that, Tommy?'

Keeping his gaze on the pavement, Tommy didn't answer.

Eva waited.

'I'd *like* her to be my friend,' he admitted eventually, 'but she won't let me.'

'I know.'

'I ain't done nuffin' to upset her neither.'

'I know that too.'

'Me mam were moody an' all.' He kicked a stone out of the way and thrust his hands into his pockets, shivering. 'Brr! It's bleedin' freezin', ain't it?'

'What do you mean, about your mam being moody?' This was the first time he'd spoken in that way about his mother, and Eva hoped he might open up to her.

Tommy shrugged his shoulders. 'Dunno. I didn't mean nuffin'.'

Eva thought it best to make no comment, believing that people were more likely to confide if you didn't push them too hard.

Not Tommy though. Tommy changed the subject. 'Patsy wouldn't even know if we'd had some pie.'

Eva laughed out loud. 'I wouldn't count on it.'

'Olive might not offer us any. She might not even be there.'

'That's true.'

In fact, Olive was there and she had just taken a delicious rhubarb crumble out of the oven. Eva couldn't resist it. When she was finished, she was so full she could hardly breathe. 'That's the best rhubarb crumble I've ever tasted,' she told the smiling Olive, who had to be restrained from spooning out another helping.

As for Tommy, he had his mouth crammed full. Grinning appreciatively, he showed a mangled mixture of rhubarb and crumble. 'Close your mouth, Tommy!' Eva told him, and he did.

'I don't know what's going on next door,' Olive chatted, 'but there have been all kinds of people coming and going. One big fellow in a duffel coat and boots went all over the grounds, taking pictures. He seemed to be here for an age. This morning, two others turned up in a big red lorry. They were in the house for ages. Afterwards, they stood at the bottom of the garden making notes and talking. Then they drove off, and I haven't seen them since.'

Eva told her about the auction, and Olive said

she was glad that the house might be renovated. 'It's such a terrible waste.'

'Eva wanted that house,' Tommy butted in.

'Oh, dear!' Olive thought she might have said the wrong thing, but Eva put her mind at rest.

'I couldn't afford it,' she said.

'It would have been lovely having you next door, but I believe in fate. It seems to me you weren't meant to have it.'

'That's what Patsy said.' Tommy had finished his crumble and was feeling talkative.

'Who's Patsy?'

'She's Eva's best friend, but she doesn't like me.'

When Olive looked surprised, Tommy went on, 'If Eva was my mother like you thought before, then Patsy couldn't make her leave me behind when they go.' Olive looked even more bewildered.

Eva intervened. 'That's enough, Tommy. Why don't you go and find some holly?'

Tommy nodded and went outside.

Olive watched him through the window as he foraged. 'Oh, look,' she said suddenly. 'That man's there, the one I told you about who went all over the grounds, taking pictures and measuring.'

Eva joined her at the window and saw the man, talking to Tommy. 'I'd better go,' she decided, knowing how Tommy let his tongue run away with him, 'but I'll come and see you again.' Olive was delighted.

Outside, just as Eva suspected, Tommy was relating his life story. 'Me dad's a Cockney too,' he was saying, 'but he couldn't settle in the north so he ran away and left me with me mam. If he came back now, I'd pretend I didn't know him.'

'I'm sorry,' Eva said to the stranger, putting a hand on Tommy's shoulder, 'we have to go.' Gripping Tommy's coat collar, she urged him away from the man and on past Acacia Lodge. 'You're too free with strangers,' she warned. 'We don't know that man from Adam.'

'He's a good bloke. He's from London, that's what he said. I were just telling him about my dad, and how he run off like the coward he was.'

As Eva turned to say something to him, she caught sight of a second man emerging from the doorway of the house. 'My God!' For a minute, Eva thought her mind was playing tricks. But then he looked straight at her, and though he was older, there was no mistaking him. 'Frank Dewhirst!' The name came from her lips like a ghost from the past.

'What did yer say?' Tommy looked from her white face to the man in the doorway. 'Who's that geezer?'

For what seemed an age but was in fact only a few seconds, Frank and Eva stared at each other, unable to believe their eyes. Suddenly he was rushing towards her. 'Eva? Eva Bereton?'

'He knows yer name!' Tommy cried.

Overcome with emotion at seeing her again, Frank hugged her to him and then held her at arm's length. 'I can't believe it,' he kept saying. 'Eva Bereton! Lovelier than ever. I can't believe it.'

Eva hardly knew what to say, she was so amazed.

Tommy thought it was like one of those films he'd seen when he'd sneaked in at the pictures. 'I'm Tommy,' he said boldly, but Frank was too preoccupied to respond.

When he asked to take Eva out that evening, she accepted. 'We can talk over old times,' he said. 'I've got so much to tell you.'

PATSY WAS SO shocked, she almost dropped the dishes. 'Frank Dewhirst, of all people! How is he? What's he doing in this part of the world? And why would he be nosing about the house on Park Street?' The questions came thick and fast. 'Ye don't think *he's* the one who's bought it, do ye? Jaysus! Wouldn't that be a turn-up for the books?'

'I don't know any more than you do.' Wiping the dishes, Eva stacked them away. 'He asked me out to talk over old times, and I've said yes.'

Pausing in her chores, Patsy swung round. 'Oh? And when's this?'

'Tonight.' Eva was wondering if she'd done the right thing. 'He's collecting me at eight o'clock.'

Patsy smiled. 'And why not?' she declared. 'He was a good friend, so he was.'

'Now I've agreed to it, I'm not sure I should have.'

'Oh? Why?'

'Water under the bridge and all that.'

Patsy frowned. 'Does he know his mother sent us packing?'

'If he does, he didn't say.'

'Then he doesn't know.' She regarded Eva's quiet face. 'He was in love with you though. You do remember that?'

Eva nodded.

'Is that why you wish you hadn't agreed to go out with him?'

Now that Patsy had spelled it out, Eva felt foolish. 'I expect so, but what does it matter now? And anyway, you're right. Frank was always a good friend, and I'm still very fond of him.'

Before Frank arrived, Eva helped Tommy put up the tree in the front room. 'It's too early to dress the tree,' Eva told him, 'but you can make some paper chains and trim the holly.'

Tommy was preoccupied. 'You won't marry that man, will you, Eva?'

'Who's talking of marriage? He's an old friend, that's all.'

'If you did get married, you wouldn't leave me on my own, would you?'

Eva laughed. 'I'll be back in a couple of hours. And when I do get back, I'll expect to see this room nice and tidy.'

When Frank arrived, the reunion with Patsy was less emotional. 'You don't look any different,' he said, though he thought she was a bit slimmer than before.

Tommy remarked on his 'big posh car', Patsy said how good it was to see someone from the old days, and in minutes Eva was whisked away. 'You look beautiful,' he said, opening the car door for her.

Eva had brushed her blonde hair into a glowing frame about her face, and her green eyes shone with excitement. She wore a light-grey, long coat, and beneath that a straight-cut black dress. The high-heeled shoes accentuated her slim ankles, and altogether she made a very attractive figure.

'I've found this lovely old inn,' he told her as they drove out of town. His hand wandered from the steering wheel to take hold of hers. 'Oh, Eva, you can't know how excited I am at finding you.'

After all this time, and two disastrous relationships, he still had marriage on his mind. But there was time enough for that, he thought. He guessed Eva had no man in tow now, or she would not have accepted his offer to take her out. So, what had she been doing all this time? What had brought her to Blackburn, and what were her future plans? He and

Eva needed to catch up with the past. So, for now, that would have to suffice.

The inn was indeed lovely. It was on the outskirts of Preston, old and beamed, with small windows and intimate rooms. The restaurant backed on to a river. Frank asked for a table by the window.

Eva was enjoying herself immensely. 'It's a long time since I came to a place like this,' she told him. In fact, she had never been to a place like this.

She thought Frank had not changed much; his appearance was slightly more rounded, and he had a few more lines round the eyes, but he still had that scrubbed, fresh-faced look and, with his smooth hands and expensive suit, he looked the picture of affluence.

Her first question took the smile from his face. 'Are you still running the hotel with your mother?'

'Mother died six years ago.'

'Oh, I'm sorry.' Eva felt awful.

'The hotel was left to me,' he said. 'It's been totally refurbished, and now caters to an elite clientele. In fact, I've made a speciality of catering for top businessmen – company directors, high-level conferences, that sort of thing.' The smile returned. 'You might be surprised to know I own eight top hotels right across the country.'

Eva was not surprised, and told him so. 'I always believed you would do well.'

'Acacia Lodge will be my ninth hotel.'

'You bought it?' So Patsy was right.

Frank nodded.

'It's so strange,' she said. 'I had plans of my own to turn Acacia Lodge into a hotel.'

'Did you?'

'I was at the auction. I had no idea it was you who bought it.'

'If I'd known you wanted it, I might have backed off.'

'It wouldn't have made any difference,' she confided. 'I couldn't raise the money for it. I just went out of interest.'

'We have so much to talk about, don't we? What's happened to you in the years since you left? Is there a man in your life still, Eva? Have you any children? What are your plans for the future?'

Eva laughed. 'So many questions!'

'Oh, there are many more,' he confessed. Not least of which was asking her to marry him. But first things first. He raised his glass to hers. 'To you and me. May we be blessed with everything our hearts desire.' Now that he had found her again, all he wanted was Eva.

Eva clinked her glass with his, and they drank a toast.

'Tommy!' patsy's voice sailed through the house. 'Answer that bloody door.'

Running to the window, Tommy looked out. 'There's no one there!' he yelled back; whoever it was must have gone away.

In the other room, Patsy was drying her hair by the fire. Irritated now, she rubbed the towel hard into her scalp. 'It's them damned carol singers, so it is! I swear they start earlier every year.'

When the knock came again, this time louder, she wrapped the towel round her head and marched to the front door. Flinging it open, she glared at the lad standing there; a round-faced fellow about the age of Tommy, but twice the size. 'What the devil d'ye want?' she demanded. 'Carol singing, is it?'

'No, missus.' Looking the essence of innocence, he smiled at her. 'I've come to see Tommy. He promised me a game o' marbles.'

Patsy continued to stare at him. In the half-light from the street light, he seemed fairly well dressed, and he had a friendly sort of face. 'Tommy's friend, eh?' There was something about him that bothered her, but she couldn't put her finger on it. 'Ye shouldn't be out at this time of night on yer own,' she chided.

'It's all right,' he answered with a sweet smile. 'Me mam knows where I am.'

'I see.'

'So will you please tell him Mike's here?'

Patsy nodded. 'Wait there.' Half closing the door, she went to the front room where Tommy was surrounded by strips of paper and mountains of holly trimmings. 'There's a lad here to see you.'

'Who is it?'

'You'd best go and find out, hadn't ye?' Her hair was dripping wet and she had no shoes on her feet; Eva was out enjoying herself, while *she* hadn't been out in so long she'd begun to feel her age. She'd almost forgotten what it was like to lie in a man's arms and feel the thrust of his body on hers. And now, as if that wasn't bad enough, she couldn't even have a peaceful evening indoors without some bloody kid banging on the door at all hours.

'Just get rid of him,' she snapped, 'or bugger off out, I don't care what ye do.' With that she stormed off, back to the fire.

Slipping his shoes on, Tommy ran to the door. 'Hello?' It was pitch-black outside, and there was no one in sight. 'Who's there?'

'Tommy, it's me.' From across the road, a young figure stepped out from behind a parked van. 'I was told this was yours.' He seemed to be lifting something from the back of the van. 'You'd better come and help. I can't carry it on my own.' The voice sounded vaguely familiar but Tommy couldn't be certain.

'What is it?' Cautiously, he stepped down from the doorstep, and crossed the road. 'Who sent you?'

As he neared the van, the figure stepped away. 'Here, lad. Come here.' The voice was that of an older man. 'It's a present, see.'

Tommy's young heart soared. 'Dad! Is that you, Dad?' All his hatred was forgotten.

'It's me, son. We have to talk. But not here. Get inside. Quick!'

Something about the tone of voice and the furtive urging made Tommy hesitate. 'Let me see who you are,' he demanded. 'How do I know you're my dad?'

The man laughed. Tommy turned to run, but it was too late. Grabbing him by the scruff of the neck, the man hauled him into the van. No sooner was he inside, than the van drove off. Through his terror, Tommy saw the boy slam the doors shut. It was the lad who had fought him over the Christmas tree.

'Thought you'd give my boy a thrashing, did you?' The man's unshaven face was pressed close to Tommy's, his warm, booze-ridden breath like a fog in Tommy's wide, stricken eyes. 'Well now, I reckon I should give you a taste of the same, don't you?'

'Let me out!' Fighting with all his might, Tommy tried in vain to escape. 'It were *my* tree, not his! I paid for it, with work.'

The van careered round corners, throwing them from side to side and sending all manner of articles down on them – the van was packed with items of furniture, lamps and what looked like tied-up bundles of bedding. 'Steady on, you silly cow!' the man yelled. 'Are you trying to kill us all, or what?'

'I don't like this business, Josh, taking a kid from his family.' The driver was his wife. She was clearly nervous. 'If we get caught, we'll be in real trouble, have you thought of that?'

'Drive the bloody van and mind your own business!' Incensed, Josh twisted his grip on Tommy. 'Nobody beats my Billy up and gets away with it,' he growled. 'I need to set the record straight, that's all.' Addressing his son who, like the coward he was, remained at the back by the doors, he said, 'The truth now, Billy. Who paid for that tree?'

'I did! It were a surprise for you and Mam.'

'And did this little bugger sneak up on you? Is that why you got the worst of it?'

'It were just like I told you. He didn't even give me a chance.'

'Well now, that's what I thought. My boy is twice your size, so I knew you couldn't beat him fair and square.'

'I didn't sneak up on him!' Tommy was terrified. 'He's a liar! I *did* beat him fair and square.'

'Stop the bloody van!' Josh shouted at the woman.

She did as she was told, bringing the van to a halt at the side of a spinney. 'Don't do it, Josh.'

'I told you to mind your own bloody business.'

She appealed to Billy. 'Tell your dad the truth.'

JOSEPHINE COX

'I already did,' he answered rudely. 'The coward sneaked up on me from behind.'

Josh dragged Tommy into the spinney. 'Right then, we'll soon see who's the liar.' Turning to the woman, he ordered, 'Fetch the rifle.'

Both she and Tommy stared at him wide-eyed with horror. 'I'm not fetching no rifle,' she said, backing away. 'I won't be part of no murder.'

'Don't be so bloody stupid, woman.' Josh laughed out loud. 'I'm not gonna shoot anybody. I just want to make certain the coward doesn't run away from a fight with our lad.'

When she hesitated, Billy ran and brought the rifle to him. 'She's a softie,' he sneered, 'like all women.' Deep down he was shaking. Tommy was the better fighter, and Billy knew it, but he dare not admit it or his dad would have the flesh off his back.

Suddenly Tommy felt himself being thrown forward. 'It's up to you now, Billy boy!' Josh yelled, and while Tommy looked round in a daze, Billy leaped on his back.

It was a fierce fight. After only a few minutes both boys were exhausted, but Tommy stayed on his feet, ready to fight on.

'Buck up, Billy!' Josh urged angrily. 'Don't let the brat get the better of you.' Coming up behind him, he gave his son a great shove. 'Stop bloody dithering! Use your fists like I showed you. Your feet as well if you have to.'

Hurting and afraid, Tommy hit out, the well-aimed blow sending Billy sprawling. Humiliated, and knowing his dad was watching, the older boy scrambled up and ran at him. Tommy side-stepped; Billy tripped, and as he fell he knocked his head on the ground, momentarily dazing himself.

'Get up!' his father ordered.

When the boy lay there, his bloodstained face upturned, he yelled again, *'Get up!'*

Billy raised his head. 'I'm not fighting no more.' He knew when he was beaten.

Enraged, Josh darted forward, yanked him off the ground and sent him head first towards the woman. Then he stripped off his coat. The woman's frantic voice called out, 'For God's sake, he's only a bairn, and he's hurt bad. Leave him be! The boy got a fair enough thrashing – they both did.'

Tommy's legs felt wobbly, his head was throbbing and a trickle of blood was running from his hairline into his eyes, half blinding him.

Behind the woman, Billy grinned. 'Go on, Dad,' he goaded. 'Teach him a lesson!'

Stepping forward, Josh stood before Tommy's small, unsteady form. 'Oh yes, I'll teach him a lesson all right. The best lesson he's ever likely to get.'

And, as he came forward, Tommy braced himself.

Patsy looked at the clock. 'Ten thirty.' She wiggled her toes in front of the fire, trying to ignore the fact that Tommy had been gone for almost two hours. 'Eva's making a night of it.' A little smile crept over her face. 'Lucky devil, so she is.'

Beginning to grow restless, she went to the front door and looked out. 'I'll give him what for when he gets back, the little sod! All the same, where can he be until this time? Jaysus! I'm getting as bad as Eva, so I am. That boy should know better than to stay out till all hours. He'll hear from me when he gets in, so he will.'

Returning to the back room, she paced the floor. 'Come on, Eva,' she muttered. 'What the devil's keeping yer?' She didn't know what to do. She had thought of going to Maggie Bell, but so far had persuaded herself there was no need.

The van had travelled only a few miles when Josh ordered his wife to stop outside a country pub. 'I've a terrible thirst on me,' he complained. 'The landlord here is a good bloke. He's well known for serving a pint out of hours.'

A moment later, man and boy both climbed out of the van. When the woman went to follow, he turned on her. 'You stay here. Keep an eye on the boy.'

'I'm hungry.'

'Do as you're told! I'll send you something out.' He gave her an unwelcome, sloppy kiss. 'Somebody's got to watch him.'

In a few minutes Billy was back with a ham sandwich and a pint of beer. 'Dad says to get that down you,' he told her. 'We'll not be long.' With a sly glance into the back of the van, he grinned. 'Got taught his lesson, didn't he, eh?' When she didn't answer, he swaggered away.

Unable to eat the sandwich, she put it aside. But she sipped at the beer, her throat dry with shame. She glanced round. The boy lay on a bundle of bedding, one arm flung out, the other buckled beneath him. In the light from the pub window, his face had a sallow, unreal appearance. Gulping hard, she took another sip of the beer. If it came to it, she could handle her son. But Josh was a bastard without mercy. He was the one she feared.

Half an hour passed. An hour. Inside the van the silence was eerie.

Getting out of the van, she peered through the pub window. Some of the men were saying goodnight. 'Give us a call at six in the morning.' Workers, staying overnight, the woman deduced.

Josh was at the bar, talking to the landlord. They were knocking back whisky now and from the look of them had already drunk more than was sensible. Billy was slumped in a chair, sound asleep. Suddenly, Josh slid to the floor. The landlord laughed out loud.

Looking up, he saw her watching. In a minute he was outside.

'Come in,' he said. 'Your lads are staying the night, so you'll have to do the same.' He put his arm round her. 'I've a nice warm bed waiting. Your man's dead to the world. We can have a bit of fun, the two of us. He'll never know.' Pushing his arm up her skirt, he felt for her thigh. 'Ooh!' Grabbing her hand he guided it to his trousers. 'Feel that! You've made him stand up like a bloody ramrod.'

'Bugger off!' She slapped him hard across the face.

'Please yourself,' he grumbled. 'Get back in your bloody van and freeze, for all I care.'

Back in the van, she waited for the light in the bar to go out. A moment or two later, she went to the back of the vehicle. She opened the door and reached inside. The boy was icy cold. Taking two ends of the bedding, she wrapped it round him, afterwards gently stroking his face.

She glanced across at the pub. All was in darkness. It was now or never, she decided.

Quietly, she closed the van doors and climbed back into the driving seat. Keeping the lights switched off, she turned on the engine and waited, her eyes raised anxiously to the pub window, fearing a light might come on and someone would see her.

Upstairs, the landlord drew back the curtains

and looked out. 'Running the engine to keep warm, eh?' he laughed. 'She'll be knocking for me to let her in before the night's through.' Still laughing, he dropped on to the bed and fell into a deep, drunken stupor.

After a while the woman drove slowly away. At the end of the lane she accelerated, speeding along the road and praying that she would not be stopped by the law.

Beyond all pain, Tommy didn't move or make a sound.

<hr />

EVA WAS BESIDE herself with worry. 'Tell me again, Patsy. Who did the boy say he was? What did he look like?'

For the umpteenth time, Patsy went through what had taken place.

'And you say he didn't tell you he was going out?'

'Not a word. Like I said, I told him his pal was at the door, then I came back in here. I just assumed he'd decided to go off with the lad.' Like Eva, she was beginning to feel very uneasy about the situation. 'Eva, what are we to do?'

'You stay here, Patsy. If he comes back and the house is empty, he'll only panic.'

'Why? Where are ye going?'

'I'm going to look for him.'

'What? At this time of night? You don't know who's prowling about. Let me come with you.'

'No, Patsy.' Throwing on her coat, Eva hurried to the door. 'Keep a lookout for him, and whatever you do, don't leave the house.' Only when Patsy had promised did Eva set off.

Frozen to the bone, she searched the streets, looking in every nook and cranny, calling his name, but he was nowhere to be found, and her heart was in her boots. The further away from Albert Street she got, the more she wondered whether Tommy really wanted to be found. Recalling how concerned he was about being left on his own, she murmured, 'I would *never* leave you on your own, Tommy, you should know that.'

Thoughts of going to the police crossed her mind, but she thrust them away. Numbly, she continued to search.

Back at the house, Patsy sat in her chair, her eyes like lead weights. 'Stay awake, Patsy, my girl,' she told herself. 'When he knocks on that door, he'll get the length of my tongue an' no mistake!'

It was nerve-racking, waiting for Tommy, looking out for Eva. Worried and angry at the same time, Patsy paced the floor. 'Ah, sure, I knew the little sod would be trouble the minute I clapped eyes on him.' The strange thing was that now, when she believed he might be in trouble, Patsy felt a surge of love for him.

Some time later, when there was a knock on the door, she fled along the passage, excitedly calling out as she ran, 'Eva! Have yer got the boy? Jaysus! I thought I'd never see the pair of youse again.'

Close to tears, she flung open the door. She was astonished to see there was no one there. 'What the devil!' Staring into the night, she thought she saw a figure running, but with the night so dark, she couldn't be certain.

'Kids!' Tossing her head, she snorted angrily. At the top of her voice, she yelled into the street, 'Little monsters! There'll be a bucket o' water waiting if yer try it again, so there will!'

As she closed the door, her gaze fell to the step. For a moment she couldn't make out what was lying there; must be something left by the kids who'd knocked on the door, she thought.

Stooping to examine what she suspected was a bundle of dirty rags, or something filthier from the gutter, she froze with horror. 'Oh, Jaysus Mary and Joseph!' It was a boy, bloodstained and looking like death itself. Shaking her head in disbelief, she knelt beside him.

A light went on in the house opposite and Maggie hurried across the street. 'What's all the yelling and shouting? Folks are trying to get some sleep.' When Patsy looked up, her face stricken, Maggie fell silent, her gaze going from Patsy to the bundle she had lifted ever so gently into her arms. 'God Almighty, it's our Tommy!'

When they got him inside and saw the extent of his injuries, both women were moved to tears. 'There's nothing we can do for him. The lad needs hospital treatment and quick!' Maggie rushed to the phone. 'Mind him gently now while I call an ambulance.'

'No!' Patsy stopped her. 'We can't wait for an ambulance. We'll take him by taxi. It'll be quicker. We'll get one easily down the road.'

Maggie nodded. 'You're right. It's the weekend, and the ambulances might be out on all manner of calls. Besides, the infirmary is only three miles away.'

While Maggie went to fetch a taxi, Patsy sat holding Tommy. Wiping the blood from his face she whispered, 'Who did this to ye? Who was it, Tommy?' But he was silent, and she could not stop her tears. She loved the boy. All this time she had rejected him because of something not his fault, and now she would give anything for him to be all right. The truth rose up in her like an angry, beautiful thing. She could let the feelings loose now, and not be afraid. Only Tommy mattered now. *Not the other one.* Only Tommy.

Bending her face to his, she asked him in the softest whisper, 'Will ye ever forgive me?'

WHEN EVA RETURNED, weary and concerned, she found the note left by Patsy:

> Eva, me darlin',
>   I'm taking Tommy to the infirmary. The boy's suffered a terrible beating. Maggie's going with me.
>   Come quick.
>   Patsy

Shocked to the core, Eva ran out into the street. She didn't stop to call a taxi or ask for help. Instead she ran all the way to the infirmary, a prayer on her lips the whole journey.

———<del></del>———

FOR THE NEXT few days, Tommy hovered between life and death. Distraught, neither Eva nor Patsy left his side and, from the moment Frank was informed, he was a great source of comfort to both women, especially Eva. 'I won't leave you,' he promised.

As good as his word, he stayed with them, a rock of strength; suffering their distress, tending to their needs, while they tended to Tommy's, and sharing their delight when the doctor announced, 'Tommy's out of danger.'

After that, but only when they knew he really was

recovering well, Patsy and Eva took turns to go home of a night.

When it was Eva's turn, Frank would stay a while and make sure she was comfortable, before reluctantly leaving. What he really wanted was to stay and hold her through the night, but Eva never encouraged that, and he wisely did not outstay his welcome, always believing there would be a time when it was right.

And, just as he had hoped, the time came soon enough.

The lack of sleep was showing on them both. Eva was at her lowest ebb, and he sensed she would not refuse if he suggested that he stay. 'Don't send me back to an empty hotel room,' he pleaded. 'It's a soulless place, Eva. I'd rather stay here and keep an eye on you. You look so tired and washed out.'

Eva looked at him, studying the pale features and the unshaven face, and she felt ashamed. 'You've been such a good friend,' she said with a quiet smile, 'and I do know how bleak a hotel room can seem when you've no one to talk to.' In fact, she felt lonely without Patsy and Tommy. Suddenly the house was cold and unfriendly, and her heart was not in it.

'Are you saying I can stay?'

When Eva nodded approval, he couldn't believe his luck.

Worming his way into her affections, he made

a cheery fire, ushering her to sit in the big arm-chair beside it, while he busied himself making a pot of tea.

Afterwards, they talked well into the small hours, until Eva fell asleep in the chair. Seeing his chance, he carried her up to her bed.

As he was laying her down, she woke and looked up at him. 'I love you,' he said and, tenderly caressing her, he lay down beside her. When she made no effort to move away or protest, he kissed her softly. 'Do you have any feelings for me, darling Eva?' he whispered and, weary and lonely as she was, Eva could not think of an answer true to her heart. But, he was here, warm and comforting, and she had always liked him.

Encouraged by her silence, he kissed her again; this time touching her breasts and daring to go further.

Eva had forgotten how wonderful it was to have a man love you. And here was a good man, who had seen her through a bad time, without asking for anything in return. She could send him away. But she had come to accept and enjoy his company. Besides, right now, she didn't want to be alone.

He grew bolder. Peeling off her clothes, he touched every part of her body. Cupping her small firm breasts, he lapped his tongue round the nipples, sending shivers of delight all over her.

When he felt she was ready, he entered her.

Eva clung to him, wanting his love . . . *not* wanting his love. But he was the only one; for the moment.

And the moment was wonderful.

Chapter Eleven

THE NURSE PEEPED out through the office window. 'Just look at those two.' Drawing her colleague's attention to Patsy and Tommy, she smiled with pleasure. 'It's a joy to see them.'

The plump nurse followed her gaze. 'You're right.' Patsy was helping Tommy with his model aircraft. Every now and then they would erupt in fits of laughter. 'To look at them, anybody would think they were mother and son.'

'I'll be honest with you, I didn't think the lad would pull through when they brought him in.' She recalled the night. 'Like death he was – four broken ribs, a fractured arm, and multiple internal injuries. Whoever did that to him must have been out of his mind.' She sighed. 'The police will never catch him now. He's long gone.'

'I'd like to get my hands on the swine!'

'So would the other woman, Eva Bereton. Beside herself, she was. I tell you, Lilian, I wouldn't want to be in his shoes if she ever catches up with him.' Turning away, she dipped a thermometer into a beaker of blue liquid.

'Still, all that really matters now is that the boy has recovered. He might be small for his age, but he's a tough little monkey.' The nurse's face beamed with pleasure. 'Nearly three months it's been, and now, at long last, he's going home.'

A few moments later, Eva appeared. Maggie Bell was with her. 'I'll go and sign him out,' she told Eva. As his aunt, she was the only one who could legally arrange his discharge from the infirmary.

'There you go.' Eva dropped a bag containing Tommy's new clothes on the bed. 'Me and Maggie have been shopping. There's even a pile of comics for you to read on the way home.' Bending to kiss him, she studied his face; pinker now, with bright, alert eyes. Thankfully, the memory of what had happened to him seemed to be fading. Eva thought it amazing how resilient children could be. 'Are you ready to come home now?'

Patsy gave Eva a wink. 'Whatever makes ye think he wants to leave here? Sure, the lad won't want to come back to a poky little house when he can be waited on hand and foot in this lovely place.'

'I *do* want to come home!' Tommy cried. 'I've had enough of being in here.' Then, when he saw the two of them smiling, he laughed out loud. Grabbing the bag, he unpacked it. There was everything he needed. 'Can I get dressed now?' he asked eagerly. 'Can we go?'

At that moment, Maggie returned. 'Everything's done,' she told them and, smiling at Tommy, said, 'Soon as ever you're ready, we can take you home.'

Tommy was ready in record time. 'Why did Maggie go to the office instead of you?' he asked Eva as she wheeled him to the lift. 'It's you and Patsy who look after me, not her.'

Eva had wondered how she would explain Maggie's involvement and had an answer ready. 'I asked Maggie if she would fetch your medicines, that's all.'

Later that evening, Eva popped over to Maggie's house. 'Why don't you tell Tommy you're his aunt?' she urged. 'It'll be a comfort to you both.'

'No.' Maggie was adamant. 'I'll always look out for Tommy, but it's best to leave things as they are. He wouldn't understand. I could have helped when his mother needed me, and I didn't, God forgive me.'

'Because she wouldn't let you, that's why.'

'I know that, and so do you, but it might look different to Tommy. She told him things about me – nasty, untrue things. Even when I helped to keep him from being taken into care, he was always wary of me. I could sense it, but I expect he thought I was the lesser of two evils. Besides, I'd be no good to him. Not now.'

'You do yourself an injustice, Maggie.'

'It's a sad thing when a family falls apart like ours did, but it happened and there's no going back now.' A slow smile crept over her kindly features. 'You and Patsy have taken the boy to your hearts, and you'll never know how grateful I am.'

'He's easy to love,' Eva answered softly. 'You need never worry about him. Patsy and I will always take care of him.'

'Isn't it wonderful how Patsy has taken to Tommy?' Maggie remarked. 'There was a time when I thought she actively disliked the boy.'

'Yes, it is wonderful.' Eva, too, had delighted in the growing affection between Patsy and the boy. 'They spend so much time together these days, Patsy and I haven't even got round to thinking about looking for a little business.'

Patsy never mentioned finding a place of their own any more, and Eva was glad of it. But they would soon have to think about earning a living, or they'd have no savings left.

When she got back to the house, she broached the subject with Patsy.

She had been having similar thoughts. 'You're right, we've got to do something. Then there's this house, and Tommy.' She took a deep breath. 'If

Mary's father left it to her, and now she's gone, who does it belong to?'

'Maggie thinks it might belong to Tommy, by rights. But unless Mary left a will saying so, and I don't think she did, it belongs to Tommy's father.'

'But the bugger's done a bunk!'

'Makes no difference. He is still her legal husband, so I think the house is his.'

'It's a crying shame, so it is.'

'What are you getting at?'

'Just thinking.'

'Come on, out with it.'

'I thought, if the house belongs to Tommy, and we've been putting aside all our rent for whoever might claim it, why not make the money over to him? And, while we're at it, why not buy the house from him and put the money into a trust or something so he'll have a tidy sum to look forward to when he comes of age?' These days, Patsy always put Tommy's interests first.

'It's a good idea, but if I'm right in thinking the house is legally Fred Johnson's, there's no question of us buying it. The rent money we've been putting aside for whoever might come and claim it is earning good interest, so we can always put that away for Tommy. So we're back where we started, with no house of our own and no business. If we bought a place, it would mean moving away from here, with Tommy, and I know Maggie wouldn't want that.'

'If she won't be honest with the boy, why should we give a sod about what she wants?'

'She's been good to him, Patsy. Don't forget he might have been put away if it hadn't been for her. And when he was hurt, she was never far away.'

Patsy relented, feeling a little ashamed. 'So, what do we do?'

'Tommy has to go to school after Easter,' Eva reminded her. 'We're very lucky the authorities were so sympathetic to his case. Why don't we leave it be until then? It's only a matter of a few weeks.'

'Fine by me.' She then voiced another worry that had been chewing away at her. 'Is it getting serious between you and Frank?'

Taken aback, Eva replied cagily, 'Why do you ask?'

'Because you've been seeing a lot of each other.'

'I'm not denying that. He's been a godsend while Tommy's been in hospital. He was there almost every other day.'

'All the same, I'm beginning to wonder if it was more to see you than Tommy.'

'That's unfair, Patsy. Frank is a good man, and he really likes the boy.'

'I'm not saying he isn't a good man. I'm just saying Frank loves you. He always has.'

'I know.'

'Do you love him?'

'I'm not sure.' She blushed deep pink. There were things Patsy didn't know.

'Can I say something you might not like?'

'I expect you will anyway.'

'It's about Frank.'

'What about him?'

'He's insanely jealous about you. That could be a dangerous thing.'

'He's no need to be jealous about me.' Unless he can read my mind, she thought wryly. Because if he could read her mind, he would see another man there – Bill Westerfield, the man she loved with all her being.

'All I'm saying is, be very careful, me darlin'. He set his cap at you once before, and I've a feeling he won't let you escape him twice.'

'I thought you just agreed he was a good man.'

'And so he is. Rich, too. Sure, Frank is a good catch for any woman.'

'But not for me, is that what you're saying?'

Patsy quietly regarded her; in her thirtieth year, Eva was a stunning beauty. Her long hair was still corn-coloured, her eyes the loveliest sea-green, her skin soft and clear, and her smile shone through the dullest of days, and yet there was always the faintest regret in those eyes. Patsy had always known the reason for that regret. Wisely, she had kept quiet over the years. Now, though, she felt compelled to speak. 'Do you ever think about Bill?'

For a moment it seemed as though Eva might not answer, she was so still and silent. Presently, she looked up. 'Yes, I still think about him,' she confessed. 'I always will.'

'Even though you know you can't have him?'

'Even then.' Her lovely eyes glistened with tears. 'I know Frank isn't Bill, and I know I can never love him the way he deserves, but I'm lonely, Patsy. So lonely.' Not Patsy, or even Tommy, could fill the void in her heart.

'Tell me something, Eva. Does Frank make you happy?'

'Sort of.'

Patsy's smile told Eva she understood. 'Sometimes that's all we can expect.'

'Maybe.'

Patsy stood up and went to where Eva sat. She put a friendly arm round her. 'You deserve a bit of happiness, me darlin',' she said, 'and if Frank can lift your heart, then who am I to spoil it? But don't make mistakes you might regret later on.'

Eva smiled up at her. 'You're like an old mother hen.'

'Not so much of the "old", if ye don't mind!'

They chatted a little longer, about nothing in particular, each keeping her own secrets.

'Ye look tired, so ye do.' Patsy yawned. 'An'
yer not the only one.' She struggled out of her chair.
'I'm off to me bed. Goodnight, Eva. Sleep well.'

'A minute, Patsy.'

'What is it, me darlin'?'

'You don't know how glad I am that you and
Tommy are such good friends now.'

'I'm glad too, so I am,' Patsy confessed. 'It
took a terrible thing for me to realise how much
I love him.'

'I never understood why you set yourself against
him.'

Patsy shook her head. 'Goodnight, Eva.' Some
things were best left unsaid.

———————

T HE NEXT FEW weeks saw many changes.
Tommy went from strength to strength
and actually began looking forward to the day he
would, belatedly, start school again.

Eva saw more and more of Frank, and Patsy
worried about that, especially when Frank twice
questioned her about Eva's past men friends. Of
course Eva had gone out with other men, and some
of them were serious, but as far as Patsy knew, Eva
had never felt the same way about any of them.

How could she, Patsy thought, when she had
only ever loved one man in the whole of her life?
Bill Westerfield was etched in Eva's heart for all

time, and no one, however attentive and loving, would ever take his place. Patsy knew that, even if she knew nothing else. But her lips were sealed where Frank was concerned. She had a feeling he would not be able to handle the truth.

Acacia Lodge began to take shape. Frank's plans for it had changed. He had not told Eva, but he meant it to be their home, after they were married.

One Saturday afternoon in March, Maggie kept an eye on Tommy while Patsy and Eva went to the market. Passing the winkle stand, Patsy made an astonishing revelation. 'I'm going to London,' she told Eva, 'and I'm not coming back until I've found Tommy's dad.'

'But *why?*' Eva knew something had been brewing.

'Because Tommy needs his dad, and because . . .' She paused, pretending to inspect the winkles.

Eva waited.

'It doesn't matter.' Patsy clammed up. 'All that matters is that Tommy needs his dad, and I mean to fetch the bugger back where he belongs.'

'You wouldn't even know where to look.'

'I can try.'

'Does Tommy know what you're thinking of doing?'

'No, and you mustn't tell him, d'ye hear? He thinks I'm going to Cardiff.'

'What?'

'I've made up a story about an old friend needing to see me.'

'Did he believe you?'

'Of course. And why shouldn't he?'

'I think it's a crazy idea.'

'Whatever ye say, I'm off first thing in the morning.'

Sure enough, Patsy was ready to leave at 8 a.m. sharp the following morning. 'The train leaves in half an hour,' she told Tommy. 'You look after yourself and I'll be back before you know it.'

'I don't want you to go.' Tommy had come to adore her, and now to lose her, even for a short time, was painful.

Eva gave him a hug. 'You've still got me,' she reminded him. 'And Patsy's right. She'll be back before we know it.'

The parting was brief and soon the taxi was drawing up at the door.

'Mind ye take care of each other now,' Patsy said as she climbed into the taxi.

'Don't forget to telephone when you get there.'

'I will.'

'And don't stay away too long.'

Patsy didn't hear. The taxi was already out of sight.

Eva dedicated the day to Tommy. In the morning, he helped her with the housework, then the two of them worked on the jigsaw puzzle Maggie had bought him. 'I'm glad you didn't go with Patsy,' he told her gratefully. 'I wouldn't like you both to be away at the same time.'

'And we won't be,' she replied. Not if she could help it, she thought, and Patsy was so attached to the boy now that she would never contemplate leaving him. Even her trip today was on Tommy's behalf. 'What shall we do this afternoon?' she asked him.

'I'd like to go to the fish market.'

She grimaced. 'Not my favourite place, the fish market.'

'We won't go if you don't want to.'

'I'll be brave for your sake.' Oh, how she hated that fish market, all those dead things lying there, staring up with flat, unseeing eyes.

An hour later, wrapped up against a keen wind and threatening rain, she and Tommy walked down Albert Street and on to Penny Street; the boulevard was just a few steps away. 'Tell me if you begin to get tired.' Though he was very much stronger now, he still had a tendency to get weary very quickly.

The bus ride was fun. There were two ladies in front who argued the whole way, and a boy with a yo-yo, which had Tommy mesmerised. The conductor sang at the top of his voice, making the worst sound Eva had ever heard, though it did cause laughter among the passengers when an old man in a flat cap complained, 'My cat makes a better noise than that when she's after her supper.'

As always, the market was packed. The stench of fish reached them before they even rounded the corner. 'While I'm here, I might as well get a nice piece of fish for our tea,' Eva decided.

'And chips?' Tommy's mouth watered. 'Make some of your nice fat chips.' It didn't take much to please him.

They had a wonderful afternoon. Instead of buying fish, Eva decided Tommy had earned a treat, so she took him to a nearby fish and chip shop where they cooked and served at table to order. 'Cod and chips twice,' she ordered. 'And mushy peas swimming in their own gravy.'

Tommy wolfed his food down, and Eva was delighted to see how his appetite had recovered. They talked about school, and how much he was looking forward to it, and afterwards they strolled along the canal to see the barges.

The day was beginning to close in when Eva decided it was time they made a move towards home. 'I ain't tired.' Tommy wanted to roam round the shops.

But Eva could see the red rims round his eyes. 'Well, *I'm* tired,' she lied, 'so take me home.' And he did.

'I ain't going to bed until Patsy rings.' Tommy was adamant. He bathed and got ready for bed

JOSEPHINE COX

but, tired though he was, there was no budging him. 'She promised to ring, and she will.'

'All right,' Eva conceded, 'but only until half past eight. If she hasn't rung by then, it's bed for you, young man, and no argument.'

The clock struck the half hour. Then it chimed eight times, and still no phone call. Tommy sat by the fire, his nose stuck in a comic, ears tuned to the phone.

Eva watched an animal rescue programme on television. After a while she switched it off and made them both a drink. 'If she rings after you've gone to bed, I'll tell you everything she says in the morning.' Her eyes went to the clock. It was almost eight thirty.

Reluctantly, when the clock struck the half hour again, Tommy dragged himself upstairs. He was on the landing when the phone rang. 'It's her!' he yelled, and much to Eva's dismay he ran down the steps two at a time. Breathless and excited, he got to the phone before she did. 'Patsy!' he shouted down the receiver. 'Patsy, it's me, Tommy!'

He talked to her for ages while Eva waited patiently, until she thought he looked tired and drawn. 'That's enough for now, Tommy.' She took the receiver from him. 'Off to bed now. I'll be up later to say goodnight.'

This time, Tommy didn't argue. 'Goodnight,

314

Eva,' he said, kissing her fleetingly. 'I've 'ad a lovely day.'

Patsy had no news. 'I've been up and down all over London,' she groaned. 'I've asked everyone who I thought might know something, and I've searched every bar in the East End, but so far nothing. It's like Fred Johnson has disappeared from the face of the earth, so it is.'

Eva asked if she ought not to make her way home. 'You've done your best,' she said, 'and Tommy is missing you. We both are.'

'Ha! And so ye should.' There was the sound of a coin being dropped into the box, and then, 'Look, me darlin', that was me last coin. I'll stay another day or so, and keep looking for him. I've found cheap lodgings and they're clean enough, so don't you worry about—' The line went silent. Patsy's money had run out.

Replacing the phone, Eva climbed the stairs and peeped into Tommy's room. He was fast asleep. Drawing the covers over him, Eva bent to kiss his forehead. Satisfied that he would sleep through the night, she went back downstairs.

No sooner had she washed her and Tommy's cups than there was a knock on the door. Fearing Tommy might be woken, she went quickly down the passage.

Eva was not surprised to see Frank on the doorstep. 'Come in,' she invited him, opening the door wider. 'But be quiet. Tommy's only just got off to sleep.'

As she closed the door, he took her in his arms. 'Two days away and I've missed you like the devil.' He kissed her on the mouth. 'It's good to be back.'

Eva led the way back to the sitting room. 'Did the Manchester opening go well?'

'Fantastic. The hotel is up and running, and already the bookings are flooding in.'

'That's wonderful.'

'It would have been more wonderful if you'd been there.'

'It's just as well I wasn't.' He had asked her, and under other circumstances she might have accepted, but she'd had a little job to do, which was best done on her own. 'Patsy's gone away.'

'Gone away? Where?' He hung his coat on the back of the sitting-room door.

Before answering, she went to the door and softly closed it. 'She's gone to find Tommy's dad.'

'Does she know where he is?'

Eva laughed. 'You know Patsy. She's scouring the East End of London for him.'

Clearing Tommy's comics off the chair, she glanced towards the door. 'Even if she found him, I'm not sure it would be a good thing. Tommy's been through so much, I dread to think what might happen if his dad walked in. Tommy believes he ran off. He doesn't know his mam threw him out.'

'Maybe someone should tell him.'

'What, and soil his mother's memory?'

'Difficult, eh?'

'You could say that.' Eva had something even more difficult to tell Frank, but first she needed a dash of courage. 'I've got some brandy, left over from the Christmas we never had,' she said. 'Would you like a drop to warm you up?'

'Why not?' Seated in the chair, he looked very much at home. The firelight played on his face and gave it a little boy look, and his brown eyes were filled with such pleasure at seeing her again, she felt moved.

While she bottomed the two glasses, his with brandy and hers with advocaat, he came to her and slid the most beautiful bracelet round her wrist. 'Do you like it?'

Startled, Eva looked down. The bracelet was exquisite, with a hem of tiny diamonds and a ruby clasp; she had never seen anything like it. 'It's beautiful.'

'Like you, my lovely.' Swinging her round, he told her softly, 'I wanted something really special to bring back to you.' Putting his finger beneath her chin he raised her face to his. With the greatest tenderness, he kissed her full on the mouth, and then he held her as if he would never let her go.

'I don't want to be parted from you ever again,' he whispered. 'From now on, everywhere I go, I want you with me.'

'You're so good to me, Frank,' she told him gratefully. 'The way you've pampered Tommy, and kept an eye on all of us through this bad time, I don't know how to thank you.'

'Love me.'

'I do.'

'Not enough.'

'So you say.'

'Let's make love, here and now.'

'Sit down, Frank.' Drawing away she took the glasses and placed them on the coffee table between them. 'I've got something important to tell you.'

As always, he did as she asked. 'What's wrong, sweetheart?' Concerned by the serious expression on her face, he leaned forward to hold her hand. 'Is it Tommy? Is there a problem?'

'No. Tommy's fine.'

'So, what's wrong?'

She didn't really know how to begin. 'A few weeks back, when I was worried sick about Tommy and . . . everything, you and I made love.'

'I haven't forgotten. How could I?' It was the most wonderful thing that had ever happened to him, making him all the more determined to marry her. 'Are you telling me you regret it, Eva? Is that what you're trying to say?' Suddenly, he looked haggard.

Anxious, she looked him straight in the eye. 'Yesterday I went to the doctor. I'm having your child, Frank.'

For what seemed an age he sat there, stunned, his eyes staring and his hands trembling. Then he gave a shivering groan. 'Oh, Eva! Eva, that's marvellous!' Leaping out of the chair, he grabbed her to him, half laughing, half crying. 'I don't know what to say. I can't think straight.'

Eva was ashamed. She had feared he might put all the blame on her and walk away from the responsibility. She didn't trust him enough. 'I thought you'd be angry,' she said.

His eyes were filled with tears. 'Angry?' He gently shook her. 'Oh, Eva, it's what I've always wanted, you and me, and a family of our own. All these years I've gone from one relationship to another – women who had a look of you, women who I tried so hard to settle down with. But I never married, Eva, because none of them ever measured up to you.'

Eva was shocked. 'I didn't know.'

'Just now you said you loved me. Maybe not as much as I love you, that would be asking too much. But I'll always look after you.'

A shadow of regret crossed his features. 'When I got that letter, the one you left with Mother—' even now, it was painful to remember – 'I felt as though my whole world had turned upside down.'

'What letter?' Eva was puzzled.

Astonished, he stared in disbelief. 'Surely you remember?'

Eva shook her head. 'No, Frank. All I remember is that your mother wanted rid of me.'

The truth struck them simultaneously, but it was Frank who voiced it. 'My God! *She* must have written it! She gave me a letter, supposedly from you . . . you were going away, to someone else, that's what the letter said.' Groaning, he covered his face with his hands. 'I was a fool. I should have known it was her.'

'It's all in the past,' Eva told him. 'Besides, it was time for me to leave, I can't deny it. You were getting serious, and I wasn't ready for that.'

He hugged her so tightly she could hardly breathe. 'Oh, Eva, you can't know how long I've loved you.' Holding her at arm's length, he smiled into her troubled eyes. 'Say you'll marry me.'

A moment of doubt; a moment when Patsy's words ran through her brain – 'Jealousy can be a dangerous thing.' And Frank did have a jealous nature. Look how he questioned her about her every move each time he returned from a business trip.

'Eva, don't be afraid of the future. We were meant to meet again because we are made for each other. I knew it from the very first.' He kissed her softly. 'No man could love you more than I do. Marry me, Eva. Say yes.'

The doubt was growing. The child too, but gentler, warm and amazing – *Frank's* child. In her heart she knew he meant every word he said. Frank was a good man, even Patsy had admitted that. He loved her, that was no lie, and just now he had promised he would take care of her and the child.

His voice penetrated her thoughts. 'Eva, say yes. You'll never regret it.'

Torn two ways, Eva hesitated, trying to reason, trying to persuade herself that it was the best, the only way. She was coming up to thirty and life seemed to be passing her by.

Suddenly like a ghost from the past, Bill rose in her thoughts, in her heart. Bill. Always Bill. But he was gone, and she was here, carrying Frank's child. Frank, a man who had loved her from the start.

'Eva? Please.'

Anger welled up in her like a vicious tide. Anger with Bill; with life. Most of all, with herself.

In that moment, she looked into Frank's brown eyes and nodded. 'Yes, Frank. The answer is yes.'

'SOD AND BUGGER it, if he's not here, I'm going home on the next train.' Patsy had trodden the streets of London relentlessly until her feet felt like two suet puddings.

First one person sent her this way, then someone else sent her another. She'd been lost a thousand times, and now she was standing outside the King's Arms with her heart in her mouth.

'Bleedin' cold, ain't it, gal?' A toothless old woman poked her face at Patsy. 'Who're you lookin' for, dearie?'

'I'm looking for a man.'

The old woman laughed out loud. 'We're *all* lookin' for a man,' she cackled. 'Trouble is, there ain't none to be 'ad.' With that she waddled inside the pub, still chuckling as she closed the door.

Patsy had to laugh. 'Silly old cow, so she is.'

The door of the pub opened again and out came a big fat man wearing a greasy overall. He glanced at Patsy, walked away, then, curious, turned round to have another look. 'Are you lost, gal?'

This time Patsy was careful how she phrased her answer. 'I'm looking for Fred Johnson,' she said. 'His ex-landlady said I might find him here.'

'She'd be right an' all. The crafty bastard's just had me for five quid at cards.' Pointing to the doorway, he said, 'You'll find him at the bar, celebrating his ill-gotten gains.'

Delighted, Patsy thanked him.

Now that she had found him, what should she say? How could she explain her presence here? How would he feel about Tommy? How would he take it when he knew his wife was lying in the churchyard? And, more importantly, would he come back with her to Blackburn?

'Don't lose yer courage now, Patsy me girl,' she told herself.

Squaring her shoulders, she marched into the pub. 'I'm looking for a man by the name of Fred Johnson.' Her voice sailed above the chatter. Amid the ensuing silence, all eyes turned to stare at her.

One pair of eyes in particular searched her out. With his pint halfway to his mouth, the big rugged feller froze. 'Christ Almighty, it can't be. *Patsy Noonan!*'

Patsy smiled. 'Did ye think you'd seen a ghost, Fred, me old darlin'?' She laughed. 'Ah! Yer sins have caught up with ye, so they have.' Stretching out her arms, she told him tenderly, 'No more running now. Sure, we've done enough of that already.' The tears filled her eyes. 'I'm here to take ye home, so I am,' she murmured.

And he went to her like a child.

——⟶•⟵——

THERE WERE TWO reunions that day.

Away from prying eyes, Patsy and Fred Johnson sat in the corner. Like two star-struck lovers, they held hands and looked into each other's eyes. 'I can't believe you're here,' Fred told her, his eyes moist with emotion. 'All these years, you bugger, and you just turn up out of the blue like that.'

'All that time wasted, ye mean. But Fred, I just wasn't ready then. I was too young.'

'How did you find me?'

'With great difficulty!'

'Why are you here, gal? What made you search me out?'

Patsy told him everything; how she and Eva had come from Wales to make a new start; how fate had directed them towards the woman he married, and who was now lying in the churchyard. 'It's been a difficult time,' she admitted, 'and I've got more reason than most people to be ashamed.'

Shocked by the news that Mary had died and Tommy had been left alone, he remarked, 'It's not you who should be ashamed, Patsy, gal. It's me.' His expression became puzzled. 'Hang on a minute, how did you find out that the Johnsons were my family? It's a common enough name.'

'By accident,' she answered. 'It was a shock, so it was.'

'Tommy told you, is that it? He let out that his

old dad was in London, you heard what name I
went by, and you put two and two together. You
always were good at figures.'

'No, it wasn't Tommy who told me,' she confessed. 'No sooner had we arrived than he threw
a fit and ran off. Eva went to look for him, and
while that was going on, I went inside.' She turned
scarlet. 'I've always been a nosy bugger, so I have,'
she admitted. 'Well, I was prying around, and I
found an envelope. Inside was a photograph of you
and her – Mary, your wife.'

'I see.' He stroked her hand. 'That's nothing
for you to be ashamed about, gal. It's only natural
that you wanted to find out about the boy and his
mam. If your friend hadn't found him, you might
have had to look for information anyway. So, don't
be ashamed.'

Patsy shook her head. 'Sure, ye don't understand.' Taking a deep breath, she revealed, 'I turned
me back on the boy. For a long time I wouldn't talk
to him. I pretended he didn't exist.'

'Why in God's name would you do that?'

'Jealousy. Like I told Eva, that's a terrible thing
to be eating away at you. But it ate away at me.
I saw the photograph, with you and her, smiling
and holding on to each other, and I thought, "That
should have been me!" The boy was your son – he
was *her* son. Can't ye see, Fred? It should have been
me standing beside you. Not her.'

'All the same, I can't believe you punished the boy for it.' He seemed to draw away, a look of disgust on his face.

Patsy's shame turned to anger. 'And what about you, eh? Where were you when the boy needed you? When he got beaten half to death by some monster of a man – where were you, tell me that!'

'What?' Curling his fists, he pushed out of his chair. 'Tommy was beat up, you say? Who did it, gal? What bastard beat him half to death? I swear to God I'll break his bloody neck.'

'Sit down, Fred. I can tell you nothing because I know nothing. Tommy claims it were gypsies, but we don't know.' Leaning towards him, she persisted, 'Why did you go, Fred? Why did you leave the boy?'

He sat down; his head bowed. 'She threw me out and pride kept me away. Not a day has gone by since when I haven't thought, "*This* is the day I'm going back for the sake of the boy."' He paused, a look of regret flooding his rugged features. 'I'm sorry she's lying in the churchyard. I wouldn't have wished that on her for the world. But it never worked out. We were wrong for each other from the start. You're right, Patsy. It *should* have been you in that picture. You should have been the one who brought Tommy into the world. But you weren't, you didn't. And all because you couldn't face up to life.'

'You wanted too much from me, and I couldn't give it.' Hopeful, she squeezed his hand. 'Not *then*, I couldn't. But it's a different story now. I love Tommy like he was my own son, and he loves me too. We could be a family, Fred – if you want it.'

'More than anything, gal.' He sighed from deep down in his boots. 'I found it hard, moving away from London. But if I've got you and the boy, wherever you are will be home.'

Rising from her chair, she took him by the hand. 'Let's go home then, before you have me crying in me beer.'

———◆◦◆———

TOMMY WAS INCONSOLABLE. 'Get him out! I don't want him here!' When Eva tried to restrain him, he kicked out. 'He ran off and left us. If he'd been here, me mam wouldn't have thrashed me all the time. She were frightened, that's why!' Looking up at his father, he cried, 'You didn't want me any more, did you, Dad? *Why* didn't you want me?' He could hardly talk for the sobs that racked his frame. And looking on, feeling his pain, Eva could not hold back her own tears.

'Ssh!' Pressing him to her, she whispered, 'Listen to him, Tommy. Listen to your daddy.'

'No!' Burying his face in Eva's shoulder, he said brokenly, 'I don't want him here, and I don't want Patsy, because she lied. She said she was going to Wales, and all the time she was looking for him.'

Fred stepped forward, his voice shaking as he confessed, 'You're right, son, I should never have left you. I didn't know your mammy was ill, or I swear to God I would never have gone away. We had a terrible row and she asked me to go. I thought after a time I'd come back and everything would be all right. But then I got to wondering if it wouldn't be better for the pair of you if I stayed away altogether.' Daring to reach out, he was surprised and encouraged when Tommy didn't recoil. 'I love you, son. That's God's truth. I did wrong in not coming back, and I'm sorry. But I'm back now, and I'll never go away again if you don't want me to.' Growing bolder, he slid his hand over Tommy's shoulder. 'Will you forgive me, son? You and me, and Patsy, let's all make a brand new start. Yer mustn't blame her, son. It ain't Patsy's fault.'

Tommy was listening but he made no response.

'Tommy? Please, all I'm asking is the chance to make it up to you.'

Suddenly Tommy was in his arms, the sobs taking his breath away.

'It's all right, son.' Fred held him close. 'It's gonna be all right now.'

All this time, Patsy had waited in the background, anxious but wise enough to make no move.

In that moment, Eva caught her eye and gestured that she should go to Tommy. Fred held out his arm, and she went to him.

With big wet eyes, Tommy stared up at her. 'I'm sorry,' he said, and she slid her arm round him.

Eva stood back, her soft gaze enveloping them – Patsy enclosed in one arm, Tommy in the other and, head bowed, Fred between. It was a sight to gladden her heart.

Chapter Twelve

ON 31 MARCH 1966, Eva and Frank were married.

On the actual morning, Eva had misgivings but pushed them aside. 'You're nervous, that's all,' she told herself. 'Frank really loves you. He's transformed the house on Park Street just for you. You'll have a secure life, and a family to call your own. A child . . .' The softest of smiles lit her face. 'Oh, think of it, Eva, a new baby.' That was what had finally decided her.

She rubbed the flat of her hand over her tummy; the small rise was not noticeable beneath the cream satin dress. Late at night when she lay in bed, Eva imagined she could feel the child moving inside her. Knowing a new life was forming there was the most wonderful and satisfying thing.

Getting up from the stool where she had sat these past twenty minutes, going through every kind of emotion imaginable, she stood sideways on, observing herself in the mirror. 'No one would ever know,' she murmured, twirling round to see

herself from all angles. Still, what would it matter if
people did know she was carrying a child? All that
mattered was that her child should have a father,
and that she should settle down with Frank and
not crave a man she lost long ago.

Suddenly the door burst open and Patsy rushed
in. 'Aren't you ready yet?' she demanded. 'The car
will be here any minute and here you are, fancying
yourself in the mirror.'

'I've been thinking.' Seating herself on the stool
once more, Eva regarded Patsy in the mirror. 'I
wonder if I'm doing the right thing.'

'Huh! It's too late for second thoughts now, me
darlin'.' Down-to-earth as ever, Patsy nevertheless
felt misgivings about this particular match herself,
and before she discovered Eva was pregnant she
had said as much to her. Now, though, she thought
it wiser to keep her mouth shut. There was nothing
to be gained from upsetting the apple cart at this
late stage, she reasoned.

'Yes,' Eva agreed, 'it is too late.' She laughed.
'I must look a sketch. I didn't sleep much last night.
Wedding nerves, I expect.'

Patsy took a long, hard look at her friend.
'You look stunning, so ye do,' she answered. With
her corn-coloured hair rolled under, and only the
suggestion of a fringe, Eva was the picture of
loveliness; never one for too much make-up, she
had touched her eyelashes with the softest brown,

a smudge of eyeshadow above, and on her full generous lips the subtlest of pink lipstick.

'I was just thinking,' Eva said thoughtfully, 'whether to pin the coronet on top of my hair, or have it further back so it doesn't flatten my fringe.' Eva had chosen not to wear a veil, but instead had bought the prettiest rosebud coronet.

'Sure, it won't matter which way ye wear it, you'll be so lovely nobody will notice.'

Eva laughed at that. 'I'm not a young girl with starry eyes,' she reminded her. 'I'm thirty years of age and my belly's already beginning to swell.' Twirling once more before the mirror, she remarked, 'It's a lovely dress, isn't it, Patsy? I've never worn anything off the shoulder before, but I'm glad I took your advice. It was a good choice.'

'That's an understatement, so it is. The dress was made for you!' Patsy sighed, thinking how she could never have got away with a dress like that; she was too clumsy, too round and plump at the shoulders. 'Let me look at you.' Standing back, she took stock of Eva, and thought she would never see a more becoming sight.

Fashioned in cream figured satin, Eva's dress was discreetly off the shoulder, with a V neck and long, close-fitting sleeves. Narrowing to the waist, it then flared out into a swinging ankle-length skirt with ivory lace at the hem above pale blue satin shoes. It brought out all of Eva's best assets. Patsy smiled at her. 'You'll steal the show. They won't notice anybody else.'

'You underestimate yourself, they'll notice you,' Eva answered. Patsy looked very pretty; in the long lemon dress, and with her vivid red hair, she looked striking. 'Wait until Fred sees you. Tommy too. You'll knock 'em dead.'

'Never mind me.' Patsy picked up Eva's bouquet. 'If we don't go now, we'll be late for the church.'

'Brides are allowed to be late.' All the same, Eva quickly put the finishing touches to her make-up, took her bouquet, and followed Patsy down the stairs.

Eva was right. Fred and Tommy thought Patsy looked terrific. They were as nervous as kittens as they arrived at the church. 'Everybody's looking at us,' Tommy said.

'Ssh!' Taking charge of his son, Fred hurried to the front of the church where the two of them sat silently, eyes trained on the impeccable Frank who stood ready, shifting from foot to foot. Beside Frank stood one of his colleagues, a short, round man with a red face – probably the result of a few pints of best the night before.

Outside, Eva and Patsy waited for the organ music to start.

'It's like waiting for a hanging,' Eva declared, visibly trembling.

'Sure, that's no way to talk on your wedding day!' Patsy chided. 'All the same, I wish they'd hurry up. I'm bloody freezing, so I am!' Rubbing her arms vigorously, she peeped inside the church. 'Apart from half a dozen people, I don't know anybody.'

Suddenly the music started. Everyone turned as they came down the aisle. 'I feel like a film star,' Patsy whispered, smiling to one and all as she passed by.

Eva looked straight ahead, her heart lurching with every step. 'Am I doing right?' she murmured. Her gaze rose to the magnificent stained-glass windows above the altar, depicting the Crucifixion. 'I hope so. Dear God, I hope so.'

In that moment, Frank turned to smile on her, his love lighting his face, and reached his hand towards her.

Eva smiled back, and the bond was forged.

In an incredibly short time, it was all over.

Now, as she walked out of the church, arm in arm with her husband, Eva felt a sense of belonging which she had not felt in a very long time. It's going to be all right, she told herself as Frank, smiling, helped her into the limousine.

She could not know how shockingly wrong she was.

Chapter Thirteen

EVA LOVED THE coming of summer. It reminded her of the happy days she and her mother had spent together on the farm. She said as much now to Patsy who, as always, had joined her on a trip to the Saturday market.

They always went by way of Corporation Park; here they could skirt the lawns and enjoy the early blossoms – rhododendrons and roses were already showing their colours. The lake was beautiful, with gliding swans and noisy geese, and excited children playing close by.

Corporation Park was a haven for Eva; when she felt lonely, and when life seemed to be getting her down, she would come into the park and stroll about, or sit and watch the world go by, and it never failed to gladden her heart. 'I do love this park,' she told Patsy now. 'Whenever I come here I'm always transported back to the farm and the orchard where we had such happy times.'

'I know what you mean.' Patsy had not forgotten those times either. 'We've come a long way since then, Eva. And sometimes it doesn't help to look back.'

'I still miss her, you know.' A child kicked a ball into her path; pausing, she kicked it back. 'Not so much my father. But I miss my mother every minute of every day. I always will.' Mingled with her joy in her pregnancy was a great sadness that her mother would never see her grandchild. 'She would have been so excited about the baby.'

'Ah, sure, it's only natural you feel the way you do.'

'If it's a girl, I'd like to call her Colette.' She hadn't yet mentioned it to Frank, but there was no reason why he shouldn't agree. 'You know, Patsy, I have a feeling that if it is a girl, she might look like my mother.'

'Sure, it's possible,' Patsy said. 'I mean, you look like your mother, so ye do. Like two peas in a pod, the pair of youse.'

In reflective silence, they strolled along the narrow pathway. Eva felt unusually nostalgic, but maybe, she thought, that's how all women get when they're pregnant.

The walk into Blackburn town centre usually took about half an hour but today, for some reason, they seemed to get there in no time at all.

The two of them headed straight for the linen stall. Eva needed towels, and Patsy complained that Fred had scorched another of her best tea towels. 'As fast as I replace them, he spoils the buggers.' There were green-striped ones and blue-striped. She couldn't make up her mind, so bought half a dozen of each. 'I'll swing for the bugger if he spoils these,' she declared.

The man on the stall told her she needn't worry, because she could always come back and buy another dozen.

'Cheeky sod!' she snapped, then accidentally dropped the lot into a dog puddle. 'Jaysus! If it's not one thing, it's another.'

'You're accident prone, that's your trouble, missus.' The stallholder had taken a fancy to her and offered to exchange them.

Patsy went away happy. 'He's got some hope.' Chuckling, she nudged Eva in the ribs. 'Even if Fred did spoil them, I wouldn't come here again. The man on the Thursday market sells 'em sixpence cheaper.'

The next stop was the cockle stall. 'Half a tub of winkles,' Patsy said, 'and the same for me friend.'

Eva took one scoop and was almost sick. 'There are things I can't stomach just now,' she apologised, tipping them into the nearest bin.

'Well, all I can say is, if it's a choice between having a tub of winkles or a baby, give me the winkles every time.'

They went away laughing, especially when the winkle man called out, 'If you ever change your mind, give us a shout, and I'll be happy to oblige.'

At the crockery stall, Eva bought a new teapot. Patsy paid for three eggcups. 'Tommy keeps accidentally throwing them in the dustbin with the shells,' she said. 'I've told the little sod to be more careful but will he listen? No, he will not! Honest to God, Eva, what will I do with the pair of them, eh?'

'You'll cope.' Eva knew how Patsy loved to complain.

'What will you call it if it's a boy?' Patsy asked.

'I haven't really thought too much about that but I suppose Frank might have a few ideas. He really wants a boy.'

'What do you want, Eva?'

'I don't mind, as long as it's a healthy baby.'

'I didn't mean the baby.'

'Oh? What did you mean then?'

'I'll tell you over a barm cake and a pot of tea. What do you say?'

'Lead on, that's what I say.' Eva was glad of a break. The shopping bags weighed heavy and her feet hurt. 'I'm that thirsty my tongue's stuck to the roof of my mouth.' The May sunshine was hot, and the market was packed with people searching for bargains. All in all, it was a tiring experience when you were nearly four months pregnant.

———⊰◈⊱———

S TRUGGLING INTO KENYON'S tea shop, they chose a table in a quiet corner. Eva dropped her bags and fell gratefully into a chair.

Like a hawk, the waitress swooped.

'Two teas and two barm cakes, if ye please,' Patsy ordered. 'I feel ninety,' she said to Eva, and Eva nodded in agreement.

'D'you want your barm cakes toasted?'

When Eva answered yes, the tiny waitress scurried away scribbling into her notepad.

'Now then, what did you mean when you asked me what I wanted?' Eva asked.

Patsy looked at her. 'You know very well what I meant.'

'Oh, that.' Eva might have guessed. 'I wish I'd never told you about it now.'

'Well, you did, and now I'm worried about you, so I am.' Patsy paused while the waitress served them, but the minute she was gone, she persisted, 'Sure, it can't be any fun when he keeps on at ye all the time – where've ye been? Who've ye been with? What did you buy?'

'Not now, Patsy, please.' Eva didn't feel like going into all that. It was bad enough knowing that if

Frank found out she'd been 'wasting time' in town, he'd spend half an hour interrogating her.

'Sure, it's not fair. You're looking tired and worn, so ye are, an' no bloody wonder, being questioned every time you set foot outside the door. Does he not realise there are times when ye feel the need for an hour out in the fresh air? Or to stroll round the shops and enjoy a chinwag with yer old friend?'

'He's jealous, that's all. When I come to think about it, the signs were all there.'

'I hate to say it, Eva me darlin', but I did warn ye.'

'I haven't forgotten.'

'Sure, the way he's carrying on, you'd think ye weren't to be trusted.'

'I won't deny it gets me down sometimes,' Eva admitted. She knew Patsy wouldn't drop the subject, and in a way it was a relief to talk it through. 'The other day it seems I took too long paying the coalman – you know, old Tom with the yellow teeth and a laugh like a donkey. Anyway, when I came back to the sitting room, Frank accused me of flirting. He laughed and played it like a joke, but underneath he was serious.'

'Frank can't have much of an opinion of himself if he thinks ye fancy old Tom.'

'I know.' Eva recalled how astonished she'd been. 'Tom, of all people. Can you imagine?' She laughed. 'It caused an awful row. Afterwards, he was full of apologies, like always. It's beginning to fall into a pattern – accusations, a flaming row, apologies, and next day an expensive present.' She sighed. 'Maybe it's my fault, Patsy. I've never really loved him. Not in the way he expects me to. The trouble is, if he keeps on like this, I'm afraid I'll end up hating him.'

'Oh, Eva!' Concerned, Patsy leaned nearer. 'Has he ever got violent with ye? Tell me the truth now.'

'Frank is not the violent type.' Then she added, 'He prefers mental torment.'

Grabbing her hand, Patsy said, 'Now you look here, me darlin'. If it ever gets too much for ye, the door at Albert Street is always open, ye know that, don't ye?'

'Frank may be over-possessive, but deep down he's a real softie. He'll be all right once the baby's born. Oh, Patsy, I can't wait for the day when I hold the baby in my arms.'

'Listen! Did ye hear what I said? I mean it, Eva. If he goes too far, you're to come straight to me, d'ye hear?'

'Thank you, Patsy, but it won't happen. Frank would never hurt me, not in the way you mean.' Laying her hand over Patsy's, she told her softly, 'I know you mean well, and I really am grateful, but there's no need.'

'Do you wish you hadn't married him?'

Taken aback, Eva drew her hand away. 'Look, Patsy, it's silly to think like that. Oh, all right! If I hadn't been expecting his child, I might not have married him. But, like it or not, I'm his wife now.'

'It's not written in blood, though, is it?'

'It might as well be.' She and Patsy had different values. 'Look, Patsy. It's no good harping on about it. I've made my bed and I'll have to lie on it. It's no use thinking about what might have been. That only leads to heartache.'

'And won't it lead to heartache the way it is now?'

The question was one Eva had asked herself many times these past weeks, but she refused to look on the dark side. 'I hope not,' she answered.

Privately, she felt differently. In the early days she had made so many plans, and now they might never materialise. Nowadays she felt a deep sadness that wouldn't go away. Even the joy of this miracle growing inside her could not shake off the feeling that her marriage to Frank was starting to go horribly wrong.

They stayed awhile in the tearooms. They talked about Maggie, and how she had kept her distance since Fred had moved back into Albert Street. 'Sure, I can't blame the old cow for feeling cheated,' Patsy remarked. 'When all's said and

344

done, the house should have been hers by rights. I'll give her her due, though, she's friendly enough when we see her in the street, and she always has a good word for Tommy. But since Fred came back she hasn't once stepped foot over the threshold.' Her mind skipped back to Tommy. 'Sure, *that* little bugger grows by the minute!'

'Given time, he'll make a strapping young man, I'm sure.' Eva had been surprised to see how Tommy was springing up in height, and filling out with it. 'How does he get on with Fred?'

'He's like a puppy dog with two tails, so he is. Every day after school he's down to the bus stop and waiting for Fred to come home from the brewery. The two of 'em come in arm in arm, talking about this and that, and I hardly ever get a word in.'

Eva didn't believe it for one minute. 'I can't see that somehow.'

'Ye cheeky bugger!'

'And how's Fred liking his job at the brewery?' A mischievous smile lifted her lovely face.

'He's not drinking the profits, if that's what you're askin'. Sure, he seems content enough to go out on a Saturday with his mates. Sometimes I go along, and we have a good time, so we do. That's when Tommy goes over to sit with Maggie. She really looks forward to it.'

'I still can't believe it – you and Fred.' When

she heard how Patsy had known him long before they came to Blackburn, Eva had been amazed. 'And you never said a word to me.' At first that had hurt her, but now she fully understood why Patsy hadn't wanted to talk about it. Sometimes there were things a woman could not bring herself to discuss, even with her best friend.

'I can't believe it myself,' Patsy replied with a grin. 'I was too young and stupid when I fell for Fred Johnson. He was big and strong, full o' the ol' blarney. He charmed me right off me feet, so he did. You know the rest, Eva. He got me pregnant; I was too young to cope and drove him away.' Her voice shook. 'I only saw the baby for a few minutes – a lovely little lad, it was. Had the look of his daddy, so he did. Me mammy made me give him away; she'd always been a hard-hearted old biddy. I pleaded with me father, but he sided with her. "It's all for the best", that's what he said. I never saw the child again.' Her expression hardened. 'God help me, Eva, but I'll never forgive them.'

'Are you sure about that, Patsy? Never is a long time.'

'Oh, I'm sure right enough, me darlin',' Patsy answered. 'All me bridges are burned. Sure, I suffered nightmares for too many years to forget or forgive. Not a day passed when I didn't wonder where the lad was, or if he was happy.' She paused. 'I'll tell ye something ye *didn't* know, shall I?'

'Not if you don't want to, Patsy.' It was obvious to Eva that the memory was very painful for her.

'I went to see him.'

'Who? The boy? Your son, you mean?'

Patsy smiled. 'I spent a whole year tracking him down. It wasn't easy, but I kept at it, asking questions, raiding me parents' private papers, following leads, and getting people to trust me. In the end, I discovered his address in Kensington. Very impressive it was too. Big posh house, fancy car and all that. I went back three times before I had the courage to knock on the door. I stood outside, looking up the drive and wondering if I might get a glimpse of him, but it never happened. I couldn't leave it at that. I *had* to see him.'

'But how?' Eva's heart went out to her.

Remembering, Patsy had to smile. 'I always fancied meself as an actress, so I did. I devised a little plan. After spending a whole week's wages on cosmetics, I put it all in a suitcase, wore a smart two-piece and knocked on the door, bold as ye please.'

'Honestly, Patsy Noonan! What then?'

'I got sent on me way, so I did! The snotty little bugger who answered the door probably thought I was a confidence trickster.'

'Why ever would she think that?'

'Ah, now, don't be so bloody cheeky, young madam!' Patsy had got the poison out of her system long ago and could now see the funny side of it. 'Anyways, like I say, I got shown the door. But I got to see the lad. Oh, but he was a bonny thing. As I went away down the drive, I heard a sound behind me – like a child laughing, you know?'

When, serious now, Eva nodded, Patsy went on, 'I went back up to the side gate that led to the garden, and there they were, all three of them. The man was a very distinguished gent, and the woman had the kindest, loveliest face.' Pausing, she regarded Eva. 'Matter of fact, I've always thought you had a look of her.' Taking a deep breath, she continued, 'The lad was playing round the woman's feet. At first I was shocked to see how much like Fred he looked. For just one awful minute I had the urge to run in and snatch him away. I tell ye, I don't know how I stopped meself.' Suddenly her voice broke and she looked away, the tears bright in her eyes.

Gently, Eva said, 'Do you want to go?'

'I want you to know how it was.' Composing herself, Patsy went on, 'I just watched for a time, hidden behind the shrubbery. Oh, Eva, they were such lovely people, and the lad was so happy with them. His new parents would always cherish him, I could see that. And it was plain to see that he would never go short of anything in his life. What could I offer him? Nothing, that's what. I was too young to look after him properly, and I had no money at all. I'd already turned my back on me parents, like they turned their backs on me and my baby. I was living in a one-bedroom flat and was already two weeks behind with the rent. Oh, I had a job, but it paid next to nothing.'

Eva could only imagine how Patsy felt. In her heart, she thought Patsy must have suffered like she had when both her parents died in that fire. 'Oh, Patsy. I'm so sorry.'

'For the first time in me life, I put someone else before meself. I knew that where the lad was he must be better off, so I walked away.'

'That must have been so hard.'

'What would you have done, Eva?'

'The same.'

'Thank you for that.'

'And you never made any attempt to see him, or your parents, ever again?'

Patsy shook her head. 'Like I said, I burned all me bridges.' Her face crinkled in a smile. 'Soon after that, I came to work for your mother, and I swear to God, Eva me darlin', I'd never been so happy as I was in that lovely place.'

'What about now, Patsy? Are you happy now?'

'Oh, I am that! But it's a different kind of happiness. I'm older now, so I am, and mebbe a bit more tolerant. I have a lot to make amends for. That night, when we arrived in Albert Street and you ran after the boy, I went inside and nosed about a bit, like I do, you know?'

Eva smiled. 'I know.' In fact, Patsy had already told her, but it seemed as if she needed to talk it through, so Eva let her go on.

'When I found the photograph upstairs in the bedside drawer, sure it was a terrible shock, I can tell ye. Tommy was Fred's son! Not mine. Oh no! *My* son was given away.' She gave a deep, withering sigh. 'Oh, Eva, I did a shocking thing, so I did. The poor boy was innocent in all of it; on top of that he'd lost his mammy, and his father had run off. But I took it out on the boy. I was jealous, d'ye see? So jealous I couldn't see straight. Now I've come to love the boy like my own. Isn't that a funny thing?'

'No, I don't think so, Patsy.' Eva had never felt closer to Patsy than she did right now. 'It's a strange world, and what do we know? You had one child taken from you, and you did the right thing in giving him every chance of a better life. And I believe with all my heart that you were given a second chance with Tommy. You're as good as his mother now, and he adores you, anyone can see that. Life has turned full circle for you, Patsy, don't you see? Fred too. You've both come back to each other, and you've got Tommy. Oh, Patsy, you can't know how happy I am to see you so content.'

'You're such a good friend to me, Eva. What would I ever do without you?'

'Will you ever tell Fred about his other son?'

'Would you?'

'I don't think any good would come of it, Patsy,' she answered honestly. 'But you're the one who has to live with whatever decision you make. Can you do that?'

'I've lived with it for so long now, it can stay between the two of us.' Quietly she added, 'I only wish to God you were as happy as I am, Eva. Ah, sure, it doesn't seem fair. You've lost so much, and ye still haven't found contentment. What are we gonna do with ye, eh?'

Not wanting to mar Patsy's new-found joy with her own troubles, Eva told her brightly, 'You can stop fretting and carrying on about me. I've been lucky. I've found a man who adores me. I've got a beautiful home and money enough never to worry about a single thing.' Her smile was incredibly beautiful as she added softly, 'And I've got the most precious gift of all to look forward to.' Tenderly caressing the growing child beneath her skirt, she told Patsy, 'In here, there's all the contentment I need.'

THEY ORDERED ANOTHER pot of tea and chatted about Eva's hospital check-ups and the knowledge that all was well.

'Don't you forget, Eva me darlin', when Frank goes away on another of them business trips, you can always come and stay with us. Or, if you'd rather, I'll come and stay with you at the big house. I don't like ye being on your own up there.'

Eva gratefully refused. 'You've got your own family to look after now,' she reminded her.

'And what are you if not family?'

'Honestly, Patsy, I'm perfectly all right on my own. Anyway, if I needed anything, there's always Olive next door. Staying at the house is better than going with Frank on his business trips.' The one and only time she'd allowed him to bully her into accompanying him to Scotland, he had asked her to charm his clients, then watched her like a hawk, and afterwards put her through sheer hell. She had seen a side to Frank that night that had shocked and frightened her. Now, nothing on God's earth would persuade her to go with him.

THAT EVENING, FRANK returned from London, greatly excited about a new venture. 'I think I've got a buyer for the land behind us,' he told Eva over dinner. 'Once he's seen it, I'm sure he'll sign on the dotted line.'

Anxious, Eva asked, 'What does he plan to do with the land?'

Frank shovelled food into his mouth. With his eyes on her the whole time, he chewed the mouthful for a few minutes before answering, 'Sometimes, Eva, you can be really stupid.' He said it as though he was talking to an imbecile.

'What do you mean?' Anger rose in her, of a kind that she had never felt before.

'What I mean, my sweet, is this. I'm a developer. The buyer is a developer. What the hell do you think he's going to do with it?'

Pushing her chair back, she stood up and faced him with equal contempt. 'You told me only a few days ago that you meant to keep that land. "Leave it for nature to shape," you said. "A wonderful legacy for our baby," you said. You went into great detail to explain how it would never be built on, by you or anyone else. "The house would have to be pulled down if the land was built on," you said, "because it's the only feasible access." So you can hardly blame me if I ask what this buyer means to do with it.'

'Whatever is the matter with you, Eva? You don't usually take things so much to heart.'

He was genuinely shocked that she should have taken it so badly. But then he didn't know how she felt these days. He hardly ever bothered to ask. He assumed that she was content with her lot, proud to live in this beautiful big house, with a chequebook of her own and an expensive car parked in the drive. Being the materialistic man he was, Frank could not imagine any woman being dissatisfied with what he had given his precious wife. She had his undying love; she was carrying his baby. What more could she want?

'I thought you would be delighted,' he said, looking like a boy chastised; and the pity of it was, he actually meant what he said.

Leaning across the table, Eva looked him straight in the eye. In a hard voice she said, 'And another thing, Frank, don't ever call me stupid. I may be a lot of things – too trusting maybe, badly misguided, and sometimes very, *very* wrong.' Especially in my judgement of you, she thought. 'But not stupid, Frank. Never that.'

Calmer now, she excused herself and left the room, inwardly cursing herself for ever having married him.

She had been up in the bedroom for only two minutes when he came in. 'I'm sorry,' he apologised. 'It's me that's stupid, and you're right. I did tell you the land would never be built on because that would mean pulling down the house, and yes, I had intended the valley to be our baby's legacy, but we stand to make a great deal of money. Think about it, Eva. We'd be crazy to turn it down.'

'Why does everything have to centre on *money*?'

Suddenly she felt as if all the fight had been knocked out of her. It had been a long day. The baby was kicking fitfully, and she felt overwhelmingly tired. 'Leave me be, Frank,' she said. 'Do whatever you like. It's your land. Your money. And your decision. I have other things to think about right now.' Like how I can make myself love you when you make it so bloody hard for me. Into her mind came another face. Bill's. He was the man she loved. He was the man she would *always* love; damn it!

Coming to where she sat on the edge of the bed, he slid his arm round her shoulders, either not caring or choosing not to notice how she cringed at his touch. 'Look what I've bought you, sweetheart.' Dipping into his pocket, he drew out a slender black box. 'Open it.' Placing it on the bed beside her, he waited.

To his dismay, Eva didn't even glance at it. Instead she got up and walked to the window where she leaned on the wall, staring out across the valley. This place was so beautiful, she thought, the idea of bulldozers and trucks, and all manner of habitat being ripped up, was nauseating. And so was the realisation that he had lied to her. 'How long have you been planning to sell the valley?' She couldn't even bring herself to look at him.

'I only want the best for you. That's all I've ever wanted, you know that.'

'How long, Frank?'

'I didn't exactly plan it, sweetheart. I just mentioned it to a business acquaintance and he made me a tentative offer, subject to seeing it.'

'And if I don't want it sold? What then?'

'Look, Eva, I don't want you to worry about this, and I certainly don't want us to argue.'

Swinging round, she confronted him with troubled green eyes. 'Answer me, Frank. What if I don't want it sold? What if I want us to keep it? To let nature reclaim it, like we planned? A legacy for our children, that's what you said, and behind my back you're busy making other plans. You lied to me, Frank. Why?' She felt cheated, left out, as if she didn't matter.

'Please listen to me, Eva.' He came to her. 'I would never deliberately hurt you.' His voice was persuasive, his smile full of contrition. 'I'll ring him right now and tell him the deal's off.' He kissed her on the forehead. 'I had no idea you loved this place so much. Trust me, sweetheart. I would never do anything that you didn't agree with. I should have told you, and I'm sorry. From now on, I promise I won't keep you in the dark.' Nuzzling her neck, he murmured, 'Am I forgiven?'

Eva's first instinct was to thrust him away, yet she couldn't help but wonder if she had overreacted. He seemed genuinely sorry, and he had not only apologised but offered to turn the deal on its head. It would be churlish of her to fuel the argument further. Besides, she didn't feel it would change anything, and even if it did, what would it matter?

It struck Eva that she was not in fact hitting out because he had schemed behind her back but because she didn't love him, and that angered her but it was anger with herself. The only thing Frank had ever wanted from her was her love, and she couldn't give it. Maybe it was she who should be apologising. Guilt swept through her. If Frank knew she fantasised about another man while she lay in his arms, he would be devastated.

Guilt tinged her face as she turned away. 'Leave me for a while, Frank. I don't feel like talking right now.'

'Are we friends?' Always like a puppy dog, she thought sadly.

'Of course.'

'Kiss then?' Putting his finger under her chin, he turned her to him. When she didn't resist, he grew bold, kissing her long and hard. 'Don't go quiet on me, sweetheart,' he pleaded. 'I hate it when you go quiet.'

Eva knew exactly what he meant. There were times when he might be talking to her and she would be miles away – back at her mother's farm, or on the road with Patsy. And sometimes she imagined herself in Canada with Bill at her side. That was the best, and worst, of all.

Now, when she felt Frank begin to remove her clothes, she made no effort to stop him. When he steered her to the bed, she lay there, hating his touch yet needing his love, for she had no other.

She felt him climb on her; she felt his stiff, warm member gently enter her. The rhythm of his movements made the bed dip beneath them, slow at first, then faster. She even responded.

Growing excited, he gripped her tight, and she thought of Bill. When he thrust hard, climaxed, and crumpled on top of her with a long, drawn-out sigh, she imagined it was Bill. And it wasn't at all unbearable.

———◆———

LATER THAT NIGHT, when Eva was sleeping, Frank slunk downstairs.

Creeping into the study like a thief, he picked up the phone and dialled.

'John, is that you? There's been a slight change of plan. Between you and me, when you come here, the reason for your stay will be the same, but when my wife is around, you are simply an old business colleague here for a social visit. She's very fond of the house, and I don't want her to know about our little agreement. Do you understand what I'm saying?'

Obviously it was understood; a broad grin spread across Frank's face. 'I knew you'd see it from my point of view. That's right, next weekend as agreed. I'm looking forward to it, and I'm sure you'll be delighted when you see the site. It's prime, I tell you.' Glancing anxiously towards the door, he lowered his voice. 'If I wasn't planning on cracking the markets abroad, you wouldn't even get a sniff at it.'

While the other man talked, Frank kept a wary eye on the door. 'Yes, I do know it could mean us moving abroad. To be honest, that's the whole idea. A fresh start will be good for both of us, what with the baby and all. No, I won't be selling my interests here, merely expanding internationally. That's where the really big opportunities are.' He smiled slyly. 'Oh, and John? I know I can trust you not to mention this to my dear wife. I want it to be a lovely surprise. She tends to get excited, you see. You're right. Women have no idea about the mechanics of big business, bless their hearts . . . Indeed, that's what I thought – keep it simple. I'm glad you understand why I won't be telling her until it's all settled.'

Chapter Fourteen

BILL WAS TALKING on the telephone when Sheila came into the office.

Realising he was talking to his mother, she turned to leave, but Bill beckoned her to come in and close the door. When she was seated opposite him, he gestured that he would only be a minute.

'Okay, Ma,' he smiled at Sheila, 'no, don't you worry about a thing.' The smile slid away. 'Don't antagonise him. You know what a mean devil he can be. I know all about the deal – heard it on the grapevine yesterday, and no, I'm not bothered at all. If he's moving in that direction he's making a big mistake, but he'll do whatever he wants, regardless. He always has.' He listened for a while, nodding occasionally, and glancing at Sheila. 'Look, Ma, if he wants to trust Todd with that kind of responsibility, that's up to him, but he may live to regret it. It's always been the same, Todd can do no wrong in his eyes, but there's no need for you to worry. If the firm goes broke, you'll always be looked after, I can promise you that.'

Another moment of listening, and then, 'I know it's late to be at the office, but there are things I have to do. Yes, I'm almost finished for the day. No, I won't overdo it.' Raising his eyebrows at Sheila, he smiled. 'That's right, Ma. I'm about ready to close shop now – just one or two things to clear with Sheila first, then I'll be heading home.'

However busy, Bill always had time for his mother. 'Yes, I'll tell her.'

He looked at Sheila, who mouthed the words, 'Sheila sends regards to you too.'

'Okay, Ma. Look after yourself now. See you Tuesday as arranged. 'Bye now.' Replacing the receiver, he told Sheila, 'Seems like the old boy has bitten off more than he can chew this time.'

'I got the gist of the conversation,' Sheila replied. 'I can't believe he's given Todd more responsibility, especially when he lost half a million on that riverside site.'

'He's a fool.' Getting out of his chair, Bill walked round the desk, where he stood, leaning nonchalantly against the filing cabinet, his active mind going over all his mother had said. 'Apparently Dad shrugged it off. "Just bad luck", that's what he called it.'

'He must be losing his marbles.' Thoughtful, Sheila leaned back in her chair. 'Even I could have done a better deal. That riverside location was always dubious. No wonder he had to offload it at a loss.'

'If he'd done his homework, Todd would have discovered how the river spills over at that particular point.' At one time, Bill had been interested, but he soon backed off. 'And if he'd only taken the trouble to check with the authorities, he would have known there was planning approval to build industrial units right next door.'

'What's going on, Bill? Why is your father handing over more and more responsibility to Todd?'

'Who knows?' Bill had wondered himself. It was something that had happened over the past year. 'All I do know is that if Todd keeps making expensive mistakes like this, the company won't last another six months.' Turning, he took a file from the cabinet. 'I don't care what happens to that pair,' he said bitterly. 'As for Ma, she'll want for nothing while I'm able to provide for her.'

Seating himself at the desk, he scanned through the documents before him. After making a few hasty notes, he looked up. 'Right. Let's see what you've got for me. It's been a long day. Time I took you home, young lady.'

'Not so young these days,' she sighed, handing him the folder. 'I might think of retiring next year.'

Perusing the papers in the folder, he laughed.

'You've been saying that for the past four years.' Serious now, he looked her in the eye. 'You're not ill, are you?'

'Fit as a fiddle.'

Visibly relieved, he declared mischievously, 'In that case, you *can't* retire. I'd sink without trace if you left me.'

'Not you. You'll outlast them all, and die a rich old man.'

'A *lonely* old man, isn't that what you mean?'

For a time they sat, Bill signing letters and Sheila watching him. Two very dear friends, each with their own quiet thoughts.

After signing the last letter, Bill handed back the folder. 'That's it. The rest can wait until Monday. Get your coat. I'm taking you home.'

June was his favourite month. Though it was gone eight o'clock, the skies were still the most beautiful turquoise blue and, judging by the songs emanating from the trees, even the birds were reluctant to go home. 'Your carriage awaits.' Opening the door of his new Jaguar, Bill waited for her to climb in.

In the car, Sheila picked up on his remark about being 'lonely'. 'Have you decided what to do about Eva?'

Day or night, Vancouver was a busy city. With his mind on the road and a junction looming, he didn't answer straight away.

Impatient, Sheila persevered. 'Just now you said you would die a lonely man. What about Eva?'

'Not now, Sheila. Please.'

But she persisted. 'I'm glad you told me about her . . . though I know sometimes you wished you hadn't.'

'You're wrong. Who else could I turn to?'

'Then turn to me now, Bill.' Her voice softened. 'I'll ask you again . . . what about Eva?'

'What about her?'

'Some time ago, you wondered whether you should make an effort to find her.'

'I decided against it.' Easing the car to a standstill at the traffic lights, he kept his gaze straight ahead. 'I've put it right out of my mind.'

'Why would you do that?'

Shrugging his shoulders, he gave her a sideways glance. 'You know things haven't been too good between me and Joan these past years, but what with the death of our son, and then a miscarriage two months ago, she came close to a nervous break-down, and she needs me now more than ever.'

'I understand that.' What she didn't understand was Bill's devotion to a woman who was obviously no good to anyone. 'But Joan isn't the only reason, is she?'

'Oh?' When you were afraid it was always easiest to plead ignorance. 'And what's that supposed to mean?'

'It's your pride, isn't it? Eva asked you not to find her, and you've done what she asked all these years. Now, when you really would like to find her, you're afraid.'

'Is that so?' Sometimes Sheila knew him better than he knew himself.

'You're afraid she might reject you. Afraid she won't return the love you feel for her.'

He laughed softly. 'You're a very perceptive lady.'

'I'm also your friend.' What she wanted to say was, 'I'm your mother and I haven't got long on this earth.'

Oh, how she yearned for him to be happy. And the only person who could bring him real happiness was Eva Bereton. But he would never seek her out, Sheila knew that. He was too fine and loyal a man. Bill had old-fashioned ideals and a deep belief that the marriage vows given in church were sacred. Joan's drinking had almost destroyed her, but now that she had dried out and was beginning to enjoy life again, he would never break her heart, whatever sacrifice it cost him.

———⊰⊙⊱———

TODD WAS NO stranger to his brother's house, or his brother's wife. 'You're a wicked tease,' he laughed. 'A woman like you could drive a man crazy.'

Naked and wanton, Joan stood before him. She was in her thirties, tall and slim, and very desirable. With her long, dark hair and beckoning eyes, she had a thirst for men, which was not easily quenched. 'How much do you want me?' Taunting, she laughed in his face, staying just out of arm's reach.

Red in the face and aching with need, Todd would have snatched her to him, but with a laugh that put murder in his heart, she moved away. 'You little bitch! I warn you. Don't torment me.'

'Now, now, it's just my little game.'

For a moment they regarded each other, he with a kind of hatred in his eyes, and she basking in her power over him. 'How much do you want me?' she asked again, leaning brazenly against the bedhead.

'Too much, and you know it.' He edged towards her once more. This time she didn't move, until he took hold of her. Fighting him off, she laughed in his face.

Together they rolled on to the floor. 'I should kill you,' he murmured, his two hands round her throat.

Her eyes bathed his face, and there was madness in her smile. 'You'd rather mate with me though, wouldn't you?' Like a thing possessed, she reached down to play with him. The hardness of his erect penis excited her. Closing her eyes, she pleaded, 'Now! Take me now!'

For one long, excruciating moment, he made her wait. 'You're crazy,' he hissed. And she was. But that was why he needed her. That was why she played on his senses like a powerful, intoxicating drug.

———⊷◆⊶———

'MIND HOW YOU go.' Sheila waved to Bill as he drove away. 'Take care, son,' she murmured.

She watched him go left at the bottom of the road, waited a while, then turned her back on the house where she had lived these many years and walked away down the street.

She wasn't in the mood for being alone. Not tonight. This morning she had seen her doctor and the news was not good. Suddenly, sunshine and birdsong were gifts to be cherished. A walk in the fresh air will blow away the cobwebs, she thought; and besides, she had some very important decisions to make.

Full of quiet thoughts, Bill made his way home. There had been something about Sheila tonight that worried him. It wasn't just the light-hearted hint about her retiring. It went deeper than that. She wasn't ill, she said, but he felt she was hiding something from him.

It was strange how she could almost read his thoughts, he mused. Especially where Eva was concerned. But then, Sheila knew the score. Eva was his dream. Joan was his reality. Joan needed him. Eva did not.

He considered that for a moment. Maybe Eva did need him. How would he know? He prayed she did, then he prayed she didn't, because it would serve no purpose. He was tied to someone else, and no doubt Eva had her own family, her own responsibilities. After all this time, he ought to be able to accept that.

But he couldn't. His love for Eva was as strong as ever.

Normally, he would leave the car outside on the drive and go in through the front door, but tonight, for no particular reason, he drove it into the garage and made his way into the house through the side door, silently cursing because he found the door unlocked. 'For God's sake, Joan,' he muttered, coming into the kitchen, 'how many times do I have to tell you, there are burglars operating in this neck of the woods.' This week the police had posted warnings everywhere.

Thinking she was in the lounge, he went through. When he saw no one was there, he thought she might have gone next door – Cath Parker was her one and only friend.

Going to the fridge he took out a carton of orange juice and poured himself a generous measure.

He was raising the glass to his lips for the second time when he heard a noise. 'What the devil's that?' Cautiously, he followed the sound through the kitchen and on up the stairs. 'Burglars?' He cursed Joan again for leaving the door unlocked.

At the top of the stairs he realised the sounds were coming from the bedroom he and Joan shared. Fists clenched, he approached the door on tiptoe. The best way to deal with a burglar was to take him by surprise, he thought. Cautiously he edged open the door and peered inside – and froze. His wife and a man were thrashing about on the bed, both naked, and so deeply entangled in each other they seemed to be one and the same.

Joan saw him at the door and began screaming that she'd been attacked. 'I couldn't stop him. Honest to God, Bill, I couldn't stop him!' For effect she started hitting her 'assailant' who by this time had turned to see Bill charging towards him, his face black as thunder.

'She's a liar!' he yelled. 'She's crazy!'

His words were lost in the crunch of Bill's fist as it landed with a sickening blow on the side of his face. '*You!*' Yanking Todd off the bed, he threw him across the room. 'You filthy bastard!' White with rage, Bill advanced on him again.

Behind him, Joan cried, 'I begged him to leave me be but he wouldn't listen.'

Like the coward he was, Todd hid behind a chair. 'I swear to God, she's lying!'

'Get up!'

'Listen to me, Bill.' Todd was crying like a child now. 'Ask her how many times we've been together. Ask her where she went when you thought she was away at a health farm – she was with me, I can prove it if you'll only give me a chance. She's cheated on you all along, Bill. First with Father, then with me. She hates you – deep down she hates you.'

Bill kicked aside the chair and drew him out. 'You're a filthy liar!' What he had just heard was too terrible to believe.

'Hit me, I don't care. It's the truth. Go on! Ask her!' The sweat was pouring down his face. 'Ask her about the baby you thought she'd miscarried. It wasn't yours, Bill! Father arranged for her to get rid of it.'

From behind them came the most terrible of screams. Bill turned, startled, to see Joan crouched at the bottom of the bed, her gaze fixed on him. Trembling from head to foot, she was sobbing uncontrollably.

In that moment, Bill knew. It was written in her eyes.

It seemed to take an age for it to register. When it did, and he realised that everything Todd had said must be the truth, Bill felt as though he had been hit with a sledgehammer. For a long, terrible moment he continued to stare at her. Behind him he could hear Todd whimpering. He looked from one to the other, and saw them for what they were.

'Please, Bill, I do love you.' Joan crawled along the bed towards him.

'My God!' His voice was like gravel, his face contorted with disgust as he stared at the two of them. 'How could I have been such a bloody fool?'

As he walked out of that place, he could hear her calling, 'Please, Bill, don't leave me.'

'Your lies won't work,' he murmured. 'Not any more.'

Chapter Fifteen

Eva had been primed all week about their imminent guest. 'John's an old friend. I haven't seen him since our college days,' Frank lied. 'Funny how we bumped into each other after all that time.'

'How long is he staying?' Eva thought it would be nice to have another face around the house. Frank had a strong dislike of visitors, particularly when the visitors were Patsy and Tommy, who regularly came to see her, preferably when Frank was out. As yet, Fred had not found the time to visit, but he was always welcome, Eva had assured him of that.

'A few nights,' Frank answered, buttering his toast. 'He'll be gone Monday morning.'

'What's he like, this old friend of yours?' Somehow, she had never imagined Frank having a friend. He was a loner, who trusted no one, especially her.

'Much like me, I suppose. A dedicated businessman, with a certain degree of success, and aspirations to do even better.'

Eva reached for the marmalade. 'What kind of business is he in?'

Looking up, Frank smiled. 'Why do you need to know?'

Sensing suspicion behind his smile, Eva answered cautiously, 'Just curious, that's all.'

'Mmm.' Putting down his toast, then dabbing his mouth with his napkin, he answered, 'John is into all sorts. Mostly shares – gilts, that kind of thing.'

'Not property then?'

'Why do you ask that?'

Eva shrugged. 'I don't know really. I just thought you might have met up through one of your business deals.'

'Ah, well, in a way you're right, sweetheart. You remember I told you about the new company I've taken on, to refurbish the older hotels, bring them up to date, introduce conference and leisure facilities?'

'Yes, I remember.' Eva had thought it an excellent idea.

'Well, John has major interests in that particular company. That's how we came to meet up again.'

'What's he like?' Eva asked again. It was so rare to get a real conversation out of Frank, she was beginning to enjoy herself.

Frank's patience was running thin. 'I've already told you. He's a businessman, much like me.'

'No. I mean how old is he? What does he look like? Is he married? Has he got children? That kind of thing.'

Containing his anger, Frank stood up. 'You want to know a great deal, don't you?' His voice had an edge that Eva had come to recognise. Realising she had touched that jealous chord again, she wisely dropped the subject.

'You're right. What does it matter?'

He nodded approvingly. 'As long as he's fed and made welcome, that's all that matters. This visit will be a one-off. I've no doubt we will never see him again.' He had no liking for men in this house. Eva was *his* property, not to be shared or ogled. She had come to mean more to him than life itself, and however much she resisted, he must protect her from the bad things. It was his goal in life to love her with all his being and always take the utmost care of her, shower her with expensive gifts and take her twice round the world if that was what she wanted.

Rounding the table he bent over her from behind. Kissing her tenderly on the top of her head, he murmured softly, 'There's nothing for you to concern yourself about, sweetheart.' He thought it was time to tell her what he had done. 'So you don't overtax yourself while he's here, I've arranged for some help.'

In a minute Eva was on her feet. 'What? *Domestic* help, you mean?'

'That's right, and before you say anything, I'm only thinking of you.' He tapped her bulge. 'And the baby, of course.'

Eva was furious. Stepping away from him, she said, 'You had no right to do that. You know how I feel about looking after this house myself. And now you bring one visitor to see us and suddenly you think I can't manage.'

Equally determined, he took hold of her by the shoulders. 'No argument, sweetheart. It's all arranged.'

'Then, it can be *unarranged*.' This was the second time he had gone behind her back, and she didn't like it one bit. 'I mean it, Frank. I don't want to be treated as if I'm incapable. It's only a house, for God's sake, and there are only two of us. One more won't make much difference. All right, I'm pregnant, and I get a little tired now and then, but I'm not an invalid. If I can't care for three adults over a couple of days, what use am I?'

'Entertaining is not easy, any hostess will tell you that. I don't want you wearing yourself out. There are all the meals to prepare, an extra bedroom to sort out and keep tidy. In your state it's too much to burden you with.' What he really wanted was a spy in the camp.

'Of course it isn't,' Eva insisted. 'And don't forget, Frank, I did run a hotel at one time.' Well, near enough, she thought. She would not allow him to push her aside as if she couldn't cope. Nor was he going to rule her like he might a child.

Taking her two hands in his, he said, 'Sorry, sweetheart. I really didn't know you felt so strongly.'

Eva drew her hands away. 'Yes, you did! You know I've fought all along against having help here. If I didn't have this house to tend, I'd be bored out of my mind.'

'All right, sweetheart. I'll cancel it.' Kissing her on the mouth, he promised, 'In fact, I'll do it right now.' With that, he hurried away.

Eva sat in her seat, looking across the breakfast table, and wondering if she would ever come to love him. 'I don't belong here,' she sighed. 'I have nothing to occupy my mind, and Frank is hell bent on wrapping me in cotton wool.' She knew he loved her, but it was a strange kind of love that gave a woman no freedom. She was an accomplished person. There was a time when she had plans, and a life. Now, all that was sliding away, and the longer she stayed, the more hopelessly trapped she felt. 'I don't belong with a man like Frank.' Closing her eyes, she let her mind wander. 'With a man like Bill,' she whispered, 'that's where I belong.'

'All done.' Frank had come back, startling her.

'What?'

'I've cancelled the help.' Standing there, he

gazed down on her pink, guilty face. 'It's not a good idea, you know.'

'What isn't?'

'Talking to yourself.'

Before she could answer, he swept her, laughingly, into his arms. 'After John's left, I think I'll take a week or so off. We could go away – a cruise maybe. It would do us both good.'

The idea was so abhorrent to Eva that she remained silent; at the back of her mind she suspected he might have heard her say Bill's name.

Walking with her to the front door, he gave no indication that he had heard. 'Behave yourself while I'm away now. No making eyes at the postman.' He gave a small laugh, kissed her lightly, and was soon disappearing down the lane in his car.

At the bottom he turned to wave, as he always did.

Eva did not wave back. In her heart she prayed he would stay away for ever.

⋙•◆•⋘

FOR A LONG time after he'd gone, Eva sat in the garden, looking out across the valley. 'It's so beautiful here,' she murmured.

Grateful to Frank for ruling out the sale of this land to a developer, she felt her heart soften towards him. 'He means well,' she sighed. 'Deep down, I know he means well.' She actually laughed. 'If he had his way he'd surround me with guards and prison bars. Oh, Frank, yours is a funny kind of love.' But it was love nevertheless. He cared for her more than he cared for anything in his life, she was aware of that. And if she didn't have Frank, who else was there? Only the baby, she thought, and the baby was Frank's.

After a while, she glanced at her wristwatch and was ashamed to see how the hour had flown. 'Come on, Eva,' she chided herself. 'You've only just got through telling Frank how you're able to cope on your own, without help. And here you are, letting the dishes lie dirty, and the bed unmade. There's washing to be done and hung out, and endless little tasks to be finished before you go to Albert Street.' The thought of seeing Patsy put a smile on her face.

She tore into the work. The dishes were washed and stacked away, the washing finished and hung out on the line, a chat with Olive before going back inside. Then she ran the Hoover round and dusted. Upstairs, the bed was quickly made, the curtains tied back and Frank's robe put tidily away. A last look round, and it was time to get washed and ready.

It was eleven thirty.

A short time later Eva emerged from the bathroom to towel her long hair and comb it through. Having already sorted her clothes for the day, she got dressed. The pretty cream underwear had been bought from Marks and Spencer the week before; Patsy had bought the same, but in black. The shoes were sensible, in view of her condition. The brown trouser suit only just fitted across her middle but it was comfortable, and quite attractive. A touch of make-up, mostly round the eyes and lips; a quick comb through her hair, which was almost dry, and she was ready for the world.

Looking in the full-length mirror, she observed herself with a wry little smile. 'Not bad,' she said, cocking her head to one side. 'Considering you're past thirty, and about to be a mum.' The bulge was not too prominent, but it was there all the same, and Eva was beginning to notice it more and more by the day.

Patsy thought she looked lovely. 'Ye look like a film star, so ye do!'

Embarrassed, Eva shoved her inside the house. 'I think you need glasses,' she said. 'I'm fat and spotty, and my breasts are beginning to sag.'

Inside the sitting room, Patsy boldly regarded her. 'Whatever ye say won't alter the fact that ye look lovely.' With a giggle she added, 'Even if your breasts *are* sagging.'

Eva threw a cushion at her and the two of them collapsed with laughter. 'It's so good to see you,' Eva said. 'I feel like I've been let out of prison.'

The pattern was always the same. Eva would put the kettle on and make the tea, Patsy would get out the biscuits. When the tray was ready, they would make their way back into the sitting room and place themselves either side of the fireplace, whether winter or summer.

In winter the fire would be cheery, with the flames roaring up the chimney; in summer, like now, a pretty flowered screen stood in the hearth to hide the black grate.

Once they were settled, they would catch up on the gossip and pass on any moans, groans, or news. Today, Eva told Patsy about the scene with Frank earlier.

'Sure, the way he treats ye, anybody would think ye were helpless,' she tutted. 'He loves ye too much, that's the trouble. He's afraid you'll blow away in the wind, that's what it is.'

'So you don't think I was being ungrateful?'

'Not at all! If it had been me, I'd have knocked him aside the head with the frying pan, so I would.'

The talk went from one thing to another. 'Maggie took Tommy to the pictures last Saturday, did I tell ye that?' She hadn't, and Eva was delighted that Maggie was growing ever closer to the boy.

'I have some other news, so I have.' Looking shy, Patsy grinned from ear to ear. 'Me an' Fred were gonna tell ye when we were together, but I can't keep it to meself a minute longer.'

Seeing the sly little look on Patsy's face, Eva almost dropped her cup. 'Patsy Noonan, you're pregnant, aren't you?' Patsy nodded and threw herself into Eva's arms. The chair rocked on its feet and they laughed and cried, and couldn't believe how things had turned out.

'What happened to all our plans?' Eva laughed. 'The little business we wanted, and all that hard work to save enough money?'

'Aye, an' here you are living in a fancy house and married to a monster, an' there's me, coming up to me pension and having a bairn!' She couldn't stop giggling. Eva asked her if she'd been at the gin, and Patsy answered, 'What do you think?'

'The money we saved is still invested,' Eva reminded her. 'You can leave it there or you can take it out. I've already signed it all over to you, so it's for you to decide.'

Patsy had had no idea Eva was planning to do that. 'Why, ye little bugger! You'd no right to sign it over to me. We *both* worked for that money. I'll not have your share. Thanks all the same, but I'd feel like I were stealing it from ye.'

'Take it for your baby, Patsy. Don't refuse me. Please. You know I don't need it.'

So it was decided.

Patsy told Eva how Fred had got some time off work. 'I was going to phone and tell ye,' she said.

'First thing tomorrow morning he's taking me and Tommy to Blackpool to celebrate the new baby. Oh, and Tommy's been promised a job at the paper mill when he leaves school next year.'

'Oh, Patsy, that's wonderful!'

'I can't believe it. Everything's come right for me, and in spite of your feller being too possessive, ye seem to be taking it all in your stride, so ye do. You've always been able to handle the rough times, and now, me darlin', I'm beginning to think it will all come out in the wash. Besides, I've got a feeling you'll be happy as a pig in muck when your baby's born.'

Eva raised her cup of tea. 'To *both* our babies.'

'Aye. And now you've told me about your half of the money, that's something else to celebrate.'

When, some three hours later, Eva left for home, she felt a great deal happier than when she had arrived.

But then, she always did.

Her spirits dipped when she thought about the weekend ahead and Frank's visitor. She suspected Frank might have been lying about this John being an old college friend. But she had no real cause to doubt his word. All the same, she and Frank were going through a bad patch, and it was very worrying. Was Patsy right? she wondered. Would it all come out in the wash?

'It has to.' She found herself talking aloud as she turned the car into the drive.

She had a strange kind of feeling about this weekend. A kind of premonition that something bad was about to happen.

Chapter Sixteen

FRIDAY EVENING ARRIVED, and got off to a bad start.

All day Eva had worked hard, and now, just as she was turning the joint, a knock came on the door. 'Frank!' Twice she called his name but there was no answer. 'Damn and bugger it!' Taking off her pinafore, she set it down on the table and rushed to answer the door.

It was a young girl, small and trim, with big eyes and a bold, well made-up face. 'I've come from Delton's Domestic Agency,' she said. 'I'm to stay the weekend and carry out general duties, as directed by the lady of the house.' She handed Eva a long, folded card. 'At least that's what it says there.'

'There's been a mistake,' Eva answered, returning the card. 'The booking was cancelled.'

Frank arrived. 'What's the problem?'

'I've come from the agency,' the girl explained. 'This lady thinks the booking was cancelled, but it couldn't have been. If it had been cancelled, I wouldn't be here, would I?'

Turning to Eva, Frank assured her he had cancelled the booking himself. 'There's obviously been some mix-up. But never mind. As long as she's here, I'm sure you could find something for her to do.'

It was obvious to Eva that he was lying. 'Sorry, Frank,' she answered stiffly, 'there is nothing at all for her to do. Everything is under control, just as I said it would be.' Addressing the young lady, she apologised. 'I'm sorry you've come unnecessarily,' she said, 'but if the booking was not cancelled before, I'm cancelling it now. If there is money to be paid, I'm sure my husband will deal with it.' With that, she excused herself and returned to the kitchen, leaving Frank to sort it out.

A few moments later he followed her into the kitchen. 'You didn't have to do that.'

'And you didn't have to lie to me. You didn't cancel the booking at all, did you?'

For a moment he toyed with the idea of lying yet again, but he knew she wouldn't believe him. 'I did it for you,' he said sheepishly. 'I don't want you overtiring yourself.'

'Oh, Frank. Why don't you let *me* be the judge of whether I'm overtiring myself? I don't need cosseting every minute of every day. I'm a grown woman. I can take care of myself.'

'Sorry, sweetheart.' When he went to kiss her, she turned away.

Bristling, he stood there a moment longer, then left without saying another word.

Eva followed him into the lounge where he was sulking. 'We're not going to have an atmosphere all weekend, are we, Frank?' she asked. 'Because if we are, you can call the agency and get the girl back. I'll go and stay with Patsy until your visitor's gone.' She knew Patsy was in Blackpool for a few days, but he didn't.

He had been standing by the fireside with his hands in his pockets. Now he turned and stared at her, his face set in a hard expression. 'Would you really do that?' He sounded hurt, like a child denied his sweets.

'Sometimes you drive me to despair.' Eva had to say what was on her mind, and the devil with the consequences. 'You lie to me. You make plans behind my back. You've cancelled the papers because you thought I was flirting with the paper boy – a lad young enough to be my son. And you did your level best to make me sell my car because you were afraid I'd be involved in an accident.'

'I'm only looking after you.'

'Oh, Frank! You smother me. I know you do it for all the best reasons. But I need space. I need to be able to breathe.'

He gave a long sigh that seemed to make him shrink. 'I love you, Eva, so very much.'

'Do you think I don't know that?'

There was a silence while he studied her, thinking how lovely she was and how he would kill, with his bare hands, anyone who tried to take her from him. 'I'm sorry, sweetheart. Really.'

Lost for words, she put out her hands in a gesture of frustration. He didn't understand what she was saying. Worse, she realised, he would never understand.

When, a few moments later, he came with her to the kitchen, asking if he could help, she found him a task in the dining room. Out of her way.

———— ✥ ————

JOHN WAS DIFFERENT from what Eva had expected. Slimmer and younger than Frank, he had a bright smile and a charming manner that put her at ease straight away. Frank introduced them. 'Eva, this is John, my old friend from college.' When he said that, he gave John a crafty wink. 'John, this is my lovely wife, Eva.'

'She's certainly lovely.' He didn't extend his hand in a greeting. Instead, to Frank's dismay he leaned forward and placed a very polite kiss on Eva's cheek. 'It's a pleasure to meet you,' he said. 'Frank is a lucky man.'

Apart from Frank's little spans of silence, the

dinner was a success. The conversation was lively, and the food cooked to perfection. Eva served homemade potato soup, followed by thick, juicy slices from a succulent joint of gammon dressed with pineapple rings, accompanied by vegetables done lightly in minted water. Dessert was strawberries laid on a bed of choux pastry and topped with fresh cream, with coffee and brandy to follow.

'That was one of the best meals I have ever tasted,' John said appreciatively. 'To get a meal like that in London would cost a small fortune.' Beaming at Frank, he said, 'She's not only lovely, she's a real gem. You'd best hold on to her, Frank. There aren't many like her out there.'

Frank merely smiled, but underneath his smile he was fuming. He had made a bad mistake bringing the fellow here, and he was frantically thinking of how he might get rid of him. Eva too was annoying him. Instead of ignoring the man's absurd praise, she seemed to be enjoying his attention – flirting with him even!

The whole thing came to a head the following evening. After a day of cat and mouse during which he and John went down to the valley, John seemed to be showing more interest in Eva than he was in the deal he was here to secure. Eva was upstairs getting changed when Frank confronted John in the drawing room. 'I want you to leave.' Frank had come to the end of his tether.

John was astonished. 'What do you mean, you want me to leave? We haven't talked the deal through yet. I like the look of it, Frank. You were right in everything you said – executive houses should go a bomb in this location. Bulldoze the house, and you've a wide, attractive access in the making. But there's more to it than that. You can't expect me to commit good money without going into all the smaller details. You know how it works, Frank. I need to see papers, deeds, outline planning and that sort of thing. You have got them, haven't you?' He stared at Frank with suspicion. 'I hope you didn't bring me down here on a wild goose chase.'

'I've changed my mind. I'm not selling after all.'

'Bugger you, Frank, you can't do that!'

'I can do what the hell I like. Now get out. You're not welcome here.'

It occurred to John that the reason for this show of temper was nothing to do with the deal, and everything to do with Eva. 'I see. Afraid she might take a fancy to me, is that it?' He laughed, but the laugh caught in his throat when Frank took hold of him by his shirt collar. 'All right! All right!' Wriggling loose, he realised that Frank was not the amiable fellow he'd thought he was. In fact, the look on his face just now had been frightening. 'I'll go, but you've wasted my time, Frank. I won't forget that in a hurry.' As he spoke he walked to the door. 'I'll get my things.'

'No.' Afraid that he might speak to Eva, Frank brushed past him. '*I'll* get your things. You wait here.' Before John could protest, he was on his way up the stairs.

Eva heard him coming. One look at his face and she knew something was wrong. 'What's happened?'

'Nothing for you to worry about. Our guest is leaving, that's all.'

'But I thought we were all going into town this evening?'

'Well, now we're not, so you can take off your glad rags.' Eva had on a straight black dress with blue trimming, and blue shoes to match. Her hair was wound back, and she looked wonderful. It only served to antagonise Frank further.

As always, he hid his anger beneath a layer of charm. 'On second thoughts, stay as you are. You look lovely, sweetheart. We'll go out if you like, just the two of us. After I've got rid of him.'

———❖———

A T THE FRONT door, he warned John, 'Remember what I said. I'll ruin you if I hear you've breathed a word of this to anyone.'

'Don't worry, I won't.' Glancing over Frank's

shoulder, John was surprised and pleased to see Eva at the top of the stairs. He raised his voice slightly, just enough for her to hear. 'I wouldn't want anyone to know how you lured me here with the promise of a deal, and once I got interested you pulled the rug from under my feet.' He laughed cynically. 'I'd look a right bloody fool, wouldn't I?'

'You know your way, down the street and turn left at the bottom. Once you get into town, there'll be signs all the way.' Frank opened the door wide. 'Now, get out.'

John lingered. 'This is a lovely place, Frank.' He looked about the spacious hallway, with the beautiful panelling and high ceilings. 'In a way I'm glad we haven't gone through with the deal. I don't know if I could bring myself to bulldoze a grand old house like this. But then, it's a case of making money, isn't it, Frank? Nothing can be allowed to stand in the way of profit, isn't that right?'

As Frank bundled him out of the door, John glanced up to see Eva's face, white with shock. He smiled, and then he was gone.

A S FRANK PEERED through the window to make sure John was on his way, Eva ran back to the bedroom where she took a suitcase from the cupboard and began packing a few basic items. She wanted nothing more.

'What the devil do you think you're doing?' Frank stood in the doorway, blocking her path.

'I'm leaving you, Frank,' she said quietly. 'I should have done it long ago.'

'What's wrong? What's upset you, sweetheart?' His face was grim. 'Is it because he's gone, is that it? I saw the way you flirted behind my back. Shameful, the pair of you!'

Eva pushed past him. 'You're mad! You're also a born liar.' At the top of the landing, she spun round. 'He's not an old friend, is he?' When he opened his mouth she put her hand out to stop him speaking. 'No, Frank, don't make it worse. I heard you downstairs just now, and I know. You brought him here to do a deal. You had every intention of going ahead with your plans to sell the valley and raze this house to the ground. It doesn't matter what I want. It never has. What sort of a marriage is that?'

He took her by the shoulders, holding her so tightly she couldn't move. 'It's a *good* marriage and you know it. We can go abroad, make a new start, you and me, and the baby. I want to get you away from everything you knew before. Patsy's a bad influence on you. She's not the kind of woman I want you mixing with. Then there's the boy, Tommy. I don't want him here. I don't want *any* of them here. I don't want them to be any part of your life, or mine. A new life. New people. That's what we need.'

'No, Frank, what you need is to keep me all to yourself. Well, that's not possible. You can't cocoon me, as if I'm a specimen in a glass case. I'm alive, with feelings and needs, just like you. You go off to work, and I stay here. I'm entitled to some sort of a life, just like you are. As for Patsy, she's more of a friend to me than you will ever understand. I won't turn my back on her or Tommy just because you think I should.'

'You don't need them.'

'That's for me to say, Frank. What I *don't* need is you trying to mould me into something I can never be.'

'Oh, but you're wrong.'

Eva could never remember what happened after that. She vaguely recalled turning away; Frank called out; there was a sharp pain in the back of her neck, and the vision of a suitcase cartwheeling down the stairs. Then darkness closed in.

A T EIGHT O'CLOCK on Sunday morning, Bill and Sheila sat down to breakfast.

'I shouldn't be imposing on you like this,' Bill said. 'I'd be quite happy in a hotel until I find a house.'

'Don't be in such a rush to move out,' Sheila pleaded. 'If you mean to buy a house, it has to be the right one for you, and that takes time. And anyway, I love having you here, you know that.'

'I know, and I'm very grateful.' Bill glanced round the homely little kitchen, at the blue gingham cosy over the teapot, and the colourful little pictures of fat chefs, the hanging copper pans and wicker baskets. It felt so right. 'You have a lovely home, Sheila. No wonder you've never wanted to leave here.'

'It's taken me a long time to get it together,' she replied. 'But it's never really been a home. Not without children.'

Ever since he had turned up on her doorstep after finding his brother with Joan, she had wanted to tell him, 'You're not alone. I'm your mother, and you're always welcome here.' But common sense prevailed and the secret remained.

Bill had been concerned about her these past weeks. He was concerned now. 'You're looking pale,' he observed. 'Are you sure you're all right?'

'I've had a few bad days,' she admitted, 'but I'm fine now.'

'I can't have helped, bringing my troubles to your door like this.'

'You're like family to me,' she murmured. That was the closest she could come to telling him the truth. 'I'm glad you're here. Besides, it gets very lonely on your own.'

Getting up from the table he made a suggestion. 'Look, I've got an idea. Why don't you help me find a house? You don't have to stay here on your own. You could stay with me.'

She smiled, her heart leaping with joy. 'I see. You think I'm getting old and frail, do you?'

'Of course I don't. It's just that I don't like to think of you being lonely.'

'I know someone who's even lonelier.'

'Who?'

'You.'

'I can handle that.'

'Bill, why don't you find her?'

Turning, he gazed at her, his heart in his mouth. 'Eva, you mean?'

Sheila nodded.

He looked away, his mind going back to Eva. She filled his soul like a bright, burning light. 'What if I find she's happily married, with half a dozen kids? Maybe some things are best left as they are.'

Sheila knew he was saying one thing and meaning another. 'Life is so short,' she told him. 'Find her, Bill. Find her and be sure.'

Laughing, he kissed her on the cheek. 'Why would I want to find another girl when I've got one right here?' Funny, how he could laugh and joke when his heart was aching.

'I won't be here for the next few weeks,' she told him. 'I took your advice and went to see the doctor. He thinks I need a complete rest. So, if it's all right with you, I've decided to take a holiday.'

Immediately concerned, he said, 'I knew you were doing too much, but you wouldn't have it, would you? And of course you have to do as your doctor says. Have a long rest, and if you'll just tell me where you want to go, I'll have it all arranged for you.'

'Let me worry about that. I'm not senile yet, you know.'

Later, while Bill went out house hunting, Sheila read the letter she had received this morning once more:

I'm sorry to report that the woman you asked me to trace was killed in a traffic accident some twenty years ago; she and her adoptive parent.

I've enclosed the photograph and documents you sent me, together with a copy of the death certificate, and details of where she is buried in England.

I know this information is not what you

wanted to hear. I'm sorry I wasn't able to bring you better news . . .

The rest was irrelevant.

She looked at the photograph of two babies, a boy and a girl, and cried at her loss. 'I'm sorry,' she murmured. 'It's hard to know I'll never see you again. But I found your brother, and I thank God for that.'

———»•«———

THE FOLLOWING MORNING, on Bill's strict instructions, she stayed at home. 'I'll get a temp in,' he told her. 'You're not to worry about a thing.'

She allowed an hour for him to arrive and get settled into his work, and then she rang the office. 'I've booked a holiday,' she told him. 'A few weeks, and I'll be as good as new.'

Predictably, Bill wanted to know where she was going, and how he could keep in touch.

'It's a long leisurely cruise,' she told him, 'and I don't want anyone bothering me, not even you.'

'I see. Well, promise me you'll get in touch if you need anything – anything at all.'

'There's nothing I need,' she said, 'but if something should turn up, I know where you are.'

'God bless then. Get lots of rest, and take care of yourself.'

'I will.'

With a deep sigh, she replaced the receiver, then picked it up again and made another call. 'I'd like to come in this morning, if that's all right?' she said to the person who answered.

A short time later she left, carrying only a small overnight bag. It was a long drive. When she got there, the doctor greeted her like an old friend.

'I'm ready,' Sheila told him. 'It's time to make my peace.'

Chapter Seventeen

———— ⇒‣•○•‣⇐ ————

W**HEN SHE CAME** to, Eva found she couldn't move.

At first she didn't understand, but then, as her senses slowly returned, things became clearer. The awful cold, and the penetrating damp. The unfamiliar gloom, infiltrated only by the daylight coming through the grating above. In the shaft of light she could see small black particles dancing and sparkling like diamonds. With a feeling of horror she realised where she was.

'God Almighty! Frank? Frank, where are you?' She remembered the weekend visitor, the things he'd said at the door, and afterwards, when she and Frank had rowed at the top of the stairs. Frank had been behind her – *behind her*. 'Oh, my God!' She hardly dared think it. Had Frank pushed her down the stairs? Why was she here? What was happening?

'Frank!' Feeling weak, she began to struggle, but it was too painful. Ropes were bound, viciously tight, about her wrists and ankles. With every movement she made, they sliced into her flesh.

For a time she lay there, shivering from the cold, and hurting all over. Fear for the baby was paramount. 'Please, God, don't let any harm come to my baby,' she pleaded. At the back of her mind was the knowledge that Frank had been looking forward to the baby, just as she was. He would never hurt it. She kept telling herself that, over and over. 'Frank won't harm the child.'

But then she was filled with another dread – that he could be so eaten up with hatred and jealousy that he might think the baby would steal her affections.

The door swung open to admit a beam of torchlight. She knew it was him. Instinctively, she kept very still.

'It's no good pretending, sweetheart.' His voice increased her terror. 'I heard you calling my name, and here I am.' He gave a small laugh. 'I always try to please you.' Shoving some bread into her hands, he ordered, 'Eat up now. It'll make you strong.' When she didn't respond, he snatched the bread away and replaced it on the tray. 'There's water too. See how I look after you?'

'Let me out of here, Frank,' she pleaded. 'Think of the baby.'

His voice hardened. 'What baby?'

'*Our* baby, Frank, yours and mine.'

'Oh no, you can't fool me any more.'

'What do you mean?'

'You know very well what I mean. Whose baby

is it really?' In the half-light his face took on a sinister expression. 'You can tell me because it doesn't matter any more.'

Believing her only chance was to stay calm and appease him, she asked, 'Why doesn't it matter any more, Frank?'

He shifted closer, his breath on her face. 'Because the only thing that matters is that we'll be together now, you and me. What happens to the baby is no concern of mine.'

'Please, Frank. Let me out of here.' It took all her self-control not to scream for help. 'We can talk.'

'No!'

'Don't you trust me, Frank?'

He laughed. 'I don't trust myself.'

'How long do you mean to keep me here?'

'A week, a month – for as long as it takes.' Reaching out, he took hold of her cold hand. 'You've been here three days, and in all that time I had to keep you alive. You see, we never got to have our evening out, did we?' He smiled, a childlike smile that curdled her heart. 'It's all right now, though,' he murmured, 'because now you're awake, and I can start to make plans.' He sighed, a long, weary sigh. 'You look so lovely in that dress.'

'Which restaurant are we going to, Frank?' She had to humour him. It was her only chance.

'Why *here* of course.' He stretched his arms out to encompass the cellar.

'Don't you want to show me off, like you always do?'

He grabbed at her then, his face close to hers and his mouth actually touching her lips, in his excitement coating them with a film of spittle. 'You flirted! I saw you.'

There was no use denying it, he wouldn't believe her, and anyway it would antagonise him. 'I'm sorry, Frank. I didn't mean to.'

'You're mine,' he whispered. 'I don't want other men looking at you.' Now, as he took her two hands in his, he shivered. 'You're so cold.'

'Let me come upstairs, to sit in front of the fire.'

Like a scalded animal he fell back. 'You're trying to trick me.' He scurried to the door. 'Sleep now. We'll talk in the morning.' He went out and bolted the door behind him.

Eva thought he must have pressed his mouth close to the keyhole, because when he next spoke she could hear him clearly. 'Tomorrow I'll get everything ready for our special evening. It won't be long, sweetheart. Soon, we'll be together for all time, where no one can hurt us.'

GROANING WITH EVERY step, Patsy hobbled into breakfast. 'Will ye look at me!' When Fred pulled out a chair for her, she fell into it. 'Four days into our holiday, and me ankle's up like a balloon.'

Fred tutted. 'Well, if you don't mind me saying so, me beauty, you did ask for it. I mean, a woman of your age, riding the bleedin' ghost train.'

'Morning all.' The stout landlady had taken a liking to this down-to-earth family. 'Let me see.' She went round the table with her pencil. 'Eggs, bacon and two sausages, smothered in fried tomatoes, for the gent, scrambled eggs on toast and a pint mug of tea for the lady, and everything that's going for the boy. Is that right?'

'No food for me,' Patsy groaned. 'Just a mug of tea, and an aspirin if you've got one. Sure, I've not had a wink of sleep all night with this bloody ankle.'

'Hmh! A cold compress, that's what you want.' The landlady prided herself on knowing all about these things. 'Right. Two breakfasts then, tea all round, and an aspirin for the lady.' Softly whistling, she ambled away to the kitchen.

'I'm sorry.' Sheepishly, Patsy looked from Fred to Tommy and back again. 'We'll have to cut short the holiday, so we will.'

Fred was understanding. 'Well, it'll save us a bob or two, that's for sure. And anyway, the forecast says rain all day today.' He winked at Patsy, and she knew he was only trying to make it easier for Tommy.

Tommy saw the wink. 'It's all right,' he said. 'If my ankle was up like a balloon, I'd want to go home an' all.'

Patsy hobbled round to give him a hug. 'Ah, you're a little angel, so ye are.'

'Will I have time to get Eva's present before we go?'

'We'll make time so we will!'

And Fred promised, 'Next year, we'll come to Blackpool for two whole weeks, if you like.'

'I've always fancied going to Rome,' Patsy announced, 'and having a ride in one of them gundolis.'

'Don't you mean Venice and gondolas?' Fred said.

'Well, whatever, just so long as I get a ride with one of them pretty men on the back singing me a love song.'

'You'll not catch me going near no water, I'll tell yer!' Returning with the tray, the landlady joined in the conversation. 'I've only ever been on a boat ride once, and it were nothin' but a disaster from start to finish. I lost me best shoe in the water, and when me late husband bent down to grab it, the boat capsized. I tell you, we were bloody lucky we didn't all get drowned. That's not all neither. They made us bloody *pay*! Can you imagine that? There we were, soaked to the skin and me with only one shoe, and the buggers made us pay!' Snorting with disgust, she went off tutting, leaving the three of them cracking up with laughter.

'I think I've gone off the idea of a gundoli ride,' Patsy chuckled, and that set them all off again.

———⟩⟩•○•⟨⟨———

PATSY AND HER little family were home by late afternoon. By the time they'd unpacked and had something to eat, it was going on for eight o'clock. 'Can I take Eva's present now?' Tommy was itching to go up to the big house. 'I can't wait to show her what I've got.'

'Well, you'll have to wait,' Patsy told him. 'Your dad's got to take the car to a mate of his. The damned thing's been playing up all day. And I need you to come with me to the doctor's, but we'll not be long.'

'Then can I go to Eva's?'

'Aye, when you've seen me safely home again. And only if you promise not to tell her I hurt me ankle riding the ghost train. She thinks I'm daft enough as it is.'

'And she's right.' Fred had done all he could to persuade her not to go on it, but when Patsy made up her mind, there was no stopping her.

———⟩⟩•○•⟨⟨———

AT EIGHT THIRTY, Frank returned to the cellar for a third time. 'I'm sorry I had to gag you,' he apologised, 'but I couldn't have you shouting and carrying on, now could I? I even had to turn up the volume on the television in case anyone heard you. Whatever would they have thought?'

Quite casually, and with an air of disapproval, he went on to describe how he had seen Olive next door going out. 'With a gentleman, no less. Seems she's got herself a boyfriend while the mistress's back is turned.' He rolled his eyes. 'Love is a funny thing, don't you think, sweetheart? I mean, look at us. I know you could never love me, not the way I always hoped you might. Oh, I'm not blaming you, it's just one of those things. The way I see it, there are only two options. You either love me, or you leave me, and I really think you were on the point of leaving me. I couldn't allow that, now could I?' He scratched his head, as though thinking his way through a dilemma. 'It's better this way, don't you think, sweetheart? This way we'll always have each other.'

Dressed in full evening wear, he carried a bottle of wine and two glasses. 'Now, you see, I kept my promise, didn't I?' He left the wine and glasses just out of Eva's reach, before heading back through the doorway. 'I said we'd have our romantic evening, and we will.'

A few moments later he returned with a tray, beautifully set out with sausage rolls and dainty sandwiches. Round the edge of the tray were tiny iced biscuits. 'I'm not very good at this,' he apologised, setting the tray down. 'But this is all I could find. There was a lot of food left over from the other evening, but it was all covered in fungus. I didn't think you'd want that.'

Eva stared at him, unable to say a word. She felt desperately ill. Every bone in her body was screaming, and she was so cold she couldn't stop shaking. All her efforts to reason with him had failed, and so, too, had her plans to escape. The cellar walls were two feet thick, and the only likely escape routes were the door leading into the house, and the grating above the coal chute. Even if she hadn't been trussed up the way she was, escape was impossible. The grating was heavily padlocked, and the door leading into the house had a foot-long bolt on the other side. Eva was beginning to believe she might well die in this place.

Tucking a napkin under her chin, Frank said quietly, 'I'm going to undo your gag, so you can join me in our celebration dinner. If you scream out, I'll have to kill you here and now, and that would be such a shame, especially when I've gone to so much trouble for our special evening.'

Suddenly, he laughed. 'How thoughtless of me, sweetheart. I know how much you enjoy your music.' Kissing her lovingly, he departed through the door. 'I won't be long,' he promised.

Eva heard the music, soft at first, and then very loud. It was one of her favourite songs. While it played, she closed her eyes, feeling her senses slipping away.

'Oh no!' A sharp slap on her face brought her round. 'You can't sleep. Not now.' He took the gag from her face. 'Remember what I said. If you scream out, you'll leave me no choice but to kill you now.'

In his blind madness, he couldn't see that Eva was already dying, that she had no strength to scream, no strength even to plead with him any more.

With great tenderness, he removed the gag. Taking up a sausage roll between finger and thumb, he put it to her lips. When, nauseated, she managed to turn her head away, he tutted impatiently. 'All right, you may have a drink. But if you want to dance with me, you have to eat first.'

<hr />

TOMMY CONTINUED TO bang on the door. 'Eva! It's me, Tommy!' he yelled over the music. 'Bleedin' Nora, what a racket! No wonder they can't hear me.'

Curious, he peered in through a window. All the lights were on but there was no one to be seen. 'Eva!' Clenching his fist, he banged hard on the window, but it was to no avail.

Never one to give up, he went round to the back. Here, he peered in through the drawing-room window. The curtains were open, but again, there was no one in sight. 'That's funny.' A cheeky grin crossed his face. 'Happen they're upstairs and don't want to be disturbed.'

He began to tiptoe away when he saw flickering light coming from the side of the house. 'Hello, what's that?'

Softly, he approached the grating.

Sure enough, there was a light of sorts down in the cellar. Getting down on his knees, he squinted through the grating, and what he saw made him reel with shock. Trussed up and white as a ghost, with her head lolling to one side, Eva was in Frank's arms, being dragged round the floor in a weird dance to the music. Lying on the ground was a torch which sent shadows flickering up the walls every time they swept past it. 'Gawd Almighty!' It was obvious to Tommy that Eva was unconscious, and in great danger.

'What have you done to her, you bastard!' Yelling through the grating, he screamed for Frank to let him in. But Frank didn't hear him. He was smiling with pleasure, engrossed in the dancing.

Scrambling to his feet, Tommy fled next door. Banging and shouting brought no one; no one was there. The same the other side. In the garden of that house was a bicycle. Tommy stole it and, as though his own life depended on it, he raced to the police station where he poured out his story.

The constable would have ignored him, thinking he was either crazy or a mischief-maker, except for one very important factor. The boy was in tears, sobbing so hard he could barely answer his questions.

The constable put out an alert. 'It's all right, lad, you stay here. We'll need to talk to you.'

In minutes, the cars were out and racing down the street, sirens full on. Only minutes behind, Tommy followed on the stolen bike, praying they would not be too late.

PART FOUR

AUGUST 1966
THE
RECKONING

Chapter Eighteen

MONDAY MORNINGS WERE always busiest in the offices of Dollond and Travers, the old and well-respected firm of Bedford solicitors.

The older partners had retired long ago, and a new generation had taken over. Leonard Dollond was the senior partner now. 'It never rains, but it pours,' he said, drawing his secretary's attention to the letter he had just read. 'Take a look at that.'

The meticulously dressed young lady scanned the letter, a two-page account of what had taken place right here in these offices many years ago.

'That's strange,' she looked up, 'it's almost identical to the one we received last week, all about the tragic death of that couple, and about their daughter, Eva Bereton, who was turned out of her home by her uncle, Peter Westerfield.'

'My father had an idea that the girl might have been the one who burned the cottage down. I was a junior clerk here when it all happened, and I remember he never voiced his suspicions to anyone except me. His sympathies were always with the girl.

As far as I can recall, he didn't have one good word to say about her uncle.'

'If I remember rightly, the letter last week was from a Bill Westerfield.'

'Peter's adopted son. They never got on.'

'He was looking for Eva Bereton. And now this.'

'Did you discover her whereabouts?'

'A last known address, that's all. I'm afraid the trail runs cold after that.'

'Have you replied to Bill Westerfield?'

'Not yet. It's taken me a while to locate the information. It's on my list to reply to him this week. But it's not our policy to give out private information like that.'

Taking the letter from her, he said, 'What I suggest we do is this . . .' And he outlined what he saw as a satisfactory solution.

<hr>

E va had been in hospital for two weeks. She had severe bruising and a gash to her wrist that needed several stitches. When they brought her in, she was emaciated and shockingly weak, and they had little hope for her full recovery.

Also, the knowledge that she had lost her child took away her reason for living, and for many anxious days she gave no visible signs of rallying.

Patsy stayed by her side day and night, with Tommy running errands and saying little prayers whenever he was allowed to sit beside her. 'Come on, gal,' he'd plead. 'We all love you, so don't leave us. Don't you dare leave us.'

And, in the end, she didn't.

TODAY, THE DOCTOR had given her the all-clear and Patsy had come to take her home. 'You've actually got some roses in your cheeks, so ye have.'

Eva smiled, a sad little smile that betrayed her sorrow at losing the baby. 'I'm really looking forward to coming home with you,' she said. 'Are you positive it's all right with Fred?'

'Ah, sure, he's the one who's insisting. If he had his way you'd stay with us till the cows came home, so ye would.' She watched Eva putting on her stockings. 'Let me help you, me darlin'.'

'I'm okay. I'm stronger than you think.'

'Eva?'

Eva looked up.

Patsy backed down. 'Nothing. I were just thinking.'

Eva smiled knowingly. 'If it's about Frank, I already know. He's been committed to a psychiatric hospital.'

'Who told you?'

'Inspector Marshal. He was here this morning.'

'And are you all right? I mean . . .'

'I know what you mean, Patsy, and you've no

need to worry. I'm fine. I can put it behind me.'
But not for a long time, she thought. It was too
horrendous to forget in a hurry.

———————◆———————

IT WAS STRANGE living with Patsy's family, and
both comforting and disturbing to see Patsy growing larger with child by the day. Patsy had been
advised by the doctor to encourage Eva to talk
about all her troubles. And, after just a few days, it
seemed to be working really well. Not only was Eva
beginning to sleep well at night, she was smiling more
and taking a real interest in everything that went on
around her. Tommy played cards with her, and she
always lost. 'You're a cheat,' she complained, and he
laughingly admitted it.

On her first weekend home, Eva had a visitor.
'It's an old friend,' Patsy explained.

Eva's first thought was of Olive, who apparently
had been away staying with her new boyfriend but
was home now, having given him the push. 'He's got
some very nasty habits,' she told Eva in a letter, and
it was plain to see the relationship would not last
much longer.

All day Patsy had been hopping about with
excitement, and now, when the doorbell rang, she
ushered Tommy and Fred out of the room. 'We're
off to the pub for a pint,' she told Eva. 'You'll be all
right with your friend till we get back, so ye will.'

As she answered the door, she instructed Tommy and Fred just to say hello and then to be on their way, and that was what they did, Fred with a wink and a nod and the advice, 'Go easy on her, mate. She's been to hell and back.'

Looking lean and fit in dark trousers and a pale blue shirt open at the neck, Bill promised he would take good care of her. Addressing Patsy, he asked, 'Does she know it's me who's come to see her?'

Patsy shook her head. 'I haven't told her. To be honest, when I wrote to the solicitors I never thought anything would come of it, but then when I heard from you, I knew it was meant to be.'

He looked down the passage. 'I think it's time I said hello, don't you?'

'Go on then, and God go with ye.'

With a pounding heart, he went inside and softly closed the door. As he went on hesitant footsteps towards the sitting room, he was actually trembling. He had waited so long for this moment and now that it was here, he felt desperately afraid.

Eva was in the kitchen putting the kettle on when he came into the room. 'I won't be a minute, Olive,' she called out. 'I'm just making us a pot of tea.'

The sound of her voice was like heaven to him. For one precious moment he stood quite still, eyes closed, thanking the good Lord for bringing them together again.

'Sit yourself down,' Eva was saying.

Quietly now, he went to the kitchen door, and there he stood, unobserved, watching her as she busied herself making the tea. She still looked the same, he thought wonderingly; somewhat thinner, but that was understandable after what she'd been through, but still incredibly lovely, with the same long, corn-coloured hair. As she swung round to stare at him, he saw those wonderful wide green eyes and his heart turned over.

'Hello, my love.' The tears welled in his eyes and he could hardly see her. The fear rose again. Would she want him? Would she turn away? Dear God, don't let her turn away.

Eva felt as though she'd seen a ghost. She wanted to go to him, but she couldn't. It was as if a great hand was holding her back. As she stared at him, she shook her head from side to side, the tears rolling down her face. 'Bill, oh . . . it really is you,' and in that wonderful moment he took her in his arms.

'I've loved you for so long,' he whispered, and her joy was like a great tide, washing away all the pain of those long years.

With his arms round her, she felt safe. For the first time since they had parted a lifetime ago, she felt as though, at last, she had come home.

Chapter Nineteen

THREE MONTHS LATER, after much legal hassle, during which they justifiably secured their freedom from their respective partners, Eva and Bill were married. It was a quiet affair, in a small, local church, and attended only by Patsy's family, Olive, and Maggie.

It was a beautiful late-October day, with the sun shining, and only a light breeze blowing. Eva looked lovely in a pastel-blue two-piece. Patsy was wearing a cream dress with bolero jacket, Fred was choking in the high-necked shirt Patsy had made him wear, and Tommy looked very grown-up in his new suit.

Bill was just Bill, standing beside the woman he loved, feeling as though his every dream had come true. He could think of nothing he had wanted more in the whole of his life than this day – himself and Eva being married. God had been good to him. Eva felt the same, and even now Bill hardly dared believe it.

Eva had wanted a small, intimate reception,

and everyone had a wonderful time – except Fred who copped it in the neck from Patsy for drinking too much.

Afterwards, they said their goodbyes. 'Mind you write now, and phone me the minute you get there.' Patsy had cried all morning, but now she was full of smiles. 'Ah, sure, you'll have a wonderful life, me darlin',' she said brokenly. 'And I'm that happy for ye, so I am.'

They hugged, and for a precious moment or two, Eva and Patsy stood aside. 'I'll never forget what you did for me,' Eva told her. 'I do love you, Patsy.'

They cried, and held each other, and Eva told her she would never be far away. 'Go on with ye now,' Patsy shoved her into Bill's waiting arms, 'before you have me blubbering all over again.'

As they drove away, Eva waved out of the window. In her heart she would always carry the picture of them standing there. Patsy dabbing her face with a handkerchief; Fred looking emotional and shuffling his feet from side to side; and Tommy, that scruffy little Tommy, now tall and fine, and every inch a man in the making. She loved them all.

As she looked, Bill reached out to hold her hand. 'They'll be all right,' he promised. 'We'll look after them, my love.' And she knew he would.

'How long will it take us to get to the airport?'

'We're making a detour.'

'Oh? Where are we going?'

'You'll see. But it's a long drive, so maybe you should get some sleep.'

She looked at him, at this man who was her husband, and her heart swelled with love. Just now, when she asked where they were going, she was certain he had a quiet, secretive smile on his handsome face. 'Are you up to something?' she asked laughingly.

'I might be.'

'But you won't tell me, will you?'

'Nope.'

'I might as well get some sleep then.'

He gave her a sideways grin. 'Good idea.'

———⟡———

THEY STOPPED ON the way for refreshments and to stretch their legs. In the cafe, they sat hand in hand.

'I bet they've just got married,' said one waitress to another.

'How can you tell?'

'Don't be daft, anyone can see that,' she replied. 'I mean, they've let their teas go cold for a start!'

Eva was asleep when they got to their destination. When Bill woke her, she looked out and her heart leaped. 'It's the old farm!' she cried, scrambling out of the car. 'Oh, Bill! You didn't forget, after all.' She had mentioned to him that she would like to see the old place and visit her parents one last time before leaving the country, and here they were.

They stood for a moment, surveying the magnificent landscape. 'I've kept something to show you,' Bill said and, reaching into his wallet, took out the photograph of her mother. 'I found this on the floor of the cottage, many years ago.' He put it in her hand.

Eva caressed the photograph, and wept. 'It was me who burned the cottage down,' she confessed.

'I know.'

'What else do you know?'

'Only that I love you.'

On tiptoe she kissed him.

The sight of what remained of the house, slowly being reclaimed by nature, brought more tears. Walking to where the old range used to be, she tenderly laid her mother's charred photograph on the place. 'It belongs here,' she said, covering it over. 'She loved this place. I don't need my mother's picture to remember her. I'll always have her here.' She pointed to her heart. Then she wiped her tears and suggested brightly, 'Let's go and see the barn.'

Astonishingly, though sagging dangerously, the old barn still stood. They went inside.

'The farm is yours now, Eva. Father went broke

last year, and everything went to auction. I bought this for you, to do with as you like.'

Eva was thrilled. She went outside to look across the meadows; all around, the hills seemed to embrace and protect them. 'Let it stay just like it is now,' she said. 'Let no one ever touch it.' And so it was decided.

━━━━━➤◆◄━━━━━

HAVING BEEN TOLD by Sheila that she was going on holiday, Bill became concerned when she didn't get in touch. He found her, too late, in the hospital, where he learned to his horror that she did not have long to live. Shocked and saddened, he wanted to take her home and be with her, but she dissuaded him. Sheila had so much to confess, and what she revealed was bitter-sweet to him.

She told him he was her son, and that when his father was killed she was forced to give him and his sister up. It was a terrible thing for her to have lived with all these years . . . being so close to him yet not daring to tell him in case he turned her away. Now though, at long last, she knew how much he loved her, and her joy was complete.

Sheila died a contented soul, her hand clasped in that of her son, and her eyes shining with a mother's love.

Bill had been broken-hearted, but he consoled himself with the knowledge that at least he had known the truth, and been able to reassure her. It gave him great comfort.

Frank was never released from hospital.

Poorer but wiser, Peter Westerfield and his son returned to England. Bill's mother went with them. 'It's where I belong,' she said, but Bill kept a close eye on her all the same.

Eva and Bill made their home in the Rockies. Wherever they went in the world, they always came home to Whistler.

They lived a long and happy life, and were blessed with three children, two sons who made them proud, but first a delightful daughter who fell in love with Tommy. Despite the difference in their ages they made a perfect couple and gave Eva and Bill four beautiful grandchildren.

Patsy lost her baby, due to 'trauma and age', the doctor said. Patsy told him he was talking out of his arse. 'I'm still a young woman!' and he knew better than to argue. In truth, Patsy had always believed she was too far past her prime to be a mother. She had never learned to be patient, and a baby would have tried her to the limit.

But she enjoyed being a grandmother, and spoiled the children rotten. 'Sure, you're the apple of yer granny's eye,' she used to say, and they loved her dearly, just as they loved Eva, the quieter one; the one who told them of their great-grandmother, Colette, and of their colourful history.

Eva's wishes for the old farm were written into that history. As it passed down through the generations to follow, it was known as 'Eva's Meadow'.

Through all the years to follow, Eva Bereton was never forgotten.

Headline hopes you have enjoyed reading LOVE ME OR LEAVE ME and invites you to sample the beginning of Josephine Cox's compelling new saga, TOMORROW THE WORLD, out soon in Headline hardback . . .

Chapter One

'Are you afraid of me?'

'Never!'

'Then trust me?'

A charming, confident fellow, Peter Doyle had the mistaken idea that every woman in the world fancied him. 'The snow's coming down heavy,' he told Bridget. 'You'll never get through on foot.' He'd had his eye on Bridget ever since she came to work at Weatherfield Grange. 'I insist on taking you home.'

'No, thank you, sir.' Wise beyond her years, Bridget always felt nervous in his presence.

'You *are* afraid of me!' His smile was wonderful, but he had a certain naughty gleam in his eye, and – judging from the way he moved his hand inside his trousers – a rising bulge that would not be contained. But then, she always did that to him and, besides, it was a long time since his wife had shown him any favours. Consequently, a man had to get his pleasures wherever he could.

As a rule he had no difficulty in persuading even the shyest of creatures into his bed. But Bridget

Mulligan was not like the others; at only twenty years of age, she was delightfully fresh and different. It was no wonder he wanted her but, as yet, he had not managed to worm his way into her affections . . . or her bed, more was the pity! Still, he promised himself slyly, there was time enough yet. And he was known to be a patient man.

'It's very kind of you, sir,' Bridget answered. 'But I don't need to put you to any trouble, because my father's collecting me any minute now.'

'Really, my dear?' Suspicious, he scrutinised her pretty features. 'I wasn't aware of that. When did you manage to get word to him?'

'It's a standing arrangement.' When needs must, Bridget lied beautifully. 'Dad's always told me that if it snows, like today, I'm to wait for him at the gate . . . and I must not accept a ride home from anyone else.' She blushed deepest pink, her face shining like a beacon, hot and aflame. 'So, I'd best be on my way . . . thanks all the same, sir.'

'Your father's right, my dear,' he grudgingly conceded. 'Not to accept a ride from anyone . . . yes, quite right!' Secretly, he thought it was downright wicked . . . especially when he could have been giving her the best 'ride' of her life.

'I'm sorry, sir. You don't mind, do you?' She was suitably apologetic, but, seeing how frustrated he was, Bridget felt the urge to giggle.

'Of course I don't mind!' Damn her eyes! he

cursed, and damn her father with her! For what seemed an age he stared at her; the smile frozen to his face like a mask, and his trousers straining to burst right open.

When she nervously returned his smile, he gave a shrug, a little laugh, then turned abruptly and was out of the room before she realised. 'Good shuts!' she giggled, relieved that he'd given up. 'Randy old bugger, I know what you're after, but you can whistle in the wind till kingdom come, for all you'll get from me.'

She was still smiling as she fought her way down the back path to the servants' gate. Once outside, though, she was shocked to see how the weather had deteriorated since midday. Now, at half past six of an evening, the wind was sharp and bitter-cold. The snow fell out of the skies with a vengeance, settling soft and thick on the ground.

Wild and spiteful, the night air cut through her clothes, like a knife through butter. 'By! It's bloody freezing!' Drawing her coat tighter about her, she glanced back to the house; warm and cosy, the lights blazed a path through the night. 'Happen I should have let him take me home after all.' Thinking of his disappointed face made her smile. In truth, she would rather run naked in a storm than let a man like Peter Doyle have his way.

Coming to the gate in a hurry, she lost her footing and slid over. 'Damn and bugger it!' Now she was wet to the bone, her boots letting the snow in, and her hooded-coat no match for the driving cold. And, to make matters worse, as she tried to struggle up she realised with a sinking heart that she had turned her ankle.

Taking stock of her situation, she realised she had two options. She could either bear the discomfort of her ankle and press ahead, or she could try and get back to the house.

A pleasant thought struck her.

If she was to go back to the house, *Harry* might be there. But, no, she remembered . . . Harry wasn't back from Manchester yet. She knew that, because she'd been watching for him all day. It was strange how she missed him whenever he was away.

Feeling ashamed, she chastised herself. 'Bridget Mulligan, shame on you! Here you are . . . thinking pleasant things of Harry, and you a married woman these past four months.' She had no right even *looking* at another man, let alone missing him. Not when she had a loving husband like Tom.

'Aw, well!' Brushing herself off, she sighed, 'I'm not going back to the house, not with the squire after me at every turn, and I don't mean to sit here and freeze to death.' Foolish though she knew it was, her mind was made up. 'There's nothing else for it,' she reluctantly decided, 'I'll have to go on.'

As she struggled on, Bridget was afraid she might fall down some deep ditch and be lost for ever. With the landmarks rapidly disappearing beneath a mountain of snow, it was becoming increasingly difficult to keep to the lane. 'The squire was right after all,' she groaned, her teeth chattering uncontrollably. 'Though I would never give him the satisfaction of telling him so.'

With the wind howling and the snow lashing down, Bridget didn't hear the cart coming up behind her.

'Woa, boy!' Catching sight of the small, forlorn figure in front, Harry Little drew back on the reins. 'Easy there . . . woa!'

A strong young man in his early twenties, Harry had no trouble bringing the horse to a halt. Dropping the reins, he leaped from the cart and hurried forward. By the time he reached her, Bridget had turned to face him, curious to see who it was that had drawn up behind her.

'Bridget!' Harry was astonished. 'What the devil are you doing out in this weather?' He was angry, but that was nothing new. Bridget had a way of making him angry; mostly because she was married to someone else.

Relieved, and utterly exhausted, Bridget fell into his arms. 'Harry! Oh, Harry, you don't know how glad I am to see you.'

'Don't you worry, sweetheart,' he told her. 'I'll get you home.'

'I know you will.' Harry had a habit of calling her sweetheart. Tom never did, and that was a shame because when Harry called her sweetheart it made her feel warm all over. But then, Harry and Tom were like chalk and cheese. Harry was twenty-two, and Tom was only four years older, but there was a world of difference between them. Harry was full of life, always smiling and happy, while Tom took life too seriously, rarely smiling, and always looking for the next problem.

Conversely, the thought of Tom was strangely reassuring. Bridget did love him, she told herself. In fact, she told herself that time and again, as though wanting to believe it. Somehow it helped her through the long, lonely days.

Miss You Forever

THANK YOU, HILARY.

Some time ago, my friend Hilary Joel told me about
an old woman who was found wandering the streets.
She died in hospital alone, a pauper. Sadly, the
authorities were unable to trace any friends or relatives.

Try as I might, I could not get the old woman out of
my mind. Imagine being all alone in the world, with
no one to care whether you lived or died.

In my imagination, I began to weave a story around
her.

The woman is Kathleen.

This is her story.

CONTENTS

PART ONE

1912
THE OLD
WOMAN'S TALE

Chapter One

'GO ON, YOU old hag. Get back to the slums where you belong!'

The taunts rang in Kathleen's ears. Tripping and stumbling over the cobbles, she hurried away, wincing beneath the onslaught of abuse and objects that followed her.

'You'd better run, old woman.' The jeers were merciless. 'If you're not out of sight in two minutes, we'll set the dogs on you.' As if to endorse the threat, the two bull mastiffs growled threateningly, straining at their leashes, mouths dripping saliva at the thought of sinking their fangs into her soft, ancient flesh.

'What you got in that bag, then, eh?'

'Huh! Crown jewels I shouldn't wonder, by the way she's clutching it.'

The dogs went crazy to be loosed. 'They fancy that scraggy mongrel of hers for dinner,' someone yelled, and they fell about laughing.

As she fled, Kathleen prayed the thugs would not carry out their threat. She knew the danger, for they were no different from many others who had made fun of her along the way.

The old woman had lost count of the times when she'd been jeered at, spat at, laughed at, or chased away at the sharp end of a pitchfork. People were wary of newcomers, especially 'newcomers' with no fixed abode or means of earning a living. Generally, they tended to pour scorn and contempt on such as Kathleen. Being made unwelcome was something she had learned to live with. There were times when she met with kindness and compassion, but these occasions were few and far between.

Too old and too tired to run any more, she yearned to put down roots, but with each passing year the prospect grew more unlikely.

In her lonely treks Kathleen Peterson had travelled the length and breadth of Britain. She had tramped across the green fields of the Emerald Isle and climbed the hills of Scotland. She had stayed in the Welsh valleys, travelled every nook and cranny of England, but her heart always brought her back to her native Blackburn.

Yet Kathleen had neither home nor family, no one who would miss her if she never returned. Her life was in the diaries she so jealously guarded, and in the mangy old dog she had found snuggling up to her when she awoke in an alley one cold February morning.

He was a dolly mixture of black and brown, with a long, meandering splash of white down his nose, and a speckle of grey round his whiskers. He had one black ear that had been broken in a fight and hung sadly over his head like an eye-patch, while the other ear remained upright and finely tuned to every sound. He reminded Kathleen of an old man she had known as a child; he, too, had had a black eye-patch and grey speckled whiskers that twitched when he talked. His name was Mr Potts. 'What else can I call you?' she had asked the dog, and so he was given the old man's name.

The two of them became fast friends. They made a comical sight as they walked the streets, Kathleen in her dark shawl and boots, with a threadbare tapestry bag over her arm and her long grey hair in thick plaits that reached down to her waist, and the odd Mr Potts, head cocked to one side as he peered from under one ear, his body so close to her heels as they went that he might have been attached.

Having been on the road since first light, Kathleen had arrived in Liverpool. She had fourpence in her purse, earned from sweeping an undertaker's yard in Sheffield. She was hungry and cold, and, having consulted with the wise old Mr Potts, had decided that Liverpool was as good a place as any to stay awhile. 'The market should be opening soon,' she explained. 'With a bit of luck we might go away with a bag of sweet potatoes.' She hadn't tasted a sweet potato in ages and her mouth watered at the prospect.

'Are you still 'ere, old woman? I thought we told you to piss off!' The four thugs who had taunted her earlier had followed her to the docks. 'What'ya got in yer bag, eh?'

Kathleen didn't have to look round. She recognised the voice. 'Come on, Mr Potts,' she urged. 'Let's be off, before they come after us.'

In spite of her scruffy, neglected appearance, the old woman spoke in a soft, genteel tone that might have shocked the rough crowd who saw her only as an object of derision. Like many others who had never taken the trouble to know her, they would have been astonished to learn that Kathleen Peterson, the unkempt and aged vagabond who tramped the roads and carried all her worldly possessions in a grubby tapestry bag, was once a fine, respected lady.

Gasping and exhausted, she came to a busier part of the docklands. Here, men hurried at their labours, talking, shouting and whistling, great ships waited to be loaded and offloaded, trolleys were pushed back and forth and there was an air of hustle and bustle. One of the men, catching sight of her, touched his cap and bade her a cheery 'Morning, luv.'

Kathleen turned nervously, wondering if her pursuers were following. They were, and her heart sank. If only she was younger, stronger, she might give them a run for their money.

The man paused in his work. He had seen the fear in her eyes and noticed how the thugs hovered a short distance away. He bristled. 'Bothering you, are they, luv?' When she nodded, he walked away, spoke to a mate, and together they approached the four thugs. On seeing the burly dockers, Kathleen's pursuers made off like the curs they were.

'They'll not bother you any more,' the man promised. 'Where are you headed, luv?'

'Nowhere in particular.'

He regarded her with concern. There was an air of dignity about the old woman that startled him. Her smile was bewitching, and her dark brown eyes were arresting, deep and troubled yet filled with the brightness of a summer's day. He bent to stroke the dog, who backed away. 'Not very friendly, is he?'

'He's hungry, that's all.' Kathleen fussed Mr Potts, and he sidled up to the docker, his tail wagging.

The docker laughed, ruffling the dog's ears. 'Pity he's not fierce though,' he commented, 'or them devils might not have been so keen to tail you, eh?' Mr Potts rubbed so hard against him he nearly lost his balance. 'By! He's a funny-looking dog an' no mistake.'

Kathleen laughed. 'That's because he's not a dog,' she joked. 'He's an old man in disguise.'

'You ought to be more careful, lady,' the docker warned. 'This area is known for thuggery and such. Anyway, what brings you out on a cold January morning? I should have thought you'd be tucked up in yer bed.' The old woman was cold, he could see. With only a thin skirt and a ragged old jumper covered by a shawl, she was trembling. She and the cur were both pitifully thin, he noticed.

Kathleen's answer shamed him. In a soft, genteel tone that shocked him, she explained, 'Some of us don't have a bed to tuck up in.'

'I'm sorry,' he murmured, digging in his pocket

7

and taking out a coin. 'It's all I've got on me,' he apologised, 'but yer welcome to it.'

Putting up her hand she smiled. 'I don't want your hard-earned money. You've been kind enough. I'm very grateful, but now we'd best be on our way.' She turned, heading away from the docks.

'Wait a minute!' With her soft smile and independent manner, she reminded him of his old mother, though the old dear had been rough and ready to look at, with a cavernous mouth and kind, wrinkled eyes, while this old lady had clear, striking eyes and a set of teeth that would put a younger woman to shame. 'Where will you go?' he asked.

'Here and there.' Experience had taught her to be careful with strangers. Even with the kind ones.

Heading towards the old cobbled square where she knew the market was held every Saturday, Kathleen took a detour which brought them into a back alley. 'Might as well find a warm place to have our breakfast,' she said, peering into the back yards as she passed the tiny terraced houses. 'Folks are still abed,' she noticed, looking up at the bedroom windows and seeing how the curtains were still tightly drawn. 'It's Saturday,' she muttered with a little smile. 'Hard-working folk deserve a lie-in, and who can blame them?' Still wary of the thugs who had threatened her, she glanced nervously behind. 'Looks like we've lost the devils,' she smiled. 'We'll be safe enough now.'

One of the yards was open. Its tall, wooden gate was split from top to bottom and hung from its hinges as though it might have been ripped off by some marauding drunk. From the house could be heard raised and angry voices.

'As long as they don't come out for a bucket of coal, we should be safe enough,' Kathleen decided, with a wry little smile. 'Be quiet and no one will be any the wiser,' she said, wagging a finger at the mongrel. She noticed the coal-hole door was ajar. Cautiously, she went inside; it was dark and cold, but not as cold as the street outside. 'Seems cosy enough,' she remarked. 'I'm sure no one would mind if we made ourselves comfortable for a while. And we can finish off the last of that pie, before it goes sour on us.'

Finding an old sack lying on the ground, she took it out and shook it, sending the black dust flying through the air. Then she laid it in a clean corner of the coal cellar and sat herself down, with the dog at her feet as always. As the cold struck through her thin skirt, she shivered. 'It's a hard life, Mr Potts,' she sighed.

Waiting for any little titbit she might have for him, Mr Potts sat on his bony haunches, eyes bright and ear cocked, intently listening to every word the old woman uttered.

'It's not like it used to be, is it?' the old woman pondered softly. 'There was a time when you could walk the streets and be safe, when you could pass the time of day and not be afraid somebody might snatch your bag or run you through when your back was turned.' She chuckled. 'It doesn't matter to you though. All you're concerned about is having a full belly and a warm place to lay your head, and nobody can blame you for that, can they, eh?'

Her kind brown eyes misted over, her voice falling to a whisper. 'As for me, what does it matter? Who is there left to care about a silly old fool like me?' She gave a sad little grunt. 'Nobody, that's who. Never mind,' she remarked wisely; she was not one to dwell on the downside of life. 'When the time comes, we can say that we were here, and we made a difference. In the end, that's all that counts.'

Smiling into the dog's eyes, she cradled his hairy face between her two hands. 'You might be a funny-looking thing, and you might have very little to say for yourself, but you've been a friend to me, and I'm grateful for that.'

Impatient now, the mongrel began to whimper, scratching at her with his paw.

She rummaged in her bag. 'Let's see what old Kathleen's got for you.' Laughing, she confessed shamefully, 'I weren't the only one watching the butcher throw his leftovers away. I'll have you know I fought off a hungry cat for this particular juicy bit, though in the end I couldn't see the cat starve and gave him a piece. So, you see, your dinner isn't as big as it might have been. Mind you eat it slowly,' she cautioned, taking out a muslin cloth and opening it to reveal a half-eaten meat pie. 'It might be all we get between now and tomorrow morning.'

The dog enjoyed his titbit. Kathleen was delighted to find another treat skulking in the bottom of her bag; the fat muffin had been given to her by a grateful woman whose purse she had retrieved from the pavement only yesterday. 'I'd forgotten all about that,' she said with a laugh. 'I must be going senile.'

She shared the muffin, and afterwards took a drink from a small stone jar. 'There's nothing better than a drop of cider to finish off a meal,' she declared, licking her lips in appreciation.

From somewhere in the distance, a clock chimed the sixth hour. 'Too early for the market yet. We'll be all right here for another hour. By then the traders will be set up and the ground rolling with fruit and veg that's fallen from the barrows.' It might be bruised and battered, but it was good enough for the two of them, she thought.

The light from the house shone into the coal hole. 'I think I'll write for a while,' she murmured. 'Lord knows it's been a curious day.' From her bag she took out a pen and a small exercise book. In the half-light she could see well enough, though not without squinting.

Using her bag as a desk, she opened the book and began to write in fine, meticulous lettering.

KATHLEEN PETERSON
SATURDAY THE 12TH JANUARY,
IN THE YEAR OF OUR LORD, 1912.

Another year, another journey. Another day, another trial.

I've travelled a long way since Christmas, and now find myself here, in Liverpool. This time, God willing, I plan to stay.

Maybe here I will find a measure of peace, a way to forget. A way to leave it all behind and never think of it again.

Oh, if only I could, if only it were possible . . .

Overwhelmed by a surge of emotion, she could not go on. Instead she sat a while, head back and eyes closed, while the past came again to haunt her.

Kathleen could not say when it all began to go wrong. There had been times when life was good, and times when she despaired. She had known love and laughter, and sadness of a kind that would stay with her until her dying day. Once, a lifetime ago, she had a promising future, a family, and reason to hope.

Now, it was all gone, and she was reduced to foraging for a living. Yet she still had her pride. She mended her clothes and washed them in the brook. She bathed in the stream, combed her hair into tidy plaits and retained a semblance of dignity. When there was work she took it, and when there was not, she lived off the land. She never begged and took no favours, and always believed that something better would come along; that somehow, life would get easier.

But it never did, and with each passing day she grew older and more weary. Her bones ached in the winter, and her skin burned in the summer. At the end of a particularly bad day, her feet might be blistered and her spirit close to being crushed, but Kathleen didn't complain. What was the use of that?

She gave a long, withering sigh, opened her eyes and stared at the page before her. 'So much to tell,' she murmured, 'and no one to listen.' Memories swamped her. So many. Too many.

She placed the pen between the pages, then closed the book, and carefully returned it to her bag. 'My old eyes aren't what they used to be,' she whispered, 'I'll wait till the light's better.'

In the house the row continued. 'Somebody's certainly got a temper,' she commented. 'Hope they leave us be.' Undaunted by the raging voices, she slid down and crossed her arms over her precious tapestry bag. 'I'll just close my eyes for a minute.'

This was always a sign she was settling to sleep. The dog knew it, and normally when she closed her eyes he would curl down beside her. But not this time. This time he remained wary, one ear cocked and a low, hostile growl issuing from his throat.

The old woman didn't hear it, for she was already asleep, warmed by the cider, and dreaming dreams of long ago.

While she slept, the four thugs crept up on her.

'The old hag's asleep,' the ringleader hissed.

'With no interfering docker to save her this time,' chuckled another. 'Let's get a look inside that precious bag of 'ers.'

INSIDE THE HOUSE, Rosie was being subjected to the same old threats and bickering that had peppered her marriage from day one. 'You're always the bloody same! What does a man have to do to get his rights? It's been three days since you let me get anywhere near you. What's the sodding excuse now, eh? Have I to knock you down and help meself?' The man paused, his grip tightening on her arms and making her squirm. 'If it's roughing up you want, why don't you bloody well say so?'

'If you forced yourself on me, you might live to regret it.' She realised the burst of defiance might cost her dearly.

She wasn't wrong.

Without warning, he raised his fist and knocked her to the ground. 'Sod you!' He stood over her, eyes blazing. 'Now are you satisfied? Can you see what you're doing to me?'

Rosie Maitland was a small, pretty woman, with a soft heart and caring ways, while her husband Jake was a big brawny fellow. In his own selfish way he loved her, but he was possessed of a terrible jealousy and a hard, spiteful nature. When roused to anger, like now, he made a formidable sight.

He stared down on her, his face twitching with emotion. 'I provide for you, don't I?' he demanded. 'I pay the bills and keep everything straight. I never refuse if you want something for the house, and I work bloody hard, don't I?'

When she didn't answer immediately he gave her

a nudge with his boot and raised his voice. 'I said, I take care of everything, don't I? I never deny you anything reasonable. ISN'T THAT SO, WOMAN?'

In that moment, Rosie hated him. 'No, you never deny me anything.' He never denied her anything, as long as it met with his approval, she thought bitterly. But he denied her the things she craved, like the smallest measure of independence, pretty clothes and the friendship of other women. Oh, she had friends at the charity hospital where she worked but she was not allowed to have anyone back to this house – the house she worked to furnish and maintain; and if she didn't immediately tip her wage packet up the minute she came through the door on a Friday night, there was hell to pay.

A terrible look of suspicion came into his eyes. 'You're not cheating on me, are you?' he hissed. 'Because if you are, I swear to God I'll swing for the pair of you.'

Her soft, honest voice made him feel ashamed. 'You can trust me, Jake. You know I would never cheat on you.' The defiance had gone and in its place was a degree of resignation. But the hatred remained. The hatred always remained.

Astonishingly, his manner changed. Reaching down, he took her in his arms and held her close. 'I don't mean to be hurtful,' he apologised, nuzzling her neck. 'But you shouldn't deny me my rights. It drives me crazy.'

She tried not to cringe from his touch. 'Tonight,'

she promised. 'I'll be feeling better by then.' Anything to appease him.

'Why not now?' He licked her mouth with the tip of his tongue.

'No, Jake. Tonight.' She looked at the mantelpiece clock. 'You'd better go or you'll be late for work.' A tough, unforgiving foreman, Jake was one of the most despised men on the docks.

Squeezing her face between his rough hands, he whispered into her mouth, 'God! I wish I didn't love you so much!' Then he kissed her abruptly, grabbed his coat and strode out into the yard, and straight into the ruffians. 'Hey! What the hell's going on out here?'

The thugs might have stayed and fought, but one look at this big, powerful man with a face as dark as thunder and fists the size of hammers and they were off in a rush, over the wall and down the alley.

'You thievin' buggers!' Jake yelled after them. 'I know yer faces. I'll be looking out for yer!'

Rosie ran to the door. 'What is it? What's going on?'

He returned to give her a parting kiss, so hard and demanding it bruised her lips.

'Nothing for you to worry about,' he told her. 'A few louts prowling about, but they'll not be back, I can promise you that.'

'What did they want?'

'Whatever they could lay their hands on, I expect.'

'But there's nothing in the yard worth stealing.'

'There you are then. Like I said, nothing for you

to worry about.' He held her for a moment. 'Don't forget what you promised,' he whispered fondly. 'I'll be looking forward to it.'

'You'd best hurry,' she said, drawing away. 'You know how you like to start the shift before anybody else.' He insisted on being there first, to see the men arrive, to glare at them and make certain they would be penalised if they were even half a minute late. He liked it when they were late. It justified his existence.

'Till tonight then, me little beauty.' A quick, spiteful tweak of her breast, and he went off to his work, whistling merrily.

Inside the coal hole the old woman lay unconscious, her faithful friend lying beside her, his head bleeding. Only the occasional flickering of one eye gave a small sign that there might still be life.

As the old woman regained her senses, she called out for him. There was no reply; no familiar whimpering or nuzzling of a wet nose against her. Only a terrible stillness, a silence that was frightening.

As Rosie turned to go back into the kitchen, she thought she heard a noise. Swinging round, she called nervously, 'Who's there?' Indignant now, she warned, 'You'd better clear off! The police are on their way.' Rosie waited and listened. There were no more sounds. 'I must be hearing things,' she snorted.

She was just about to close the door when she heard it again, a soft, agonised moan. Aware that one of the ruffians might still be lurking, she took up a heavy shovel and went cautiously towards the coal hole. She found the old woman crouched over the dog. 'Mr Potts, it's all right, I'm here . . .' The old woman's voice trembled with fear. A sob catching her words, she turned her eyes to Rosie. 'They've hurt him,' she croaked. 'They've hurt my dog.'

Horrified, Rosie dropped the shovel and ran to her. 'Dear God!' Gently, she helped the old woman into a sitting position, shocked when her hands were warmed with blood. 'Oh! You're hurt too.'

In the half-light the old woman stared up at her with surprised brown eyes. 'Help him,' she whispered.

Rosie followed the old woman's troubled gaze. She feared the mongrel was past all help. 'I'll see to him,' she promised, 'but you mustn't try to move any more. I need to go for help, but I won't be long, trust me.'

<hr />

THOUGH RETIRED FROM work these many years, Bill Soames was strong as an ox and had a heart of gold. He and his good wife Amy were the best of neighbours. 'Course I'll help,' he said, on answering the door to a frantic Rosie. 'You're the nurse. Just tell me what to do.'

It took only a minute for Rosie to explain what had to be done, and while she ran back to the old woman, he brought his old flat-cart round to the alley. 'She's badly hurt,' Rosie warned. 'You take her weight while I keep her still. Gently now.'

Together they carried the old woman outside where they wrapped her in one of Rosie's blankets and made sure she was safe for travelling. 'I'll stay with her,' Rosie said. 'You'll have to take it slow, Bill. Go by way of the canal, that way we'll avoid the cobbled roads.'

Bill's wife stayed behind to close up the house and keep an eye on the sorry Mr Potts. 'Poor little devil,' she murmured, stroking his soft fur. 'What kind of monsters did this? Attacking an old woman and killing her dog? They should be hanged.'

When Mr Potts seemed to sigh, she drew back, astonished. 'Lord above! I thought you were done for. You must be tougher than you look. Like the old woman, eh?' Delighted that he still drew breath, Amy took it upon herself to tend Kathleen's brave little friend.

———◦◦◦———

THE RUFFIANS WERE never found, and after eight long days it was still touch and go whether the old woman would survive the vicious attack. She had lost consciousness on the way to hospital and remained in a coma.

Rosie worked long hours to watch over her. She sat by her bedside and talked to her as though Kathleen could hear. She described the weather, and she read from the pages of the newspapers; she sang softly, and picked out the humorous incidents at the hospital in an effort to amuse Kathleen. But it was all to no avail. Kathleen slept on. And with every day that passed, it seemed the old woman's life was disappearing with it.

The ward was quiet now. Beyond the curtain the sky was darkening into evening. Above the door, the big round clock rhythmically ticked away the seventh hour.

Rosie arrived to take over the shift. This was her favourite time. Behind her she left a husband whose appetite to satisfy himself on her was insatiable and obnoxious, while here in this place there were people who valued her, people who trusted her. It was a good feeling.

Taking off her coat, she made her way along the ward, checking that everything was as it should be. That done, she hurried towards the far end of the ward where the doctor and the other ward nurse were in discussion by the old woman's bed.

'In a way it might be a blessing if she goes,' Dr Naylor remarked as she approached. A kind old gent, disillusioned with the way things were, he had developed his own philosophy. 'She doesn't appear to have any family, and she's old and apparently homeless.' He sighed from his boots.

Leaning forward he gently prised open her eyelids. 'She won't last long in my opinion. It's a pity, I know, but there's nothing more we can do.' He looked at the old woman's face. 'Amazing what a bit of soap and water will do, don't you think?' he asked softly. 'When she was brought in she looked like any other old vagabond, but now . . . Well, I mean, she has a certain, oh, I don't know . . . a kind of gracious beauty – the look of a lady.' He laughed at his own ramblings.

'Who knows, she might be worth a fortune, and here she is, ending her days in a charity ward.'

'She does have a fine face, doesn't she?' Rosie agreed. It was a good face, with strong features, high cheekbones and a full, plump mouth. The eyes were closed, but the long dark lashes and gently arched brows gave the impression of vitality beneath.

When she was brought in her hair had been covered in coal dust and her hands were blue with cold, but now, with the long grey hair combed into deep, shining waves about her shoulders, and her slim hands stretched out on the blanket, Kathleen had the look of a woman who had been a real beauty in her time. 'How old do you think she is?' Rosie asked, intrigued.

Dr Naylor shrugged. 'It's hard to say. She may have been living rough for some time, and such a life will age a person. But her skin is surprisingly good, and her hair has a remarkable sheen.' He picked up one of her hands. 'See here, how firm and clean her nails are? Whoever she is, and however she came to be a vagabond, this lady took great care of herself. Normally we find months of dirt ingrained in the nails, and the same beneath the breasts; the feet, too, are usually diseased, but not this woman's.' He laughed softly. 'She has healthier feet than I have, and God knows how many miles she may have trudged along the roads.'

'How old though?' Something about the old woman had stirred Rosie's heart.

He shook his head. 'She could be in her late fifties, early sixties. Like I say, it's difficult to be precise.'

'I wonder if she has a family somewhere.'

'Who knows? We're not paid to do detective work, my dear. We're here to mend bodies if they can be mended. She received a vicious battering. I believe she may go in her sleep, and that would be a merciful thing. I suspect it won't be too long before we have the use of her bed.' With those words, he moved on to the next patient.

As Rosie considered his harsh comments, her colleague stepped forward. 'Ain't no good dwelling on it.' A scrawny creature with a dark scraping of hair beneath her white cap, Nell Salter had a thin, whining voice that made cats want to mate.

Rosie didn't answer.

'That old woman's been here over a week,' Nell persisted. 'The doctor's right. There's nothing else we can do for her, and you can't deny we do need the bed.'

Drawing her aside, Rosie was sharp. 'That "old woman" is a charity case, and this a charity hospital. It's gentry with consciences who keep this place open,' she reminded Nell. 'Spoiled gentry with fat wallets and purses, who make themselves feel good by helping the less fortunate. Not one of them has ever shown their face through these doors. They have no idea of the terrible things we see here, and by and large they don't want to know. But I'll tell you this, Nell Salter, for all their privilege and arrogance, I don't believe there's a single one of them who would want to see this old woman thrown out to die on the streets.'

Feeling aggrieved and inadequate, Rosie was hitting out at everything and everybody. She was incensed by Nell's casual attitude. Here was a woman who had taken on the responsibilities of nursing yet was incapable of administering a few kind words to those in her care. Most of all, Rosie was hitting out at the way things were between her and Jake. Life was a bag of tricks, and whatever trials it set her, she was never ready. Maybe it's me, she thought bitterly. Maybe I'm the one at fault and everyone else is right. It wasn't the first time she'd questioned her place in the order of things. No doubt it would not be the last either.

'I know the old dear is gravely ill,' she said to Nell, 'and I know we've done all we can, but she's strong and might just surprise us all – if you and the good doctor aren't too hasty in writing her off!'

'Whoa! Don't go mad at me.' Nell was taken aback by the outburst. Usually Rosie was quiet enough. It was true she cared more than most, even at times being reduced to tears, especially if the patient was an infant. But to see her fly off the handle like this was something altogether new. 'Don't take it so personal. You're not blaming yourself because she was attacked in your yard, are you? We take patients like her all the time. Drunks, paupers, orphans – destitutes who don't have a soul in the world to care what happens to them.' She cast a glance at Kathleen. 'Like her,' she added thoughtlessly. 'Tramps and suchlike.'

Rosie rounded on her. 'People! Not once have you called them people, but that's what they are, just like you and me.'

Nell shook her head. 'Oh, no,' she snapped. 'Not like you and me, Rosie. We work bloody hard for a living, and if you ask me, so could most of the rabble who are brought in here. Like you, I do my job. I nurse their wounds and I fetch their bedpans, and I loathe every minute of it. I do it because at the end of the week I get paid, and that's all.' Red-faced with anger, she cursed herself for revealing the truth.

Rosie had always suspected as much but she was still shaken by the admission. 'If that's how you really feel,' she accused angrily, 'you shouldn't be here.'

'And neither should *she*!' Nell waved a hand at Kathleen. 'That old nobody is taking up valuable space. The sooner she goes the better, and it can be out the back door in a box or out the front door on her own two legs. Either way will do, as long as it's soon!'

Conscious that the old woman might be able to hear what was being said, Rosie moved to the desk in the centre of the ward and Nell followed. 'Is there anything new that I should know about?' she asked.

Nell handed her the clipboard. 'Nothing,' she replied curtly. 'Except Mrs Tyler seems to have developed a raging thirst. You'll need to watch her or she'll have you running yourself ragged.'

Rosie glanced through the clipboard. 'Thanks,' she said, and before she could go on, Mrs Tyler began calling for a drink. 'I'll see to her.' Rosie's shift didn't start for another ten minutes but she was never a clock-watcher. In fact, if truth be told, she would rather be here than at home with Jake.

It took only a few minutes to help Mrs Tyler to a drink of water, but during that time Nell Salter took the opportunity to rifle Kathleen's bedside cabinet. Something the doctor had said earlier had made her curious – 'Who knows, she might be worth a fortune,' that was what he had said, and it made her wonder what the old woman carried in that tapestry bag she had been clutching when she was admitted.

When Rosie returned to the desk she noticed the screen drawn round Kathleen's bed. Quickly, she went up the ward and there, on the other side of the screen, was Nell furtively going through the old woman's tapestry bag. 'For God's sake, Nell! What do you think you're doing?'

Red-faced and excited, Nell continued to turn things out of the bag, on to the bed. 'D'you remember how she clung to this bag when she was brought in?' she whispered excitedly. 'Like it had valuables inside.'

Rosie couldn't believe her eyes. 'Have you gone out of your mind?'

'You heard what the doctor said,' Nell hissed. 'What if she really is worth a fortune? The old hag's on her way out so she'll not need it any more. We could help ourselves and no one would be any the wiser. It's only what we deserve, Rosie.'

Stepping forward, Rosie challenged her. 'Put it all

back,' she ordered in a harsh whisper, 'and we'll say no more about it.'

'Don't be daft!' Defiantly Nell turned the bag upside down, spilling its remaining contents on the bed: a torn notebook with a pen tucked inside; food crumbs; a twig shaped like a hook with a bit of twine on the end for fishing; a bone comb; and various other bits and pieces.

'You disgust me!' Gathering up the old woman's belongings, Rosie made a grab for the bag. In the tussle, a small bundle fell to the floor with a gentle thud.

'Christ, Rosie!' With trembling fingers, Nell bent to pick up the package. 'I bet this is stuffed with money.' In a frenzy of greed she pulled at the ribbon that held it secure.

Over the years the ribbon had frayed and as Nell tugged at it, the whole thing came apart in her hands. 'Christ Almighty!' Angrily, she flicked through the books, throwing them to the ground with anger. 'Notebooks!' she cried hoarsely. 'Nothing but notebooks and pages of scribble!'

While Rosie bent to her knees to retrieve the books, Nell picked up the bone comb; a handsome thing, it had marbled teeth and a slim, gleaming backbone inlaid with mother-of-pearl. 'Looks like it might be worth a bob or two,' she said, eyes glittering. 'It won't be a fortune but it's better than nothing.'

'Steal it and it will cost you your job,' Rosie promised.

'I don't think so,' Nell sneered. 'One word about this and I'll make out it's *you* who's the thief.' She smiled. 'I'm a very convincing liar. You'd best think on it, Rosie Maitland. I've got two brothers who would turn the world upside down for me. They wouldn't take kindly to you spreading lies about their little sister.' Her face darkened. 'Keep it shut or you'll pay dearly.' As quickly as her face had darkened, it brightened again with a smile. 'I'm feeling a bit peckish. I'll get off home now and see what me mam's got for supper.'

Shaken by the events, Rosie gathered up the exercise books. 'Brothers or not, I won't keep quiet about what she's done,' she muttered. 'Stealing from patients who can't defend themselves!'

A small voice made her sit up. 'Rosie?'

Grabbing the books and scrambling up, Rosie was astonished to see the old woman looking straight at her; astonished, too, at the timeless beauty of her dark brown eyes. 'How long have you been awake?' It shamed her to think the old woman had heard every word.

Kathleen smiled. 'Rosie . . . lovely name.'

'Did you hear . . . everything?'

Kathleen's next words confirmed it. 'Is it true? Am I really on my way out?'

'Don't let her upset you.'

'Please, is it true?'

Rosie couldn't find the words to answer but her silence spoke for her.

'Mr Potts?'

'He's recovering. Don't worry, he'll be well looked after, I promise.'

Her smile became a sigh. 'I'll miss the silly old scruff.' Suddenly, two plump tears sprang from her eyes and trickled to the pillow. 'So much to tell,' she whispered. 'So much.'

'Sleep now.' Rosie held her hand for a moment, and when she believed the old woman was asleep, she began piling the books up, her intention to tie them with the frayed ribbon as best she could before returning them to the bag, and the bag to the cupboard.

'The comb was given to me by a boy I used to know.' Kathleen's memories grew stronger. Oh, what a glorious summer's day it had been, and how much in love they were. In her mind, it was only yesterday.

'I'll get the comb back for you if I can,' Rosie promised. It was obvious the comb meant a lot to the old woman.

With a surge of strength, Kathleen raised herself on to one elbow. Looking into Rosie's surprised eyes, she told her, 'I want you to know . . . about me.' Falling back on to the pillow, she reached out and placed her long fingers over Rosie's small, workworn hand. 'In the books.' She paused, her old heart glowing. 'It's all there,' she whispered. '*Everything.*'

'Have you no family?' Rosie was deeply moved.

'Only you,' came the sad reply. 'The books are all I have to give,' she murmured. 'They're yours now.'

Still Rosie made to return them to the cupboard

but Kathleen saw. 'Cherish them,' she pleaded, her eyes brimming with tears. 'For me.'

Worn by the effort, Kathleen drifted into a fretful sleep. With the books on the bed before her, Rosie sat by her bedside, her gaze sweeping the old woman's face. 'You must have been very beautiful when you were young,' she mused. 'Who are you? How did you come here?'

From somewhere down the ward a voice called out. Rosie went to investigate. It was Mrs Tyler, wanting another drink. 'I'll 'ave a gin, if yer please,' she grinned with her toothless mouth.

Rosie had to smile. 'It was too much gin that brought you here in the first place,' she chided. 'You can have a cup of water and then you can go to sleep, before you wake the whole ward.'

'I want a piss!'

'You want a lot, don't you?' For all her irritating traits, Mrs Tyler always made Rosie smile.

'It's all that bloody water.'

'So you don't want it then?'

'I want a drop o' gin.'

'Sorry.'

'Bugger off then. I can't get any sleep wi' you standing there.'

Rosie 'buggered off', back to Kathleen who appeared to be peacefully sleeping. 'Sleep well,' Rosie whispered, and was about to return the belongings to the cupboard when she paused. 'So much to tell,' the old woman had said. 'Yes, I can imagine,' Rosie murmured. Fingering the notebooks, she thought for a moment, and then nodded. 'All right, I'll read them, but I can't promise when I'll have the time.'

It was quiet on the ward that night and Rosie laid the books out on her desk. They were tattered old things of a kind used by schoolchildren or clerks, or the foremen at the docks – she had seen the very same type curled into Jake's overall pockets. The books were numbered from one to twenty, with the name Kathleen Peterson written on each one. 'Nell was wrong,' Rosie murmured. 'There was a fortune in the bag after all. Not a fortune in money or jewels, but a hoard of memories, the precious memories of one woman's life.' And now they were entrusted to her. The responsibility suddenly seemed overwhelming.

She took up the first book and opened it.

There, in that quiet place, in the soft glow from the lamp, Rosie settled into her chair, turned the page, and began to read.

PART TWO

1855
THE GIRL

Chapter Two

TREMBLING WITH FEAR, Kathleen hugged her rag doll close to her heart. 'Adam's been naughty,' she whispered. 'Father's whipping him again.' Placing a finger over the doll's lips, she urged, 'Ssh! He mustn't hear us.'

Crouched inside the closet, the five-year-old child quivered at the sound of her father ranting and raving, the crack of the whip as it rose and fell, and her brother Adam's cries. 'Adam's hurting,' she told the doll, a tumble of tears creating a smudged trail down her white face. 'It's all my fault,' she quietly sobbed. 'Adam's being whipped and it's all my fault.'

Upstairs in her room, Kathleen's mother heard it too. Arms folded and face pinched with fear, she paced the floor. 'I should go down,' she muttered, 'but God forgive me, I'm too afraid.' She continued to pace, back and forth, to the window, then to the door, agonising over whether she should intervene, fearing that if she did it might be her on the receiving end of that whip.

Years before, when she first met the man who was now her husband, she had been courageous and bold.

Over the years he had eroded her self-confidence until now she was little more than a coward.

In the town of Blackburn, Elizabeth Peterson was a fine example of what a squire's wife should be. When the sun came up, she spent the long lonely days doing what was expected of her. She performed her duties with grace and accomplishment; she displayed active interest in her husband's work; ran a big house with no apparent effort; marshalled and supervised the servants and made certain her children had the best nanny and governess money could buy.

When the sun went down, she lay in her bed while her husband took his satisfaction. At times, and because it seemed to pleasure him, she even feigned a measure of satisfaction herself. But the truth was she hated every minute of her existence, seeking her happiness wherever she could find it, at whatever cost.

Her husband had a foul and vicious temper which he often vented on his only son. Robert Peterson had longed for a son who might take after himself; a son who would grow tall and strong, with a fierce and ruthless nature to match his own. When he first cast eyes on his newborn son, the disappointment showed in his eyes. 'No matter that he's weak and puny,' he vowed, 'if I have to punish him every inch of the way, I'll make him the man I want him to be.'

The baby slept and his father woke him. The infant loved to walk and his father made him run. The boy loved to paint; his father made him climb trees. When his son was four years old, Robert Peterson rallied the servants to show them how fearless his son was. Demanding their attention, he hoisted the small boy on to the back of a stallion, parading him round the grounds. Then he sent the animal into a frenzy by slapping it hard with a crop. It shot forward at a gallop, with the boy clinging on for dear life, obviously terrified and begging his father to get him down.

Laughing, the man took the boy down, carried him indoors and then viciously beat him. 'Don't ever again humiliate me in front of the servants!' he thundered. 'Like it or not, you are my son – though I wish to God you weren't. Puny coward that you are, you carry my name. Robert Adam Peterson is a proud name, with centuries of tradition behind it. Don't ever forget that!'

The boy was afraid of water, so when he was eight, his father threw him into the sea and watched him almost drown before he sent a servant in to rescue him. 'Another disappointment!' he declared, striding away in disgust. 'Another humiliation!' It was an incident the boy was never allowed to forget.

The latest 'humiliation' had taken place this after-noon, when young Adam, now ten years old, was in the garden with his sister Kathleen, whom he adored. They had been swinging from the lower boughs of an apple tree when Kathleen dropped her doll, which fell on to an area of rockery some ten feet below.

Horrified, Kathleen would have gone after it, but her brother made her wait while he went down to retrieve the doll. The doll was broken, and he was cut and bruised. Kathleen was distraught. The whole episode was witnessed by the governess, who rushed out and took them both inside. Inevitably, the tale was related to the master and, in spite of all protests that Adam had been brave in clambering down to recover his sister's doll, the boy was blamed and viciously punished.

Now, trembling as though she herself was receiving the terrible blows, Elizabeth Peterson remained in her room, knowing that she was a greater coward than her son would ever be.

Her son's cries ceased and a terrible silence permeated the house. 'Oh, dear God, let him be all right.' She went to the door and gingerly opened it. Burying her head in her hands, she began to sob. 'I daren't go to him, I'm afraid. God help me, what kind of woman am I?'

Suddenly a piercing scream rent the air. Quickly Elizabeth slammed shut the door and leaned against it, her arms spread out as though to fend off an intruder. 'Don't kill him,' she kept saying. 'Please, don't kill him.' Yet she made no move to stop it.

Pressed deep in the closet, Kathleen felt the silence, and she too was startled by the sudden, high-pitched scream.

Suddenly she could bear it no longer. With immense courage, she flung open the door of the closet, ran to the drawing room where she burst in, her eyes filling with horror at the scene before her.

Adam was small for his age, with a shock of fair

hair and dark, blue eyes. Now, though, his eyes were closed in pain; he stood against the wall, his arms reaching up and out against the wood panelling. From the waist down he was naked, his blood-stained legs and buttocks criss-crossed with a weird pattern made by the lash.

When the beatings stopped, he made no move. It was as though he was welded to the wall, his small body only barely managing to keep upright, his heart infused with a strength that only made his father more determined to break him. He wanted Adam to beg for mercy. Exasperated that not once had his son shown any sign of doing so, he had paused to rest his arm and then wielded the whip one last time with all the power he could muster. It was this that had made Adam scream in agony.

Robert Peterson didn't even look to see who had burst into the room. He kept his eyes on the boy and yelled, 'Get out, damn you! *Get out!*'

Kathleen stayed by the door, tears rolling down her face at the plight of her brother, who was her only friend. So shocked was she that her tongue wouldn't say the words that rushed to her mind. She remained quite still, clutching her broken doll, her gaze focused on Adam and only the soft sound of her crying permeating the awful silence.

Robert swung round, his features crumpling with shame when he saw who stood there. 'Oh, Kathleen!' He rushed across the room. 'No, sweetheart, you mustn't see this.' He reached out to her, his face suffused with love. 'Come on, let Daddy take you out of here.'

Holding the doll close, Kathleen backed away. 'Go away. I don't like you.' For the first time in her young life she knew hatred. It was a bitter thing, but not as bitter as seeing her brother cut and bleeding. 'You're hurting Adam!'

'Don't be silly, darling.' He loved her so very much. In many ways she had been some measure of compensation for the son he craved but could never have. 'Adam has been bad and he has to be punished.' When she didn't move, he picked her up and strode out of the room with her.

She fought him with such ferocity, he was taken aback. Hitting out with fists and feet, she could only think of her brother. 'Leave him alone! I hate you! I hate you!'

He put her down, and when he looked into her tear-filled brown eyes, a great tenderness overcame him. 'You don't understand,' he said. 'This is men's business, and you're not supposed to see.' While she quietly sobbed, he went on, 'Don't ever say you hate me, Kathleen. I couldn't bear that.'

Kathleen wasn't listening. With a determined twist of her arm she broke free and before he could stop her she had run back to the room and her beloved Adam. She found him slumped on the floor, face down. 'It's all right, Adam,' she sobbed, falling to her knees and stroking his hair. 'I won't let him hurt you. I won't let him.'

In two strides her father was across the room. Taking her by the arm, he propelled her into the hallway and on up the stairs, yelling as he went, 'Elizabeth! Elizabeth, where the hell are you?'

Like a frightened mouse she came scurrying out of her room. 'I'm here, Robert,' she said in a remarkably calm manner. 'Whatever is it?' She had grown adept at feigning ignorance when the occasion warranted. The less she pretended to know about what went on, the easier it was to strike it from her conscience.

His eyes swept her pretty face. 'I thought I told you to keep Kathleen away from the drawing room.' As he spoke he came closer, making her tremble.

'But I thought the governess had her safe.'

'You're bloody useless! You've allowed Kathleen to see a punishment. Damn it, Elizabeth! You know how I feel about that.'

'I'm sorry. It won't happen again.'

For a moment he was silent, his gaze intent on her face. Kathleen was like her mother, he thought; the same chestnut-brown eyes and long dark hair. He loved them both. Hated them too, for the power they had over him. The girl was still innocent, but the mother was knowing; too knowing. There were times when he could have willingly killed her, and times when he loved her until she cried out for mercy. 'The governess,' he demanded drily. 'Where is she?'

'I thought she was in the garden with the children.'

'When I'm finished with the boy, find her. Send her to me in the study.'

'Let me take Kathleen.' She reached out but did not make a move towards him.

He kept hold of Kathleen. Suppressing the rage inside him, he bent to address her in soft, loving tones. 'You never have to be afraid,' he promised. 'I would never punish you.' When she cowered away from him, he persisted, 'I love you, more than anyone else in the world. You know that, don't you, sweetheart?'

She raised her small face to his dark, passionate eyes. 'You hurt Adam,' she accused brokenly. 'I don't love you any more. I only love *him*.'

'Don't talk like that. Come on now, give your daddy a kiss.'

'No!' Kicking out, she caught him on the ankle with her boot. Insane jealousy took hold of him.

'Adam is a coward,' he hissed, shaking her. 'I don't want you to love him, do you hear?' Damn and blast that boy, he soured everything. 'He broke your doll, didn't he? He had to be taught a lesson.' He made himself smile. 'If you forget what you saw downstairs just now, Daddy will take you shopping in London. We can go on the train, or we can go in the carriage. You can choose. Just you and me, sweetheart, and I promise you, we'll find the best, most expensive, most beautiful doll in the world.' Foolishly he took hold of her broken doll. 'You don't want this old thing any more, do you? Adam's spoiled it – like he spoils everything!'

Nothing could console her. Snatching back her doll, Kathleen tore away from him and ran to her mother who, startled and afraid, tolerated the child clinging to her skirt. 'What am I to do?' she asked nervously, keeping her hands clasped. 'I honestly thought the governess had her safe.'

He glared at his wife. 'The governess,' he reminded her. 'In my study in ten minutes. See to it!' Inwardly fuming, he turned and went down the stairs.

He didn't return to the drawing room. Instead he stormed into the kitchen. 'It seems I pay people for doing nothing,' he snapped at the three servants he found there. 'Where is the housekeeper?'

Being the boldest and least expendable, Cook spoke up. 'I believe the housekeeper went up to inspect the bedrooms, sir.'

He looked around the room. As usual it was spotless, with food on the table and sideboard in various stages of preparation; and a particular favourite of his cooking in the oven. The aroma of steak and onion pie filled his nostrils and made his stomach rumble. 'Get her,' he ordered. 'I'll be in the study.' With that he strode out, leaving them gasping with relief that they still had their jobs.

'It ain't often he shows his face in 'ere,' Cook remarked, brushing a whisper of baking powder from her eyebrow.

'What d'yer reckon he wants with Mrs Glover?' With her thin face, thick lips, and wispy hair escaping from beneath her cap, Nancy Tomlin made a comical sight. She wasn't too bright but she was a wonderful worker with a heart of gold, and Cook had a special place in her heart for her.

'It isn't for us to question the master,' she said curtly. 'Run upstairs now and tell Mrs Glover the master's been here looking for her, and that she's to make her way to the study.'

While Nancy ran to find Mrs Glover, the butler stepped forward, his face dark with anger. 'You know why he wants her,' he said quietly. 'You heard the lad's cries as well as any of us. He's taken a terrible thrashing and now Mrs Glover will be made to shut him in his room until the master is ready to let him out again.'

Cook was a round, homely woman with kind eyes and a kinder nature behind her sharp tongue; she had seen things in this house that touched her deeply. 'It should be the governess who deals with that, not Mrs Glover,' she snorted with disgust. 'The governess!' she declared haughtily. 'Jumped-up nothing, if you ask me, not fit to take charge of a dog. What's more, I shouldn't be at all surprised if she gets paid more than all of us put together.'

'I didn't know you were so set against her, Mabel. You've never said before.'

'That's because I know when to keep my mouth shut.' She glanced about, ever nervous they might be overheard. 'It's true though,' she went on in a quieter voice. 'That young madam is paid good money to mind the children. Oh, I'm not denying they've learned their tables and the pair of them can read and write as good as any I've seen afore. But she doesn't care for them like she should. Since the master got rid of the nanny and gave the task to this one, she's neglected the children shamelessly. They're put at all manner of risk. Time and again they go off on their own, across the fields and down to that fast-flowing brook. My God, anything could happen, and her nowhere in sight.'

'Aye, well, happen that's not such a bad thing, the young 'uns going off on their own, I mean. Being left to their own devices has taught 'em to look after theirselves. I bet you could set 'em down in the middle of a jungle and they'd find a way of surviving. Still, you're right, the brook's a dangerous place for the children to be. I've said as much to the master and was swiftly told to leave such matters to them as know.'

'The master's a fool!'

'If I were you, I shouldn't worry too much. And anyway, the boy swims like he were born to it. As for the lass, well, she's not afraid of anything.'

'Aye, John, I'll not deny they're a capable pair, God love 'em. But they're too young to be wandering off on their own. That fancy madam should be doing the job she's paid to do.' Sighing, Mabel wiped her nose with the back of her hand. 'She's worse than useless. Never anywhere to be found when she's wanted, except when the delivery men call. Oh aye, she's to be found then, right enough. Making cow eyes and showing off her ankles to all and sundry.'

John gave a grin. 'Well, you must admit she has got a well-turned ankle.'

Being round and lumpy, and never having had her ankles complimented, Mabel snorted disapprovingly.

'If it was up to me, I'd have her out the door before she knew what day it was!'

'Yer not jealous, are you?' John teased. 'Because you needn't be. Haven't I told you before, Mabel Down, you're the finest woman that ever walked on two legs – pretty or not.'

He had thought to please her. Instead he got a sharp tap on his knuckles with the rolling pin. 'My legs are as good as anybody's,' Mabel retorted, adding with a chuckle, 'for getting me about, that is.'

The butler's mind was already on other things. 'Mind you, we all know why he keeps her on, don't we, eh? She's his fancy bit, that's why. Time and again young Nancy's heard him creeping up the back stairs to her room, and many's the time he's not come out till morning.'

'Be careful what you say,' Mabel warned. 'Walls have ears.'

John shook his head in anger. 'The way he thrashes that lad, we should shout it from the rooftops!'

'What good would that do? I know he's a bad-tempered, merciless devil, and I know he takes it out on that poor boy, but when all's said and done, he is the boy's father.'

'More's the pity. Adam is a good lad. He'd die before he'd let any harm come to that little lass, and the master knows it.'

Mabel nodded. 'There's a lot of jealousy there, I reckon,' she murmured. 'The master dotes on the girl, and he can't stand anybody else near her, especially the boy, who he seems to hate like poison. And for no good reason that I can see, other than he's never going to make a master huntsman because he doesn't like riding the horses. The lad hates the idea of killing things. I mean, look how the master went berserk when the boy refused to lay traps for the rabbits. And there was nearly murder when he caught the boy down by the brook with an easel and paintbrush.' She shrugged her ample shoulders. 'It's true the lad's not the same strong build as his father, and he prefers painting to killing. But there's nowt wrong with that.'

'If he only opened his eyes he'd see how Adam is a son any man could be proud of. He isn't built big, I'll give you that, and he doesn't have the same killer instinct his father has, but he's no coward. He has the heart of a lion and he knows the difference between right and wrong. In my book, he's a better man than his father will ever be.' John nodded his head, as though agreeing with himself. 'The master knows it too, and that's why he whips the lad until he draws blood.'

'I'm well aware o' that. We *all* are.' Her heart went out to both the children. 'But we're only paid servants in this house, John.' She squared her shoulders. 'Don't forget what happened to old Mr Potts. That man tended the gardens for nigh on twelve years but he were sacked in a minute when he made a comment to the master about the boy being too small to take a man's punishment.'

'Aye, but he had the guts to speak up.'

'It didn't help though, did it? What can any of us do, eh? Who could we tell that might believe us? And how long do you think we'd be in a job? Once we opened our mouths we'd be out of here quicker than you can draw breath, and there wouldn't be a lady nor gent in the country who would ever give us work again. Troublemakers, that's what they'd call us, and likely we'd starve to death in a gutter somewhere.'

'Hey, now, that's a bit strong.'

'It's the truth. What's more, even if we did stand up and tell the world, the gentry would stick together like they always do. The master would still flog the boy, and the law would still be on his side.' Mabel rolled up her sleeves, plunged her arms into the baking bowl and sent a fine spray of flour into the air. She sneezed. 'Tell me I'm wrong. Go on. Tell me I'm wrong.'

Frustrated and angry, John slammed his fist on the table. 'If you ask me, it's not the boy who should be flogged, it's that bastard.' He blushed. 'If you'll pardon the strong language, Mabel.'

Shaken by the ferocity of his outburst she turned to regard him. He was a small man, white-haired and ferret-like. But there was something about him that made him tall among other men; a strong, good-looking face and elegance that made him attractive to her. 'It's all right, John,' she said kindly. 'I know how you feel.'

'All the same, I shouldn't let my tongue run away with me, not in front of you, I shouldn't.'

When he smiled, she was afraid her deeper feelings might show. So, setting her features into grim disapproval, she sharply rebuked him. 'You're right! In future mind your language. I'm partic'lar who comes in my kitchen!'

Bowing his head, John muttered something incoherent. He had a secret fancy for this big, bustling woman. She was kind and generous, and knew how to laugh. What's more, she made the best meat pie and veg he'd ever tasted. It made him determined that one fine day he would take Mabel for his wife. It was something to look forward to and it kept him going. It kept him here, in this house, waiting on a man he detested, when he would rather be a million miles away. He would have been gladdened by the cheeky twinkle in Mabel's eye, as she looked away. Since John's fleeting kiss under the mistletoe, many a foolish dream was raised in her old heart.

<hr />

Mrs Glover made her way towards the master's study at a smart pace. A tall, trim lady, with strong, proud features and her white cap fluttering as she went, she might have been a galleon in full sail.

'Come!' As always after administering a beating, Robert Peterson was in a state of great excitement.

Mrs Glover knew of the beating. Like everyone in the house, she had suffered the boy's punishment as if she herself was on the receiving end. 'You want me to take the boy to his room,' she said without preamble. She had done it so many times before.

'You know the procedure,' Robert snapped. 'See to it.'

Only when Mrs Glover had departed the room did he relax. 'Damn her!' he snarled, downing a glass of whisky. 'Damn them all!'

It was only a matter of minutes before there came another, softer knock on the door. 'Go away, bugger you!' He was in no mood for visitors.

The voice was so low and vibrant it seemed to be in the room with him. 'I was told you wanted me.'

At the sound of the voice, Robert laughed out loud. 'Come in, you slut,' he replied jovially. Stretching out his legs, he raised his feet to the desk, awaiting her entry with the air of a gentleman at ease.

The door opened. He kept his gaze down, staring into the bottom of his glass.

The door closed. He smiled, but still did not look up. 'You have a lot to answer for,' he murmured.

She made no move, but answered softly, 'Don't be angry with me.'

'Lock it.'

'What?'

'The door. Lock it.'

'You won't beat me, will you?'

'Lock it, damn you!'

The click of the lock made him glance up. He liked what he saw. Connie Blakeman was neither short nor tall; she was fair-haired and pleasantly feminine, with soft features and pale eyes that were sometimes blue and sometimes green. She was both cunning and naive, and had a way of winding men round her little finger. She took one cautious step into the room.

'The boy has had a thrashing.' His smile was evil.

'I know.'

'Your fault.'

'I know.'

'Come here.'

Just a little afraid, but knowing she only had to smile and he would be at her mercy, she went to him. 'I wasn't far away,' she said. 'I wandered into the spinney. I really thought the children were right behind me.'

Swinging his legs down, he let her fondle him. 'I should have known you were too young to look after them.' Opening her blouse, he kissed her bare breasts. 'Only eighteen.' He grinned at her. 'Elizabeth was right. You're too young for such a responsibility.'

She was kissing him, sending him wild. 'You've never complained before.'

'That's because I don't give a sod what anyone else thinks.' Clutching the neck of her blouse, he tore it from her shoulders. For a long, awful moment he stared at her breasts, small ripe fruits, pointed to a dark, erect nipple. Stirred deep inside, he caressed them like a man starved. 'You're always warm,' he murmured, rolling his face over the pink, supple skin. 'Warm and soft.'

She laughed softly. 'You've ruined my blouse.'

He didn't smile. 'You'll have to go,' he said, peering at her from beneath heavy eyelids. 'You know that, don't you?'

Uncertain whether it was the drink talking or the man, but either way feeling confident that he would never send her away, she teased, 'Do you want me to go this very minute?'

'Not yet,' and now he did smile. 'We haven't finished our business.' His mouth covered her nipple and his hands moved up her skirt. Suddenly he was pushing her to the floor, his weight bearing down on top of her. 'What will I do without you?' he moaned, pushing up her skirt and feasting his eyes on her bare flesh.

While he watched, she drew down her underwear, sending him wild when she exposed the darker, more secret area. 'Do you want me?' she invited, spreading her legs. 'Go on then, take me.' Bold and unashamed, she arched her back and waited, eyes and fists closed, limbs trembling, anticipating the unbearable rush of pleasure.

She wasn't disappointed. 'You little witch!' With a swift, brutal movement, he tore away his own garments and was into her with one long, direct thrust. In their wild and frenzied passion, they were oblivious of the fact that their cries could be heard outside the room.

'Cor!' It wasn't the first time Nancy had burst into the kitchen with eyes sticking out like hat pegs and hair flying. 'You should hear the noises coming from the master's study,' she exclaimed. 'It's like there's murder going on!'

Mabel grabbed her by the arm and propelled her to the range. 'There *will* be murder going on,' she promised, 'if you leave this kitchen again without my say-so. Now stir that pot until it bubbles. If just one piece of meat sticks to the pan, my girl, I shall want to know the reason why.'

With that she returned to her baking, one eye on Nancy, the other on the door. 'They're like a pair o' dogs on heat!' she muttered, dropping generous dollops of plum jam into the pastries.

At that moment John returned from his tour of the house. He, too, was well aware of what was going on in the master's study, and he arrived in a fluster. The sounds rose to a climax. Mabel reddened; John coughed and rolled his eyes with embarrassment, then with the calm dignity that set him apart, he closed the door and asked, 'Is there a cup of tea going?'

'There might be,' Mabel told him, 'but you'll need to make it yourself. Us women are too busy.'

But she wasn't too busy to sit and enjoy a cup with him afterwards, and even Nancy was allowed to join them.

'It's frightening, ain't it?' Nancy said, looking from one to the other with her big round eyes.

'What is?' John asked curiously.

'Never you mind!' Mabel intervened, reddening again. 'There's been enough said on that partic'lar matter. Now eat your cake or I'll throw it out for the birds.'

Threatened with having her cake taken away, Nancy tucked in, trying to forget all about the 'frightening' noises coming from the master's study. They sounded like the noises her mam and dad made and soon after there was always a baby. But the master wasn't like that, she thought. He and the mistress were gentry, and everybody knew that gentry were different. And anyway, the mistress was upstairs with the girl. She knew that because just now she'd been summoned to take up a tray of tea and dainties.

⤜⤛●⤚⤝

Upstairs, Elizabeth sat by the window, her sorry gaze fixed on the far-off hills. On the settee behind her Kathleen slept fitfully.

'You don't know how lucky you are,' Elizabeth murmured, shifting her gaze to the child. 'You're unhappy now because your brother has been hurt, but you don't know anything yet.' She sighed, letting her gaze linger a moment. 'Poor little Kathleen.' She smiled sadly. 'All too soon you'll be a woman, and then your heartaches will really begin.'

She turned away, quiet for a moment, then spoke aloud, letting her feelings flow from within. 'I should never have got married,' she whispered. 'That was a bad thing.'

Having few people to talk with, Elizabeth often conversed with the birds roosting in a wide-spreading apple tree outside her window; at this glorious time of year it was in full bloom, the sweet scent of its blossom wafting in through the open window. 'I might have loved him once, but not any more.' She shuddered. 'I can't bear him to touch me.'

After a moment, she rose from the chair and crossed to the settee where Kathleen was sleeping. 'I know I'm not a good mother,' she murmured, gazing down at the girl's innocent face. 'But I have tried. You can't know how hard I've tried all these years, until now there's nothing left. I never wanted children, but he insisted. I want to leave him, but I can't. He's the one with all the money, you see. I want to leave you and your brother too, but I don't know how.'

She felt ashamed. 'None of it is your fault. You're such a lovely, generous little thing, but I can never love you as you should be loved. Maybe it's because he smothers you and I can't bring myself to go where he's been, or love what he loves.' A sob caught her voice. 'Or maybe it's because I'm afraid to love you in case he finds out. Adam loves you, and he gets beaten for it.'

She wrung her hands, alone and desperate in that great, cold house. 'I'm so afraid,' she muttered, 'so afraid of what he might do. And, oh! If he should ever find out the truth! I daren't even think about it.'

She wasn't talking about her love for Kathleen now, but about her love for another man; a man who gave her comfort and listened to her as though she mattered.

She sat down on the settee and began stroking Kathleen's long, dark hair. 'You're so pretty,' she whispered. 'One day you'll fall in love with a good man, and it won't matter that your mother couldn't love you. You'll forget about me, and the beast who thinks he fathered you.'

She clamped her hand to her lips and lowered her voice. 'Must be careful what I say, Kathleen. Let him believe he's your father, and you must believe it too, because that's the way it should be. But the truth is you were conceived in love,' she whispered, 'not out of fear, like your brother.' Now that she had spoken the secret out loud, she felt strangely free of her husband. 'No one knows, except me,' she murmured. 'And no one ever will.'

She sat awhile, dreaming and wishing, and knowing there would come a day when she might be brought to answer for her sins. But for now she had little thought for herself. 'When you leave this place, as you surely will one day,' she whispered to the child, 'I pray you will put him out of your life. And you must forget me because I've let you down badly.' A tender smile crossed her sad features. 'Not Adam though. You must never forget what Adam means to you. Unlike you, he does have his father's blood running through him, but thank God he's not tainted by it. Nor is he tainted by my weakness. Adam has taken my own father's nature, he's kind and strong. Be thankful, Kathleen, thankful that he's your brother and your friend. Adam knows you better than anyone, and he knows how lonely you are.' Taking Kathleen's fingers in her own, she put them to her lips and softly kissed them. 'Adam will always look after you,' she promised. 'No matter what happens, you must always remember that.'

Suddenly she heard angry, raised voices. Going to the door, she edged it open, silently listening but not surprised. She had seen this particular confrontation coming for some time; ever since he had brought the girl into the house. She knew it would be only a matter of time before he threw her out, like so many before her.

'You bastard!' It was Connie Blakeman's voice. 'You mean you really are throwing me out?' Trembling with rage, her voice dropped to a low, threatening tone. 'What if I open my mouth about you and me, eh? What if I tell all and sundry how you've been taking advantage of a decent, hard-working girl who wanted no part of you.'

'Huh!' His laughter echoed through the house. 'You? Connie Blakeman? Whose father's a useless nobody and whose mother sells her favours on the market corner for a bob a time? Who do you think would listen to a no-good whore like you?'

'You're the one who's no good!' she yelled. 'For all your money and fancy things, you're less of a gent than my dad is. He ain't a drunken old bastard like you. He don't beat his kids raw neither, and he don't rape his wife!'

Incensed, he took her by the hair. 'One day that

big mouth of yours will get you hanged,' he hissed, and while she continued to struggle and scream, he marched her to the front door where he wedged the toe of his boot up her backside and kicked her down the steps. She landed in a painful heap at the bottom. 'Now be off with you,' he said, staring down at her. 'And I warn you, don't try slurring my good name or you'll be very, very sorry.'

As he slammed the door on her, she continued to shout threats and obscenities. 'You'll be the sorry one, Mr high and bloody mighty! 'Cause when my brothers hear what you've done, they'll be round here, I can promise you that!'

Bruised and hurt, she hobbled away, spitting blood. Occasionally she glanced back, her face wreathed with loathing.

Like him, she was a vindictive creature. And she never forgot an insult.

⟢●⟣

LATER THAT NIGHT, when the house was quiet, only the children were awake; Adam because he was in too much pain to sleep, and little Kathleen because the image of her brother bleeding against the wall would not let her sleep.

Softly she clambered out of bed and put on her robe. Barefooted, she made her way out of the room and down the long draughty corridor. She had to see him. She had to know he was all right.

Adam had been sitting by the window, tears

streaming down his face at the memory of his humiliation. 'I hate him!' he muttered, wiping away his tears. 'I hate him!'

When the door handle softly turned, his heart turned over with it. For one awful minute he believed it was his father come to hand out more of the same punishment. Defiantly, he stood with his back to the window and his eyes on the door. 'I won't show him I'm afraid,' he muttered. 'I won't!'

When he saw Kathleen's worried face peer into the room, he sagged with relief. 'It's you!' he gasped, going across the room to draw her inside. 'What are you doing? You should be in bed asleep.'

'I couldn't sleep, Adam.' To see him out of bed and walking towards her, was too much of a relief. She began to cry; big rolling tears and racking sobs. 'He whipped you. Daddy whipped you and I don't like him any more.'

'Aw, come here.' With his arm round her shoulder, he took her to the chair and sat her down. 'You don't have to cry,' he chided. 'I'm all right, aren't I?' His back felt as tight as a drum and if he breathed too deeply the wounds seemed to pop open and it was agony. 'I want you to go back to your own room, and go to sleep. Will you do that?'

She regarded him in the moonlight that gentled in through the window. He seemed all right, but she wasn't certain. In fact there were suspicious smudges on his face. 'He's made you cry, hasn't he?' She had never seen Adam cry and the realisation was a shock.

She couldn't know that he had cried many times before; he never let her see, he had too much pride for that.

'Maybe a little,' he grudgingly admitted. He had never lied to Kathleen, and he never would.

'I don't like him any more.' As she spoke, the tears trembled over long lashes. 'Can I stay with you, Adam?'

He shook his head. 'It's best if you go back to your own room.'

'Please.' She couldn't rid herself of the awful things she had witnessed. 'If he comes to get you, I'll make him go away.'

He smiled at her then. 'Oh, Kathleen, you're a silly billy, and I do love you.'

'Can I stay then?'

'Course you can.'

After tucking her up in bed, he watched while she fell asleep. 'Does your back hurt?' she asked dreamily.

'Not too much,' he said. 'Go to sleep.'

'Cuddle me.' She held up her arms and he cradled her close, until at last she drifted into a contented slumber.

Still in a considerable amount of pain, he sat in the chair, watching her sleep and thinking he would kill his father if he ever laid a hand on little Kathleen. 'I'll never let him hurt you,' he whispered. Then he lay forward on the bed and fell asleep.

It wasn't a contented sleep. His back was on fire, and he burned with anger.

One day he would be a man. When that day came, the tables would be turned and his father would never again dare to take a whip to him.

Chapter Three

THE BLAKEMANS WERE renowned for their arrogance and aggression. Their reputation spread far and wide, from the narrow streets beneath the shadow of Blackburn's cotton mills to the fresh green lands of the Ribble Valley. On Saturday nights they scrapped outside the pubs, and in the confines of their own home they fought among themselves.

There were fourteen Blakemans. Aggie, aged forty-eight though she looked much older, was a small, wiry woman with iron-grey hair and a tired stoop to her thin shoulders. Her husband Bob, ten years older, was big and burly, a quiet, amiable fellow, content to spend his days at the mill and his nights with his feet up by the fire.

When the rowing started, as it usually did when their bellies were filled with their mam's stew, or the landlord's booze, he would close his eyes and feign sleep until it was all over. 'Let them get on with it,' he used to tell his wife when the boys were younger. 'They'll soon wear themselves out.' Now, with each one still at home and no sign yet of marrying, he wished to God he'd slung them out on their ear when they were small enough not to challenge him.

It was too late now. They'd got their feet well and truly under the table and were waited on hand and foot by their tired old mam. Even if he did ever pluck up courage to show them the door, he'd likely be the one to end up face down on the pavement.

So, much to the aggravation of his long-suffering wife, he let it all ride over him. Having fathered eleven strapping boys and one good-looking, wily girl, he felt he had contributed his lot to society.

The sons ranged in age from nineteen to thirty-two, and were as different from one another as washing on a line.

Nathan was the eldest; the biggest in size, the biggest coward, and the most cunning of all his siblings.

Then came Jack the liar, who idolised and imitated him.

Robby was named after his father but was more violent. Bold and fearless, he was also without mercy or compassion.

Steve was the handsome one. He was also a troublemaker and loved to drop poisonous suggestions into an otherwise innocent discussion until there was murder in the air.

Luke was the sensible one. Much like his father in height and build, he had the bluest eyes, the quietest nature, and was the only reasoning voice in any heated moment.

The remaining six looked to these five for guidance but invariably erred on the harder, more violent side.

Only two of the sons had regular jobs. Luke ran cargo up and down the canals. Jack worked for a local club-owner and was the dandy of the family. Both men valued their small measure of independence but neither had yet shown any inclination to move away from home and family.

Home was a converted warehouse on Penny Street. It had three floors, a cellar, and endless dilapidated rooms, many with rotting floorboards. Ten sons shared five rooms, and the eldest, Nathan, had a room of his own. The parents slept downstairs in the back room, and Connie had a small box room, kept for the few occasions when she deigned to visit, which was as little as possible because she hated the warehouse and everything in it, including her family.

They ate in the kitchen; a surprisingly sunny room, where Aggie had surrounded herself with the best she could steal, buy or borrow. There was a fine old dresser arrayed with cooking implements, peg rugs and pretty curtains, and a table made out of old doors and cupboards, smoothed down and nailed together, so it was big enough to seat the whole family at once.

At mealtimes, when everyone was seated, they made a formidable sight. While they ate, there was not a word spoken, but when the last mouthful was swallowed and the meal over, the talking would start, with everyone impatient to get a word in. Inevitably, the rows would soon follow, and one by one the family left the room, the quiet ones first, the aggressive ones last, until only Aggie was left in the kitchen, to clear away and reflect on this huge, disappointing family she had raised.

Usually Bob would sit back, enjoy his pipe and let them all get on with it. Tonight, though, he and the others had a certain matter on their minds. The matter was Connie who had arrived home unexpectedly three days ago and was saying very little.

From under heavy brows, Bob discreetly regarded her. She looked as pretty as ever, he thought, but she wasn't happy. No, not happy at all. 'You still haven't told us what brought you home, luv,' he said, sucking at his pipe. 'Is there summat you want to tell us?'

Peeved and humiliated, she gave him a scathing glance. 'I can deal with it!'

Feeling rejected, he shrugged his shoulders. 'All right, please yerself.' He got up and left the room.

'Will yer be going back to the Peterson place?' Aggie asked. She hoped so, because Connie was the hardest of her children to deal with. Whenever the two of them were in the same room together, there was an uncomfortable, brooding atmosphere. It hadn't always been that way. Right up until Connie was fifteen, they had shared most secrets. Now they didn't know how to converse without rowing. Maybe it was because Connie was no longer a girl but a woman, eighteen years old with ambitions that frightened Aggie, who was a contented, simple soul.

Connie didn't answer. Instead she kept her gaze

down and her features impassive. She didn't know whether to tell the truth dressed up with lies, or to say nothing until she had devised a plan to get back at that swine, Peterson.

Aggie turned away with a sweeping glance at the rest of her children, secretly wishing she'd never given birth to any of them – except maybe Luke, who was the best of a bad bunch.

'We're all behind you, Connie,' Steve declared, bristling. 'We're your brothers, after all, so if there's a problem, we should know about it.' He was always ready for an argument with somebody.

Robby, too, was itching to punch someone. 'That's right,' he snarled. 'If the bastard's been trying it on, we'll have to teach him a lesson, won't we?' He glanced about, looking for reassurance.

Connie wasn't sure if that was the right way to go about it. Oh yes, she wanted Peterson beaten to a pulp, and she knew Steve and Robby would do it for the pleasure, but there was always a chance that she might get back in Peterson's good books. If she was wrong, then her brothers could do their worst, but she had to try. Returning here had been a trial. After three days, she couldn't wait to get out again. Another chance, that was all she wanted. She still had plans for herself and Peterson and couldn't, wouldn't, believe it was all over.

Steve was insistent. 'If he has been trying it on, you'd better tell us. We've a right to know.'

'Mind your own bloody business!' she snapped. 'If I want your help, I'll ask for it.'

'Leave her be,' Luke ordered. 'Connie's right. She'll let us know when she's ready.' He read Connie better than most and thought she might have Peterson well in hand.

A short time later, they all went their different ways. Aggie looked around at the dirty plates and the piles of washing-up still to be done. 'Sometimes I wonder why I bother,' she groaned, collecting up the dishes and going back and forth until everything was piled into the big pot sink. 'Lazy buggers, that's what my lot are, every bloody one!'

She had rolled up her sleeves and made a start when Connie returned. 'I'm sorry I snapped at everybody, Mam,' she said. 'Only I don't want them knowing what happened.' She didn't really want her mam to know either but she needed to talk to somebody. With no friends to confide in, that left only her mother.

Aggie paused to look at her, at the small slim figure and the bold brassy face that made men go weak at the knees. God forgive her but she didn't like her own daughter. 'He hit yer, didn't he?' she remarked, returning to the washing-up. 'I saw the bruises when you were coming out of the washroom the other day. Like you say though, it's none of our business.' She had enough on her own shoulders without taking on the weight of Connie's troubles.

Dejected, Connie threw herself into the nearest chair. 'You don't give a bugger, do you?'

'Course I do. Same as you gave a bugger for me when you took yerself off to greener pastures.'

'I'm not like you, Mam. I've got ambitions.'

'Oh yes, and don't we know it.'

'I mean to be a lady. I mean to have fine clothes and a carriage to run me about. The only way I can manage that is to marry a man who's loaded.'

'Well now,' Aggie remarked acidly, 'Peterson is loaded, that's for sure. He's also married.'

'Being married don't matter.' Growing excited, Connie gave away more than she intended. 'Robert Peterson owns eight cottages and endless acres of farmland. He's got interests all over the city, and more money than he knows what to do with. He fancies me rotten. There's nothing between him and that stupid wife of his. She won't give him what he wants but I will, and one day I'll get my reward, you see if I don't.'

Aggie turned to stare at Connie with disgust. 'I married yer father for better or worse, and I bore him an army o' sons that took me figure and took me strength. There were times when I could have gone off and left him to it, times when I never knew where the next penny were coming from, and all of you small and hungry, wanting clothes, wanting things I couldn't give yer. Me and yer dad had a hard life, and things ain't so much better now, even with more money coming in. More money in, more money out, and never enough, that's the story of my life.'

'It's not much of a life to be proud of, is it?' Connie remarked spitefully.

'Mebbe not, but you've nothing to be proud of

either, young lady. The minute you turned of age, you walked out that door when you could have been helping me and fetching another wage into this house. But oh no. You chose to go swanning off to yer fancy man and yer precious ambitions.' There was a sob in her throat as she went on, 'I'll tell yer this an' all, you think yer pretty, don't yer? But I were prettier than you. I could have had any man I wanted – even the ones with money. I could have left yer dad and made my life easier, but I never did, and shall I tell yer why? Because I had respect for meself, that's why.'

With immense cruelty, Connie told her, 'Peterson says you sold yourself on street corners.'

For a moment it seemed as if her mother had not heard, but then she lowered her gaze, took a deep breath and said very softly, 'Sometimes, when the money's short and you've nothing in the cupboard to feed the young 'uns, a woman might be driven to . . . desperate measures. I'm not denying I did things I'm ashamed of, but that were a long time ago, and I hope I've paid me dues.'

'You bloody old hypocrite! Who the hell d'you think you are to preach at me? What I'm doing ain't no different than what you did.'

Rage coloured Aggie's face. 'That's where you're wrong, my girl! You're whoring for greed, for yerself, and what you can take a man for. I whored because my kids were hungry and there was no other way. It were a long time ago, and it stopped soon as ever your dad got better pay. Now I'd sooner starve before I'd sell my body to any man, rich or poor.'

'Any man would be better than Dad. What's he ever done that you can be proud of? What's he ever given you, eh? And when will he provide you with the things a woman should have – money put away and clothes you might be proud to walk the streets in? When did you last go on a holiday? When did he buy you a present? Huh! You'd have been better off staying with one o' the men who *paid* for your favours.'

'You ungrateful little swine!' Striding across the room, Aggie took Connie by the shoulders and shook her hard. 'You don't know what you're saying. Your father's been good to me in his own way. He's worked his fingers to the bone, and he's done all any man can do for his family. And you have the bloody nerve to compare him with the no-goods *you* ferret out! He's worth ten o' the buggers. I'll grant you he's not rich and never will be, and he's not able to give me fine things, even if I wanted them, which I don't. But he's hard-working, and he's never raised a hand to me in all the years we've been wed. So don't you ever think he's less than the cowardly creature you've been bedding.'

'Get your hands off me.'

'Think on then,' Aggie warned, releasing her daughter and feeling ashamed. It wasn't in her nature to be violent, but this arrogant little sod brought out the worst in her. 'Your father never knew what I did all those years back, so keep your mouth shut or I might have to flay you alive.'

There was a moment of quiet, during which Aggie returned to the sink and Connie reflected on her mother's anger. 'If he *had* hit you, what would you have done?'

Aggie thought a moment. 'Much as I love him, I'd have packed me bag there and then. I would never stand for any man nor woman raising their fist to me.' She looked into Connie's small, cruel eyes and thanked the Lord she was not made in the same mould. 'Like I said, I have respect for meself.'

'And you think I haven't?' Her mother's words had managed to make her feel ashamed and that made her angry. 'You think I have no respect for myself, is that what you're saying?'

'If you like.'

'Well, you're wrong! Why do you think I've come home?'

'I wish you'd tell me.'

When Connie hesitated, Aggie answered for her. 'You've come home because he's thrashed you, and then he's thrown you out. I'm right, aren't I? The grand man used you for his own ends and now he's had his fill and doesn't want you any more. Come on, now. Own up and shame the devil.'

'We had an argument, that's all.'

'Just an argument, was it?' Aggie knew Connie was fooling herself. 'And now here you are to lick yer wounds before you go, cap in hand, begging him to take yer back in. But he won't want you back now, will he? Yer soiled, aren't yer? He's dirtied his hands on yer and now he's washed 'em clean.' A wave of pity overwhelmed her. 'Oh, Connie, why don't yer come home for good? I'm sure we could try not to murder each other.'

'No!'

'Yer only fooling yerself if yer think he'll have yer back. Rich man Peterson is rid of you, and now he's off looking for the next conquest.'

Leaping to her feet, Connie raged, 'Shut up, damn you!'

'Face the truth, my girl.'

Bristling with hatred, Connie shouted, 'All right, he did thrash me. So what? Maybe I deserved it. Time and again he had his way with me, and I enjoyed it. What d'you think to that?'

'I think you're a damn fool.'

Relentless, Connie went on, 'Me and Robert Peterson have been lovers right from the first, and it's been bloody wonderful. But then we had a silly argument and, yes, he called me a whore and threw me out. I suppose you're satisfied now.'

'No, gal. I'm just sorry you can't see him for what he is.'

'You're jealous, that's all. Because your life's been one long drudge, you can't bear to see me making something of myself. Well, I don't give a monkey's what you say. I'll wait a few more days, till he comes to his senses, then I'm going back, and nothing you can say will change my mind.' With that she flounced out, straight into her brother Steve. 'And you keep your

nose out,' she ordered, realising he must have heard
every word. 'If I find out you've been anywhere near
him, you'll be sorry.'

'Wouldn't dream of it,' he said softly. But as
she went on her way, he had a cruel gleam in his
eye.

———————◆———————

'So!' ROBERT PETERSON stood by the fireside,
hands clasped behind his back and a look of
disdain on his face as he addressed his gamekeeper.
'The poachers got away yet again?'

'Empty-handed though,' came the reply. 'Half a
dozen rabbits and a string of fine, plump fish abandoned in the escape and now delivered to your own
kitchens.'

'That's not the bloody point, man!' Robert hated
the idea of his lands being plundered. 'I want these
poachers caught and punished.'

'They will be. They're a cunning bunch but it's
only a matter of time before I have 'em red-handed.'

'One month.'

'Beg your pardon, sir?'

'I'll have these poachers caught and punished, or
I'll have your job away. Got that, have you?'

'Yes, sir.'

'Good. See to it then.' He stared at Matthewson
until he had backed out of the room and closed
the door. 'Useless bastard!' Robert Peterson hated
everything and everyone at that moment.

Elizabeth was in the hallway when Geoff Matthewson came out of her husband's study. 'Good morning, Mr Matthewson,' she said politely.

Acutely aware that the maid was waiting by the door, he returned her greeting in the same polite manner. 'Morning, ma'am.' He nodded his head and gave a quiet, knowing smile. Then he waited for the maid to open the door, passed through it and went on his way.

Wasting no time, Elizabeth hurried up the stairs to her room where she ran to the window, her eager gaze following his progress across the fields.

The gamekeeper was a fine figure of a man, with fine brown hair and kind blue eyes. The very sight of him did her heart good. When he was gone from her view, she sat on the window seat, her eyes closed and her heart racing. Another hour, that was all. Just one more hour.

Exhilarated, she went to the wardrobe, where she rifled through every garment, until she found the one she wanted: a simple, pretty gown in fine white fabric with a low, sweetheart neckline and tiny red rosebuds trimming the hem and sleeves.

Quickly, she put it on and admired herself in the long mirror. 'Why shouldn't you have someone to love you?' she asked herself softly. She stepped out of her shoes and into her ankle boots which she laced tightly. She brushed her hair until it shone and then tied it into the nape of her neck; she touched her mouth with colour and her cheeks with rouge, and gave herself one last look in the mirror. 'I hope he likes my new dress,' she murmured. 'But then he seems to like me in anything. Not like Robert, who only sees what's underneath.' Her pretty features crumpled with sadness.

A few moments later she rang for the housekeeper. 'I have a crippling headache, Mrs Glover. A walk in the sunshine might do me good.' She had learned to lie beautifully. 'I shall be gone for about an hour, maybe a little more.'

'Quite right, ma'am. It's a glorious day.'

'With the governess dismissed and no one to take her place, I'm sorry you've been burdened with extra responsibilities.'

'I understand, ma'am.' Oh, she understood all right. The master had had his fun and now everyone else was paying. 'I'm sure it won't be for too long.'

'I'm interviewing a young woman for the post in the morning. Let's hope she will take some of the weight from your shoulders.'

Mrs Glover nodded, but she had reservations. If the new candidate was young and pretty, she wouldn't last any longer than the one before, and the one before that.

Elizabeth saw the look of disillusionment cross the older woman's face. 'I know what you're thinking,' she commented wryly, 'but rest assured, if I can arrange it, the new governess will be of a more mature and responsible nature.'

Mrs Glover smiled. 'Thank you, ma'am. Go for

your walk and don't worry. I'll keep an eagle eye on the children, see they don't come to any harm.'

'If the master wants me, please explain how I'm taking the air to rid me of this terrible headache. And that I should not be too long away.' If she only had the courage she would be gone and never return to this house, or the man, or, God help her, the children.

'Of course,' said the housekeeper and took her leave.

Downstairs in the kitchen, Mabel set the children outside with a picnic, close to the window where they could be seen. 'Mind you don't go wandering off now,' she chided, 'or you'll get a tanned arse an' no mistake.'

'You said arse!' little Kathleen giggled. 'That's a naughty word.'

Mabel was unruffled. 'Yer right,' she agreed. 'It is a naughty word, but you'll still get it tanned if yer run off.'

The children settled to their picnic and Mabel went inside chuckling. 'I've just been given a wigging by the little madam out there,' she said as Mrs Glover came into the kitchen.

'Did you deserve it?'

'Aye, I expect so. I mean, I did say a naughty word, after all.' With a few moments to spare, and it being a time when the servants gathered in the kitchen for their tea, she then put out the goodies on the kitchen table. 'Help yerself,' she told the others. 'Heaven only knows we've earned it.'

Settling down, they discussed the recent business of Connie Blakeman and the master, which consequently led on to the matter of a new governess. 'The children are a delight,' Mrs Glover said, 'but I can't do them justice with their learning.'

'Nor should you,' the butler reminded her. 'You get paid for housekeeping, not being governess to the children.'

'There's a woman being interviewed tomorrow for the post,' Mrs Glover informed them. 'Let's hope she stays longer than the last one.'

'Only if she's old and toothless,' Cook snorted.

Nancy Tomlin had a face stuffed with cake, but was so intrigued she had to ask and set them all laughing, 'Why would the mistress want to tek on somebody who were old and toothless? And anyway, wouldn't she frighten the children?'

'Yer a joy, Nancy Tomlin,' Cook told her in a fit of giggles. 'Yer might be daft as a brush, but yer a joy all the same.' And Nancy beamed so wide that all you could see was mangled cake. Until Cook told her to close her mouth, 'Before yer put us off our tea!'

Subdued by the ensuing laughter and feeling a bit of a fool, yet not really knowing why, Nancy closed her mouth and didn't speak again for an hour; much to Cook's delight.

⊷∢●∢⊶

AFTER LEAVING PETERSON's office, Geoff Matthewson did a quick tour of the spinney; he followed the path to the river and here he came across two men. One of them was Connie Blakeman's brother, Steve. 'What are you doing here?' Taking his gun off his shoulder, Matthewson held it loosely over his arm. 'This is private property. Be off with you!' Still smarting from the confrontation with Peterson, his tone was sharp. His job was at risk, and though he could soon get other work, he preferred to stay where he was. He had no liking for his employer but Elizabeth was another matter. While he worked here, he was close to her, and that was important to him.

Steve was quick to reply. 'Sorry, mate, we were just taking a short cut home. Me an' me mate here, we work at the mines – or we did till an hour back when we were given our cards and told to piss off. We ain't got no work at all now.' He paused. 'Don't suppose you've got work we could do, 'ave you?' he asked innocently.

'No,' said Matthewson curtly. 'And don't let me catch you here again,' he added.

The two men made their way off Peterson's land. 'By! That was close!' The older man, whose name was Ned, had been persuaded to the river against his will. 'If he knew we'd skipped work just to fish the river, we'd have had our collars felt an' no mistake. All the same,' he went on, 'we were caught on private property. Funny that gamekeeper didn't march us up to the house, don't you think?'

'Naw. He could see we were honest blokes,' quipped Steve. 'And anyway, he'd have to be a heartless bugger to haul us in when we've just lost our jobs.'

Ned laughed. 'How you came to think that one up, I'll never know.'

'Well, I weren't about to tell him that we were skiving work and fancied making a bob or two off the poacher's back.'

When Steve took another turn, away from the river and deeper into the woods, Ned was alarmed. 'Christ, Blakeman, where the hell are you going?'

'I fancy a fat rabbit for me tea.'

'Don't be so bloody daft, man. The gamekeeper can't be far away. He's probably watching us right now.'

'You're free to go.'

'You'll get us both hanged, you bugger.' But the prospect of a rabbit stew was too tempting, so he stayed. 'I've heard Peterson is a bastard.'

Steve nodded. 'You heard right.'

'From what I understand, he likes his women fresh and young. Treats 'em like dirt under his feet, so I'm told.'

Steve stayed quiet for a time, remembering his sister confessing how Peterson had bedded her time and again, and what was more she'd bloody well enjoyed it. Well, now she knew what he was like, and served her right. But what about his mam? Been a whore in her day, she had, and kept it quiet all these years. That had really got to him. Filled with contempt and disgust, he would never feel the same way towards either of them again. Yet he didn't altogether blame his mother and Connie. He blamed men like Peterson. Men who had it all, and still wanted more. Jealousy crept through him, trembling in his voice. 'That bugger Peterson needs teaching a lesson.'

'Maybe he does, but I'll leave that to others. It's all right for you, taking risks like this. You're footloose and fancy-free, but I've a wife and kids to worry about.'

Steve wasn't listening. 'If you knew your sister had been taken advantage of by a man who should know better, what would you do?'

'Cut his balls off, an' no mistake.' He'd hardly got the words out of his mouth when the sound of footsteps caused them to dive behind a shrub. 'It's a woman,' Ned whispered. 'By! She's a bit of all right an' all.'

'Ssh! It's Peterson's wife.'

'How do you know that?'

'Well, just look at her, man. She ain't the bloody gardener's wife, is she, eh?'

They ogled her from their hiding place. Her hair was loose and blowing in the breeze and the sun lit her face. She was enough to tempt any man, but Ned was nervous. 'Jesus Christ. Peterson's wife. And only an arm's reach away.' Trembling with fear, he clutched Steve by the arm. 'What if she sees us?'

'She won't.'

Ned wasn't convinced. 'I should never have listened to you in the first place. I must want my brains tested, coming on to Peterson land.'

'Ssh!' Elizabeth had stopped to look around. 'She must have heard you,' hissed Steve.

While the men crouched low, their hearts beating for fear of being discovered, Elizabeth remained quite still, her quiet eyes searching the immediate area. She had not heard them, but they didn't know that. Neither did they know that in fact she was afraid of being discovered herself and was only satisfying herself that she was not being followed. Presently she moved on, quickening her footsteps.

'That were too close for comfort, Blakeman.'

'Curious, weren't it?'

'What d'you mean, curious?'

'I mean she seemed to be looking for somebody.'

'Aye, she bloody were! She were looking for *us*. I'm off, mate, and if you had any sense, you'd do the same.'

Steve shrugged. 'Bugger off then.' He smiled. 'And mind how you go. I hear Peterson has mantraps set all over these woods. They'll tear your leg off like it were a twig.'

He watched Ned until he had disappeared from sight. 'Now then,' he muttered, his shifty eyes peering in the direction Elizabeth had taken, 'why would Peterson's wife be skulking about in the woods, I wonder? What if she's playing him at his own game, eh?' The thought was very satisfying. 'While he was bedding my sister, what if his lovely wife was being bedded by some other bloke?' He chuckled. 'Happen I should find out what she's up to.' With that he softly made after her and soon caught sight of her a short distance ahead. 'Easy, boy,' he told himself. 'Don't scare her off now.'

⟹━◦◦◦━⟸

ELIZABETH KNEW THE way by heart. Through the fringe of trees that bordered the woods, then down into the valley where the shepherd's hut nestled with its back to the trees and its face to the land. There was a time when the hut was used regularly, but not any more. Not since Robert had sold off all the sheep and concentrated on crops.

Her face lit up when she saw Geoff Matthewson standing at the door, and she ran to meet him. 'Oh, Geoff, Geoff, I do love you so.' She laughed like a child as he swung her round. Then he wrapped his arms round her and kissed her long and passionately.

'I'm so glad you're here,' he whispered. 'I was afraid you wouldn't be able to meet me.'

'Nothing would keep me away. Don't you know how much I love you?'

He held her to him. 'It's just that he was in such a foul mood, I thought he might take it out on you and somehow keep you from me.'

She shook her head. 'Never.'

'Are you ready to go inside?' He was ready. He was always ready.

'Can we go for a walk first?'

'We have to be careful, Elizabeth.' He glanced nervously about. 'We mustn't be seen. At least not until we've finalised our plans.'

'I know, but it's such a beautiful day, and I need to talk.' She gave him a little smile. 'I talk better when I'm walking.'

'Sounds serious.'

'It is.'

'About us?'

'Yes – and him, and the children.' A deep frown creased her pretty face. 'What we mean to do, and when. We have to be clear about it, Geoff. I need to talk it through.'

His face lit up. 'Are you saying you're ready to come away with me?'

'Yes, but I'm not sure what to do about the children.' She turned and started to walk away. He followed. 'I know I told you I didn't want to take the children, but now I'm not so sure. He's such a cruel man, and he hates the boy. He has an unhealthy obsession with Kathleen, and it frightens me.' She shivered. 'The children are so young, Geoff, so vulnerable. I don't know if I could bear to leave them with him.'

He caught her to him. 'Oh, Elizabeth. It's only right you should bring the children. They'll have a better life with us, you know that.' He smiled. 'Adam will make a fine young man, and Kathleen is such a delightful little soul.'

Shame suffused her face. 'I'm not a good mother,'

she murmured, unable to look him in the eye. 'It shames me to say so, but I have no talent for it.'

'I'll help you.'

'I'm afraid.'

'Don't be.' Taking her by the hand, he led her back to the hut. 'You know I would never let any harm come to you or the children.'

They moved out of earshot, but Blakeman had heard enough to have his suspicions confirmed. 'Well, I'm buggered!' He was beside himself with delight. 'So they're planning to clear off, eh? And take the kids an' all. By! I shouldn't think Peterson will take very kindly to that, no sir.' Going carefully so as not to be discovered, he backtracked towards the river. 'We'll have to see what the big man has to say about all this, won't we, eh?'

Laughing out loud, he began running and rounded the river bend straight into the arms of the man himself. His face coloured with fear. 'Mr Peterson!'

Robert Peterson was taller and far stronger than his quarry. He was also enraged at finding a stranger on his property. 'What the blazes are you doing on my land?' He grabbed Steve by his jacket. 'Who the hell are you?'

Filled with the knowledge of what he had just seen, and feeling the taste of revenge so close, Steve grew bolder. 'I'm Connie Blakeman's brother,' he said arrogantly. 'And I know all about you and her.'

Startled, Robert almost let him go, but then he tightened his grip and gave him a shaking. 'Blackmail, is it? Well, you can go to hell. Your sister knew what she was doing. She got what she wanted, and no more. She's just a whore, like all the others, and as for you, you're trespassing on my land.' His eyes glinted with malice. 'I'd be well within my rights to shoot you. I mean, you're a poacher, you ran away, I had no choice but to stop you.' With a sudden movement that took Steve by surprise, Robert flung him to the ground, dropped his gun from his shoulder and took aim. 'The only good poacher's a dead one,' he muttered.

Afraid for his life, Steve cowered before him, arms crossed over his face, babbling, 'It's not my sister who's the whore. It's your own wife. I've just seen them, her and the gamekeeper.'

There was a moment of silence, during which Steve didn't dare look up. Then pain exploded in his groin as Robert's booted foot slammed into him. 'You're a liar!'

'I'm not. I swear to God.' Still he didn't have the courage to look up. 'I'll take you to 'em if you want. Honest to God, I saw the two of 'em with me own eyes, kissing and canoodling, talking of running off an' taking the kids with 'em.' He felt the cold bore of the gun against his head and for a long, terrifying moment he thought Peterson would shoot him anyway. But then the gun was pressed into his back and he was viciously propelled forward.

'Move!' ordered Robert.

And move he did. As fast as he could, Steve led the way to the hut, every now and then glancing back at the gun which stayed unnervingly close, pointing right at him. He had never been so near to the barrel of a gun before and it was a terrifying experience. More than once he wished he'd gone with Ned when he ran off. But it was too late now, and he had to use his wits or never see his mam again. Suddenly that was important. He thought he was a man, but right now, in the face of losing his life, he was just a shivering, pitiful little wreck.

As they approached the hut, Steve pointed. 'There,' he said excitedly. 'They were just there.'

'Well, they're not there now.' Robert was past patience. 'I did warn you,' he said, and his meaning was clear.

'No! They're inside!' As there was no immediate sign of the woman and her lover, it was all he could think of. 'I swear! They were making plans and he said they should take the children, that you were a cruel bugger, and it would be wrong to leave them with you. She was afraid, but he said he would never let any harm come to her.' His life was at stake, and he had nothing to lose by telling the truth now. 'He asked her to go inside and she said she wanted to walk. But they're inside now. They've got to be!'

As if in answer to his prayers, the soft, pleasant sound of a woman's laughter rang out.

Robert was visibly shocked. 'Elizabeth!'

'I told you!' Steve was jubilant. 'I said they were inside!' Seeing how Robert had dropped his guard Steve broke away, and ran like the wind. 'You won't shoot me, you bastard!' he shouted bravely. 'If you're itching to shoot somebody, shoot them!'

It was only a matter of minutes before he heard two distinct shots. 'Jesus!' Gasping for breath, he stopped to look back. All around him the trees gave cover, but he felt naked and threatened. 'He's shot 'em!' He ran on, ignoring the flailing branches that cut and bruised him as he fled, dodging and weaving, getting deeper and deeper into the woods and growing more fearful with every step. 'He shot 'em!' he kept saying, over and over. 'The bastard shot 'em!' He knew how close he had been to the very same fate, and his soul quivered.

Suddenly his heart was almost stopped by the sound of Robert Peterson's voice calling, *'Blakeman, listen to me!'*

It was close. Too close. 'God Almighty, he means to kill me an' all!' He had seen too much, he couldn't be allowed to live.

'I only want to talk. I won't hurt you.'

Steve had no intention of stopping to 'talk'. He made himself go faster, his lungs burning. He had no doubts whatsoever that Peterson meant to shut his mouth once and for all.

'Blakeman, don't be a bloody fool, man. I only want to know what they said.'

God, but he was close.

'Blakeman?'

Visibly shaking and dripping with sweat, Steve flattened himself against the trunk of a broad oak tree, silently praying. 'Don't let him find me. Dear God, don't let him find me.' In all his life he had never been so frightened.

'We can do a deal. What do you say?' An eerie silence, then, 'Money in your pocket, Blakeman. More money than you've ever seen. What do you say to that?'

Steve was shaking so hard he thought Peterson must find him.

Robert feverishly hunted the area, poking his gun into the undergrowth and softly swearing under his breath. He came so close to where Steve was hiding that one sound, one breath too loud, and it would all have been over. But he didn't see him, and was eventually forced to conclude that Steve had run off, and was still running. 'Damn his eyes!' he cursed, and angrily strode away, leaving Steve almost collapsing with relief.

'Don't count your chickens,' he told himself. 'The bastard could be waiting anywhere for you.'

He was. Coming to the edge of the woods, Steve was shocked to see him patrolling up and down, obviously hoping he might still catch a glimpse of his quarry. 'The bugger ain't giving up easily,' he mused. 'I'd best keep down and go by way of the river.'

But in that moment when he believed he had cheated death, greed got the better of him. 'More money than I've ever had,' Peterson had said. '*They'll* have money on them, I'll be bound, her and her fancy man. What's more, if I remember right, the gamekeeper were carrying a very 'andsome shotgun. Happen I'll need it if I come face to face with the big feller again.' The prospect of being able to defend himself by the same means as his enemy was too tempting. 'Once I'm safely home, that shotgun should fetch a pretty penny, I'll be bound.'

Without delay, he turned and made his way back to the hut.

What he found sickened him to his stomach.

The man had obviously been shot first; he was at the far end of the hut and partway covered by the woman, who lay on her back with her arms flung wide, as though trying to shield him from her husband. They were both partly unclothed, not completely naked. Blood patterned the wall, and for a moment Steve was morbidly fascinated by Elizabeth's dress on which small splashes of blood had caused the tiny rosebuds to blossom into full-blown red roses.

'Can't blame him for wanting you,' he murmured, admiring her beauty. 'If I'd known you were going for the asking, I might have made a play for you myself.'

He bent to ease her aside and turned back the gamekeeper's jacket. Dipping into the pocket, he sighed with satisfaction. Just as he thought, the wallet was bulging. Quickly, he slipped it into his own pocket and was about to turn away when he was startled almost out of his wits as Elizabeth's hand reached out to take hold of his trouser leg. 'Help . . .' she whispered, her stricken eyes looking up. 'Please . . . bring help.'

Frantic, he didn't know what to do. Snatching

away, he stared down at her. 'You brought it on yourself,' he croaked miserably. 'I had to tell him or he'd have shot me. I had to tell him, I had to!' Tears ran down his face at the sight of her. She wasn't dead, like he thought. She was still alive, and he couldn't bear it. 'All right!' As bad as he was, he couldn't desert her altogether. 'I'll get help. I'll find somebody. Hang on, missus. Just hang on.'

He shifted her gently to one side, where he made her as comfortable as he could. Then he took off Matthewson's coat and laid it over her. 'Just hang on,' he said again. 'I'll be quick as I can.' Her eyes closed and he feared she was slipping away.

As he departed, he caught sight of the shotgun propped against the wall by the door. 'Don't suppose the poor bugger could get to it in time,' he remarked, snatching it up. 'But he'll pay. Me an' the woman in there, between us we'll see Peterson dangling on the end of a rope an' no mistake.'

Only then did he fully realise how much he needed to keep her alive. 'Jesus! If she croaks before I get back, it'll be my word against his. If I'm not careful, it'll be *me* dangling on the end of a bloody rope!'

Chapter Four

The sound of their boots echoed down the corridor. Silent and grim, the two officers made their way to the ward where Elizabeth Peterson lay, gravely ill and as yet unable to confirm or deny the account given by Steve Blakeman. 'If she dies without talking, we'll never know the truth,' Inspector Larch remarked as they approached the room. 'One of them is guilty. Which one, though? That's the thing. Which one?'

'For my money it's Blakeman,' his sergeant replied. 'Guilty as hell if you ask me, sir. Comes of a troublesome family, and he's been had up many a time before.'

'Minor things though.' Larch had his own strong beliefs. 'Nothing like this. Good God, man, we're talking about murder! Blakeman might be a bloody nuisance, and he'll fight with all and sundry, but murder? No, I don't reckon that. He's too much of a coward.'

'There's a first time for everything, sir. Blakeman had a run-in with the gamekeeper earlier, he admitted as much. Peterson himself said he caught Blakeman poaching on his land. And what about the sister? When

Peterson sacked her because she was no good at her job, she threatened to send her brothers round. What's more, the servants heard her make the threats.'

'I'm not denying Blakeman was poaching. That's about his style, and his workmate admitted that. But I still don't think he's guilty of murder.'

Then you're a bloody fool, thought Sergeant Armitage.

'What about his claim,' Larch went on, 'that Peterson's wife was having an affair with the gamekeeper? It has to be true. I mean, they were found together, weren't they? And why would Blakeman try and save her if it was him who shot her in the first place? It doesn't make sense.'

'It does if you're a cunning bugger like Blakeman. He probably didn't realise she was still alive and ran for help to make himself look good. As for finding the two of them together, who's to say Blakeman didn't somehow arrange all that, just to support his story? Who's to say he didn't shoot her elsewhere and then carry her to the hut? And think on this. If he did stumble across them, what was he doing so far into Peterson land? And what was he doing with the gamekeeper's gun?' Armitage shook his head, a smug little smile on his face as he concluded, 'He's as guilty as they come.'

'He told us why he took the gun. He said Peterson was after him, to shut him up because he'd seen too much. And what makes you assume Peterson had no motive for killing them both? What makes you think they *weren't* having an affair, just like Blakeman claims?'

'Because Blakeman's a liar, sir, and Peterson's not. I know which man I believe. I've dealt with his type before.'

'There's something strange about this whole business. When Blakeman burst into the police station, he was still carrying the gamekeeper's gun. He made no attempt to hide it, which makes me believe his story, that he took it for his own protection. Besides, we know now it wasn't that particular gun that fired the shots. So where's the weapon that did the damage? We've searched everywhere but we've still not been able to turn it up – unless Peterson's got it hidden away. If you ask me, that gent is making fools of us all.'

'If the murder weapon is hidden away, then it's *Blakeman* who's hidden it.' Sergeant Armitage was a man who looked at the immediate facts, made a fast opinion, and clung to it. 'Blakeman did it all right, but his dirty little plan backfired and now he's locked up where he should be. If there's any justice, he'll be hanged and we'll all be well rid of him.'

In the three weeks since she was brought to Blackburn Infirmary, Elizabeth Peterson had received the very best of care, and still she showed no sign of recovery.

'Please make it very brief,' the nurse instructed the officers as they entered the private room. Then she left them alone. She went no further than the corridor, where she chatted to the constable on duty.

'A terrible thing,' she commented. 'With the poor woman at death's door and her husband spending every minute God sends by her side.'

'I don't know what the world's coming to,' the constable replied. More than that he was not allowed to say.

'He's a creepy sort, though, don't you think?' She was glad Peterson wasn't *her* husband.

The constable coughed politely. 'Under the circumstances, I don't think it's wise for me to pass an opinion on the gentleman.' In truth, though, he didn't care much for Peterson. He didn't care much for Blakeman either. As far as he was concerned, the world would be a better place without both of them.

The sound of footsteps in the corridor made them turn.

'Well, I never,' said the constable under his breath. 'Talk of the devil,' and he gave the nurse a wink, to imply nothing she had said would be repeated.

Pale and gaunt, Robert Peterson looked in need of sleep and sustenance. The nurse went to meet him. 'Excuse me, sir, but the police are in with your wife.'

'Police?' Robert stiffened. 'You had no right letting them in to see her!'

'I had no choice, sir. It's only for a moment and I was never far away.'

'Out of my way.' Rudely shoving her aside, he burst into the room, demanding that the two men leave immediately. 'What kind of people are you?'

he said angrily. 'My wife is seriously ill. You can't just barge in here. I'll have your jobs for this!'

Inspector Larch tried to calm him. 'I'm sorry, sir, but we're not here to disturb your wife in any way, only to sit quietly and hope she may be able to tell us something.'

'How the hell can she do that? Talk sense, man!' After nights without sleep, his nerves were frayed, but he had to be careful. One slip and he might give himself away. 'You've no idea how distressing this is for me,' he said more calmly.

'We do understand how you feel, sir. But you have to understand our situation too. We're in the middle of a murder inquiry. The doctor informs us that your wife is not beyond regaining consciousness, if only for a moment or two. Anything, the smallest detail, might throw light on what happened.'

'You already know what happened. Blakeman and his sister did this, to teach me a lesson.' Robert bowed his head and ran his fingers through his hair. 'God Almighty, haven't we suffered enough,' he groaned. 'I want you out of here. I need to be alone with my wife.'

'Of course, sir.' Larch nudged his sergeant. 'We'll be just outside.'

Robert followed them to the door. 'I want to see the doctor,' he told the nurse. 'According to these gentlemen he told them my wife might regain consciousness. Why wasn't I told that? I want to see him. Now!'

'I'll see what I can do.' Arrogant man, she thought. Outside she told the officer in charge, 'I won't be long. I'm sure he wouldn't mind though, if you peeped in now and then.' It was just an instinct but it made her feel more comfortable to know he was being watched.

Robert closed the door and turned to the bed. For a long moment he stared at Elizabeth's face, at the deathly pallor and the closed eyes, and he feared the awful secret that lay behind them. 'Why don't you die?' he muttered. 'You shouldn't be here. You were meant to die with him, with your lover.'

A look of hatred coloured his features. 'You and him,' he hissed. 'You little whore! I ought to finish you off here and now.' Instead he bent to kiss her. 'See?' He was half crazed. 'You might prefer him to kiss you but he can't. He's dead, and so are you. It's only a matter of time.' Exhilarated by the power he had over her, he kissed her again. 'Do you hate the touch of my mouth on yours, eh, my darling? Want it to be him, do you? Oh, I am sorry. But you see it doesn't matter to me how you feel. If I want to kiss you, I will. If I wanted to make love to you, I could climb right in beside you.' Soft laughter issued from his throat. 'I can do whatever takes my fancy and there isn't a single thing you can do about it.'

He became maudlin. 'You should never have done it, you know. You should never have taken a lover. You insulted me, and I can't allow that, can I?' He took a deep breath and the words came out in a quiet rush.

'I wanted you dead then, and I want you dead now. Only I have to be careful. There's always somebody watching. They're outside right now.'

He put her limp hand in his. 'Day and night I've been here. Day and night, guarding you, afraid you might open your mouth and tell them what really happened.' He closed his eyes. 'Oh, I'm so tired, so very tired. Everything's being neglected. The farm's crying out for me to be there, it's harvest time, there are a thousand and one things I should be seeing to, but I don't care. Let it all go to pot. I'll start again somewhere. Once you're gone, I'll take off and make a new life. Put it all behind me . . . put *you* behind me.'

Suddenly he drew back. Her hand had been loosely resting in his, but now her long, fine fingers gripped his with such startling strength that it put the fear of God in him.

Just then the door opened and in came the doctor, followed by the nurse. One look at Peterson's horrified face and he said, 'What is it?' Bending to examine Elizabeth, he was astonished to see her eyes flicker open. 'Mrs Peterson, can you hear me?' he asked urgently. 'Don't worry. You're safe.'

'Tell her to let go!' Panic-stricken, Robert was struggling to release himself from her iron grip. 'Tell her,' he cried, 'for God's sake, tell her to let go!' He was trying to prise her fingers off but she had the grip of death on him and wouldn't let go.

'Nurse!' The doctor beckoned, then gave an

instruction. An injection was administered. Still, Elizabeth would not let go of her husband's hand. 'She's in spasm,' the doctor explained. 'A moment longer, that's all.'

When Elizabeth looked up at him, he realised she was trying to say something. Bending his head to hers, he listened intently. On the other side of the bed, Robert could not move, held there by his wife's unrelenting grip. 'What's she saying?' he demanded nervously.

Outside, the officers patiently waited. Then the nurse opened the door to usher them in. 'She's awake,' she informed them. 'Please, you must be very quiet.'

Inside the room, the atmosphere was electrifying, with Robert, frozen with fear, and Elizabeth relating the tragic events to the doctor in painful, broken whispers.

It was all over in a matter of minutes. Her last words were for her husband. 'God forgive you,' she said, and long after her eyes closed for the last time, she held on to him. It took both doctor and nurse to release him from her clutch.

Inspector Larch read Peterson his rights. Quickly and quietly, he was escorted from the room, quivering like a child. Six weeks later he was hanged, the bruises made by Elizabeth's fingers still on his flesh, 'Like the mark of Cain,' one officer said.

For years following his execution, there were those who claimed his greatest fear on going to the gallows was that Elizabeth would be waiting for him on the other side. There were also those who thought it highly unlikely, because the gentle Elizabeth had gone one way, while he, with his wickedness, had gone another.

Chapter Five

THE LONG, HOT summer clung, until it seemed it might last for ever. But now, in the first week of October, the brown and rust of autumn began to show in the hedgerows. The sun dipped lower in the skies and in the evening the breeze took a chilly edge. But autumn had its own special beauty, and though it was sad to see the summer leave, the onset of winter brought its own comforts.

'By! There's nothing like a cheery fire to warm the soul.' Mabel rubbed her hands and settled down after a fine dinner of baked fish and home-reared asparagus. 'The company appeared to enjoy the meal,' she told John who was seated beside her. 'I've never seen food disappear so quickly.'

John agreed. 'They certainly had some good appetites and that's for sure.'

'The plates were so clean and shiny, Nancy could have saved herself the trouble of washing up. If she'd put them plates straight into the cupboard as they were, I'd never have guessed.'

'Oh, yes, you would,' Nancy contradicted her from the other side of the table. 'You'd have known and

I'd have got a terrible beating for not doing my job properly.'

Mabel was offended. 'When did I ever give you a terrible beating, my girl?'

'Sorry, Cook,' Nancy muttered. 'Yer ain't never done that, even though there's been times when I've deserved it.'

'Think before you speak, my girl,' Mabel reprimanded. 'I'll thank you not to make me look like an ogre.' She gave John a sidelong glance. 'Especially not in front of Mr Mason here.'

'Oh, don't worry,' he remarked, smiling from one to the other. 'I know very well you're not an ogre. You've always been kind and fair, and generous to a fault,' he gushed, always trying to get into her good books.

'Hmm. It's a pity Nancy doesn't think so.'

The sound of Nancy crying startled them. 'Whatever's the matter?' Getting out of her chair, Mabel went to the girl's side. 'You mustn't take it to heart, I meant nothing by it. You know me, I were just letting off steam.'

'It ain't that,' wailed Nancy.

'What is it then?' asked John.

'I'm worried about me job.' The tears fell thick and fast, and Mabel had to dip into her pocket for a hankie which she pushed into Nancy's hand; though instead of drying her tears with it she screwed it over and over in her fist, until Mabel was obliged to take it from her.

JOSEPHINE COX

'You never have appreciated good things,' she
chided gently. 'This was a present from Mr Mason.'
Holding it up, she pointed to her initials embroidered
in the corner. 'See? He had it done specially.'

Nancy had other, more pressing matters on her
mind. 'I don't want to lose me job,' she wailed. 'Oh,
Cook, I'm that worried.'

'We're all worried about our jobs,' Mabel said
stiffly. 'It's worrying times but we'll just have to make
the best of it.'

Nancy wasn't reassured. 'Whatever will I do?'

Straightening her back, Mabel put her hands on
her hips. 'We'll know our fate tomorrow. Until then
it's not a bit of good you fretting.'

'You don't understand,' Nancy wailed. 'Me mam
says if I lose me job I'm not to show me face at her
door again.'

'What?' It was enough to make John get out of his
chair. He knew Nancy was the eldest of a large and
poor family, but surely she would still have a home
to go to. 'That's not fair,' he said. 'It's not up to us.
With the master and mistress gone and the whole
place going to pot, doesn't your mam know we could
all be given our marching orders and through no fault
of our own?'

'I've told her that but she don't care. She says it
ain't no party with so many young mouths to feed and
a man who don't like to work, an' if I think I'm coming
back to be another burden on her then I've to think
again, because she don't want me nowhere near.'

100

'Then you'll just have to get another live-in position.' Mabel was ever optimistic.

'Who's gonna set me on, eh? I ain't no good at nuffin'.'

'What are you talking about?' Mabel exclaimed. 'Who told you such a thing?'

'You did.'

Mabel was shocked into momentary silence. Guiltily she recalled the many occasions on which she had indeed called the girl good for nothing, but that was then and this was now. 'Nonsense!' she spluttered and bristled with indignation. 'I must say, girl, sometimes your imagination runs away with you.'

'She has a point,' John intervened. 'I wonder if any of us will find another place after what's happened in this household. I mean, there's been both of 'em carrying on outside their marriage, then murder committed, then a hanging, and now it seems that he ran up bad debts all over the place.'

'Hearsay,' Mabel replied promptly. 'Until someone in authority tells me otherwise, I shall treat those nasty little rumours with the contempt they deserve.'

'Come now, Mabel,' John persisted. 'You know as well as I do, the man was no good.'

Being the superstitious soul she was, Mabel softly warned, 'Mustn't speak ill of the dead.' And all three made the sign of the cross. 'All the same, you're right,' Mabel conceded. 'These past months the estate has been going downhill fast. I blame the solicitor myself. When the manager took off, he should have got someone else in the very next day. Instead the crops were left to rot and now the creditors are queuing up.' Nancy started crying again but this time Mabel took no notice. 'I wonder, when the debts are settled will there be enough money left to pay what *we're* owed?'

John had been thinking along the same lines. 'I've always guarded against something like this,' he said proudly. 'A few shillings here and there over the years. I'm pleased to say it's mounted up to a pretty penny.' To Mabel's extreme embarrassment, he eyed her curiously. 'I imagined you might have been doing the same.'

'Maybe I have and maybe I haven't,' Mabel retorted. 'If I haven't, I dare say it's my own fault, and if I have, it's no one's business but my own.'

John felt well and truly put in his place and there followed a moment's silence while each of them reviewed their own particular situation.

It was Nancy who broke the silence. 'Yer lucky to 'ave a nest egg,' she said. 'I ain't got a farthing to call me own.'

The other two stared at her.

'Not even tuppence to get you from here to any position you might be offered?' Mabel asked.

Nancy shook her head. 'Not a farthing. Not a penny. And even if I were offered a position, I couldn't present meself, 'cause I ain't got no decent clothes, nor money to buy 'em.' In fact she thought the best solution was for her to climb on Blakewater Bridge and throw herself over.

'Where's all yer wages gone then?' John was so frugal he couldn't believe anyone could squander everything they earned.

'Gone to me mam.'

Mabel was shocked. 'What? All of it?'

'Every penny. Every week, reg'lar as clockwork, and now, if I can't send money, she don't want me.'

'She don't deserve you!' Mabel had a mind to pay Nancy's mother a visit, and she said as much. But Nancy was filled with such horror at the idea that she had to promise not to do it.

'Right then.' Taking charge, John began pacing the floor. 'This is the situation as I see it.' He took a deep breath. 'As Cook rightly said, the manager went some time back and since then many of the farmhands beside. We've lost old Tom the gardener, who struck lucky and was offered a place with the Henshaws in Langho. And then there's Mrs Glover who's staying only out of loyalty to the children. Little by little this household is falling apart. It's been dragging on for weeks, but now, what with the gathering of officials, it seems some sort of decision is about to be made.'

'D'yer think they'll throw us out?' Nancy was still in a fright.

'There's no telling.' He didn't want to alarm the women but felt it his duty to point out the possibilities. 'Anything could happen. We shall just have to hope they want the household to remain intact. No doubt we shall be the last to know. We might be fortunate, Nancy, so don't go worrying yourself half to death.

The solicitors might decide in their wisdom to keep the house up and running for the sake of the children – though who will be in charge of it all, God only knows. On the other hand, if the rumours of bad debts are true, the children might be taken away and the house sold. If that turns out to be the case, every man jack of us will have to fend for himself.' He smiled at Mabel. 'Of course there are those who will never want for a home or someone to take care of them.'

Embarrassed, she looked away, her face pink.

'So there you are,' John concluded. 'That's the way I see it.'

'I do wish we knew for sure, one way or the other,' Mabel said quietly. 'It's so unsettling.'

Squaring his narrow shoulders, he tucked in his chin and sounded very official. 'It's out of our hands. We should get a good night's sleep and hope tomorrow brings favourable news for us all.'

'It's them children my heart goes out to.' Mabel shook her head forlornly. 'Poor little buggers. With both their parents gone and the house filled with strangers to decide their future, heaven only knows what they're going through.'

<hr />

UPSTAIRS, SEATED BESIDE Kathleen on the window seat, Adam tried not to let her see how afraid he really was. 'They won't let us come to any harm,' he told her. 'We'll be taken care of, you're not to worry.'

'I don't like that man.'

'Which man?'

'Mr Ernishoam.'

Adam smiled. 'You mean Mr Ernshaw.'

'Yes.'

'Why don't you like him?'

'Because he'll take you away from me.'

'I won't let him!' The idea that he and Kathleen should be separated was unthinkable. 'He and the others are here to see how they can keep us together.'

'Who are those men, Adam?' So much had happened so quickly, Kathleen's young mind could hardly grasp the implications.

'Mrs Glover already told you.' So many questions, and so much to think about.

Tears trembled in her eyes. 'Don't be cross with me.'

He put his arm round her shoulder and drew her close. 'I'm not cross.'

'Are you afraid?'

'Of course not!' Yet he was only a boy, and it was hard, being strong enough for both of them.

'Who are they, Adam?'

'Mr Ernshaw is Father's solicitor. I don't know who the others are.'

'I want them to go away.' Small and frightened, the only time she felt safe was when Adam was here.

'They'll all be gone tomorrow.'

'And will they never come back?'

'I don't suppose so.'

'Will Father ever come back?'

The question took him by surprise. 'Do you want him to?'

'No.'

'Then he won't.'

'Why are those men here, Adam?'

In as kind and careful a way as possible, Mrs Glover and Mr Ernshaw had outlined the situation to Adam. Not the true situation, however. No one had had the courage or seen any reason to explain that his mother had taken a lover and when his father had discovered them together he had killed them both. Instead, the boy was told a simple tale. 'Your parents were killed in an accident on the highway,' they said. 'Nobody's fault. Just one of those dreadful things.'

Once again, Adam explained it to his sister in the same careful way he himself had been told. 'So we're orphans now. The men are here to decide our future.'

Kathleen was too young. 'If Father comes back, we'll have to run away, won't we, Adam?' In her mind she could see the rage on her father's face. She could feel the cruelty and loathing; smell it, as if it was a perfume that clogged the brain. It was something she would carry with her all her life.

'He *won't* come back,' Adam promised. 'People can't come back if they're killed.'

'He hurt you.' Another image, another reason to be afraid.

'He can't hurt me any more.'

'Mummy was pretty, wasn't she, Adam?'

'Yes.' But she was distant. They could never love her.

'Why did she never cuddle me?'

'Maybe she didn't know how.' He felt her tremble. 'Are you sorry she's not coming back?'

'I think so.' Raising her face, she looked at him; a small, trusting little face, the sad eyes filled with confusion. 'Adam?'

'Yes?'

'Are *you* sorry?'

'What about?'

She shrugged her shoulders. 'I don't know.'

He thought for a moment. Yes, he was sorry. He was sorry he could never reach his father. He was sorry his mother had been like a stranger to them. He was sorry for his little sister. 'I'm sorry they wouldn't let us go to the funeral,' he said; that bothered him more than anything.

'Why?'

'Because they were our parents.'

'Mrs Glover didn't want us to go, and Cook didn't want us to go either. I heard her telling Nancy.'

'Nobody asked *us*.' That was the bit that hurt. He was the man of the house now, and nobody had asked his opinion about going to his own parents' funeral. 'We should have been there. It was our place to be there, Kathleen.'

'I'm tired, Adam.'

'Get into bed then.' He walked across the room with her. 'I expect we'll have to be up early in the morning. Mrs Glover said we might be sent for.'

Kathleen was too tired for all that. 'Goodnight, Adam.'

'Goodnight.' He gazed down at her, then softly left the room and went to his own bed.

But he didn't sleep. With both his parents gone and strangers in charge, he didn't know what to expect. 'I'm frightened too, Kathleen,' he murmured. 'Frightened of what might happen to us. Frightened they might send us away from each other.'

It was a terrible, crippling fear.

———◆———

MORNING BROKE IN a blaze of glory. 'By! What a day for the sun to shine,' Mabel exclaimed. 'It should be pouring with rain, and a sky so black and thick you'd think it were a pie crust over the world.'

Nancy nodded in fervent agreement.

'Away with you!' After a sleepless night, John looked ragged. 'We must look on the sunny side, Mabel. It won't do to get ourselves in a state before we even know what the verdict is.'

'I had bad dreams, an' now I'm fit for nuthin'.' She dropped into the armchair. 'If they think I'm cooking breakfast, they can think again. I'm not budging from this chair until someone tells me whether I'm safe enough here or whether I'm out on the street.' She folded her arms and set her features.

John was unperturbed. 'Is that freshly brewed?' he asked, pointing at the big brown teapot.

'Course it is!' She had no patience, not even with him.

He took a moment discreetly to regard her. She didn't look her usual self, he thought. There were bags beneath her eyes, and a tight line to her mouth that suggested she meant every word she said. It was plain she needed something to distract her from the matter that was to be finalised in the drawing room after breakfast.

With this in mind, he went to the table and poured himself a cup of tea. With great deliberation, he took a mouthful, immediately grimacing. 'I thought you said this tea was freshly brewed?'

Both Nancy and Mabel stared at him in astonishment. 'What's the matter with you?' Mabel demanded, ready for a fight. 'I made that tea meself not two minutes afore you walked through that door.'

Taking his life in his hands, he bravely confronted her. 'All I can say is, you must be losing your touch. This tea's stone cold.' To underline his point, he strode to the sink and threw the offending liquid into it. 'In fact it might be as well you're not cooking breakfast for our guests or you might poison them before they've a chance to secure all our jobs.'

'You devil!' Mabel was beside herself. 'In future you'd best stay outta my kitchen. D'you hear?'

As he left he could hear the pots and pans being slammed down. 'I've never known anything like it,'

Mabel complained loudly. 'Coming into my kitchen and telling me I can't make tea. The very idea!'

Unable to resist a peek, John inched open the door and poked his head round it. Mabel was standing at the range, sleeves rolled up as she arranged the bacon rashers in the pan. Nancy stood at the table, slicing bread and looking like the tousle-headed mop that stood outside the back door.

She looked up, and was so startled by the sight of John's face she gave a squeal. The squeal startled Mabel, who splashed herself with hot fat and flew into a tantrum. 'What have you done now, you silly, useless girl?' she shrieked. 'Get over here and see to the bacon. I'd better slice the bread afore you cut your skinny arm off.'

As she exchanged places with Mabel, Nancy shot a look at John, who winked at her. 'Cook?'

'What now, for heaven's sake?'

'I think the butler fancies me.'

'What?' Swinging round, Mabel glared at her. 'How did that foolish notion get into your silly head?' Mimicking the girl, she said, '"I think the butler fancies me." Good grief, girl, have you lost your mind?'

'Just now,' Nancy revealed, 'he was at the door and he winked at me.'

'Winked at you?'

'He were there, I tell yer. He were the one who made me squeal. I didn't mean to do it, only he winked, d'yer see?'

Mabel was indeed beginning to see. 'Are you

saying he was watching from the door?' she asked softly. 'That he never really went after he threw away his tea?'

'That's right, Cook. An' he were smiling, like he were really pleased about summat.'

Mabel burst into laughter. 'Why, the crafty little bugger! The tea weren't cold at all. It were just a ruse to get me in a temper so I'd feed the devils out there.'

And feed them she did, with tureens filled to the brim with bacon and sausage, and mushrooms and tomatoes. There were kippers and porridge, and freshly squeezed orange juice; piping-hot coffee and tea, and thick slices of toast dripping with butter. All in all, it was a feast for kings.

'Splendid!' After such a meal, Mr Ernshaw was ready for battle. 'If you've finished, gentlemen, shall we retire to the drawing room?' He looked round the table, taking in the stern expression of a rival solicitor who was here to represent irate creditors who were demanding the sale of all land and property. There was also an appointed judiciary to weigh up all the considerations and arbitrate as necessary, and finally there was Mr Ernshaw's own partner who was here to lend support to the unlikely prospect that maybe the house and lands could be saved and thereby perhaps secure the future of the unfortunate children.

It was a very delicate situation, and one which would tax all their skills.

Impatient to get started, Mr Ernshaw beckoned to Nancy, who was attending table and looked quite presentable in a clean white apron over a dark frock, with her hair firmly pushed under a pretty cap.

'Yes, sir?'

'Please advise Mrs Glover that we will expect her in the drawing room in one hour from now.'

'Yes, sir.'

'And kindly bring a pot of tea through.' He patted his rotund stomach. 'We've thirsty work ahead.'

'Yes, sir.' Nancy knew what thirsty work he was talking about. When these men came out of the drawing room, she and everyone else would know the worst, or the best.

<hr />

M RS GLOVER WAS in the kitchen, talking to Mabel and John. 'You'd think they might have come to a decision yesterday,' she was saying. 'Half the day walking the grounds, taking notes and looking into every nook and cranny, then another four hours locked in the drawing room. Four long hours talking it through, and not one of them prepared to give way.'

'What makes you so sure they'll come to a decision today?' John's anxiety was echoed on everyone's face.

'Because I've been told as much.'

They all turned as Nancy entered. 'Mr Ernshaw says you're to see him in the drawing room in an hour.'

'There you are then,' said Mrs Glover. 'One hour. They must have thrashed out most of the business yesterday after all.'

Nancy brought some shocking news back with her when she returned from taking in the tea tray. 'Mr Ernshaw was saying how the children were orphans now, and there was a danger of them being sent to the orphanage.' She was so upset she could hardly talk. 'If they don't care about the children, why should they care about us?'

John calmed her down. 'I expect they were looking at the worst possibility,' he said. 'It wouldn't surprise me if Mr Ernshaw was just being clever. He's the one who wants to keep the house and land, don't forget.'

'Will it be all right then?'

'Of course it will,' he assured her. 'Now then, get about your work and put it all out of your head.'

While the servants waited inside the house, the children sat in the orchard with Mrs Glover who was reading a favourite storybook to them. 'I have to go inside now,' she told them when Nancy came to remind her of the time. 'Adam, read to your sister while I get back, will you?' Adam read well, and Kathleen, too, had an excellent grasp of the written word.

When Mrs Glover walked into the kitchen she found Mabel, Nancy and John lined up by the hallway door, looking at her as if silently pleading for their jobs to be saved. 'I'll do my best,' she murmured as she swept by; for wasn't her own position at stake too?

A sharp tap on the drawing-room door and she was quickly summoned inside. 'Ah. Mrs Glover.' Ernshaw gestured to a chair. 'Please, sit down.' When she did so, he went on in sombre voice, 'We have finally managed to reach agreement,' he informed her, 'but I'm afraid it isn't the news you might have hoped for.'

Suddenly, to her shame, she had thoughts only for herself. 'Tell me at once,' she said boldly. 'Is my position safe here?'

He studied her for a moment, thinking how human nature could be so disappointing. He had truly believed that Mrs Glover, above all people, would want to know how the children were to fare in this dreadful situation, and here she was, concerned only for her own situation. 'The decision we have reached affects everyone in this house,' he said sternly. 'Perhaps it might be as well if you were to sit quietly and listen to what I have to say.'

While Mrs Glover listened in silence in the drawing room, Mabel sat without speaking at her big kitchen table drinking tea, Nancy nervously bit off every fingernail, and John paced the floor, hands behind his back and a look of determination on his face.

Some time later, Mrs Glover went to fetch the children. 'You're to see Mr Ernshaw in the drawing room,' she told them, and when they had gone, she silently wept. 'I let you down,' she whispered. 'You trusted me, and I let you down.'

By the time she came into the kitchen, she was composed enough to impart the news. 'The house is to be sold to satisfy the creditors, and I'm afraid we are all out of work.'

Nancy cried, and Mabel looked at John with sorry eyes. 'What about the children?' he asked, voicing the question that was on everyone's lips. 'Surely to God they won't send those two bairns to the orphanage?'

'You may recall a visitor here some time ago, not long after little Kathleen was born. A small, wizened old dowager, who was sent packing by the master after only two days.'

'Widow Markham!' Mabel cried at once. 'I remember. She was the strangest little thing I've ever clapped eyes on.'

Even Nancy recalled the odd visitor. 'She just turned up one day and never left her room until the master kicked her out.' She rolled her misty eyes. 'She were ninety if she were a day. I expect she's dead and gone by now.' Even in her misery she had to chuckle. 'When she were going, she told the master how she'd be back and then he'd have to pay what he owed her. Shouted at 'im all the way to the carriage, she did. What a funny little thing she were.'

'No funnier than you, my girl!' Mabel remarked. 'By! You've got a lot to say for yourself all of a sudden, haven't you? Sit still and be quiet while we hear what Mrs Glover has to tell us.'

Mrs Glover continued, 'It seems that Widow Markham was Mrs Peterson's aunt, and consequently the children's great-aunt and only living relative.'

The news came as a great surprise to one and all. 'Mind you, we shouldn't be all that surprised,' Mabel decided. 'If I remember rightly, she arrived as if she were part of the family. There was a lot of arguing, like families sometimes do, and when the old dear left, Mrs Peterson did seem upset.'

'So the children have a great-aunt,' John said. 'Does that mean they won't be going to an orphanage after all?'

'No orphanage,' Mrs Glover confirmed. 'According to the solicitor, there won't be much money after all the debts are paid, but apparently enough to satisfy their modest needs should their great-aunt agree to have them.'

'I bet she won't!' Mabel was convinced. 'I mean, the master threw her out of here so she ain't likely to want his childer, is she?'

'Time will tell.' John always tried to be optimistic. 'And what will you do, Mrs Glover?' he asked politely.

'I expect I shall find a post. Mr Ernshaw says he'll give me the highest references.' She hadn't expected that after showing that streak of selfishness. 'What about you?'

'Oh, I have plans,' he said cagily with a twinkle in his eye. 'I mean to get married and open a guesthouse by the seaside.'

Mabel was astounded. 'Married?'

'That's right,' he confirmed, 'if you will please do me the honour, Mabel my love.'

She went all shades of red. Nancy screamed out loud, and Mrs Glover beamed with pleasure. 'Oh, how romantic,' she sighed, thinking it could never happen to her.

Flustered and thrilled, Mabel accepted and everyone had a drop of best sherry. 'Here's to us,' John said, raising his glass.

The only one with a frown on her face was Nancy. 'I wish I were going with yer,' she muttered.

John put the matter to his betrothed. 'What do you think, Mabel? Will you need someone to change the beds in your little guesthouse?'

'I dare say I will,' she chuckled. 'There'll be rugs to beat and washing to be done, tables to be waited on and all manner of household duties to see to.' Winking at Mrs Glover, she said wryly, 'I'm not sure Nancy has it in her. I mean, she's such a little thing, don't you think?'

Everyone laughed when Nancy jumped up to show off her muscles. 'I can fetch and carry better than *anyone*!' she protested, then burst into simultaneous tears and laughter when Mabel told her she'd better start getting her bags ready, 'If you're coming with us.'

PART THREE

1855
THE LEAVING

Chapter Six

KATHLEEN WAS AFRAID. 'I don't want to go,' she sobbed as Mr Ernshaw hurried her along the hallway to the front door. 'I want Adam! Where's Adam?'

Impatient to get the difficult task over and be on his way, Mr Ernshaw gave her a little shake. 'Behave yourself, child!' he reprimanded. 'You know very well Mrs Glover has gone to fetch him.'

'Poor little bugger.' Peering from the kitchen door, Mabel wiped the tears from her own face. 'She's only a bairn,' she muttered to John, who was standing beside her. 'She's lost her mam and dad, and now she's being shipped off to some strange old woman she's never met in her life afore.'

As always, John looked on the bright side. 'Let's be thankful they're not being shipped off to some awful orphanage. At least they'll be with blood kin.'

Nancy joined them. 'That ain't allus a good thing neither,' she told them. 'See how me mam's turned on her own daughter. Since I lost me job, she'll not even look at me in the street.'

'Aye, but you'll be all right,' John replied kindly.

'God willing, you'll have a good home with me and Mabel.'

Mabel had something to say about that. 'Mebbe. So long as she keeps her nose clean and earns her keep,' she said. 'At our age, we can't afford to carry no lazy good-for-nothings.'

Nancy was indignant at the slur on her good character. 'That ain't fair, Cook,' she replied sulkily. 'I ain't *never* been a lazy good-for-nothing.'

'Aye, well, think on you never are,' Mabel warned.

Suddenly Kathleen broke free from Mr Ernshaw and flung herself at Mabel. 'I want to stay here,' she cried, holding on to her skirt for dear life. 'Me and Adam don't want to go away.'

Deeply moved, Mabel swallowed her tears and painted on a smile. 'You'll be fine, bless yer,' she told the child. 'You're going to yer Aunt Markham's house, and you'll have Adam there with you. Be a good girl now, won't you, eh?'

'I don't want to go,' Kathleen wept. 'Don't want to go.'

Pulled away by Mr Ernshaw, she cried all the more. 'You're a bad girl!' he declared, marching her to the front door. 'It took time and a great deal of effort to squeeze enough money out of this estate to see that you children were well placed.' Red with anger, he let his temper get the better of him. 'I've a good mind to send you to the workhouse. You'd have something to cry about then, I'm sure.'

John stepped forward. 'There's no need for threats,'

he said angrily. 'Can't you see, the child is frightened enough.'

Furious, Mr Ernshaw drew to a halt, keeping a firm hold on the struggling Kathleen. 'I'll thank you not to interfere, my good man. Especially as you have not yet received your severance pay.'

It was enough to silence them all. Without their severance pay it would be difficult trying to build a new life elsewhere.

'Shame on you, sir.' Mrs Glover had not heard the warning but she'd heard the child sobbing, and she'd heard Mr Ernshaw shouting at her to stop. 'I did warn you. It would have been kinder to bring the children down together.'

'I'm here to carry out my duty,' Mr Ernshaw told her acidly. 'With other urgent business to attend to, I have no time to waste. I want the children away so we can finish up here before the auctioneers move in.'

His words had a deep effect on all those present. Whether he meant it to be or not, it was a stark reminder that their work here was finished and, like the children, they were about to embark on an uncertain future.

'Lord help us,' Mabel muttered and scurried into the kitchen to shed more tears. Nancy followed and sat dolefully at the table. John remained where he was, head bowed and heart heavy. 'Before this is over,' he said, 'we'll all need a slice of good fortune.'

Adam ran downstairs to his sister. 'Don't cry, Kathleen,' he urged. 'We'll look after each other.' He took hold of her hand and, with great dignity, walked her to the waiting carriage.

When the luggage was loaded, Kathleen looked at Mrs Glover. 'I wish you were coming too,' she said forlornly. 'I wish Cook was coming, and Nancy, and everyone.' While she spoke, she held Adam's hand so tightly her knuckles ached.

'Bless you.' Mrs Glover's voice wavered with emotion. 'Remember what Adam said,' she urged gently. 'You can look after each other.' Cupping the child's face between her hands she tenderly kissed it. 'Your aunt will love you both,' she promised. Yet deep down she wondered. Would their lives be any better for their change in fortunes? Or would they be worse?

The other servants gathered round and said their goodbyes. 'God luv 'em,' Mabel trembled as the carriage drew away down the drive. 'Let's hope they're going to a better place, eh?'

'Aye.' John knew exactly what she meant. 'They've not known much love in this house, that's for sure. Let's hope to God they'll be cherished by their aunt, however strange she may be.'

Nancy had been thinking about her own particular situation at home. 'If there's any justice in the world, they will be,' she said with such feeling that they were all subdued.

They made their way back into the house and a moment later Mr Ernshaw joined them in the kitchen. 'Now then,' he said, seating himself at the table and unfolding a large leather file, 'let's get this over with.'

Half an hour later he rose to leave. 'You have your dues,' he said, pointing to the envelopes each one clutched, 'and you have your orders. The house is to be left spotless from top to bottom, and all of you are to be gone by four o'clock today. Mrs Glover, you are to oversee the leaving and then to deposit the keys at my office.' He looked from one to the other. 'Be warned, I've taken an inventory of everything, so I shall know if even the smallest item goes missing.'

There was a chorus of protest.

'Are you calling us thieves?'

'You've no call to say a thing like that!'

He was unmoved. 'So long as you understand what I'm saying.'

When they silently glared at him, he grunted. 'Right. I'll be off then. Good luck to you all.'

After he'd gone, they all remained in their seats for a moment. 'The house seems dead with the children gone,' Mabel mumbled, and Nancy shivered.

The first to rise was Mrs Glover. 'We might as well get on with it,' she suggested. 'I'll check the upstairs, if you'll check downstairs,' she told John. 'Once that's all done, we can pack our bags and meet back here in an hour.' She glanced at Mabel. 'Is that all right?'

'Sounds fine to me. There's nothing to be done that I know of. I had Nancy cleaning the upstairs all morning, and there isn't a speck of dirt or dust in my . . .' She stopped. 'It isn't *my* kitchen any more, is it?' she whispered brokenly.

John put his arm round her. 'Come on now,' he

said fondly. 'We've a number of guesthouses to view, so with a bit of luck and some canny bargaining on my part, you'll have your own kitchen soon enough.'

'Not before I've a ring on me finger!' she told him.

'And that will be taken care of before you can say Jack Robinson,' he promised.

The house was checked and nothing was amiss.

One hour later, they each returned to the kitchen carrying their bags. 'Well, this is it.' Mabel looked round the kitchen and her heart sank. 'I shan't see this again,' she said. 'I hope the next person to come in here takes care of it. I couldn't bear to think of it all going to rack and ruin.'

Overcome, Nancy muttered, 'I'll wait outside,' and made good her escape.

There was nothing more to be said, so the others followed her outside. Mrs Glover locked the doors. They all shook hands, wishing each other well, and then went their separate ways – John, Mabel and Nancy to the bottom of the lane to catch the bus to the railway station and a train to Blackpool, to view the first guesthouse on their long list, Mrs Glover to the offices of Ernshaw, Trial and Bottomley, Solicitors, where she would deliver the keys and wash her hands of the Peterson place for good and all. Once her duty was done, she meant to go straight to the agency on King Street; they had promised to find her a place with a suitable family in Manchester.

Just before she turned out of Penny Street, she

glanced back, to see the others waving her off. 'Good-bye,' she murmured, waving back. 'And good luck.'

As she continued on her way, two other faces entered her mind; small, innocent faces with young, sad eyes. 'Mr Ernshaw should have let the children meet their aunt before packing them off,' she muttered. 'But then she wasn't interested in meeting them, was she? If you ask me, all Widow Markham wants is the money that Mr Ernshaw enticed her with.'

It was a very worrying situation, but not one she was paid to worry about, she reminded herself. She had her own uncertain future to cope with. All the same, she couldn't help but wonder what sort of life was awaiting the children. How would they be received? Most important of all, would they be given the love they so desperately needed?

Mrs Glover sighed. It was all very unsettling and worse, she would never know what became of them.

Chapter Seven

THEY WERE LEAVING.

Kathleen and he would never again climb the aged oak trees in the grounds of that big old house. They would never again see the new lambs being born, or play in the corn when it was so high they could hide from the world. They wouldn't sit at Cook's table, eating the delicious tarts that spilled over with warm raspberry jam. Nor would they be taken into town by Mrs Glover, to gaze at the shop windows and later stop at the pretty little café in the railway station for a plump muffin and a glass of dark-brown sarsaparilla.

All that was gone. But then, so were the beatings and the fear. So were their parents; the pretty mother with the cold heart, and the father with his hatred and obsessions. All were gone.

'Where are we going, Adam?' The small, familiar voice broke into his mind. At least she's still here, he thought. We still have each other.

'You know where we're going.' He tried so hard not to be impatient with her. She was only a baby, and he had to take care of her now. 'We're being sent to Lytham St Anne's.'

'What's the lady's name?'

'Great-Aunt Markham.' Very carefully, he pushed aside a lock of hair that was falling over her dark eyes. 'She was Mummy's aunt, and so she's our great-aunt. Mr Ernshaw says she's promised to look after us.'

'She's never seen us.'

'She did, once, when we were small. I think Father threw her out.' It was only a dim memory. He remembered being woken by angry voices, and when he started down the stairs, this little woman was being bundled out of the door. 'Mummy was crying, and Father was in a really bad mood. When he slammed the door shut, he told Mummy her aunt was never to visit the house again.'

'I don't remember that.'

'You were too small to remember. I was nearly six.' He didn't go on to tell Kathleen how his father had found him hiding on the stairs and he had received a terrible beating.

'What if she doesn't like us?'

'Why would she not like us?' He shrugged his shoulders. 'It wasn't us who threw her out.'

'What if we don't like *her*?'

'We *have* to like her, Kathleen. Mr Ernshaw said if it wasn't for Great-Aunt Markham, we might have been sent to the orphanage.'

'Oh.' The very word 'orphanage' made her shiver. 'We won't have to go now, though, will we, Adam?'

'No.'

'Does she live on a farm?'

'No. She lives west of here, at the seaside. Mrs Glover says we're very lucky.'

'I'd rather live at home.' With the fields and the trees, and the pretty flowers all around. She could see it all in her mind's eye. She would always see it.

Adam knew what she meant. 'We have each other,' he said, and that brought back the smile to her face.

Lost in thoughts of what had been and what might be, the children fell silent, sombre faces turned to the rear window, gazing out as the familiar landscape disappeared into the distance.

The carriage took them through the lanes and into the smoky grime of Blackburn itself, past the many inns and churches; cobbled streets and long rows of tiny houses; cotton mills and factories that rose up like great monsters, belching smoke and fumes across the sky.

As they went, the wheels played a merry tune against the cobbles, clickety-clack, clickety-clack, almost as though they were singing.

Suddenly, the landscape was changing. The autumn sun shone down, the road opened up, and suddenly, there were green fields on either side.

Soon they were travelling through the fringe of the Ribble Valley. All around were lush fields and sparkling brooks, and trees with wide-spreading branches, beneath which the many cattle rested. The land rose and fell like a green ocean, and the autumn sun bathed it in a special glow. 'I like it here,' Kathleen whispered, and Adam promised they would come back again one day. 'When we're grown up,' he said, and Kathleen couldn't wait.

The journey took a little over an hour. The children talked themselves out, and slept awhile. When they were woken by the driver, they realised with a sinking feeling that they had arrived at their new home.

'Where's Great-Aunt Markham?' A long, lazy yawn showed Kathleen was still sleepy. 'Do you think she's run away?'

'She's very old,' Adam said wisely. 'Maybe she's having a little nap – you know, like Cook used to do.'

'Cook said she was only resting her eyes.'

'Nancy told me Cook said that because she didn't want people thinking she was getting old.' He climbed out of the carriage and helped Kathleen down. 'Be on your best behaviour,' he warned. 'Mrs Glover said we have to make a good impression.'

'Is Great-Aunt Markham *very* old?'

'I heard Mr Ernshaw telling Mrs Glover, "Widow Markham must be going on eighty."'

'How old is that?'

'Older than Cook, I think.'

'Will she be able to play with us?'

'I don't suppose so.' His eyes lit up. 'But she might have a dog. Father would never let me have a dog but, oh, if only I could have one now.'

'Why do you want a dog when you've got me?'

He laughed out loud at her. 'It's not the same,' he told her. 'Every boy wants a dog.'

'I do too.' If Adam wanted a dog, then so did she.

While the driver unbuckled the luggage from the rear of the carriage, the children stood side by side, looking towards the sea. It stretched as far as the eye could see, vast and endless. There were little ships bobbing up and down, and a stretch of golden sand beyond the promenade where laughing couples strolled and looked into each other's eyes. 'Can we go to the beach, Adam?' Kathleen felt better already.

'We shall have to ask Great-Aunt Markham.' He swung round to look at the house, and Kathleen did the same.

'It's scary,' Kathleen declared, and Adam was inclined to agree.

A grand old place, the house had seen better years. The stonework on the three steps up to the door was crumbling at the edges. The timber on the gable was flaking with age, and there were several tiles missing from the roof. There was a big, panelled oak door, with a lion's head knocker in the middle, and eight long windows across the front of the house, all dressed with faded lace curtains; like the house, they were past their best.

From the top step to the pavement and along the width of the house ran a rusty old wrought-iron railing. At the far end of this was a stairway leading down to a small wooden door. 'Where does that go,

Adam?' Nervous though she felt, Kathleen was filled with curiosity.

'I expect it goes to the cellar,' Adam answered.

They were both startled when a high-pitched voice called out, 'That's right, young man, and if either of you give me any trouble, I shall lock you in there till kingdom come.'

The woman was small and wizened, with a pointed face and a wild halo of silver hair. She carried a silver cane with splayed feet and a large eagle on its top, its big glittering eyes staring down as though it was about to swoop on something tasty.

Instinctively, Kathleen took a pace backward. 'That bird wants to eat me,' she whispered, much to the amusement of her brother.

'It can't eat you,' he assured her. 'It's not real.'

'Is that Great-Aunt Markham?' she asked tremulously.

'I think so,' Adam answered softly. 'I can't be sure.'

'I don't like her, Adam. Tell her to go away.'

The high-pitched voice shrieked out, 'You! Driver! Put that luggage down. I'm not giving you good money to carry it in when there's a perfectly healthy boy here.'

Affronted by such treatment, the driver boldly gave her a piece of his mind. 'I weren't looking for no money,' he protested. 'I were paid at the start of the journey, by a Mr Ernshaw, so yer can keep yer money in yer pocket, missus.' Under his breath he added,

'Bleedin' little shrew!' He kept hold of the bags, one in each hand and two tucked under his arms. 'Well? D'yer want the luggage or don't yer? I ain't got all day.'

'I want you off my pavement!' she squealed. 'Leave the bags there. The boy can fetch them in.' Pointing to Adam, she ordered, 'Hurry up then, before he thinks to charge me waiting time. It's hard enough making ends meet without paying for a job twice.'

'I already told you, I don't want yer bleedin' money.'

'Clear off, you scoundrel, before I set the dogs on you.'

'Hang on a minute, missus.' He wanted to see the children safe inside, as was his duty. What's more, he didn't think the lad was strong enough to carry all the luggage, and he said as much.

Unperturbed, the little woman turned away, flung open the door and yelled, 'Here, boy! Here, Jake. See him off!'

Not wanting to be torn limb from limb, the driver dropped the bags and leaped into the carriage. Urging the horse away, he was soon careering down the street, cursing. 'Off yer rocker, missus, that's what you are, off yer bleedin' rocker! I pity them kids having to stay with an old bat like you.'

With the driver gone and the baggage lying on the ground, an odd silence remained. Silently, the widow regarded the children, and the children regarded her. Kathleen remained half hidden behind her brother, who was trembling in his shoes.

For what seemed an age, the silence continued, and so did the mutual regarding, until at last the little woman pointed a bony finger at Kathleen. 'You, girl! Come out of there!'

Far from coming out, Kathleen shifted further away, with only her big, dark eyes peering round Adam.

Adam stood firm, one hand by his side, the other holding Kathleen safe. 'Leave her alone,' he pleaded. 'She's afraid of you.'

Suddenly, a shrill peal of laughter sent the seagulls soaring with fright. 'Look at the brave little man,' she pointed at Adam, 'protecting his sister as though his life depends on it.' Wagging a finger at him, she added, 'You'd better be warned, young man, I won't stand for any disobedience. And I won't have you talking to me like that. How dare you raise your voice to me? Noisy, and insolent too. Whatever will the neighbours think?'

Always brave when her brother was under attack, Kathleen stepped out from behind him and confronted the little woman. 'It wasn't Adam being noisy,' she said quietly. 'It was you.'

For a dreadful minute Kathleen thought she might be given a spanking there and then. Instead, much to the surprise of both the youngsters, the old woman threw back her head and roared with delight. 'You're right,' she spluttered. 'I do tend to make a lot of noise. But then I'm entitled. I live here. What's more, I've lived here a lot longer than anyone down this street.' She eyed Kathleen with interest. 'They're a curious lot of devils. The best thing is to pretend they're not there.'

Kathleen gave her her answer. 'We don't want to stay here.'

'Oh?' Widow Markham wasn't quite so amused now. 'And why's that, young madam?'

'Because you're not nice.'

'Not nice, eh?' Keeping her beady eyes fixed on Kathleen's face, she made her way down the steps towards them. 'I'm not paid to be nice. Unfortunately, I'm your only living relative and it seems you are now my responsibility. Nice or not, you're stuck with me, and I'm stuck with you. As for me being nice, as I'm the one who's been put upon, I shall be whatever I choose to be.' Quickening to anger, she turned to Adam. 'Don't just stand there, boy. Fetch the luggage, and be quick about it.'

The little woman led the way and with great difficulty Adam struggled up the steps after her with the bags. Kathleen walked behind him.

'Not nice indeed!' rambled the widow. 'I don't suppose you think I'm pretty either,' she said, her voice falling to a softness that was strangely pleasant. 'It doesn't matter though. I don't really care what you think. I stopped caring what people think a long time ago.'

Kathleen was sorry she had made the remark, and she said so. 'I didn't mean to offend you, Great-Aunt Markham, only you shouldn't blame Adam when it isn't his fault.'

'I shall blame whom I please, young know-all!' Anger coloured her face. 'It's no good you being sorry either. You said what you said and you can never take it back. What's more, I don't think *you're* nice – you *or* your brother. I suppose it's not your fault you happen to be children. The thing is, I don't like children. I don't want children in my house. But I was approached by Mr Ernshaw and he reminded me I have a duty towards you. I explained how I couldn't possibly take such young children into my care, but he was persuasive, told me how you would otherwise be taken away and deposited in some institution.' She tutted and shook her head. 'After the way your father treated me, I ought to let them take you away. What should I care? But, because of your poor, foolish mother, I couldn't say no, and now I'm stuck with the pair of you.'

At the door she swung round. 'Your mother was a silly creature, with no thought for anyone but herself. She married that man against my advice. I warned her, but would she listen? No, she would not.'

Gazing at the children, she suddenly saw how tired they seemed, how weary and small, and afraid. She saw the look on Adam's face, a look that said, 'You can send us away if you like, and we'll manage.' She saw Kathleen's tortured little face and realised that here was a tiny soul with a big heart. She looked at these two remnants of a terrible situation and knew instinctively that they were made of much sterner stuff than either of their parents, and for one, aching moment they melted her heart; a quiet, lonely heart, which until now she had determined to harden against them.

Drawing in a deep breath, she let it out noisily through her narrow nose. 'Unfortunately, your mother was my niece, and now she's gone and left me with a problem. That's what you two are, a problem to an old woman who doesn't care tuppence for you.'

Adam remained silent, but Kathleen was outspoken. 'If you don't care tuppence for us, why are you looking after us?'

Widow Markham thought about that for a moment, her gaze roving the girl's lovely features. There was something about Kathleen in particular that touched her old, mad heart. She had been intrigued by a letter from Mr Ernshaw that had arrived that very morning, and now she was intrigued by the girl. She was tempted to hurt her by revealing the letter's contents, but she didn't.

Instead, with a crafty little smile and a wink of the eye, she answered, 'Because, like the man said, I must be "off me bleedin' rocker", and because Mr Ernshaw paid me to have you – though not as much as I deserve.'

Adam muttered something under his breath, and her mood immediately changed. 'Bring the bags inside,' she snapped, turning away to enter the house.

Inside the gloomy hallway, she pointed to the wide stairway. 'Up there,' she told Adam. 'You're in the first room on the right.'

Kathleen's voice piped up, 'Where's the dog?'

'What dog?'

'The one you wanted to bite the man.'

The old shrew regarded Kathleen with amusement. 'That was just to get rid of him,' she confessed. 'I can hardly afford to keep *myself* at times, let alone a dog.' She turned to Adam. 'The girl's room is on the left, two doors down. Next to mine.'

Alarmed, Kathleen appealed to her. 'I don't want to be next to you,' she pleaded, her face white. 'I want to be next to Adam.'

'That's too bad, my girl, because I've made up your room, and it's the best one, after mine of course. It's at the front of the house, and if you press your face to the window, you can see the sea.'

'I don't want to see the sea.' She did, but not if it meant sleeping next to someone who was 'off 'er bleedin' rocker'.

'You're an ungrateful girl. I've a good mind to let Mr Ernshaw collect you straightaway.'

'She doesn't mean to be ungrateful.' Adam felt the need to intervene. 'It's just that she's really very frightened. Please don't send her to an orphanage, Great-Aunt Markham.'

'Why not?'

'Because she will sleep in the room you've got ready.' He stared at his sister. 'Won't you, Kathleen?'

'If you say so, Adam.'

The little woman bristled with satisfaction. 'Good!' She looked from one to the other. 'One more thing before you take your bags upstairs.'

Adam looked her in the eye. 'Yes, Great-Aunt Markham?'

'There! You're doing it again. Great-Aunt Markham this and Great-Aunt Markham that.' A deep frown swallowed the many wrinkles in her tiny face. 'What idiot told you to call me that?'

Kathleen giggled. 'Mr Ernshaw.'

'Hmm! Well, I don't like it at all. I haven't got time for all that nonsense. Kindly address me as Markham. It's short and quick, and I won't have to wait half an hour before I know what you're trying to say.'

The children couldn't make head or tail of her. She was odd, and weird, and a little scary, yet she was sweet and funny, and already they were beginning to like her, just a tiny bit.

'Right then. Off up the stairs, and get a move on. We have things to do before the day is out.' As they went away, she ran after them, clapping her hands and crying, 'Come on! Come on!'

Never having met anyone quite like her before, and not knowing what else to do, the children looked at each other and giggled.

They had gone only a short way up the stairs when Adam had to stop and shift the luggage. No sooner had he put down the bags than the little woman was scurrying up the stairs. 'What next?' she shrieked. 'Have I to carry the things myself? Have I to unpack them and treat you like babies?' Taking two of the bags she marched ahead. 'Quick now,' she called, 'before I throw you and the bags back out on the pavement.'

Carrying the remaining two bags between them, the children dutifully followed, across the dingy landing and along the passage, until they came to Adam's room. It was a large room, with bulky dark pieces of furniture: a dresser with six drawers and big wooden knobs; a tall fearsome wardrobe, and a wide iron bed. The dark tapestry curtains at the window were moth-eaten and ragged. 'You're in here,' she told him. 'Once a week you take out the rugs and beat them. You keep the furniture dusted and the room generally clean. Right. Which bags are yours?'

'The brown one and this one I'm carrying.'

Markham slung the bags on to the bed. 'Follow!'

She went out of the room, down the corridor, and into a smaller, prettier room, with a narrow brass-headed bed, a small light-wood wardrobe and a dressing table with an oval mirror. 'You do the same,' she told Kathleen. 'Keep the room clean, and everything in it. There are no servants in this house.'

With that she marched out, leaving Adam to unpack Kathleen's things and then his own.

'You really can see the sea,' Kathleen said, with her nose squashed against the windowpane.

'There you are then.' Adam knew they had to make the best of it here. 'She might be crazy, but she doesn't tell lies.' In fact, if anything, she was too truthful.

Downstairs in the drawing room, with its heavy old furniture, yellowing lace and smell of lavender, Markham listened a moment at the door. 'Hmm. That should keep them busy for a while,' she muttered. Fishing out a long silver chain hanging round her neck, she selected one of the small ornate keys hanging on it and unlocked the bureau. She opened the flap and took out the letter that had arrived this morning from Mr Ernshaw. The neat handwriting filled two pages.

This letter is formally to execute my duties as instructed.

Adam John Peterson, and his sister Kathleen Beth, being the surviving children of Robert and Elizabeth Peterson, are to be given into the care of their great-aunt, Judith Markham, until they come of age.

Should Judith Markham die or, for whatever reason, become unable to continue her duties with regard to her wards, then it falls upon the writer of this letter to seek other guardianship; or, if deemed to be the only solution, to place the children in a suitable institution.

The sum of fifty pounds has been paid over to Judith Markham, to be returned in the event of her not carrying out the appointed duties.

> *Yours faithfully,*
> *Frederick Ernshaw*
> *OFFICE OF SOLICITORS*

The letter had a postscript, and it was this that had caused Markham to regard Kathleen with interest.

Some years ago, the writer of this letter was made party to a confidence he would rather not have been entrusted with.

In a state of distress, Elizabeth Peterson told how she had taken a lover, and that she was carrying a child fathered by this man.

The man in question was the same man who, together with Elizabeth Peterson, was later shot and killed by Robert Peterson, for which crime he was hanged. The bastard child was named Kathleen Beth.

Having kept this secret for too long, the writer of this letter takes the opportunity to unburden himself of it.

This privileged information is now entrusted to the girl's appointed guardian who, in turn, must do as her conscience bids.

'Stupid, foolish woman!' muttered Markham. Hearing the children approach, she quickly thrust the letter back into the bureau and slipped the silver chain inside her blouse. There was a tap on the drawing-room door. 'Come!' she called, making an effort not to look guilty. 'Finished, have you?'

'Yes, ma'am.' Adam led the way into the room.

'No! No!' She shook her head vigorously. 'Not ma'am, not Great-Aunt Markham. Have you forgotten already, damn you? What have I told you, boy?'

'We're to call you Markham. I'm sorry.'

'Sorry is not good enough.'

'No.'

'I'm sorry too.' Kathleen did not want to be left out.

'Be quiet, girl.'

Kathleen did as she was told.

'Close the door.'

Kathleen ran and closed the door.

'Come over here. I have something to show you both.' Markham beckoned them to the far side of the room, to where a piano stood. 'Shift it,' she told them, and they stared at her in disbelief. 'It's got wheels on,' she informed them. 'You just need to get your backs behind it and push,' and she illustrated the action for them.

They obeyed and it was as she said, it was no great effort to move the piano aside.

'That's far enough,' she said. 'Now you, boy, turn the rug back and raise the floorboard beneath. You'll find a box hidden there.'

It was a small, iron cash box.

She took it from Adam's hands and carried it to the table. 'This is a small fortune,' she told them, revealing a wad of bank notes and a cache of coins. 'Part of it was given me by Mr Ernshaw to take care of you, and part of it I've managed to save over the years. I'm an old, old woman,' she confided, 'and I won't live for ever. If there should come a time when I'm very ill, or taken away to die, I want you to take this box and run – run as far and as fast as you can. Because if they ever find you, you'll be locked away and might never be seen again.'

Kathleen was alarmed. 'Don't die, Markham,' she pleaded. If she had to choose, she would rather stay with Markham than be locked away and never seen again. 'I don't want to live in an orphanage.'

'And you won't.' Markham was adamant. 'Why do you think I let myself be persuaded into taking on a pair of brats like you? I'll tell you why. It was because of your mother. She may have been stupid and fickle, and she may not have loved you like she should have, but she was my only kith and kin, and I know my duties.' She wagged a finger at them both. 'It was a pity she didn't know *her* duties or none of this would ever have happened. Now look what she's done. Both your parents gone, and the pair of you farmed out to a mad, crotchety old woman who should know better. The plain truth is, after what your mother did, she should have been hanged, along with the other culprit. I, for one, will never forgive her.'

Realising she was saying too much, she briskly changed the subject. 'That's enough of that,' she snapped. 'Just remember what I said about this box, if anything should happen to me.'

Adam had always suspected there was more to their parents' deaths than they had been told. And now the old woman had as good as confirmed his suspicions. 'What did Mummy do?'

'Never you mind.'

'Please. I need to know.'

Slamming shut the box, she handed it to him. 'Put the box back.'

When the box was safely tucked away and the piano returned to its place, she led the children to the cellar. 'Down you go,' she said. Thinking she was about to follow, they went ahead, jumping with fright when she shrieked from the top of the steps, 'Markham does *not* like to be questioned. Your mother's mistake was marrying that oaf of a man, and that's all there is to it.' As she closed the door she could be heard shouting, 'I warned you the cellar was for naughty children, and now you can stay there until I think to let you out!' With that she turned the key in the lock and stormed off.

<hr>

I T WAS A long night. 'When will she let us out?' Like her brother, Kathleen had slept fitfully, wary of the dark, and shivering with cold in that damp place.

'Soon.' Maybe never, he thought, and there was no way out, because he had searched while Kathleen slept.

'I don't like it in here.'

'Try not to think about it.'

'Will it be morning soon?'

'I think so.'

'Will she let us out then?'

'Maybe. When daylight comes, and she's punished us enough, she might be sorry.'

Adam was wrong in one way and right in another. She did arrive with the daylight, to let them out. But she was not sorry. 'Just remember,' she told the wary pair, 'Markham will tell you as much as she wants you to know, and no more.'

She ordered them to wash and change, and when they came downstairs, she put a dish of hot porridge before them. 'Mind you eat it all up. This is good, wholesome food.'

When their dishes were scraped clean, she told them to wash up, while she fetched her hat and coat. 'You don't need to wrap up,' she told them, eyeing the cardigans they both wore. 'You'll do as you are. Your bones are not as thin and worn as this poor old woman's, and anyway there's still a bit of warmth in the sun.'

Out in the street, a group of boys shouted obscenities. 'Ignore them,' Markham said. 'They don't like me, and I don't like them. I've learned not to take any notice.'

Adam was all for giving them the same treatment but Markham told him that would make him as bad as they were. 'You're a gentleman,' she said. 'Hold your head high and walk right by, as if you can't even see them.' And, remembering the cellar, that's what he did, much to the louts' frustration. There was one boy, however, who stood aside from the others. Tall and well built, with fair, unruly hair, he smiled at Kathleen who, taken by surprise, smiled back.

'Where are we going?' she asked Markham.

In that unpredictable manner they had already come to know and respect, the frown disappeared from Markham's face and an impish grin lit up her features. 'Why, we're going to the beach,' she answered. 'You took your punishment well, and now it's time to enjoy yourselves.' She tutted at their puzzled faces, her eyes wide and surprised as she asked impatiently, 'Isn't that what children do . . . enjoy themselves?'

And that was exactly what they did. In fact they had the best day of their lives. In spite of the slight chill in the air, they rode the brown-eyed donkeys and ate the largest ice-cream cornets they had ever seen. They played on the beach and buried Markham up to her waist. And afterwards, tired and weary, and very happy, they made their way home.

At the end of that eventful day, two things were clear.

Great-Aunt Markham was like no one they had ever known. Peculiar and frightening, she was also funny and childish and, in spite of their ordeal in the dark cellar, the children were already beginning to warm towards her.

It was clear, too, that for as long as Adam and Kathleen remained in her dubious care, no two days would ever be the same.

Chapter Eight

Nancy was like a dog with two tails. 'Oh, Cook! Is this where we're going to live?' Her eyes were like saucers in her head. 'Oh, I do want to live here, I really do.'

Mabel was in no mood for Nancy's silly banter. 'Be quiet,' she told her. 'You're driving me mad with yer chatter. All the way up on the train yesterday, and then in the hotel lounge all evening long. And now, here we are, looking round the first house of many and all I can hear is you and yer bleedin' chatter.'

Nancy was downcast. 'I'm sorry, Cook,' she muttered. 'Only it's the first time I've ever been anywhere, and I've allus wanted to come to Blackpool. Now here we are, an' I'm that excited, I can't stop meself from talking.'

John chuckled, but Mabel was not amused. 'You'd better stop yerself,' she warned, 'or I swear to God, I'll gag yer.'

'Sorry, Cook.'

'Sorry nothing. Don't start that again, and don't keep calling me Cook. I've left all that behind. Besides,

I'm a married woman now, so you'd best call me Mrs Mason.'

Nancy giggled. 'Funny, ain't it?'

'What?'

'You, being called Mrs Mason.'

'There's nothing funny about it. You're a silly, brainless girl!'

'Sorry, Cook.'

'God help me if I won't strangle yer with me own hands, Nancy Tomlin!'

Nancy hung her head and shuffled her feet.

Mabel looked at her husband, and he shook his head, as if to say, 'Don't let the girl suffer too long.'

Dropping her weight into the nearest chair, Mabel sighed. 'Don't sulk, Nancy,' she chided. 'Look at me.'

Nancy raised her head.

'I didn't mean to bite yer head off, only you do go on. You must learn how to contain yer excitement.'

'Yes . . . Mrs Mason.' She nearly said 'Sorry' and she nearly said 'Cook'. And the fright showed on her face.

John chuckled again. 'I think it's all too much for her, Mabel,' he said kindly. 'Would it really matter if she went on calling you Cook? After all, you'll still be doing the cooking here, won't you?'

'Well, I'm certainly not trusting *her* to do it, that's for sure. Anyway, she'll have her own work cut out.'

'Well then?'

Seeing she had an ally, Nancy made the most of it. 'Please,' she pleaded. 'I'm used to calling yer

Cook, d'yer see? I can't never get used to new-fangled ideas.'

'Oh, all right then. I've been Cook for most of me life, an' I expect I shall still be cooking the day they carry me off.' She looked up at John. 'I can't think straight,' she complained. 'I'm hot and bothered, and gasping for a decent cup of tea. There's half the day gone already, and still four houses to be looked at.'

'It's my fault,' John said, concerned. 'I haven't given you time to get your breath. We got married in a hurry, and now I'm rushing you into making other important decisions.' He felt guilty. 'If you like, we can leave it until tomorrow. Tonight, we'll sit and discuss whether we really want Blackpool or whether we should look at other seaside places.'

'No.' Mabel was having none of that. 'Whatever we've done, we've done with our eyes wide open and I don't regret one single thing.' Giving him an encouraging smile that lifted his heart, she went on, 'I always hoped you and me would get wed, and now I'm proud to be yer wife, John Mason. As for looking elsewhere, what's wrong with Blackpool?'

'Nothing, as far as I can see.'

'Right, then. Blackpool it is. What's more, we'll look round this partic'lar house, and if we like it, we'll look no further. What do you say?'

'I say that's a grand idea.'

'And then we'll find a café for a cup of tea and an Eccles cake. What do you say to that?'

'Even better.'

'Come on then, you two.' Struggling up, she stretched her back and groaned. 'Might as well make a start upstairs.'

The house was lovely. A grand old place built in 1800, it was situated on the promenade, overlooking the sea. In its lifetime it had been a gentleman's residence, a home for retired folk, and, more recently, a small hotel catering for holidaymakers who thronged to Blackpool in the summer months.

Painted white, and with every room beautifully decorated, it was a spacious and desirable property. Catching the sunlight for most of the day, the rooms were bright, with tall ceilings and pretty cornices. There were good carpets on the floors, handsome lightshades hanging from the ceilings, and all the furniture was of a tasteful, sturdy kind. 'Some of this stuff's for sale with the house, ain't it?' Mabel stared round the sitting room, her mind leaping ahead with ideas. Particularly attracted to a long walnut sideboard with a mirrored back, she commented thoughtfully, 'This would be more useful in the dining room.' She fingered the deep carving on the drawers. 'The top is big enough to take any number of tureens, and the bottom cupboards could house all the usual paraphernalia – plates, condiment sets and suchlike.'

John thumbed through the details. 'Yes, this one is open to offers,' he informed her, 'but we might have to lower our sights, love. I mean, the house is more than we thought to pay, and there are other things we have to get. Besides, we don't really know how the business will go at first, so we need to keep back a bit for a rainy day.'

Mabel didn't agree. 'If you ask me, we have to start out right,' she said. 'It's no good scrimping and scraping and ending up with only half what we need, or the cheap, nasty stuff got from down the market. We need good stuff, like this. First impressions are important, and if we're to build up reg'lar customers, we need to offer comfortable beds, good food, and a feeling of wellbeing. It has to be the kind of place where folks will want to come back again and again. I say we should throw caution to the winds and jump in with both feet. Sink or swim, that's what I say.'

John was impressed. 'You really think we can make a good business, don't you?'

'If we don't, then we don't deserve the chance.' When they had first learned that they were to lose their jobs, Mabel had been worried, but now she truly believed they would never look back. 'It's just under four weeks to Christmas,' she said. 'Do you think we could be installed in time for Christmas? Oh, I know we won't be up and running, but we could have our own Christmas in our very own place, and in the New Year we could start the decorating and planning. Oh, wouldn't that be wonderful?' Her eyes sparkled.

'Sounds to me like you've set your heart on this place.' John glanced round the room. 'Don't you even want to see the others?' He hoped not, because he, too, had taken a fancy to this grand old place.

She shook her head. 'This is the one,' she replied decisively. 'It has a good feel about it.'

It was settled. 'Right then, Mrs Mason,' he beamed at her with affection, 'make a list of the bric-a-brac you want and we'll get straight back to the agent's office to thrash out a deal.' He winked mischievously. 'I've a feeling that cocky young feller behind the desk won't know what's hit him.'

Nancy was overjoyed. 'We might even bump into the children one day.'

'Why do you say that?' Mabel asked.

'Because I heard Mr Ernshaw tell Adam that they were going to the seaside. Blackpool isn't far away, that's what he told him.'

'Well, I never!'

'Wouldn't it be grand if we came across them one day?'

'It would, Nancy,' Mabel agreed. 'It'd put my mind at rest to know the children were happy enough in their new life.' A great sigh seemed to travel from her boots to the top of her greying head. 'Lord knows they deserve a bit of happiness.'

Chapter Nine

IT WAS TWO days before Christmas 1861.

Six years had passed since the orphans were
delivered to Markham's door, and with the passing of
the years, the boy had matured with confidence, the
girl had grown tall and softly beautiful, with a nature
as lovely as a summer's day. The old aunt, however,
was madder than ever, unpredictable as the English
weather, and shrivelled with age.

Perched on the edge of her seat, she gazed at
Adam. A handsome fellow, with a tall, capable figure
and blue honest eyes, he made the old woman proud.
She had learned to respect him as someone who knew
his own mind and did not hesitate to say what he
thought, even if it got him into hot water, as it so
often did. Between the boy and herself there reigned
a constant, silent tussle for supremacy.

Mr Ernshaw was seated beside Markham and
directly opposite the children. 'Everything is most
satisfactory.' He smiled at Markham with approval.
'The girl is an independent, intelligent creature, while
the boy has made good at school, so much so that it
seems he may qualify for a higher education.' His

smile broadened. 'Well done, Mrs Markham, the children certainly seem to have prospered under your care.'

'I do my best.'

Addressing the children, he informed them, 'I have received several complimentary notices from your school. It seems you both have a remarkable ability for learning.'

Adam felt obliged to speak for himself and his sister, who was unusually quiet. 'Thank you, sir.'

Mr Ernshaw rose to leave. 'You're a young man now. Sixteen years old, and I have no doubt you have a fine future ahead of you. I see I shall have no more cause to visit. My duty is ended.' Very grandly, he shook Adam by the hand.

He was less gracious to Kathleen, recalling how she was not a true Peterson but a bastard, born out of a tawdry affair between her wayward mother and the gamekeeper. 'You do as your great-aunt instructs,' he said sternly. 'You're out of my hands now.' Thank God, he thought.

'Yes, sir.' Kathleen had not forgotten how he had man-handled her out of the old house and made her cry. She hadn't liked him then and she found no reason to like him now.

Sensing her animosity, Ernshaw was abrupt. 'Goodbye then. It's time I was on my way.'

'Just a minute,' said Markham. 'I'd like a word before you go.'

'Of course.' He was impatient to depart, and it

showed. 'But please bear in mind I do have a train to catch.'

Dismissing the children, Markham got right to the point. 'I need more money,' she said bluntly. 'With the children being older, everything costs more – clothes, food. The boy may have prospects but the girl has a few years left at school. She's required to wear a uniform, and there are other expenses which try my allowance to the limit.'

'I'm sorry, but there are no more funds,' he informed her coldly. 'You must either manage or commit the girl to an orphanage.'

'Never!'

'Then I'm afraid there is nothing I can do.'

On that sombre note, he departed.

Later that evening, when the three of them were seated round the kitchen table drinking tea, Adam wondered how he should broach a particular, thorny matter – the matter of Christmas and a certain promise made by Markham, which she appeared to have conveniently forgotten.

'I was wondering, Markham,' he began, 'whether we shouldn't start to look for a tree.'

Markham took a nibble out of her scone. 'No tree,' she said, and a blob of red jam landed on her chin. She snaked out a long narrow tongue and flicked the jam into her mouth. 'Don't bother me, boy.'

'But a tree isn't much to ask for,' he coaxed, 'not when it's Christmas, and you promised Kathleen we could have one this year.'

The old woman was stubborn as ever. 'There'll be no tree in this house, young man. In all the time I've lived here, I have never seen the need for a tree, and I don't see the need for one now. You've done without one these past six years. What's so different about this year?'

'Please, Markham,' said Kathleen. 'You said we could have one, as long as it didn't dirty the carpet. The man at the market said if we put it straight into a bucket, there wouldn't be a mess, and if the needles fall, I'll clean them up, I promise.'

'There'll be no mess, girl, and there'll be no needles because there'll be no tree, even if it means me going back on my word.'

'That's not fair.' Kathleen had set her heart on a tree. When she had first mentioned it to Markham, the old woman had not seemed to mind. Now, though, as always, she was going back on her promise. 'Cook used to say if you told lies, no one would ever trust you.'

Markham regarded her through narrowed eyes. 'You may be coming up twelve years of age and growing wiser by the minute, but don't get too big for your boots, young lady. I don't give a tinker's cuss for what Cook said. What's more, I can see I've let you two get away with far too much. I won't have you talking back to me, and I will not have you telling me what I can or cannot do in my own house.' She wagged a bony finger at the girl. 'You've got far too much to say for yourself, young madam.'

Kathleen certainly had come out of her shell.

It had happened about the time that rascal from Adelaide Street had started hanging about the house, and Markham had had to send him on his way. 'I knew it was wrong to let that young ruffian come to your birthday party,' she said now. 'Murray Laing comes of a poor family. There was a time when they had money but the father gambled it all away when his pretty wife ran off with some sailor. As far as I can tell, the lazy fellow hasn't done a day's work since. There was talk at one time that he sent the boy out thieving in the dead of night, breaking into houses and the like, and I for one am quite ready to believe it.'

Kathleen held her head high. 'Well, *I* don't believe it,' she declared. 'Murray would never break into people's houses.'

Murray Laing was the tall, fair-haired boy who had smiled at Kathleen that first day when she and Adam had left the house to go to the beach with Markham. After that, Murray had often loitered near the house, waiting to give her a smile whenever she left the house, and she had begun to look forward to seeing him. She had begged Markham to let him come to her eleventh birthday party, and to her surprise and delight the old woman had eventually agreed. He brought her a present, the prettiest thing Kathleen had ever owned – a small bone comb, edged with mother-of-pearl. 'I didn't steal it,' he told her earnestly. 'I saved hard to buy it for you.' And Kathleen never doubted him.

The old woman shook her silver head. 'Murray Laing is five or six years older than you are,' she tutted, 'and he's charmed you with his beguiling smile. Where does he get his money if he doesn't steal it, tell me that? He told us here in this very house that he was sixteen years of age, and if that's the case, why isn't he working, eh? I'll tell you why. It's because he finds it easier to pick other folks' pockets, that's why. He wants to pick your pocket too, I dare say. I've no doubt the boy's father put him up to getting to know you. He probably thinks you're worth a penny or two, and that he can get his hands on your money through his son.'

'I haven't got any money.'

'He'll be disappointed then, won't he?' These past weeks the old woman had felt closer to her maker than she would admit, and when her time came to face him, she meant to see that the children would not be left penniless. Though she would rather they had not been placed in her care, she had come to rely on their company in a way she never envisaged. There was a brightness about this old house that had not been there before. These two unfortunates had taught her how to laugh again. They had brought sunshine into her empty life, and not a day went by when she didn't thank the good Lord for sending them to her.

All the same, she must not let the children get the better of her. They seemed to grow taller by the minute, they were strong, capable characters she had secretly grown proud of, and she was sometimes tempted to lean on them in her times of need, when she felt so old and tired she could hardly put one foot before the other. But that must not be allowed to happen, she thought. She couldn't let them feel responsible for her. It wouldn't be right. She had her pride, and young as they were, they still relied on her. She must be strong. For all their sakes, she must always be seen to be in charge.

'If you ask me, that young fellow is not to be trusted. He's too much like his father ever to make good, he's lazy and ignorant, and you've got too keen an eye for the blackguard, my girl.'

'I like Murray, and I want to see him again.' In fact Kathleen had taken him to her young heart. He was warm and funny, and he made her laugh. Moreover, he was the first real friend she had ever known, and she couldn't bear the thought that she might be forbidden to see him again.

Her affection for the boy only strengthened the old woman's determination to take a firm line. 'You'll do as you're told,' she snapped. Her manner was unyielding, but still her heart was sorely touched by Kathleen's young, generous face.

It was a face to turn any boy's head, she thought bitterly. The girl had the makings of a beauty, with her long dark hair and those dark, desperate eyes. She was tall and slim, and filled with a zest for life that made the old woman feel breathless just watching her. 'And don't tell me I made promises when I didn't,' she said angrily though she clearly recalled doing so in a moment of weakness. 'I've an idea you and your brother would like me to think I'm growing senile. And anyway, even if I did promise, it doesn't matter because I've changed my mind. I'm an old woman. I can change my mind whenever the fancy takes me.'

Kathleen would have argued the point, but Adam saw the danger signs. 'Leave it, Kathleen,' he warned. 'We'll talk about it later.' Over the years, he had come to recognise the old woman's moods and knew when not to press a point.

Kathleen was bitterly disappointed. It was going to be such a wonderful Christmas, and now it was being spoiled, like all the other times. 'We need a tree to put the presents under,' she said sadly.

'Presents?' the old woman shrieked. 'What presents?'

'Adam and I have bought each other a present, and we've bought you one as well.'

'Where did you get money for presents?' Markham sat up, her whole body bristling.

'We bought them out of the pennies you paid us for doing the housework,' Adam explained.

'Then I've paid you too much. "Presents" indeed! From now on you can do the housework for your board and keep, and you can go without supper tonight. That'll teach you to argue with me.' Aching for her afternoon nap, she closed her eyes. 'Now go away.'

Obediently, they went upstairs to Kathleen's bedroom. Later, as she gave herself up to sleep, the old woman thought of the children and was filled with a warm and wonderful sense of belonging. In the space of a heartbeat, the sensation became a feeling of deep-down love which, in all her lonely existence, she had never known before.

'Markham's crazy, isn't she?' Kathleen said, setting herself on the window seat. Adam sprawled on the bed.

'Mad as a hatter,' he smiled. 'But she's harmless enough, though I sometimes wonder if she's ill.'

'Why do you say that?'

He shrugged his shoulders. 'Sometimes, when she thinks no one's looking, she holds her side and her face is filled with pain.'

'Is that why she's so grumpy?'

'Maybe.'

Kathleen felt bad about that. 'If Markham's ill, I don't really care if we have a tree or not,' she lied. A terrible thought occurred to her. 'Markham won't die, will she, Adam? I know she's cruel sometimes but I don't want her to die.' Her voice shook with emotion.

'She won't die,' he answered. 'She'll probably live to be a hundred. Maybe we should have let her sleep before we asked her about the tree. When she's tired, she gets irritable and stubborn.'

Kathleen's mind turned to something else Markham had said. 'Adam, do you think Murray Laing is a thief?'

'I don't know,' he answered truthfully. 'He seems decent enough to me, but we don't know whether his father might bully him into doing something he doesn't want to do.'

'He's not a thief,' she insisted. 'And I will see him again, whatever Markham says.'

The next morning they woke to the smell of freshly cooked omelettes and sizzling bacon. Kathleen leapt out of bed and beat Adam to the bathroom. 'Brr! She's filled the jug with cold water,' she gasped as she splashed her hands and face.

She emptied the used water into a bucket while Adam waited patiently, before refilling the bowl from the water jug. Gingerly cupping a generous measure into his hands, he threw it over his face, spluttered loudly, then briskly rubbed himself dry. 'That'll do,' he declared, leading the way downstairs.

Markham greeted them suspiciously. 'Did you wash thoroughly?' she demanded, hands on hips and guarding the table. 'Did you scrub yourselves clean, you dirty pair? Did you use the soap?'

'Yes, Markham.' Kathleen could hear her stomach rumbling.

'Let me see your hands, young lady.'

Stepping forward, Kathleen held out her hands, palms up, then turned them over. 'See,' she said boldly. 'Satisfied now?'

'Not yet.' Markham swept back Kathleen's hair and examined behind her ears. 'All right,' she said. 'Sit at the table. But don't start until I say.'

She put Adam through a more vigorous inspection. 'You don't look to me as if you've had a thorough wash,' she said, stretching up and sniffing his face. 'You don't smell as if you've used the carbolic either.'

'I did,' he protested. 'Ask Kathleen.'

The old woman looked at Kathleen and got an affirmative nod. 'All right,' she relented. 'Sit down.'

Relieved, Adam drew out a chair and sat opposite his sister. She gave him a little smile that did not go unnoticed by Markham's small, busy eyes. 'What are you grinning at, young lady?'

Fearing she might be sent from the table, Kathleen put on her most innocent manner. 'I'm not grinning.'

'You *were* grinning.'

'I didn't mean to.'

'And don't talk while you're having breakfast.'

'No, Markham.'

'And no leaving food. It's a sin and a shame to leave food when I can hardly make ends meet.'

'Yes, Markham.'

In spite of Markham's constant chirping, breakfast was hugely enjoyable. There were fluffy omelettes and crispy bacon; delicious shop-bought scones and heapings of strawberry jam. And to top it all, Markham produced two glasses of dark sarsaparilla. 'Just this once,' she said, 'as a special treat.' In fact the whole breakfast had been a special treat. Normally, they were fortunate if they had toast and jam.

Their pleasure and contentment lasted only as long as breakfast did because for the next three hours Markham made them earn the food. First they had to wash up while she paced the room, pausing occasionally to make sure they were doing it properly. Then they had to take out every rug and mat in the house, which, under strict instructions, they hung over the line and beat until their arms ached. Next they had to take down every ornament in every room, only returning them to the shelves when Markham was satisfied that each one had been polished until it shone.

Finally, when the house sparkled from top to bottom, Markham ushered them into the drawing room. 'Think yourselves fortunate,' she told the suffering pair, 'you're about to hear me play the piano for the first time in many a year.'

This was the worst 'punishment' of all, because, while Markham's piano playing gave her immense pleasure, it was half an hour of sheer purgatory for the children.

'There!' Having played herself into a frenzy, she slammed down the piano-top and turned jubilant to smile on their crestfallen faces. 'Right! Coats on, you two.'

'Where are we going?' asked Kathleen wearily. She felt exhausted and just wanted to sit somewhere quietly out of reach of Markham's constant demands.

Markham grinned. 'We are going out for some fresh air and exercise.' She paused, and Adam groaned inwardly. The last thing he felt like was exercise, after all that running about the house. 'And while we're out,' Markham went on, 'we'll buy a Christmas tree.'

'Oh, Markham!' Delighted, Kathleen ran to fling her arms round the little woman's waist. 'Thank you!' She could hardly believe it.

'Not a big one, mind,' Markham warned. 'The big ones are far too expensive.'

———⟶⟵———

I T WAS GROWING dark and still they had not found a suitable tree. Now they were standing outside a shop with numerous trees displayed on the pavement. Wearied by a long, tiring day, Markham lost no time in choosing one she thought could be easily carried home. 'This one looks all right to me,' she announced. She was tired. Her old legs ached, and she longed for the warmth of her cosy fire.

The short, round shopkeeper had been watching the little group. 'That's a good choice, missus,' he told Markham. 'It's stout and full, with more at the bottom than the top, so it won't fall over when you stand it in a barrel.'

Giggling, Kathleen whispered to Adam, 'It sounds like him,' and Adam had to agree.

Markham eyed the fellow with her birdlike stare. 'How much is it?'

'A shilling.'

'Too much.'

'Ninepence then.'

Markham was having none of it. 'Come along, children. There are plenty of shops who'll be glad to get rid of their trees so near Christmas.'

''Old on, missus!' The shopkeeper stepped in front of her. ''Ow much then?'

'Threepence, and not a penny more.'

'Daylight robbery!'

'Is it a deal?'

'Go on then.' He scratched his head and looked bemused. 'I must be losing me bleedin' marbles,' he groaned.

Adam hoisted the tree on to his shoulders and they made their way home. 'It's a lovely tree,' Kathleen exclaimed. 'And we don't have to buy any trimmings because I've made some paper chains and rag balls. They'll look ever so pretty, you'll see.' It made her feel that at long last they had a proper home, and a real parent to care for them.

She thought of her mother and father, and her heart grew heavy. But it was only momentary. They had never loved her or Adam. Not really. They only looked after them. Like Cook looked after Nancy. She thought about them, and realised how much she still missed old Cook and the rest of the servants. Markham had made up for a lot though. She did some strange and frightening things, but she did love them and in spite of the times when she and Adam were locked in the cellar or were sent to bed hungry, Kathleen dearly loved the old woman.

'Don't loiter, girl!' Markham was eager to be off the streets. 'It's late. We should have been back home ages since.' Gathering up her skirt hem, she stepped off the pavement, almost under the wheels of a carriage and four.

'Yer want to look where yer going, yer silly old bugger!' came the shout from the driver's seat.

'That's no way to speak to an old lady!' Markham yelled back. 'I should get my man here to teach you some manners.'

The driver looked at Adam and roared with laughter. 'I'd 'ave more trouble fighting the bleedin' tree!'

'Ignorant devil!'

Markham's mood was not improved when they were confronted by the louts who habitually jeered at her when she ventured out.

'Well now!' It was the same big, untidy fellow, with the same big, loud mouth. 'If it ain't the crazy old bag who thinks she's better than the rest of us.' He and two others barred her way. 'Cat got yer tongue, 'as it?' Pressing his face to within an inch of hers, he hissed, 'Give us yer purse and we'll be on our way.'

Kathleen had been lagging behind with Adam, but now she ran forward. 'Leave her alone!' she cried. 'Get away from her!' A swift kick on his shins made him cry out, more with astonishment than pain. Markham laughed in his face and Adam dropped the tree and ran forward too.

'You'd best be on your way. Now!' He glared at the offender, who squared his shoulders and glared back.

'That yer sister, is it?' he sneered.

'I told you to clear off.'

'Bit of all right, ain't she?' He grinned nastily at Kathleen. 'Wouldn't mind 'aving an armful o' that.'

Adam lunged forward and in a moment the two were rolling about the ground, with Kathleen kicking the lout at every opportunity and Markham urging her on in the background. But then the other two joined in, and it was soon obvious that Adam was getting the worst of it. One lout grabbed hold of Kathleen. 'Give us a kiss then,' he demanded, holding Kathleen's arms tight by her sides.

Suddenly a young man sprang on the lout's back. 'Get yer dirty paws off her!' Murray Laing had been keeping his distance, but the lout's treatment of Kathleen had incensed him. Adam, meanwhile, had been kicked to the ground, momentarily stunned.

Concerned at the developments, Markham suddenly began shouting, 'Police! Police! Oh, there you are, officer.' She seemed to be addressing someone in the shadows. 'The ruffian's after my purse. Grab him, officer, before he gets away.'

Alarmed, the ruffians took to their heels with Murray in pursuit. All four were soon lost in the dark.

'There!' Markham pointed after them. 'Did you see who that was? That was your friend Murray Laing. Did you see him? Did you?'

'He was trying to help.' All the same, Kathleen had to admit to herself that he had seemed to be part of the gang, until the lout took hold of her.

'He was one of them, I tell you! In fact he's their ringleader. If that lout hadn't threatened you, Murray Laing would have stood by while they took my purse.'

'We don't know that for sure.' Kathleen didn't

want to believe it, but she had lost some of her faith in Murray. She would have to confront him when next their paths crossed.

'You must have nothing at all to do with that ruffian, do you understand?'

'Was there really a policeman?' Kathleen asked, hoping to distract her aunt.

'Course not,' said Markham. 'I was just pretending, and it worked a treat. Ran off like the cowards they are,' she chuckled. 'They're not so big, letting an old lady hoodwink them. They'll not get the better of me.'

———◦∘◦———

THAT NIGHT KATHLEEN lay sleepless in her bed for what seemed an age.

The muted chiming of the downstairs grandfather clock filtered through the house. It chimed the evening out and the morning in, and still she couldn't sleep. 'Maybe he really is bad,' she mused. 'Maybe he's everything Markham says he is.' The thought of Murray as a thief and rogue made her young heart ache. So much so that she had to get out of bed and sit by the window, her sad, dark eyes searching the night.

At first she thought it was a trick of the dark. Then she realised there really was someone moving about outside, directly beneath her window. Anxious, she quickly stepped back and hid behind the curtain.

He called out to her. 'Kathleen. I need to talk to you.'

'It's Murray!' Her heart soared. 'I was thinking of him and now here he is.'

'Kathleen!'

Quickly now, before he woke the others, Kathleen opened the window. 'Go away, before Markham hears you.'

'I'm not part of that lot,' he said, 'I swear to God.'

'I saw you.'

'I know, and I'm ashamed. I didn't think they were out for trouble, but after tonight I'll steer clear of 'em, I promise.' He smiled his easy lopsided smile. 'I've brought you a present.' He placed a small package on the wall.

'Markham says I'm not to see you ever again.'

'I'll talk to her.'

'It won't do any good. She's made up her mind.'

'What about you, Kathleen? Have you made up your mind?'

'You should never have gone with them.'

'I know that now.' He dropped his head and stared at the ground, his next words only just audible. 'Believe me, I didn't know they were out for trouble.'

'How do I know you're telling the truth?'

'I am!' He flung out his arms in frustration. 'Look, Kathleen, I know why your aunt doesn't like me, and I don't blame her. I'll not deny I've been running with a bad lot, and I'm not surprised she tars me with the same brush. On top o' that, she doesn't like it because I'm five years older than you, and you're too young. But I need to see you . . . until we're old enough to court proper. I'll wait, Kathleen, for as long as it takes. We've got a lifetime to find out about each other, ain't we?'

In the lamplight from her bedroom, his face shone with affection. 'Yer do like me, don't yer, gal? I mean, just to be friends, till we know what we want. I swear to Gawd I ain't never looked at any other girl. Me dad says I should be looking, on account of me coming up seventeen and close to being a man.' He grinned. 'If he had his way, I'd be married with a dozen kids as quick as the drop of a hat.' The grin faded and he was penitent again. 'I'm really sorry,' he apologised. 'I wouldn't have let them hurt her.'

'My aunt says you're the ringleader. Are you?'

There was a pause. 'I *was* the ringleader,' he confessed, 'but that was a long time ago. Now I just hang around sometimes 'cause there's nothing else to do, but I don't go along with them. Not any more. It's different now. I've changed, Kathleen. I've changed because of you.'

'Have you, Murray?' Her voice was kind. Her heart was warmed by his declaration though she couldn't understand the deeper implications. 'I'm glad.'

'Tomorrow I'm going for a job in the market. I'm gonna work hard and save every penny I earn, for when we get married.'

He might have said more but he was grabbed from behind and shaken like a rag doll. 'Get away from here!' Enraged, Markham had heard every word. 'Married indeed! She's only eleven years old. And even if she were a grown woman, I'd give her to a travelling circus before I'd see her with a ruffian like you.' Swiping him hard across the ear, she yelled, 'Now be off before I set the authorities on you!'

'All right, missus, I don't want no trouble.' He moved off down the street. 'But I meant what I said. One day I'll prove meself, and if she'll have me I mean to marry 'er.'

'Over my dead body!' Markham's words echoed in the night. 'Keep away from her, do you hear me?'

'All right,' he promised, 'but only until she asks for me.'

Markham marched upstairs to confront Kathleen. 'I blame you, my girl!' The old lady shook with anger. 'You deliberately defied me! You talked to him after I ordered you not to. That scoundrel came here like a thief in the night, and you encouraged him.'

'He's not a scoundrel,' Kathleen protested. 'He's changed. He's even going for a job in the market tomorrow.'

'I heard what he said.' She was done with arguing. 'There will be no tree. No rag balls or paper trimmings. And no more mention of Christmas in this house.' Until then she had kept her right arm behind her back, but now she brought it forward, to show the cane clutched in her hand. 'It's such a shame, I have to punish you now when you were doing so well.'

The punishment was cruel.

Made to stand with her face to the wall, Kathleen tried hard not to scream when the cane cut into her legs time and again. But she was only a child, and soon she was crying out in pain.

Her cries brought Adam from his bed, but by the time he burst into the room, it was all over. Quietly sobbing, Markham was cradling Kathleen in her arms. 'I had to punish her,' she said brokenly. 'It was for her own sake.'

Later, when Kathleen was sleeping, she ordered Adam to take the tree outside and burn it. Reluctantly, he did as he was told. There were things here beyond his understanding. He couldn't be sure who was in the right, Markham or his sister, but there was no denying Kathleen had an unhealthy liking for Murray Laing.

Inside the house, Markham found Kathleen's trimmings and destroyed them. 'She has to learn,' she told the shocked Adam. 'The whipping hurt me more than it hurt her. But I know I've done right, and in your heart you know it too.' Wiping the back of her hand over her brow, she sounded weary. 'When the Lord sent you to me, he sent me a heavy burden,' she said. 'I've never had children, and maybe I'm not very good at being a parent. But I do love you both.'

It was an admission that shook him. 'You've never said that before,' he responded quietly.

'And I'll never say it again,' she told him.

Chapter Ten

CHRISTMAS CAME AND went. Kathleen's wounds healed, and her fondness for Markham was not wholly diminished by the treatment she had suffered at the old lady's hands. Markham, however, was not her usual, commanding self.

'What's wrong with her, Adam?' It was plain to them both that their aunt was not well. 'When I ask her she tells me it's nothing and that I shouldn't worry.'

'Then don't.' Adam wouldn't admit that he, too, was concerned. 'You know what she's like. She hates to be fussed over. If she needs a doctor, I'm sure she'll send for one.' Head down, and pushing against the bitter wind, he hurried across the yard. Having just spent half an hour in the bitter cold tipping coal into the coal hole, he was eager to get back inside. But he paused to glance up towards the old lady's bedroom window. 'All the same, it's not like her to lie in bed day after day.'

'What did you say?' Kathleen had been hanging washing on the line. She turned to look at him with a frown. 'Adam, what did you say?'

He walked on. 'I said hurry up with that washing before you catch your death.'

Kathleen's mind was still on Markham. 'It's New Year's Eve. She's stayed in her bed for almost a week. It's not like her. Do you think it's my fault? Do you think she's ill because of what happened with those louts, and then afterwards, when she saw fit to punish me? You told me yourself she said it hurt her more than it hurt me.'

'I dare say it upset her.' He knew it was more than that. He'd seen the way the whole series of events had affected the old lady, and yet he had not entirely forgiven her for whipping his sister like that.

'I should have listened to her about Murray Laing. I shouldn't have riled her like I did.'

'There's no blame.' The cold reached his bones and made his teeth chatter. If anything, the blame lay with his parents, he thought, for doing what they did and saddling a tired old lady with two children she never wanted. 'Markham is a tough old bird, but she's very old. It's to be expected that she might have an off day or two. She'll be fine. Finish what you're doing, then you can take her tray up. She'll feel better with some hot food inside her.'

Ramming the last peg home, Kathleen let go of the line which instantly sprang upwards in the wind. Markham's nightshift billowed like a cloud and her bed socks did a comical tap dance one against the other. 'Wait for me, Adam.' Collecting her wicker basket from the flags, she followed him into the kitchen.

'I wish she would eat some hot food,' she remarked, dropping the basket to the floor. 'This morning, I made her two soft-boiled eggs, and she didn't even touch them.'

'Like I said, she'll be fine.' Placing the coal bucket in the hearth, he began banking up the fire. 'I'll go up and have a word with her when I've done this.'

'And I'll serve up a good helping of that baked fish. I've done it exactly the way she likes it.' Markham had shown her how to bake a cake and cook a ham, and do all the things her mother had never taught her. 'I'll have it ready in half an hour. You tell her that, Adam. And tell her I'll never talk to Murray Laing again, if only she'll get better.'

'Don't make rash promises, Kathleen.' He stood up, his face rosy-red from the heat of the fire.

'It's not a rash promise,' she protested. 'I really mean it. That's what all the trouble was about. That's why it's all my fault.'

Washing his hands at the sink, suddenly he knew how enormous a responsibility Markham had taken on, because now it was his responsibility. Kathleen had no one but him to rely on if Markham should die. He daren't let himself think about it.

Kathleen noticed his preoccupation. 'Adam, you will tell her what I said, won't you?'

'Tell her yourself,' he answered impatiently.

A small voice startled them both. 'Tell me what?'

Kathleen was thrilled to see the old lady standing by the door. 'Oh, Markham!' Running to her, she put her arms round the frail shoulders. 'Are you better?' Carefully, she helped the old soul forward.

Adam pushed the armchair nearer to the cheery fire. 'You look better,' he lied. He wished it was so, but in truth Markham looked grey with pain.

'I'm perfectly all right. Stop fussing.' Her small face crumpled in a smile. 'You're worse than a pair of old hens,' she chuckled.

'It's good to see you out of your bed, Markham.' Greatly relieved, and certain now that her aunt was on the mend, Kathleen was close to tears.

Markham saw how anxious she was. 'I smelled the fish baking,' she declared with a sly wink at Adam. 'I remember the last fish your sister put in that oven. It started out as a fat, juicy trout and ended up looking like a roasted sprat.'

'I think you'll be pleasantly surprised with your supper tonight,' Adam said with a smile. 'You've taught her well.'

He was right. Supper was delicious: slowly baked fish steeped in cider and slightly browned, small potatoes in their skins, and dark green cabbage lightly done. A dish of jelly topped with custard followed.

Having eaten a good measure, Markham gave her approval. 'You've done me proud, my girl,' she said, and Kathleen blushed with pleasure.

The evening was spent leisurely, with Markham tucked up in a blanket in front of the fire. Kathleen sat at her feet, and Adam reclined in the chair beside them. 'This last lot of coal is really good,' he remarked, shoving his chair back a way. 'It throws out more heat than the scrapings we had delivered last time.'

Markham loved the heat on her face. It made her feel safe and cosy. 'Since old Laurence gave up the coal round, it's not been the same,' she said. 'He's been delivering coal round these parts for nigh on fifty years, and now any old Tom, Dick or Harry turns up on the doorstep.' The long drawn-out sigh made her physically shrink, until she seemed like a doll in her chair. 'They say he'll not last long, poor thing.'

All this was news to Kathleen. 'What's wrong with him?'

Markham shrugged her narrow shoulders. 'No one seems to know for sure. I heard people talking in the grocer's shop the other week. Some say he's crippled, and others say he's too tired to work any more. I'm not surprised. Years of carting heavy sacks of coal on his back can cripple a man.' She liked old Laurence. When he called to collect his money on a Friday night, he'd always have a broad smile and a word of cheer. Another familiar face gone for ever, she thought sadly.

'I wouldn't mind being a coalman,' Adam confessed. 'Nobody to tell you what to do and a wage in your pocket every week.'

Kathleen sat up and stared at him. 'I thought you wanted to be a rich farmer. With land and cattle and everything.'

He shook his head. 'That was when I was young. I know better now.' He was thinking of his father, and of how the land had not brought his family happiness.

Markham smiled at his worldly comment. 'You're still young now,' she laughed. 'Sixteen is a prime age. I wish I was that young again.'

She let her mind wander over the years, to when she was Adam's age and loved a young man who went away and left her lonely. All her life she had never forgiven him for it. If she was young again, she would not make the same mistakes. She would not end up old and alone. But she wasn't young. She was crotchety and ancient, and her old bones creaked when she walked. Still, she couldn't complain. There were always people worse off than she was.

She looked at her companions and her spirit brightened. Because of these two, she thought, her quiet life would not end in loneliness.

'*I* wouldn't want to be a coalman,' Kathleen piped up. 'And I don't care if I'm not rich. I want a pretty cottage with roses round the door, like that one on the way to the church. I want a white pony and trap, who'll take me where I want to go. Two big dogs to play in the garden, and six noisy children – three boys and three girls.' She swept her audience with a wonderful smile. 'You two could come and stay for as long as you wanted, and when the circus comes to town, Uncle Adam could treat us all.' Funny how she hadn't mentioned her husband. But the shadowy figure at the back of her mind resembled a young man she had been forbidden to see ever again.

Adam smiled at her daydreams. 'I hope you get what you want one day, sis,' he said, 'but I don't know if I'll have the money to treat six children to the circus. I'm not interested in making a fortune. All I want is enough money never to have to beg, steal or borrow.'

Markham nodded approval. 'Your brother's right.' She knew how money brought its own curses. 'Making a fortune isn't everything. It's far more important to be content in your work.' She regarded Adam with affection. 'You may find yourself making a fortune without meaning to,' she said. 'You're a very bright young man. The headmaster says you have a natural aptitude for figures and, if you wanted, you could have a brilliant future in the business world.' She thought it a pity for him to waste such talents and said so. 'Having money isn't always an evil,' she concluded. 'It depends on the man.' She thought of Adam's father, and it was obvious that Adam had him in mind also.

'We'll see,' he mused. 'I haven't really made up my mind what I want to do with my life.'

'What about me and Markham?' Kathleen suddenly felt left out of her brother's future. 'When you're a businessman and you travel the world, you won't forget about us, will you, Adam?'

He gazed at her and the love lit his face. 'How could I ever forget about either of you. You and Markham are all I have.'

Markham's next words were sobering. 'Whatever happens, you must always watch out for your sister.

Once you're out in the big wide world, anything can happen. Kathleen, too, will have a life of her own, but you two must always be close, Adam. You've been through so much together.' Leaning down to stroke the girl's long dark hair she went on softly, 'Don't worry about me. I'm old. I won't always be around.'

At eleven o'clock Markham bade them goodnight and made her way upstairs. 'No, I'll be all right,' she told them as they offered to help. 'And you two should get off to your beds. It's very late, and I've kept you talking too long.'

Half an hour later, Kathleen went upstairs and soon afterwards she heard Adam close his bedroom door. She knew it was his door because it was ill fitting and when it scraped the carpet it made a swishing sound.

Contented, she turned on her side and went to sleep.

Outside, the night thickened.

It was in the early hours when they arrived; three burly louts who had not forgotten their confrontation with the old lady. They had been seen off shame-faced and empty-handed, and now they were out for revenge.

'Seems quiet enough to me.' The dark-haired fellow with big, crooked teeth edged forward. Looking up at the bedroom windows, he whispered, 'No lights. Not a sound to be heard. Seems to me like the little darlings are all asleep.'

'Which room is the girl's, d'yer reckon?' The ringleader couldn't get Kathleen out of his mind. He'd been cheated last time, but this time he meant to have a taste of her. 'Once we find her, she's mine. Understand?'

Tongues hanging out like a pair of curs, the other two nodded. 'We can watch though, can't we?'

'Don't see why not. So long as yer keep yer hands to yerself.'

The third one had his mind on other things. ''Ow much d'yer think the old bat's worth?'

'Don't know for sure, but we'll soon find out.'

'What makes yer think she'll 'ave it tucked under her mattress?'

''Cause that's where they all hide it.'

'Fair shares when we find it then?'

'That's what we agreed, ain't it?' Pointing to the thin fellow, he told him, 'You keep watch while we ransack the place for anything worth taking. Stay hidden, and be quiet about it. If you hear anybody coming, whistle like I said.' Addressing the one with the crooked teeth he hissed, 'Any sign o' trouble, and we leg it outta there. Understood?'

'What if the bloke sets about you?'

'He'll be sorry, won't he? Last time he had help from that traitor, Murray Laing.' His features thickened to a scowl. 'I'll deal with that one when the time comes. As for the bloke here, he'll soon find out he ain't no match for me on his own.' With that he put his fingers to his lips and crept forward. Used to entering other people's houses, he soon had the back door open, and the two of them crept inside.

—————————

THE FIRST INDICATION Markham had that someone was in her room was when thick, rough fingers gripped her face and covered her mouth. 'Do as you're told, yer old bugger.' A face leered at her from above; in the moonlight from the window it looked like the devil himself.

The lout pulled her to the floor and, with surprising ease, tore two strips from the bedsheet. One he fastened tightly about her mouth, the other he used to bind her to the foot of the bed. With her hands and feet secured, and her mouth cruelly gagged, she was unable to move or call out.

Helpless, she watched with wide, angry eyes while he ransacked the room. She saw him turn the mattress over and rip it from top to bottom, growling like an animal when he found nothing valuable. He searched beneath the bed; he emptied the drawers and turned out the wardrobes, all done softly, so as not to wake anyone. 'Where d'yer keep yer val'ables?' he demanded, grabbing her by the throat and raising her from the floor. 'Tell me, or I swear to Gawd I'll tear yer limb from limb.'

As the neck of her nightshift tightened on her throat, the old lady feared she might be murdered there and then, leaving Kathleen and Adam at the mercy of this foul creature. Trembling, she nodded and he let her loose. 'Where is it? And you'd better not lie to me, old woman.' Quickly, he loosed her hands and feet and thrust her forward. 'Get it!'

Seeing a cradle of matches and a candle on the bedside cupboard, he ordered, 'Light the candle.' With stiff, shaking fingers, she did as she was told. He kept hold of her while she went slowly across the room.

Going to the chimney breast, her mouth still tightly gagged, she reached inside and drew out a small dirty bag. 'There ain't but a few guineas in 'ere!' he growled, throwing the contents into a chair. 'Don't tell me this is all you've got! Where's the rest of it?'

The old lady shook her head.

Enraged, he hit her.

She shook her head once more, her eyes now wide with fear.

'Useless old biddy!' He hit her again, so hard her nose was broken and the force of the blow sent her in a heap to the floor. 'Happen this is all you've got.' Sniggering, he gave the small limp figure a spiteful push with the toe of his boot. 'I don't think you'd take a battering like that for nothing.' Reaching down, he grabbed her by the hair, grinning in her face. 'No matter. There's bits and pieces downstairs might fetch a bob or two. I'll be off in a minute, yer old bag, but first I've a date with a pretty dark-eyed beauty. You might have liked to watch, but I can see you're not up to it.'

Stretching to his full height, he chuckled, a low, grating sound that stirred her senses. 'Which room is she in, eh?' he mused, thoughtfully stroking his chin while he glanced this way and that. 'Never mind, I'll find her. And if I should come across the feller-me-lad, happen I'll teach him a lesson he's not likely to forget in a hurry. If it hadn't been for that traitor Laing, I'd have dealt with him afore. Laing's gone all soft on that gal o' yours. Because of her, 'e wants no part of his old pals. Mind you, 'e were never any good at stealing. He's a fighter though, I'll give him that. Got a pair o' fists like sledgehammers, an' knows how to use 'em. But he ain't got the killer instinct, not like me.'

After stashing the money into his pockets, he bent down and caught hold of Markham's hair. Summoning all her courage, the old lady kept her eyes tightly closed and her body perfectly still. Her face beneath the blood was as white as chalk. Momentarily frightened, he whispered, 'Yer ain't dead, are yer?' In the candlelight he stared hard at her face, but then a smile crept over his rough features. 'It's no matter if yer 'ave snuffed it. The buggers won't catch me, not in a month o' Sundays, they won't.'

Snorting angrily, he let her fall to the floor. 'To hell with yer! A few minutes with the girl an' I'll be on me way.'

Unaware that the old lady had partly regained her senses and was catching snippets of what he was saying, he bound her hands again, muttering all the while. 'Can't have yer waking up an' making a fuss, can we, eh? Can't 'ave yer waking the feller neither, though I'm not frightened of him, I can tell yer that. But y'see my dilemma. I've got certain business to attend to, and I wouldn't want nobody finding their way into the girl's room just when we're enjoying ourselves.'

Eager for her to hear what he was saying, he bent closer. 'Laing says you've told the girl she ain't to 'ave no truck with him. Well, yer might be sorry about that, 'cause now she's anybody's, ain't she, eh? I dare say 'e won't like it when he finds out I've had her before him. But then he wouldn't take her against her will. Like as not he'd hold her hand and whisper sweet nothings in 'er ear.' His expression hardened. 'But then he's pretty an' I'm ugly, an' the ladies don't take kindly to me whispering in their ear. Don't matter to me, 'cause I ain't got time for such—'

A hard fist came crashing down like a hammer blow to his head, knocking him to the ground and stunning him.

Murray Laing's first thought was for the old lady. Stooping, he quickly released her. 'It's all right,' he murmured when she looked up at him with stricken eyes. 'You're safe now.'

Returning to the other man who was still dazed, he pulled him up by the neck of his shirt. 'Think yourself lucky you won't be swinging on the end of a rope. Another few minutes and it might have been a different story, you bastard!'

Murray Laing had left the other two beaten senseless downstairs, and now he intended to teach this one a lesson. He covered his mouth with one hand while with the other he twisted his arm up his back. 'I warned you about the girl,' he whispered. 'I said I'd do time if you laid one finger on her, and I meant every word.' Forcing him forward, he told him, 'It seems you're hard of hearing. Outside! We'll sort this out, once and for all.'

As they went out on to the landing, Adam came running down the passage, with Kathleen behind. On seeing the two men, Adam launched himself at them while Kathleen ran to check on Markham.

In the uproar that followed, the lout managed to get away. Realising he might be implicated, Murray Laing, too, made good his escape. The two he had laid into downstairs had scarpered as soon as they'd regained their senses.

Adam chased after Murray and the other thug, but they knew every alleyway and escape route and soon disappeared from sight. 'I know who you are!' Adam called out. 'You won't get away with it!'

Dejected and bruised, he returned to the house and went upstairs to the old lady's room.

'She's badly hurt.' Kathleen was on her knees, her arms round the small, frail figure. 'Oh, Adam, I'm frightened.'

He knelt by her side and lifted Markham into his arms. 'I'll stay with her,' he told Kathleen. She was too young to see this, he thought, too dear and vulnerable. It would be better if he stayed and Kathleen went. 'Run and get help. Quickly!'

The sound of his familiar voice filtered through the old lady's pain. She had to tell him how that young man had helped her, how he had saved Kathleen from terrible harm.

Opening her eyes, she looked up at him, her lips moving, but no sound emerged.

'What is it, Markham?' Tenderly, Adam took hold of her hand and bent to hear what she was trying to say. Kathleen paused at the door.

'Murray . . . Laing,' Markham managed.

'It's all right. He can't hurt you now.'

She shook her head. He didn't understand. Wearied, she closed her eyes and was silent.

Kathleen heard her say his name, and her heart hardened against him.

When help arrived and Adam heard them hurrying up the stairs, he assured the old lady she would be all right.

'Don't . . . leave me,' she pleaded.

'We won't leave you.'

'The young . . . man . . .'

'Murray Laing? He'll be caught, don't worry, and he'll pay for this. They *all* will.'

As the ambulance men came into the room, her hand tightened on his. 'No! He . . . helped me . . . saved Kathleen . . . Not him . . . Not him . . .' She saw the look of realisation dawn on his face and knew he had heard. Contented now, she rested.

Kathleen heard her frantic whisperings but was not near enough to decipher the words. She saw the thoughtful look on her brother's face. 'What did she say, Adam?'

Markham was being carried out on a stretcher and the two of them followed close, Kathleen anxiously waiting for an answer, Adam struggling with his conscience.

He knew what Markham had been trying to say. He knew that it was not Murray Laing who had done this terrible thing to her. And yet he wondered whether he should keep the information to himself. There had been awful arguments in this house because of that fellow.

He made up his mind. Kathleen's admirer might not have been guilty of anything here tonight, other than being in this house where he had no right to be, but one way or another he had caused a lot of trouble and deserved to be punished.

'Hush now, Kathleen.' Winding his arm round her shoulders, he drew her close. 'There'll be time for questions later.'

━━━►►◄◄━━━

For two days and nights, the old lady remained oblivious of all around her. 'Your aunt's very ill.' The doctor was brutally honest. 'She may not last another day.'

From the same, uncomfortable chair where she had slept and sat and guarded the old lady, Kathleen gazed up at him. 'Don't let her die,' she pleaded brokenly. 'Please, don't let her die.' She put her hands over her face and quietly sobbed. Adam gently held her. 'I don't want Markham to leave us,' she whispered.

Though he, too, was heartbroken, Adam knew he must be strong for her sake. 'There must be *something* you can do,' he entreated the doctor.

He shook his head. 'I'm sorry.' He looked at Kathleen, and his heart went out to her. 'When do your parents return?' The astonished look on Adam's face puzzled him. 'Before she lost consciousness, your aunt told me you were staying with her for a short time. Until your parents return from abroad, she said.'

Adam did some quick thinking. Of course! Bless her old heart. Right to the last she only had thoughts for them. If the authorities knew they were orphans, they might be taken away. 'That's right, sir,' he lied confidently. 'Our parents are due back soon, and then we'll be going home.'

'Your aunt said it was not possible to contact your parents. Is that right?'

'Yes, sir.'

Eyeing Adam with concern, he asked, 'How old are you?'

'Eighteen, sir.' It was what the doctor needed to hear.

'I see.' Certainly he sensed nothing untoward here. Indeed, the young man and his sister seemed more capable than a good many older people who had frequented this infirmary. 'And are there no other relatives?'

'No, sir.' Adam stood up, a tall, fine young man with an air of proud confidence. 'Our parents would want us to be here with our aunt,' he assured the doctor. 'She has no one else.' That much at least was true.

The doctor was humbled. 'Of course.' At times like these, he felt like an intruder. 'I understand.' More relaxed now, he asked with a smile, 'And are the nurses looking after you both?' His question was put to Kathleen.

'Yes, thank you, sir.' She wiped her eyes. He must not think her a baby.

'Good. That's good.' He spoke to Adam now. 'Your sister looks washed out. Why don't you and – Kathleen, isn't it? Why don't you go and stretch your legs for a while? Your aunt will be in good hands, I can assure you.'

Adam wasn't convinced. 'What if she needs us?'

'If your aunt needs you, we'll find you quickly enough,' he promised. 'Meanwhile, it will do you both good to walk in the fresh air. In fact, if you go by way of the office, I've no doubt Sister will have a pot of tea in the making.'

Adam nodded. 'Thank you, sir.' He glanced at Markham's quiet face. 'Don't leave us, Markham,' he murmured. Then he led Kathleen away down the ward.

━━━━━➤●ଐ━━━━━

TIRED THOUGH SHE was, Markham could not rest. There was still so much to do. 'The children?'

'The children have been sent for.' The nurse was a homely soul, small and prim as her patient. 'Are you sure there's nothing I can get you?'

Markham shook her head. 'I need . . . the children.'

'The children will be here any minute.' Plumping up the pillows, she caught sight of them. 'Here they are now.'

The nurse pulled the screen round the bed and left them alone.

'Oh, Markham, you're going to be all right!' Kathleen was filled with hope.

Markham smiled sadly. 'I don't think so,' she whispered. 'But you mustn't be sad.' Pausing to gather her strength, she went on to tell Adam, 'The house was never mine, just rented. But you know where I keep the money. It's yours, yours and Kathleen's. Take it and go away, before anyone gets suspicious.'

Adam was taken aback. 'We don't want your

money, Markham,' he told her gently. 'I thought the thieves made away with everything anyway.'

'That's what ... they thought too.' A coughing bout took hold of her and brought the nurse running. 'I'm all right,' she argued. 'Please ... leave us alone ... a minute longer.'

Reluctantly, the nurse did as she was asked, remaining close by, in case she was needed.

Hard though it was, Markham went on, occasionally pausing to take a deep, grating breath. She had to make certain the children were safe. 'Mr Ernshaw must not know,' she told them. 'Take the money. Get away ... don't let them put you in ... an institution.'

Kathleen could hold her grief no longer. 'No, Markham, don't leave us!' Sobbing, she wrapped her arms round the dear soul. 'Don't die,' she pleaded, the tears rolling down her face. 'Please, Markham.'

Tenderly, Adam put his hand on Kathleen's shoulder and drew her aside. 'Come away,' he murmured. 'We have to do as she says.'

Helpless in his arms, Kathleen kept her stricken gaze on the old woman's face.

'Come here, sweetheart,' Markham bade her. 'Come here, child.'

When she was close again, Markham stroked her young face. 'You know I love you both ... don't you?' A little chuckle escaped her throat. 'I've locked you in the cellar, and I've had to punish you time and again, but you must know ... I always loved you.' In Kathleen she saw herself as a child. She felt a deep empathy with the girl, this poor little bastard who, thankfully, would never know the truth. 'Do you love old Markham?' she asked.

Kathleen's tears blinded her, but not to the abiding love she had come to feel for this woman. 'Yes,' she said firmly, 'I do love you.' She always would, even if tomorrow Markham was not here. Even if she never saw her again, she would always love and remember her.

'Will you do . . . what old Markham wants then?' She felt her life ebbing away. It was not a sad thing, but for these two who had come to lean on her, it would be hard. It was in her power even now to help them, and help them she would, or be ashamed to meet her maker. 'Go with your brother now,' she said. 'Will you do that?'

Filled with emotion, Kathleen could only nod. The tears burned her eyes, blurring her vision. When she was able to see Markham more clearly, it was with the stark realisation that the little woman was struggling to breathe. 'Adam, quick!' Instinctively, she stepped away.

The nurse came running at Adam's call. 'Best you wait outside,' she told the children. 'I have to get the doctor.'

She hurried away, and Markham grabbed Adam by the arm. 'Get away!' she urged. 'Now!' When he hesitated, she shook her head. 'Please go,' she begged, her gaze going to Kathleen's sad face. 'Take her . . . away from here.'

'I won't go!' Kathleen said stubbornly. 'I won't leave you.'

Markham appealed to her goodness. 'You promised.'

Adam knew they had to leave. 'You did promise,' he told his distraught sister. 'You said you would do what Markham asked.'

Markham closed her eyes. 'Take her. Quickly.'

As they left, passing the doctor and nurse on the way, Markham murmured after them, 'God go with you.'

<hr />

ADAM FOUND THE money beneath the floorboard under the piano.

'It's like stealing,' Kathleen said. 'When Markham gets better, she'll need it herself.'

Adam sat her down. 'Kathleen.' He ran his fingers over hers, his heart heavy. 'Markham won't get better. That's what she was trying to tell us, to get away from here, before news gets to Mr Ernshaw and he comes looking for us.'

'I don't care.'

'Don't you care if he puts you in an orphanage? Markham cares. That's why she's helping us.'

'I want to go back.'

'Back where?' For a moment he thought she meant to the old house, to where they had lived with their parents. The thought made him shudder.

'To the infirmary. I want to be with Markham.'

'We won't be able to stay.'

'Why not?'

'Because they'll start asking questions. Because Markham doesn't want us there.' He swallowed hard. 'Because, whether we like it or not, Markham is leaving us, and we have to get away.' For the first time he couldn't hold back the tears. 'We have to do as she asked.'

Distressed to see him crying, she promised, 'I just want to see her once more.'

'All right, but then we must leave.'

'I know.'

By the time they got back to the infirmary, it was too late for goodbyes. 'I'm sorry,' the nurse said, 'but there are forms to be filled out. The police have questions, and we need more information.' She spoke briefly to the clerk at the desk, before hurrying away. 'I'll only be a minute,' she told Adam as she went. 'Then we can talk in Sister's office.'

Fearful that they might be detained, Adam told Kathleen, 'We have to go.'

Kathleen, too, was keen to leave, but first there was something she had to do. Going to the desk, she told the clerk, 'It was Murray Laing.'

The round-faced woman smiled and it seemed as if the full moon had risen. 'Pardon, dear?'

'The people who robbed Markham and hurt her, it was Murray Laing and his three friends.'

'Did you tell this to the police?'

'No. But I want you to tell them. Murray Laing and his friends broke into my aunt's house and attacked her. Tell the police to find them. They have to pay for what they did!'

To the woman's surprise, Kathleen turned and ran out of the building. Adam thrust a fistful of money on to the desk and told her, 'This is to bury Markham.' Then, without another word, he hurried after his sister.

Outside, he caught her by the shoulders and spun her round to face him. 'Why did you say it was Murray Laing who attacked Markham?' Up until now, no names had been mentioned, not even when the police asked them a number of questions.

'Because it was. You heard Markham say so, didn't you? She said it was Murray, didn't she?'

With a rush of shame he recalled how Markham had in fact cleared Murray of the crime, but that he had let Kathleen believe she was accusing him instead. What had happened to Markham was a wicked and evil thing, but by not telling Kathleen the truth, he himself had done something even more wicked. But they couldn't go back now. It would raise too many awkward questions about their circumstances.

'Adam!' Kathleen's anxious voice disturbed his thoughts. 'Markham said it was Murray, didn't she?'

'You know she did,' he assured her. 'You were there, weren't you?' He felt angry. Guilty.

'They killed her. I hate them! I hate *him*!'

'Come on,' he said, urging her forward. 'Let's get out of here.'

<hr />

A S THE DARKNESS closed in and weariness overwhelmed them, they found refuge in an old warehouse in Blackpool's back streets. 'Where will we go, Adam?'

'We'll decide in the morning.'

Curling up in a corner, she drew her coat tighter about her and settled down to sleep.

Fishing in his pocket for the brown paper bundle he'd found in Markham's hiding place, Adam took out an official-looking envelope. Opening it, he began to read.

The letter was from Mr Ernshaw. It revealed how Kathleen was conceived by her mother in an illicit affair with the gamekeeper. It also revealed exactly how his parents had died. He could hardly take it in. His senses reeled as if he'd been punched repeatedly. 'Kathleen, not my full sister but my mother's bastard! And my father! Hanged as a double murderer! It can't be true,' he cried out.

Kathleen stirred. 'What's wrong, Adam?' Peering through the half-darkness, she saw the letter in his hand. 'What's that?'

'Nothing,' he managed to say. 'It's nothing.' As

she watched, he tore the letter into shreds. It was too much to bear. He felt utterly drained. He was the son of a murderer, and his sister – his *half*-sister – was the bastard daughter of a gamekeeper. He couldn't come to terms with it.

He gazed at Kathleen, this delightful creature who looked up to him, loving him with an innocence that tore at the heart, and a great compassion and strength filled him. She was no more responsible for the circumstance of her birth than he was. A piece of paper with some words written on it didn't change anything; it didn't suddenly turn her, or him, into a creature to be shunned. 'It's all right,' he told her, more composed now. 'It's just an old letter, of no consequence.' Standing up, he resolutely stuffed the torn pieces through the broken window. 'Go to sleep,' he said, watching the bits of paper disperse in the breeze. 'We've a long day ahead of us tomorrow,' he reminded her. 'I need to get work.'

'Me too,' she replied.

He smiled. 'We'll see,' he said. 'We'll see.'

Curled up on the floor, Kathleen's thoughts went to the woman they had left behind, and she wept softly.

She wondered about the future. She thought of Murray; that tousle-haired young man who had wormed his way into her young heart; she thought of his winning smile and the mischievous way he would wink at her. She recalled how they had talked, and laughed, and shared their foolish, childish dreams.

These were the good things.

Then she thought of Markham, and sorrow swept over her like a dark, suffocating blanket.

———◆———

KATHLEEN WAS THE first to wake. Something had stirred her out of a restless sleep, and now she saw the reason. Far from alarming her, it brought a smile to her face. 'Hello,' she said, winking sleepily at the tiny mouse perched on her arm. 'Where have you come from?'

Its beady little eyes stared back at her, its face so near she could see the silky whiskers twitching. 'I've got nothing for you to eat,' she apologised, 'so you'd better go and look elsewhere.'

The creature cocked its head to one side, as if to say, 'I can wait.' And for a while they looked at each other, the mouse studying Kathleen and she studying the mouse. 'You're a pretty little thing,' she murmured. When it sat back on its haunches and brought up its tiny fists to wash its face, she reached out to touch it, half fearing it would scurry away. But it stayed, even when her gentle fingers stroked its small, smooth back. 'I won't hurt you,' she smiled. 'You know that, don't you?'

It was Adam who scared it away. Hearing her voice, he woke with a start. 'Who's there?' Sitting up, he rubbed his eyes. 'Are you all right, Kathleen?'

'I didn't mean to wake you.'

He scratched his head and looked around. 'I thought I heard you talking to someone.'

'We had a visitor.'

Alarmed, he glanced around. 'Where is he?'

'Stop worrying,' she chuckled. 'It was only a mouse. The poor little thing was hungry.'

He laughed. 'Talking to a mouse! Whatever next.' More serious issues filled his mind. 'Come on, Kathleen. We've a lot to do. We need somewhere to live and I need a job.'

Scruffy-headed and still yawning, she stood before him. 'But how?'

'I haven't made up my mind. Maybe we could find work in a Blackpool hotel. That way we would have a wage and a roof over our heads. Or we could go south, into the country. Get work with lodgings, in one of the big farmhouses.'

Kathleen shook her head. 'I'm not going any-where until I've seen what they do with Markham.'

'Have you gone mad? It was Markham who told us to get away. There's nothing we can do, Kathleen. I know you loved her, and so did I, but she's gone now. I left money for her to be buried, and there's nothing more we can do.'

'If there was no money, what would happen to her then?'

He shrugged, trying hard to recall what happened when people had no money to be buried. 'I'm not sure. I think they put them in a pauper's grave.'

'What's a pauper's grave?'

'It's a place outside the church grounds. Sometimes, if people don't have money, the authorities open up somebody else's grave and put them in there.'

She fell silent, obviously troubled, and he did his best to reassure her. 'But that won't happen to Markham. I left more than enough money.'

'What if somebody steals the money?'

'Who would steal it? These are doctors and nurses.' The idea that they would steal a person's burial money was unthinkable.

Kathleen was not satisfied. 'I'm not leaving until I know what they're going to do with her.'

He knew that when she had made up her mind about something she was stubborn to the last and there was little anyone could do. 'All right. But don't blame me if it all goes wrong.'

In a way he felt the same as Kathleen, but not for the same reasons. He just wanted to see the old lady put to rest. 'We're taking a risk,' he reminded her. 'If they find out Markham was all we had in the world, they'll want to put us away, and they might separate us. Do you understand what I'm saying, Kathleen? If that happens, we might never see each other again.'

The idea made her feel physically sick, but the thought that Markham might be put in a pauper's grave was too shocking. 'We'll have to be careful, that's all,' she said. 'We'll have to stay out of sight. Afterwards, we'll go wherever you want.'

He paced the floor, thinking. 'How can we find

out what's happening? I mean, we can't go in and ask, can we?'

'We could ask that nice nurse.'

He shook his head. 'She'd call the authorities.'

'What about somebody who works there, like a cleaner, or one of the women who take away the bed linen?'

'We could try, I suppose. They must know what's going on. Just as long as nobody else sees us.'

'They won't. Especially if we wait until dark. I expect the cleaners and laundry women leave the infirmary by the back. We could wait there.'

He regarded her with admiration. 'You've given this a lot of thought, haven't you, sis?' Calling her 'sis' came without thinking, but to his dismay he was reminded of the contents of that letter. He thrust it away. 'I don't expect they waste much time once a person's dead, so let's hope we can sort this out tonight. We'll have to spend another night here but with any luck we'll be able to get away tomorrow.'

'Thank you, Adam. But we don't have to hide in here all day, do we?'

'No, we don't. We must get something to eat, too. I'm starving.'

The day was cold and crisp, with a keen wind and a biting chill, but they were well wrapped up and didn't feel the cold. They bought some buns at a baker's shop and spent the day on a deserted beach, losing themselves in memories of when Markham had taken them to Lytham.

Balancing precariously on the narrow wall which protruded into the ocean, Kathleen looked back at Adam who was lying on the sand, his long legs crossed, his face towards the sky and his eyes tightly closed. 'Are you thinking, Adam?'

He didn't move. 'Yes.'

The wind was gaining strength, forcing her to raise her voice. '*What* are you thinking?'

'Things.' Still he made no move and his eyes remained tightly closed.

'What things?'

'None of your business.'

'I've been thinking too.'

'Oh?'

'About Markham.'

'What about her?'

'I'm just remembering Lytham. We ate our ice cream, and we buried her up to her waist in the sand. It made us all laugh.'

'I remember.' He blinked, stared at the sky and closed his eyes again.

Kathleen's voice trembled just a little, and her eyes grew moist. 'People stopped and stared.'

'I remember that too.' He gave a little laugh.

The wind was raging around them, so strong that Kathleen had to cup her mouth in order to be heard. 'That man with the bowler hat thought she was a crazy old woman let loose from the asylum. He said people like her ought to be locked up.'

'It's people like him who should be locked up.'

The wind receded a little. The sea calmed and everything became eerily quiet for a moment. She watched the sea awhile, frothing and raging and seeming like an angry, tortured soul. 'I'm afraid of the sea,' she murmured, but Adam didn't hear. Her dark eyes grew troubled. 'Remember how she told us the sea was alive?' she said more loudly. 'How we should never be afraid of it but must always be respectful?'

'Did she say that?'

'She said the sea could think. That it could be kind, and angry, just like a person. She said if it grew angry, it could rise up and take you, and you would never be seen again.'

Forced to shout above the elements, he replied, 'I don't recall Markham saying that. But then you only hear what you want to hear. You're a lot like Markham. You have strange ideas about things.'

'I think she was very wise.' She had learned more from that old lady than from anyone else she had ever known. 'Markham said this was a world of mystery, and that nobody would ever know what secrets it held.' Kathleen had been fascinated. 'Do you believe that, Adam?'

Adam could hardly hear her. Wondering why she sounded so far away, he opened one eye and was horrified to see her balancing on the far end of the wall, waves battering at her feet. 'For God's sake!' Darting forward, he grabbed her by the hair and pulled her off the wall. 'Have you no sense?' He was shaking with fear. 'You could have been swept in and drowned!'

Rubbing her sore scalp, she retorted, 'I was safe enough.'

'Stronger people than you have been dragged under. Stay off the wall or we'll leave right now.'

'Can I dip my feet in the water?'

'No!'

'Please, Adam. Just for a minute.'

'I said no!'

'Just to paddle, that's all.' She gazed longingly at the ocean. 'It might be years before we come to the seaside again.'

'One minute,' he conceded. 'Then we'll have to go.'

She took off her shoes and socks. Mindful of how defiant she could be, he went with her to the water's edge and stayed close by. 'Don't go in higher than your ankles,' he warned, catching hold of her skirt hem and keeping her in check. 'There might be undercurrents.'

Bravely, Kathleen dipped in a toe. 'It's freezing!'

She squealed and paddled, and splashed the water in his face. 'You're mad,' he told her with a laugh. 'And look at the pair of us. We're soaked.' But it didn't matter. For that one precious moment in their young, innocent lives, nothing else mattered but that they had each other, and a whole life's adventures before them.

Soon it was time to leave. 'We'd best make our way to the infirmary,' Adam said, and they retraced their steps along the beach and up the steps near the windmill. Here, Kathleen sat to put on her shoes and socks.

'I didn't realise it was so late,' Adam said, glancing at the darkening sky. 'Move yourself, Kathleen. It's a fair walk to Lytham.'

By the time they had walked the length of the promenade, the night was closing in fast. Adam was striding out, with Kathleen running behind, trying to keep up. Every now and then she would call and he would wait, but soon he was striding ahead again. 'It was your idea to wait outside the infirmary,' he reminded her. 'By the time we get there they'll all have gone home. Hurry up, Kathleen!' It was dark and cold and he was impatient.

As he walked he twisted round yet again to check how far behind she was; he didn't see the woman who got up from the bench and bent to pick up her bag. He walked straight into her and sent her and her bag sprawling.

'Get off, yer scoundrel!' she yelled. Scrambling to her feet, she attacked Adam with her umbrella, forcing him to fold his arms across his face to protect himself.

When he gallantly tried to pick up her handbag for her, she smacked him hard across the head with the butt of the brolly. 'Thief!' she cried. 'Knock a woman down and steal her bag, would you?' Angry and indignant, she tore into him.

'Adam's not a thief!' Kathleen threw herself between them. 'He's only trying to help. He didn't see you, he was looking out for me.'

In an instant the woman stopped, brolly held high and an expression of astonishment on her face. In the yellow halo of lamplight, she stared at Kathleen, then she stared at Adam, astonishment giving way to uncertainty.

Kathleen wasn't certain. The years had marked the woman's face but the features were still scraggy and the body still thin and waif-like. 'Nancy?' She could hardly believe it. 'Nancy Tomlin!'

Nancy screeched with delight. 'It *is* you! Oh, my God!' To Adam's relief, she threw down the brolly and flung her arms round them both. 'Wait till Cook finds out. I told her we might see you one day, on this very promenade.' She cried and laughed, and there was so much to talk about, but they couldn't stand there in the dark and cold. 'Come on,' said Nancy. 'Cook and Mason are waiting back at the house.'

As they hurried along the street, Kathleen and Nancy chattered excitedly. Adam kept silent. He was pleased to see Nancy again, and meeting Cook would be wonderful, but he couldn't help wondering how this would affect their plans.

The guesthouse was only a short walk. 'I can't wait to see Cook's face,' Nancy said as she opened the door with her key. 'She won't believe her eyes.'

When the three of them came into the parlour, a cosy domestic scene greeted them. A cheery fire warmed the room and on one side of the fireplace John Mason was slumped in a big flowered armchair, fast asleep with his mouth wide open and the newspaper spread out on his lap. Mabel's chair had its back to the door, and as Nancy entered, her voice sailed from its depths, 'Is that you, Nancy Tomlin? Where've you been till this time? I've told yer time and again not to stroll that promenade after dark. There are rascals out there as 'd cut yer throat for a shilling.'

Glancing at Kathleen and Adam, Nancy put her finger to her lips. Trying hard not to giggle, she said sombrely, 'You're right, Cook. I should've listened to you, 'cause I came across a pair o' rascals tonight. I even had to fight one of 'em off with me brolly.'

'What!' Mabel leaped out of her chair. 'Are yer all right, yer silly woman?' Being a big lady and not given to leaping, it took a moment before she was steady on her feet and looking Nancy in the eye. 'Yer just won't listen . . .' Her gaze went to Adam first. 'Who the devil's this?'

From Nancy's side, Kathleen stepped forward. 'Hello, Cook,' she said softly. 'Don't you know us?'

Mabel stared at her. As realisation came, her hand flew to her mouth and the tears sprang to her old eyes. She gazed into Kathleen's dark eyes and the years fell away. 'Oh, my goodness.' That was all she could say. 'Oh, my goodness.'

Nancy was beaming from ear to ear. 'These are the rascals I were telling you about,' she said proudly. 'I thought you'd want me to bring 'em home.'

Unable to contain her emotion, Kathleen ran forward to fling her arms round that familiar, podgy figure. Overwhelmed by the occasion, she couldn't speak.

Adam was more restrained. 'I'm sorry if we're intruding,' he apologised. After all, it wasn't Cook who had invited them into her home.

'Intruding?' Mabel was flabbergasted. 'By! Yer a sight for sore eyes, that's what yer are.' Having recovered from the shock, she caught hold of him and, much to his embarrassment, crushed both him and Kathleen to her ample bosom. 'Yer can't know how glad I am to set eyes on yer again,' she cried. 'It does me old heart good to know yer both all right.'

Nancy was glad she'd done something right after all. 'I knew you'd want to see 'em.' With a dark shawl flung haphazardly over her shoulders and flyaway hair framing her thin, bony features, she resembled a scarecrow.

'Tidy yerself up, woman,' Mabel told her. 'Yer enough to frighten the dead.'

With the hugging done for now, Mabel proudly regarded Kathleen and her brother. 'By! Just look at the pair of yer,' she said. 'All growed up and looking more handsome than ever.' She saw how Adam was a young man now, and how Kathleen was on the verge of changing from child to woman. 'You'll break a few hearts along the way, I'll be bound,' she observed. 'Oh, my goodness!' She sniffed and wiped her eyes, and startled everyone by yelling at the top of her voice, 'Mr Mason, wake up. We've got visitors!'

Through sleepy eyes he peered at the little group.

It took a moment, but soon he was on his feet and greeting them with excitement. 'I never thought we'd clap eyes on you two ever again,' he said, his own eyes popping with astonishment. The questions fell thick and fast, until Mabel put a stop to it. 'There's time enough for all that,' she reprimanded. 'Let them get through the door first.'

Taking charge as always, she settled Adam on the settee, with Kathleen beside him, and then she sent Nancy off to the kitchen. 'We'll have a pot o' tea, an' some o' them little scones I baked today,' she ordered, and Nancy went away in great excitement.

'Are you still with your great-aunt?' John asked Adam. 'We weren't told all that much, only that you'd gone to live with her, and that Mr Ernshaw would be keeping an eye on things. Still, I expect you're at that stage now where you'll be deciding whether to go to college or look for suitable work.' He was amazed at how confident a young man Adam had become; it was heartening to see, especially when he'd had such a bad start.

Adam was saved from having to reply because John turned to address Kathleen.

'And you look lovely as ever, my dear,' he said. 'I hope you've been happy. You seem to have been well looked after and all that. But whatever were you doing in Blackpool after dark? And won't your aunt be wondering where you are?'

Mabel was exasperated. 'For heaven's sake, John,' she exclaimed, 'leave the children alone.' Nancy came into the room and she gestured for her to set the tray on the low table between them, and to sit herself down on a chair. 'We've a lot to talk about,' she said. 'It might not be good manners, and I dare say the old aunt wouldn't approve, but we'll enjoy our tea as we talk.' Handing round the scones, she informed Kathleen, 'I made these special, for the guests, you understand.'

Kathleen wondered about the guests. 'Won't they mind?' Normally she would never eat a scone belonging to someone else. But then again, she and Adam had been out all day and she was so hungry her stomach was playing a tune.

Mabel chuckled. 'I made the scones and I say who eats them. The other buggers can 'ave crumpets instead.'

Kathleen took a bite out of her scone. It melted in her mouth. 'You make the best scones in the world,' she said, and Mabel's face lit like a beacon.

Adam had one eye on the clock and the other on Mabel. 'I'm sorry, Cook,' he apologised, 'we didn't realise you had guests.' Like Kathleen, he was starving hungry. Biting eagerly into the scone, he sent a shower of crumbs down his front.

'Oh, bless yer! They ain't guests like family or friends, nor anything like that. They're more like lodgers that come and go. This is a guesthouse, y'see. I'd like to call it a small hotel, but in truth it ain't that grand.' She shrugged her shoulders and smiled easily. 'Still, it's a fine little place, and it gives us a living.'

She was rightly proud of her business. 'I'll show yer both round when you've had yer tea.'

Adam didn't know how to excuse themselves without sounding ungrateful, especially when he dearly would have liked to stay and talk, and learn what Cook and the others had done with their lives. 'Thank you,' he answered, 'but we'll have to be going quite soon.' He shifted his gaze to the mantelpiece clock. 'It's quarter to six,' he said, and he gave Kathleen a swift, knowing glance, discreetly reminding her of their urgent errand.

John had been quietly watching and listening. He was wondering about these two: what were they doing wandering Blackpool in the dark? Where was the aunt, and why did they seem loath to mention her? Moreover, they looked unkempt, as if they hadn't washed or changed in days.

When he saw the glance that passed between them, his suspicions heightened. 'There's something wrong here,' he remarked, at the same time gesturing for Mabel to remain silent when she seemed about to protest. 'Are you two in some kind of trouble with the old lady? Have you deliberately stayed out and now you daren't go home, is that it?' He smiled. 'You can tell us. You're among friends here.'

The colour drained from Adam's face. He was tired, and a little afraid, but it was his problem and these kind people must not be dragged into a bad situation. 'We have to go, sir.' More than that he wouldn't say.

Mabel wasn't having it. In that firm, authoritative voice they knew so well, she declared, 'Yer neither of yer leaving this house till somebody tells me what's going on.'

Silence greeted her.

Undeterred, she addressed Kathleen in a warmer voice. 'Is Mr Mason right, luv? Have yer stayed out too long, and now yer worried what yer aunt might say when yer get back?'

Kathleen glanced at her brother. 'Tell them, Adam,' she pleaded. 'They might be able to help.'

'Of course we'll help,' Mabel said firmly. 'Isn't that what friends are for?'

Since Kathleen had already given the impression that they needed help, and since he was unsure whether her plan would have worked anyway, Adam felt he could do a lot worse than trust these people who had played such an important part in their childhood. 'We haven't done anything wrong,' he began, 'but you're right, we are in a bit of trouble.'

John nodded, his smile reassuring as he regarded them. 'You really are among friends here,' he affirmed. 'A trouble shared is a trouble halved.'

When Adam hesitated, Mabel prompted him. 'Whatever kind of trouble you're in, I promise we'll do all we can to help.'

Kathleen was nervous. 'You won't go to the police, will you?'

'Never!'

'And you won't take us back to the house?'

'I can't promise that. Let's hear what you have to say first, then we'll decide what's best to do.'

She and John and Nancy sat, quiet and thoughtful, as Adam told how they had been unhappy with Markham when they first arrived, but then they had come to love her. 'Even though she was a little bit crazy,' Kathleen added, her young heart filled with pain.

Mabel chuckled. 'I knew that already,' she told them. 'Right from the time she stayed at the big house and the master threw her out.' Realising she had said too much, and being silently chided by a fierce look from John, she apologised. 'Sorry. Go on, luv. If yer came to be fond of her, why is it yer don't want to go back?'

Adam took a moment to compose himself. In his mind's eye he could see Markham lying in that hospital bed, and he ached with loss. If only he had been able to do something. If only he'd heard those thugs earlier, she might still be alive.

He told of how the thugs had victimised Markham long before he and Kathleen had come to stay with her. He explained how Markham treated them with contempt and how that only seemed to make them worse. He described how, on that fateful night, he was woken by a commotion. When he went to investigate, he found the thugs had attacked the old lady. He fought them, and they ran out of the house, himself in pursuit. But they escaped, and the old lady was rushed to hospital where she had died.

Mabel was appalled and Nancy chewed her bottom lip to stop from crying. John stood up and came to where Adam sat. 'I'm sorry,' he said. 'If there's anything we can do, you've only to ask.'

'We need to make sure she has a proper funeral,' Kathleen told them. 'We left some money, but somebody might steal it and I don't want her to go in a pauper's grave.'

'Bless your heart, child,' Mabel cried. 'We won't let them do that to such a fine old lady.'

Adam confessed how they meant to waylay one of the hospital cleaners or a laundry woman to try and find out what had been arranged for Markham.

'First of all,' said John, 'do the authorities know she was your great-aunt and that you've got no one else in the world except her? Do they realise you're left as orphans? And secondly, you said you left money for her funeral. Where did you come by that? And what's happening to the old lady's belongings – her house and suchlike? Did she make a will, and if so are the two of you mentioned as beneficiaries?'

'Really, John.' Mabel thought he was being insensitive. 'The children have just lost the only person left to care for them, and here you are talking about wills and such.'

'I'm being practical, that's all,' he protested.

'She didn't own the house,' Kathleen piped up. 'It was rented. She told us that. She said she owned nothing worth selling, just bits and pieces, and furniture that was past its prime even when she bought it.'

'She hid some money away and told us where to find it,' said Adam. 'I have what's left of it here.' He tapped his jacket pocket. 'It should be enough to keep us from starving while I find work.'

'Work, eh?' John looked at the young man, thinking how he was too fine to be a manual worker. 'What have you got in mind?'

'I don't care what it is. I'll do anything, as long as we have a roof over our heads as well. Maybe a labourer on a farm, or a porter in a hotel.'

'If I remember rightly, you had a particular leaning towards numbers.' John winked at Mabel. 'You could add up a shopping list before Cook got to the second column.'

'I might go into accounts later, when Kathleen is older. For now, I'll have to take what's on offer and be grateful. I've got Kathleen to think of now. We'll need to get away from these parts, in case the authorities find us and tell Mr Ernshaw we're on our own again.'

'If he finds us, he'll put me in an orphanage.' Kathleen's voice trembled.

'He'll do no such thing!' Mabel declared. 'Mr Ernshaw won't know, 'cause we won't tell him. And as for having a roof over yer heads, you need look no further.'

Excited and appalled by the turn of events, Mabel had let her tongue run away with her. If they were to let these two stay, it meant turning away other, paying guests, and that meant a considerable drop in income.

The same thought had crossed John's mind. Alarmed but not surprised by her outburst, he gave her a warning look. She knew he was concerned, but she had made the promise, and now she must keep it. 'We'll work it out 'atween us,' she said, and when Kathleen ran to her, overjoyed at the prospect of staying here, John had no choice but to agree.

As for Nancy, she was so thrilled, she danced on the spot. 'We'll have such fun,' she told Kathleen. 'Adam can get a job, and I'll meet you every day from school.'

Adam was still worried. He was sure the only way to keep out of Mr Ernshaw's clutches was to leave Blackpool. 'It's very kind of you,' he said, 'but we couldn't put on you like that. Besides, we've made our plans, and please don't worry, I'll see Kathleen comes to no harm.'

'We'll discuss all that later,' John told him. 'Right now I'd best get down to the infirmary and see what's being done. I'll say I'm a neighbour of your parents or something, and have just heard the news about Markham.'

⟫►◆◄⟪

T HE NURSE AT the desk was most helpful. 'I'm very glad the children are back with their parents,' she said. 'Of course, the authorities did question them but they couldn't throw much light on the matter.' She paused. 'Although, come to think of it, later on the girl did point a finger at someone, and she must have been right, because he's been arrested.'

She leaned forward as if to impart a secret. 'Mind you, the old lady did say to the nurse who tended her that this particular young man had tried to help, but what I'd like to know is, what was he doing in the old lady's house? Tell me that? Up to no good, that's what. If you ask me, he's every bit as guilty as the others.'

'I dare say.' John knew nothing of this, and didn't want to know. But he had information to ferret out, so must show a degree of interest. 'Terrible thing, though.'

'Still, she had two good friends in those children. They even brought money in, to pay for her funeral.'

'So the old lady is to be given a decent burial, is she?'

'Good enough. At least she'll be laid in consecrated ground.'

'Where?'

'I'm not sure.'

'Do you know when?'

'I'm not sure about that either.' He was asking too many questions. 'Surely the children's parents can tell you.'

'Yes, of course,' said John quickly, 'but I've only just heard what happened, and since I was passing the infirmary I thought I'd get the details here. I'd like to pay the old lady my respects, and I don't want to trouble the relatives at this sad time.'

The nurse nodded in understanding. 'You'll need to speak to the chaplain.' She pointed along the corridor. 'To the end, then turn left. You'll see his office there.'

<hr />

FOUR DAYS LATER, beneath a flurry of snow, Markham was laid to rest in a pretty old church close to the railway. 'She'll like it here,' Kathleen said. 'She always enjoyed standing on the bridge, watching the trains go by.' Somehow it made losing her more bearable.

'Let's get home out of the cold,' Mabel urged, her shawl flying in the wind. 'This is no place to linger.' She felt the need to sit by the fire and feel the warmth on her face. At that moment, after laying the old woman in the ground, she felt her age and it weighed heavily upon her. 'I'll have a lazy evening,' she declared, 'with the fire up the chimney and a spot o' gin in me tea.'

The small party of mourners made their way out of the churchyard. 'Tired, are you, me dear?' Linking his arm with Mabel's, John walked her to the waiting carriage. 'We'll have an early night, eh?' he suggested.

222

'I don't fancy an early night, thank you. I'm in no hurry to climb the stairs tonight,' she informed him.

'Well, I am.' Nancy had a bad habit of butting into their conversations. It was an irritating habit which Mabel had failed to cure. She glared at her, sending out a message that anyone else might have taken note of, but not Nancy, who was delightfully unaware of her own shortcomings. 'It's been a long day. I need to put my feet up,' she groaned. 'They feel like two swollen loaves.'

'That's too bad,' Mabel snapped. 'There's work to do.'

There were three paying guests staying at the house; an old man by the name of Jed, and a recently married couple with eyes only for each other. These two stayed in their room most of the time, and came down for meals looking bleary-eyed and in a kind of trance. 'Young love!' Mabel said, wishing she was thirty years younger, and much to John's amusement old Jed would wink at her in a suggestive manner.

This evening was no different from any other, except for Kathleen and Adam's presence. They all sat round the table and enjoyed one of Mabel's special meals: a grand stew of meat and vegetables with her own homemade gravy, so thick you could stand a spoon up in it. There was jam tart and cream for afters, and a pot full of piping-hot tea to swill it down.

Afterwards the guests retired to their rooms, where the couple would cavort for a while until they were so exhausted they'd fall into a state of unconscious rapture. The old man would read until his eyes began to close, then he would climb into bed and wake only when the smell of Mabel's sizzling bacon teased his hairy nostrils.

When the dishes were washed and returned to the cupboard, Adam, Kathleen and Nancy went off to their beds too. Mabel sank into her favourite chair in the parlour, beside a banked-up fire, with the warmth playing on her face and the gin playing on her senses. John read the newspaper for a while, then he sat, watching her and thinking.

'I need to talk to you,' he said eventually. 'About a certain matter that's been worrying me.'

Mabel sat up. 'Then get it off yer chest,' she urged. 'We've never kept things to ourselves, and we mustn't start now.'

A few moments later, Adam made his way downstairs for a glass of water. The stew had given him a raging thirst. The parlour door was ajar, and hearing an intense conversation taking place between John and Mabel, he tactfully turned to retreat. He paused, however, on realising that the conversation concerned himself and Kathleen.

'We can't just turn the poor little devils out, not after what they've been through.'

'But you must know they can't stay here indefinitely. They're taking up two rooms, and we've already turned guests away because of it. That's money out of our pockets. Money we can ill afford.'

John felt guilty, but the running of this household was ultimately his responsibility, and he had never been afraid to make difficult decisions when duty called. 'Much as I'd like to keep them here, they're not our responsibility,' he insisted. 'We've helped them out of a sticky situation, and now they'll have to look after themselves. After all, Adam is of an age when he can earn a living. By the same token, he's old enough to look after his sister.'

Mabel was not easily persuaded. 'The lad's already been out looking for work. He's bound to strike lucky this coming week, and when he does, I'm sure he'll pay his dues.'

'It won't be enough.' John sounded exasperated. 'At his age he'll be paid a pittance. Even if he does contribute to his board and lodging, it can't possibly make up for what we lose. And we'll still have to keep the girl for some years before she's earning.'

There was a pause in the conversation, during which John could be heard pacing the floor. 'It's not what we planned, Mabel. We're getting on in years, and we neither of us know how to raise children, even if we wanted to.'

'I don't think I've the heart to ask 'em to leave.' There was a pitiful break in her voice. 'I'm sure the lad can take care of himself, but what about the girl? She's only a child.'

'Exactly.'

'Oh, John. She's such a trusting young thing. It

would be a crime to turn her away just when she's found some kind of security again.'

'I'm not denying she's a lovely girl, and I no more relish the idea of turning her away than you do, but I don't see what choice we have. We can't run this place as a charity home. It's hard business that puts the bread and butter in our mouths.'

'God forgive us. The poor lass.' Mabel was on the verge of tears. 'Do you think she knows?'

'How can she? I've said nothing to her. I wanted to discuss it with you first.'

'No, I don't mean what we've just been talking about.'

'What then?'

'Do you think she knows that Peterson wasn't her father?'

'I shouldn't think so. The secret went to the grave with her mother. As far as I know, there's only you and me left who has an idea of what was really going on in that house.'

'I hope you're right, John. It would be a terrible shame if the truth got out. Being born out of wedlock is a bad thing. It can scar a body for life.'

'We none of us know for certain,' John reminded her. 'A little knowledge can be a dangerous thing. It might be wise not to mention it ever again. Not even among ourselves.'

Adam was dismayed by what he'd heard. He had thought nobody but himself and Ernshaw knew about Kathleen's parentage, now that Markham was dead.

He toyed with the idea of telling Kathleen before anyone else did, but then he wondered how she would take it. Maybe she would be happy to know that Peterson was not her father, but how would she feel about being born a bastard? How would she cope with the knowledge that he was not her full brother? Wouldn't she feel that he was under no obligation to take care of her? Would she believe him if he told her differently? He was all she had to cling to. And she was about to be turned out on the streets.

Adam knew he couldn't tell her.

As he turned to creep back up the stairs, his heart stood still. John was at the parlour door. Standing on the stairs directly opposite, Adam could go neither up nor down without being seen. He stood quite still, holding his breath, praying John would not glance up. He did not. He quietly closed the door and returned to his conversation.

Adam had heard enough to know that he and Kathleen must leave that very night.

Upstairs, he gently shook his sister awake. 'Get dressed,' he whispered. 'We have to go.'

She stared at him through sleepy eyes. 'Why?'

'Do you trust me?'

'You know I do.'

'Then get dressed and move quietly. We don't want anyone to know we're leaving.'

'Has something happened?'

'Ssh!' He looked anxiously towards the door,

convinced he'd heard footsteps. 'Get dressed,' he urged. 'Quickly.'

While Kathleen did as he asked, he went to the dresser and scribbled out a note. He wouldn't leave without a word of thanks or reassurance for Mabel.

A moment or two and Kathleen was ready, with more questions. 'Adam, what's happened? Why do we have to leave?'

'Later,' he answered softly. 'Keep quiet or they'll hear us.'

As they approached the door, he suddenly halted, putting his finger to his lips. There *was* someone out there, he was certain. With a sudden movement he flung open the door, and there was Nancy, hand over her mouth and her eyes wide with shock.

'Ooh! You gave me a terrible turn,' she cried. 'I've been waiting for you.'

'What do you mean?' Quickly, in case they were overheard, Adam took hold of her arm and unceremoniously pulled her inside. 'Why were you waiting out there?'

Nancy's gaze fell to the floor. 'I was in the kitchen,' she explained. 'I saw you come back upstairs and I knew you'd be leaving tonight.' Tears rolled down her face as she looked up. 'I 'eard what they said. Yer mustn't be too 'ard on 'em. They do love yer. Only this little guesthouse is all they've got, and it's terrible hard to make a living. Honest to God, I know they'd keep yer if they could.'

Now Kathleen understood. 'Are they turning us

out, Adam?' She looked at him and the truth was written on his face.

Nancy was distraught. 'Whatever will yer do? How will yer manage?'

Kathleen took hold of her hand. 'We'll manage all right, Nancy,' she said softly. 'Please don't worry.'

Adam was impatient to be gone, but first he had to be assured of one thing. 'You won't let them know I overheard, will you, Nancy?' he pleaded. 'I'd rather they thought it was our decision to leave. That way they won't feel so bad.'

Nancy's gratitude was obvious. 'Course I won't tell 'em,' she whispered. 'And I'll not forget you – either of you. God bless yer, and take care, eh?'

Adam folded the note into her hand. 'Give this to Cook,' he said, and she promised she would.

She watched them go softly down the stairs and past the parlour, like a pair of thieves in the night. 'Look after yerselves,' she murmured. 'God willing, happen we'll meet again in better circumstances.'

The door opened to let the night in. Then it closed, and they were gone.

In the lamplight, Nancy unfolded the note and read it through a blur of tears:

Dear Cook,

 Thank you for having us.

 We're very grateful for all you've done, but now we have to move on. I must find work where we're provided with board and lodgings.

*Once we're settled, Kathleen will need to finish school.
I'll look after her, don't worry, and we'll be in touch when
we've found a suitable place.*

Thank you again for all you've done.

Adam

Outside, the night closed in around them. There was
a coldness in the air that pinched at the face and
stiffened the fingers. 'Stay close to me.' Adam kept
to the houses as they hurried along; the walls were
a welcome buffer against the elements.

They had dressed sensibly and so were protected
from the biting wind, but there had been no time
for anything else. They had no food, or change of
clothing, and the money Adam had would not last
for ever.

'We'll make for the railway station,' he told
Kathleen. 'It'll be warm there, and we can decide
what best to do.' He had an idea to go south, but
he needed a plan of sorts and, before deciding, he
wanted to talk his ideas through with Kathleen.

Kathleen was feeling sad at leaving Cook and
the others behind, but she tried to look eager and
even managed a smile. 'All right,' she answered.
'I'm hungry. Maybe the hot-potato man will still
be there.'

'You had a huge helping of Cook's stew,' he
reminded her. 'You must have hollow legs.'

Two lost souls, they hurried through the night,
heading towards the station and a promise of warmth.

The snow was falling thickly now, driven by a fierce wind that made it difficult to see. 'Keep close to me,' Adam urged as they crossed the main road. Even at this time of night there was a steady flow of traffic through the town.

Blinded by the snow and pushing hard into the wind, they didn't see the carriage and four as it came careering towards them. In that last split second before it sent Kathleen hurtling backwards, Adam lurched forward to grab her, but he was too late.

While pandemonium broke out, with passers-by chasing after the carriage, shaking fists and abusing the driver, Kathleen lay on the ground, white-faced and still. 'Gawd Almighty, he's killed the poor lass!' one shocked woman uttered.

Adam was on his knees, talking to his sister, rubbing her cold hands and trying to ease her back to consciousness. In the lamplight she looked as grey as marble. For one awful minute he feared the woman might be right. 'Kathleen. Look at me, *Kathleen. Please.*' He had to believe she would be all right.

'Help is on its way,' a man in the crowd promised. There were others, though, who thought she was beyond all that.

'Kathleen.' With the tears blinding him, Adam continued to call her name. 'Kathleen . . .' When he sensed she might be responding, he urged in a stronger voice, 'Open your eyes, Kathleen.'

Suddenly, someone was pushing through; a tall gentleman, clad in cloak and hat, and with a look of anxiety on his handsome face. 'Let me through,' he ordered authoritatively, and people instinctively moved back. There was even a mark of respect for him, until an onlooker called out, 'It's the gent from the carriage! The murdering bleeder!'

There was a fierce scuffle. The man's hat was knocked into the gutter and, if it hadn't been for the burly carriage driver who accompanied him, the distinguished gentleman might have been rolled in the gutter with his hat. In the event, the carriage driver put out his big arms and held back the crowd, and in a moment anger was replaced by apprehension, and a morbid curiosity.

'Let me take her to my house,' the man said to Adam. 'I know a good doctor. I can have him with her in a matter of minutes.'

Incensed, Adam turned on the man. 'If she dies, I'll kill you!' he yelled. 'I swear, I'll kill you!'

'She won't die if we get help quickly. My home is only a short distance away. Please. Let me help.'

His anger spent, Adam nodded numbly. Carefully he picked up Kathleen and carried her to the carriage. The gentleman ordered his carriage driver to take them home, telling him sharply to watch his speed. In a few minutes they reached their destination, a grand house, situated high above the town in a row of fine houses, with long, small-paned windows and heavy curtains keeping out the night. A broad run of four stone steps led to the front door; it was an impressive door, of solid oak, with four deep panels and a huge brass knocker in the shape of a lion's head.

As Adam carried Kathleen up the steps, he was only vaguely aware of the house but sensed an air of grandeur and opulence here. As they approached, the door inched open and then swung back to reveal a small man of advancing years, with a thick mop of snow-white hair and a round, protruding belly that looked as if it had been stuffed for the Christmas table. His face wrinkled with curiosity. 'Whatever's happened, sir?' His eyes were on Kathleen. 'Shall I get the doctor?'

'Straightaway, James.' The urgency in his voice sent James rushing into the house and out again, with his long coat on and wearing a pork-pie hat that sat on his head like something dropped from a great height. He made off down the street, heading for the big house at the end where the doctor resided.

'Take her into the front room,' the man instructed Adam. He would have taken Kathleen into his own arms but Adam held her fiercely to him. As he laid her on the couch, she opened her eyes. 'Hello, sis.' Adam tenderly raised her to a sitting position. 'Easy now.' To see those lovely brown eyes alive and inquisitive was an indescribable joy to him.

'Adam?' Dazed and confused, she could recall nothing of the accident. She had been walking along, there was a lot of shouting, and now she was here, aching from head to toe. Her unsteady gaze reached beyond Adam to where the gentleman was standing. Who was he? Was this his house? Why was she here?

By the time it was explained that she had been involved in an accident, the doctor had arrived, together with the butler who was wheezing and gasping and seemed to be more in need of medical attention than Kathleen. 'For heaven's sake, man,' snapped his employer, 'go and get yourself a nip of brandy. It'll warm you up.' The gentleman turned to the doctor, who was tending Kathleen. 'I was a passenger in the carriage that knocked her down,' he explained. 'The driver's had a roasting but I dare say it won't end there.' He addressed Adam. 'Say the word, young man, and I'll have him reported to the police station.'

Kathleen heard all of this, and her first thought was that if the driver was turned over to the police, then so too might they be. If that happened, the authorities might ask all sorts of awkward questions. 'I'm all right, sir,' she said, though she felt as if she really had been run over by a carriage and four. 'Please, I'd rather you didn't cause a fuss.'

Somewhat bemused by this, and fascinated by Kathleen who he thought was an extremely attractive girl, he smiled at her. 'I'm sure your brother thinks differently.' Shifting his attention to Adam, he wondered about these two. The young man was what? Sixteen, seventeen? And the girl probably no more than twelve years old. They appeared to be hiding something. Certainly they were nervous, frightened even, and if he knew anything about human nature, it was little to do with the accident.

He was intrigued, especially when Adam gave the same answer as Kathleen. 'We don't want any trouble. As long as Kathleen's all right, that's all that matters.' He knew why Kathleen had answered the way she did, and he was proud of her.

'You surprise me. Anyone else would want that man punished.'

Kathleen answered for them both. 'We can't stay in these parts,' she told him. 'Reporting the incident would only hold us here. Besides, I should think the man's learned his lesson. I expect he'll drive more carefully in future.'

'I see.' Yes. These two were definitely afraid of something. 'Let's hear what Dr Jarvis has to say first.'

What he had to say put all their minds at rest. 'Like all young things, she must have rubber bones because there appears to be nothing broken, and apart from a few bruises and a bump on the head where she hit the pavement, I'd say she's had a very lucky escape.'

Adam was relieved. 'We'll be on our way, then, just as soon as she's able.'

'I'm able now, Adam.' Suppressing the discomfort she felt, Kathleen struggled to stand up, but when she almost lost her balance, it was plain to all that she was far from able.

'You've had a nasty shock,' the doctor reminded her. 'If you value my advice, you won't attempt any travelling for a day or two at least.'

'I suggest you stay here the night.' The gentleman stepped forward. 'There are enough rooms in this house to sleep an army.' He smiled and Kathleen thought him very handsome. He looked to be in his early thirties. Tall and lithe, he had a commanding presence. His face was proud but kind, and his blue eyes seemed to shine with goodness. She felt he could be trusted. After all, he'd brought them here to safety, hadn't he?

Similar thoughts were running through Adam's mind and after only a moment's hesitation he graciously accepted the gentleman's hospitality. 'Thank you, sir,' he said.

'Wonderful! James will take good care of you. Chief cook, bottle-washer, and wicked wizard in the making, he knows what I'm thinking even before I do.' He laughed out loud; it was a warm, pleasant sound. 'There are times when he thinks I'm the servant and he's the master, but I don't mind telling you I wouldn't know what to do without him.'

Adam held out his hand. 'I'm Adam Peterson,' he said. 'This is my sister Kathleen. We're in your debt, sir.'

The gentleman shook hands with them both. 'Glad to help,' he said. 'Westerfield is the name, Maurice Westerfield. I dabble in anything that makes money, and I must be doing something right because

I'm disgustingly wealthy. I import mostly – buy cheap, sell at a profit, that's the way I work. I'm also a widower, with a son who thinks work is for fools and a daughter who spends money faster than I can earn it.' When James coughed meaningfully, he chuckled. 'My butler thinks I talk too much.'

'I'm sorry, sir.' Behind James's apology lay a stern tone of disapproval. 'I was only wondering whether you would like refreshments now.'

'Of course, and I hope you'll join us, Dr Jarvis. Though knowing you, I shouldn't be at all surprised if you'd prefer a drop of good brandy.'

The good doctor accepted the brandy, knocked it back in one gasp, then took his leave. 'I left an important dinner engagement,' he explained. 'Now we know the young lady is all right, I'll make my way back. Will I see you before you return south?'

'What? Afraid I might make off with your fee?'

The doctor rolled his eyes. 'God forbid! Then how would I afford my brandy?'

Later, the other three sat round the small table, enjoying the hot tea and sandwiches James brought. The atmosphere was friendly and relaxed. They exchanged small talk, until Maurice's curiosity got the better of him. 'Have you no parents?' he asked.

Adam shook his head. 'We've been staying with an aunt but she died recently.' He glanced at Kathleen. 'I won't let them put Kathleen in an orphanage. That's why we have to keep travelling. I must find work.'

Maurice regarded them both with interest, particularly Kathleen; he could hardly take his eyes off her.

'Are you good at figures, Adam?'

'So I'm told.'

'And are you ambitious?'

'I like to think so.'

The next question was put after some quiet deliberation. 'Would you be interested in working for me?'

Adam thought quickly. 'We must have a place to live, sir.'

'And so you shall. I have a house and land in the south, not too far from London. You and your sister could live there. You'd be paid according to your work, with free board and lodging until you feel the need to find a home of your own.' His smile was warm and honest. 'Does that suit you, young man?'

'It sounds wonderful!' Exactly what he wanted.

Maurice's warmest smile was bestowed on Kathleen. 'Good. That's settled then. As soon as you're up to it, the three of us will travel south.'

Chapter Eleven

MAURICE WESTERFIELD WENT to great lengths to ensure that Kathleen was well cared for on the journey south the next morning, with blankets tucked round her legs and a pillow on which to rest her head. He ordered a picnic hamper to be set inside the carriage and, to Adam's irritation, personally took charge of her wellbeing.

They stopped twice along the way, each time at a reputable inn where every assistance was lavished on them. At two o'clock on a bright, cold day, they arrived in Ilford. Kathleen was mesmerised. 'Why, it's beautiful!' she cried, and while she gazed out of the window at the sights that greeted them, Maurice Westerfield gazed at her. And as he gazed, his heart was filled with a sadness he could hardly bear.

'Look, Adam!' Kathleen pointed to the street name. 'Beehive Lane,' she read. 'There was a street named Beehive Lane next to Markham's house.'

Maurice was interested to know about their past. During the journey Kathleen had referred to Markham several times. 'This Markham seems to be an important person in your life,' he observed. 'Was this the aunt you told me about?'

Adam replied. 'Yes,' he said shortly. They had trusted Maurice with the information that they were orphans but Adam was reluctant to divulge any details that might lead to Mr Ernshaw. If things didn't work out with Maurice Westerfield the less he knew about them, the better. 'I think we should forget the past and start afresh. That's what Markham would have said.'

'Of course,' Maurice conceded. 'And I should mind my own business.'

There was an uncomfortable silence until they came into Cranbrook Road overlooking the wash and Kathleen spotted two puppies playing on the bank. 'Oh, look! Aren't they lovely?' She smiled straight into Maurice Westerfield's watching eyes and his heart turned over.

'You'll be pleased to know I have two dogs,' he told her. 'They're not puppies, I'm afraid. I bought them from the meat market six years ago. It was the end of the day and, being unsold, they were about to be put down.' He shook his head. 'I couldn't leave them to such a fate.'

In that moment, he grew tenfold in Kathleen's estimation.

At the bottom of Cranbrook Road the carriage came to a halt. 'This is it, guv.' The driver jumped down and opened the door. Maurice climbed out and helped Kathleen down; Adam followed, a little peeved.

'I thought you said you had land.' He glanced up and down the road. All he could see were grand houses. One thing was for sure, he thought, there's a deal of money in these parts.

'The land lies beyond here. At the moment, the only access to the house is along the lane.' Maurice pointed to a narrow gap between the last house and a small wooded area. 'Unfortunately it's impassable to vehicles in winter.' An impish grin creased his handsome face. 'Mind you, that can be a Godsend,' he declared. 'It keeps out the undesirables.'

'Such as us,' Adam quipped. He felt irritated, jealous even. And he couldn't understand why.

'Oh?' Maurice gave him a curious look. 'Are you and your sister undesirables then?'

Adam was saved from having to reply by Kathleen.

'Why did you buy this house if you can't get a carriage up to it?' she asked, ever curious; he was obviously wealthy enough to buy whatever he wanted.

While the driver unstrapped the cases from the back of the cab, Maurice directed them towards the lane and, as they walked, he explained, 'I searched far and wide for a house I could spend the rest of my days in. Although the access was not altogether suitable, I liked the place. I was not told that the lane was impassable during winter; I found that out for myself. This is my first winter here. Mind you, it's only a temporary obstacle.'

'What will you do?'

'Fortunately, a parcel of land between the road and one of my meadows came up for sale and I snapped it up. I can now build my own driveway straight to the house. The workmen began constructing it about a month ago. It winds through the cherry trees up to the house and then branches off to the stables at the back.' He waved his hand in a grand gesture. 'There are two hundred and sixty acres all told.'

Kathleen was glad they had come, it sounded lovely. 'Are you a farmer then?'

'I don't have time to farm. The land is all leased. It brings in a great deal of money and I don't have to lift a finger. There are two cottages, but they're kept for my house servants. The handyman lives in one, the other is vacant. When the drive is finished, I'll take on a driver for my own carriage and four. The cottage will be his, rent free. I did have a driver when I first came here but he went away to be a sailor. God knows how anyone could prefer the ocean to the land.' He smiled directly at Kathleen. 'Still, each to his own, that's what I say.'

'Do you have horses?' Kathleen had visions of herself leaping over fences on a black stallion.

'Why do you ask?'

'You mentioned stables.'

'Yes, we have four carriage horses and a large grey gelding belonging to my son.' A dark frown crossed his face as he thought of his son, Christian. That young man had been a heartache for too long now.

Quiet in their own thoughts, they trudged towards the house, Kathleen with the blanket wrapped securely round her shoulders, Adam with his arm round her to keep her steady. The driver brought up the rear loaded down with baggage.

As they rounded the bend, Adam stopped in his tracks. 'Is this your house, sir?'

'It is.'

Kathleen stared, and couldn't believe her eyes. 'It's like a palace!' she cried, and felt very foolish when the driver gave her a sidelong glance.

The house was a mansion. Built of white stone, it was wide and high, with many large windows and round bays, and numerous chimneys reaching to the sky. The walls were criss-crossed with sleeping ivy. The wide steps that led up to the entrance were flanked by tall stone urns, spilling over with the sad remains of autumn blossoms.

For all its great size and presence, there was something about the house that exuded a welcome, and also a certain calm in spite of the uproar of work going on. Immediately before the house, the ground was in upheaval, but it was possible to discern a wide, sweeping track taking shape.

'Why don't you live in the house up north?' Kathleen asked. 'Nobody needs two houses, do they?'

He led the weary party up the steps to the front door. 'I have business interests in the north as well as in the south. Besides, much as I love the north, this is home.' He sighed, reflecting on the way it used to be.

In a quiet voice, heavy with emotion, he murmured, 'They say the heart is where the roots are, and that's certainly true in my case.'

At the door he turned to survey the scene before him, the ravaged earth and the beautiful, untouched land beyond. 'From here you can see the rooftops of Ilford. This is where I belong. I was born in Ilford and I've no doubt this is where I shall die.'

On seeing Kathleen's face fill with horror, he laughed that warm, engaging laugh that set everyone at their ease. 'Not for some years yet, I hope,' he said. 'I'm not yet forty, and there is still so much I want to do.'

He turned and fumbled in his waistcoat pocket, eventually producing a key that opened the front door. 'Leave the bags in the hall,' he told the driver as they went inside. 'My son will see to them later.'

While he paid the driver, Kathleen's interested gaze went round the hall. There was the usual rack for umbrellas and cloaks, a tall and beautiful grandfather clock, a dark-wood dresser as high as the ceiling, and rugs beneath their feet that were soft and mellow.

Through a high, wide arch, she could see another richly furnished room, with crystal and silver ornaments, and plush, red velvet curtains framing floor-to-ceiling windows. There were tapestries on the wall, and deep floral-covered armchairs. In the marble fireplace, a roaring fire threw out warmth and cheer. Altogether, Kathleen felt that this was a good place, a place where she and Adam might find contentment.

Adam, too, felt this was a good house. One thing puzzled him, though, and while Maurice was busy with the driver, he voiced his concern to Kathleen. 'It's strange,' he whispered. 'Where are the servants?'

No sooner had the driver been shown out than there was a loud, excited shriek. 'Daddy! Daddy!' Along with two dogs and a woman, the girl raced down the stairs, her arms stretched wide. She was a pretty thing, aged about twelve, with long fair hair and huge blue eyes. 'I didn't know you were coming home today,' she cried, throwing herself into his arms. 'You said you wouldn't be home for a week.'

Catching hold of her, he swung her round. 'And *I* thought the house would be empty,' he laughed. 'You were supposed to be staying in London – shopping and all that.' He fondled the two dogs jumping up at him, one a big black creature with drizzling mouth and floppy jowls, the other a tall, thin animal with sad red eyes and feet the size of meat plates.

'Down!' The woman's voice intervened, a sweet, invasive voice which had the dogs running to sit obediently at her feet. Addressing Maurice, she explained. 'The trip to London was planned for tomorrow,' she said, 'but now that you're home,

I don't suppose I'll be able to drag her away. No matter, we can visit London another time.' The woman was slim and attractive, and obviously very much in charge. Her voice was disturbingly familiar to Adam, though he couldn't immediately place it.

She stepped closer. 'It's good to see you, sir,' she said, smiling into Maurice's eyes. 'Melinda does so pine when you're away.'

'It's good to see you too, Emma, my dear.' Yet he seemed less happy to see her than she was to see him. 'I concluded my business early.' He gestured for Adam and Kathleen to come forward. 'I've not returned alone. This is Adam and his sister Kathleen.' A wave of regret flitted across his features. 'I'm afraid we didn't meet under ideal circumstances. I had the misfortune of choosing a maniac for a driver. He lost control of his carriage and four, sending Kathleen hurtling across the pavement.' He stroked Kathleen's hair, a simple, instinctive action marked by all of them, with varying unease. 'Thankfully, she wasn't too badly hurt,' Maurice went on. 'However, I feel a certain amount of responsibility so I want our guests treated very well while they're under this roof.' He looked at his housekeeper. The nod of her head and the ready smile on her face suggested she was happy to comply with his wishes. His gaze shifted to his daughter, who also smiled back at him. 'That's settled then.' He was satisfied. Yet the minute he looked away, the girl's smile was replaced by a sour expression. Adam noticed it, and his unease increased.

Maurice completed the introductions. 'This is my daughter Melinda, and Emma Long, my housekeeper and Melinda's governess.' He gave her an appreciative glance. 'She's only been with me since I bought this house, but I really don't know how I ever managed without her.'

Emma had been paying particular attention to the visitors. When she had first laid eyes on them, she had had a feeling they were known to her. Now, after hearing their names, she was positive. She was shocked to her roots but she managed to keep calm, and even to appear delighted. 'I'm so glad you weren't badly hurt,' she told Kathleen. In truth, she would rather the girl had been trampled to death.

'They'll be staying here with us,' Maurice told her. 'Kathleen will be taught alongside Melinda, and Adam is to be trained under my guidance.'

'Very well, sir.' She turned to them. 'I'm sure you'll be happy here,' she smiled, but there was a glint in her eye that said otherwise.

Kathleen shrank from her. Something about Emma disturbed her.

The housekeeper took a moment longer to stare at Adam. He was so like his father, it was unnerving. 'I'm sure we're going to get on very well.'

Introductions over, Maurice led the way into the drawing room. As they filed in, with Adam and Kathleen bringing up the rear, Adam suddenly realised who the woman was. 'I know her!' Gripping Kathleen's arm, he held her back. 'And so do you.'

'There is something familiar about her,' Kathleen replied softly, 'but I don't know anybody called Emma.'

'Anyone can change their name.'

At that point Emma turned, her small, beady eyes enveloping them. She lingered, her gaze going from one to the other. It was obvious she had overheard their conversation.

'She knows,' Adam whispered, horrified. 'She knows I've recognised her.'

Emma smiled and placed her fingers to her lips as if to say, 'It's our secret.' In a moment she had turned away and was chatting to Melinda as if nothing had happened. 'You have two new friends, Melinda,' she said. 'We must make them feel at home.' Out of the corner of her eye she glanced back. And winked.

That bold, intimate wink and the easy, arrogant way she walked were unmistakable. 'It *is* her!' Adam muttered. 'It's been years now, and she's changed. She's cut her hair and got herself a new name, but it's her all right.'

Kathleen was alarmed. 'Who, Adam?'

'Connie Blakeman. She was—'

'Our nanny from the big house, before Father threw her out,' Kathleen finished for him. 'I remember now.'

AFTER BEING SHOWN their rooms, which were situated in the east wing of the house, they were taken to the kitchen and fed. Connie, or 'Emma' as she was known to the others, did the cooking, and it was a filling, wholesome meal.

'We don't have a cook yet,' Maurice explained. 'Before buying this house, my children and I travelled a great deal. I bought it on the spur of the moment. I do that sometimes, buy on the spur of the moment. It's in my blood, you know. You might not believe it, but I used to be a barrow boy in my youth.'

Adam was astonished. 'You? A barrow boy?' And here he was, with a mansion to live in and all the trappings of a gentleman. In an instant, Adam saw himself in the same situation. If a former barrow boy could do all this, then so could he.

Maurice laughed. 'It's hard to believe, isn't it? But it was easy enough really. I'm not ashamed of my background, and I'm not a proud man, although having said that, I am proud of what I've achieved. I could say it was hard. I could claim that every step of the way was a nightmare, but I'd be lying.' His face clouded. 'I might be a lot of things but never a liar.'

Leaning back in his chair he surveyed the faces before him: his own daughter who was more ashamed of his background than he was; his housekeeper, an attractive, secretive woman who pretended to be genteel but in fact was no more a lady than he was a gentleman. She was good with Melinda, however,

249

and she had also proved herself to be a very competent housekeeper. He had a sneaking suspicion she fancied being the mistress of this house, but that would never happen, not in a million years.

Then there were his two house guests: the young man, Adam, who, he could tell, had the hard-nosed makings of a good businessman; and the girl, Kathleen. Oh, the girl! The dark, intense eyes, and that long flowing hair that he ached to run his fingers through. But he mustn't. He must never frighten her away. She belonged in this house, and if he had his way she would stay here for as long as he drew breath.

'Daddy?' Melinda's voice shook him back to the present moment. 'Are you all right?'

'I'm sorry, I let my thoughts carry me away.' He finished his tale. 'I've always had an instinct for buying at the right time and selling for a profit. I do the same now, only on a grander scale. I import goods at a bargain price and sell them on at a profit. There's no secret to it. No matter what you have to sell, if you're prepared to travel, you'll always find a ready market.' He wagged a finger at Adam, who was listening intently. 'But you do need money to get started, and you need the courage to buy when everyone else is looking the other way.'

'How do you mean, sir?'

'Here's an example. Last summer a business acquaintance mentioned that he'd been offered a consignment of trees from Norway. He turned it down because we were enjoying a heat wave and, like many other traders, he was too busy concentrating on parasols, garden furniture, and suchlike.'

He took a moment to savour the memory. 'I made extensive inquiries, bought the timber consignment at rock-bottom price, and stored it until the winter when I made a very handsome profit. Like I said, I have an instinct for buying at the right time and knowing when to sell. It's important to read the market for months ahead. Not everyone can do that. I can. That's why I'm a wealthy man. Some say I'm an entrepreneur, others say I'm a very clever, shrewd businessman. In actual fact I'm still a barrow boy, but dealing in larger quantities.'

Realising he had wandered off the point, he shook himself mentally and told them in a crisper voice, 'As I say, I've travelled a great deal, and have only recently acquired this house. I am in the process of hiring servants and by the end of the week, we should have a full complement.'

He dabbed at his mouth with his napkin, his gaze falling to the table. For a long, awkward moment he seemed to be far away, but then in a soft voice he continued. 'I'm afraid I've been a little neglectful, disorganised even,' he confessed. 'You see, I lost my dear wife after a long illness.' He looked at Kathleen, and his eyes were pleading. 'After that, I couldn't settle. I couldn't think, and I couldn't work. So I sent my son away to college and took my daughter to see the world; of course she had a governess to tend to her schooling, so I did not fail in my duty on that count.' He took hold of his daughter's hand. 'I sold my previous house before we sailed for America. I lost the heart to live there – too many memories.'

While he was speaking, Connie sat with her hands crossed on the table, listening closely.

Adam and Kathleen were embarrassed and surprised that he should confide such private matters to them, while Melinda sat protectively by her beloved father's side, her blue eyes bright with malice as she looked at the two guests he had brought home. She did not take kindly to their presence, and she did not think that her father should entrust his life story to these strangers.

Unaware of the tension, Maurice went on, 'I'm home now, and life must go on, as they say.' He straightened his back and sat up. 'Eat and drink,' he urged. 'We'll talk again later. You must be wondering what I expect of you, Adam. You, Kathleen, will work hard at your schooling, I hope.' The smile slid from his face, and his gaze became more intense. 'I have great plans for you, my dear,' he told her. 'You have no parents or relatives to take an interest in your welfare other than your brother, of course, who must be commended for the way he's looked after you.' Sensing Adam was about to protest, he added quickly, 'But now your brother's of an age when he needs to concentrate on his own future.'

'Kathleen is my future, sir,' Adam retorted sharply.

'Of course. All I am saying is, your sister will

be cared for in every way, while you may pursue a career and look forward to a secure future. You seem a bright young man, and I mean to do everything in my power to see you reach your full potential. I do hope I haven't offended you.'

Adam was bone-tired. They were all tired, he reasoned, and Maurice Westerfield did seem genuine enough even if he was rather high-handed in his assumption of responsibility for Kathleen. Adam wondered about that, and he resented having his own place in his sister's welfare brushed aside so lightly. Nevertheless the fact was, Westerfield was offering them both a unique opportunity, and for that they should be immensely grateful. 'No, sir,' he answered. 'You haven't offended me.' But Maurice's words had created a small barrier between them.

'Good.' Maurice rubbed his hands together, as though ridding them of something unpleasant. 'Finish your meals, and then I suggest an early night. Tomorrow, my son will be home. The day after that it's back to business, and I can assure you that next week this house will be bustling.' Again his brightest smile was for Kathleen. 'There is much to look forward to,' he promised.

They all heard his promise. But it was not meant for them. It was meant only for Kathleen.

A T NINE THIRTY, they went to their rooms. The housekeeper led the way. At the top of the stairs she turned to glare at them, the real Connie Blakeman shining out of her eyes. 'If you've any sense you'll keep your mouths shut,' she hissed, her face looking garish in the halo of lamplight. 'I've worked long and hard to get where I am, and I don't mean to lose it all because of you two brats.' Leaning forward she held the lamp forward to look at them more closely. 'D'you understand what I'm saying?' She spat out the words.

Adam was not afraid. 'We understand.'

She looked him up and down. 'Quite the little gent, aren't you?' she sneered. 'And look at madam here.' She eyed Kathleen with a surge of grudging admiration. 'I'm buggered if she hasn't turned into a right little beauty.'

Kathleen met the hostile glare with indignance. 'We won't tell him about you,' she said, 'if you don't tell him about us.'

'What could you tell him about me, eh?'

'That you were our nanny and Father threw you out because you were no good.'

Adam knew more. 'I heard Cook say you and Father were "dancing a pretty tune together". I didn't know what it meant then, but I do now.'

'Then you know enough to finish me here, don't you?'

'I think so.'

'And is that what you have in mind?'

'Not unless you give us reason.'

'I won't give you reason, you little bastard.' Her face was contorted with rage. 'Since your precious father threw me out, I've suffered some terrible times. I've travelled the length and breadth of this country, and I've skivvied in many a big house. I've cleaned boots belonging to people no better than me; I've scrubbed the spit off kitchen floors and I've taken care of brats that should have been strangled at birth. There have been times when I've almost starved.' She threw back her head and stared at the ceiling, and for one awful minute Kathleen was convinced she was crying.

The minute seemed to go on for ever. Just as Kathleen was about to ask if she was all right, she lowered her head and looked at them. 'I've had some bad times,' she said, her voice not quite steady, 'but I've picked myself up and I've done well. I've got prospects here. Mr Westerfield has respect for me. He pays me well, and who knows . . .' Suddenly she was the old Connie, grinning wickedly and making plans that once before had proved to be her downfall. 'One day, I might even fill his late wife's shoes and be mistress of this place.' She flicked a glance up and down the stairs. 'So think on, you two. I can be a good friend, or I can be a bad enemy. Give me trouble and you'll get more back than you can handle. Do you hear me?'

'We don't want trouble either,' Adam said.

'What about you, young madam?' She glared at Kathleen. 'Is he speaking for you as well?'

Kathleen nodded. 'We won't tell.'

IN THE EARLY hours, Adam was awakened by a commotion downstairs.

He got out of bed, flung on the robe which Connie had draped on the chair, and in a minute he was out on the landing, peering towards the stairway and thinking all hell had been let loose. There was a fierce row raging downstairs; shouting and swearing, and the sound of things being knocked about.

He was about to investigate further when a sound behind him startled him. When he saw that it was Kathleen, he visibly relaxed. 'What are you doing out of your bed?'

Tousled-haired and bleary-eyed, she was relieved to see him there. 'The dogs are going mad. It sounds like somebody's fighting down there.'

'I don't know what's happening. Go back to bed. I'll go and see.'

He might as well have saved his breath. Kathleen was not the sort to lie in bed while her brother investigated the row. She was too curious. Too rebellious. 'I'm going with you,' she stated, and he knew nothing he could say would change her mind.

Cautiously they made their way towards the head of the staircase. There was the sound of scuffling. 'Don't be a bloody fool, man!' That was Maurice Westerfield's voice, and he sounded furious.

Creeping along the landing, they stretched their

necks to see over the top and down into the hallway. There were signs of a struggle: a vase smashed on the floor; a picture hanging crooked on the wall; and, directly beneath the picture, red stains on the wallpaper.

'That's blood!' Kathleen instinctively recoiled. 'Adam! There's *blood*. On the wall.'

'*Ssh!*' Putting a hand over her mouth, he drew her back. 'Be quiet. I don't want them to know we're watching.' Her big brown eyes stared back at him. She nodded, and he let her go.

At that moment there was a screech of laughter and a man's voice said, 'Don't care much for me, do you? Think I'm no good, don't you?' Another screech of laughter, followed by a curious silence. Even the dogs were stilled.

Connie Blakeman's voice could be heard asking, 'What do you want me to do, sir?'

Maurice answered, 'Help me get my son to his bed. There's little else we can do tonight.' In the background the barking of dogs could again be heard. 'Keep hold of him,' he said. 'I'd better quieten the dogs before they wake the whole house.' It took only a moment, and he was back. 'I've given them some food,' he said. 'That should keep them quiet.'

Up on the landing, Adam drew his sister away. 'Get back,' he whispered. 'They're coming up here.'

Crouched down against the balustrade they could see without themselves being seen.

Three people emerged from the drawing room;
between Connie Blakeman on one side and Maurice
Westerfield on the other slumped the limp form of
a young man not much older than Adam. His head
lolled and his thick mop of brown hair obscured his
face. His jacket was open and his shirt smattered
with blood.

'So that's his son,' Adam whispered. 'Doesn't
amount to much, does he?'

'Is he dead?'

'Either that or he's so drunk he can't walk on his
own two feet.' Disgust marbled his voice.

The trio were mounting the stairs now. 'Keep
still,' Adam warned. 'Don't say a word.'

They had climbed only three steps when the
young man suddenly threw out his arms and turned to
face the hallway, as if performing to an audience. Loud
and abrasive, he launched into a bawdy music-hall
medley.

The awful racket made the dogs start barking again and Connie Blakeman smile, but Maurice
Westerfield was beside himself with rage. Grabbing
at his son's arm, he pulled him onwards. 'Have you
no shame?' He glanced up, towards the bedrooms, his
eyes momentarily closing in anguish when he saw his
daughter standing at the top of the stairs. 'Go back to
bed, Melinda,' he pleaded. 'There's nothing for you
to worry about.'

Melinda's expression stiffened. Her brother's
behaviour made her angry.

'Do as I say, Melinda,' Maurice called. 'Go back to your bed.'

She made no move, and continued to watch as, in a sudden convulsion, her brother threw himself towards the banister and spewed up the contents of his stomach.

While Connie ran to the kitchen to collect a mop and bucket, Maurice fought with his son, telling him what a useless being he was and wondering how he ever came to spawn such a creature.

Having seen enough, Melinda turned away, a look of utter disgust on her face. She had seen it all before and no doubt she would see it all again.

Out of the corner of her eye she caught sight of the two figures crouching there, shame-faced and at that moment wishing the earth would open and swallow them whole.

They waited for the recriminations, but there were none. Instead, Melinda softly laughed, regarding them with sly eyes, before walking away, quietly smiling.

Closing his eyes and gritting his teeth, Adam groaned. 'Damn! I wish she hadn't seen us.'

'She doesn't like us, does she?' Kathleen had sensed that from the first moment they met. 'She wants us out of here.'

'Well, she'll have to want on. This is her father's house. He was the one who invited us here, and so he should after almost killing you.'

'I've got a gash and a few bruises, that's all,' Kathleen reminded him.

'That's not the point. You could have been killed.'

'All the same, I'm not sure I want to stay here. If she put her mind to it, she could make our life a misery.'

'She could, I suppose. But we've got nowhere else to go, and no one to help us. Maurice Westerfield has given us a roof over our heads. He's offered me a job, the chance to earn money and better myself. He's also promised to give you a good education. I'm buggered if we'll turn it all away because of that spoilt brat!'

Shocked to hear him swear, Kathleen regarded him with amazement. 'You *like* her, don't you?'

'Don't be silly.' All the same, he couldn't look Kathleen in the eye. 'She's about the same age as you are.'

'What does that mean?' She was remembering how much she had been drawn to Murray Laing. She recalled how her heart had lifted whenever she saw him, and how devastated she was when Adam had confirmed he was partly responsible for Markham's death.

'It doesn't mean anything in particular.'

'If you mean younger people can't be attracted to someone older, then you're very wrong.'

He knew she was thinking of Murray, and the guilt tormented him. 'Come on, sis.' He nodded down the stairs, where the trio were making headway. 'We'd better get back before anyone else sees us.'

Suddenly all hell broke loose. The young man began to yell and shout, fighting like a tiger when his father tried desperately to urge him forward. Barking frantically, the dogs sprang from nowhere. The big black one bounded up the stairway. Launching itself through the air, it landed with a thud on the young man's chest.

Startled, he lashed out at the dog, screaming abuse. With one mighty sweep of his arm he sent the poor animal flying through the air to land in a crumpled heap in the hallway below. The other dog trotted over to it and nudged it with its head, then sat, whimpering, beside it.

'You bastard!' Flinging his son aside, Maurice went down the stairs two at a time, but it was no good. He knew the dog was dead before he reached it.

White as a sheet, he made his way back upstairs. 'You drunken swine, you've killed the dog. He didn't deserve that.' But there was no regret in the young man's eyes, no trace of compassion. 'One of these days, you'll get your dues,' Maurice vowed, and roughly shoved his son up the stairs as if he could hardly bear the sight of him.

Horrified, Adam and Kathleen crept swiftly to their rooms. 'Don't cry,' Adam said, seeing the tears flowing silently down his sister's face. He gave her a hug. 'We'd best stay clear of that one. He's as bad a lot as I've ever seen.'

Kathleen nodded.

'Don't think too much about what we've seen tonight,' he suggested. 'You have to try and put it out of your mind.' He smiled into her sad brown eyes. 'All right?'

She nodded again.

'Quickly then. Get to your room.'

'Goodnight, Adam.'

'See you in the morning, and remember what I said, try not to think about it.'

She hurried away. Witnessing that poor animal's death had made her sad and angry. Besides that, memories of Murray were breaking her heart.

Safe in her room, she climbed into bed and closed her eyes, but it was a long time before she gave herself up to sleep. In her mind's eye she could see the dog lying on the floor. She thought of the young man responsible. She wondered how he could have done such a terrible thing, and she recalled what Adam had said. 'He's as bad a lot as I've ever seen.' Adam was right. Adam was always right.

Her mind shifted back, to Markham, and Murray, and how he had left that helpless old woman lying on the floor, just like that young man had left the dog there. In that moment she wished Murray was here so she could tell him what a bad lot he was. Just like Maurice Westerfield's son.

'You lied to me, Murray,' she whispered. 'You're wicked too, just like they said.' She cried for a while, her heart hardening. 'I hate you for what you did to

Markham,' she murmured. 'I'll never forgive you, as long as I live.'

Adam, too, was struggling with his emotions. Torn by his feelings, he paced the floor. 'How can I tell Kathleen?' he asked himself. 'Especially when I deliberately let her believe Murray was guilty? Because of it, she even gave his name to the authorities? Good God! It must have torn her apart to do that! If she was to find out what I'd done, she would despise me.'

Another thing plagued him. He was only just beginning to realise there was a very real possibility that Murray might be hanged.

There was no contentment for the master of the house, either.

After seeing his son to his room, Maurice Westerfield left his trusted housekeeper to undress him and put him to bed. 'I must bury the dog,' he told her. 'I'm very grateful for your help. I hope the events of this night will stay within these four walls.'

She smiled at him in that sly, seductive manner she had. 'You can trust me, sir,' she said.

And he did.

He fetched a spade and dug a grave for his dog beneath one of the cherry trees. Its companion stayed there, howling its lament into the night. When the task was done, he led the sorry animal into the house and then went back outside, to sit by the naked lady, a statue that had come with the house. Tall and elegant, with perfect limbs and coiled hair that resembled sleeping snakes, she looked down on him with cold arrogance.

'You're lucky,' he told the silent stone lady. 'You have no feelings. You can't be hurt, or shamed, and you'll never feel the loss of a loved one. You don't know what it's like to have a longing that you can't shake off, or to want affection so badly you can't sleep or work.'

His soft voice touched the night but had no effect on her; hard and unyielding, she continued to look down on him with unseeing eyes. The night closed in, deeper and darker, echoing with strange sounds, the clicking, whispering sounds of another world. A weird and wonderful world that came alive when humans slept.

He wondered what it might be like to feel nothing, to survey the world and not be part of it; never to be hurt, never to love, or hate.

He laughed softly. 'No,' he murmured. 'I'm the fortunate one.' He touched her hand, the stone fingers like ice against his skin. 'I'm alive. I don't envy you, because however hard life can be, it is also immensely precious.'

He moved away, walked awhile, and eventually returned to the house. He took the lighted lamp from the hallway table and carried it up to his room. On the landing, he paused to listen. There was no sound to disturb him. Satisfied, he went into his room and closed the door.

Inside the sanctuary of his own quarters, he went

directly to the dresser where he looked at the painting above. It was of his late wife; young and strikingly beautiful, with her long, chestnut hair, pixie face and dark, smiling eyes.

Gazing on her face was a torment to him. 'I miss you, my love,' he murmured, his long, sensuous fingers reaching up to stroke her features.

The pain of remembering was too much. He put his head in his hands. 'I'm so alone,' he groaned. 'I have wicked thoughts, and I'm so ashamed.'

Sighing, he looked up at the portrait once more. In the halo of light from the lamp, she seemed almost to be alive. 'Have you seen her?' he asked softly. 'Have you seen the girl?' A small smile flickered over his face. 'When I first saw her, I thought I was looking at you. And when she spoke, she so reminded me of you, I could hardly breathe. She has that same soft manner, and a certain way of looking at me, with those familiar dark eyes. Oh, you can't know . . . It's as if I've been born again. It's as if you've come back to me. I can hardly wait for her to grow up. But I will wait. I can't let her go. I *won't* let her go. I'll make her happy. She'll learn to love me, I know. And I won't neglect our daughter, or turn out the son we brought into this world, though God knows he deserves nothing from me.' His voice grew hard. 'I have to love him because he's our son. But I can't like him.'

Thinking of Christian brought a shadow to his face. 'He shames us, my love. Our own son is like a stranger to me.' His kindly eyes glinted with unshed tears. 'I've been so sad,' he confessed. 'But now I've found a reason to go on. I look at the girl and my heart sings like a bird.'

He gazed on the face, as if waiting for it to smile, or answer, or give approval of some kind. But it remained passive, and in his heart of hearts he knew she would never smile on him again, or talk to him, or look at him with approval. He had never been able to accept that before, and it was something of a shock to him now.

'I know you're gone from me,' he murmured. 'And I will never forget you.' The smile lit his face. 'But if I have the girl, she can bring you closer. That's why I can't let her go.' He touched the features again; the eyes, the mouth, his fingers lingering there. 'Fortune sent her to me.'

Turning his back on the painting he looked out of the window, into the dark night. Into the future. For the first time in ages, he felt a surge of real hope.

PART FOUR

1868
THE LOVER

Chapter Twelve

THE SOUND OF her laughter sailed across the lawn, making him laugh too. 'It does my heart good to hear it.' Stroking the old dog at his side, he raised his eyes to a blue, unblemished sky. 'I'm a happy man,' he mused, 'and it's all because of her.'

Maurice Westerfield couldn't recall a time when the sound of Kathleen's laughter didn't echo round this house, or fill his heart with joy. 'It will soon be time,' he told the old dog. 'Next Saturday is Kathleen's eighteenth birthday. It shouldn't be too long after that before we're man and wife.'

The thought of putting a ring on her finger and the two of them exchanging marriage vows was a dream he had cherished ever since she had come to live here. More than that, the idea of her lying beneath him, naked and yielding, was enough to take his breath away. 'She knows nothing of my plans,' he murmured. 'Not yet. Soon though, very soon.'

At that moment, Kathleen came running round the corner, with Melinda hard on her heels. Screeching with laughter, they fled across the lawn towards the house. 'You cheat! You're not having it!' Kathleen called, and Melinda ran all the faster.

'Give it back!' she cried. 'It's mine!'

Excited by their antics, the dog scrambled to its feet and chased after them. He'd gone only a few paces when he decided it was all too much and lay down beside the willow tree. 'Come back, you silly old thing.' Maurice laughed aloud. 'I'm afraid you're a bit like me, too old and dignified for such carrying-on.'

Connie Blakeman's voice made him turn towards the house. 'The dog might be old,' she said kindly, 'but not you, sir.'

'Oh, I don't know. I'm in my fortieth year. Soon my bones will start to creak.'

'Your bones will never creak, sir,' she told him. 'You head a thriving business, and your energy outpaces many a younger man's.'

Maurice smiled and gestured for her to be seated. 'All the same,' he said, 'I must seem old to those young ladies, Kathleen and Melinda.' The thought worried him, and he was looking for reassurance. Connie's response did not really supply it.

'I hope you won't think me bold, sir,' she said, 'but I'm sure there are plenty of women who would give their eye teeth to have you walk beside them.' She certainly would. She would give her right arm if it meant she could have him and all his fortune. But she was no fool. The passing years were sapping her beauty. Her mother had been a beauty when she was young but she had aged before her time. Connie felt she was going the same way. In her early thirties, she thought she looked much older. Her breasts were not so round, not so firm. Her waist was beginning to thicken, and there were permanent shadows beneath her eyes. The days were long gone when she could count on her looks to snare a man. If she was to build a nice little nest egg for the future, it would be through her brains and cunning. Thankfully, these had not been dimmed by the flow of time.

Maurice was silent for a while. He seemed to have gone into a little world of his own. 'Would you like me to leave, sir?' Connie felt uncomfortable. She also realised he was looking at Kathleen with the eyes of a man in love. But then, she had seen him look at Kathleen like that before. At first it had bothered her, but not now. Now, she saw it as an advantage to herself. After all, if she couldn't snare the man, why not let Kathleen do it for her?

He returned his attention to her. 'I'm sorry. I was deep in thought.' When he smiled, like now, the years fell away from his handsome face. His gaze found Kathleen again. Having settled their differences, the two young women had resumed their croquet match. 'She's grown into a beautiful woman.' He spoke softly, almost as though he'd forgotten anyone else was there.

'Your daughter or your ward?' Connie asked slyly.

Startled, he jerked round. 'Well, of course they're both lovely, but in fact I was referring to Kathleen.'

'Yes, sir. She is a beautiful woman, with a quick, intelligent mind too. She does you proud, sir.'

'So do you, my dear.'

'Beg your pardon, sir?'

'Over the years, I mean. You've been with me ever since I bought this house, and I don't know what I would have done without you. There have been times when I've been at my wits' end, times when I might have thrown my son out bag and baggage and you dissuaded me.' He grimaced. 'Though, God forgive me, I often wonder whether I shouldn't have done it anyway.'

'Christian is stubborn, but I don't think he's bad, sir. Some children just take longer to grow up. I'm sure he'll make you proud of him one day.' Connie didn't believe that would ever happen. Christian Westerfield was not of the same mould as his father. He was clever, but the cleverness was of a devious, mercenary kind. Much like myself, she thought with amusement.

Maurice didn't believe it would ever happen either, and he changed the subject. 'I was thinking about Kathleen in particular,' he explained, 'because I was just now recalling the dreadful scenes when she first came here. For a long time, Melinda refused to accept her into this household, yet you managed to persuade her that the two of them could become good friends. I don't know how you did it, but you were right.' The two young women were now seated on a bench, deep in conversation. 'Look at them,' he remarked. 'Whoever would have thought it?'

Connie was delighted. 'You have a soft spot for Kathleen, don't you, sir?' Her best bet was to encourage it. In the long run, his infatuation with Kathleen might work to her advantage.

'Oh yes,' he answered. 'She means a great deal to me.'

'I can see that, sir.'

He looked at her consideringly, then took a deep breath and confessed, 'I mean to marry the girl.'

Connie could hardly contain her excitement. 'I'm not surprised, sir,' she said carefully. 'I've seen the two of you together, and I've always thought you would make a wonderful couple. It's plain you adore her, and, if you don't mind me saying so, sir, I believe she feels the same way about you.' What a liar you are, Connie Blakeman, she chided herself. Kathleen would run a mile if she knew what he had in mind.

He beamed with delight. 'Do you really think so? I honestly thought you would be shocked. I think most people would be if they knew I meant to marry her.'

'People will always stand in your way if you let them, sir,' she chirped. 'I mean, I've no doubt your own son and daughter might be against the idea.'

'Quite so. And probably Adam won't take kindly to it either. I'm sure he has ambitions for his sister, and they don't involve marrying her off to a man more than twice her age.'

'But surely, sir, such an important decision has to rest with you and Kathleen, doesn't it?' She laid

273

the seed and watched it grow. 'I mean, a man like you makes powerful decisions every day. I wouldn't have thought you were likely to let others make this particular decision for you.'

At that moment the dog came ambling back and dropped at Maurice's feet. Bending forward, he tickled its ears, and Connie couldn't see his expression. 'I suppose it was very remiss of me to confide in you like this,' he said awkwardly.

'Not at all, sir. Not a word of it will ever be repeated.'

'I meet people every day, all kinds of people in all kinds of places. I travel the world and I'm never alone. But I'm always lonely.' He looked at her and smiled that wonderful smile of his. 'Does that make sense to you? Don't you think it odd that a man can be surrounded by people and yet still be lonely?'

'I'm a little like that myself, sir.' He had touched a raw nerve with his sad remark.

He sensed her pain and was immediately concerned. 'I hope I haven't upset you, my dear.'

'No. It's just that sometimes we forget old friends and family. A chance remark can bring it all back.' She was thinking of her estranged mother who had died some years back. She was thinking, too, of Kathleen's father, and how it had been between them. In her foolish girlish dreams, she had really believed he would always look after her. She must never make that mistake again.

'You know this family as well as I do,' he

told her. 'I look on you more as a friend than a housekeeper.'

'Thank you, sir.' She knew now. Being a 'friend' was all she could ever hope for. To be a 'lover' would have been better. To be a 'wife' better still. However, a small bone was better than a big nothing. For now, anyway.

Seeing Kathleen and Melinda coming towards them, they stood up. 'I'm proud of them,' Maurice said. 'Considering they had no mother to raise them, they've turned out quite well, wouldn't you say?'

'They're a credit to you, sir.' There had been times during the past six years when she had hated the sight of them both. But that feeling had mellowed, and another took over; a feeling of superiority. She knew things they would never know. She had experience of life, and they were innocent babes. She soon learned she had no reason to fear them. Instead, she saw how she might worm her way into the master's good books by nourishing these two. And, to her satisfaction, it had worked. Maurice Westerfield valued her. He valued her opinion and, according to what he had just now said, he valued her as a friend. It wasn't much, and it wasn't what she had hoped for, but if she kept her wits about her, it offered a measure of power over them all.

'They're also a credit to you,' he told her. 'You have guided them well through some very difficult times.' He looked at her with a warm smile. 'You can't know how grateful I am.'

Oh, I do, she thought cunningly. And there'll come a time when I take my reward.

They watched the two young women approach, and he had eyes only for Kathleen. Connie saw this and secretly smiled. Through Kathleen she would get what she deserved. 'They look hot and tired,' she commented. 'Would you like me to arrange a cool drink for all of you, sir?' Always the good servant, always at hand, she thought slyly.

'That's an excellent idea,' he said, and she hurried away to her tiresome duty.

His face glowed with pleasure the closer Kathleen came. She was so beautiful. It wasn't a glamorous beauty, or a bold beauty. She was warm, and kind, and lovely at heart. Her long chestnut hair flowed behind her as she ran, and her eyes sparkled with the joy of life. When she laughed, as she did now, her teeth shone white and perfect in the summer sunshine, and her face lit with happiness. And yet, for all her generosity of heart, Kathleen had a fiery temper. She loved all animals and hated to see a less fortunate being hurt or used in a way that might cause pain or distress. When that happened, her temper caused sparks to fly.

Only that spring she had found Christian shooting rabbits caught in his traps; the wicked snares had maimed two baby badgers, one with its leg hanging off, the other spiked across its back. In danger of being shot herself, Kathleen released them and carried them back to the house. Maurice ordered Christian not to set any more traps, and he was furious at being slighted by the girl.

Lovingly, Kathleen tended the badgers until they were recovered enough to be returned to the wild. They never did completely leave her though. Even now, she would sometimes sit and wait by the kitchen door in the early hours, and the three of them would meet and renew their acquaintance. Once, Maurice saw them from his bedroom window, and he was captivated.

She championed the underdog, and he loved her for it. He loved her temper, and he loved her laughter. There was nothing she could do that would ever stem his love for her. Rightly or wrongly, he believed Kathleen was everything a woman should be. She was his late wife, his lover, his partner and his friend all rolled into one. The intensity of his devotion sometimes frightened him, for Kathleen had become his very life.

Melinda, too, delighted and surprised him. As a girl she had been too possessive of him; too quick to turn on anyone who threatened to come between them. Now she was more tolerant. She had taken to Kathleen, as he had. As everyone did. It gladdened his heart to see how they were the best of friends. Melinda was pretty in her own way, like a small, precious doll with her blue eyes and golden hair. Yet beneath that babyish appearance she could be hard and tough, even a bit of a bully when the occasion warranted. She was a good daughter, though.

'If only my son had turned out half as good as his sister,' he mused. 'But he's not like her, not like any of us. He's hard and peevish, with a wicked, selfish streak.' He sighed deeply. 'God only knows what's going to become of him.'

As the girls came on to the porch, he smiled and kissed first Kathleen, then his daughter. 'Sit with me,' he invited. 'Tell me what you've been up to.'

'Women's talk.' Bright with sweat, Melinda flopped into a chair.

'Your daughter's a cheat,' Kathleen teased. 'The ball wouldn't go straight for her, so she moved the course.' Hitching herself on to the rail, she winked at him, and his heart quickened.

'It's the only way I can win,' Melinda protested. 'She's too good for me.'

A small, brown-haired maid arrived with a tray on which was a huge jug of cordial and three glasses. Carefully she placed it on the low table before the chairs. 'Will there be anything else, sir?' As she looked up at Maurice, her face grew a peculiar shade of grey. It was all she could do not to burp in his face. That morning she'd had too much porridge, and it weighed on her stomach like a sack of coal.

'Are you all right?' Kathleen had seen the colour drain from the girl's face.

'Yes, miss. Thank you.'

Maurice gave her a curious look. 'A plate of sandwiches, I think,' he said, 'and three big slices of Cook's gooseberry pie.'

'With lashings of cream,' Melinda added. 'I've worked up a huge appetite.'

The maid hurried away, heading straight for the outer loo, to throw up the contents of her stomach. The thought of sandwiches and gooseberry pie, with lashings of cream, was the last straw.

From his comfortable wicker armchair, Maurice regarded the two young women. 'So.' He looked at his daughter but his mind was on Kathleen. 'Women's talk, eh? I don't suppose I'm allowed to know what it was about.'

Melinda tutted. 'No, you're not.'

'It was about my birthday,' Kathleen volunteered. 'Melinda wants a big, glamorous party, and I don't.'

'I see.' He was disappointed because his plans coincided exactly with those of his daughter. On Kathleen's eighteenth birthday, he wanted the biggest and finest party this house had ever seen; not least because he had another little surprise in mind. 'And what do you want, Kathleen?'

'Family,' she answered without hesitation. 'I just want my family round me. You and Melinda and Adam . . .' She hesitated. 'And Christian of course.' Even the mention of his name made her cringe. 'I thought maybe the servants could have a little party too.'

Melinda was horrified. 'Servants are for serving,' she retorted. 'Giving them a party would only embarrass them.'

Maurice seized on the idea. 'No, she's right,' he declared. 'Let them have a party.'

Kathleen was delighted. 'Do you mean it?'

'On one condition.'

'What's that?'

'You let me organise a big, wonderful party for you, and we'll invite everyone who wants to come.'

'I don't want a big party.' She hated crowds. If all the others could be here, she would not have hesitated – Markham, and Cook, John Mason, Nancy. But Markham was long gone. She had no idea whether the others were still in Blackpool. Adam had written to them, as he had promised, to reassure them that he and Kathleen were well and living in the south in some comfort. But he hadn't included a return address in his letter. Finding Connie Blakeman at Westerfield House had made him more cautious.

Maurice persisted. 'I thought you wanted the servants to have a party.'

'I do.'

'Well then. It's up to you.'

Kathleen thought of all those in the past who had cared for her. She hadn't been able to give them a party but there were others, here and now, who had also been kind; good, ordinary people who might never be fortunate enough to attend a party except as servants. Now she was being given the opportunity for them to have something special, away from their daily grind. 'All right,' she conceded. 'You can plan my party if Melinda and I can plan the servants' party.' She looked at her companion. 'You will help, won't you?'

Melinda was tempted to refuse, but then she changed her mind. 'I think you're mad, but it might be fun.'

Maurice was not convinced about the servants' party. In fact he was against it. But if it was the only way he could persuade Kathleen to have the party he wanted, where he could show her off to the world and maybe make that special announcement, then so be it.

'When shall we have this splendid party?' Melinda asked excitedly.

'When Adam comes home,' Kathleen said wistfully. These days he seemed always to be travelling and she missed him so.

Maurice came to stand beside her. 'He should be home by mid-August,' he said, placing a hand on her shoulder. 'I know it's hard for you when he goes away, but there are vast untapped markets abroad. Adam has taken to merchandising as if he was born to it. Tea, tobacco, silk or calico, it doesn't matter what cargo he buys, he makes us all a handsome profit.' If only my own son was as enterprising, he thought. But he wasn't, and never would be.

'Mid-August it is then.' Kathleen was beginning to look forward to it. 'Who will be your partner, Melinda?'

Melinda twirled on the spot, pretending to hold someone in her arms. 'I don't know yet,' she replied.

'But whoever he is, he'll be tall and impossibly handsome, and he'll dance like an angel.' She threw a look at Kathleen. There was mischief in her face, but also a hint of serious rivalry. 'And you'd better keep your eyes off him.' The trouble was, with Kathleen around, nobody looked at her. It was a sore point. 'What about you?'

Maurice froze. Did Kathleen have an admirer he knew nothing about? She had never shown any interest in any of the young men she had met through his business acquaintances.

Kathleen laughed. 'Don't be silly, Melinda. What do I want with a partner at my own birthday party?'

Maurice breathed a silent sigh of relief. I shall be your partner, he thought. For life.

Chapter Thirteen

I T WAS ALL ready.

On this glorious summer's day, the rhododendrons and hydrangeas provided a galaxy of reds and
blues down the west side of the sweeping lawns. Placed
along the east side and shaded by the old cherry trees
were five long tables. Each was spread with a white
cloth which hung to the ground and was laden with
all manner of sumptuous food: whole fishes baked in
their own juices; joints of pork and plump chicken;
slices of ham off the bone, piled high and decorated
with segments of orange. Strategically placed among
the main dishes were dishes of nuts and sweetmeats,
and little titbits to whet the appetite.

On the centre table stood a remarkable selection
of desserts – jellies, trifles, scones aching with currants
straight out of the oven that very morning, and the
daintiest, prettiest fruit pies.

The beverage table boasted a splendid display of
fresh fruit and a long array of silver coolers housing
fine wines, some of which Adam had acquired on his
travels, others brought from the wine cellars beneath
the house. There was a huge crystal bowl filled to the

brim with punch and hung with crystal cups. Beside this were numerous fruit juices, and, set aside on its own small table, a large urn with china cups and saucers for anyone who fancied a cup of tea.

'Wonderful!' Maurice had watched the preparations all day. 'All we need now is the music and the guests.' He looked at Kathleen with adoring eyes. 'And you, my dear, the star of the evening, looking as lovely as ever.'

'I don't know about that.' Kathleen had been anxious about such a big event, but now her excitement grew with every passing minute. 'I've hardly had a wink of sleep this past week, what with Adam being caught up in rough seas and not knowing from one day to the next whether I'd ever see him again.' The fear momentarily shadowed her dark eyes. 'I was so afraid.'

'Understandably so.' He placed a comforting arm round her shoulders. 'When the report came in, I was afraid too,' he confessed. 'The sea is unpredictable. One minute it can be calm and beautiful, lulling you into a false sense of security, and in the next it can be wild and mountainous, and you know in your heart that your life is in her hands.'

'It sounds terrifying.' The thought of crossing vast oceans had always frightened her.

'It is.' He smiled, that handsome, winning smile of his. 'But there's something wonderful about the sea. She's magnificent and alive. Sometimes wild, yes – like any woman.'

'You love travelling, don't you, Maurice?' For a long time she had felt uncomfortable calling him by his first name, but that was what he had insisted on, and now she addressed him like an old friend. 'Doesn't the sea ever frighten you?'

'I'm a born sailor,' he replied, 'and after the thousands of miles he's travelled these past five years, your brother is as fine a sailor as any man I know.'

She was proud of Adam, and she said so now. 'You gave him a future, and I'll always be grateful to you for that,' she told him. 'We both owe you so much.' She laughed aloud. 'Oh, he does love the sea. He always comes home excited and raring to be away again. Last night he told me such wonderful tales, of India and America. He told me about the people there and the way they live, and oh, it sounds so wonderful.'

'Don't you ever want to see for yourself?' Lately he had been thinking of a honeymoon at sea. It would be wonderful to take her to those new and exciting lands.

She shook her head. 'No, thank you.' She was emphatic. 'You and Adam may love sailing the oceans, but I mean to keep my feet on firm ground. I wish I had Adam's pioneering spirit, but I'm just a homely girl at heart. Sails in the wind and a horizon that never seems to come closer is not really my idea of heaven.'

'What is your idea of heaven, Kathleen?'

For one strange, nostalgic moment Murray Laing came into her mind. Murray, with his laughing eyes and lopsided grin that filled her with joy. She would have given anything to have him near. But then she thought of Markham, and the image was gone.

'My idea of heaven is four walls about me and a floor that doesn't roll about when I move. It's a garden filled with flowers that waft their scents on a summer's breeze; where the bees flit from one blossom to another, where I can stroll and sit, and quietly think of the future. Heaven is sitting on a fallen tree in the woods and watching the animals at play. Heaven is a house to come home to, with a roaring fire in the winter and the windows flung open to the breeze in the summer. Above all, it's having the people I love all about me.' She moved away, her dark eyes thoughtful. 'It's not worrying about whether the sea will take someone away from you for good.'

He was deeply moved by her words. 'Are you really that afraid?'

'Of the oceans, yes.'

'You never told me.'

'I'm telling you now.' Suddenly her mood changed, and her smile was bright and bold as ever. 'I'm glad you've given Adam something that satisfies him. He has such a wonderful sense of adventure.'

'So have you.'

'Maybe.' Her mind flashed back to when she and Adam had had to fend for themselves, sleeping rough, wondering where the road would lead them. Those unhappy times would live with her for ever. Maybe it was the uncertainty of her past that made her want a certain future. Yet there were times when she felt like taking off and going where her heart led her. Unfortunately, her heart might take her straight to Murray Laing, and that would never do. 'I'm content enough for the moment,' she said. 'Adventure can wait.'

She laughed. 'Look at me! The guests will be arriving all too soon, and I'm not even ready. Adam and I stayed down talking well into the early hours. I expect he snored like an old dog when he went to bed, but I could hardly sleep for thinking about the party.' She tweaked her hair and grimaced. 'I'll probably look like a wreck by the time the first guests arrive.' Kissing Maurice fleetingly on the face, she ran indoors. 'See you later.'

Upstairs, she bathed, washed her hair, dried and brushed it until it shone. Then she hunted through the wardrobe, choosing a gown of darkest blue, with a slim neckline, pretty ruffled sleeves and a hem that danced when she walked. She brushed her cheeks with the merest flush of rouge and touched her lips with warmest pink. Finally she fastened a single string of pearls round her neck and slipped her small feet into her favourite blue shoes. Then she regarded herself in the mirror. 'Shadows under your eyes,' she tutted, 'but you'll do.'

With that, she ran out of the room and all the way down the stairs. 'What do you think?' she asked Melinda, who was ready before her.

'You look as if a good night's sleep wouldn't hurt,' Melinda answered flippantly.

'I ought to say the same to you,' Kathleen chuckled.

'But honestly, you do look lovely.' Her own dark-brown locks hung loose about her shoulders, but Melinda's golden hair was piled up and fastened with a silver comb. She wore a burgundy gown which fitted her dainty figure perfectly and showed more ankle than her father might think proper. 'Has anyone arrived yet?' Kathleen asked nervously.

Melinda shook her head. 'One or two early birds, but Father is keeping them entertained, I think. It would serve you right if they all arrived in a rush,' she teased. 'Imagine a hostess who wasn't there to greet her guests. The social circle would talk about you for weeks.'

Kathleen shrugged carelessly. Leading the way outside, she stood on the verandah, viewing the scene before her. 'I got ready as quickly as I could.'

'You're a fool, Kathleen.'

'Oh, and why's that?' She knew what was coming.

'If you hadn't insisted on the servants having a day off for this ridiculous party of theirs, Maisie would have been there to help you get ready.'

'I'm perfectly capable of getting myself ready.'

'It's so mean. I had to bring a stranger in to do my hair, and I really missed having my back scrubbed.'

'You should have called me.'

'And have the skin taken off?'

'Oh, stop moaning.' Kathleen looked on Melinda as a sister now. In the early days it had been very difficult, and at one stage she despaired of ever befriending her. 'Look.' She pointed to where servants were busy putting the finishing touches to the tables. 'The domestic agency sent us some good people, so everything's turned out all right.'

'Well, I agree with Father. The idea of servants having a party is shameful. On the same day as you have yours too! Whatever will the guests think?' The matter of the servants' party had been a bone of contention between them since it was first mentioned. 'We'll never live it down.'

Under constant pressure from Melinda, Kathleen had conceded one point. 'Since you insisted they should have their party two miles down the valley, our guests won't even know.'

'I should hope not!'

'Aren't you even the teeniest bit curious to know how they're getting on?'

'I have more important things on my mind.'

'Such as?'

Melinda hesitated, but she had to say something or burst. 'I have a secret.' Her devious smile alerted Kathleen.

'I knew it!' she cried. 'I just knew you'd been up to no good. Going out night after night when your father was away on business, and sneaking back at all hours. It's a man, isn't it? Come on! Own up, Melinda, you've got yourself a man, and he's such a bad lot you daren't let your father know about him.'

'Don't be silly.'

'What then?'

'You know what Father's like. He thinks there's no man on earth good enough for me.'

'This man, what's he like?'

'You'll meet him later.'

'Who is he?'

'Wait and see.'

'Is he here?'

'Not yet. About nine thirty, he said.'

'Is he good-looking? How old is he? He's not one of your father's pot-bellied friends, is he? What does he do for a living?'

'I said, wait and see.' Melinda giggled. 'I'll introduce you when he arrives. Meantime, I'm off to enjoy myself. There was a good-looking fellow down by the food tables just now. I might go and say hello.'

She never ceased to amaze Kathleen. 'Wait a minute! So you're not serious about this other mysterious man then?'

Melinda appeared to be shocked. 'I adore him,' she said softly. 'He's everything I want in a husband. He's wealthy and handsome, and he's generous with it. But, apart from all that, I really do love him. I've loved him for months now, from the first minute I saw him.'

'Months!' Kathleen wondered how she'd managed to hide it for so long. 'You've been seeing him as long as that?'

'It seems like for ever.' She smiled dreamily. Kathleen had never seen her like this before. 'He bumped into me when I rushed for cover in that dreadful rainstorm – middle of March, you remember, the wind blew some of the rooftops off and I was caught out in it. He took me into the hotel and bought me a drink to calm my nerves.'

'He sounds like a real gentleman.'

'He is.'

'If he is, and you love him, like you say you do, why in God's name are you still making eyes at other men?'

'It doesn't mean anything.' She was taken aback by Kathleen's condemnation. 'And anyway, tonight will be my last fling before I settle down. It frightens me, but once we're married, I won't cheat on him. Honest, Kathleen, I really do love him, and when I'm wearing his ring on my finger, I mean it, I'll never deceive him.'

'I know how to keep you out of mischief. Let's go and see how the others are getting on with their party.'

'What?' Her mouth fell open. She stared at Kathleen with horror. 'You mean the servants?'

'I want to make sure they have everything they need.' Cook had been working like a slave but, like everyone else, she was thrilled they were having their very own party. No one had ever given them such a treat before.

'You must be mad!' Melinda had no intention of making sure the servants had everything they needed. Her horror was replaced by relief when she saw a carriage approach. 'You can't go, your guests have started arriving. You'd better go and greet them. And do try and behave like a lady.'

'Yes, ma'am.' Kathleen gave a wonky curtsy.

Melinda had to laugh. 'Now, where's that good-looking fellow got to?' Kathleen's concern showed on her face. 'One last fling,' Melinda promised. 'That's all it is.'

'I wish you wouldn't. What if he arrives before you get back?' She had a bad feeling about Melinda's last fling.

'Don't worry. I'll be back before he gets here.' She took hold of Kathleen's hand. 'You'll like him, Kathleen. When you meet him, you'll see why I want to spend the rest of my life with him.'

Kathleen realised that Melinda really was serious. 'He must be very special,' she said wonderingly. No man had come into her life that she cherished in such a way. Only Murray, and he was long gone.

'He is. Later on tonight, we mean to speak to Father and ask for his permission to be married. I know he'll say I'm too young and that we should wait, but I'm not a child. It's time I was married and responsible for my own life. I want my own home, and lots of children – we both do.'

'It sounds as if you've made your mind up, whether your father agrees or not.'

'I won't take no for an answer.' Winding her arm in Kathleen's, she said softly, 'I've found the man I want, and I won't let anyone or anything take him from me. He wants the same things I want, and I'll be happy with him, Kathleen, I know I will.' She sounded sure. Desperate even.

'Then don't go chasing after other men.'

'Just this once.' Bending forward, she whispered wickedly, 'In the long years ahead I might need a memory or two to keep me going.' She giggled like a naughty schoolgirl. 'I like to compare the men – if you know what I mean.'

Kathleen choked back her laughter. 'I know what you mean, and I think you're wicked.'

'Tonight will be the last time, cross my heart.' Making the sign of a cross on her breast, she rolled her eyes to heaven, as if offering a prayer.

They left the house and crossed the lawn, Kathleen to her guests, and Melinda to the Irish musicians who were still setting up with their fiddles and bows. 'We want soft music, until the wine starts to flow,' she ordered. 'After that, we'd like music to set the feet tapping.'

They knew what she meant, and exchanged a merry word or two when she departed. 'Be Jaysus! There's young stuff here.' One of the men caught sight of Kathleen talking to her guests. 'Sure, I wouldn't mind a dance with that little beauty.'

His colleague looked to where Kathleen was and he, too, was struck by her presence. With the sun playing on her long dark-brown hair, her tall, slim figure and lovely, laughing face, she was a desirable and sensuous woman. 'Hands off, Seamus,' the little flute-player muttered. 'Sure, she's a lovely lady but she's not for the likes of us.' And he should know, because hadn't he tried time and again to make it with the ladies?

'If you've been turned down afore, it's because yer an ugly ol' bugger,' Seamus quipped. 'I'm young and handsome, and there's where the difference lies, me ol' mate.' He puffed out his chest and drew in a noisy breath. If he did strike lucky today, it wouldn't be the first time he'd had his arms round a good-looking lady.

'Keep yer eyes on the job, Seamus, me ol' son.' That was the old fellow again. 'Sure, you'd be wise not to poke yer fingers – or anything else – where they don't belong.'

The young man laughed. He shrugged his broad shoulders, picked up his fiddle and started to play.

The music was enchanting. Music was his first love. Women came a close second.

Soon the party was in full swing, and much to her disappointment, Kathleen had no chance to see how the servants' party was faring. Deciding to slip away later, she poured her boundless energy into playing the dutiful hostess.

The music played and the wine flowed, and soon everyone was in high spirits. 'Are you glad I persuaded you to have a party?' Keeping an eye on the needs and pleasures of the many guests, Maurice's watchful gaze followed Kathleen wherever she went. He was never far away and once again she found him at her elbow when she turned.

'Oh, I am! I am! You were right, and I was wrong.' She hadn't had such a good time in ages. There were people here she had never met, and others whom she'd met at Maurice's business dinners. He liked to gather important men around him and show off his family.

Kathleen's eyes roved over the many people gathered for her party. 'How did you manage to persuade them to come?' she asked with interest. 'I don't know any of them well, and they don't know me.' Some of them looked as if they were ready for their last, long sleep. Yet there were others young and lively enough to make the party fun.

'Everyone loves a party,' he answered. 'And I wanted to make certain you were noticed.'

What he really wanted was for them to see his future wife and be filled with envy. He wanted them to know how beautiful and intelligent she was, and how excellent his judgement. But even if, for whatever reason, they disapproved of her, it would make no difference. He was painfully aware of the difference in their ages, and he knew she could probably have any man she wanted. The fact that she didn't seem interested in men in that way only fired his confidence. He knew also that his own son would be the first to condemn a marriage between himself and Kathleen. To hell with them all if that was the way they felt, he thought bitterly. He loved Kathleen too much to let anyone ruin his plans. He would take her for his wife, come what may. Even if Kathleen herself had her doubts, he would overcome them, somehow.

Kathleen's voice interrupted his thoughts. 'They're a mixed bunch, and no mistake.' When she was a child and Cook was preparing a dinner party for her father, Kathleen had heard the old dear make the same remark. Now here she was saying it herself. Strange, how you subconsciously mimicked someone you had lost, she mused.

Remembering was painful. Amusement turned to regret, and her spirit was dimmed for the moment.

'Kathleen?' Maurice had sensed she was a million miles away, and he felt left out. He didn't like that. 'What are you thinking, my dear?'

She forced a smile. 'Nothing. I was just looking at the guests, wondering who they all were.'

He chuckled. 'You're right,' he admitted. 'They are a mixed bunch.'

There were young merchants dressed in long coats and bright cravats; old men with young things on their arms and wallets bulging under their coats. There were a number of attractive, middle-aged women, all dressed to the nines, obviously on the loose for a man, and two newcomers to the merchant line, who, so Maurice informed Kathleen, 'had great promise'. They all threw themselves into the spirit of the party. The more they enjoyed themselves, the more Maurice smiled. While they were entertained, he could stay beside Kathleen – except now and then some daring young scoundrel would infuriate him by taking her on to the lawn to dance to the strains of an Irish ballad.

As the evening wore on, Kathleen became anxious.

Adam had gone out to look for Christian and they weren't back yet. She sought out Melinda, to see if she knew anything.

'They're old enough to take care of themselves,' Melinda said haughtily. 'What's more, I'm enjoying myself too much to care about anybody else. Before too long my future husband will arrive, and I'll have to behave myself. Until then, I mean to make the most of it.' And, without further ado, off she went with a young man in tow.

Kathleen went in search of Maurice. 'Adam and Christian still aren't here, are they?'

'I shouldn't worry,' Maurice told her. 'Adam's a sensible young man. I'm sure he'll find Christian without getting himself into any kind of trouble.' He didn't say so, but he was in fact concerned about the kind of places his son frequented and the shady people he seemed to know. He glanced at his pocket watch. 'It's almost nine,' he said. 'I'll give them an hour. If they're not here by then, I'll go looking for them.'

'I'll come too.' It wasn't like Adam to miss her birthday party. She was worried about him.

'You'll do no such thing!' Maurice glanced around at the many people chatting, laughing and dancing, all of them happy to be here. 'In half an hour you must stop the music and send the people towards the food tables. It's your birthday party, Kathleen, and your place is here. As I said, if your brother and Christian aren't back in an hour, I'll go and find them. On my own. All right?'

Kathleen nodded, but she wasn't reassured.

At a quarter past nine, she decided to take her mind off Adam by going to see how the servants' party was faring. 'I'll walk you there,' Maurice said at once.

'No. I'd prefer to go on my own,' she said gently. 'I'll only be gone a short time. I can run there and run back, and while I'm gone you can make sure no one misses me.' She needed to get away. She needed a few moments' peace and quiet, under God's quiet sky.

'As you wish.' Clearly, he was disappointed. 'Later, when your brother and Christian appear, I'll find a moment to pay a call myself. After all, it's only courteous.'

Her answer was a peck on the cheek, and before he could say anything else, she lifted her hem and set off at a run. In a moment she was gone from his sight. 'Hurry back,' he whispered.

Kathleen sped over the meadow and across the small brook that ran between the two fields. Here she sat and caught her breath, feeling exhilarated and happy, and wonderfully free. 'It's not that I don't like parties,' she told a curious water rat disturbed by her arrival. 'It's just that sometimes I feel hemmed in.' Leaning back on the wooden strut of the bridge, she wished Adam hadn't gone looking for Christian. 'That one is bad, through and through.'

There it was again, that awful sense of dread. 'I'd best get a move on,' she muttered, taking off again.

'Whether Maurice likes it or not, I'm going with him to find Adam.'

She could hear the music ahead of her, and she could hear the music behind. The two different, distant strains of melody made a weird, haunting sound.

Quickly now, she ran past the big barn, pausing when she thought she heard something inside. 'Rats,' she muttered, going on across a field. 'The little devils are everywhere.'

Inside the barn, Melinda giggled. 'You'd best hurry up,' she told Seamus. While he took down his trousers, she slipped the silver watch out of his pocket. In the light of the moon through the open window, she could just make out the time. 'It's quarter past nine already. I must be back by half past.'

'Won't take me long,' he panted. 'Open yer legs, there's a good girl.'

'Don't be too quick, though, will you? I don't want it to be over before I've had my money's worth.'

'Will twice do you then?'

'Three times if you've the energy.' She laughed out loud, and then sighed with pleasure as he rolled on to her. A series of groans and squeals was followed by a long, exquisite, shivering sigh.

———⟶◦◦◦◦⟵———

K ATHLEEN WAS WELCOMED with open arms. 'Oh, miss, it's wonderful!' Cook was merry on cider. 'I ain't never had such a rousing time since we buried Uncle Willie.'

Accepting a glass of Cook's homemade rhubarb wine, Kathleen was glad to stay awhile. She emptied the glass and was warmed through. She ate a generous helping of chocolate cake and tapped her foot to the tune of an accordion. With regret she realised she ought to get back. 'Mr Westerfield will be calling on you later,' she said, though they were too merry to care. 'I'll try and get back too.'

With that she was off again, running across the field, though maybe not as fast as when she came because now she was full of rhubarb wine and chocolate cake. 'Serves you right,' she chuckled, resting by the big barn. 'You shouldn't have had such a big slice.'

Suddenly she was aware of noises coming from inside the barn. 'That isn't rats,' she whispered. 'There's somebody in there.'

Softly, she crept up to the window and stretched her neck to see over the ledge. The sounds intensified. She could tell there were two people, one groaning as if in pain and the other making small unintelligible sounds. 'Sounds as if some poor devil's being murdered.' Afraid yet determined to help if she could, she put her two hands over the ledge and drew herself up. Peeping over the top, she couldn't believe her eyes.

The man was facing her but he was too far gone to know she was there. Rising and falling in a frenzy, he pushed in and out of the woman, holding her legs wide apart while she gripped his bare buttocks. As his movements grew more feverish, the sweat dripped down his face on to her bare breasts, his face creased with arousal.

Suddenly he reared up, pushing hard into her with the whole of his body, and as he did so his eyes opened and he looked straight into Kathleen's shocked eyes. 'Jaysus, Mary and Joseph!' In an instant he was on his feet, his member sticking out like a ramrod, his eyes bulging with disbelief. 'It's a Peeping Tom! Sure, we've a bloody Peeping Tom looking through the window!' Panic-stricken, he snatched up his trousers, and while he hopped about trying to get them on, his still-swollen member getting in the way of his buttons, Melinda swung round.

She gasped with shock to see Kathleen at the window. 'What the hell are you doing here?' she demanded. 'Bugger off!'

Kathleen had no intention of 'buggering off'. 'Get out of there this minute!' she cried, and ran round the side of the barn to the door. 'I don't know who your man is,' she yelled, 'but he'd better be the one to bugger off and quick, because your husband's on his way.'

The man came rushing out, carrying his coat and shoes. 'Run for your life!' Kathleen cried. 'Her husband's got a temper like a mad bull, and a loaded shotgun too. If he catches you, you'll never be able to enjoy another woman, I can promise you that.'

By the time Melinda emerged, red-faced but fully dressed, Seamus was out of sight. 'You bitch!' She wasn't pleased. 'You spoiled it all. What did you want to do that for?'

'To stop you from going to your "special man" carrying someone else's baby.'

'That won't happen.'

'How can you be so sure?'

Melinda wouldn't meet her eyes. 'That woman on Albert Street has potions,' she said evasively.

'Oh, Melinda! Things like that are no good. They might even do you harm. What if they don't work?'

Melinda was silent.

Afraid for her, Kathleen pleaded, 'Please, Melinda. Promise me you won't use anything like that again.'

Melinda straightened her corset. 'I don't need to promise,' she replied slyly. 'I've already told you, from now on I'm saving myself for my future husband, and we both want a whole lot of children.' She regarded Kathleen warily. 'He's not really looking for me, is he?'

'Not as far as I know.' Putting her hand beneath Melinda's elbow, she propelled her forward. 'But he will be if you don't get back.' As they hurried away, Kathleen glanced over her shoulder. 'Who was that man, anyway? The last time I saw you, you were with one of your father's promising young men.'

'Not my cup of tea.' Melinda grinned. 'The Irishman knew what I wanted.'

'I know I've seen him somewhere before. Who was he?'

'Seamus, the musician.'

'Of course.' Now she remembered. 'I saw him earlier, making eyes at the women. Just now, though, it was hard to recognise him. I mean, it was difficult to look anywhere else but . . . down.' She had to ask, 'Are *all* men as big as that?'

Melinda turned to stare at her. 'You mean you've never seen a man's . . . *thing* . . . before?' When Kathleen shook her head, she gasped. 'Good God! You don't know what you're missing!'

The image was still alive in Kathleen's mind. 'I couldn't very well miss *his*, could I?' she chuckled. The chuckle grew into a laugh, and suddenly the whole incident seemed wildly funny. Soon she was bent double, tears of laughter streaming down her face. 'Did you see him trying to get his pants on?' she cried.

The humour of the situation hit Melinda too, and as they went on their way, the sound of their laughter echoed across the valley.

In the far field, Cook took another swig from her cider jar. 'Did you hear that?' Trying desperately to keep her balance, she informed anyone who was interested, 'That was the first cuckoo.' She then keeled over and had to be carried away to sleep it off.

<hr />

MAURICE DIDN'T HAVE to go out after Adam and Christian. 'They turned up five minutes after you'd gone,' he told Kathleen.

Melinda's attention was on the milling guests. 'He

isn't here,' she said distractedly, 'and it's gone half past nine.'

Maurice was curious. 'Who isn't here?'

'A friend,' she said. 'Someone very special to me, Father, and I so much want you to meet him.'

'Him?' This was the first he'd heard of it. 'And who is this friend?'

'You'll like him,' she answered warily. 'You'll all like him.'

'I think you and I had better have a talk. Who is he, and when did you meet him?' He could recall no mention of a young man in Melinda's life; though she had so many friends, it was difficult to keep track. However, this one sounded different.

'You can ask him all your questions when he gets here,' Melinda said. 'Please be patient, Father.'

Hoping to distract Maurice, Kathleen said, 'I can't see Adam and Christian anywhere.'

'They're both inside,' Maurice told her. 'Unfortunately, Christian is hopelessly drunk and Adam is freshening himself up. I'm afraid there was a skirmish. Christian was with some undesirable people. Apparently he owes them money – gambling debts or some such trouble. Adam insisted they turn him loose and was caught up in a fight.'

Kathleen turned, intending to hurry into the house. She stopped at the sight of her brother emerging from the drawing room. 'Adam! Are you all right?'

He came and hugged her, just like he used to when they were small and she was frightened. 'Still worrying about your big brother, sis?' Adam had grown into a very attractive young man. He hadn't changed much, except he was taller, and broader, and his thick, fair hair was longer than he used to wear it. His eyes especially hadn't changed. They were still the same darkest blue, clear and honest, and now they crinkled in a smile. 'Haven't had a good fight in ages,' he laughed. 'It never ceases to amaze me where Christian finds these people. They're all muscle and mouth.'

'You shouldn't keep putting yourself in danger for him.' Kathleen found it hard to feel charitable towards Christian. She still hadn't forgotten their first night at this house when Christian had caused the death of that lovely dog. 'Just look at you.' She reached up to the swelling on his face.

'It's just a bruise.'

Melinda met his gaze. 'You could have been knifed, or kicked to death in the street,' she said. 'He wouldn't have cared.'

Adam looked at her for a long, intimate moment. He loved Melinda. He had always loved her, even that first night when she saw them hiding on the stairs and looked at them with contempt. But she didn't love him, and so he kept his silence. 'Christian is Christian. Bad as he is, we can't leave him to the wolves.'

'You may not be prepared to leave him to the wolves, but I am,' Melinda retorted. 'It's what he deserves. He's a no-good drunkard, and he doesn't care what happens to any of us, especially Father, and God knows he's caused him enough pain over the years.'

Maurice hated to see what his own son was doing to his family, but he had given up. He had tried everything and now he found it easier to turn a blind eye. 'Don't think like that,' he begged. 'It doesn't solve anything.'

Melinda's eyes blazed with anger. 'What am I supposed to think?' she demanded. 'I'll tell you, shall I? I think he'll never be any good, and I think he'll drive you into an early grave, that's what I think. And I wish to God he was dead. Do you hear me, Father? I wish he was dead!' Breaking into a sob, she ran into the house.

Kathleen would have followed but Maurice caught hold of her arm. 'No,' he murmured. 'Stay with your guests.' He turned to Adam. 'Please, Adam.' He felt old, and haggard. Christian always did that to him. 'Will you go to her?' Adam was more of a son to him than his own. It had been his dearest wish that Adam and Melinda might get together. But it didn't seem as if that would happen now. He consoled himself with the thought that at least they were the best of friends.

Adam nodded and went after Melinda.

'They didn't see Christian,' Maurice told Kathleen. 'The guests, I mean. They didn't see him drunk. I managed to get him out of sight and up the stairs before anyone realised.'

Kathleen's heart went out to him. 'I'll talk to him tomorrow,' she promised. 'Maybe he'll listen to me.'

'My son listens to no one.'

Kathleen had seen the truth of that time and again. Always at the root of any trouble, he seemed beyond redemption. 'I'm sorry,' she said, and she really was.

'You're a good person, Kathleen.' Taking hold of her hand he softly kissed it. 'What would I do without you?' The answer, he knew, was that he would shrivel and die.

She smiled brightly. 'No frowns please. It's my birthday party and I want everyone to be happy.' She was immensely fond of this kindly man, and it hurt her deeply to see what his son was doing to him.

'I wouldn't spoil your party for the world,' he said.

'Come on then.'

'Lead on, my beauty.'

They went down the steps and across the lawn to the dancing area, where Maurice caught her to him in a waltz. All eyes turned to them. 'Look at them,' he said, his head high, his handsome face wreathed in a proud smile. 'There isn't a man here who wouldn't swap places with me now.' Winking at her, he chuckled, 'Let them wait.' He swung her round with panache, declaring firmly, 'It's *my* turn to dance with the birthday girl.'

As they danced, Kathleen caught sight of a group of women watching them. And *they* wouldn't mind changing places with *me*, she thought wryly.

U P IN HER ROOM, Melinda stared out of the window, watching her father dancing with Kathleen,
and wishing she could be out there enjoying herself too.
Her father had been very attentive towards Kathleen
this evening. He always was, but tonight Melinda
couldn't help but notice his love for her shining in
his face. She had long suspected that her father's
feelings towards Kathleen were more than simply
paternalistic; now she was convinced. She was both
shaken and pleased. It might be a good thing if
her father's attention was taken up with Kathleen,
especially just now.

She gazed miserably out of the window. Oh, where
was he? *Why* wasn't he here? 'Maybe he doesn't
want me any more,' she mused worriedly. 'Maybe
he's changed his mind about getting married.' The
thought was unimaginable.

There was a tap on her open bedroom door. 'Am
I welcome?' Adam asked, poking his head round. 'Or
would you rather be left alone?'

Melinda wiped her eyes. 'Of course you're welcome,' she said. 'Come in, Adam.'

He entered the room but kept his distance. This
was the first time he'd been in her room, and he felt
stupidly self-conscious. 'I came to take you back to
the party.'

'In a moment,' she said. 'Come and stand beside
me.'

He crossed the room and stood so close she could
feel his warm breath on her face.

'What's wrong?' he asked. He had come to know her very well, and he sensed her unhappiness wasn't only because of Christian. 'If there's something troubling you, I wish you'd tell me.'

She laid her head on his shoulder, taking him for granted, as she had done ever since he had come to live in her father's house. 'You're a good friend, Adam,' she murmured. 'You're always there when I'm in trouble.'

'Are you in trouble now?'

She drew away. 'No, of course not. Forget I said that.' She pressed her nose to the windowpane, her blue eyes still searching. '*You* wouldn't let me down, would you, Adam?'

'Never!'

'You wouldn't arrange to meet me and then not turn up?'

'You know I wouldn't do such a thing.' He swallowed hard. 'Is it a man?'

She nodded but didn't look at him.

'Is he special, Melinda?' He held his breath, letting it out in a gasp when she answered truthfully.

'I love him, Adam. I really love him.' She turned to him and her eyes were shining. 'Oh, Adam, I can't wait to be his wife.'

He took a moment to compose himself. 'Does he feel the same way about you?'

'Oh, yes. He was coming to the house this very night, to ask Father if we could be married.' She didn't see how her words tore him apart. 'But he isn't here.

He told me half past nine, and he still isn't here!' She gabbled on, 'Oh, Adam, if he doesn't want me any more, I'll throw myself in the river. He has to come for me. He *has* to!'

She would have gone on, but she glanced out of the window and there he was, striding towards the house. 'Oh! He's here! Adam, he's here!'

Screaming with delight she ran out of the room and down the stairs, alight with joy, laughing as she ran into his arms.

From the window, Adam saw it all. 'I've lost you,' he whispered brokenly. 'I've missed my chance.'

He lingered there a moment longer. 'You're a lucky fellow,' he murmured, his gaze falling on the man below. 'I hope you know how to take care of her.'

Suddenly his face paled. 'My God!' He pressed closer to the window, his eyes wide as he took in the man's face; older, yes, and more lined with experience, but there was no doubting who it was.

The man Melinda was walking towards the house with was Murray Laing.

Chapter Fourteen

MELINDA GATHERED HER father and Kathleen together in the drawing room. 'Stand there, and don't move,' she told them. 'I've got a surprise for you.' As she ran out, the sound of her laughter made them smile.

'What's she up to now?' Maurice wondered.

'Whatever it is, she's happier than I've ever seen her.' Kathleen suspected she was about to produce her boyfriend. 'Be kind to him,' she whispered to Maurice. 'She really likes this one.'

Maurice smiled. 'I see. It's him, is it? All right, I'll be kind, but he'd better be good enough for her. I'll soon know if he's not.'

They were still smiling when Melinda came back in. 'This is Murray Laing,' she told them. 'We've been courting for two months.'

Kathleen heard the name and her heart skipped a beat. The smile slid from her face and she could hardly breathe. She was looking straight at him, and still she couldn't believe what she was seeing: Murray Laing, the man who was responsible for Markham's death, right here, in this house, looking at her as if he, too, couldn't believe what was before him.

'Murray?' Her whisper was heard only by Maurice, who glanced curiously at her.

'Do you two know each other?' he asked, addressing Kathleen.

Kathleen opened her mouth to speak, but Melinda answered first.

'Of course they don't!' she said. 'It's the first time Murray's been to this house.' Neither Kathleen nor Murray corrected her. 'Well? Aren't you going to welcome him, Father?'

'I think you both owe me an explanation.' He was a man of principle, a man who valued the old traditions and who expected his daughter to do the same. 'You say you've been courting for two months. I don't recall anyone asking my permission.' His back stiffened. 'What have you to say for yourselves?'

His question was directed at Murray, who met his gaze coolly. 'We owe you an apology, sir.' Before he could say more, Melinda again intervened.

'It's my fault, Father. Murray insisted I should tell you, he even threatened to call on you without my knowledge, but I begged him not to.' She looked at her father with those big blue eyes. 'Please don't be angry,' she begged. 'I do so want you to like each other. You *must*. You really must!' There was desperation in her voice.

'Oh?' Maurice raised his eyebrows. 'And why is it so important that we like each other?'

'Tell him, Murray. Please tell Father what we planned.'

Hesitating now, his glance going nervously to Kathleen who stood white-faced and motionless, he confessed, 'Melinda and I had a mind to be married, sir, with your permission of course.'

'I see.' Maurice's voice was authoritative, his manner stern, though in truth he had taken an instinctive liking to Murray who appeared to be prosperous and well mannered. It was painful, but he had come to compare every young man with his own son.

'You have to say it's all right.' Melinda was growing nervous. 'Please, Father.'

Maurice's face stiffened. 'You'd better come through to the library.' He ushered them both towards the door. 'Excuse me, my dear,' he said to Kathleen. 'I'm sure this won't take too long.'

The moment before he left the room, Murray glanced at Kathleen. It was a forbidden moment but later, when the shock of seeing him subsided, she held that moment in her heart, and, through all the years to come, it never left her.

———⟫●⟪———

Connie Blakeman watched Kathleen slowly leave the drawing room and go into the garden. Connie hadn't joined the other servants at their party; somebody had to oversee the people the domestic agency had sent, and as she had made no real friends among the other servants she was quite happy to do so. She had spotted Melinda run out of the house to throw herself into the arms of a stranger. Her curiosity aroused, she had followed them back inside, where she had seen and heard everything from her vantage point in the shadows of the hall. She was delighted to learn that Melinda was hoping to be married. It all fell in very nicely with her own plans. With Melinda out of the way, she would have a freer hand. But she was puzzled by Kathleen's reaction.

'Strange,' she mused, a look of cunning on her still-attractive face. 'She didn't seem too delighted by Melinda's happy news. I should have thought she'd be overjoyed because, when all's said and done, they have turned out to be the best of friends.'

In her mind, she ran over the scene she'd witnessed. 'Come to think of it, there was a moment when Maurice thought Kathleen and that fellow knew each other.' A devious little smile crept over her features. 'I wonder.'

<hr>

A DAM FOUND KATHLEEN standing apart from the party guests, beneath the cherry trees. Drawing close, he saw how distressed she was; her face was turned to the sky and tears were rolling down her cheeks. He took her hand in his. 'Come and sit with me here.' As she meekly followed him to a bench beneath the trees, he breathed a silent sigh of relief. It seemed Murray had not yet said anything which might cause Kathleen to question the circumstances surrounding Markham's death. 'I'll get us a drink,' he suggested. It wasn't just his sister who needed a drink. 'We have to talk. Stay right there.'

Adam had waited upstairs in an agony of suspense and turmoil while Melinda introduced the man she intended to marry to her father and Kathleen. Pacing up and down, he had prayed that whatever happened, Kathleen would not find out he had deceived her about Murray's role in Markham's death. How in God's name had the man found them? Did Melinda know he was an ex-convict? No, surely not. That wasn't the sort of information he'd be likely to divulge to anybody, let alone the daughter of a wealthy household he was hoping to marry into. Did he want revenge? Of course he did, but was he using Melinda as a means to achieve it, to gain her father's trust and then tell him he'd taken a couple of liars into his house, hoping they'd be thrown out in disgrace? Or did he just see Melinda as a route to easy money? In his well-tailored suit and polished brogues he didn't look short of money. Adam shied away from the thought that Murray might genuinely love Melinda. There was harsh justice in the fact that he should lose the woman he loved to a man he had wronged so utterly. And there was cruel punishment in the knowledge that if Kathleen found out the truth, he would lose her, too. What he had done to Murray, and to Kathleen, was unforgivable. But Murray didn't know Markham had cleared him of all blame. And in that, Adam thought, lay his only hope.

Seated on that bench, in the twilight of a beautiful evening, Kathleen tried to come to terms with seeing Murray again. Alone in that quiet corner, she thought how far away her childhood seemed. She recalled growing from child to woman, a slow, surprising change, when powerful emotions seemed to chase away all else. She remembered when she first saw Murray, the tousled-headed boy with the wide, cheeky grin and laughing eyes.

In all her memories one thing stood out above all others. She believed she had put it all behind her, but now it rose before her like a phantom from the past. Her love for the boy who was now a man was stronger than ever. Now, that man was in love with Melinda, and Kathleen was bitterly torn between the two.

Could she let Melinda marry him? Or should she tell her the dreadful thing Murray had done? If she came between the two of them, Melinda would hate her. Then again, if she didn't tell Melinda and later it was discovered that she had known all along that Murray was responsible for an old woman's death, Melinda might still hate her. Love was a powerful thing. It made people blind to the faults of others. Kathleen knew that better than most. She had named him as a murderer to the police and yet, God forgive her, she still dreamed of being in his arms.

Adam returned with a cordial for her and a whisky for himself. He sat beside her and told her he had seen Murray with Melinda in the garden. 'I've never said anything, but I had hoped Melinda and I . . .' He took a gulp of his drink. 'I'm a bloody fool!'

Kathleen laid her hand on his. 'I've always known you love her,' she murmured. 'I'm so sorry, Adam.'

'What are we going to do about *him*?' He jerked his head towards the house.

Kathleen knew what she must do. Despite her own feelings, she was determined not to flinch from it. 'There's only one thing we can do,' she said sternly. 'Melinda has to be told. We owe her that much at least.'

He was afraid. 'Wait until he's gone,' he pleaded. 'Don't tell Melinda in front of him. He might lie, worm his way out of it.'

'What's wrong with you?' She couldn't understand him. 'There's no reason to wait. He can lie all he likes, but the truth will out, and Melinda will know the kind of man she wants to live with for the rest of her life.' She recalled Melinda saying those very words. 'Come with me or stay here. It's up to you.' She put her glass on the ground and stood up. But she had no chance to carry out her intention because Melinda came running across the garden.

'Father said yes!' she laughed. 'Murray and I are to be married, as soon as it can be arranged.' She threw herself into Kathleen's arms. 'Oh, Kathleen, isn't it wonderful?' Running to Adam, she kissed him full on the mouth. 'Be happy for me, Adam,' she said. 'Say you'll be best man. Please.'

Taking her by the arms, Kathleen made her sit down. 'Are you really saying your father has agreed you can be married?' She couldn't believe it. Maurice had been so guarded when he went into the library with the two of them. 'I was sure he'd insist you court a while longer before making any decision.'

Melinda shook her head. 'He was all for it. Murray and I are to be married as soon as arrangements can be made.'

Suspicions were already stirring in Kathleen's mind, but it was Melinda's secret little smile that gave it away. 'Oh no!' Kathleen closed her eyes in anguish. 'You're with child, aren't you? *That's* why your father's agreed. That's why he wants it done as quickly as possible.' Her heart sank. How could she tell Melinda now?

'The doctor says I'm almost two months pregnant.' She proudly stroked her stomach. 'And you can't even notice.'

Adam was so shaken by the news, he stared at Melinda as if seeing her for the first time. 'You shame yourself,' he said coldly. 'You shame us all.'

Melinda pouted. 'I'm sorry you feel like that. I was sure you of all people would stand by me.'

Kathleen drew her aside, whispering so only Melinda could hear. 'Is Murray really the father?'

'I swear! If it wasn't Murray's, I wouldn't be marrying him.' She looked the picture of offended innocence. 'You do believe me, don't you, Kathleen?'

Against her better instinct, Kathleen nodded. Her reward was a hug and a kiss. 'I must get back to him,' Melinda declared, and ran off as merrily as she had arrived.

'Maybe you deserve each other,' Kathleen murmured.

The knowledge that Melinda had been fornicating with another man that very evening even though she was already pregnant by Murray nauseated her. But then, she wasn't at all certain that Melinda was telling the truth when she swore that the baby was Murray's.

'Well,' said Adam bitterly, 'you can't tell her now, can you? The bastard's made her with child, and there's nothing we can do.' He drank his whisky and went for another, leaving Kathleen alone.

She wasn't alone for long. Soon a group of guests joined her, and for the next hour she was caught up in their laughter and chatter.

Midnight came, and the guests began leaving, each one searching out Kathleen to thank her for a lovely evening. Maurice was nowhere to be seen, and she explained he had been unexpectedly called away on a family matter.

By one o'clock the guests had all gone, and still there was no sign of anyone emerging from the library. 'Now the work really starts.' Connie

Blakeman marched by with her little army of servants in tow. 'You there, and you, clear the tables and then fold the cloths,' she instructed, quickly organising the clean-up.

Kathleen went in search of Adam. She hadn't seen him since Melinda had told them her shocking news. She eventually found him by the brook, seated on the grass, his back to a tree trunk, his head in his hands. Beside him was a half-full jug of ale. 'Adam!' She ran down the grassy bank to him. 'I've been looking everywhere for you.'

'Well, now you've found me.' He looked up at her and his face was haggard in the moonlight. 'I know she has lovers and I'm insanely jealous, but I was sure in the end I would have her all to myself. She's a bitch, isn't she?' His voice rose and the words slurred. 'No! She's wonderful and lovely, and I want her so much it hurts. Can you believe that, sis? Can you believe I would still want someone like that?'

Kathleen believed it, for didn't she feel exactly the same way about Murray?

Folding herself beside him, she entreated, with a world of love in her voice, 'I know exactly how you feel, but it won't help to get drunk. Come inside, Adam. Get a good night's sleep. In the morning you might see things differently.'

He was crying like a child now. 'Oh, sis! I've lost her. Sleeping or waking, nothing can change that. Melinda's gone, and I want no one else.'

She put her arm round him and he laid his head

on her shoulder. 'Tell her,' Kathleen suggested. 'Tell her how you feel.'

'No. I can't do that. Not now. Maybe I should have done it a long time ago, but not now. Not when she's carrying another man's child. Besides, if she had ever loved me, I'd have known. I suspect the plain truth is, Melinda sees me only as a substitute brother.' He laughed wryly. 'God knows, she needed a better one than Christian.'

He drank deeply from his ale jug. 'Leave me. I don't want anyone near me right now, not even you, sis.' Especially not you, he thought, because now I know how you must have felt when you lost Murray. 'I have things to sort out in my mind.'

'What things?' She didn't want to leave him here, so close to the brook, in his sorry condition.

He waved the jug in the air. 'The wedding, of course! I need to think about Melinda's wedding. Have you forgotten I'm to be best man?' He laughed and spluttered, choking on his words.

'There may not be a wedding.' The cool firmness of her voice made him stare.

'What do you mean?'

'Being the kind of man he is, Maurice is bound to make inquiries into Murray's background. He'll dig deep. Money won't matter, you know that. Melinda is precious to him, and there won't be a stone left unturned. Once he learns the truth, he'll know what to do for the best, I'm sure.'

'Does he realise we knew Murray before?'

'I don't think so.' As far as she could tell, Murray had kept silent about that, and no wonder, she thought bitterly. 'But it's bound to come out. There are records – he'll know I turned Murray in. I'm not ashamed of that.'

'I am,' Adam muttered, turning away.

'What did you say?'

He mentally shook himself. 'I'm tired, that's what I said,' he snapped. 'You'd better take me to the house before I fall in the brook and drown.' He groaned as she helped him up. 'It would solve everything though, wouldn't it, eh? If I were to drown, we'd all be better off.'

'Don't talk like that.' Supporting his considerable weight as well as she could, she led him back to the house. 'Things really will seem different tomorrow,' she promised. But she didn't believe it, and neither did he.

<hr>

MAURICE STOOD BY the window, listening to an account of Murray's life. 'That's all I can tell you, sir,' he finished. 'I learned how to be a commercial broker the hard way. There have been times when I've had to be ruthless, but I have never gone out of my way to harm anyone.' It was the truth as he saw it.

'I see.' Not altogether satisfied, Maurice stared out of the window, hoping he might see Kathleen. The party was over and he still hadn't declared himself to her. He had so wanted to be able to announce their engagement tonight. Instead he was being forced to agree to his daughter's. My God, the girl ought to be whipped. He turned back to Murray. 'I won't deny I've heard of you, and as far as I can tell you have a decent reputation.' He raised an accusing finger. 'But it's a pity you weren't capable of being decent where my daughter was concerned.'

'I won't shirk my responsibilities, sir,' Murray said boldly. 'I never have.' Not even when he was sent to prison for harming that old lady when in fact he had not touched a hair on her head. He had followed the others, suspecting they were up to no good and concerned for Kathleen. If only he'd dealt with them earlier, all might have been well. For that he accepted part of the blame. The others were never charged. The police knew he had not been alone in the house but they didn't have any names, and Murray hadn't enlightened them, reckoning that it was safer not to. Those thugs would only have tried to save their own necks by pointing the finger at him. Without any witnesses to prove he had been the one actually responsible for attacking the old lady, he had calculated – and prayed – he would be spared the hangman's noose. And so it was.

Murray shook off the memory of that time and looked at Maurice levelly. 'I'm always prepared to face the consequences of my actions, sir.'

Maurice was impressed with his sincerity. He returned his attention to the outside, his eyes lighting up when he saw Kathleen coming towards the house with Adam, though Adam appeared to be leaning rather heavily on her. 'Excuse me a moment,' he told the other two.

He went out of the room, closing the door behind him. Hurrying to Kathleen, his worried gaze went to Adam who was swaying slightly, his eyes half-closed and the remnants of a song issuing from his lips.

'I'm afraid he's drunk.' Straightforward, without excuses; there was no other way to say it.

'Drunk? I've never seen Adam drunk before.'

'Neither have I,' Kathleen said. 'I expect we all fall from grace once in a while.' She didn't mean anything by it, but Maurice obviously assumed she was alluding to Melinda.

'She told you then. I saw her run across the lawn to where you and Adam were sitting.'

'Yes, she told us, and I'm very sorry. I know it isn't what you wanted for her.'

'What do you think of the young man?' He valued her opinion. 'Do you think he would make a suitable son-in-law?'

She could have told him everything, but wisely decided not to. There was no need to alienate Melinda when Maurice was bound to find out anyway. 'It's what you think that matters,' she said diplomatically. 'Anyway, if I know you, you're already planning to have him thoroughly investigated.' She hoped so.

'I have that in mind, yes.' He felt better for

having talked to her. 'Here.' He slid Adam's weight on to his own shoulder. 'I'm sure we can get Adam to his room without bothering the servants.'

'He'll have a roaring headache in the morning,' Kathleen said, 'and it'll serve him right.'

Between the two of them they got Adam to his bed. Then Kathleen went to her own room while Maurice returned downstairs. As he went he smiled fondly at her. 'Goodnight, my dear,' he said. 'Don't worry about Adam. I'm sure he'll be full of remorse in the morning.'

'And so he should be,' Kathleen said, though her heart went out to him.

In the privacy of her room, she looked at herself in the mirror. Surprisingly she appeared as fresh as a daisy, her face glowing with health and her eyes sparkling. 'Must be the fresh air,' she told herself. 'Poor Maurice. I wonder what he'd say if he knew how much Adam loved his daughter?'

She knew what he would say: he would much prefer Adam as a son-in-law.

She undressed, washed all over, and brushed her long hair. That done, she put on her pretty blue nightgown and climbed into bed, wanting to put the whole business out of her mind.

It was impossible. When she lay awake it played on her mind, and when she slept it haunted her dreams.

There was a lovely church, bedecked with flowers and ringing to the sound of bells. Melinda and

Murray, arm in arm, were walking back down the aisle. He saw her there, he smiled, and suddenly it was her walking arm in arm with him, it was her wearing the wedding ring. Then out of nowhere came the small, familiar figure of Markham, and suddenly it was snowing; there was no church, no Murray, and even Adam had deserted her.

Twice she woke with a start, and each time she turned over, desperate for sleep. Finally, when she could fight the tiredness no longer, her mind relaxed, the images disappeared, and she slipped into a deep, sound sleep.

<hr />

IN THE FURTHEST wing of the house, Connie Blakeman was also restless. She lay on top of the bed, the lamp still alight on the cupboard, and her eyes wide open, counting the wrinkles in the curtains. Behind the eyes was a shrewd, mischievous mind. Almost all her life she had lived by her wits, until now she was as sharp as a tack.

'The buggers must be asleep by now,' she reasoned. Still, she mustn't be hasty.

Five minutes passed.

Getting off the bed, she tucked her feet into soft slippers. Her elbow knocked the lamp, making it rock. 'Whoa!' Carefully she righted it. 'Quietly does it. Mustn't get caught.' Taking her robe from the back of the chair, she put it on and tied the belt tightly. Then she took up the lamp and made her way across the room. Softly she opened the door, peering out to make certain there was no one about.

Satisfied, she went along the landing, down the back stairs and through the house towards Maurice's study. She had done it so many times before, she knew the route by heart. That's why she was now able to quench the light from the lamp and leave it safely on the hall table.

She pushed open the study door and went inside. She lit the table lamp and made sure the curtains were closed. Then she pulled out the bottom drawer of the desk, placed it on the carpet and stretched her arm into the gap it had left. 'Ah!' There was a small click as the hidden door sprang open. 'I still haven't lost my touch.'

Drawing out the wad of notes, she counted them. She liked nothing better than counting money – unless it was having a well-endowed man roll on top of her. She was disappointed. 'Only twenty-five pounds! Why doesn't he keep more money hidden here? The bigger the wad, the more I can sneak away without him suspecting.'

How much should she take this time? A daring thought presented itself, and not for the first time. 'Why not take the lot?' she asked herself. 'With this, and the notes I've already stashed away, I could live comfortably.'

It was a temptation, but there was more to be gained by staying, she reasoned. 'Another year and I could have enough trickled away to see me right into my old age. Then again, if I can get him and Kathleen together, I could name my price. Once the old fool's tied the knot, I can tell him a few home truths that would rock him in his shoes. Like how his pretty bride comes from a mother who was nothing better than a whore, and a father who was hanged for two murders. On the other hand, once she's wed to him, the lovely Kathleen will have the keys to more money than I'll ever see in a lifetime. Happen she'd be prepared to pay more for me to keep my mouth shut than he'd pay for me to open it.'

It was intoxicating to think of being in such a fortunate and powerful position. 'I'll take two of these here notes now,' she decided. 'I'll put the rest back and wait for my chance of a bigger pot.'

Deftly she tucked two notes inside her slipper, replaced the drawer and blew out the lamp. Departing the room, she headed in the opposite direction from which she'd come.

Whenever she went robbing, it gave her a crippling thirst. Just now the roof of her mouth was so dry, her tongue was sticking to it. 'A drop of cool sarsaparilla, that's what I need, and then I'll be away.'

In a moment she was in sight of the main kitchen. There was no light on. The house was quiet. She felt safe enough.

She entered the kitchen. The curtains were open and the moonlight broke the darkness just enough for her to see where she was going. Careful as a mouse, she took the sarsaparilla jug from the pantry and popped out the cork. It rolled away across the floor. Leaving the cork, she raised the jug to her parted lips. 'Mmm!' The rich, brown liquid slithered down her throat, warming her all over. Her thirst not yet quenched, she took another drink. Sheer heaven. A drip escaped from her mouth. She wiped it away, then licked the tips of her fingers.

From his seat at the table, Christian watched her, his face creased in an evil smile.

He, too, had come down to quench a raging thirst; it was always the same when he'd had too much to drink. The booze got in his blood and the blood boiled, until he cooled it with a hair of the dog.

He let her drink, and made not the slightest move. There was something very gratifying about watching someone who had no idea you were there. Especially when that someone was not bad looking, with tousled hair that hung down and a figure not too displeasing to the eye.

As she moved, her legs parted. The night sky filtered through her robe, silhouetting her figure: small-waisted, with breasts that were still round enough to cup in the palm of a man's hand. Her face was upturned, her mouth open to the spout of the jug.

His avaricious eyes took in every wonderful, tantalising detail.

He could wait no longer. Silently, he rose from his chair and stepped away from the table. Like a cat he went towards her, his loins burning with desire. In all the time she had been in this house, he had never seen her in such a way before, never wanted her like he wanted her now, nor thought she was worthy of his attention. But he was still giddy from a night of revelling and wasn't thinking straight.

When he was just an arm's reach away, she stooped to retrieve the cork from the floor. This was his moment.

With surprising agility he lunged forward and grabbed her, one hand over her mouth, the other sneaking up her nightgown. 'It's all right,' he whispered. 'It's me, Christian.' When the horror had died from her eyes, he took his hand from her mouth. The other hand continued to caress her warm, smooth flesh. 'I saw you. Just now, in the moonlight, I *saw* you.' He smiled knowingly. 'I never realised you were so beautiful.' Lies would get him what he wanted. Tomorrow, he would be lying to someone else. To him, women were all of a kind.

She was passive in his arms, delighted by his attentions, knowing that he was yet another means to a small fortune. 'What do you want with me?' Her voice was the smallest whisper, but her eyes shone with triumph. Bastard! she thought. Take me, and I'll make you pay! She knew what he wanted all right, and she was more than prepared to oblige. Yet it might pay her to behave like a lady, or at least not to appear eager. To that end she struggled, but not very effectually.

'I don't want to hurt you,' he said, stroking her hair. She wasn't struggling now. 'I wondered if you were lonely, like me.' His hand crept to her thigh, to that soft, warm, pulsing corner. 'Are you? Are you lonely, like me?'

She nodded, but remained silent.

He kissed her then. It was a moment before she kissed him back with any passion, but when she did, it was all he needed. Sometimes when he'd been drinking he could not be aroused easily, but now he was as hard as he had ever been.

When she wrapped her legs round him and drew him in deep, he laughed softly. 'Bitch! You want it too, don't you?'

She didn't answer. She was too busy kissing him, licking him, moulding herself into his body.

It was a wild and hungry coupling. Two people gratifying themselves for their own selfish reasons. Fast and furious now, he brought her to a climax, before he too was satisfied, the pleasure coursing through his senses.

When it was done, he rolled away and left her there on the floor. 'Keep your mouth shut,' he warned. 'One word of this and you'll wish you'd never been born.'

When he'd gone, she made her way back to her own quarters. Once inside, she twirled round and round, softly giggling, as if demented. After a moment she fell on the bed, pressing her hands over her face to muffle the laughter. 'You've done a good night's work, Connie, you clever thing,' she flattered herself. 'One way or another, Christian Westerfield will be made to pay for his naughty little pleasures.'

***

A DAM WAS WIDE awake. He was sitting by the window in his bedroom, deep in thought. Slowly and painfully he came to a decision.

Once the decision was made, he lost no time in carrying it out. It didn't take long to throw a few things into an overnight bag. He checked his wallet. It was enough. Over the years he had amassed a considerable bank balance. 'The days are long gone when I might go hungry.' It gave him a great deal of satisfaction to know that every penny he owned had been earned by the sweat of his brow.

Seating himself at the desk, he took up pen and paper and wrote a long, careful letter. This he sealed into an envelope, addressing it to 'My sister, Kathleen'.

He wrote a second, shorter letter, this one for Maurice.

As he sealed it, his resolve faltered and for one weak moment he almost tore the letters up. But he knew that the alternative was worse. Stay and watch Melinda marry another man, see it tear Kathleen apart? He couldn't do it. And he couldn't go on living a lie. His immediate reaction on seeing Murray had been how best to keep Kathleen from suspecting the truth. Recalling that now, his shame only increased. His sole option was to make a clean breast of it.

He made his way to Kathleen's room where he slid both letters beneath her door. 'God bless you, little sister,' he murmured. 'We've been through some bad times, you and me, but you'll be fine now. You don't need me any more.'

This was the worst moment of his life. He lingered there, making the agony last, touching the door and wishing he had the courage to tell her face to face. 'Forgive me,' he whispered. Then he departed, leaving behind everything that made life worth living.

———❖———

KATHLEEN WOKE FEELING refreshed. A moment later her spirits dipped as she recalled Murray's presence in the house last night, and the reason for it. 'Leave it to Maurice,' she decided, shutting her mind to it all. Even so, it wasn't easy.

She selected a sage green blouse and white skirt. 'First a brisk wash at the basin, then dress for breakfast.' Yet she couldn't shake her mind free of the knowledge that soon Melinda and Murray would be married. And before long there would be a child. 'Put it out of your mind,' she told herself in the mirror. 'No matter how much you might wish it, the child isn't yours. However much you love him, he was never for you, and never could be.'

A short time later she was washed and dressed, and ready to meet the world. She threw open the window on the August sunshine, then quickly made her way to the door. 'Best foot forward, Kathleen, my girl,' she declared. 'You may not fancy breakfast, but you'll have to show willing, for Melinda's sake, if nothing else.'

She almost stepped on the letters. They lay side by side half under the door, half out. She picked them up, turning them over in her hands. 'Looks like Adam's writing.' Her insides grew cold. 'Why would Adam be writing letters when he's just down the corridor? And why put this one under my door?' she wondered, reading Maurice's name on the second letter.

She rushed out of the room and down the corridor. The door to Adam's room was open and the maid already tidying the room. 'Yes, miss?' Startled by Kathleen's unexpected arrival, the maid looked up from making the bed.

Kathleen sensed the awful emptiness of the room. 'I'm sorry,' she said lamely. 'I'm looking for my brother. Have you seen him this morning?'

The maid shook her head. 'No, miss.' She gathered the laundry and excused herself. As she went, she muttered under her breath, 'No wonder I'm late doing me chores, with folks rushing about all over the bleedin' place!'

With the letters still in her hand, Kathleen went out on to the landing. Seating herself on a tall, upright chair beside the jardinière, she opened the letter addressed to her.

My dear Kathleen,

I hope you will forgive me for what I'm doing, but I see no other way. I have to leave this house and find work abroad. I don't have the kind of courage to stay and see Melinda married to another man.

There is something else, Kathleen. Something I've kept to myself all these years, though it has haunted me every minute.

I know how much you liked Murray, right from the very first day you saw him. I know, too, how the liking turned to love, and how it broke your heart to name him as Markham's attacker.

The shameful truth is, I did you, and Murray, a terrible wrong, and now I can't keep silent any longer. I feel I owe it to you and Melinda, for he is not the devil he appears to be. You see, Kathleen, it wasn't Murray who attacked Markham. In fact, she told me herself how he tried to save her from the others.

I didn't tell you because I thought it was for the best. I know now I had no right to let you go on believing he was the cause of her death. It was wrong of me to keep the truth from you. It was wrong of me to stand by when you gave his name to the nurse at the hospital. Because of me, Murray must have served a long term of imprisonment.

I wouldn't blame you if you told him and sent him after me, but I know it isn't in your nature to do such a thing. Maybe he already knows anyway. Maybe he's a more honourable man than I could ever be.

I had no right to do what I did, and I offer no excuses.

A better man might have stayed and told you both face to face. It's ironic that I should lose Melinda to a man I wronged. That is my punishment.

I know this will be a terrible shock for you. I only hope there may come a time when you can feel it in your heart to forgive me.

I'm going far away. By the time you read this, I will be aboard a ship bound for foreign parts. It will be many a year before I see these shores again, if ever.

Please, Kathleen, don't think of me too harshly.

Take care of yourself.

Your loving brother,

Adam

Kathleen fell back into the chair, anguish flooding her soul. Her eyes were tightly closed and her hands lay loosely in her lap. The letter fluttered to the floor. Dear God, Adam had stood by while she had labelled Murray a murderer. *No!* Oh no!

'Oh, Adam. How could you?' She covered her face with her hands and cried bitterly, wishing herself a million miles away. But she was still here, having to face them all while he was gone, run away like the coward he was. 'It was *me* who put Murray away for all those years. I daren't even think about it. What if they'd hanged him? Oh, dear God!'

The thought was horrifying. 'You're right, Adam,' she muttered harshly. 'I wouldn't send him after you, though God knows you deserve it. But I can never forgive you. Not as long as I live.'

Shakily she dried her eyes and picked up the letter. The other one was tucked in her skirt pocket. She took it out and stared at it for an age. 'I expect you've told Maurice the truth. I hope you have. But the truth won't erase the years Murray spent in prison.' She couldn't begin to imagine what he must have gone through. She had heard tales of the cruelty meted out to prisoners. 'The truth won't give him back the peace of mind he lost. Nor will it clear the way for Murray and me to find each other again.' That was what cut most deeply. She had lost him, and in such a wicked, wicked way.

A feeling of disgust came over her. 'Shame on you, Adam! You may have run from it all, but I won't. Someone has to stay and face him. Someone has to say sorry, futile though it sounds, and as you're not here, it falls to me.' She shivered at the prospect. 'God help me, I'll do what's right, with as much courage as I can muster.'

A strange calm settled over her. She stood up and went down the stairs straight to Maurice's study.

'He's in the breakfast room, miss.' It was the same maid she'd encountered earlier, in Adam's room.

'Is Miss Melinda with him?' She had things to explain to them both.

'Yes, miss.' A little grin crinkled her homely

features. 'With her young man, miss. They're having breakfast with the master.'

'Thank you, Sally.'

On her way to the breakfast room, she paused, her heart beating wildly. For one faltering moment she was afraid she might not be able to go through with it.

The moment didn't last long. She carried on, and the nearer to the breakfast room she came, the stronger grew her courage. She had to be brave. Adam had left her little choice.

When she entered the room, Maurice stood to greet her. 'Kathleen, my dear. As you see, we have a guest. Do come and join us. I'll get you some fresh tea.' He turned to the maid. 'A pot of fresh tea, if you please, and some hot muffins.'

Kathleen remained standing at the head of the table. Maurice was on her right, the other two on her left. Her gaze went from Maurice to Melinda, who was too interested in Murray to notice any-one else. Then, with a heart-rending effort, she brought her gaze to Murray. He smiled at her, slowly, fondly, looking at her with those wonderful sincere eyes. Kathleen's heart turned over. What she felt for him was reflected in his gaze. The same love. The same regrets. The same memories and longing. The realisation shook her. His love for her had survived the years, in spite of everything, just as hers had for him. It made her task all the more painful.

Maurice was puzzled. 'What's wrong, my dear? Please, come and sit down.'

Kathleen said, 'There is something I have to tell you.' She was looking at Maurice but was acutely aware that the other two were paying close attention. 'Adam has left this house for good.' Before they could respond to the startling news, she went on, 'He had things to tell you but was afraid he might never be forgiven. Now I have to tell you these things. Afterwards, I too may be asked to leave this house.'

'You will never be asked to leave,' Maurice assured her. 'For pity's sake, Kathleen, what is it? What's happened?'

'I can't believe Adam's gone!' Melinda's impatient voice broke in. 'Why would he do that?' Her small fist banged the table. 'I want him at my wedding. He promised to be best man.'

'Quiet, child!' A stern glance from Maurice and she was instantly sullen.

Shifting her gaze briefly to Murray, Kathleen said quietly, 'What I have to say mostly concerns you.'

She took a deep breath. 'I've no doubt that Murray was preparing to tell you this himself.' She had to keep all possibility of blame from his shoulders. 'Adam and I knew Murray years ago, when we were children. After our parents died, Adam and I were sent to live with Great-Aunt Markham. We saw Murray often on our walks across the park or along the beach, but he only ever came to the house once. All the same, we might have been

339

very good friends, only . . .' She gulped, choking back the tears.

'Murray used to hang around with a gang of young hooligans, but then he left their company for good and got himself a job. He meant to do well, that was what he said, and I always knew he would. Right from the start, I knew he didn't belong with those people. Aunt Markham told us his father was a bully; it wasn't surprising he got mixed up with a bad lot because he was not encouraged to do anything else. He had faith in himself though, and I was proud of him.' I loved him, she thought. I believed in him even then.

At that moment the maid arrived. 'Not now!' Maurice was totally absorbed by Kathleen's tale.

'These same hooligans broke into Aunt Markham's house. We don't know exactly what happened but she was badly hurt and later died from her injuries.' Once again she had to swallow the rising emotion. 'Murray was there, but I didn't know until this day that he was trying to save Markham. I know now he wasn't involved in the break-in, and had nothing to do with the attack on my aunt.' When she glanced at him, he looked away, his eyes downcast.

She went on, 'My brother knew this because Markham told him before she died. For reasons I won't go into, I was never told of Murray's innocence, and so, to my undying shame and in a fit of rage, I gave his name to the authorities. Needless to say, he was arrested and imprisoned, for something he didn't do.'

'My God!' The colour had drained from Melinda's face. Maurice sat rigid in his chair, speechless with shock.

Kathleen felt Murray's eyes on her, and faced him with courage. 'There is nothing I can do or say to make up for what I did or to convey how sorry I am. All I can say in my defence is that I had no idea you were innocent until this morning, when I found this letter from Adam beneath my door.' She held up the letter for them to see. 'He knew Melinda's father would search into your past. He was afraid I might find out that he'd deceived me all along. That's why he went away, because he couldn't face the consequences of what he'd done.'

She made no mention of Adam's love for Melinda, or that he couldn't bear to stay and see her married to another man. Nor did she confess how she loved Murray with the same passion. There was nothing to be gained from revealing all this. Instead, she said simply, 'I'm as guilty as my brother. I'm so very sorry.' The shame and heartache threatened to suffocate her. 'I should have known you weren't capable of such a thing.'

The silence was profound.

She gave the second letter to Maurice. 'He left you this,' she explained. When he opened the letter and began reading, she quietly left them. She had no right to stay. How could any of them want her there?

———————⟫•⟪———————

KATHLEEN WAS OUT in the garden when Maurice came to her. 'No one blames you,' he said. 'And please, Kathleen, don't ever talk of leaving. This house would be empty with you gone.'

He sat beside her on the bench and put his hand over hers in a gesture of friendship. Above them the boughs of the cherry tree were heavy with fruit. In the clear blue skies birds swooped and from the woods came the plaintive sound of animals calling. Yet Kathleen could find no solace in the beauty that surrounded her.

'Will you let them marry?' She prayed her confession had not spoiled Melinda's life. At the same time, she wished those two had never met. Maybe then, somehow in the future, there might still have been a chance for her and Murray.

'I have no choice,' he answered. 'You know Melinda is with child. Even if she were not, and I truly believed those two were in love and wanting to marry, I think I might still agree. He seems a good choice. Melinda is strong-willed but I don't think she'll get the better of him. He's a good man. Intelligent and ambitious, and in view of his background his success is all the more remarkable. We've talked at great length. I like him.'

'Will you investigate him?'

'Of course. I wouldn't be doing my duty as a father if I didn't probe into his past. But now that I know the worst I doubt whether I'll find anything but good.'

'I'm glad you won't stand in their way.' She wasn't glad. She was desperately unhappy.

'Adam going like that.' He shook his head. 'I never would have believed it. One of the things I admired most about him was his courage.'

But you don't know, she thought bitterly. You don't know how much he loves your daughter, and how devastated he was when he discovered she was to be married – and to the man he'd wronged all those years ago.

'Why didn't he come and explain his mistake?'

'It wasn't a mistake. He let me send Murray to prison and he knows I will never forgive him for it.' She wondered if he really would never return.

'Never is a long time not to forgive someone.' He sensed something here that was too secret, too deep to be spoken about, yet he had to ask. 'Tell me, Kathleen. Was there ever anything between you and Murray?'

'We were only children,' she prevaricated. 'When Melinda brought him here it was the first time I'd seen him in all those years.' It wouldn't do if Maurice thought Murray meant anything special to her.

'I'm sorry, my dear. It was a foolish thing to ask.' He tucked his fingers under her chin and raised her gaze to his. 'Kathleen, promise me you'll never again speak of leaving.'

She smiled, and for the briefest moment she forgot the pain. 'As you said, never is a long time.'

Feeling foolish, he stared at the ground. 'With Adam gone and Melinda leaving soon for a home of her own, I can't imagine being here without you.'

'I thought I might take up secretarial work or something useful like that. I won't waste my life.' For some time she had been considering asking Maurice if she might be involved in his work. Now, though, she wouldn't be so direct.

'If that's what you want, we can talk about it, but promise me you won't leave, at least until after Melinda's wedding.'

It wasn't much to ask. 'All right.' But she must find work. Only busying herself would keep her sane.

'Thank you, my dear.' Realising she needed to be alone, he made his excuses and returned to the house. There would be time enough later to put his ideas to her. This was not the moment.

The old dog came to sit at her feet. 'Hello, old feller,' she murmured, stroking his head. 'Are you lonely too?' Until that moment, she had never known what it was to feel utterly and completely alone.

Another voice answered, a voice she knew immediately. 'I'm lonely,' it said. 'Even more so since I came to this house and saw you again.'

Her heart leaped. 'Murray!'

'Don't run away,' he begged, sitting down beside her. 'I only want you to know I don't hold you responsible, or your brother come to that.'

'But it was Adam who let me believe you were responsible for Markham's death, and it was me who gave your name to the authorities. For God's sake, Murray, you were innocent.' She was crying now, hot, burning tears streaming down her face. 'How can you not hold us responsible?'

He gazed at her for a while, his warm, anxious eyes quietly regarding her every beloved feature. 'Don't cry.' Raising his hands, he thumbed away her tears. 'I did a lot of bad things before I realised what a fool I was – stealing and fighting, halfway to being a thug every bit as bad as the others. If it hadn't been for you, I might have gone on to even worse. Oh, I won't deny the long years in prison were sheer hell, but they taught me a valuable lesson. I've become a good citizen. I earn my living through legitimate means, and I'm a very wealthy man.'

'Oh, Murray. Will you ever forgive me?'

'For sending the authorities after me, yes. For sending me away from you, no.' There was a world of regret in his voice.

His warmth and tenderness moved her deeply. 'I missed you,' she confessed. 'After we went away, and even though I thought you were to blame for Markham's death, I couldn't stop thinking of you.' She laughed, embarrassed. 'Isn't that silly?'

He held her gaze, his voice trembling with emotion.

'No, Kathleen, it's not silly. In that prison, and ever since, not a day has gone by when I haven't thought of you.' Taking hold of her hand he pressed it to his face. 'Oh, Kathleen, Kathleen. You can't know how much I still love you. When I came out of prison, I searched far and wide for you. I asked everywhere. But it was as though you'd vanished into thin air. When I saw you here, I thought I was going mad. I still love you, Kathleen. I've never stopped loving you.'

Fearful now, she drew her hand away. 'It's too late,' she reminded him. 'You're marrying Melinda. She's carrying your child.' She would have given anything for that not to be so, but it was. And nothing could turn the clock back.

'There's no love there. I was lonely, at my lowest ebb. One night Melinda was there, lovely, willing, and I was weak.' He shrugged, as if casually dismissing the episode. 'It was just one encounter, short-lived and quickly forgotten. It meant nothing, not to either of us, I thought. Just two unhappy souls comforting each other.'

He drew in a long breath. 'Now she's having my child. Oh, I'll do the right thing by her. I hope I haven't lost my sense of decency altogether. I helped make that innocent child, and a child needs its father. I'll care for Melinda, and I'll give her all she wants.' He paused, his voice a soft caress. 'But it's you I love, Kathleen. It will always be you.'

He loved her! She wanted to shout it from the

rooftops. Instead she remained silent, and more than a little afraid. 'You'd better go. She'll be wondering where you are.' She wanted him to stay, or go away with her. But that was impossible, she knew.

'Melinda and her father are in the library.' His smile was mischievous, delightful. 'No doubt they're discussing the shocking news you dropped in their laps just now.' He stood up. Leaning easily on the trunk of the cherry tree, he remarked kindly, 'I'm sorry about your aunt. She was a strange little thing, but she was always a lady.'

'Yes, she was always a lady.'

'Life couldn't have been easy for you after she died.'

'We had plans, me and Adam.'

He sat down beside her again. 'Tell me about your plans,' he urged. 'I want to know everything about you.'

In the years to come, he would remember these precious moments.

<hr>

MELINDA WAS ADAMANT. 'No, Father! I won't forgive her. And I won't forgive Adam for going away.' The truth was, she had always been fond of Adam, and the idea that she might never see him again was too upsetting.

Maurice was equally adamant. 'I will not have bad feelings in this house. Kathleen has been a good friend to you. Either you show her some compassion now, or I might have to think again about this young man of yours!'

. Stamping her feet, Melinda showed a fierce temper. 'You heard what she said, Father. Murray was innocent of the charges against him.'

'Exactly. And if it hadn't been for Adam confessing to that, and Kathleen having the courage to tell us, I might have discovered Murray's prison sentence and that would certainly have put an end to any marriage between you.' Taking her by the shoulders, he warned angrily, 'Your shame, and mine, would have been tenfold. Think of that, my girl, and be grateful to her.'

She fell silent, realising that what he said was the truth. But the truth was, she was wildly jealous that Kathleen had known Murray first, all those years ago. And from the way Kathleen had spoken about him, they had obviously formed a close bond. Why didn't Murray tell her last night that he knew Kathleen? Was he hiding more than just his prison sentence? Whatever her father said, and however unreasonable it might be, she would never again be able to feel the same about Kathleen. She blamed her too for not stopping Adam from leaving. That distressed her more than she liked to admit.

'Go to her now.' Maurice turned her to face the door. 'Kathleen must not leave. Where would she go? How would she live?'

'She's capable enough. Anyway, why should you

care?' She knew the answer to that well enough, and her jealousy deepened.

'It's enough that I do care, and so should you,' Maurice said, exasperated. 'You must let her know she still has a friend in you. Tell her you don't blame her for any of this.' His patience at an end, he thrust her forward. 'Go on, child! Do as you're told.'

She wasn't sure, but as she approached Kathleen and Murray, Melinda felt they were sitting too close together, talking too quietly and, when they got up on seeing her, looked almost guilty. 'What are you up to?' she asked, painting on a smile. To Murray she said, 'Father would like a word with you. He's waiting in the library.'

As he came close, she took hold of him and bent his head to hers. 'He won't bite you,' she murmured. Then she kissed him on the mouth, her eyes open and looking over his shoulder at Kathleen. Embarrassed, Kathleen stood up.

'It's getting chilly,' she said. 'If I'm wanted, I'll be in my room.'

Taking Melinda by the shoulders, Murray stood her away from him, his eyes on her but his message for Kathleen. 'I think Melinda would like you to stay awhile.' His voice was firm as he then addressed Melinda. 'Isn't that so?'

Realising she had no option, Melinda ran and linked her arm with Kathleen's. 'We need to talk,' she said. 'I don't want you to think we can't be friends any more.' Gritting her teeth, she sat down on the bench and waited for Kathleen to do the same.

When, just before entering the house, Murray glanced back, it was to see the two of them deep in conversation. 'At least I haven't come between you,' he murmured. 'God willing, we won't be strangers over the coming years.' Though, in a way, it might have been less painful if they were never to see each other again.

He would have been less easy in his mind if he'd heard what his future wife was saying.

'You won't tell, will you?' Melinda was pleading. At first, when her father had insisted she should show compassion to Kathleen, she hadn't considered the possibility that Kathleen might be the one to withdraw her friendship. 'I know I've had too many men friends, I'm not denying that. But that's all over now. I'm in love for the first time, and I'll be a good wife. I'll never again cheat on him. He's a wonderful man, rich and handsome, and he knows how to take care of a woman.'

Her words cut into Kathleen's heart.

Unaware, Melinda went on, 'Murray is the kind of man any woman would die for. If he should find out how many men I've had before him, he wouldn't feel the same way about me any more. He'd call off the wedding, I know he would. You won't tell, will you, Kathleen?' She wished to God she hadn't boasted about her many conquests. Now, if she wanted to, Kathleen could cause her untold hardship. 'Please, Kathleen, promise you won't tell.'

Grateful still to have Melinda's friendship, Kathleen said warmly, 'It isn't for me to tell. If anyone should tell Murray about your previous lovers, it ought to be you.'

'Never!'

Kathleen wondered if Melinda was right to be so afraid that Murray would desert her if he knew the truth about her. He might still go ahead with the wedding, if only for the child's sake. But if he did choose to walk away, Melinda would be left a mother with no husband. The scandal might persuade Maurice to send her from this house for good, though he would undoubtedly see she never wanted for anything. That gentle, kind man had already suffered one shock after another: his only daughter carrying a child out of wedlock; the revelations about Murray; the bitter disappointment of Adam going away. For his sake, as well as Melinda's, Kathleen knew she could never betray Melinda, though she couldn't help but wonder whether her silence wasn't a betrayal of Murray. 'You must do as you see fit,' she told Melinda quietly. 'I won't tell, you have my word.'

Melinda hugged her. 'I knew you wouldn't turn your back on me,' she laughed, secretly triumphant, 'and I won't turn my back on you. It must have taken a lot of courage to admit how you sent Murray to prison,' she grudgingly admitted, and then, with astonishing arrogance, 'it was a wicked thing you did, but I forgive you.' A sly grin curled the corners of her mouth. 'We all have our little secrets. In a way, you're no different from me.'

Kathleen burned to wipe that smirk off her face with the sharp edge of her tongue, but she let it go. 'Tell me one thing, Melinda.'

'Ask.'

'The child, is it really Murray's?'

Melinda laughed softly. 'Like I said, we all have our little secrets.'

'Are you saying Murray *isn't* the father?' Damn Melinda and her games.

Melinda replied warily, 'I'm not saying any such thing, and even if I was, it can never be proved either way. All I am saying is, I slept with Murray, and we made love like I've never known before.' Bunching her fists and thrusting them out before her, she sighed ecstatically. 'It was wonderful!'

Kathleen's silence urged her on. 'Seriously though, there's no doubt in my mind that Murray is the father. When our child is born, you'll see for yourself.'

It occurred to Kathleen that maybe Melinda herself did not know who the father was. God knows the girl had had enough lovers.

Melinda sprang to her feet. 'I'm going inside, to make sure Father isn't bullying my husband-to-be.' Reluctantly, she added, 'Are you coming?'

Kathleen shook her head. 'I think I'll stay out here for a while. I have a lot of thinking to do.'

'Father says you're not to leave. He won't stand

for it, and neither will I.' At least, not until I'm safely married to Murray, she thought. 'You're not planning to leave, are you?'

'I haven't got as far as making plans.'

Satisfied, Melinda touched on another issue. 'Do you know where Adam went?'

'No.'

'Will you make an effort to track him down?'

'No.' Her heart was hardened against him.

'I'll miss him.'

'I expect you will.' It struck her that Melinda might have been more fond of Adam than she'd ever admitted. A rush of spite drove her to say something she instantly regretted. 'Was Adam one of your little secrets?'

For a moment Melinda was shocked, yet she knew it might have been true, if only Adam had shown her the way. 'If you're asking whether he was a lover, no, he wasn't.'

'I'm sorry. I shouldn't have said that.' She recalled what Adam had written about his love for Melinda, and she was overwhelmed with shame.

'Can I tell my father we're friends again?'

Kathleen began to understand. 'Did your father send you out here?'

'Of course not!' Melinda was an accomplished liar.

'Go on in, I'll follow in a while.'

'Just now, when I came out, what were you and Murray talking about?'

'Oh, nothing much.' Everything, Kathleen thought.

'It didn't look like it was nothing.'

'Oh? What did it look like then?'

'Like two lovers whispering.' Bristling with jealousy, Melinda demanded, 'You wouldn't be keeping something from me, would you?'

'Like what?' Anger rose in Kathleen.

'I don't know. Something.'

'Please, Melinda. We've made our peace, and now I'd like to be left alone for a while.'

'I'm sorry if I've made you angry.'

'You haven't.'

'I'll see you later then?'

'Yes. Later.'

Connie Blakeman had witnessed the meeting from an upper window. Intrigued, she watched Melinda as she walked back to the house. She could see the young madam's dark expression. 'Nastier piece of work than I'll ever be,' she muttered. 'Smiles on one side of her face and spits on the other.'

Bringing her gaze to Kathleen who sat dejected on the bench, she warned, 'Watch her, my beauty. She knows her dad's fond of you. Whether she marries her rich young man or not, it'll never be enough. If she thought for one minute you might get your hands on her father's fortune, she'd cut your throat soon as look at you.'

After a while, Kathleen made her way to the house.

As she passed the library, she could hear voices,

intense, deep in discussion. Probably making plans for the wedding, she thought, going on up the stairs.

Suddenly the door opened and Melinda came out, her arm linked with Murray's. He seemed pre-occupied but she appeared to be bubbling over with happiness.

As Kathleen paused, looking down, her gaze met Murray's and, for a moment, time stood still.

She turned away and carried on to her room. As she closed the door, her heart was like a clenched fist inside her.

Chapter Fifteen

IT WAS THE sort of day any woman would wish for her wedding. The September sun shone gloriously, the gentle breeze was wonderfully refreshing, and everything was ready for the big event.

From the upper reaches of the house came Melinda's shrill, peevish voice. 'If only I wasn't so fat!' She was now almost three months pregnant and it was beginning to show. 'Everyone will know,' she wailed. 'They'll stare at me.'

Kathleen had been up since five o'clock that morning, helping where she could and soothing Melinda's frayed nerves. 'Nobody's going to stare at you.' Laying Melinda's beautiful wedding dress on the bed, she tried hard not to wish it was hers. 'Honestly, Melinda, you're never happy unless you've got something to moan about.'

'But what if they *do* stare?'

Kathleen rolled her eyes. 'They won't! And even if they do, it'll only be your lovely dress they're looking at.'

'Oh, thank you very much!' She gave Kathleen a disdainful stare. 'You're not much help. I think you'd better go and see what's going on down-stairs.'

'Gladly,' Kathleen replied, and she hurried off before Melinda could change her mind. She could hardly bear to be actively involved in preparing another woman to wed the man she herself loved so desperately. As she went, she could hear Melinda shrieking at the two unfortunate women who had been summoned to make her beautiful for her big day.

Kathleen shut her ears to the angry cries. Today was going to be enough of an ordeal without Melinda doing her best to be a miserable, obnoxious little pig! She ran down the stairs, pushing all upsetting thoughts out of her mind. 'You're on trial, Kathleen,' she told herself. 'Don't let yourself down.'

Connie was downstairs, checking that everything was in order. Over the years she had honed her skills as a housekeeper until now she excelled at her job. When Kathleen came into the dining room, she was alone there, setting out the crystal. 'Chased you away, has she?' Flicking an indignant stare towards the ceiling, she muttered, 'It's a pity she can't realise how much of a friend she has in you.'

'What exactly do you mean by that?' Kathleen asked. She was always uncomfortable in Connie's presence, hating the familiarity she had shown to herself and Adam from their first day here. And she always seemed to be watching and listening.

Every word she uttered, every look and insinuation

suggested this woman knew more about what went on here than she ever revealed.

Connie shifted her attention to the flower display. 'I'm not trying to say anything,' she said. 'I'm simply remarking on what an ungrateful, selfish devil she is.'

'She's nervous, that's all. Any woman would be.' Feeling the need to defend her, Kathleen put her own feelings aside, though they were remarkably close to those of the housekeeper.

'Would *you* be nervous?' Connie didn't look up, but the sly smile still shaped her mouth.

'I suppose so, yes.'

'Of course you would.'

'I'm not sure what you're trying to get at but I don't like your attitude very much.'

'I'm sorry.' Unusually contrite, Connie stepped back to admire the flowers. 'Maybe you'd better go and get ready, leave me to my work.'

'You're right. It wouldn't do for the bride to be without her maid of honour.'

She was halfway across the room when Connie's next remark stopped her in her tracks. 'I expect you'd rather be the bride.'

She swung round. 'What did you say?'

'I saw you last night. You and him.'

Stiff with anger, Kathleen clenched her fist and for one awful moment was tempted to slap that sly, brazen face. 'If you have something particular to say, you'd better come right out and say it.'

Connie fiddled with the flowers. 'I can't imagine why you're getting in such a state. I only said I saw you and him – having a chat as far as I could tell.' Facing Kathleen now, she said softly, 'Isn't that how it was?'

'You know perfectly well that's how it was. If I hear you saying otherwise, you'll answer to me.'

'Such a temper,' Connie remarked casually. 'Anyone would think you had something to—' Suddenly she clutched her stomach, her face as white as a sheet.

Kathleen stared at her, wondering whether she was genuinely ill or just playing some bizarre trick. But when she groaned and slumped forward across the table, her legs buckling beneath her, Kathleen darted across the room. Putting her arms round Connie's shoulders, she helped her up into a chair. 'Sit here,' she said. 'I'll get you a drink. Will you be all right?'

Connie nodded. 'But please,' she gasped, 'don't say anything to the others.'

'I won't,' Kathleen promised, hurrying out of the room.

The house was a hive of activity as servants rushed about putting the finishing touches to the preparations. In their best bib and tucker, they went about their duties with a smile on their faces. Even if Melinda wasn't the nicest person they'd ever worked under, a wedding was always cause for celebration. Besides, she and her husband had bought a house in

Kent. After today, the master's daughter would be far enough away not to bother them.

Kathleen went swiftly towards the kitchen. The hallway was filled with flowers – a beautiful, trailing rose bouquet for the bride, a smaller, less formal one for the maid of honour, and a selection of corsages for anybody in need of one.

'My goodness, miss!' exclaimed Cook as Kathleen entered the kitchen. 'I would have thought you'd be upstairs, getting ready. Maisie's been up and down wondering where you are. Look at the time, miss!' She waved a hand at the clock. 'In a few hours the carriage will be here to collect you.'

'When it comes I'll be ready – done up like a princess, don't you worry.'

Maisie was bold enough to remark, 'You're always like a princess, miss.'

'Why, thank you, Maisie, and so are you.' Wasting no time, she poured a glass of water from the jug. 'Nerves,' she explained coolly, and pretended to take a sip.

As she left the kitchen, the glass still in her hand, Maisie ran after her. 'Are you going upstairs now, miss?'

'You go on up, Maisie. Get everything ready, and I'll follow you up in five minutes.'

'Very well, miss.' And off she went, softly singing to herself.

When Kathleen made her way upstairs ten minutes later, it was by way of the back stairs. Connie leaned heavily on her arm. 'Thank you for getting me past without anyone seeing,' she said. 'I don't want them thinking I can't do my job.' Connie had two rooms in the upper reaches of the house, at the front and some way from the servants' quarters.

'Are you sure you'll be all right now?' Kathleen wasn't certain she ought to leave her. 'I could send Maisie,' she suggested. 'She's a good girl, not prone to gossip.'

Connie sat in the chair, her colour slowly returning, and her breathing almost back to normal. 'No, no. I'm better on my own. I'm not ill . . . as such.' She seemed to blush a little. 'You go on. You've got to be ready when the carriage comes. Maisie will be waiting.'

'If you're sure.'

'Just one thing. Why did you help me after the way I goaded you?'

Kathleen smiled. 'Because I'm not sure you meant anything by it. And anyway, shouldn't we all help each other?'

'You make me feel ashamed.'

'Good!' She laughed, and so did Connie.

On her way downstairs, Kathleen recalled what Connie had said. 'I'm not ill . . . as such.' It intrigued her. What did she mean? Still, there were other, more pressing matters to attend to now, and time was running short. 'Like it or not, I've promised to be there, and I will. Smiles and all.'

While Kathleen got ready with Maisie's enthusiastic help, Connie leaned over the bowl, retching and spewing, and feeling like death warmed over. 'There's no doubt about it now, my girl,' she said, splashing her face with cold water. 'You're carrying Christian Westerfield's bairn.' She hadn't been certain until now. 'It couldn't have worked out better if you'd planned it yourself,' she told her mirror image. 'But take your time. Be sure when you make your move. That drunken devil's as cunning as you ever were.' She leaned on the dresser, staring at her reflection. 'You might be past your bloom,' she muttered, 'but at last you've got your ticket to an easier life.' Patting her stomach, she grinned. 'This little bugger is the way to a fortune. Or my name's not Connie Blakeman!'

Going to the wardrobe, she put away the pretty lemon blouse and blue skirt she'd originally chosen to wear to church. Instead, she took out a grey dress and a sensible pair of shoes. 'Mustn't look like the sort of woman who would lead a man on,' she laughed.

Suddenly she was looking forward to attending the church, even if it did mean she had to stand at the back with the other servants. 'You won't be a servant for too long now, Connie, my girl,' she declared. 'Wait until after the wedding. A few days at the most, and then we'll see.'

In spite of last-minute crises – Cook dropped a tray of meringues and the butler skidded across the floor on them; Melinda trod on her bouquet and the crushed gypsophila had to be replaced; Kathleen lost two hairpins and had to borrow from Maisie – the wedding went smoothly.

The church was ablaze with colour; flowers decorated the pews and lined the aisle, and a myriad blossoms made long, meandering trails down the centre columns. The bright autumn sunlight filtered in through the windows, and when the bride came in, all eyes turned to gaze on her.

Melinda looked very glamorous. In her long dress and wearing an exquisite pearl tiara, she looked almost regal. A gossamer veil of lace and silk flowed from her head to the ground behind her, moving gracefully as she walked, slowly and sedately, to the tall, handsome man waiting at the altar.

It was only a moment before all eyes turned to Kathleen. Dressed more simply, in a straight-cut primrose-coloured gown, she looked almost like a bride herself. Her long dark hair was swept up, leaving trails of tiny ringlets framing her face and neck. In her ears she wore small, pear-shaped drops of gold, and round her neck a single gold chain. Her feet were clad in silver slippers and her hands in gloves of the same, finer material. She carried her flowers low, moving with grace and confidence towards the altar – and the man whom she, too, loved with all her heart.

Maurice walked his daughter up the aisle, proud

to do so but ashamed of the reason for it. At the altar, he turned to glance at Kathleen. Her beauty took his breath away. She smiled, and his heart tightened with love. Quickly he looked away. She must not see the longing in his eyes. He must be patient a while longer. Once Melinda and Murray were settled in Kent, his time would come.

Kathleen couldn't stop her gaze from rising to Murray's profile, strong and serious, his dark hair smoothed back, one small lock straying across his forehead. He looked so proud and fine, the way any man should look when he was making his vows. But Kathleen sensed his pain. When he made his vows, his tone was clipped and cold, not warm and soft like that of a man in love. There was no hint of nervousness, and no sign of pleasure either. His back was stiff and straight, and he held his bride's hand as though it was a necessary duty.

Melinda didn't notice. Too wrapped up in herself, she smiled demurely, and when the service was over, she kissed him the same way.

Christian Westerfield made a handsome best man. He carried out his duty, and, to all those present, he seemed a good son and brother. Maurice had warned him unequivocally that if he did anything to disgrace the family or upset the united front they were presenting to the world, he would cease to be part of that family. And so he carried out his duty with dignity and presence. It was a small price to pay for a life of comfort.

After the formalities, the servants returned to Westerfield House, leaving the gentry to follow at their leisure. 'Can't say the groom looked very happy,' Cook remarked.

'I'm not surprised,' Maisie retorted. 'Who'd want to wed an uppity madam like her?'

'I reckon she's having a bairn,' the scullery maid said. At that everyone was silent, except Cook who instantly reprimanded her.

'That kind of talk will get you in trouble, my girl!' But her anger was mild. The girl was only saying out loud what she herself thought in private.

The reception went on into the evening, with music and dancing and a great deal of wine. Christian drank too much but he managed to remain sober enough to keep his advances to another man's wife reasonably discreet. The young wife was flattered, and her husband remained blissfully unaware of the flirtation, so no ugly scenes disturbed the proceedings.

Kathleen was danced off her feet by two persistent young men and then by Maurice, who was insanely jealous but managed not to show it. While they danced, Murray swept by with Melinda in his arms. Kathleen knew she should look away but couldn't, and his eyes met hers. The longing in them shook her to the core.

There was one forbidden moment of magic when she escaped out into the garden for a breath of fresh air. The relative quiet soothed her frayed nerves. Out here, under a star-decked sky, she could think more clearly. It was such a beautiful evening she decided to stroll to the cherry trees. She stood beneath them, her eyes raised to the sky. 'Help me forget him,' she whispered. The music gentled through the night air, touching her soul, freeing her mind.

Startled by a sound behind her, she swung round, and there he was.

He didn't speak, and neither did she. For a long, anxious moment, they gazed at each other, not sure what to do. Then, stepping forward, he took her in his arms and pressed her close. Looking down on her lovely face, he didn't have to say how much he adored her. There was no need for words. It was there, in his eyes, a love so profound it would last all her life.

They held each other close, and danced, hidden by the trees. When the music was over, he bent his head to hers and kissed her long and tenderly.

Another glance, one more kiss, and the heartfelt whisper, 'I love you, Kathleen. Always remember that.'

She watched him stride away. He turned only once, his gaze searching her out. A warm smile, a look of regret. Then he was gone, back to the celebrations. Back to the woman who was already wondering at his long absence.

Kathleen's stricken eyes followed him to the last. 'Goodbye, my love,' she murmured. Through the window she saw Melinda claim him. 'You belong to her, and the child. As for me,' she smiled through her tears, 'I will miss you for ever.'

━━━━➤●◄━━━━

'I HAVE TO find work,' Kathleen declared, restlessly pacing the kitchen, much to Cook's disapproval. 'But I don't know how, or what I'm capable of.' Right now, anything would do. Anything that would keep her busy and take her mind off Murray and his new bride. They had gone to Venice for their honeymoon. Kathleen couldn't imagine a city with canals instead of roads. It sounded magical. Oh, if only—

'No good asking me,' Cook interrupted her thoughts, dumping kneaded dough on to the table and pushing her bunched fists into it. 'All I know is how to cook and bake, and anyway, what do you want to go working for when you have all you need right here?'

'I know, and I'm thankful for that. But it isn't enough. I need something to occupy my mind.'

'Talk to the master. He'll know best.'

'I've often thought I wouldn't mind learning about the world of merchandising.'

Cook was gently scornful. 'Oh no, miss, you wouldn't want to do that, handling money and suchlike. Best leave that sort of thing to the men.'

'I see,' said Kathleen with a grin, 'you don't think I'm capable, is that it?'

'Now, I never said that. I said it were best to leave such things to the men, and I meant it. Women are for getting wed and bearing children, not sitting at a desk

poring over accounts and chasing after merchandise.'
Thump went the dough as she threw it down again.
'Women ain't made for sailing the seven seas looking
for treasure neither.'

'Maybe not.' Kathleen didn't entirely agree, but
there was little point in arguing with Cook, who always
had the last word.

'No maybe about it.' Eyeing Kathleen with concern, Cook asked tentatively, 'Is there any word from
your brother, miss?'

'No.' Kathleen couldn't help but wonder what she
might do if Adam did get in touch. Rightly or wrongly,
she found it hard to forgive what he had done.

'I expect he's off on some adventure or other. He'll
be back when he's found a fortune.' She pummelled
the dough until the table shook. 'He'll be back before
you know it,' she declared with conviction. 'You see
if I'm not right.'

Kathleen smiled, but inside she was sad. 'I'm
going out. If Mr Westerfield asks after me, would
you tell him I've gone for a walk?'

'Course I will, miss.' Cook flopped the battered
dough into a bowl, where it lay, limp and exhausted.
'A walk will do you good, if you don't mind me saying.'
She draped a cloth over the bowl and then called out
for the scullery maid, who pattered into the kitchen
like a scared rabbit. 'Where the devil have you been?'
Cook demanded.

Smiling to herself, Kathleen crept out. In the
hallway, she collected a shawl and draped it loosely

over her shoulders. She left the house and walked down the lane, towards Ilford High Street; past the White Horse public house, and the butcher's shop next door. Here she hurried her footsteps. The butcher's was a sight to turn her stomach, with its many pig corpses hanging outside, dripping blood on to the pavement and staring at her with big, dead eyes. Poor things, she thought, and hated herself for having enjoyed one of Cook's pork chops last night.

She bought a bobbin of cotton in the draper's, and two ounces of bull's-eyes in the grocer's two doors down. Kathleen had always been partial to bull's-eyes.

Sucking her sweets, she went on towards Valentine's Park, where she often sat and let the world go by.

She wandered over the crooked, rustic bridge and down to the stream. On the bank she sat and stretched out, not caring who might see her. In fact there was no one. She was alone, as she often was in this particular spot. 'Nobody can find me here,' she mused, closing her eyes to the autumn sunshine. 'This is my place. My very own private garden.' For the best part of two hours, she was undisturbed. Lying there, visited only by the birds and the bees, she could have stayed for ever. Eventually though, the daylight faded and evening began to creep in.

'Time to go,' she sighed. She brushed herself down and slowly retraced her steps back to Westerfield House, pausing at the bridge to mull over what she and Cook had talked about earlier. 'It's not a bad idea for me to learn a trade,' she said. 'I'll talk to Maurice this very evening, ask him if he can take me under his wing and show me the world of finance. After all, Adam's natural flair for figures only really came to light when he started working for Maurice.' The idea wouldn't go away. 'Maybe I'll find I'm as good as he is. Why not?'

In the event, she had no chance to discuss it with Maurice that evening. As soon as she entered the house, he came hurrying towards her. 'Kathleen. Oh, thank goodness,' he exclaimed. 'Can you come to the study?'

'Are you all right?' she asked, thinking he looked ill.

'As soon as you can,' he said distractedly, and hurried away, back to his study.

Losing no time, Kathleen hung up her bonnet and shawl and followed him.

'Come in, my dear,' his voice called out when she tapped on the door.

Maurice was seated at his desk, his face grey with worry. On the opposite side of the desk, perched uneasily on the edge of her seat, was Connie Blakeman, her eyes wet with tears, and her face a picture of anxiety.

'Is anything wrong?' Kathleen asked, looking from one to the other. The question seemed foolish; it was painfully obvious that something was dreadfully wrong.

'Sit down, my dear.' He indicated a chair and then turned to Connie. 'Tell me again, please, in front of Miss Peterson.'

Connie played her part well. 'I'm not a liar,' she cried, appealing to Kathleen. 'Everything I've said is the truth.'

'I'm not calling you a liar,' Maurice assured her. 'I just want you to tell me again.'

Wiping her nose on her best linen hankie, Connie sniffed. 'You've been good to me, sir, and it grieves me to bring you such distressing news. But, as I stand before God, I'm telling you the truth. Some weeks back, your son took advantage of me, and now I find I'm carrying his bairn.' She glanced at Kathleen who was staring with shock. 'Miss Peterson knows how ill I was on the day of the wedding, sir. It was her who took me to my room.'

'Is this true, Kathleen?'

'Well, yes. But I didn't know she was . . . I mean . . .' Lost for words, she lowered her gaze. She was shaken by Connie's story. What a terrible thing. And yet, she wasn't surprised that Christian was capable of something like this.

'Nobody knew,' said Connie. 'I wasn't even certain myself until very recently.'

Maurice rubbed a hand over his face. He could confidently lead a board meeting with a dozen or so men in fierce debate and still win the day; he could shake a good deal out of thin air, when the competition was baying at his heels; and there was no ocean he was afraid to cross. But here and now, confronted by a woman accusing his own son of violating her, he was utterly out of his depth.

'I'm truly sorry, sir,' Connie wailed convincingly, 'but it wasn't my fault. I swear on my mother's grave, I did nothing to encourage him.'

Kathleen felt the need to intervene. 'When did all this happen? Have you told Christian you believe you're expecting his child?'

Connie answered in a small voice, looking from one to the other and seeming exhausted by the ordeal. 'I haven't told anybody outside this room. I felt I owed it to the master to speak to him first.'

'And I'm very grateful for that,' he said. Turning to Kathleen, he asked solemnly, 'Could you please find Christian and bring him to me?'

Kathleen was on her feet in an instant. 'Of course,' she said.

When she returned with a puzzled and rather sullen Christian, Kathleen made to leave, but Maurice asked her to stay. Christian resented it but said nothing. As soon as he saw Connie seated there, looking forlorn, he was instantly on his guard. 'What's this all about?' he demanded of his father.

Maurice was blunt. He relayed Connie's claim, and then, in a voice that shook with anger, he asked, 'What have you to say for yourself?'

The row that followed was heard by everyone in the house. Christian vehemently denied the charge, while Connie accused him of creeping up on her that night when she was in the kitchen. 'He tore off my nightgown,' she cried. 'He was drunk out of his mind, and strong as a lion. I didn't stand a chance. I'm ruined.' Falling into Kathleen's arms, she sobbed her heart out. 'He's ruined me,' she said brokenly. 'What will I do now? No man will take my word against his son's.'

'Take her out!' Striding across the room, Maurice flung open the door, his face set like stone. Only when he looked at Connie's face did he soften. 'You're wrong, my dear,' he said. 'No other man has a son as wicked as mine.'

Kathleen took Connie to the drawing room, leaving her there while she went to the kitchen.

'You should have rung through,' Cook chided. 'But then, you never have, so why should you start now?' While Kathleen got a tray ready, Cook set the kettle to boil for tea.

Kathleen could hear Christian's voice, yelling abuse and denying everything. 'I'm sorry you have to hear all that,' she told Cook.

'So am I, miss.' She clicked her teeth. 'Dreadful business, if you don't mind me saying.'

Kathleen picked up the tray and carried it into the drawing room, where she and Connie waited, Kathleen anxiously walking back and forth, Connie noisily gulping her tea and silently congratulating herself.

Suddenly there was a lot of shouting, much closer now. Then a loud, rattling bang. 'Stay here,' Kathleen told Connie. She hurried out of the room and across to the study. The door was wide open, almost split from its hinges where Christian had flung it back in his rage.

Maurice was standing leaning on his desk, his hands spread in front of him. 'He's gone.' Looking up at Kathleen as she came into the room, he seemed like an old, old man. 'I never thought I would have to throw him out. My own son.' He sank into the chair and covered his face with his hands. 'Oh, Kathleen, Kathleen. What else could I do?' Into his mind came the image of his lovely wife, and how they had been a happy family once. Now, in his awful loneliness, only Kathleen gave him a reason for living.

She went to comfort him. 'Don't reproach yourself,' she said softly, putting her arm round his shoulders. 'You did what you felt was right.'

'He admitted it.' His voice was heavy with pain. 'She was telling the truth.'

'I'm sorry.'

'I couldn't turn him out penniless. He may be a weak, useless coward, but he's still my son. I've made him a generous allowance, but if he hasn't got work inside twelve months, he'll get no more. I've told him that. Now it's up to him.' He sighed. 'I'd better speak to her now.'

While Kathleen went to collect Connie, he took the brandy bottle and a glass from the cupboard, poured a small measure and quickly drank it down.

He was not a drinking man, but now and then a small nip took away the heart's chill.

Connie listened while he told her what he had decided. 'In view of the fact that my son reluctantly admitted his part, and Kathleen witnessed how ill you were, I've decided not to submit you to a medical examination.'

'I should think not!' she spluttered. 'I want no man, medical or otherwise, putting his hands on me.'

'I shall make one, generous, single payment, to see you through until the child is born. After that, there will be an adequate allowance. However, I will not leave myself vulnerable to blackmail by any—'

'Never, sir!'

'And to that effect, you will be required to sign a document, drawn up by my solicitor.'

'Yes, sir.'

'As for the child, he or she will be my own flesh and blood but I shall be the one to decide whether or not I want to make contact. Do you understand?'

'Yes, sir.' Pity. She wanted him to be the loving, generous grandfather all his life, and maybe leave a hefty legacy when he was gone.

'At this point, I have no wish to see or hear of the child.' He glanced at Kathleen, who was visibly surprised by this. 'I've been disappointed enough in my own children.' He squared his shoulders and suddenly he was a man of authority again, tall and straight, his face expressionless. 'You must make no attempt to contact any member of this family, or let it be known to anyone who the father of your child is. Before I make a settlement on you and the child, I must have your agreement on that.'

Connie's quick mind calculated that, in the end, she might be better off doing it his way. 'How will I know the child and myself will always be cared for?'

'The document my solicitor will draw up will be legally binding on both of us. You and the child will be provided for all your lives as long as you keep to the terms I've outlined.'

'I'm very grateful, sir.'

His manner softened. 'So you agree to the terms?' She nodded. 'Then I suggest you leave this house as soon as arrangements can be made. Say nothing to the servants. They may guess, but if we all keep our silence, no one will ever know for certain.'

Kathleen was concerned that any woman should be left to bear and rear a child alone. 'Will you be all right?' she asked Connie as she prepared to leave the house two days later.

Connie was humbled by her kindness. 'After the way I've behaved towards you in the past, I'm surprised you don't want me kicked out and left on the streets.'

'I wouldn't want that for anyone.' Kathleen knew what it was like not to have a home and to search the streets for a roof. 'Take care of yourself,' she said as she waved her off, a small, pretty woman whose rage at the world was now tempered by the knowledge that soon enough she would be the sole person responsible for another human being, her own child, and because of the honourable generosity of her child's grandfather they would never want.

<hr />

IN THE WEEKS that followed, Maurice learned to smile again, but he had lost some of his self-confidence, and he felt his age keenly. It seemed almost as if fate frowned on him, and he held back from declaring his love to Kathleen although his dream of marrying her remained undimmed.

Kathleen talked to him about learning the business of merchandising, and he was delighted. 'A woman in the business,' he laughed. 'It might raise a few eyebrows.' But he loved the idea, especially since it meant they would spend more time together. 'I have an important business meeting in Liverpool next week. Come with me, Kathleen.'

Thrilled, she accepted. This would be her first real introduction to the world of business.

But fate, yet again, intervened.

The morning before they were due to leave, Maurice came to her in the garden. Kathleen knew from the look on his face that something was wrong. 'What is it?' she asked nervously. 'Tell me.'

He took hold of her hand. 'It's Adam,' he said. 'I've just got news.'

From the kitchen window the servants saw him

relay the news. 'God help us,' Cook sobbed, 'if it ain't one thing it's another.'

'Maybe he ain't drowned,' Maisie said hopefully. 'Maybe they've got it all wrong.'

The butler intervened. Shifting them from the window, he said quietly, 'They haven't got it wrong. The ship went down in treacherous seas, that's what the master told me before he went outside. "The ship was lost, and everyone with it. Including Adam Peterson. His name was on the passenger list."'

It was the worst week of Kathleen's life. Maurice set in train investigations, gleaning information from every possible source. Eight days after the initial news, official confirmation came through that the ship, bound for New York, had broken apart in a storm and sunk, taking every soul on board with her.

Unable to eat or sleep, Kathleen saw it as a punishment for her unforgiving anger towards her brother. In her mind's eye she saw his face, the way he used to laugh, the way he would look at her as a child when she'd done something wrong. At the service held in the local church, her grief was crippling.

One day ran into another, and when there was nothing to distract her, the quiet was unbearable. She walked a lot, and kept to herself. She cried herself to sleep, and in her every waking moment she cursed herself for being so wrapped in herself and Murray's sudden appearance that she had not seen how deeply troubled Adam was. And so he had gone without a word of love, or forgiveness. She imagined his loneliness, and her own was tenfold.

Maurice's heart ached for her. He knew she needed time and space to come to terms with her loss on her own, without interference from him. But he cancelled all business trips and made sure he was never far from her, should she need him.

One warm October evening, she was strolling in the garden and caught sight of him at the drawing-room window, watching her. He smiled and waved to her. To his joy she beckoned to him to join her, and at last she spoke to him of her feelings, her sense of guilt. 'Adam knew I would never forgive him, that's why he went away. If it hadn't been for me, he would never have gone.'

'You know that's not true.'

'How can you say that?' She looked at him, and suddenly she realised what he meant. He knew. He had known all along.

'Your brother was always in love with Melinda,' he said softly. 'I knew that, and so did you.'

She gulped back the tears. 'But he left thinking I would hate him, and now he's never coming back.'

Gently, Maurice took hold of her hand. It was cold. Cradling it between his own, he fed back the warmth. 'I have no doubt your reaction to the knowledge that he had deceived you about Murray was something he did not relish having to face, but the truth is, Adam was driven from this house because of his love for Melinda. I don't believe he would have

379

stayed even if you'd gone down on your knees and pleaded with him. You see, my dear, love is a powerful thing. I know.'

Something about the way he spoke made her ask, 'Are you lonely too?'

'Yes, I am.'

'Why have you never married again?' She shivered, and he put his arm round her and drew her close.

'You're cold, my dear. Do you want to go inside?'

'Not yet.' She felt warm in his arms, safe, protected from the outside world. 'You still haven't told me.' She moved in his arms. 'Why have you never married again?'

The moment seemed to go on for ever. He gazed down on that small upturned face and those lovely dark eyes, and his love for her was like a beacon inside him. 'Why do you think?' he murmured. All his need rose up in him, and it seemed so natural to lean forward and kiss her. When his mouth touched hers, it was as if his very soul took flight. He kissed her with all the love and tenderness of a man who would cherish and protect her always. 'Marry me, Kathleen.' Drawing away, he held her face between the palms of his hands. 'I won't ever let you down.'

She started to tell him, 'I'm not in love . . . with . . .'

'Don't say it,' he whispered. 'All that matters is that we're two very lonely people. We can stay that way, or we can make each other happy. Please, Kathleen. Will you say yes?'

'Yes,' she murmured. 'If you think I can make you happy.'

Overcome with emotion, he raised his head and looked to the sky, giving a silent prayer of thanks. When he looked at her again, he was smiling like a man at peace. 'You've made me happy since the first moment I saw you,' he said brokenly. 'And I've loved you . . . all my life.'

Kathleen didn't fully understand what he was saying. She saw the love in his eyes, and it warmed her. Murray was beyond her reach. Adam was gone for ever. She had no close friends and the loneliness stretched before her like a never-ending road. Maurice was all she had in the world, and he needed her. He loved her. She owed it to him, and to herself, to give back some of the happiness he had given her.

Strangely content, Kathleen nestled into his arms. She vowed to heal the wounds his own children had inflicted on him. She would be a good wife and, if there should be children, she would be a good mother.

At last, she had a worthwhile purpose.

PART FIVE

1892
THE
PRODIGALS

Chapter Sixteen

THE SCENE WAS one of domestic bliss.

On this balmy summer's evening, the windows were open wide to let in the cool night air and the chink of crystal heralded a celebration. 'Happy birthday, Kathleen, my love.' Raising his glass, Maurice drank a toast. 'To the woman who made me the happiest man on God's earth.'

Kathleen smiled. 'You're a very easy man to please.'

'No.' He shook his head. 'That's where you're wrong. Only you could have made my life complete.' He gazed on her with deepest love. 'Forty-two years old, and still the most beautiful woman I've ever seen.' The idea that his first wife might live on through Kathleen was long ago forgotten. Each of them was lovely. Each of them gentle and kind, but so very different.

'You flatter me,' she chided, a little embarrassed. 'Only this morning I found two grey hairs.' She laughed. 'I plucked them out so you wouldn't see them.'

He smiled. It was said that some women never

realised their own special beauty. Kathleen was such a woman. He looked at her now. She had worn the years well. Her skin glowed with health, and her long dark hair shone as it did on the day he found her. The neck was firm, the dark eyes soft and wondrous, like those of a child. She carried her sadness deep down and never spoke of it. There shone from her face only a kind of contentment, and every day, every moment he was with her, he never forgot how fortunate a man he was.

For a moment Kathleen observed him across the table. Though only in his early sixties and working harder than ever, Maurice had grown old before her eyes. Still tall and handsome, still possessing a certain commanding presence, he had become slightly stooped at the shoulders, his hair was marbled with grey, and to her observant eyes his attractive face showed signs of stress. Though he never burdened her with his troubles, Kathleen knew he was saddened by the absence of his children and weary of the demands of his work.

'Are you tired?' she asked, hoping he might say no.

'No. You?'

'I'm too excited for sleep.'

He walked the length of the table and taking her by the hand led her to the fireplace, where he sat on the couch. Kathleen sat by his feet, as she often did. 'It's been a lovely day, Maurice.' She fingered the pearls round her neck. 'Such a beautiful present. Thank you.'

'Kathleen.'

She looked up.

'If I ask you something,' leaning over, he kissed the top of her head, 'will you be honest with me?'

'I always am.' But then he had never asked her the kind of questions where she might feel the need to deceive him.

There was a moment while he wondered if he should broach a subject so close to both their hearts. But tonight for some reason he couldn't fathom he needed to know if he had failed her in any way.

Inexplicably, Kathleen suddenly felt afraid. 'What's wrong, Maurice?'

'Nothing's wrong,' he assured her. 'I was just thinking.'

'About us?'

'Do you ever regret not having children?' There. It was said.

Stunned by his question, and wondering what had brought it on, Kathleen gazed into the empty fire grate. She didn't answer right away because she didn't want to make him feel guilty. Yes, she would have loved children, but they weren't to be. It was a bitter disappointment.

'I'm sorry.' Mortified, he drew her close. 'I should never have asked you.'

She looked up then. 'You have every right to ask me,' she told him. 'But why now? We've been married for over twenty years and you've never asked it before.'

'I had to know,' he answered simply. 'Don't ask me why, but I feel the need to know if I've failed you.'

Her smile was convincing. 'You haven't,' she lied. This was the first time she had ever deliberately deceived him. It gave her no pleasure. 'What about you? Do you regret we never had children?'

'Children can be a blessing,' he admitted. 'They can also be heartache.' He shook his head. 'All I've ever wanted is to make you happy.'

'And you have,' she said. Her assurance was all he needed.

They were quiet for a time, he leaning forward with his arms round her neck and his head close to hers; and she with her long legs stretched out over the rug, her hands enclosed in his, and a feeling of contentment filling her soul.

'I wanted it all to be so perfect for you.' There was a sense of urgency in his voice.

'What is it, Maurice?' Scrambling up, she sat beside him. 'You sound so strange, as if it's all going to end tomorrow. Something's worrying you. Is it work? Is it because you lost the shipment you so desperately wanted?'

'No. I did want that cargo of silk, but it wasn't the first and it won't be the last. I've come to accept I can't win all the time, and lately I've been thinking of taking a year off.' He chucked her under the chin.

'Maybe we'll sail round the world, what do you say to that?'

'I say if you haven't got your work, you'll be lost.'

'Ah, but there isn't the excitement like there used to be. Or the opportunities. In the old days I could buy a shipload of tobacco in the morning and sell it on in the afternoon for twice what I paid. You know that. You saw it for yourself – before you decided it wasn't the kind of work you wanted and took yourself off to do voluntary work at the hospital.'

Kathleen recognised his evasive tactics. 'Is it Christian?' she persisted. 'Have you heard from him? Is he in trouble? Is that what's worrying you?' Strange how when she thought of Christian, she always assumed he was either in trouble or causing trouble.

'I haven't heard from Christian since the day I threw him out. If I never hear from him again, it won't lose me any sleep.'

'What about Melinda? You miss her, don't you?'

He bowed his head. Then, as if winning a fight within himself, he sat up, straightened his shoulders and answered with conviction, 'If she chooses to move to the other side of the world, there is nothing I can do about it.'

'It's my fault she went away. If I hadn't said yes when you asked me to marry you, she would still be here.' Their wedding had been a very quiet affair. Neither of his children attended the service. Rumours reached them that Christian was sinking deeper and deeper into a seedy world of crime and as for Melinda, she persuaded Murray to accept a post overseas, in Australia, as far away as she could take her husband and son.

Kathleen suspected that Murray had needed little persuasion. On the day Maurice told them that he and Kathleen were to be married, she had seen the pain on Murray's face. And she felt in her heart she would never see him again.

'I offered Murray a good position in the business, but he turned it down,' Maurice recalled. 'I know she was behind that, and I know it was her who stopped me from seeing my grandson.'

'It's him you really miss, isn't it? Not so much Melinda but David, your grandson.'

Torn between love and fear, he didn't know how to answer. 'I'm not sure if he should be anywhere near me.'

'You're too hard on yourself.'

Maurice didn't think so. 'What if he turns out to be like Christian? What if he has the same selfish tendencies as his mother? I don't know where I went wrong but for both my children to turn out the way they did, it must have been my fault.' There was anger in his voice. 'I sometimes wonder if David even knows he's got a grandfather. Perhaps his mother has told him I'm a monster to be avoided at all costs, or that I'm dead. David was only a baby when they sailed away. He'll be almost twenty-four now, and he probably doesn't even know I exist.'

Kathleen was shocked. All these years he had never once spoken so openly about his grandson, or so bitterly. 'You never told me how strongly you feel about this. Write to your grandson,' she urged him. 'Tell him how much you want to see him.'

'And have her come between us? I'd rather he never knew me than got caught between the two of us. I don't want to be the one who causes him to choose between his grandfather and his mother. And she would make him choose, make no mistake about that.'

'He's your grandson, Maurice. He has a right to know. Why don't you find out exactly where they are? You know they settled in Melbourne. With your contacts it shouldn't be too hard to find them.' Briefly she wondered about that other grandchild, Connie's son – or was it a daughter? It troubled her, not knowing how mother and child had fared, or even if they were alive. As far as she knew, Maurice had made no attempt to find out, although presumably his solicitor, who was responsible for ensuring the allowance was paid, could have told him. Maurice never mentioned the subject, and Kathleen did not feel it was her place to probe.

Maurice seemed to be considering her suggestion, and she was glad. He was such a good man, he deserved to have the love of one grandchild at least, and maybe, just maybe, that young man might be the means of bringing the family back together again.

She smiled to herself. That young man – Murray's

son. Was he like his father? Did he have the same wayward fair hair and warm green eyes? Did he smile in a way that touched your heart? Was he quick to laugh, and did he have a mischievous twinkle in his eyes?

'I'm tired, my dear.' Maurice's voice shattered her thoughts. 'You don't have to come up if you don't want to.' He stood up. 'It's been a long day, and I'm not as young as I used to be.' In that moment he looked years older than his age. 'Shall I ask Cook to send you in a hot drink?'

'No, thank you. I'll just sit here awhile.'

'Goodnight then, my dear.' He held out his arms and she went to him. They kissed, a gentle, loving kiss. 'You've given me so much,' he murmured, 'and I've given you so little.' He cradled her face in his hands. 'Sometimes I fear I stole you from life. So young. So innocent. I wouldn't blame you if you resented me for it.'

Kathleen couldn't understand his melancholy mood. 'I could never resent you,' she said fiercely. 'You and I have given each other contentment and love. We made each other happy, and we've been good companions over the years. It was what we both wanted. Please, Maurice, don't regret what we've had together.'

'I don't think you'll ever know how much I love you,' he whispered. He kissed her again and left the room.

It was one o'clock in the morning when she

climbed the stairs to bed. These days, Maurice slept in his own room, but she always went in to kiss him goodnight before she crossed the landing to her own room.

She went in now, tiptoeing across the room so as not to wake him. 'Goodnight,' she whispered. 'Sleep tight.' He stirred, glanced up, and smiled. 'And you're wrong,' she said. 'I *do* know how much you love me.'

'God bless you, Kathleen,' he murmured.

It was when she went to close the door behind her that Kathleen sensed something different. She stared across the room to where he lay, and suddenly, like the gossamer wings of an angel in flight, there came the softest, most beautiful sigh. It was unnerving, making every hair on her neck stand on end.

Instinctively, she hurried back to him. 'Maurice?' She looked into his face, and she knew instantly. 'Oh, no! Dear God, *no!*' Falling on the bed, she took him in her arms, rocking him back and forth, her cries filling the house.

Maurice had gone. And she was all alone.

———⟶⬥⟵———

THE HEAVENS OPENED and it poured with rain on the day they buried Maurice Westerfield.

The news of his departure from this world had spread far and wide. People from all walks of life came to pay their last respects. 'Maurice Westerfield was a pillar of our community,' the vicar told his congregation. 'He was a respected businessman and a kind soul who cared for his friends and servants with equal compassion.'

His gaze fell on Kathleen who was seated in the family pew, head bowed and veil down to hide her red, raw eyes. 'Our thoughts and love go out to his widow and family,' the vicar concluded. He closed his prayer book and led the procession behind the coffin as it was carried on the shoulders of four strong men to its last resting place.

Kathleen came next, then Maurice's son and daughter. His grandson walked sedately with his father, two men out of the same pod. David was the same build as his father, with the same long, easy stride; the same green eyes and wayward hair. Kathleen had not noticed. She had been aware of very little since Maurice was taken from her.

As they walked in silence, huddled under their umbrellas, the sound of the rain seemed to echo their grief.

When the prayer was said, and the earth sprinkled, they made their way back. Kathleen climbed into her carriage alone, while Christian accompanied his sister and her family. 'She's beautiful,' David remarked. Like his father, he had not been able to take his eyes off Kathleen.

They followed her now, the carriages moving slowly, respectfully. 'Why was I not told about her?' David asked his mother. 'Why did I never get to meet my grandfather?'

'This is not the time.' The years in Australia had done nothing to dim Melinda's jealousy and resentment of Kathleen. In fact her bitterness had grown in proportion to her disillusion with her empty marriage to Murray, until now she hated her with a passion so strong she could taste it.

'You never told me I had a grandfather. Why, Mother? Why was I not told?'

Murray intervened. 'Not now, David,' he said in a firm voice, his eyes flickering a warning. 'Like your mother said, this is not the time.'

At the house, everyone gathered round Kathleen, offering their condolences, comforting her with their fond memories of Maurice.

At a distance, Christian and his sister stood in a corner, talking in whispers and occasionally glancing in Kathleen's direction. When she looked up and caught their gaze, she smiled at them sadly, thinking that at least in their common grief they could be united. But her smile was not returned. Nor did they seem too grief-stricken. In fact, at one point Melinda let out a peal of laughter, drawing astonished looks from everyone there and a sharp, private rebuke from her husband.

When the formalities were over, Murray brought his son to meet her. 'This is David,' he said proudly. He stood back while his son stepped forward.

'He's so like you,' Kathleen said, and her heart was broken all over again.

Holding out his hand, David said warmly, 'It

isn't the best way for us to meet, but I'm very glad to know you.'

'Thank you,' she said. 'And I'm very glad to know you.'

While she and David talked, about Australia, about the grandfather he had never known, Murray could not take his eyes off her. Seeing her now was like a knife through his heart. He devoured her beauty, her presence, her every word like a man starved for too long.

After a time, the guests began to leave, forming a little queue to wish Kathleen and the family the best for the future.

All this time, the servants had been weaving in and out, doing their duty and hiding their sadness. Now, however, they returned to their own private places, quietly shedding their tears for a man they had loved and respected, and wondering what would happen to them, and to the mistress.

'That Christian,' said Maisie unhappily, 'he told his sister that the mistress wouldn't get a penny. "If she thinks she's getting his fortune, she can think again." That's what he said.'

'You're not to carry gossip, my girl!' Cook warned. 'You heard nothing, do you hear? You heard nothing!'

Maisie went off in a huff, but when she'd gone, Cook told the butler, 'I've never known that girl to tell a lie. If she's right, and I'm certain she is, the mistress had better watch out for them two grabbing buggers!'

The butler was inclined to agree. 'There's bad feelings, running deep,' he muttered. 'If I know them two from old, they'll show their hand sooner or later.'

———◆◆◆———

THEY SHOWED THEIR hand the very next evening, when the solicitor came to read the will. After outlining some minor bequests, he came to the bulk of the estate and the Westerfield fortune: 'Three thousand guineas to my son Christian; the same amount to my daughter Melinda. My grandson David is to have my collection of silver sailing ships, and the sum of one thousand guineas, to be invested until he reaches the age of thirty. To his father, Murray, with my thanks and gratitude, I leave my coveted chess set.'

The solicitor looked up, his stern gaze travelling over the faces of those present. 'Now, to the bulk of the estate,' he said. 'As directed by the will of Maurice Westerfield, it goes in its remaining entirety to his widow Kathleen.'

'No!' Melinda was instantly on her feet and accusing Kathleen. 'Cunning bitch! You did this! You got him to turn against his own family. It's our money! Mine and my brother's.'

Incensed by her outburst, Murray leaped up and grabbed her by the shoulders. 'Get a hold of yourself,' he muttered, desperate to retain some kind of dignity. 'You don't know what you're saying.'

'She knows what she's saying right enough, and so do I.' Christian launched himself at Murray, sending him stumbling to the ground. 'I've seen you making eyes at that bitch. Is it *her* you want, or are you after getting your paws on my father's money?'

As Murray tried to get up, Christian knocked him down again with a vicious kick to the stomach. 'Want to fight, do you? Come on then!' He was about to land another kick but this time Murray was too quick for him. Grabbing his ankle, he tossed Christian aside.

'There'll be no fighting here.' Murray picked him up and held him by the scruff of the neck. 'Do you understand?'

Kathleen stepped forward, her eyes hard and unforgiving as she told Christian, 'You're a disgrace to your father's memory. All his life you caused him sorrow, and now that he's dead you tarnish his memory. Get out. And don't ever come back.'

He clenched his fists and tried to move towards her, but Murray still held him fast. 'You heard what she said,' he growled.

'Oh, I heard what she said right enough,' Christian sneered. 'I'll go, and gladly. I can't stand the sight of her. But you haven't heard the last of me.' Glaring at Kathleen, he told her in a trembling voice, 'None of this is yours.' Opening wide his arms, he embraced the house and land, a wicked smile creasing his face. 'Be on your guard, *Mrs Westerfield*.' He spoke her name as though it was a curse. 'I *will* be back, and when I am, *you'll* be the one thrown out of the house, for good.'

Melinda moved towards him. 'Go away, Christian,' she said. 'You shame us both.'

Shocked, he glanced up. He saw the look in her eyes and, without another word, took his leave.

Kathleen was grateful for her intervention, and for Murray's. 'Thank you,' she said to them both. 'I'm sorry it had to come to this.'

'No,' Melinda was kindness itself, 'it's us who should be sorry.' Turning her blue eyes on Murray, she said, 'Please, take me back to the hotel.'

'You know you don't have to stay in a hotel,' Kathleen said. 'I've told you, you're more than welcome to stay here with me.' It would be nice to have company. She might even get to tell David more about his grandfather.

Melinda graciously refused. They quickly left, with Murray giving a backward glance as he climbed into the carriage.

'Goodbye, Murray,' Kathleen whispered. 'It seems we're destined to be always parting.'

The following morning David asked his parents to take him into London and show him the sights. 'I've never been there,' he reminded them, 'and you've told me so much about it.'

Murray was delighted, but Melinda begged off. 'I had a mind to do some shopping here in Ilford before we go back,' she said. 'I need a new hat, and

my blue jacket is way past its best. You go ahead. I'll
see you both when you get back.'

'If you're sure.' Murray had grown used to her
impulsive whims and fancies.

'Of course I'm sure,' she said, kissing them in
turn. 'You know I always like to shop on my own.'

The two men left, Murray's arm draped over his
son's broad shoulders. 'Right, son, where would you
like to go first?'

'The docks,' came the immediate reply. 'I want
to see where you and Grandfather started out.'

Once the men were out of the way, Melinda
took a carriage to the far side of Ilford. After giving
the driver an address, she settled back to renew
her acquaintance with all the sights and sounds
of the town; past the old post office, down Barley
Lane; along Oakfield Road where the authorities had
earmarked a site for Ilford's first fire station, then out
to the edge of town where the driver manoeuvred his
carriage down a narrow street. Flanked either side
by rows of terraced houses, the street was loud with
playing children. Mothers watched from a distance,
babes at their feet, and tattered shawls round their
shoulders.

Bringing his carriage to a halt, the driver jumped
down to open the door for his well-dressed passenger.
'Are you sure this is the right address?' he asked. 'It
doesn't seem the sort of place a lady like yourself
should be visiting.'

Ignoring his comment, she gave him a steely

glare. 'Wait here,' she instructed, going at a smart pace towards number twelve.

'Get orf, yer buggers!' The driver ran at a number of ragged children who were stroking his horse. 'I don't want him catching no bleedin' fleas from the likes o' you lot.'

Inside the house, Melinda held a handkerchief over her nose. 'How can you live in a place like this?'

'Don't you come here with your high and bloody mighty ways,' he warned. 'I'm living here because I've got nowhere else to live.' He swaggered across the room. 'But don't worry, soon I'll be living in splendour. I'll have servants and a carriage and all the booze and women I want.'

'You're drunk.' Disgusted, she wafted the smell away. 'I thought we agreed there'd be no more drinking until it's settled.'

'I've only had one, to settle my nerves, that's all.'

'Make it the last, until all this is over.'

'Trust me.'

'I've got no choice. I can't be seen to be involved. Murray would never stand for it. Neither would David, come to that.'

'I'll need money. If I have to consort with solicitors and suchlike, I'll need to look the part.'

Digging into her bag, Melinda took out a fat wad of notes. 'This should be enough to begin with.' She flung the money on the table. 'You'll

JOSEPHINE COX

have all you need, but keep your mouth shut and stay sober.'

'She's really got under your skin, hasn't she?' Sneering, Christian grabbed up the money. 'Is it just because she married Father and cheated us out of our inheritance, or have you got it in for her because Murray looks at her the way he's never looked at you?'

Her face went white, and for a moment he thought she might hurl herself at him. Instead, she came a step closer, her eyes boring into his.

'*Ruin her!*' Her voice was quiet, shivering with emotion. 'I don't care how you do it, or how many years it takes.' She paused. 'I want her left with nothing but the clothes she stands up in.'

Chapter Seventeen

'THEY'RE HERE!' Red-faced and anxious, Maisie came rushing into the kitchen. 'I've shown them into the drawing room.'

'How many?' Like everyone else, the butler thought it was a sorry business but there was nothing he could do about it.

'Four of 'em.' Maisie counted on her fingers. 'There was the awful Christian, a lady friend of his, and two men in dark suits and bowler hats.'

Cook gasped. 'They'll be the bailiffs, may God forgive 'em!'

The impact of what was about to take place sent the strength from her legs. 'I'll have to sit down,' she said, dropping into the rocking chair. 'I can't believe it's come to this. It's been four years since the master died, and she's not had a minute's peace in all that time.'

The butler stood with his hands behind his back, staring out of the window at the two parked carriages. 'I wonder what's going on in there,' he mused.

'You know very well what's going on,' Cook exclaimed. 'The same thing that's been going on these past four years. Right from the start, Christian Westerfield was determined to get his claws on this place, and every penny the master left. Anybody who's followed the court cases and read the newspaper articles knows that.'

Maisie peered through the window. 'Who are all those folk gathering outside?' she cried. 'What do they want?'

'News travels fast round these parts,' Cook said with satisfaction. 'The local shopkeepers and trades-men want to send her on her way with their good will, that's what they want. They all know what a disgrace it is. That good lady in there is besieged by them that aren't fit to wipe her boots. And them folk outside are waiting to show their displeasure.'

They didn't have to wait long.

'She's coming!' Maisie had been peering through the door and now she slammed it shut and ran to stand beside Cook. 'She's got 'er bags packed and everything, and she did it all by herself.'

'Course she did.' Cook's ample bosom rose with pride. 'She were never one to be waited on hand and foot, weren't Miss Kathleen. Sometimes I think she's more one of us than one o' them.'

'Aye, and it's them who's turned on her, damn their souls to hell and back.' The butler was not one for strong words but at this particular moment he felt like a fighting man.

When the door opened they all stood to attention. 'Sit down, please.' Leaving her bags outside, Kathleen came in and closed the door. 'Is there a cup of tea going begging?' she asked, and Cook had one in front of her in no time at all.

'Bless you, ma'am,' she said, wiping the tears from her eyes. 'Whatever will yer do?'

'I'll find work, and I'll do very well, I'm sure. There's no need for you to worry either. I've fought hard for you to keep your positions here. The solicitors and I have come to an agreement. Your jobs are safe.'

'How can we ever thank yer?'

'No need for thanks.' Kathleen was just grateful that she had been able to insist on that small clause.

Before she departed, the butler told her how sad they were to see her go in such a spiteful manner. 'The place won't be the same without you here.'

'Thank you,' said Kathleen simply. 'I shall miss you all.'

When she emerged from the house carrying a large tapestry bag in one hand and a small portmanteau in the other, a great cheer went up. 'You don't deserve to be thrown out of your own house and home!' they yelled. 'Shame on them that did it to yer.'

As she went down the drive, head high and heart full, they called after her, 'God bless yer!' Cries of encouragement and anger followed her to the gates. Here she turned, her stricken eyes going over the house and the grounds, the home where she and Maurice had spent so many happy years together.

In the autumn she had planted narcissus and daffodil in the flower urns outside the front door. Now, in the warmth of spring, the shoots could be clearly seen from where she stood.

'Goodbye, Maurice.' She raised her eyes and found herself looking straight into the triumphant face of Christian Westerfield. 'Badness never prospers,' she whispered.

With that, she went on her way. Out of the past and into the future, with only a few personal belongings. And the clothes she stood up in.

When she was lost from sight, her enemies began to disperse. The woman went off to roam the house. One of the men hurried to the carriage, anxious to escape the baying crowd. The second man remained behind, huddled in a deep and furtive conversation with Christian Westerfield.

'You're to follow her wherever she goes,' Christian instructed him, just as he himself had been instructed, by Melinda. 'You're to spoil every chance she has of work or lodgings. You'll hound her, day and night, until she has no friends, nor reason for living.'

'By! Yer asking me to ruin 'er!'

'Does that bother you? Because if it does, I'll get somebody else.'

'No, it don't bother me. As long as yer make it worth me while.'

Christian thrust a roll of banknotes into his sweaty palm. 'That's more money than you could earn in a year. If I'm satisfied with your work, you'll get more.'

The man grinned wickedly. 'Oh, you'll be satisfied, I can promise yer that, guv. She'll come up against all kinds of obstacles. When she thinks she's sailing before the wind, I'll set up a storm to send her down, and when she seems to be striding too far ahead, I'll put the skids under her. Everywhere she turns, there'll be bad luck and misfortune. There'll be no let-up.' Feeling bold, he nudged Christian, sniggering into his face. 'I reckon that should do the trick, don't you, guv?'

'Oh, yes,' Christian murmured. 'I think that should do it.'

Mutually satisfied, they parted company.

Christian lingered on the front step, watching as the people began to drift away. 'This is a good day's work,' he told his woman when she came to him. 'It makes a man feel good to know he's done something worthwhile.' Melinda would have been proud of him, he thought. It was one favour in return for another. She would not press for her share of the inheritance if he did as she asked. Ruining the lovely Kathleen seemed to be all she wanted.

Chapter Eighteen

ROSIE MAITLAND SAT back in her chair, the old lady's diary open on the desk before her. Her eyes were sore from reading in the gaslight but, like last night and every other night she'd been on night duty in the hospital, she felt compelled to finish the chronicles of the old lady who seemed destined to end her days here in a charity ward.

'Nurse Maitland!' Matron's soldierly voice startled her. 'Reading again?' She would have peered at the diary, but Rosie was too quick. Snatching it up, she rammed it into her apron pocket.

'Sorry, Matron,' she gasped. 'I was just about to do the rounds. Everything's quiet so far. Nothing to report.'

'Good.'

'Matron?'

'Yes, what is it?'

'She won't suffer, will she?' Rosie glanced down the ward. 'The old lady, I mean.'

'According to Dr Naylor, she'll probably just sink quietly away. Her injuries are slowly mending but she seems to have lost the will to live.' She marched briskly towards the door. 'Get on, nurse,' she whispered harshly. 'Get on.'

Rosie's first call was to Kathleen who was sleeping soundly. 'I don't understand,' she whispered. 'Maurice Westerfield was a rich and powerful man who adored the ground you walked on.' She observed the sleeping face; not young any more, but still a proud and lovely face. 'What happened to you? If you had all that, and the love of a good man, how in God's name could you have come to this?'

She finished her rounds and went back to her desk. Here she sat, watching Kathleen from a distance, and wishing she had known her when she was younger. 'What a life you've lived,' she murmured. 'What a tragic, exciting life. So many relationships of one kind or another, and yet here you are, all alone at the end.' It was difficult for her to accept. 'What happened?' she muttered. 'What happened to you, Kathleen Peterson?'

'Talking to yourself, are you?' The hours had passed and now the new shift was starting. 'That's a real bad habit, Rosie Maitland. Some people might think you were going out of your mind.'

'Maybe I am.' She prepared to leave. 'Miss Leatherhead wet the bed twice,' she reported.

The other nurse wrinkled her nose. 'From the smell wafting down the ward now, I'd say she's done a bit more than that.'

'She must have seen you coming,' Rosie laughed. 'It serves you right for confiscating her knitting yesterday.'

'She could have hurt herself with those needles, you know that.'

'Tell her, not me.' Swinging away, Rosie chuckled, 'I'm off to my bed.'

Normally the walk home took her only ten minutes at a brisk pace, but tonight she loitered, thinking about Kathleen. 'I can't understand it,' she kept saying. 'Where are they now? All the people she knew. Why have they deserted her?'

As usual when she got home, he was waiting. As usual, he wanted to row. Afterwards, he wanted to make up and use her in the same old way. 'No!' She was done with all that. 'Not tonight,' she told him, 'I'm too tired.' Sick and tired of *him*, that was the truth.

'Sod you, then!' Grabbing his clothes, he stormed out of the room.

'Good shuts to you.' Rosie settled down to sleep.

But she couldn't sleep. 'I have to find out what happened,' she decided. 'Maybe there's something I can do to help Kathleen. There must be somebody, somewhere, who still cares what happens to her.'

With that in mind, she took up the diary and began leafing through it. As she did so, she made notes. Names. Places. Anything and everything that might help her unravel the mystery. The hospital owed her some holiday and the ward wasn't too busy at the moment. It might end up being a complete waste of time, but she couldn't let Kathleen just fade away in hospital without doing something to try and track down a relative or friend.

    —————>◦<—————

ROSIE HAD NEVER been to Blackpool before. Fascinated by the wide promenade and glittering sea, she leaned over the balustrade. It was a beautiful spring day. The sun was on her face and the wind in her hair. Here, in this place, the hospital seemed a million miles away. So did her husband, and what a blessed relief that was. He thought she was staying with her sister in Cleethorpes. She'd told him Dora had been taken suddenly ill and she had to go to her. He'd been so taken aback by her spirited insistence, he'd hardly argued. It made her wonder why she hadn't done it before. In fact, it made her wonder why she shouldn't do it again, for good. Serve the bugger right if she just up and walked out on him.

She watched the many children playing on the sands. 'This is where Kathleen came as a girl,' she mused. 'This is where Markham brought her and Adam, and now here am I, trying to piece her life together.'

Turning round, she looked up and down the front. All the buildings looked the same: three storeys, bow windows with pretty curtains, and a narrow flight of steps leading up to each front door.

She consulted her notebook. 'If my instincts are right, Mabel's place should be around here.' She walked the length of the promenade and back again.

In Kathleen's notes there was no address. Only a description, and a mention of the windmill.

Deciding to ask for help, she went into a quaint little teashop that straddled a busy corner. It had two entrances, frilled nets at the windows and clean white tablecloths. 'Tea, please,' she told the elderly waitress. 'And a buttered scone.'

When the refreshment was delivered, Rosie asked, 'I don't suppose you know of a man by the name of Mr Mason, do you? He has a small hotel round these parts. There's a wife who used to be cook at a big house, and a young woman by the name of Nancy.'

'I'm not sure,' the woman answered. 'There was a family at number fourteen, used to take in guests. I've a feeling they were called Mason but I can't be certain. It don't really matter anyway, being as he died, oh, years since. His wife went soon after.'

This was a blow to Rosie. She hadn't anticipated that Mabel and John Mason might not be alive any more. She should have thought of it, though; they weren't young when they took on the hotel, and that was more than fifty years ago.

'And their names were Mason?'

The waitress scratched her chin. 'I think so, yes. And now I come to think of it, there *was* another woman, but I don't know as how she's young. More like in her sixties now, I'd say. Funny little thing an' all. Kept herself to herself after the other two passed on. Might have passed on as well, for all I know, or gone from the area altogether.' She shrugged her shoulders. 'Folk come and go,' she said casually. 'Can't keep track of 'em.'

'In her sixties, you say?' It sounded about right. Nancy must have been what? Eight, nine years older than Kathleen?

Rosie finished her tea and made her way to number fourteen. The house looked very much as she might have expected, but more downtrodden. The curtains were grimy and the door panels painted with dust. The whole place looked ready for demolition. 'Doesn't look like there's anybody living here,' she muttered, but knocked on the door anyway.

No answer.

She knocked again.

Not a sound.

Rosie put her mouth to the letterbox. 'Hello!' she called, coughing when the dust flew down her throat. 'I'm looking for Nancy. Is anybody home?'

Silence.

'Empty,' she muttered.

Turning away, she thought she heard a noise. She opened the letterbox again and called out, 'The lady in the teashop on the corner said Nancy might live here. My name's Rosie. I'm Kathleen's friend. She's in hospital.'

Nothing.

'I must be imagining things.' She shivered. 'Ghosts maybe.'

Returning to the teashop, she left her name and

address. 'If you hear anything at all that might help me find her, I'd be grateful.'

Her next stop was Lytham St Anne's. She wanted to see where Markham had lived.

Waiting for the tram, she consulted her notes. 'Westerfield House sold last year, to a mystery buyer. Christian Westerfield killed in a bar fight, and Connie Blakeman nowhere to be found.' Frowning, she closed the book and replaced it in her purse. 'Not much for my troubles, is it?'

'Pardon me, dear.' An old woman cupped her ear and grinned toothlessly at her. 'Are you talking to me?'

Feeling embarrassed, Rosie shook her head. 'Just thinking out loud,' she said lamely. Three days left before she returned to work. After that there'd be no time for searching out Kathleen's friends.

There was still one avenue she hadn't explored. 'I have to find Murray.' Her fighting spirit returned. 'There must be a way.' Suddenly, a light flickered in her mind. 'Of course!' It was staring her in the face and she hadn't seen it. 'You stupid thing, Rosie! Why didn't you think of that before?'

'Beg yer pardon, dearie?'

'Sorry.' She wouldn't be at all surprised if the woman thought she'd escaped from an asylum. When the old dear gave her a funny look and shuffled away, Rosie had to bite her lips to stop from giggling.

NANCY STAYED HIDDEN in the staircase cupboard for a long time after Rosie had gone. 'That were Rosie,' she told herself, 'Kathleen's friend.'

She came out of the cupboard like a mouse, bent low and nervous. 'I should 'ave gone to the door. Cook said I were never to be afraid.' A smile lit her eyes. 'Cook liked Kathleen.'

Coming to the door, she peered out of the letterbox, recoiling when a man glanced her way. 'Rosie.' She liked the sound of that name. 'She said Kathleen were in 'ospital.' She began pacing the floor. 'Kathleen. Kathleen . . . so pretty.'

⸻⸻◆⸻⸻

THE TRAM ARRIVED and Rosie got on. 'A tuppenny ticket, please,' she said, handing over the coins.

The conductor waited for the others to board the tram. 'Hurry along there, please,' he shouted impatiently. 'Hurry along.'

As Rosie turned to accept her ticket, she saw a ragged woman running down the road, a small, wizened little thing, with flyaway hair and a pixie face, and she knew her at once from Kathleen's diary. 'Nancy!' Her voice sailed out of the window and across the road. Nancy came to a halt. Staring this way and that, she couldn't tell where the voice had come from.

Rosie leapt off the tram and, dodging the traffic, ran towards her. 'Nancy!' she called. 'Stay there!'

Nancy stayed and Rosie fell into her arms, laughing and crying all at the same time. 'If you only knew,' she said, the tears running down her face. 'Oh, Nancy, if you only knew!'

They sat in the café for an age, going back over the years and reminiscing. Rosie told her all about Kathleen and the diaries, and Nancy told her about Cook and Mr Mason, and how they'd gone to heaven and left her behind.

Chapter Nineteen

R OSIE LEANED OVER the bed. 'Listen to me,
Kathleen.' Her voice shook with excitement.
'There's someone here to see you.'

Kathleen opened her eyes. 'Hello, Rosie.' Her face
lifted in a smile, but oh, she was so tired. 'Where've
you been?'

Holding out her hand, she felt the warmth of other
fingers, strong fingers, not like Rosie's at all. 'I missed
you,' she murmured, her dark eyes half closed.

'Did you, my lovely?' The voice shook Kathleen
to her very roots. 'I missed you too. More than you'll
ever know.'

In a heartbeat, Kathleen was transported back
over the years to when she was young and beautiful.
In her tired old mind she saw herself standing with
him in the garden of Maurice's house. That was the
night they had said goodbye, when she told him she
would miss him for ever. And she had. Every minute,
every day and night since.

'No, it can't be,' she whispered. Her heart was
beating so fast she feared it might leap out of her
chest.

'Look at me, Kathleen.'

Slowly, she opened her eyes, desperately trying to focus on the face before her. It was a moment before she saw it, the same strong face and warm, green eyes, the wayward fair hair that fell over his forehead, and the voice, so soft, so loving. 'It's me, Kathleen. I've been searching everywhere for you.'

With a little cry, she covered her face, the chin dimpling with the effort of keeping back the tears. But the tears came anyway, spilling through her fingers and blinding her.

'Look at me, Kathleen. Please.'

It was a moment before she dared peep through her fingers. At first she couldn't speak, but then her eyes shone and her arms opened, and she knew she wasn't dreaming. 'Oh, Murray! Is it really you?'

Taking her in his arms, he whispered, 'It's been a lifetime, hasn't it?'

She clung to him and he held her tight, as though his very life depended on it. 'I'm taking you home, sweetheart,' he said, and her heart soared.

TWO MONTHS LATER, her will to live restored and her body responding in kind, Kathleen went home.

In the carriage Murray sat beside her, holding her hand and thinking how their lives had turned full circle. He looked on this woman who had been his one and only love, and he could still see the girl.

Though older and marked by the years, Kathleen was still Kathleen, with striking dark eyes and long hair, now grey and dressed into a long thick plait down her back. The smile was still the same. Kathleen touched his heart with a magic that no other woman had ever been able to do.

Kathleen, too, took stock of her companion. He was older, but straight and proud, and still possessing his fine handsome looks. His hair might be grey and his stride not so brisk, but she saw only the young man who had swept her off her feet all those years ago.

'Close your eyes,' he told her as they came down Ilford High Street.

Laughing like a girl, Kathleen did as she was told.

When the carriage came to a halt, he carried her out and, standing with her in his arms, said softly, 'You can look now, sweetheart. This is your new home, yours and mine.'

She opened her eyes and when she saw where he had brought her, she was filled with astonishment and delight, for she was looking up at Westerfield House, and wondering if she was dreaming after all.

Inside the house they waited for her: Rosie, Nancy, and Murray's strapping son David.

'Oh!' Kathleen walked in on uncertain footsteps, with Murray at her side. 'Oh, look!' she cried, and the tears started again. She shook her head and cried and laughed, and when Nancy ran forward, calling out her name and telling her, 'Bleedin' hell, miss, you ain't changed a bit!' everyone laughed and clapped. Then they were hugging and kissing, and Murray stood back, letting them take her for a while. But she was his, and he would never let her go again.

Kathleen couldn't take it all in. She turned once to glance at her man, and he smiled encouragingly. 'You're home, sweetheart,' he said. 'Now all you have to do is get strong and well.'

Rosie had already explained how she brought it all about. 'I found Nancy in the same guesthouse where she'd lived with Cook and Mr Mason all those years,' she told Kathleen. 'I had lost all hope of contacting Murray, but then I began thinking about the mysterious man who'd bought this house. After that, it wasn't too hard to find him.'

'Melinda never really settled in Australia,' Murray told her simply. He saw no reason to burden her with the details of his wretched marriage. 'After Maurice died, she was never the same. She seemed somehow consumed by devils. I don't know how else to put it. I couldn't reach her at all. Then when Christian was killed, she took her own life. I brought David back to England two years ago. We set up a merchandising company and now David is taking over the running of it.'

That evening, Murray made a speech. 'I want to give thanks for Kathleen's promising recovery,' he told them, 'and for Rosie Maitland who brought us all together again.' Here he paused, dipped into his pocket and brought out a small box which he gave to

Kathleen. 'This is for you,' he said. When she opened it to find a sparkling engagement ring, he murmured, 'I think it's time we got married. What do you say, sweetheart?'

'I say yes.' She gave her answer wholeheartedly, and a rousing cheer went up.

'To Kathleen and Murray!' David announced, and everyone raised their glasses. He turned and discreetly put his arm round Rosie. 'To us,' he whispered.

Kathleen saw the special way they looked at each other. It was too soon yet, she thought, but in her heart she knew that Rosie and David would find a way.

The celebrations were interrupted when the doors opened and in strolled a mangy, grey-whiskered old dog. Kathleen knew him instantly. 'Oh, look! It's Mr Potts!' Holding out her arms, she waited for him to come to her.

Just then a shadow fell across the doorway. Curious, she glanced up and for a moment she thought her mind was playing tricks on her. The hair was grey, and the figure seemed a little shorter than she remembered, but . . . No. It wasn't possible.

But then he grinned, and there was no doubt. 'Hello, sis,' he said, and the years rolled away.

She wasn't aware of the others watching; they'd all known he would be here. Adam had not been on the ill-fated ship bound for America. He was on the passenger list because he'd bought a ticket, but before the ship sailed he was suddenly and unexpectedly offered a job in India, which he promptly accepted. There he had made a new life, believing that Kathleen would never again want to see him. He had never married. Murray had managed to trace him, and when he learned of Kathleen's fate, he had vowed to be with her.

Now, as they held each other, no words could describe the joy in their hearts. 'We're together again, sis,' he murmured in her ear. 'Doesn't it seem like only yesterday?'

Through her tears, Kathleen answered. 'Someone up there's been good to us,' she said.

She looked round the room, at Rosie and David, Nancy and the little dog at her feet. Beside her stood the only man she had ever truly loved, and here before her was the brother she had prayed for every night since he'd gone.

It's been a long and difficult road, she thought, but, for all that, I would not have travelled any other.

As she gazed on her loved ones, Kathleen knew they would be together, for a long, long time.

Bad Boy Jack

Josephine Cox

Deserted by the two women in his life, Robert Sullivan is left to raise three-year-old Nancy and her seven-year-old brother Jack. Unable to cope, Robert is driven to abandon his children to those who he believes can provide them with a better life. However, he quickly has a change of heart and decides to go back for them. But on the way there, he is involved in a horrific accident.

Unbeknownst to him, Jack and Nancy are placed in the brutal regime of the Galloway Children's Home, where Jack's fierce devotion to his sister and fiery temper land him in more trouble. Clinging together, the two children find themselves at the mercy of the corrupt Clive Ennington, who splits them up and sells Nancy off to the highest bidder.

When Robert begins to recover in hospital he is determined to find and reunite his family. But he soon begins to realise the terrible consequences of his own cowardly actions.

Praise for Josephine Cox's writing:

'Cox's talent as a storyteller never lets you escape' *Daily Mail*

'Driven and passionate' *The Sunday Times*

Bad Boy Jack is also available in an audio edition.

0 7472 6640 9

<u>headline</u>

Jinnie

Josephine Cox

Jinnie is the child from a one-night liaison between Louise Hunter's husband, Ben, and Louise's sister, Susan. When Ben takes his own life, and Susan deserts her newborn child, Louise puts aside her own heartache and adopts little Jinnie as her own. Louise's solace down the years is little Jinnie, and their close relationship. But what will happen when Jinnie finds out the truth? And then, one day, a letter arrives from Susan, saying she intends to get Jinnie back.

There are others whose lives are badly affected by the tragic events of the past: Adam, who witnessed his mother's murder, and his sister, Hannah, inwardly traumatised by what she too saw that night. And their beloved grandmother, who longs to keep them safe, but knows in her heart that the day will soon come when she must take them back to the place where it all happened. It seems Fate is already taking a hand.

Jinnie is the heart-rending new novel from the number one bestselling author of *The Woman Who Left*; both novels follow the dramatic and compelling fortunes of the Hunter family.

'Cox's talent as a storyteller never lets you escape the spell' *Daily Mail*

'Driven and passionate' *The Sunday Times*

0 7472 6639 5

headline

The Woman Who Left

Josephine Cox

Riddled with guilt, she was far from being sleepy. Because even when he held her as close as any man could hold his woman, her mind was filled with thoughts of another man.

Louise and Ben Hunter have a happy, loving marriage, marred only by their unfulfilled longing for a child. Living and working with Ben's father, Ronnie, they quietly accept their uneventful but contented lives. But when Ronnie dies, their whole world changes.

News of his father's passing brings Ben's lazy brother, Jacob, back on the scene, in the mistaken belief that he stands to inherit Ronnie's small fortune. Added to which he means to have his brother's wife; though just as she did years before, Louise warns him off. Jacob, however, is not so easily dismissed.

When he realises it is Ben who will inherit everything, Jacob is beside himself with rage, and commits a terrible deed, one that threatens to destroy everything his brother and Louise hold dear – their home and their family, their friends, their marriage and even their very lives . . .

Praise for Josephine Cox's writing:

'Cox's talent as a storyteller never lets you escape the spell' *Daily Mail*

'Impossible to resist' *Woman's Realm*

'Driven and passionate' *The Sunday Times*

0 7472 6634 4

headline

Now you can buy any of these other bestselling books by **Josephine Cox** from your bookshop or *direct from the publisher*.

FREE P&P AND UK DELIVERY
(Overseas and Ireland £3.50 per book)

Bad Boy Jack	£6.99
Jinnie	£6.99
The Woman Who Left	£5.99
Let it Shine	£5.99
Looking Back	£5.99
Rainbow Days	£5.99
Somewhere, Someday	£5.99
The Gilded Cage	£5.99
Tomorrow the World	£6.99
Love Me or Leave Me	£6.99
Miss You Forever	£6.99
Cradle of Thorns	£6.99
A Time for Us	£6.99
The Devil You Know	£6.99
Living a Lie	£6.99
A Little Badness	£6.99
More Than Riches	£6.99
Born to Serve	£6.99

TO ORDER SIMPLY CALL THIS NUMBER

01235 400 414

or visit our website: www.madaboutbooks.com

Prices and availability subject to change without notice.